PATRIOT PINN'S PEARL

PATRIOT PINN'S PEARL

Horace Rice

Copyright © 2015 by Horace Rice.

Library of Congress Control Number:		2015906730
ISBN:	Hardcover	978-1-5035-6528-9
	Softcover	978-1-5035-6529-6
	eBook	978-1-5035-6530-2

All rights reserved. No part of this book may be reproduced or transmitted in any form or by any means, electronic or mechanical, including photocopying, recording, or by any information storage and retrieval system, without permission in writing from the copyright owner.

Scripture quotations marked KJV are taken from the King James Version. © 1982 by Thomas Nelson, Inc. Used by permission. All rights reserved.

Scripture quotations marked NIV are taken from the *Holy Bible, New International Version. NIV.* © 1973, 1978, 1984 by International Bible Society. Used by permission of Zondervan. All rights reserved. [Biblica]

Any people depicted in stock imagery provided by Thinkstock are models, and such images are being used for illustrative purposes only.
Certain stock imagery © Thinkstock.

Print information available on the last page.

Rev. date: 11/06/2015

To order additional copies of this book, contact:
Xlibris
1-888-795-4274
www.Xlibris.com
Orders@Xlibris.com
672726

Contents

Prologue		xi
Chapter 1	The Great Man of Wiccocomico	1
Chapter 2	Indentured Servitude	24
Chapter 3	Home on the Ridge	45
Chapter 4	Minute Men	66
Chapter 5	Wiccocomico and Cherokee Heritage	81
Chapter 6	A Compassionate Heart	101
Chapter 7	Shadow of Yorktown	126
Chapter 8	Human Hostilities	141
Chapter 9	Men as Trees Walking	149
Chapter 10	The Siege	164
Chapter 11	The Battle of Battles	187
Chapter 12	I Will Come Again	205
Chapter 13	The Road Not Taken	232
Chapter 14	The Pearl: The Heritage	247
Chapter 15	Documents, Past Tense	257
Chapter 16	Dreams of the Distant Future	268
Chapter 17	One Pearl of Great Price	278
Chapter 18	Sacred Ground	291
Chapter 19	Free People of Color Registration	305
Chapter 20	The Census	327
Chapter 21	Shalom	344
Chapter 22	Is It Possible?	370
Epilogue		391
Recommended Reading		395
The United Cherokee Indian Tribe of Virginia (UCITOVA)		403
Works Cited		519
About The Author		529

To my wife Gloria Jean, my daughters Joylyn
and Holli, other descendants of
Raleigh Pinn and pillar ancestors of
the Ridge and Stonewall Mill,
and *Daughters of the American Revolution*
sisters of Central Virginia.

Synopsis

Patriot Pinn's Pearl, a historical fiction account, chronicles the lives of a rare Native American tribe of mixed Cherokee and Wiccocomico, unique and distinctive by its extraordinary ingenuity and strength to survive several hundred years, despite colonial settlers' racial hatred and attempts to take its lands and destroy its aboriginal heritage. The most prominent character during the eight generations noted in this account is Chief Raleigh Pinn, a Wiccocomico and Cherokee from Wiccocomico Indian Town in the Northern Neck area of Virginia. Having been an indentured child servant for English settlers who confiscated his ancestors' official reservation lands, Raleigh learned the ways of the settlers, moved to Central Virginia at the end of his Northern Neck indentured servitude, purchased properties in Buckingham and Amherst Counties, and provided a haven for his family and other dispersed Cherokee and Wiccocomico people.

    The reader will empathize with Raleigh's and his descendants' reactions to colonial settlers and the hardships these settlers caused in the early to mid-1700s through the mid-1800s, as well as his tribe's struggles to survive in a hostile milieu. Initially hating the colonial settlers, he grapples to control his deep animosity for everything "Anglo" as he models survival strategies for his indigenous people. He purchases several hundred acres of land, becomes a prosperous farmer, joins the Amherst Militia, and participates in several Revolutionary War military campaigns, including the decisive battle at Yorktown. He establishes, unites, and protects his people in two Cherokee villages that are separated by the James River, during his years in Amherst and Buckingham Counties.

Raleigh's faith in God and his keen awareness of his royal heritage provide the essential self-confidence required to tame his animosity and teach his people how to coexist with white settlers in a world that makes survival for Native Americans almost impossible. This is a story of Raleigh's skillful ability to pass on history and heritage to his progeny and to exhibit his love rather than hatred for his neighbors, and, in the process, he serves as a model for his descendants' achievement and tolerance. This book also includes events in the life of other tribal members, Native American Revolutionary War patriots and their children and grandchildren, who are ancestors of the present-day members of the United Cherokee Indian Tribe of Virginia (UCITOVA).

At the end of *Patriot Pinn's Pearl*, the author has included a short historical chronicle of UCITOVA.

PROLOGUE

During the time that Samuel de Champlain founded the French Quebec settlement in 1608, the British captain John Smith explored the Wiccocomico villages in Northern Neck Virginia and discovered inhabitants living in serene settings. At the time, the Cherokees were living in comfortable tribal villages in Southwestern Virginia, on lands that were part of their Southeastern United States territory, including sections of the states of Tennessee, Kentucky, South Carolina, Georgia, North Carolina, Alabama, and Virginia. Cherokee bands also roamed and lived on land in Central, Southside, and Tidewater Virginia. Due to pressures as a result of settlement intrusions by British, French, and American colonists, some Cherokees and Wiccocomicos became allies and even intermarried. Actually, historical records indicate that they became one people in many settlements in Northern Neck, Southside, and Central Virginia, while their Cherokee kin in Southwestern Virginia continued to live as tribal bands in several counties.

How did this partnership between Cherokees and Wiccocomicos fare in Virginia? What were and are its social impacts on Central and Northern Neck Virginia? Is it possible that any residue of that seventeenth-century alliance remained through the twenty-first century? This is a story about several of those four-hundred-year-old families, hybrids of Wiccocomicos and Cherokees.

> To every thing there is a season and a time
> for every purpose under the heaven:
> A time to be born, and a time to die . . .
> Ecclesiastes 3:1–2 (KJV)

1

The Great Man of Wiccocomico

1734

Robert Junior, John, and Raleigh, ages five, four, and three, respectively, sat in the cold, dark parlor where their father's body had been placed in repose. Their two-year-old sister played with her tattered rag doll on the floor. Margaret Pinn, their mother, stood over the plain, inexpensive coffin and stared at her husband's remains. His facial deterioration recorded the effects of his discomfort during his month-long incapacitation and home confinement.

The three young boys sat restlessly upon a bench. John spotted a wooden whistle that had fallen from Robert Junior's pocket. He pounced on it, and moments later, the two were close to wrestling over the whistle. Raleigh, the youngest son, tried unsuccessfully to grab it.

"Boys, show some respect!" Their mother frowned fiercely upon them from across their father's plain wooden coffin. The children's faces fell, and they respectfully shifted back into well-behaved positions with backs straight and hands folded on their laps.

Robert Senior suffered from chest pains during the last month of his life. The pressures and aches had become too much for his body to bear. Margaret took comfort in knowing that her herbal medicines had been helpful, but in the end, they had not been enough. Succumbing to the effects of stress, excruciating pain, and fever, Robert Senior had died the day before, on Monday. Taking a deep breath and consciously stiffening her spine, Margaret tried to prepare herself for the days to come. Her husband's funeral would be held in two days, and she had much to do.

She shook her head in momentary disbelief. Robert—her dearest Robert—had been such a vibrant and energetic man. It did not seem possible that he was now lying unmoving in that unadorned box. What was she to do without him? What would the community do without him? Her thoughts turned to the deeds of his lifetime. As the grandson of the Great Man of Wiccocomico, Robert was as well respected for his leadership as his grandfather had been to Wiccocomico Indian Town. Court officials called Robert Pinn the "Great Man," rather than king or chief. In the 1670s, Northumberland court officials addressed his grandfather, Robert Pekwem, the "Great Man of Wiccocomico." Robert Senior was also known as Robert Pekwem before his name was anglicized to Pinn.

"Boys, what did I tell you? Didn't you hear me? Do I need to take a switch to your bottoms? Give me that cane whistle!"

Robert Junior, who had managed to wrestle the whistle from his two brothers, walked shyly toward this mother, with head and eyes aimed toward his feet. He gave his prized whistle to his mother, wondering if and when she would give it back to him.

John Pinn, the Great Man's son, was her husband's father. Margaret mused to herself that the Great Man, like his grandson, Robert, had truly been a great man.

She tidied the house knowing that more visitors would arrive soon. She gathered the cups that had been left on the table and took them to be washed. Although there were only about ten local adult Wiccocomico tribal members still living in Indian Town, three of the ten members had already visited her home to express their condolences. About thirty white neighbors had also stopped by to console Margaret.

While she cleaned the house, she pictured her husband in her mind. Robert Pinn was a tall six-foot-one prince known to Wiccocomico Indian Town's tribal members as Chief, the grandson of Robert Pekwem, or Pewem, as some called him. As she swept the floor and prepared the food, Margaret recalled the memories of a lifetime, sometimes with tears sliding down her somber face and occasionally a tender smile controlling her trembling lips. Robert was a great provider for his family as he cultivated great tobacco and vegetable crops and brought in bountiful seafood from the Wiccocomico River. He also negotiated land deals with local colonists that provided funds for Margaret to hide in her secret place in the house.

He always walked through the door after those successful real estate deals, with a big smile on his face and pounds in his hand. "Margaret, you know where to store this for hard times."

She tiptoed and managed to kiss him on his chin. "Yes, Robert."

Much later, the visitors all departed their home, but the usual atmosphere had not returned. The spirit of Robert Senior—chief, husband, father, hero, and friend—was absent. Margaret, still attired in her long dark blue English dress and her indigo and white hat, gathered her children around the casket, seating them on a long bench near the fire. Refusing to let his memory fade, she took a deep breath and prepared to give them another history lesson. She felt she owed it to her deceased husband to keep not only his memory alive but also the Native American heritage.

She gazed into the face of each of her children, wondering how best to retell their proud legacy from their father. She found her voice and began to speak.

"Children, Wiccocomico Indians have lived in the lower part of the Northern Neck as far back as thousands of years. Your people hunted from the land, planted on the land, and gathered their food from the same land. When the English first came to Wiccocomico in the early 1600s, they found at least five hundred of our people living in this area. These settlers had their own ideas about how our land should be used and did not like our style of living on the land. They had their own view of what should be planted in the rich soil. The English newcomers were supported by some financiers called the Virginia Company and wanted to use our land in a different way. Our people had been happy here as the land always supplied everything we needed to survive, but when those people came from England, they thought we were lazy and idle. They decided that we needed to be taught other ways to use the land to make money for their Virginia Company. Our ancestors wondered why the English people who came across the ocean cared about our planting methods."

Margaret paused, looking at the children to make sure they understood what she was saying. With three pairs of dark slanting eyes focusing on her face, she continued.

"The English kept coming to Wiccocomico, and this made our people very uneasy and tense. They wanted us to adjust to their way of life and give up our way. In 1644, some of the Indians fought against the English, but they stopped our people's rebellion. The Virginia Colonial Council made a treaty with the Wiccocomico that gave the English people's land, a property that they had from the York River to the Wiccocomico River, to our people. The white people moved to our more valuable Indian-held lands between the Rappahannock and Potomac Rivers, a land that was previously our people's Indian reserve."

Her anger, usually so well hidden, was evident at this point, bringing a stinging bitterness to her voice. "In the winter of 1655–1656, around the time of the Rechahecrian Indians' assault at the falls in Richmond, the court gave our people a new area—4,400 acres near Dividing Creek for the Wiccocomico and Chicacoan Indian. These 4,400 acres provided fifty acres for each of the ninety adult male warriors. There were about four hundred tribal members, but they only gave fifty acres per adult warrior," she explained. "They moved the Chicacoan Indians and the Wiccocomico southward from their previous lands and combined the two tribes on the new 4,400-acre Indian reserve."

Again, she paused, wondering how best to explain, and then slowly continued. "Children, you don't understand now, but you will learn later that the colonists knew how to make our people fight each other. After putting the two tribes together, the local colonial officials appointed the Chicacoan chief Machywap to rule over both tribes."

The children rolled their eyes at each other as if they were ready to wrestle again, but they restrained themselves as their mother constantly gave them the familiar "don't you dare do it" look.

Margaret sagely nodded her head, glancing from one face to another. "The Wiccocomico, who had more tribal members than the Chicacoans, thought it was unfair to appoint Machywap as chief." Margaret's tone let the children know that she agreed, and they nodded in accord.

"Why would they conceive such an action? Why did they make Machywap chief for both groups?" She answered her own questions. "I guess they were trying to start a fight between the two groups so that they would kill each other off. They succeeded. The Wiccocomico threatened to kill Machywap if he tried to serve as werowance—chief— of the whole group. Around 1659 or 1660, our Wiccocomico people got rid of Machywap, the colonists' man, and the Wiccocomico placed a Wiccocomico chief, your daddy's grandfather, of the whole group, both tribes. After that time, the combined group took the name Wiccocomico."

Although it was getting late and the fire burned low, the three boys remained seated on the bench, listening attentively and absorbing the words tumbling from their mother's lips. Little Ann sat on the floor beside the boys, holding her rag doll in her tiny arms.

"During those years, the colonial commissioners didn't want to call our leader king, but were willing to use the Great Man title. Now, boys, I know your daddy told you the story at least one time already, but I also want you to remember hearing my voice telling you this in the presence of your daddy's coffin. You must remember our history. It will stick in your minds better because you can associate your daddy's death with the gradual death of our Wiccocomico Indian Town."

Robert Junior, hearing the urgency in his mother's voice, reassured her. "Mother, we will never forget the story. We heard it before from daddy, and now we will remember you telling us." John and little Raleigh nodded solemnly in agreement.

She insisted, "Make sure you never forget that the English took our prime farmland and gave us less productive property because we lost our entire way of life. The English tried to force us to live according to their English ways. Soon after this, our people started disappearing like snowflakes left on the soil to melt in the sun. Now, children, we only have eight or ten Wiccocomico Indian Town residents paying their respects out of a total of four hundred members who lived in Indian Town almost eighty years ago. Why?" she asked, her voice suddenly getting louder. "It is because some of our people died and others left the area because they refused to live under English control. The English even took some of our people from the area as slaves."

She turned and gazed at the coffin. Ann, an energetic two-year-old, clung tightly to her mother's dress with her left hand. It was as if Margaret had a need to stay close to Robert's remains and was looking to him for inspiration and power to choose the correct pieces of oral heritage to share with the children. Hearing the rustling from the bench as the boys fidgeted in their seats, she turned back to them.

"Where was I, Robert Junior?" Margaret asked, smiling encouragingly at the boys.

"You said some of our people died and some people left Wiccocomico Indian Town," Robert Junior answered promptly.

"Junior, I wish I could call you Great Man, but I cannot because our tribe is so small now. Our people have faded away. All but the few that you have seen streaming though this parlor room today. There are others out there in other areas of this colony, and even in other colonies; they may be known as Indian or may be passing themselves off as either white or black. Our Wiccocomico Town is almost gone. Therefore, we might not need a Wiccocomico chief to lead the less than two handfuls of people remaining!"

John interjected, "No, Mother. I will be the chief of three of the people. Junior can lead four because he is the oldest son. Raleigh will be the chief of two also. That makes nine people and three chiefs." He was pleased with his own logic and mathematical ability.

Raleigh jumped to his feet and stopped John, "No. I want to be the chief of a big tribe like the one we had before the English came. I will try to find the people of the Wiccocomico Indian Town. I will look for them and tell them that I will be their chief. I will say, 'Follow me back to Wiccocomico Indian Town.'"

Even though he was only three, his voice rang with determination. He sat back down and rested one of his hands on his left knee and the other on his chin, as if he were thinking deeply, waiting for his mother's response.

"Children, the white people respected your great-grandfather Pewem and your grandfather John Pinn, just like they trusted and respected your daddy. Perhaps if our tribe increased in size, one day it will be your turn to have that same respect."

She had heard stories about how her grandfather-in-law was called on to be a witness to legal events at the courthouse in Northumberland. Robert Senior told her that his grandfather Pewem was a witness to the February 1662 land transaction of John Clark and his wife. Robert's grandfather put a large R as his witness mark on the court document. He was no ordinary man; he was the great and respected werowance of Wiccocomico.

"The white judges treated our people fairly, but some of the colonists did not always obey the judges."

Margaret was thinking of an incident in which, out of fear of an Indian uprising, the colonists had confiscated the guns of Wiccocomico men. The colonists had taken the guns, but the court protected the Wiccocomico people by ordering the guns to be returned to their owners. Twelve years earlier, in 1722, she checked on the accuracy of this legend about her grandfather-in-law and the Wiccocomico tribesmen by going down to the courthouse and looking at the court records. She found the notes in the official court documents and wrote the information down. Margaret kept the handwritten copy of the original court order just for such a time as this. She walked away from the coffin long enough to go to her bedroom. A few minutes later, after thumbing through papers in her cedar chest at the foot of her bed, she returned to the parlor with a small piece of yellowish paper. Standing over the boys, she showed them the handwritten copy as she read the contents slowly:

> 19 Feb 1678–79 – All persons of this county that have any guns belonging to the Indians of Wicomico Indian Town do forthwith deliver the said guns to Robert the Great Man of the said Town and by him to be delivered to their owners.

After she read the words, she displayed the paper so the children could see it. She held it reverently with both hands as the boys leaned forward to see the faded writing. As they looked at the words, she continued the story. "Out of fear of an Indian uprising, the colonists had confiscated the guns. The judge ordered them to be returned. On behalf of his tribe, Robert Pewem accepted the few guns that the colonists actually returned and distributed them to their original owners." She carefully put the paper down and the children again focused on her face.

"Children, just twenty-some years before they took the guns, the white residents had become nervous when they heard about the Rechahecrians—the Cherokees—invading the land near Richmond falls. They started picking on our people more and more with the passing of each moon. Even now, after all these years since the battle at Richmond falls, the colonists are still scared of us. They are still harassing us. It is so unfair!" Indignation rang in her voice, and once again, she glanced down at the coffin.

"They didn't return all the guns that they stole from our men. We heard that the guns trickled in slowly, but the white people kept the best weapons. Some colonists were suspicious that my grandfather-in-law, Robert "the Great Man" Pewem, would incite a rebellion in Wiccocomico Indian territory.

"Children," she said as she shook her head in disbelief, "with the way they treated our ancestors, I wonder why they didn't stir up more trouble against those newcomers. I know what I am saying is not Christian-like, but I wish they would have defended themselves more aggressively."

Raleigh asked, "Mother, can I be the chief? I will beat up those bad people. Please?"

Speaking at the same time, John said, "Mama, what's 'aggressively'?"

Margaret, ignoring John for a moment, replied to Raleigh. "Child, you need to grow older before you think about such grown-up military matters. I have seen some of the future. It has been revealed to me that you and one of your brothers, I am not sure which one, John or Robert Junior, will fight the British. Raleigh, your time will come. Just be patient."

As she contemplated her vision, other thoughts crossed her mind. *Was Robert's demise the straw that would actually break the back of the remaining Wiccocomico Indians and result in their total dispersion?*

She concluded that a number of circumstances caused the dispersion and dissolution of the aboriginal people as they originally existed. It was evident that friction and battles would occur between the colonists and her people. Some of the Wiccocomico left the area and joined other Powhatan tribes. She knew that some Wiccocomico even traveled south and west and became part of the Rechahecrian or Cherokee people. Some had been taken and moved away from Wiccocomico as slaves. She silently lamented the fact that Wiccocomico Indian Town had begun to lose its identity decades ago. With the setting of each sun, Wiccocomico was slowly ceasing to exist.

Margaret knew that some of the people died from diseases, and that not all of the diseases were brought by the colonists. Some of the Wiccocomicos, however, believed that the settlers were the root cause of their maladies and afflictions. Even the English lifestyle changes caused harm to the social and physical health of the Wiccocomico people. She shared her thoughts with the boys as they sat attentively in the parlor, which had now become a funeral parlor.

"Children, when the settlers came to our land, they brought their new ways of living, which were not always good for our people. Our people lived happily in Wiccocomico for many years with our old ways. When the new people came, their new ways hurt our people."

Then she considered the third cause of the dissolution of the tribe and speculated what would happen to the people. "Children, some Wiccocomicos joined the colonists. They joined and became white people!"

"Mother, why did our people become English people? Didn't they like being Wiccocomico?" Robert Junior inquired.

"Junior, the Wiccocomico people were happy until the colonists came to our land. Then the colonists made our life so hard with their new ways. Then our people began to be unhappy. Some left the area and others stayed. The people who stayed had to decide to stay Wiccocomico or act like white people. Your father and I decided to stay Wiccocomico. Some of our tribal members became white."

"How did their dark skin change to white skin?"

"Junior, their skin color didn't really change. They just acted like white people by the way they lived. You remember that black cat we had that slept with the dogs and acted like a dog even though he was really a cat and not a dog."

"Yes, Mother. That cat wanted to be a dog!"

"Some of our relatives got jobs like the white people and they stopped hunting and fishing in Wiccocomico ways. They lived so much like white people that Wiccocomico tribal members stopped calling them Wiccocomico and began treating them the way they wanted to be treated, like white people."

This consideration brought trepidation and consternation to her mind and heart. She was dismayed at the image of her people fusing with the colonists, adopting their lifestyles, and taking the "unite with them if you cannot defeat them" attitude.

By explaining how their ancestors lost their battles with the colonists, Margaret was preparing the boys to face the impending arrival of the English way of life, although they were much too young to really understand fully what she had told them. She was aware that the colonists had begun to seek cheap labor by making indentured servants out of the dispersed Indian children, as the slaves were not sufficient to meet all of the colonists' labor demands in the new agrarian culture. The English farmers also needed Indian people to improve production on their farmlands. Some colonists forced Indians to slave in their tobacco fields, while other colonists, who brought Indian children on their farms as indentured servants, took a more civil and legal stance to support their farm economies.

Margaret Pinn wondered about her children and the other Wiccocomico people. For the thousandth time, she asked herself, *What will happen to them?*

She meditated on the situation, conceding that the court had been fair with her people over the years even though the European settlers had been very rude. The court seemed to provide the checks and balances between the European colonists and the Indian people. Even the Church of England tried on numerous occasions to help the Indian people, but it seemed to Margaret that the king's policies and the Virginia Company's ambitions were leading the way in Virginia. The Indian people seemed destined for genocide.

Margaret knew all about the power of the English church. The Church of England made a major contribution to English culture in Northumberland County, playing a prominent role in the lives of the colonists and Indian people. The church even had the power to tax the inhabitants of the parish, including the Indian residents, some of whom had become prosperous. The funds were used for a number of purposes. The levy on the parish inhabitants provided funds for the salaries of the ministers, clerks, and sextons. The church needed funds for its upkeep as it levied tithes on landowners in the form of tobacco. Tobacco was money to the colony and the tobacco funds were also used to support the parish's work in the community. The church was instrumental in caring for the poor, needy, and indigent, as well as in burying the dead. The levies also provided funds for repairing the roads.

"The church was good to the Indian people," Margaret stated after some reflection, "but they had too many extra burdens from the English Crown. The church had the weight of the king hanging around its neck."

Margaret understood the Church of England's situation in the Wiccocomico Parish. The church members were good people, but church-state laws, as they existed at that time, required that the church act as an agent for the colony. "They had to represent the government of England and Christ," Margaret said. "They had a weight that was too much for church officials to bear. England's policies were too heavy for the mission-to-the-people-oriented church."

Tears began to trickle down her aging eyes as she remembered the shocking order that the church and court—the church-state—had sent to her husband in 1733:

> Robert Pinn of the Wiccocomico Parish being presented by the Grand Jury for absenting himself from his parish church for one month is fined fifty pounds of tobacco or five shillings . . . that the said Robert pays his said fine to the church wardens of the said parish with cost.
> Northumberland County Court
> August 16, 1733

Margaret deliberated as the tears flowed like a crystal-clear river over a waterfall. Then she shared her thoughts with the boys, who were exchanging concerned glances with one another, unsure what to do about her tears.

"Church leaders were strict with parish members. Your daddy couldn't miss four Sundays in a row. If he did, they would tax him and force him to come to church. My dear husband, my love . . . he didn't go to the parish church because he was sick at that time. There were other times when he didn't go and he really didn't have a good reason for staying at home. That time, however, he was sick. They made him pay fifty pounds of tobacco for staying at home four straight Sundays! He was sick," she repeated. "That is why he didn't go to Wiccocomico Church." Her tears started to flow again and the boys' eyes became misty. Even little Ann's bottom lip started to quiver even though she did not completely understand what was going on.

Wiping her eyes with her handkerchief, Margaret continued to tell the children about their father. "Although Robert Senior loved the Lord and our family enjoyed going to the parish church, he didn't like the way the church was administered. He thought they were too strict with the members and didn't like the way England meddled in the affairs of the church and his personal worship. While he accepted the fact that the parish was doing great work, he questioned why they had to encumber church matters with state politics and why the state seemed to side with the Anglican faith. Robert Senior and our whole family enjoyed going to the parish church. They just didn't give those Baptists and Methodists a chance to start churches."

She hoped the boys would realize the importance of what she was saying. "The parish church leaders even sent wardens annually to our house to count the number of tobacco plants in our fields, as they expected the tithes when the crops came in. They were firm with their members. If you didn't pay your tithes willingly, they would go to court and the judge would order you to do it. The church and the state worked together. Other denominations protested to the colonial officials because of the way the state seemed to be partial with the Church of England. 'Why were the Anglican Church allowed to tax people for the whole colony and other denominations were not given the same benefits?' the complainers asked. The colony had a state-approved denomination, a state-favored religion!"

Raleigh, although he did not fully understand everything that his mother was saying to them, looked at his mother closely. Even though he was young, he knew that she was taking his daddy's death very hard. As Margaret grabbed Robert Senior's shoulders in the coffin and started crying openly, Raleigh rushed over and hugged his mother. Unable to hold the tears back any longer, he began crying as well. Brushing his tears away with the back of his small hand, he offered to console her.

"Mother, do you want a glass of water? I will go get it for you. What can I get to make you feel better? You want some sassafras tea? I will make some for you, Mother."

John and Robert Junior, who were also crying by now, also jumped up and attempted to comfort her. John touched her arm and inquired, "Can I help, Mother?"

Robert Junior ran toward the kitchen, pulled out some sassafras roots and leaves, and placed them on the table. "Mother, how much water should I put in the pot for the sassafras?"

Margaret made a tremendous effort to pull herself together. She then said, "Junior, I will fix us some in a few minutes. Thank you for being so kind to think about me. You are a dear child."

She headed toward the kitchen, silently giving thanks to heaven for her family. As she passed the children, she tenderly patted each one on the head. "All of you are special striplings, and I love you all dearly. Let me leave this parlor room and fix your children something to eat before you go up to bed."

Raleigh woke up prior to sunrise, before Ann and his brothers. He had slept fitfully, and now he left his warm bed and silently crept forward so he could watch his mother. He observed her for a long time from the other room as she sat in her parlor chair near his daddy's coffin. After each fifteen-minute interval, she cried. Her grieving sound was so loud that it bounced off the parlor walls and traveled through the seven rooms in the house. She would then wail and tears would roll down her face like the rushing Wiccocomico River during a rainstorm.

"Why, Lord? Why, Lord? They will be dispersed! Why, Lord? Why, Lord? They will be a desolate people!"

After fifteen more minutes of thinking and meditation, she cried out again, "Why, Lord? Why, Lord?" Afterward she said, "If the wind blows the seeds away, the garden will perish. The plants will not grow again. Why, Lord? Why, Lord?"

Following another interval, she hollered, "No, Lord! No, Lord! Not dispersion! Why, Lord? Why, Lord? Don't let my children be dispersed! They will lose their culture! Their Indian tribe will be thrown all over the place like the windblown garden and its dispersed seeds."

She said this as if she needed to use an analogy to convince the Lord of the seriousness of what she had seen in the future, as though this would help change the Lord's mind. She connected her husband's death with the possibility of her children becoming orphans.

Raleigh trembled as he stood in the shadows for almost an hour, wondering what to do. He had never seen his mother act this way. In doubt, he remained hidden and listened.

Margaret continued her appeal to the Lord to protect her family. Speaking low, she entreated, "Lord, if you make indentured servants of my children, they will forget the great Wiccocomico traditions. Their heritage seeds will be thrown all over the colony. The swine will trample on them. Some will die. The winds will carry some of my children into wild, grassy fields of non-Indian cultures. They will be choked off from Algonquian and Cherokee culture! No, Lord! No, Lord!"

Then yielding to the inevitable, she appealed to the Lord in prayer, "Lord, if you must do this, put them in good gardens, where they will grow healthy. If I may ask one other thing, don't let Wiccocomico die! You did not bring the great Wiccocomico tribe this far to leave our people. Let it keep some semblance of the original!"

Raleigh then heard his mother close her prayer in the Cherokee language, "*Wa do, wa do!*" Thank you, thank you! His mother then stood up from her chair and wiped her face with a lacy white and lavender kerchief.

Seeing Raleigh, she rushed over to hug him. Embarrassed that he saw and heard her heartfelt secret prayers, she inquired, "What are you doing up this early? How long have you been standing here, child?"

"About a half hour or more. I heard you praying."

"I was talking to my Father, God. I don't have a living earthly father and mother, so I talk to God. He is my loving Father. You don't have a father either now that Robert Senior is dead, so I need help from the Lord to assist you children and me in getting through these rough times."

Hugging her legs with his little arms, he gazed up at her and asked, "Mother, are you all right?"

"Yes, child, your mother is doing fine, now that I have prayed to the Lord." She patted him on his head in a soothing gesture, wiping away her last drops of tears with her handkerchief before she wiped away a tear that was hanging on Raleigh's left eye.

He gave her a tremulous smile. "I will pray for you, too, Mother. I will also pray for Ann, Robert Junior, and John."

"Thank you, child, but you can pray later. Pray tonight before you get in bed, but now I want you to do something else for me. Go tell the other children to get out of bed and come to the parlor. I need to say something to you all."

She headed him in the right direction, and he almost tripped on the parlor rug in his haste to do her bidding.

A few minutes later, Ann, Robert Junior, and John stood near the door of the parlor, rubbing their eyes, half asleep, and holding on to Raleigh's arms. They stood at attention in the same spot where Raleigh had been standing earlier. Hesitating in their frozen positions as if waiting for their mother's official invitation to come into the parlor, they breathed slowly, watching intently for her hand signal to enter. Since their father's body had been placed there in repose, there was something different about that room. They looked to their mother for formal cues before they felt comfortable entering the parlor.

Margaret looked up and noticed her usually active children standing in a state of passivity. She stood up halfway and lifted both hands straight out toward the children and beckoned them to come forward. Ann, John, Robert Junior, and Raleigh waited for the bravest sibling of the four to step forward first.

John moved forward one step; first his right foot and then his left. "Mother, you sent for us?" Worry was evident in his face and his voice.

She went over and circled her arms around them, herding them into the parlor. Sitting down with them on the davenport, Margaret told them the bad news.

"I can't tell you how, but some or all of you will leave our home and go to other homes or areas. I don't know why, where, or when, but you will. It is a part of God's plan. He just told me. I know we are poor now. We have very little money after your dad's long sickness because he was unable to work. Now that he is dead, things will get even worse. Always remember, I love you now and will always love you. You may be miles away from me, but my prayers are with you. You will stay Indian in your heart. The Lord has promised me that all or some of you will travel to other areas, and one or two or three of you will keep the aboriginal traditions. I don't know which one of you will be the instrument of God's revelation to me that I will have a special, serious-minded child who will be loyal to the Indian traditions. I was assured in my vision that Wiccocomico did not come this far—thousands of years in its making—to die in 1734 with your daddy. One or two of you will be instruments of God to keep the aboriginal heritage. On the other hand, one or two of you may adopt the colonists' lifestyle in Northumberland or move to other areas and adopt the colonists' ways. God promised me that Wiccocomico will not die. It will continue. The seeds will be sewn in new areas! I don't know where or when or by whom, I just know because I have seen the vision. The tribe will live on. Maybe in the same form or a different form, I am not sure, but it will live on. The colonial wild grass will not choke the Wiccocomico blades. The English wild grass will not smother your tender roots. God will even pick up a seed or two in the mouth of a seagull, if necessary to retain the Indian culture, and take them from the coast here in the Northern Neck to the wilderness. Then a sparrow will take the seeds and fly them to a ridge or mountain. An eagle will then take them and protect them until the time of planting. The English culture will not swallow up our Wiccocomico culture like the king swallowed up our land. Always remember what I have said. One or more of you will protect the culture. You will not let the heritage die when you die. Don't let our people become white. Remember what I have said. The Indian man must live on or else we will allow the colonial genocidal practices to prevail. Don't let it happen!"

She turned toward Junior and, looking into his eyes, exclaimed, "Robert, don't let it happen!" She looked into her other children's black eyes: "John, don't let it happen! Raleigh, don't let it happen! Ann, don't let it happen! You must remember Wiccocomico. Remember the great Wiccocomico!"

Her children all remained silent and still during her long pronouncement, just like they had been trained to behave in church. Even Ann, fumbling with the bow on her wrinkled and partially unbuttoned dress, was unusually attentive. When

Margaret finished, Raleigh spoke up and assured her that he would be faithful to the Wiccocomico heritage.

Ann, even though she was just two years old, said, "I will always be Indian."

Lastly, John and Robert Junior also promised her that they intended to keep the Indian culture.

After clutching her children one more time, she told them that she would help them with their prayers and God would do the rest. She assured them, "God will not let present or future colonists hold back the destiny of the Indian people. I do not believe God will let thousands of years of Wiccocomico existence or the more recent Wiccocomico-Cherokee coexistence die at the hands of the colonists. The Rechahecrian people are special. They have a mission. God may be using several Indian groups to continue our Wiccocomico ways, only in a different form. God will do that. Nobody will hold him back from that! No man or woman or historian or politician can stand in his way to keep him from accomplishing his promise! If it takes fifty, a hundred, two hundred, or even three hundred years to achieve that end, so be it. But it will be achieved!"

Having finished her prophecy, she turned her attention to the immediate work to be done. Margaret looked at her children, and said, "Everyone get ready for breakfast. Robert, you get the plates."

Resolutely, she marched toward the kitchen with her children following her steps. She clutched her kerchief in one hand, but refused to put it to her eyes since she wanted to present a confident countenance before her children. Bracing herself, she prepared to heat up breakfast. She gave another brief prayer, this time of thanksgiving, because her neighbors brought food yesterday and she only needed to warm up some pan-fried potatoes, baked apples, and frizzled pork chops. There were ashcakes already cooling near the fireplace.

As Margaret removed the last of the dishes from the table and put the remaining food away, she turned to her children and said, "We have to get ready to receive friends and mourners. You have about an hour to dress in your church clothes before our neighbors start dropping by to pay their respects. They will come to our house off and on all day, probably until late tonight."

Still eating the last morsel of his ashcake, John asked, "Why do they pay their respects?"

"Son, paying respects means that our people and white neighbors who knew your daddy will come to our home and tell us how much they loved your father. They just want to let us know that they are sorry that he passed away. Now you all get up to your rooms! You want to look nice when they pay their respects."

Robert Junior turned away and ran to his room. Raleigh and John, rushing behind Robert Junior, moved upstairs quickly. They played the "Who can dress the fastest?" game. Ann followed her mother to the master bedroom, where they dressed in preparation for receiving their visitors.

They buried Robert Senior the following day.

> Thus saith the Lord; A voice was heard in Ramah, lamentation, and bitter
> weeping; Rachel weeping for her children refused to
> be comforted for her children, because they were not.
> Jeremiah 31:15 KJV

Samuel Garlington walked upon the porch, knocked on the door, and announced his presence. Margaret recognized him as one of the Wiccocomico Church officials. He was also the administrator of her deceased husband's property. Standing there, holding his hat and twisting the band in his big hands, he kept his eyes directed on the toes of his boots. Finally, he raised his head and cleared his throat.

"Mrs. Pinn, I am here to talk to you about the court order of May 15. I thought you would want a copy of this order. I hope this is a good time to visit."

As soon as she heard his words, she dropped her head in sorrow. Her thin, frail shoulders were bent, but only for a moment. She knew that this order was just another act in the continuing saga of a family that was being forced into dispersion for years; another chapter in the book of Wiccocomico tribal destruction. With the death of her husband, the next step was the settlement of Robert Senior's estate. She drew upon her reserves of strength. "Yes, this is as good a time as any. Thank you and come in."

"Here is a copy of the court papers." Mr. Garlington reluctantly handed them to her.

She reviewed the court order.

> Upon the motion of Samuel Garlington, said administrator of Robert Pinn, Deceased, John Gaines, Josias Gaskins, John Dameron and Andrew Chilton or any three of them are appointed to meet sometime before the next court (being first Sworn by the next Justice) and approve the Estate of the said Deceased...and Ordered that the administrator as aforesaid exhibit an inventory thereof on oath to the next Court.
>
> May 15, 1734, Northumberland Co.
> (Order Book B 1729–1737, p. 146)

Although Margaret did not tell Mr. Garlington what she was thinking at the time, she had begun to feel the weight of financial pressures coming down on her. Robert had been a very prosperous farmer until his health began to fail him. Having no idea how to manage the farm on her own during her husband's long illness, she used their savings and farm produce profits to run the household and feed her family. Since she did not have another male adult to help her, their farm's productivity went down quickly. She recalled the death of another Indian man who had passed away a few months ago. Margaret had gone to console his wife. Now she found herself in the same circumstances, with the threat of poverty and lack of male support looming over her head. She rehearsed in her mind the official court procedures, since the ritual was so well known to her. *First, the court will settle the estate of the deceased. Next, they will start figuring out a way to take the burden off the wife by having the court find upstanding citizens to take the children. Finally, the court will order the Indian children into indentured servitude.*

It all sounded so considerate and Christian. However, Margaret cynically realized that it was strange that it helped the "upstanding" white citizens more than the Indians.

"Mr. Garlington, Robert's sickness was hard on his finances," Margaret explained. "You know about his debts and what he was going through. He was a well-to-do person in Indian Town. Now look at us. We are headed to disaster. Our property will be sold off little by little. Then they will tell me how my children can be protected with this law that they have. You call it indentured servitude."

Once again, Mr. Garlington's eyes fell to his boots.

Margaret continued, "The court will start sending my children into this indentured servitude soon. The officials encourage Indian children to leave their homes when one or both parents die. They will not even wait until I am dead before they start eyeing my children. They won't have the courtesy to wait until I am dead. They will rush to make them work in their great tobacco fields."

Mr. Garlington tried to sound encouraging. "Mrs. Pinn, you have time to deal with these possibilities and work through them. You may find that you can take care of your children without letting the court assign them. I am not here to tell you what to do about those matters. I just brought you the court orders concerning your husband's estate."

Realizing that he was just the messenger, she replied, "Thank you, Mr. Garlington. I am sorry for my rude manners. I hope you can understand."

"You don't need to apologize, Mrs. Pinn. I just pray when I die that my wife does not have to go through the things that I have seen happen in Indian families during the last few years. These are bad times, Mrs. Pinn, not just for Indian people, but for all citizens. These are hard years that we are living in now, and I understand some of what you are going through.

Your husband was a good man, and I saw him as more than an Indian. He was as good as any white man. I want you to know how I feel."

"Thank you, Mr. Garlington."

"Good day, Mrs. Pinn." With that remark, he jammed his hat back on his head, turned, and marched back toward town.

Margaret sincerely appreciated Mr. Garlington's visit and comments. She heard what he had said—that remark about Robert being as good as any white man. After considering the remark, she decided that he did not realize what he had implied. She wondered, *I think he meant that as a commendation on Robert's character. I know he liked Robert, and I cannot be mad at him for suggesting that most Indian men are not as good as white men.* She did not waste any more time thinking about Mr. Garlington's remarks. Instead, Margaret set herself in the place of Rachel, the matriarch of the Bible, and empathized with her as she saw Israel's desolate state and her orphaned children. Just as Rachel wept bitterly for Israel and her heirs, Margaret lamented openly for her children. While her children played in the yard, she took advantage of the quiet time in her parlor to think about the past, present, and future.

Margaret continued to deliberate on the Wiccocomico dispersion, long after Samuel Garlington's departure from her house. She wept bitterly as she wondered what would happen to her children. Her family had suffered financially after her husband's death. Similarly, as a result of family poverty, Indian children all over the area were going into servitude. She was alarmed that Samuel Garlington arrived at her house before she had seized the moment to tell her sons that they might be living and working on other families' farms in the future. Margaret had seen some of the little children walking near the huge tobacco plantations. They were crying because they were made indentured servants. These future braves were reduced to a state of servitude on behalf of and in the name of the new English system.

On that occasion, she wondered, *How long will these children work in those large fields? A month? A year? A decade? Will they ever go back to their parents? Who will teach them to fish, to master the bow and arrow, or to track game? Surely their chief will rescue them! Will they lose their Indian culture on those colonists' farms?*

Now she shed more bitter tears as she held the open Bible with her fingers pointing to Jeremiah 31:15. She cried aloud, "Rachel, help me!" Then, immediately, Margaret realized that Rachel did not have any power to help her because she too had lamented over her own children. Margaret exclaimed, "In the name of Jesus Christ, Lord, please help my children!"

A time to get, and a time to lose; ...
Ecclesiastes 3:6

2

Indentured Servitude

1743

It was a frigid, blustery afternoon in Wiccocomico. The mid-January air, sweeping off the Chesapeake Bay, penetrated the Pinn children's skin as they worked in the barn that unusually cold day.

Robert Junior, John, and Raleigh worked briskly at their farm chores, rubbing their hands together and moving their feet in a running motion while standing in place. They kept their bodies warm by jumping around as they fed the hogs and threw hay out for the cow and calf.

Raleigh envied his ancestors, remembering stories he had heard about how warm animal skins and furs were against their skin. Raleigh remarked to his brothers, "Wouldn't it be good to have those warm animal furs on our bodies today? The windy hawk is ripping us every time we stick our heads around the barn corner." Shivering, he wrapped his arms around his chest.

Robert, the elder of the three boys, told his brothers to stop complaining. "Those Wiccocomico warriors could hunt in the forests and fish on the bay in this kind of weather even without shirts on their bodies. They didn't get cold because they knew how to cast the thoughts of pain out of their minds. John and Raleigh, try to pretend that you are not freezing, and you will find out that you are not as chilly."

Raleigh responded indignantly, "You try it. Don't try to tell me what to do when you cannot do it yourself. You are jumping around out here more than us."

The boys, wearing homemade breeches and wool shirts, wished they had warm coats to fight off the wind.

"You want to borrow my wool shirt, Raleigh? I am not cold. I am like a Wiccocomico warrior. I am tough and don't need a shirt because my skin can resist the wind. I can control pain in my mind," Robert bragged as he pointed to his chest and then acted like he was about to take off his shirt.

John spoke up. "Robert Junior, I am going in the house and tell mother that you are about to get sick out here with no shirt on your body."

"If you go in that house, we will know that you are just cold and want to get warm. I will not take off my shirt if you will promise not to tell mother what I was getting ready to do. She has so many worries in her heart, and she doesn't need you running in there with a new burden for her," Junior stated.

The cold airy house added to her worry about her children's health. It was almost as cold in the house as the windy twenty-five-degree temperature outside. While the boys were working outside, Margaret, clad in a dull brown woolen dress, appeared to be at least fifteen years over her true age of forty-eight. She heard a knock on the door and opened it to a stranger. He was a court representative bringing her more sad news as if she had not gotten her fair share of suffering already.

He came to the point quickly. "I am an assistant from the Northumberland Courthouse. I have some news regarding your son, Robert."

"Please come in," she responded hospitably, realizing how cold it was outside, still fearing the news that he was about to drop on her already overloaded mind. "I apologize for the draft in this house. I was just ready to put some more wood in the stove before you came. I guess I should have done it when I thought about it."

He hastened to reassure her. "No, don't go to any trouble to heat up the house. I am not cold, for it is much warmer in here than outside. Please let me get to the reason for my visit. I have a piece of paper here with the court order for your son, Robert Junior."

Instantly alarmed, she put one hand to her heart. Her distress was evident on her face. "What did my son do? He is a good child. I don't know why the court would fret about his behavior."

"No, Mrs. Pinn, Robert Junior has not done anything. We have an indentured servitude order here to help him with his food and clothes." At this point, he raised the document in his right hand. "This paper also guarantees that he will continue improving his reading and writing skills and get training in the cooper trade."

During the last decade, Robert Senior seemed to get further behind in his financial obligations for seed and other farm items. It is said that for years, before the settlers came, tribal members did not have to purchase seed and other occupational supplies from white men. God provided them naturally, and Robert and his fellow Wiccocomico were free to secure abundant supplies from nature. Now the family faced unpaid debts and their consequences.

Bitterly, Margaret replied, "Years ago, our people did not worry about barrels. We had everything we needed to be happy and healthy. Now they have all these new English things, and you want my son to help them make those fancy gadgets." Margaret expressed her disappointment with the order even though she herself had forecasted this very court order years ago. Now, to her dismay, she saw the long-ago vision showing up on her doorstep in the present tense.

"Let me read the order for you, Mrs. Pinn," the man offered.

Drawing herself up to her full height, she stated with rough dignity, "I can read and write too, so you don't have to read for me. I don't mean to be rude to you. I just don't like to get news from the Northumberland Court. Every time the officials bring those court papers to my house, I see darkness and dark clouds. There is never any bright, happy, rainbow kind of news. You just bring bad news."

The stranger was irritated, unable to fathom why she would not welcome the plan of the court. "Mrs. Pinn, it is good news for your son," he said earnestly. "You will miss him, I know, but you need to help us plan his future."

Margaret was offended by this visitor's remark. "Please don't tell me about planning futures. If those English people had only stayed in London or wherever they came from, my boys would have had plenty of food from the soil and the ocean. They would not be hungry like they are now. They would have warm clothing from the skins of animals, not the fancy, thin white man's clothing materials." She raised her voice and her hands found their way to her hips. "If the English had stayed in London, my boys would be skilled archers, bow and tomahawk makers, hunters, farmers, and medicine makers. Our men would have taught them skills in everything that they would need for the future."

Then her body seemed to sag, as if the weight of the world, the court order, had just been placed on her chilly shoulders. She reached for her heavy wrap shawl with trembling work-worn hands and slowly put it on. She pulled the shawl tightly against her chest, as if the cold air had chilled her bones. Her deliberate, unhurried pace was due less to the chill in the house and more to her dread in having to tell Robert Junior the awful news.

Ann, now eleven years old, came into the room. Seeing the heaviness of heart in her mother's facial expression as well as in her posture and general demeanor, she stopped and just looked down at the floor. She remained quiet since there was a stranger in the room.

As Margaret prepared to bring Robert to the house, questions raced through her mind. *How can I explain this to Junior? What do I tell Ann when I get back? What explanation do I give the other boys?* She trudged slowly to the barn, the stranger silently following her steps.

Robert and the other boys had been cutting firewood from fallen trees they found in the forest. As Margaret came around the house and headed toward the barn with the man, Robert was just putting away the axe while John and Raleigh finished stacking the wood against the barn. Robert was getting ready to pick up an armload of wood when his mother and the stranger interrupted him. The court representative seemed very tall as he looked down on the Pinn boys who were unusually tall for their ages. Robert—a spindly five-foot-eight fourteen-year-old boy—looked up at the stranger as the man came closer.

Examining the man closely from beneath partially closed lids, Robert Junior thought he had seen him before in the church. Believing that he was one of the church wardens, he was so scared that his heart began to race, and he could hear and feel blood gushing through his veins. Years earlier, Robert remembered the officials ordering his father to report to the courthouse for one thing or another. Sometimes the orders frustrated his dad and irritated his normally reserved Christian mother. Robert, John, and Raleigh were apprehensive whenever the word "court," was mentioned.

"Robert," the man stated in a formal monotone fashion, "the court has ordered you to report tomorrow morning to the Northumberland County courthouse. Your mother will come with you. I understand that you will become an indentured servant of Thomas Doggett of this county." The man paused and lowered the paper. "I should not really have told you the person that the court will put you with, but you seem so scared that I felt I must tell you the nature of the court order." He paused and then asked, "Are you all right?"

"Yes, sir," Robert replied even though it was difficult to force the two words from his mouth.

The man nodded and then moved away to allow Margaret to talk to her son.

His mother hugged him. "Robert Junior, are you scared?" His mother often called him Robert Junior on formal occasions as it was her way of revealing what she considered his nobility. She often explained that she called him Junior because his great-grandfather—the Great Man—as well as his father had both been named Robert. Although the surname Pinn had been misspelled or corrupted from the original spelling of the first Robert—Robert Pekwem or Robert Pewem—Robert Junior knew that all their names were really Robert Pinn. Therefore, he and his father always went in formal settings as the "Junior" and "Senior." If it were not for the fact that Robert "the Great Man" Pinn had a son named John Pinn instead of Robert, who named his son Robert Pinn, then there would have been four

Robert Pinns in succession. There would have been Robert "the Great Man" Pinn, Robert Pinn Junior, Robert III, and Robert IV.

Robert in an affectionate tone to his mother, replied "*Tla,* madam." No, madam. He often reverted to his Cherokee heritage in oral communication. He told her that he was not afraid.

His mother took a deep breath and said, "Robert, tomorrow you must report to the Northumberland Courthouse to meet Mr. Doggett. He will take care of you." She tried to paint as good a picture as possible even though her own heart was breaking. "He will give you more food for your tall, lanky body and teach you how to read and write better. The good man will also put more clothes on your back. The hawkish air is blowing out here today."

Robert recollected how he had just bragged about his tough skin, and now his mother informs him that he needed more clothes next to his body.

Stoically, he stood in silence, but he wanted to ask his mother a dozen questions. *What is this man doing to our family? Is he saying that mother has not been taking care of us? He must be trying to make John and Raleigh feel neglected because he never mentioned a word about what they needed. What about Mother and Ann? Don't they both need warm clothes too?* However, he remained silent.

The man walked with Margaret back around the house where they stopped and talked privately. The boys walked slowly at a distance behind them, as if their mother had given them a cue to stay back. The visitor then climbed into his buggy and told his horse, "Get up."

Margaret, hesitating at the foot of the front porch, raised a hand to the court official as his horse and buggy moved down the dirt road. She turned and walked back to where the four children waited. They stood like soldiers, waiting for their mother to give the order to move forward.

"Lord, what will I say to Robert Junior?" Margaret prayed as she deliberately walked slowly toward her children. Her eyes were fixed on her eldest son. The short walk from the porch to the back corner of the house where the children's feet were fixed to the ground seemed to take forever. Margaret hoped that the walk would be long enough to give her time to think about what she would say to Robert and the other children. She hoped in vain, for her time for speculating ran out before she could frame an explanation. She stood before her four children and all she saw were sad large black eyes looking up toward her tired, even sadder, gaze.

Margaret asked them to go to the parlor, then turned and led the way. She was sure that her children were strong-willed. They followed her steps in militia precision as she thought, *These boys are tough and will make fine workers and even soldiers one day. I know they will represent our Wiccocomico people well! Ann is also a hardworking girl.*

The children all sat on the davenport as Margaret pulled a chair closer. She spent the next hour attempting to explain why the visitor had come to Wiccocomico. Their mother was extremely open and honest with them and suggested that one or both of the other boys would also go into indentured servitude.

When there was nothing left to be said, the boys went back to their chores outside while Ann and her mother returned to their household responsibilities. They continued to work, trying to maintain an air of normalcy. It was nearly dinnertime when their mother stopped cleaning long enough to prepare supper. Shortly afterward, Margaret struck a metal triangle hanging on the porch, summoning her family to the table for their last dinner meal together. She had lovingly set the table with their best china, taking particular care to make the table look its best. After saying the blessing, Margaret passed the bowls containing their meager fare—beef and vegetable soup and ashcakes. Although the children were unusually quiet and subdued, she talked to them as she ate. The food tasted like ashes in her mouth.

They went to bed that gusty night at eight o'clock, feeling the chilly breezes invading their dwelling. Margaret agonized over Robert Junior's trip to the courthouse tomorrow morning. Throughout the unusually long night, she wept intermittently. In the meantime, John, Raleigh, and Ann cried themselves to sleep quickly. Robert kept his eyes open the whole night, hoping that the sun would not rise to announce a new day. He had Indian friends who became indentured servants and knew the horrible effect their abrupt departures had on their family members. He worried little about the cruel hard work that would be heaped upon him, but lost sleep over the breakup of his family.

"First, my daddy left by dying. Tomorrow, it is my turn to leave my home. Next, it will be John and Raleigh's turn to give up this life at Wiccocomico. The Pinn family home life is dying each day."

Despite his wishes, the morning inevitably arrived. Robert left home that morning to go to Northumberland Courthouse, not knowing if he would ever see his home again. His mother went to the courthouse with him and came back home that afternoon.

When she opened the front door, she appeared to John and Raleigh to have aged many years; they saw white streaks in her hair that previously had been dark. She stepped over the threshold and closed the door firmly behind her. Her head was bent over as though she carried the weight of the whole Wiccocomico Indian Town as well as her troubled household on her shoulders. She leaned against the door, breathing deeply as though she had sprinted rather than walked from the courthouse.

Margaret heaved a sigh, pushed away from the door, and marched forward. She seemed oblivious to her environment, as if she were sleepwalking, and sat down in her chair in the parlor. Since she did not sit on the davenport, her children got the message that she did not want them to sit beside her; they knew she desired solitude. Unsure what to do, they remained in their places, silently waiting for her to return from her reclusion.

Margaret gazed at the spot in the room where Robert Senior had lain in his coffin almost ten years earlier. Ann, John, and Raleigh continued to stand quietly. After meditating for about ten minutes—although it seemed much more to the children—she lifted her head quickly and looked straight at them. She motioned to them with her hand to come to her chair because words would not come out. Moving to the davenport to make room for them, she pulled them down beside her. Margaret sat stiffly, holding her chest with both hands as if she were trying to steady her heart, which had become increasingly wild during the last decade. Then she breathed slowly and deliberately and once again tried to express her thoughts.

"Children," she said with a quivering tone, "I had to leave our Junior Great Man at the courthouse today. He is going to live with the Doggetts. You know them. They are the nice people over . . . over . . . over . . ." She wiped her eyes quickly with her lace handkerchief, valiantly trying to stem the tide, but the tears flowed faster and faster. "He will not come back here to live with us anymore until he is twenty-one years old." She paused before adding, "They sometimes keep them longer."

In her mind, she could still see the words of the court order:

> Robert Pinn, orphan of Robert Pinn (Dec), is by this court bound to Thomas Doggett of the County til [sic] he attains the age of twenty-one years. His master is to teach him to read and write and the trade of a cooper, and to [provide] . . . lodging, and apparel and at the expiration of his service to pay and allow him as is appointed for servants by indentured or custom.
> Northumberland County Court
> January 13, 1743
> Order Book 1743–1752

Margaret saw the fear in the eyes of her children and tried to explain what the court order meant for Robert and how things would be better for him. "He will have more food and clothing. Maybe he will learn to read better and come back here to help you children with your learning." She hoped this would comfort the children.

Raleigh had begun to think more deeply about serious family matters and realized that his mother's remarks did not make sense. He thought to himself, *She is trying to make us feel like Robert will come back to help us read and write. She forgot that less than a minute ago she told us he will not come back to our house again until he is twenty-one or older.* Raleigh second-guessed her privately. *Did she give Junior away to the colonists after telling him to keep the tribe together? Why, Mother?* In his secret heart, he was very angry with her. *I wonder who is next. Ann? Me? John?*

Even though he was still a young boy, Raleigh realized that this was not the time to ask her to explain what she had done. He signaled to John and Ann to keep quiet, as he knew that they also had questions for their mother. Raleigh knew she had too much stress on her to have the will and strength to explain what she had done at the courthouse this dreadful day.

Without asking permission to leave the room, the children stood up, turned from the parlor, and went to their rooms. Feeling their anger against her rising but still wanting to spare her from having to explain why she left Junior at the courthouse, they hastened up the stairs, forgetting to eat their supper. They were strong enough to hold back their tears until they had closed the doors to their rooms. Sinking their faces into their pillows, they cried themselves to sleep.

Unable to sleep long, Raleigh awoke in the evening and went downstairs. He found his mother still sitting at the table, looking into her full bowl of vegetable soup, which had become cold and congealed. She gazed at that soup as if she were looking through the bowl. He stood against the kitchen wall waiting for his mother to acknowledge his presence, but she did not see him. She only stared into the bowl. Raleigh realized she was worried about Robert Junior. He knew he had been so angry with her for returning home without Robert that he hadn't considered her reasons. *Mother was always the one who told Robert and John to protect Ann and me and even told Robert to never leave us alone.*

At that moment, Raleigh understood exactly what had happened. During the ten minutes he had stood against the kitchen wall, he thought about his mother's actions. He had watched his mother become a very old-looking woman in just one day. Now he felt an overwhelming pity for her because she knew she could not prevent what had happened. *She did not intentionally leave Robert. She had to leave him. The judge made her leave him. That is what happened. The judge did it!*

While he stood there thinking about his mother, Ann and John came quietly from their rooms. Feeling the hunger pangs in their stomachs, they joined Raleigh and stood against the wall with their hands behind their backs, watching their mother. It took another fifteen minutes for her to raise her head. She had so much on her mind that she still did not see them standing there.

John whispered to Raleigh, "Daddy died and she tried to raise us alone. She thinks that she has failed us because she lost Junior."

When Margaret finally realized that her children were standing against the wall, she signaled to them to come to the kitchen table and sit down. Pushing her cold soup away, she put her elbows on the table. "Children, remember after your daddy died I told you that seeds would be blown and taken by fowls to different parts of the colony? Well, those seeds are you. You will be carried away from this house to other areas. I cannot help it. I do not have any control. The colonists have changed our land to some extent by making it into farms and changed our lifestyle and our customs. Now they are taking Indian children to work on their farms. They have more land than they have people to work it. Remember what I told you about table manners? When you pile more food on your plate than you can possibly expect to eat, you are going against God's law and are becoming a glutton. You will make yourself sick and take food from other people at the table."

Raleigh thought, *She doesn't eat much anymore, and I always thought she was too worried to want any food. Now I know! She is leaving half of her food portion to add to our portions.*

Margaret looked at each child in turn as she spoke. "Well, the colonists are doing just that! They have more land than they can possibly farm. Now they are bloated and fat with land and they are sick that they don't have enough people to work the farms. The colonists have their family members as well as some slaves, but now they are looking over at our farm for people to help them. They are gluttons. They are full with land and people, but they still want more land and people. Remember that time when John took more food from the serving bowls than he could possibly consume when we had plenty of food in this house? Well, you know that he got sick. He messed up the kitchen table, the floor, and his vomit made us so sick that we couldn't eat. Well, the colonists want our children. They have children and slaves, but now they want our Indian children. Now the court is allowing them to take our children. We don't have to let them go, but we are poor and hungry. They are fat and full with land and other valuable things, but they still want to consume our children. As a result, I am sick today because the colonists are gluttons. You are sick because your brother is not here with us. Our family is disappearing more and more each day. John, you will be the next one to go, and then Raleigh." She drew a big breath and glanced at the face of each of her children before continuing. "Remember what I have told you. You must retain the Indian ways. If they will not let you live as a tribe together you must have the tribe in your heart. They cannot remove the Indian from your heart. They may cut the heart out, but the Indian is still there. You are the only one who has control over what you feel in your heart. If you love the great Wiccocomico heritage, keep it. If you appreciate the Rechahecrian heritage, retain it. Tell your children and children's children about it. Don't let the Indian die. We are thousands of years old and these colonists must not destroy us, and since we know that God's promise is true, they will not kill our heritage. Protect your seeds. Don't let them go to waste. You, children, will be instruments of God to protect our aboriginal culture. Don't forget it! You can destroy your own people just by forgetting your heritage. You must remember this!"

She did not have to say anything else. Her children understood this as her apology for coming home without Robert. They nodded, indicating that they accepted her unspoken apology.

As his mother remained at the table, looking dejected and wiping her eyes, Raleigh told his siblings, "Now we know that it was beyond her control. Mother did it because she wanted to provide food, shelter, and clothing for Junior and because of our family debts. Since our old Indian ways of hunting and living have been destroyed, we must survive. Since we have to eat, and do not have enough food to feed our whole family through the winter, she did what she thought would keep us healthy and alive, and pay our debts."

At the kitchen table that night, they learned that there were some good mixed up with the bad. Robert left home, that was bad, but Robert had food to eat and clothes to wear, that was good! He had a chance to learn, write, and read more English, and that was good!

"Children, you are in a powerful colonial society, and we have to adjust to that change. The old Indian ways are disappearing. As dew dries on the grass with the movement of the sun in the east, so are our ways drying up with the movement of the English people from the East to the West. I have been told by the court officials that Robert will learn to make barrels, that he will be a cooper. That is good!" She then added, "We must coexist with the white man or die! If we don't like it, we have to leave Northumberland. Otherwise, we must start making those English barrels!"

Six months later, on a hot, humid day with the sun spiking the temperature above ninety-five degrees, Robert Junior was working in a tobacco field with several other men. Margaret and her children, by providence, elected that very day to walk to town to buy some essential household items. Her meager funds restricted any unnecessary purchases. They were strolling on the sandy dirt road that stretched between six-mile long tobacco fields. Virginia tobacco farmers satisfied the cavernous appetites that England had for American tobacco products.

The workers tended miles of tobacco plants in the moist scorching heat. Ann, in playful jest, decided to sprint about five hundred yards ahead of Raleigh, John, and their mother. Raleigh, deciding to show how swiftly his bare feet could move, caught up with her in a few seconds. As he looked over to the right side of the road, he caught a glimpse of a boy who looked just like Junior. With the sun shining over Raleigh's shoulder, he saw Robert Junior clearly.

Pointing toward the tobacco field, Raleigh turned and called to his mother. "I see Junior over there! Look, Mother!" Then he stepped toward the edge of the road and cried out to his brother. "Junior! Junior! We are over here!"

Junior did not respond because he was about one thousand yards away from the road, and the sun was shining directly into his eyes.

"Junior! Junior! We are over here! Over here!" Raleigh yelled.

Junior, however, continued to work feverishly, sweating as he worked with the plants and did not hear or see his brother.

Cupping both hands to his mouth as he attempted to shout to his brother, Raleigh felt his mother's hand on his mouth as she stopped his attempt to get Junior's attention.

"Mother, I want to let Junior know we see him."

"No, son, don't call him. He does not want you to see him in this state."

Raleigh stared up at her in disbelief.

"Junior is wiping his eyes and sweating as he digs around the plants. Can't you see that he is caught up in a cycle of crying, wiping his eyes with the back of his sweaty palm, digging around the tobacco plants, and crying again? He doesn't want your pity."

Raleigh understood what his mother meant because he knew how proud Robert Junior was. He remembered that cold day in January when Junior attempted to show them how his tough body could take the frigid air.

"I see him crying because his body is hot and tired," Raleigh suspected. "I think he wants to be home with us! That is why he is crying."

They passed by Junior without saying anything further to get his attention. As they moved away from Junior, their tears increased with each step. Margaret cried the most while they continued their walk toward town.

When they left town, Margaret told them that they must walk home on the back road to avoid seeing Robert Junior again. Justifying her reason for traveling this road, she said, "You don't want Junior knowing that we saw him crying out there in those tobacco fields. Let us just go back home so he will never know that we know he is so unhappy."

Before he fell asleep that night, Raleigh heard her crying and praying. He whispered to John, "I heard Mama crying and praying to God for Robert. She is even praying for you, Ann, and me. I heard her. She asked God to make our yoke easy. I did not understand why anyone would want to put a yoke on us. She asked God to protect us and not let us suffer with a burden of weight like Robert. I know Mother is worried about us."

After that night, John and Raleigh tried to reassure and relieve her worries and said that they would not mind being indentured servants.

"Mother, if we become servants, we will learn a trade, get new clothes, and have more food to eat. We will even learn to read and write better. The judge will make the person in charge of us teach us well and take care of us, and the judge will not let our master be mean to us like Junior's master." Raleigh said this to take a heavy burden off his mother who was now struggling to feed, clothe, and care for the family.

John told Raleigh and Ann not to eat all of the food on their plates because their mother was not eating much anymore. She gave them more food on their plates as she reduced her own portion.

Raleigh thought, *She keeps giving most of her food to us. I don't understand it. She is hungry. She is always saying, 'Eat all your food. You are growing boys!' We are growing and she is getting skinny. Mother used to be a pretty woman, but now her skin is hanging off her bony frame, and she looks so old.* Raleigh thought about John's words to Ann and him. *I thought it was because she was worrying about Robert Junior. She is starving because she saves food for us!"*

Summer 1751

Making regular visits to the county courthouse, Margaret kept abreast of her boys' servitude assignments. She always went straight to the section where the indentured servant records were kept.

In June 1751, William and Helen Downing took over the care of Robert. He had a new master. The court order read:

> Robert Pinn, son of Margaret Pinn. Consent is by court bound to William Downing and Helen his wife til [sic] he attains the age of twenty-one years. His master is to learn him to read and write and the trade of a shoemaker and to find and provide him with sufficient wholesome and cleanly diet, lodging, and apparel. At the expiration of the servitude to pay and allow him as is appointed for servants by indentured or custom.
>
> Northumberland County Court
> June 14, 1751

She carefully recorded Robert Junior's recent assignment to William Downing's home and carried a handwritten copy home. As soon as she arrived home, she called Ann to come to the parlor. "Ann, I found out today that Robert Junior is working for William and Helen Downing." Since they could not be involved directly in Robert's life, she made sure that Ann knew his current location.

By this time, John and Raleigh were also working as indentured servants. After Margaret became unable to give her two youngest boys proper clothing and sufficient food due to her poor financial situation, they were bound to masters and worked away from home. Contrary to the wishes of Margaret and her deceased husband, their boys had been caught in the acculturation process, whereby Indian children were becoming white and taking on colonial customs.

Summer 1754

On August 25, 1754, Raleigh saw John for the first time since they left home. John sat in the courtroom with a Mr. Hayden of Lancaster County, and Raleigh sat behind him with Mr. Garner of Northumberland. Raleigh was ready to leave Lancaster to go to Northumberland while John would leave Northumberland County to take up residence with the household of the Haydens in Lancaster County.

The unusually cloudy August morning seemed to accentuate the boys' despondent moods. Even the courtroom, with all its windows, seemed darker than usual. Both Raleigh and John had been there before as indentured servants waiting for their verdicts.

One of the clerks signaled to the boys' masters to come to the judge's chambers. As John and Raleigh stood up with them, the clerk told them to wait in the courtroom. Raleigh decided to walk around the courtroom to work off his tension. John remained in his seat, waiting for the judge to complete the indentured servitude transactions. The brothers kept looking at each other. Not knowing whether they should greet each other in the formal courtroom environment, Raleigh fixed his eyes on the judge's desk as if the judge had already returned. They continued waiting, hoping to talk to each other when the legal process came to an end.

John sat on the first center bench and Raleigh, by this time, stood near the back of the courtroom. John, dressed in his clean Sunday clothes, hid his bare feet under the court bench. He wore a white cotton shirt and blue breeches. His straight black hair was combed back as if he were trying to impress his new master with his clean appearance. John, occasionally turning to look at his brother, wondered when he would have an opportunity to take charge of his own future rather than have the judge decide his destiny.

Raleigh was attired in black breeches and a blue cut-at-the-elbow shirt, and he wore his own handmade brown shoes. As he leaned against the wall, rocking back and forth from his left foot to his right, he also thought of the influence that the judge's decisions would have. He bit his lips as he became stressed with pessimistic anticipations of future events.

Raleigh silently fumed, *How long are they going to pass me around from one place to another? I am not a child any longer, so why don't the judges release me from this slave work? I should have been released from this servitude a year ago. They say they are looking out for me by giving me shelter and food, but I don't need their charity. They must let me go so I can start my own family. Will it be this way the rest of my life?*

He remembered reading and reciting God's promise in Psalm 121:8:

> The Lord shall preserve thy going out and thy coming
> in from this time forth, and even for evermore.

Just then the judge returned from his chamber with William Garner and Ezekil Hayden. They called both boys forward and informed them that they would be assigned to new masters.

The judge informed Raleigh, who had been working for Richard Seldon in Lancaster County, that he would be under the care of William Garner of Northumberland County. The judge ordered that William Garner be paid for caring for "Rawleigh."

> 25 Aug. 1754 – To William Garner of this County for
> taking up Rawleigh Pinn, a servant boy belonging to
> Richard Seldon of Lancaster, 90 lbs. tobacco.
> Order Book 1753–56, p. 213

The judge told John, who had been working for Richard Hudnall of Northumberland County, that he would become an indentured servant for Ezekil Hayden of Lancaster County.

> 25 Aug. 1754 – Ezekil Hayden of Lancaster County
> for taking up John Pinn, a servant man belonging to
> Richard Hudnall of this County, 90 lbs. tobacco.
> Order Book 1753–56, p. 213

Raleigh thought it was sad that indentured servant arrangements did not permit his brother and him to live in the same county. When he left Lancaster to work for William Garner of Northumberland, John was ordered on the same day, August 25, to leave Northumberland County to work for Ezekil Hayden of Lancaster County. The officials reversed the locations as if they did not want the two brothers to come into contact with each other.

This new servitude system became the rule rather than the exception for Indian children in the area.

As Mr. Garner and Mr. Hayden walked together toward the judge's chamber, Raleigh and John hugged each other for the first time since their indentured assignments. They were able to talk together for about twenty minutes on the courthouse steps while the two white men were conversing with the judge in his chambers. They joyfully sought news about each other's adventures, their pains and joys since their parting.

"John, it is great to see you! What have you been doing? Where have you been?"

"I'm doing well. I've been working for Mr. Hudnall, a farmer in Northumberland. Where have you been?" John was eager for any knowledge of his brother's life as he and Raleigh had not written letters to each other since their assignments in the indentured servitude system.

"I worked for Mr. Seldon in Lancaster, but now I am being assigned to Mr. Garner of this county." Then Raleigh declared quickly, as if it were urgent to share the news before their new masters came back to get them, "John, we must leave the Northern Neck area and join up with another tribe or else we will lose our Indian hearts. We are becoming whiter and whiter with the passage of each calendar page. It is really strange that we are getting lighter and lighter in our heart—rather than darker—with the rising of each summer sun. Our culture is turning white! We are losing our Indian ways. For seven nights in a row I had nightmares. I saw giant gulls, much like the gulls that flew over the great Wiccocomico Indian Town, and now fly over Northumberland and Lancaster counties, only larger. The gulls came down on some seeds in the field in Indian Town, snatched them up, and flew like lightning toward the west. They traveled under the shelter of the sun. As the sun moved over an area, the gulls flew. The gulls flew in my dream over a two-night period, carrying the seeds in a westward direction. Then the gulls dropped the seeds and flew back toward the eastern ocean as if they realized they had gone beyond their natural boundaries. Then sparrows flew down and picked up the seeds that had been deposited by the gulls. They also flew in a westward direction for two nights, and then they became weary and dropped to the ground, exhausted and famished. They spat the seeds on the ground as they panted for breath. Then I dreamed for two nights that there was a mighty fight between sparrows, which would not die on the ground, and huge vultures, which waited for the sparrows to die. The sparrows fought bravely against the cannibalistic vultures that wanted to eat the dying sparrows. The sparrows resisted the vultures for two days. When they died, the seeds had taken root on the ground. The vultures consumed the sparrows and looked for the seeds to eat but could not find them. Therefore, the vultures waited for the seeds to produce plants so that they could pluck them up. They had now become herb-eating creatures rather than meat-eating fowls."

John listened thoughtfully. He knew the importance of dreams well.

"Finally, one night, just as about half of the seeds sprouted forth plants, an eagle flew down seconds ahead of the vultures and snatched the plants up with its mighty claws. The vultures pursued the eagle, but he soared up so high that the vultures became weary and dropped back to a large decaying tree and waited there for the other seeds to germinate. They would eventually consume the other plants. These plants represented the Wiccocomico tribe. The eagle with the plants, however, flew to a small mountain ridge and rested with the plants in his mouth. He dropped half of the plants in his mouth near a place known as Stonewall and the other half in a certain spot on the mountain known as Buffalo. Then I saw the book of Isaiah open to chapter 40, verse 31, before my eyes in my dream.

> But they that wait upon the Lord shall renew their strength; they shall mount up with wings as eagles; they shall run, and not be weary; and they shall walk, and not faint.

Raleigh continued, "John, the dreams and nightmares are signs from the Lord. The Lord wants you and me to keep on waiting because he has something great for us. We shall mount up with wings as eagles. We are weary now. We are working ourselves to death in those tobacco fields, but there will come a time when we shall not be weary. There will come a time when we will not faint under the hot sun in the giant tobacco and maize fields of Northumberland and Lancaster Counties. There will be a time when our fingers will not be numb and dirty from the tobacco resin. There will be a time when we will not have painful backs and shoulders in those three-mile long tobacco fields. There will come a time when we will own similar fields and the tobacco will be for our possessions. We will own livestock for our own welfare, not for the colonists."

"Raleigh, do you really think that we will ever be able to leave this area? All the other Indians are either dead, working as indentured servants or slaves, or have gone from the Northern Neck."

"We will go to a mountain region in the west. The eagle in Isaiah 40 will take us there, where the eagles live, in the mountain. I don't know where, and I don't know when. We must wait on the Lord. Let us not be weary in our hard tasks as indentured servants. God has a reason for letting us endure this hardship. Something good is going to come out of this pain like the pearl that forms in the shell of an oyster and endures great pain and agony."

Before they parted company, Raleigh hugged his brother once more.

> But we have this treasure in earthen vessels,
> that the excellency of the power may be of God, and
> not of us.
> 2 Corinthians 4:7

3

Home on the Ridge

1774

"The swamp was dreary and cold. By this time, the people had adjusted to the sad and solitary scenes. This had become their home for a while." Raleigh's brown complexion glowed, and his black eyes snapped with excitement as he shared the well-known story once again with his family. "They had to hide out in the swamps, the dismal swamps, to flee the meanness of the new invaders, the colonists from Europe." Raleigh glanced around, letting his eyes rest on each person in turn. He enjoyed telling his family and tribal members about the glorious past of the Cherokee people in general and his tribe specifically.

The oral traditions, the storytelling on the cold nights of winter and the warm evenings of summer, were the rules. This heritage had been given to Raleigh by Robert, his father, just as Robert's father, John, had given it to Robert. John received his stories from the Great Man of Wiccocomico, Robert Pewem. As he prepared to continue with the story, Raleigh thought, *My son Turner will surely pass these stories on to his descendants as his ancestors and I have done for generations.* He smiled, taking pleasure in the knowledge that the family history would continue.

Raleigh gave one of his frequent history lessons to Turner while Sarah sat quietly near Raleigh, crocheting a white cotton sweater for their son. "Turner, your Cherokee ancestors migrated from the west to the upper Ohio area over a period of many years. They were great travelers. They migrated eastward over the Allegheny Mountains to the Peaks of Otter in Central Virginia. They moved on along the Appomattox River and had sprawling settlements on the riverbanks. They had their own Cherokee chief. They lived peacefully, except for occasional battles with the northern Indians."

Turner reclined on the floor at the feet of his father, who sat in the white oak rocking chair he had made himself. Turner watched his father's face as he spoke. Deliberate in his choice of words, Raleigh carefully recited the story that his father, Robert, told him almost forty years earlier. Turner, reclining on the large bear rug near the fireplace, listened intently as his father told the stories that had been handed down to each succeeding generation. Even at the young age of five, Turner could sense the importance of the story through his father's facial expressions. Raleigh's deep, heartfelt emotions were reflected in his eyes, on his lips, and through his hand motions as he told the story. He often waved his muscular arms to make a point. Raleigh knew that Turner would eventually sit in the white oak rocking chair, surrounded by his sons and daughters. Then Turner would have his turn at the time-honored responsibility of passing the heritage on to his grandchildren.

Rocking gently, Raleigh continued, "We were in a friendly relationship with the Powhatan Indians. God created the aboriginal people from the ground. We protected his earth because we knew that he removed us from the soil. In Iroquoian, our people named themselves *Ani-yun-wiya*, which means 'real people.' The Cherokee always felt that we were God's special people. We didn't think we were better than anyone else, but we knew that God took great care in making us from dirt. The Wyandots or Hurons, who were of the same Iroquoian language group as our people and who lived in the Great Lakes and St. Lawrence Valley, called the Cherokee people *Uwatayo-rono* or 'cave people' and *Entari ronnon*, which means 'mountain people.' They knew that Cherokees were close to the earth as God's creatures of the earth and therefore often made the 'mountain' and 'cave' people references." He paused to make sure his son understood. "So, Turner, my son, never forget that you are made from clay, special clay that has been created by God."

To illustrate his point that the Cherokees are special people, Raleigh carefully picked up the family Bible and held it with reverence at his chest. He turned the pages and read from the Second Epistle to the Corinthians, chapter 4 verses 6 and 7:

> For God, who commanded the light to shine out of darkness, hath shined in our hearts, to give the light of the knowledge of the glory of God in the face of Jesus Christ.
>
> But we have this treasure in earthen vessels, that the excellency of the power may be of God, and not of us. KJV

Slowly, he put the Bible down and picked up two straight pins from the nearby table. Turner watched him closely, sitting up straight and leaning forward just a little.

"Turner, you are never to forget that you are a special creation. You are made from clay but have the real treasure not in the clay, but within the clay. You have this royal Cherokee heritage, priceless, perfected through the travels of the people, their victories in battle and wars, their sufferings and struggles. We are a mixed tribe composed of the defeated and the victorious people. '. . . We have this treasure in earthen vessels, that the excellency of the power may be of God, and not of us.' Turner, as stated in 2 Corinthians 4:7. Let your life—everything you do—reflect the power of God. Don't let any people, regardless of the color of the clay from which God made them, think that they are more special than you are." Here, his voice rose in passion. "Help them realize that they are not any better created. God just used lighter or darker clay. They are still made out of clay, regardless of the color."

Raleigh caught himself at that instance, realizing that he had begun to preach to his young son, and changed the subject to a more concrete reference. With two straight pins in his right hand, he asked, "Turner, what are these?"

"They are two pins."

"What are they?"

"Two pins."

"What are they, Turner?" he asked repeatedly with patience acquired over a lifetime.

After some thought, Turner shouted eagerly, "They can be used to stick you!" He hoped he was getting closer to answering his father's question.

Turning his pins slightly in his hand, Raleigh asked him again, "What are they, Turner? You are getting warm."

Turner smiled, and with eagerness shouted, "A cross! Put them together and you have a cross."

Raleigh wanted to know how he arrived at that conclusion. Turner stated, "Daddy, you wear the cross to church and whenever you wear your Sunday clothes. You wear it to the Cherokee Council meetings. You wear it all the time."

"You are right, Turner. Why do you think I wear the cross?" He realized that the question was a bit hard for Turner and hinted at the answer, "They represent two things that are special to me."

"The cross means Christ!" Turner anticipated that he had one of the correct answers.

"Yes. What else?"

"You love people."

"What people are loved with a special love?"

Turner guessed. "The Buffalo Ridge people, us, and the Stonewall people!"

"You are right, my son." Raleigh smiled broadly. "You are so right. You too must love them if and when you become their chief or leader. They are a special people who have suffered and are in need of protection. We who are strong must bear the infirmities, or sicknesses, of the weak."

Turner considered the words, nodding in childish agreement.

Raleigh continued the lesson, hoping to teach both history and wisdom. "When you put the two pins together they represent more than straight pins to stick in something. They mean togetherness. They mean unity. The pins touching each other represent the two groups, the Ridge and Stonewall groups, coming together. They also represent two important values we hold dearly in our hearts: our love for God and the love we hold for our fellow man. We wear the pins as one item, crossed pins representing the cross of Jesus Christ, our Christian faith, and unity between the two Cherokee bands. They also show the unity that exists between the Cherokee and Wiccocomico peoples. The two pins together represent the two bloods that flow through our veins, Cherokee and Wiccocomico."

Turner, not sure that he understood everything that his father had said, asked, "Can I wear it too, Daddy?"

Raleigh said, "Perhaps in time, Turner. Now, they will only prick you when you put them on your clothes. You need to be old enough to the point that you fully understand the symbol of the two pins. When you are old enough, I will tell you. Until then, trust me. I will tell you when the time has come." He gently laid the pins back down on the table, making sure to put them where they would not be lost. "Our fathers, who owned the land, were invaded by light-skinned, light clay people from lands beyond the ocean. They were lighter than we are and their skin did not turn dark in the summer sun. They came in large canoes from England and tried to conquer our people. First, our people, the Powhatans, had to give them food, but later they wanted our land. Our ancestors, the Rechahecrian Indians, came to help the Powhatans. Both groups were called unruly Indians, or roaming Indians, suggesting that they were Indians without a home." He raised his voice, which was charged with emotional energy. "The land was our home before they came, our special home. How could the visiting colonists call us 'people without a home'? They clouded true history and twisted their own versions to make themselves look good and our people look bad. Powhatan, the chief, died in 1618. His brother Opitchapam, who was also called Itoyatin, became the leader of the 'unruly Indians,' as the colonists called the Rechahecrians, the Cherokees, and the Powhatans. Our people only fought colonists because they invaded our home."

Raleigh rocked a little faster, and Turner, still sitting on the wooden floor, hugged his knees.

Raleigh continued, "We were here first. We were God's chosen people living in harmony with nature on the land God gave us. Then explorers came from faraway places with strange names such as Spain, Portugal, and England. Many came only to see, and then they left. The European colonists came to Jamestown. They wanted more than to observe. First, they desired our food. Next, they wanted our land. The new colonists were greedy and land-hungry. In response to these rude visitors, the Powhatans and the Cherokees formed a partnership and rebelled against the unwelcome settlers. Both groups, the Algonquians and the Cherokees, were our ancestors. They retreated to the place called *Rickahake*, or the Dismal Swamp, to hide. They were still there around 1621. It is sad that our people, who were here since earlier times, had to hide from the new visitors in that lonely place, the Dismal Swamp."

"Daddy, why were they hungry for our food and land? Did God forget to give them some food and land beyond the ocean?"

"No, son," replied Raleigh with a smile. As he gazed into his son's black eyes, alert and sharp as the eyes of an eagle, he knew that he had his full attention. "They were greedy. When we give you food, we wouldn't expect you to eat your food and also take food from your mother's plate, would we?"

"No, that would be bad!" responded Turner, shaking his head.

"So it is with the people from the ocean. They had land and food beyond the ocean. They wanted to have their land and take our home soil too. They wanted to eat their food and eat our food as well. The colonists were bad people! Many people died—Powhatan's people, the Cherokees, and the colonists—all because of the new settlers' greedy attitude. They even tricked Indian people to the extent that they fought one another."

"Daddy, what is 'tricked'?" asked Turner, turning his face up quizzically.

"It is what your friend does to you when he causes you to fight and throw river rocks at your cousins, even when you don't want to fight them," replied Raleigh.

"Yes, sir, I understand," responded Turner. "It's when he is making me fight when I don't want to fight!"

Raleigh opened his mouth to continue his story but then hesitated. He thought he would wait until Turner had reached his tenth birthday before he would tell him about the attacks by his people on the colonists, one of which marked the name Rechahecrians in legend for generations. Although the massacre of 347 colonists in March of 1622–23 seemed to have been manipulated by the chief of the Pamunkey Indians, Cherokees under the command of the successor of Powhatan had been accused of the massacre. Turner, he suspected, might have nightmares if he told him about the massacre. No, he decided he would wait to tell Turner about this part of the Cherokee and Powhatan history. However, he knew he must tell him at some point, no matter how much he wanted to spare him. In his heart, he knew the Virginia settlers would taint history in favor of the colonists. The Indians would come out on the short end of history if they had to rely only on what the colonists wrote on paper. Virginians had already begun to tell the "evil" side of history relating to Indians while ignoring the atrocities of the colonists. Even during this early period, Raleigh was aware that Virginia historians were distorting or omitting facts that would show the noble side of the Red Man. *I must tell the whole story as my father told it to me. I must not be guilty of breaking the oral heritage chain. Turner must know the whole truth, but not now,* he thought. However, Raleigh would have to wait for Turner to grow older so he could explain the rich history in more detail.

Again, he pondered the unfairness of their situation. He was full of anger because historians were clouding history against the Indians. They only recorded information that showed Native Americans in a negative light. They were portrayed in literature as savages. If only all historians could be like Capt. John Smith, the European. He was an honest historian who presented the facts faithfully. Colonial writers did not write historical details like he did, as the Cherokees passed their history down through the ages by way of oral traditions. He wondered why the colonists did not record true Native American history on paper. He was, however, proud because they could not possibly develop the oral tradition memory skills of the Native Americans.

Raleigh had often said the colonists did not have the memory skills to pass on the heritage as his people did. They had to write it down or else they would forget it, or they would lie about it or just ignore it intentionally if the history were not in their favor. Raleigh thought, *I must tell the untainted history to Turner because the colonists will surely leave out large chunks of the Cherokee and Powhatan peoples' history.*

In his heart, Raleigh harbored strong hatred against Virginia colonists because of their mistreatment of his people since their arrival in the colony. These deep personal feelings had become an obsession, influencing every part of his life. Even though he was a professing and practicing Christian, he refused to let go of his negative feelings against colonists. He dealt with his guilt by rationalizing that he had every reason to feel the way he did. He did, however, go through the motions of admitting his hatred during Sunday worship services. He had been brought up as an Anglican member at Wiccocomico and knew that he should not hate his fellow man. Yet, after confessing his wrongs on Sunday, he picked up the feelings again and lodged them in his heart each Monday morning. He could see this hatred in his own eyes when he looked at his own reflection.

Raleigh was a striking Native American, although county tax clerks had classified him as "white" for years when he visited the courthouse to pay his personal property and real estate taxes. He had been successfully masquerading as white on certain occasions, while still holding aboriginal pride in his heart because of his heritage. It was not easy maintaining friendly relations with his colonist neighbors, but he achieved harmony—at least on the outside. He had long ago realized that he must protect his family, land, and social status in the Ridge. This meant keeping a level head and acting as though all things were well with his soul. Yet peace was easier to achieve outwardly with neighbors than inside his heart. He felt the pressure to teach Turner about his past so he would have a good foundation of knowledge about their heritage to face future social and economic pressures.

His mind raced now and he had much to tell, but Turner—his flickering eyes sending out hints to his daddy that it was now close to his bedtime—could not endure any more storytelling. His eyes were now jumping between a half-moon and a quarter moon. He was getting very sleepy as the grandfather clock chimed to remind them of the late hour. Raleigh gazed down at Turner with love, seeing his dark brown complexion, straight black hair, and black eyes. He was a large boy for his age of five. He looked like a little adult as he reclined on the floor, trying to keep his eyes focused on and his ears open to his daddy. He was a precocious child and enjoyed hearing stories about his ancestors, especially since his father was such an excellent storyteller.

From her chair, Sarah, whose crocheting needle moved slower and slower with each tick of the grandfather clock, was now giving Raleigh the signal to put Turner to bed. Sitting near the fireplace, she pointed the crochet needle slowly toward Turner's bedroom and Raleigh caught the cue.

Raleigh asked, loudly, "Where did I stop, Turner?"

Opening one of his eyes, Turner said slowly, "The hungry ocean people. They wanted our food and land. They are greedy and bad!"

"Good. We will pick up where we left off tomorrow night. Now give me a hug and off you go to bed. Don't forget to say your prayers."

Turner had learned a new prayer at the Fairmount Church fellowship service last week and he recited as Sarah listened:

> Lord, now let me go to sleep,
> Please keep me from head to feet.
>   Amen.

> Oh, yeah, Lord, bless my family and
> don't let the hungry colonists take
> daddy's land and food. They can go
> home in the ocean and get their own
> land and food. God, don't let the
> greedy people be bad. Thank you.
>   Amen.

The cold mid-November winds blew outside as the fireplace flames flickered. Now that Turner was safely tucked into bed, Raleigh leaned back in his oak rocking chair, and prepared a mental list of all the things he must do the next day. He knew that he had to pay his taxes on his property across the James River in Buckingham County next week, and he expected to rise early and travel by wagon to Amherst Courthouse this week. The Virginia Assembly law of 1748 declared that all persons sixteen years of age and upward had to pay personal property and land taxes. He had lands and a building in Stonewall Mill. He decided that he and his family would make an enjoyable trip out of what would otherwise be unpleasant—paying taxes. Being a true patriot, he did not really mind paying taxes. As a frugal citizen, he had carefully guarded his resources and so was able to pay his taxes in both counties.

Still rocking slowly in the chair while Sarah prepared for bed, he planned to drive his mule wagon upon the ferry boat at Stapleton. When he returned from Buckingham Courthouse, he would soon visit the Cherokee Band in Stonewall Mill. He made weekly visits, informal and official, to his relatives and friends in the village, as he was the principal chief of both groups, the Stonewall Mill Band and the Buffalo Ridge Band. Although he lived at times in Buckingham County's Stonewall Mill as well as Amherst County's Buffalo Ridge, he also had business and tribal responsibilities in Stonewall. He needed to meet and confer with the tribal leaders of clans at Stonewall: the Fergusons, Pinns, Megginsons, and Beverlys. He also wondered how the Humbleses and Bankses were doing there. He has always enjoyed the visits across the James River. It was more than a business trip; it was exciting to greet his dear followers. They were like his children, and he their father.

Colonists, remembering the events of 1622, were suspicious of large tribes. Two Cherokee bands had been formed in the two areas to reduce the size of the tribe, and to keep down the suspicion from angry, vengeful colonists. Indians still had large tribes in this part of Virginia. Although the aboriginal people had been in the Ridge for years, Buffalo Ridge was one of the first two areas settled by colonists in Amherst County.

Under his skillful leadership, Raleigh had masterfully joined the two villages. The Virginia Colonial Council refused to allow Cherokees to settle in Virginia as an official Cherokee tribe as early as 1721. The Cherokees had petitioned the Williamsburg Colonial Council on November 3, 1721 to grant permission for the tribe to settle on the Roanoke River, so that they might enjoy the convenience of free trade. The Council noted that the request did not seem convenient because the Cherokees might disturb other Northern Indian hunting tribes. Raleigh often thought that this was a pretext to keep the Cherokees away from Virginia officially. It was a well-known fact that the Cherokees had been forced out of Virginia during the 1620s and forced to reside in scattered locations in central and southwestern Virginia, assuming identities as peaceful white or colored people, or even as other tribes, but they could never be listed as Cherokee. The Cherokee had been so powerful in Virginia in their resistance to the colonists that the very name Cherokee caused chills and shudders in the hearts of residents. The colonists disliked and feared Cherokee so much that they actually committed the heinous act of placing a bounty on the heads of Cherokee Indians.

The Pinn family and the other families in the Ridge did not show off their Native American status. Actually, Virginian colonists had committed so many atrocities against his ancestors that it was not fashionable to be Indian. They had to act white even though the tax men sometimes listed his people as mulatto and at other times white. The colonists did not use the word "Indian" on records because they did not want to document the presence of Indians in this area of Virginia. It was amusing among the Cherokees in Stonewall Mill and Buffalo Ridge that the tax people sometimes called their relatives white in Stonewall Mill and mulatto in Amherst. Raleigh would even be listed as white on the first U.S. Census.

In Stonewall, the Fergusons—or Furgeson, as they were sometimes called—the Elliotts, the Megginsons, and the Wests were descendants of Pocahontas. They held more firmly, however, to the Cherokee heritage than to the Powhatan line, although either connection was worthy of cultural pride. The local white citizens thought the people were white until the summer sun gave away their skin's secret that had been hidden in the winter—a very red color. Some white citizens in that area, however, had often suspected that they might have some Indian blood, but since they acted and lived like white people, they were not thought of as "loincloth-attired" Indian people. They were successful farmers, like other white people in Buckingham County.

In Amherst, however, the Pinns, Beverlys, Fergusons, Bankses, and Sparrows were often thought of as Indians, mulattoes, or colored even though some of the people could move to other areas and pass for white, especially in the winter season. The summer rays had a way of giving most of the Buffalo Ridge people away. The relatives in both areas—Stonewall Mill and Buffalo Ridge—did not mind if the people did not recognize them as Indian because they were keenly conscious of some Virginian colonists' negative feelings against and hatred toward Native people. The Cherokees were successful in assimilating into the general culture. While they survived by masquerading as white people in public, they lived as Indians in their communities.

When morning came, they all got into the wagon to travel to the Amherst County Courthouse. Sarah never turned down an invitation to travel with Raleigh. She always trusted him and joyfully accepted his marriage proposal. Raleigh looked at her with pride as she sat beside him on the wagon seat, for she was still a very beautiful woman. Raleigh, Sarah, and Turner always enjoyed traveling over the Ridge road, through the Glades, and into Amherst Courthouse to pay the taxes. Raleigh was a very successful farmer and land developer. He thanked God for giving him bountiful financial blessings in two locations. He had learned these skills from his Cherokee and Wiccocomico ancestors. He could not give all the credit for his farming success to his Cherokee ancestors because the Powhatans were also his ancestors. The Cherokees had lived along the Appomattox River in a friendly relationship with the Powhatan people for years.

He remembered when he had first seen Sarah. She had been attired in a deerskin dress with moccasins on her feet. Her beautiful black hair and copper complexion had immediately caught Raleigh's black eyes. His aboriginal instincts led him directly to her, and he responded instantly to her innocent smile, shyly seductive walk, and animated expression. Raleigh thought they made a nice couple. He was five feet eleven-and-a-half inches tall and very muscular. Sarah, on the other hand, was of average height, about five foot five and slender. Even from the first moment he met her, he sensed that she too had aboriginal ancestry. They married after a short courtship. Even now, as they traveled along the highway, Raleigh noticed how much attention Sarah received from the wandering eyes of male strangers.

As they journeyed, they passed the time by singing and talking of everyday events. The weather was chilly, so Raleigh and Sarah had sandwiched Turner between their bodies on the wagon seat to keep him warm. They were glad when they finally arrived at the Amherst County Courthouse. As Raleigh climbed down from the wagon, his tall frame was bent over in a half-frozen posture. He briskly straightened up his body, stomped his feet on the hard dirt sidewalk, and turned toward the courthouse. He wore his rabbit fur–lined leather coat that Sarah and he made last winter. He also wore his Sunday dress wool breeches that she sewed just last week. Turner sported his breeches, which Sarah made from the same material as his daddy's pants. Raleigh wore black-dyed deer-hide boots he made during the winter of 1772. He learned leather crafting and shoemaking in addition to other vocational arts as an indentured servant in Northumberland and Lancaster Counties. Those skills proved valuable to his farm economy and home life. These clothes had kept his body reasonably warm during the fifteen-mile trip to Amherst Courthouse. After shaking himself free from the chilly numbness of the three-hour trip, he appreciated the opportunity to stretch his legs as he walked toward the courthouse. Sarah and Turner remained in the wagon, where Sarah wrapped themselves in a quilt she pulled from the back of the wagon. Raleigh paid his taxes and headed to the local store.

Turner especially appreciated his daddy's trips to Amherst and Buckingham to pay taxes because he bought him candy at the store. Raleigh kept up the tradition on this occasion by purchasing a half-dozen licorice sticks. As they headed back toward the Ridge, Turner sucked on one stick of licorice while dust, stirred up by the swiftly moving wagon wheels, clung to his candy. Like his daddy, he had learned to save what he valued. He saved five candy sticks, held them up, and said, "I am five. Look, Daddy and Mommy!"

Raleigh thought, *Turner has done well with his history, mathematics, and geography lessons this week.*

It was Friday again, and the grandfather clock reminded the Pinn family that the morning was swiftly fleeting. It was already 6:00 a.m. and Sarah asked Raleigh if it was a good idea to take Turner to Buckingham with the weather being so cold and damp.

It had rained during the night. Although it had stopped, the November air was threatening. Turner was sleeping well now after a battle with whooping cough at 2:30 a.m. Sarah got up and prepared honey and locust bark tea for his coughing. She also added cherry bark and pine needles to the water to relieve the cough and the fever. Sarah had become a very good Cherokee drug practitioner. She was well respected among the villagers for her knowledge of the medicinal arts. Her recovering patient, Turner, was another good example of her dedication and skills. He was sleeping so well that his mother did not want to awaken him for the trip to pay the taxes. She told Raleigh to go on alone on the horse. "It would be easier for you to ride the horse and not hook up the horse to the wagon for Turner and me," she said.

Raleigh disagreed with her. He knew how she enjoyed the occasional trips to town, and he did not think Turner's cough during the night was a serious concern. She protested by reminding him that she still had a batch of the tea left, and she did not want it to go to waste. She would keep Turner by the fireplace and "doctor him with hot tea." She remembered what she had said and quickly changed the words to "nurse him with warm tea." She realized that a doctor was a man's job and, although she was excellent at her medical work and as good as any male doctor, she did not want to embarrass Raleigh, who was considered one of the village's resident medical men. Raleigh, secure in his own abilities and masculinity, smiled and gave her a nod to indicate that what she said the first time was all right. She returned the smile. He further showed his love for her and respect for her concerns by agreeing to leave Turner at home.

People of color, Indian people back on the coast, did not have to pay taxes. Part of his Indian people still lived in the present-day Lancaster and Northumberland areas, and he was not aware if they had begun paying county taxes. Raleigh gathered his gear and money and reached for his hat, but he knew Turner would be disappointed to be left behind. He was disappointed as well because he had hoped Turner would be able to witness his paying the taxes to the white tax man at the courthouse. So many of his people were poor, and he had become the motivator for the Stonewall community members by encouraging them to improve their lot through self-help, not dependency on the colonists. He imagined that Turner, if he had come on the trip, would have observed two things in his act of paying the taxes: God's material blessings on the family and his father's independence as a farmer and landowner in two counties. He cheered himself with the thought that, God willing, there would be other times to take Turner to Buckingham.

He rode his stallion proudly toward Stapleton. Near the Porridge Creek Bridge, he met a hunter who greeted him and then gave him a warning.

"Raleigh, you had better be careful and bundle up or you will catch your death in this thirty-five degree weather," the hunter said.

The wind had already begun to howl and drive the chilly air against his face. Just then, he remembered Proverbs 16:18,

"Pride goeth before destruction and a haughty spirit before a fall." As his horse turned left from the Buffalo Ridge Road and headed toward Buckingham on Stapleton Road, he thanked God for his blessings and for allowing Sarah to keep Turner at home. He believed at that moment that Sarah, the Beloved Mother of the Buffalo Ridge Band, had been inspired by God to warn him not to display a proud look in the presence of Turner at the tax office.

He wondered, *Could she have been that far ahead of me?* Then, with self-confidence, he said to himself, *No, she just wanted Turner to stay at home because of his cough.* Then he realized he had not heard Turner coughing during the night. He knew he would have heard him, for he was a master hunter and had hearing skills as good as any hound dog. *It is strange. It is very strange,* he thought, as he rode on down the road with a new and refreshing humility that was very much out of place with his economic status and high position among the elders in Buffalo Ridge and Stonewall Mill. *No, Sarah did not trick me!* he assured himself.

When he arrived at Buckingham Courthouse, he dismounted and tied his horse to a post. He took a few minutes to stretch his legs because they had a tendency to get stiff after long trips. Raleigh knew that this twenty-eight mile trip, like his long mounted hunting trips, would take a toll on his bones. After a three-minute pause, he straightened up and headed toward the courthouse. When he reached the building, he grasped the door and pulled it open. He strode in to find the building almost empty. He spoke to the clerk and stated, "I would like to pay my taxes, please. My name is Raleigh Pinn."

The clerk looked up his tax records. He then returned to the counter and asked, "You are Raleigh Pinn?"

Raleigh said, "Yes. Is there a problem?"

"No. I just thought you were a white man since you have properties in Buckingham and Amherst Counties."

"I don't understand what you are saying. What is the issue? Are you surprised that I am a colored person?"

The clerk, embarrassed, responded. "No! Well, yes, somewhat. Anyway, there is no problem."

Raleigh, feeling slightly annoyed, drew himself up to his full height, stiff legs and all, and said, "Please stop the chatter and take my money."

When the transaction was complete, he asked for his receipt. He knew that the receipt was proof of his home ownership and another document to protect his land from "baser sorts." Raleigh had begun to grow paranoid about his property, as he had heard stories from Cherokee relatives in southwestern Virginia. The Blevins and Beverley family members often shared with him horrific tales of land crimes against native people. The colonists were stealing land from Native Americans, calling them colored and making them leave the counties.

Raleigh thanked the clerk for his receipt and said, "See you next year." He made this remark to assure the clerk that he had no intentions of letting go of his land. *He had better not get the idea of doing in Buckingham what they are doing in Southwest Virginia. I will fight for my land. They need to know this before they think about trying to steal one inch of my property!* He had these precautions on his mind as he walked out of the clerk's office and moved briskly to his horse.

He was glad that the tax agent had received his money and handed him a receipt. Now, however, he considered where he would hide the receipt to protect his property against unscrupulous officials who might deny that he paid his taxes and try to take his property. Success had not come by accident but with sweat, prayer, and faith. His present level of affluence was a result of hard work on the farm—by developing and improving his lands, and managing his resources well. Foolish actions in business would assure that his resources would be wasted. Besides, he reasoned, *I am the leader of my people, and I am an example for them. I must be wise on every score, and as God gave me the wisdom, I will be wise.*

At that moment, he removed his left rawhide boot, placed the receipt in it, and slipped the boot back on his foot. He continued walking down the street until he had another thought. He needed to review the receipt closely. Quickly, he removed the boot and examined the receipt that the clerk gave him. He gazed at it for a long time and noticed a mistake.

> Rawly Pen (Mulatto) – Buckingham County – 1774 – 1 Tithable.

The clerk had written his name incorrectly. Raleigh did not have any trouble writing and reading English, and he knew his name very well. Fuming inwardly, he wondered, *Did my pronunciation with Wiccocomico and Cherokee dialects cause the clerk to misspell my name? Maybe the clerk wrote it wrong intentionally because he resented me having a noble English name like Raleigh.*

Then he questioned why the clerk listed him as mulatto. He knew about the experiences of the Fergusons, the Evanses, the Megginsons, and the McCoys; they did not have "mulatto" on their receipts. He had seen their receipts earlier during one of the tribal meetings at Stonewall Mill because they had already paid their taxes. *Some of the people looked white, but they had Indian in them, so how were they able to avoid the mulatto brand?* he questioned himself.

He looked somewhat white even though he was Cherokee. It was now November, and he did not have a deep tan. Then he remembered something. He had visited the courthouse in August of that same year to check on a Stonewall Mill deed. The clerk may have remembered his darker skin. As he walked out to the courthouse yard, he met his friend John Fields, who had a receipt in his hand.

After a few words of greeting, Raleigh said, "*O si yo,*" hello, and "*do hi tsu,*" are you well? as he looked around to make sure that they were not being observed or heard by other people. Virginia colonists did not like the idea of Cherokees walking the streets of their towns, or even being in the woods near their homes.

He then quickly asked John, comically, if he had earned the classification of mulatto on his tax document. "John, when you paid your taxes, what did that clerk write on your papers?"

John said, "The usual stuff was listed. He wrote my name, the county's name, and a number one."

"Did he write down your color?"

John replied, "Yes, yes. He jotted down that word, mulatto." He anticipated where Raleigh was heading, and added, "I am glad that they are documenting that we are not white but people of color. How could our descendants otherwise prove that they are indigenous people in years to come? They could not prove it then, with their great-grandfathers being listed as white persons. They must have some *mulatto* or *Indian*, or even the label *black* in their lineage somewhere, or else they could not be considered *Indian*."

John had a Cherokee tradition in the area and proudly pointed to the fact that he had relatives as a part of the Cherokee Nation in Tennessee. Some still lived in the Etowah River area in Georgia. Others lived in scattered areas of Tennessee—Lookout Valley and Hiwassee River. He said that they were once in one location, but they were later scattered to the two colonies and throughout many villages during the colonial wars against his people, in the mid- to late 1750s and early 1760s.

Raleigh first sent up a prayer of thanks to God for this well-planned, God-inspired visit—not a coincidental meeting—between two friends and aboriginal relatives, and then thanked his friend John for his words of wisdom. He did not elaborate to John on his use of the word "wisdom," but just kept saying thank you over and over, *wa do, wa do*, as he backed away and moved toward his horse. After he mounted his horse, he wondered, *Now where is that candy store? Where is that fancy bonnet place?* Raleigh planned to keep the recent incident in the clerk's office to himself as he told his horse to get up. As he headed toward the Buckingham country store, he realized that he had been a little hard on the tax clerk. He pledged to himself, *I will pray for forgiveness on Sunday.*

Riding his horse down the road toward Bent Creek, he finally understood why Sarah kept Turner at home. *Turner,* he imagined, *would have seen his daddy make a fool of himself back there at the courthouse.* Just as he began to cross the James River at Bent Creek, his horse slipped on the river rocks, knocked a shoe off, fell in the water, and threw Raleigh into the river. While on his back with the water soaking his fancy colonial-style, long-sleeved white shirt, he looked up at his horse's rear end as he limped on slowly ahead of the fallen rider. Then he remembered the words from Proverbs, "A haughty spirit before a fall."

While walking home with his horse, he thanked God for the experience of the day, the education from his friend John, the corporal punishment provided by his stallion, and the humbling opportunity to walk beside his limping horse all the way from Bent Creek to Buffalo Ridge. He arrived at his cozy and warm home about an hour after midnight.

Sarah greeted him at the door. "Raleigh Pinn, come near the fire before you catch your death in this cold November air." She had no idea why he was shivering, wet, and so cold.

"I am sick, Sarah. You will get the whole story later. You just doctor me with that leftover cherry and locust tea that you claimed you made for Turner last night." Raleigh sat by the fire, coughed occasionally, and picked up his Bible while Sarah made some tea. He turned to Numbers 22: 27–34. He read:

> And when the ass [donkey] saw the angel of the Lord, she fell down under Balaam...And Balaam said unto the angel of the Lord, I have sinned; for I knew not that thou stoodest in the way against me: now therefore, if it displeases thee, I will get me back again.

He then closed his Bible and prayed.

> Lord, I didn't believe before yesterday that an animal—either donkey or horse—could talk to men. Forgive me for my lack of faith in your written word. When my stallion fell under me, like the ass that fell under Balaam, I realized that you were also talking to me through my beast. You were telling me to humble myself just as you humbled Balaam. Balaam turned back toward you, Lord. I will turn my haughty spirit back toward you also. Please keep me humble here at the Ridge and at Stonewall Mill.
> Amen.

A few minutes later, Sarah gave him some locust and cherry bark tea. She quickly added some red oak logs on the charred wood that was slowly burning out in the fireplace. After he had leisurely sipped the hot herbal tea, she put him to bed and turned off the oil lamps. By the time she had put out the lights, Raleigh had already fallen asleep.

> Honour has come back, as a king, to earth,
> and paid her subjects with a royal wage;
> and Nobleness walks in our ways again;
> and we have come into our heritage.
> —Rupert Brooke

4

Minute Men

17 November 1775

Rising early in the morning, Raleigh hurried to collect all of his gear and to check his rifle one last time. As he put his equipment beside the door, he thought about the recent legislation that had been passed by the government. The Patriot Virginia Convention met in Richmond and passed an ordinance on July 17, 1775, requiring "a battalion of minutemen" to be organized in each district to drill twice a year. The Buckingham district battalion included the counties of Buckingham, Amherst, Albemarle, and East Augusta. In obedience to the order, the battalion was scheduled to meet on November 17, 1775, and to continue the military training until the sixth of December, for a total of twenty consecutive days.

Raleigh had been a faithful member of the Amherst Militia until the Patriot Virginia Convention ordered the formation of the Buckingham Minuteman Battalion. He recalled the pride that he always felt with his relatives, tribal members, and friends when he performed military service for Amherst County. Each time the militia met, it was like a reunion of aboriginal people. This reunion was not really like the close-knit Buffalo Ridge/Stonewall Mill tribal meetings that he conducted monthly, alternating between the two locations. These militia gatherings included mostly white settlers. However, a small number of the soldiers were family, either related by way of the Indian or kinship connections. Raleigh suspected that he had some white blood running in his veins, but he preferred to recognize the Indian side at the Ridge and at Stonewall Mill.

Breakfast was a strained affair with both Raleigh and Sarah pretending that this was just like any ordinary day. Turner, trying to sit up straight at the table, was unusually quiet. He kept his eyes on his plate and slowly ate his eggs and biscuits. When the meal was finally over, Sarah began to clear the table. Turner carefully carried his plate from the table, handed it to his mother, and sat quietly by the fireplace, idly playing with two three-inch Indian warriors that his father had carved out of locust wood. Raleigh, momentarily left alone at the table, slowly sipped the last of his hot coffee. As he drank, he reflected on the changing attitudes of the local settlers toward the Indian people. The county officials of both Amherst and Buckingham had begun to record his race more and more as mulatto on legal documents, whereas on previous occasions he had been listed as white. Some of his fellow militia soldiers who were aborigines preferred to be called white. Then his thoughts turned to the upcoming militia training, where he would see some of his tribal members. In a way, it would be like a gathering of many of his relatives, except this would be for military rather than tribal purposes.

Raleigh still maintained the leadership position in the military that he previously enjoyed among tribal members since the battalion leaders depended on his Indian scouting and military skills. He and his other friends and family members were essential to the success of the Amherst Militia, and in his heart, he was sure that they would perform admirably for the Buckingham Minuteman Battalion.

Finally, the cup was empty. His excuse to tarry had now expired, so he knew it was time to leave. Sarah watched as he gathered his supplies, and then she and Turner followed him outside. He turned to say his goodbyes, and he saw the look of concern in their faces. He put his hand on Turner's shoulder and smiled down at him before turning his gaze toward Sarah. He tried to reassure her that everything would be fine.

"Sarah, this is only practice. It is not really war. It is November 16 and the minuteman training only lasts a few days." Then he added, "Besides, my friends and some family will be with me, just like in the Amherst Militia."

With her hands still clasped together, Sarah inquired, "Which ones are you talking about?"

"All of them," responded Raleigh. "Abraham Cooper, Phil Going, Reuben and William Banks, John Hix, Thomas Hopper, the Pendleton boys, and Ben Megginson will be there. There will be William Megginson, Samuel Megginson, John Redcross, William Scott, Absalom Adkins, John Bowling, James Bolling, Richard Lawless, and Francis Satterwhite. John Turner and John Tyler will also be there. Abraham Warwick, William Warwick, and Francis, Bransford, and John West will be there too. Some of these soldiers have Indian background or act like Indians with their martial arts skills. They will help the battalion get the best training. James Hartlesses, the Powells, the Robertses, and Ben Rogers are also strong soldiers. John Tyler will help cover me because he knows me from the Buckingham area. You know that we are related to the Tylers by marriage. My friend and your kin, John Redcross, will help protect my back side."

He knew that his kinfolk had always been excellent warriors with the tomahawk and lance, the blowgun and the bow. Some of their ancestors had settled on the Appomattox River as part of the great Cherokee settlement there. Their descendants—some of these soldiers—had learned how to shoot birds from a tall oak twenty-five yards away with small bird-point arrowheads. Raleigh remembered that family members had discovered hundreds of arrowheads and other Indian artifacts on the Appomattox River banks, miles from the small town of Appomattox. He was aware that some Cherokees later came into the area during the war of 1760–61, when South Carolina, North Carolina, and Virginia militia troops closed in on the Lower, Middle, and Overhill Cherokee towns. He remembered oral narratives of how the troops destroyed many of the towns in the Lower and Middle settlements, and forced hundreds of survivors to flee along the Blue Ridge Mountains. Other Cherokees came into the area from the Overhill towns by way of southwest Virginia.

He smiled as he remembered the great heritage of his people. "The Cherokees and the Wiccocomicos were great warriors, and we are still great warriors, with the help of the Lord," he remarked as if he needed to reassure Sarah and himself. Raleigh thought about the Cherokee force that secured the position in Richmond in the mid-1600s and how the colonists had to beg for peace with the Cherokees. He reflected on the other battles of the Cherokees, better known as the Rechahecrians, as he had heard oral stories about their adventures as well as tales about how they withdrew to the Dismal Swamps in the early 1620s. He knew that Virginia had always been the home of the Cherokees, not just on the Appomattox River. He changed the subject, trying to distract Sarah from thoughts of war, by discussing the plans for the work he needed to do when he returned.

November 16 was unusually chilly, even though the sun was shining brightly. Feeling the chill both inside and out, Raleigh buttoned his coat tighter. Then he reached out to hug Sarah and Turner. Sarah, looking woeful and dispirited, had Turner in her arms. He too had a sad expression in his eyes.

Sarah, with her black hair shining in the sun, looked into Raleigh's eyes, trying to see into his heart—looking to see if sadness was there as well. She glimpsed some sadness for just a moment, and then he smiled as he leaned forward to kiss her on the lips, showing her without words how much he loved her and that he would miss her. He thought of their love as similar to that of Abraham and Sarah in the Bible. They too were always in danger as they lived in a hostile land.

Slowly letting her go, he said to her, "Sarah, my love and best friend, you know that I will miss you, but my devotion to you will only grow stronger." At these words, he saw a trembling smile appear on her face. "Please remember, Sarah, that for every day we are separated, our love will increase in depth and width and height."

She brushed several tears from her face, and he felt his own throat tighten. He leaned down and gave Turner a hug. Raleigh then threw her several kisses and quickly mounted his horse. As he did so, he dipped his head because he didn't want to look into her tearful eyes while he headed his horse out of the yard, riding off toward Buckingham to join his fellow militiamen.

His thoughts were already turning to his mission, eagerly anticipating the gathering of like-minded men. He thought, *We have come into our heritage! We, as the minutemen, are keeping up our aboriginal war heritage and tradition. We are the true fighters and have been given an opportunity to do what Cherokees have done best since early times—fight!*

Sarah, still holding Turner in her arms, remained motionless. The rising sun shining in her eyes prevented Sarah from having a clear view of Raleigh as he rode toward the sun. She only saw a shadow of his image, pointing back toward her feet as if God were saying, "Everything will be fine. He will join you back at the Ridge." The shadow caused her to remember Psalm 23 and the words, "Yea, though I walk through the valley of the shadow of death, I will fear no evil."

Remembering David's confidence in God, she hugged Turner, turned around, and walked slowly toward the cabin, intermittently looking back at Raleigh as his body and shadow became smaller and smaller. Eventually, he disappeared as the bend in the Buffalo Ridge road separated him from her sight. Those five minutes, from the time of the kiss to the moment that he disappeared behind the bend, seemed like eternity. Time appeared to stand still or at least caused Raleigh and the horse to move in slow motion. It was as if the sight of the horse's tail moving right to left and Raleigh's movement from right to left on his horse placed her in a hypnotic state and stopped time temporarily.

As Raleigh rode down the Buffalo Ridge road toward Stapleton, he mentally reviewed the things he had done for his people. He had flashbacks of the persecutions that his fellow indigenous people had endured because of the greed of the colonists. He thought about the settlers' insatiable appetite for land, and how they—as visitors to his homeland—had now become the hosts, and were gradually trying to remove all

Native Americans from the territory that was really their God-given land. He felt troubled with the images of his people being forced to move from Virginia because of the colonists' intense hatred for the word "Cherokee," or "Rechahecrian." He was saddened as he put himself in the position of both the Cherokee and the Powhatan people, who had been forced to remove themselves from eastern and central Virginia in the 1620s. They had often traveled together and the two peoples were close. Both groups had suffered because of their skillful and daring martial arts successes—and failures—against the settlers. Both groups had already been the victims of attempted genocide by the colonists, and Raleigh feared that this would continue.

He remembered the stories that his father told him about the Chickacoan District between the Rappahannock and Potomac rivers—land that was previously an Indian reserve for his people. In 1648, the area was annexed and Northumberland County was created. His people, in the early 1600s, numbered more than five hundred members in the Wiccocomico Indian Town, north of the head of the Little Wicomico River. They were gradually dispersed from their homeland because of the colonists' desire for good land. Like most Algonquians and Cherokees, his people in Wiccocomico Indian Town had their settlement near a major body of water and close to the marshlands for the purpose of securing food. They saw to it that they were close to springs for fresh water. They also sought sandy and silt loams for growing maize. In addition, they made sure that the land formation was elevated so that they could see all around the area for security and protection. This required that the land be formed on broad neck lands. The heart of the villages always existed near rivers, and their river tributaries provided food and transportation.

As he continued to ride on his faithful stallion, Raleigh's attention wandered from one thought to another. He reflected bitterly on the attitude of the colonists, who believed that Indians were lazy pagans who did not really know how to make the most profitable use of the land. Therefore, the representatives of the Virginia Company felt no remorse for removing them from their valuable land. In his thoughts, he noted that the

Wiccocomico Indians were strong enough in number to offer resistance to the colonists, and he wondered how they were able to get his people off their Indian reservation. He knew there were bands of Cherokees, living among the Algonquians. His father had told him stories about the military skills of the Cherokees, and how they had battled the colonists. He knew that Powhatan did not have to fight the colonists alone. The Cherokees or Rechahecrians did not mind coming to the assistance of their friends, the Powhatans, as they had in 1622–23 during the so-called massacre, and again in 1656 in Richmond. He wondered if the Cherokees had joined forces with the Wiccocomico Indians against the colonists when they forced the Indians from the Northern Neck reservation in 1648. Raleigh suspected that the colonial Virginians would continue to dislike the Powhatans and the Cherokees because both groups did not mind challenging colonists. He wondered how long it would last. Having no answer, he turned his thoughts to his family and descendants.

He passed trees, pastures, farms, and houses, but he seldom noticed the scenes as he was lost in thought. He looked toward the future and asked himself if his son, Turner, would ever have peace at the Ridge and Stonewall Mill. *Would he have to continue in his footsteps by living as a white man with brown skin in the summer sun? Would he, as an aboriginal man, have to continue dressing like the white man? Would he have to pretend to be land-hungry like his daddy to be accepted? Would he have to keep buying and selling land to throw off their true aboriginal identity from the white people? Would Turner have to deny his race—the special race that God created and placed in this land first—and live secretly as an aboriginal resident with only his tribal members having this knowledge?*

His mixed Cherokee and Powhatan ancestors had passed down to him the oral heritage. Raleigh knew that they had moved gradually and slowly—over several moons—from the Appomattox River area to Buffalo Ridge. Since they did not want to be too concentrated as Indian people in one area, they had strategically placed people on Buffalo Ridge during and after the 1700s. Amherst County's first settlers at the Ridge, the pioneers, as they were called, trickled in during the eighteenth century.

Raleigh thought, *We—my kinfolk—were already there hiding when the pioneers came in. My forefathers were not called pioneers but settlers, and the white settlers were called pioneers.* His heart was heavy, and he wept softly and wondered, *Why can't we be Cherokees? Why do we have to keep pretending that the Cherokees have been forced out of Virginia and that we don't exist in Virginia anymore? Why are we such a threat to the colonial people?*

His ancestors had told him not to trust his colonial neighbors with "The Pearls: the precious culture and history of our people." His forefathers had said that the new settlers on Buffalo Ridge in the early 1700s told their Cherokee neighbors—whom they thought were dark-skinned white people—that the Cherokee savages had the nerve to ask the Colonial Council in Williamsburg for permission to settle on the Roanoke River. They had asked Raleigh's ancestors, "Can you believe that the mongrels, after the bloody massacre of 1622–23, would dare come back to Virginia? We removed the name Cherokee from Virginia forever, primarily because of the blood that they and the Powhatans spilled from the three hundred colonists they killed. Can you believe they would be bold enough to ask to settle on a branch of the Roanoke River for convenience of trade with the white man? The Colonial Council's councilmen were very indignant. They refused, making the excuse that it would not be convenient because it might disturb Northern Indians' hunting tribes."

Raleigh had been told many times how the new settlers had continued their assault on the Cherokees. They had asked Raleigh's forefathers in the 1720s, "Would you like to live within fifty miles of those savages? My wife and I would not be able to sleep with those dirty mongrels smelling up the place that close to us!"

The irony of the situation was not lost on Raleigh. Laughing to himself, he thought, *They had lived on land near my ancestors and did not know that they were Cherokees. My folks told me not to trust settlers with our Pearl, and to always remember that the Cherokees are hated in Virginia, and I must tread lightly with one eye open and* the other eye wide open, looking at the ground with the wide-open eye, looking and smelling for snakes in the grass.

He remembered, *My forefathers told me to act like a white man— and if necessary, as a free colored man—because you have to survive in Virginia. You can act like another tribe and become the colonists' servant. The white man knows that a Cherokee will not be his servant, so don't try to be an independent Cherokee, and don't try to be a servant Cherokee. An independent Cherokee will be scalped, and a servant Cherokee will lose his own heart, self-respect, and his God-given independence! Act like a colonist and live among your kin as Indian. You may lose some of your identity, but you will keep your pride. Attempt to change your tribal name from Cherokee to something else for survival with the colonists, and you will lose your heart, your soul, and you will destroy the Pearl.*

Shifting slightly in the saddle, he reminded himself to tell Turner about the importance of protecting the Pearl, but not until he reached his tenth birthday in four years. He knew that Turner must pass down to his descendants the oral heritage of the Cherokee people in Virginia because the settlers did not want Cherokees here, and thus, they would certainly not preserve the history. Raleigh thought, *If we don't do it, it will not get done by anyone else.* He remembered the proclamation of May 26, 1765 from the Colonial Council. The council admitted that a party of Cherokees arrived at Staunton in Augusta County, and had planned to go on to Winchester after getting a pass from Colonel Lewis for that purpose. The proclamation announced that the chief and four more Cherokees were killed, and two others were wounded in violation of the treaties existing between the Cherokees and the whites. They even stated that such actions by the whites should not escape punishment. Raleigh, however, knew that they had not been punished. The Council's proclamation had merely been a ploy by the councilmen to ease their own consciences. Raleigh believed that he must always keep his eyes open and to the ground while protecting his back. "Our people have suffered greatly; the Pearl is visible proof," he groaned, "and God will give us the strength to go on."

Now Raleigh would serve Virginia as a soldier. He would serve a colony that did not even admit that he existed as a Cherokee. North Carolina, Georgia, South Carolina, and

Tennessee admit that they have Cherokees in their midst, but Virginians are fooling themselves. Raleigh felt angry because while they recognized they have skilled Indian fighters here, the Virginians remained unwilling to acknowledge them publicly. Raleigh resented that the government was using their Native American military skills as militiamen to serve the colony. The colonists had too much pride to admit that the Indians were a powerful force in the past and that they had defeated the colonists at James River falls in 1656. They did not like it now that they had been forced to stoop down and ask the Indians to help them fight the British.

The hours and miles had passed by, and Raleigh stopped to give his horse a rest and drink some water. He was no longer cold, so he unbuttoned his coat as he stretched his legs. Still, he continued to ponder his situation because he has always wondered if he should fight for the colonists. Raleigh struggled with his inner self. *Some of the colonists hate the person I really am, even though they do not know for sure that I am Native American. Some suspect that we are Cherokee, but they are afraid to ask. Perhaps they don't really care now.* Then another thought occurred to him. *Do the others know how we are being treated? John Redcross? The Bankses, John and Jacob?*

Remounting his horse, he continued on his way. Once again, his thoughts shifted. The idea of being a minuteman proving great warrior skills in battle was comforting to him while the atrocious history of Virginia's relations with the Powhatans and the Cherokees depressed him. He briefly considered at that very moment if he should just turn his horse around and go back to Sarah and Turner, back to his farm and his many chores. But he knew that John Redcross, John Tyler, and the others would be disappointed in him. Raleigh took his role as tribal leader very seriously and knew that he must represent the brave people of the Ridge, Stonewall Mill, and other areas to the best of his ability.

Raleigh deliberated on whether history would ever record his military service to the colony. Would history say that he was a Cherokee or would it make him a white minuteman? He wanted history to say that he was a Cherokee and a Wiccocomico warrior and minuteman, but he concluded that the Cherokee title could come much later in history after the constant threats on the Pearl were past.

Raleigh had a lot of time to think about his past—the good, the bad, and the horrible treatment by the colonists. Not all of the white colonists hated the Cherokee. Some of them were even very kind and friendly, but there were still a few waiting in the bushes to destroy him and what he had built at the Ridge and at Stonewall Mill. In the midst of this all, Raleigh knew that he had to maintain a cool head while a fiery zeal to preserve his rich history burned in his heart and soul. Raleigh remained constantly aware of his forefathers, and he fought to keep their legacy alive. He realized that he had to leave legal documents about his past. He knew that many of the things that his ancestors had accomplished were vital pieces of Virginia's heritage that had not been recorded by historians. Raleigh lamented that the historians devalued Native American history and focused on colonial activities such as the colonists' western movement in Virginia. While colonial historians were indifferent to the positive contributions of his people, they did everything they could to give the impression that the Cherokees were gone from Virginia. No doubt these omissions provided comfort for settlers in the new Virginia frontier.

Raleigh reasoned that as long as they believed Cherokees were not around their wives and their children, they could rest comfortably at night. This was one reason why Raleigh knew that he must keep up his disguise as a white man. Some of the tribal members at the Ridge acted white for the sake of convenience while others allowed themselves to be colored or mulattoes for survival. He had contrived a master plan for the Ridge and Stonewall. He separated the two groups by geographical divisions. The Stonewall Mill group used Pinn and other surnames; the Buffalo Ridge band had Pinns and some of the same surnames as those in the Stonewall Mill area. Raleigh realized earlier that he had to divide the Pinn family so they would not appear to be living in a tribal settlement. He would never forget the Northern Neck colonists' forced dispersion and slaughter of his Wiccocomico Indian Town ancestors.

He did not want to see his two settlements destroyed and dispersed like the whites did to the large Cherokee settlements on the Appomattox Riverbanks. Although some stayed in the area and passed as white or colored people for survival, others were scattered to many areas. Some moved to southwestern Virginia. A large group had gone into North Carolina by way of southwestern Virginia's Holston River area and Southside Virginia. Missouri had a band whose ancestors once lived in Virginia. They were descendants of the Bollings, Wilsons, Blairs, and other families of Amelia, Chesterfield, Henrico, Amherst, Buckingham, and other counties. They were forced out of Virginia in large numbers. The one advantage to this was that when they lived in Virginia, they were forced to live as Cherokees secretly. Those who moved to other states would openly celebrate their Cherokee and Powhatan heritage. Many of the tribes had moved far away—some had joined the Chickamauga Band of Cherokees, some had gone to Texas with Chief Bowles, and some had settled in Missouri.

Once again Raleigh's thoughts turned to his history, to the carnage of 1760–61 when the colonial militia had assaulted Cherokee villages. They would do so again in 1776. The militia from three states, including Virginia, stormed into the Cherokee towns of North Carolina, South Carolina, and Tennessee. Many of the Cherokee family members who had been driven away came back to Virginia. Raleigh and his kinfolk had put them up in one of the two villages. Those who survived the massacre fled to the Blue Ridge Mountain into the areas of Big Island in Bedford County, Buffalo Ridge of Amherst County, and the Stonewall Mill area of Buckingham County, which would later become Appomattox County.

So while some Cherokee had been forced to leave the Old Dominion to survive, others came into the Old Dominion to flee the massacres in other colonies. Some of his relatives had left the Wiccocomico Indian Reserve, and moved west and south when dispersed by the colonists. They would become Pann, Pan, Pinn, and Pins in the Cherokee towns. Although Raleigh did not know it at the time, some of his Native American relatives' surnames would show up on the Cherokee rolls in Oklahoma some sixty years later.

With thoughts of his people in mind, he resolved to continue to excel as a soldier because he had been recognized for his work in the militia for years. He protected the citizens around Amherst and at Buffalo Ridge and Stapleton, specifically, in fulfilling his duties in the Amherst Militia. Now he must put on a new uniform.

Tired of his depression that was brought about by heavy thoughts and long hours spent on his horse, he imagined pleasant images. With unusual vanity, the thought of whether the minuteman regalia would look attractive on him crossed his mind. He looked forward to getting the uniform in a few hours when he reported for the minutemen's drill. He wondered if Sarah would be proud of him. Suddenly, he remembered that he would have to cut his long, glossy black hair in order to be in uniform with the other soldiers. He then smiled to himself as he thought of how his friend, John Redcross, would feel when he found out that he would not be allowed in uniform until his hair had been cut. He laughed at the thought of how mad John would get. Raleigh knew they'd have to cut his hair off while he was twisting and squirming in the chair. He continued to chuckle to himself at the vision of John and the other Cherokee men reluctantly getting their haircuts. With this picture in his head, he and his horse moved ahead slowly toward the rendezvous with the Buckingham Battalion of Minutemen.

He thought of several stories he had heard about the bravery of his fellow Cherokees in South Carolina's Cherokee Lower Town settlements. There was Colonel Montgomery in 1760 assaulting the towns with his twelve hundred brave and hardy Scot Highlanders. They were reported to be the best troops around, and could fight in Cherokee towns better than six thousand regular soldiers. They would later realize that they were too few in number for the Cherokees in the narrow passes where the trails ran near the river with a steep mountain and deep valleys below. Montgomery's troops proceeded; each step weighed down with fear of losing their lives. Finally, they retreated secretly during the night and withdrew to the town called Nuquose. Later, the troops retreated to Charlestown. The following year, Major Grant out of Florida went against the Cherokees in that same location. The Cherokees were low on ammunition and used the steep mountains where the paths ran to their advantage.

Still basking in the stories he had heard, Raleigh's thoughts persisted, *The Cherokee in the Lower Town area would have whipped Major Grant too, with his big army of regulars and provincials, if the Cherokee had not used up their ammunition in previous battles. Our people were skillful in hand-to-hand combat. We always chose our places to attack and fight. The militia troops were in Cherokee country—a land that they did not know as well as the Native inhabitants. Our people knew the valleys and hills. They were aware even in the dark of night where to place their feet as they assaulted the enemy or made tactical retreats to regroup and fight again. They knew where every crevice, rock, or molehill was located. Their skills with the tomahawk caused each victim within their grasp to lose heart even before the blow had landed. The Cherokee warrior used his eyes to convey his vengeance, as if to say, 'This blow is for the damage that you brought on our neighboring villages, and this other lick is for the fire that you set in our cornfields near those villages, and this assault is because of your hatchet men's acts against our orchards.'*

According to the oral accounts passed down to Raleigh, the warriors would vault backward with somersaults after dropping their victims—moving on to other fearful soldiers who revealed their intense terror by wetting their pants and shaking their rifles in nervous motions—and using a different assault tactic on them. A Native warrior would throw a militia soldier over his shoulder with the martial arts skills of a Japanese warrior. While the fallen victim was getting his bearing on the ground, the warrior would dive on him with the tomahawk.

Raleigh took great pride in his tribal combat heritage. As he approached the training camp, thoughts of his Cherokee and Wiccocomico heritage fueled his spirit of bravery and completely prepared him for the battle he knew would come. Despite all this, he questioned whether he should have taken the gold that the British officers offered to local Indians to defect to their side. He dropped the thought as quickly as it entered his mind.

The British realized that they could win the war with the help of Indians, especially the Cherokees.

He was pleased that he had not taken their offer. He thought, *If I had taken their royal wages, I would have become their subject. I am a Cherokee, and I am subject to no one but God—not anyone else, including the king of England. I have a noble heritage in my blood and do not need royal wages to give me the boldness to fight. I fight because the spirit is in my blood already. Cherokees live to fight. They enjoy fighting. They would rather fight than eat.* He recalled how Cherokee warriors ran for miles at a sustained pace, and did not tire, stopping only occasionally to grab a berry or two from the bushes for energy while still pursuing their fearful retreating enemies. Their hunger for battle was greater than a hungry Cherokee's craving for food.

As always, his thoughts eventually turned to his family. He wondered what Sarah and Turner were eating in the cabin now, and if they were warm and comfortable. As his thoughts became more bothersome, he rode slower and slower and began to bite his bottom lip. He knew he would worry about them for the duration of the drill, twenty days, until December 6. The small voice of hope in his soul told him that all is well with the cabin at the Ridge. With his mind at ease, he dug his heels into his horse's side and picked up his pace again. It then occurred to him that there was another benefit to attending the training exercises. Whenever he was forced to travel from home, he had a stronger desire to return home to Sarah. The separation only served to deepen his love for her and make him eager to return to the cabin. He pictured Sarah in his mind and thought of how beautiful she was when he kissed her this morning, with her smooth copper skin and silky black hair. Thoughts of her occupied him for the rest of his journey.

> Give me, kind Heaven, a private station,
> a mind serene for contemplation.
> —John Gay (1685–1732)

5

Wiccocomico and Cherokee Heritage

5 December 1775

On the world scene, Benjamin Franklin went to England to present the American colonies' grievances before the parliament, and the Ministry of Trade. When he returned, he presented his draft of the Articles of Confederation to the Second Continental Congress.

Native American history began to take a more official place in the colonies when the Second Continental Congress established Indian commissioners. Congress gained centralized authority over Indian affairs rather than leaving it to the respective colonies or British discretion. Congress created the northern department under Commissioner Benjamin Franklin, the southern under James Wilson, and the middle under Patrick Henry. They had the authority to make treaties and arrest Indian agents commissioned by the British.

The Ridge, in the meantime, was a secluded, serene place with colored people controlling the land. Could Raleigh have foreseen in 1775 that the Ridge, seventy-five years later in 1850, long after his death, would have incubated a sprawling settlement of Cherokee people? Did he plan this community for the tired, hungry, and poor indigenous peoples, some drifting in from the Appomattox River area and others moving in from the south and west? It seems impossible. Yet with the connections that he had with other Cherokees in the militia and relatives in the Cherokee towns and in Northern Neck Virginia, could he have intentionally set up the Ridge and Stonewall Mill as havens for the weary?

A Cherokee tribal group would eventually inhabit Buffalo Ridge. Those inhabitants included the Bankses, Blairs, Beverl(e)ys, Bollings (Bowlings), Carters, Chamberses, Davises, McCoys, Fergusons (Furgesons), Elliotts, Evanses, Wests, Pinns (Penns, Pins), Isbells, Jordans, Christians, Jenkinses, Jewells, Johnsons, Megginsons, Greens, Coopers, Sparrows (Sparrowhawks), Warricks (Warwicks), Woods, Sorrells, Cousinses, Wests, Umbleses (Humbleses), and Tylers. They cherished their Cherokee heritage, but some also clung to the Cherokee/Pocahontas connections with the people of the Appomattox River settlements and Wiccocomico Indian Town, especially the Megginsons, Elliotts, Fergusons, and Wests.

In 1775, Raleigh and his family lived there in a small cabin in a private station among a few other Cherokee cabins scattered about the Ridge. They had a quiet refuge, which—largely due to the efforts of Raleigh Pinn—would later become a sanctuary for various Native American people.

Raleigh and Sarah had always been faithful Christians, and their cabin was a blessing for their neighbors. They often held devotions in their home with friends arriving there each Sunday to worship. The men wore two straight pins, inconspicuously arranged in the shape of a cross, on their coat lapels each Sunday, just as they did during formal tribal occasions. As they attended devotions, they took solace in the idea that they were in fellowship with their sister tribe, the Stonewall Mill folks who were also worshiping in their homes at this same time and manner. This feeling of kinship was reinforced as they secretly held monthly tribal meetings, one month at the Ridge and the next month at Stonewall Mill.

Raleigh was also a local trader and had connections with Cherokee traders from the Overhill towns on the Little Tennessee River. The Overhill country was the most powerful of all the Cherokee towns during most of the eighteenth century. As early as 1754, Virginians had been trying to win the support of the Cherokees by placing traders in contact with the Overhill Cherokees to gain and hold their allegiance. Eighteen years earlier, Virginia and South Carolina built two forts in the area. Virginians were the first to erect a fort in Cherokee territory, but it was never garrisoned by colonial soldiers.

In addition, Raleigh had connections with other traders in the Little Tennessee area as well as with the Cherokee traders who traveled from that area. They also kept him informed about what was happening with the Cherokees in the Middle and Lower towns. The people in the Lower, Middle, and Overhill Cherokee towns knew about the Ridge and Stonewall Mill villages, as they claimed the people as their Virginia relatives. Since it was removed from the beaten paths, the Ridge residents always left the cabin doors open for anyone who was Cherokee. White residents did not suspect what Raleigh was doing in the remote, off-the-beaten-path settlements. The Buffalo Ridge area was far back in the woods. The traders and warriors came up the Blue Ridge Mountain from the Middle and Lower towns, and the Overhill travelers moved in from southwestern Virginia. They had easy travel into the Ridge area from the Blue Ridge Mountains at Big Island and then traversed through the Glades area into the Ridge. Cherokees often visited their kinfolk all along the Appomattox River area in the 1600s. The Ridge Cherokee residents occasionally visited their relatives in the Stonewall Mill area also, although they were careful to dress and act like their white neighbors so as not to attract undue attention. In fact, some of the Ridge and Stonewall Mill people looked more like white people, except in the summertime, than Cherokee warriors and traders.

The Ridge location was a well-kept secret among the people of Cherokee settlements in Tennessee, North Carolina, and South Carolina. Even the Virginia Powhatan Indians knew about the Ridge, as Raleigh made regular trips to visit relatives on the East Coast. He had relatives in the Northumberland and Lancaster areas on the East Coast—the Pinns, Hursts, Coxes, Nickles or Nuckles, Sorrells, and others. Between 1820 and 1840, Virginia Indians knew how much some colonists hated the Cherokees, and due to this fact, they did not bring any undue notice to the Stonewall Mill and Ridge people. In spite of their care, the Ridge and Stonewall Mill settlements came dangerously close to being exposed as Cherokee villages later.

Because of militia invasions in the 1760s and 1776, and the rumors about the Oklahoma Removal in the early 1800s, the Cherokees from the Lower, Middle, and Overhill towns started flowing into Virginia. They primarily came into areas near the Piedmont locations along the Blue Ridge and Roanoke River area. The McCoys, Howells (Owls), Humbleses (Umbleses), Eagles, Sparrows, and others came to strategic areas of Virginia. They set up themselves as white people, and at times as colored people in order to survive economically and politically. The colored people, and for a time, the people who eagerly desired to be white, were called mulatto on official documents.

While Raleigh may have had some premonitions of the events that were to come, even he could not have known the magnitude of his efforts to protect his family and tribal members. He was a man imbued with pride in his heritage and with a fierce desire to keep them safe. This was one of the reasons why he was currently training with the militia.

Sarah attended to her household chores and saw to Turner's needs during Raleigh's absence from the cabin. She was accustomed to having him away from the house for long intervals because he went on hunting trips during the winter around this time of the year and returned a week or two later. He was a dedicated militiaman protecting residents of the county, night and day, against enemies.

She kept busy with her household tasks as there was always work to do. She cared for Turner, made clothes for the family, tended the livestock, and prepared food. Women at the Ridge usually made baskets, floor mats, and pottery items. Sarah was very good with these tasks because her mother and grandmother had taught her Native American skills. As a child, her mother and grandmother showed her how to cut white oak strips from very small trees and weave them into baskets. She also used the strips to make bottoms for chairs that Raleigh had built for the living room. She proudly displayed oak baskets in the cabin that her grandmother had made some thirty-three years ago as proof of their durability.

During the summers, she assisted Raleigh with the garden and livestock chores at the farm. When he was away, she tended to the animals alone, caring for two cows, three horses, six goats, ten chickens, six guineas, and four hogs. The hogs always fretted her more than all the other duties put together. In addition, they had two dogs—beagles that Raleigh loved because they were his partners on short hunting trips, and they were very good guard dogs around the cabin. Sarah was grateful to have them, especially with all the Indian traffic through the Ridge, and the more recent British spies' surveillance of the area. Sarah smiled as she recalled how a British agent was almost eaten alive by the beagles when he showed up one day to beg Raleigh to join his side in the war against the colonists. Although Raleigh said he would think about it and get back to him, he planned to forget to get back to him. He never did get back to him. Of course, the agent did not care to come back to the spot where he was routed by Raleigh's small animals.

Sarah, a very good cook, prepared meals as part of her household chores. Raleigh enjoyed coming in from the cold weather and finding hot, nutritious venison soup already on the table. Her turtle soup was a favorite in the Pinn family. She also prepared excellent dishes with corn, and her meals often included boiled, roasted, or fried corn. She made such good corn cakes and mush that the smell could bring Turner and Raleigh into the cabin even when the two were engaged in enjoyable activities in the yard. Her hominy and ashcakes were legendary among the residents who lived at the Ridge. Often their dogs sniffed near the front door, alerting Raleigh and Turner as they worked outside that something good was cooking in the cabin. Neighbors often dropped by the cabin, hoping to be invited to taste her current recipes. The beagles, with their keen sense of smell, had a habit of following Sarah's visitors into the cabin.

During the summer, she dried the garden beans and peas that she planned to prepare for meals during the long, cold winter. Sliced apples, peaches, and other fruits were sun-dried on the cabin roof in preparation for cold months at the Ridge. She enjoyed making mulberry and blackberry cobblers for Raleigh in the summer, but she discouraged him from asking for apple, peach, and pear cobblers because she hoped to save these dried fruits for the winter. While Turner had a special craving for the small fried fruit pies, he also liked his mother's cobblers. He enjoyed them best when she made the fried pies in the shape of a half-moon by folding half of the round flattened piece of dough over the fruit and using a fork to place fancy markings around the circled edges.

Food at the Ridge was abundant. While Raleigh was away, Sarah and Turner went down to the James River to catch catfish, the family's favorite meat. Deer, bear, wild turkey, squirrel, and raccoon were plentiful at the Ridge. Sarah added herbs and spices when frying, baking, or boiling wild meat.

In November, Raleigh usually slaughtered three or four hogs and salt-cured the meat. Beef and deer meat were more difficult to preserve than hog meat. Cured pork lasted almost the whole year even though he shared some of it with his neighbors. After he returned from the militia drill, two weeks later than the usual hog killing time, he planned to slaughter the hogs in December this year.

Raleigh had always shown his appreciation for Sarah's faithfulness as a wife and partner at the Ridge by bringing her a gift when he returned from his travels, even from short trips. Of course, he also remembered to get a gift for Turner. After a recent trading trip, Raleigh brought home some very good sewing needles. Prior to receiving these modern presents, Sarah had used very fine slit sinews to make materials for the household. Sometimes, when Raleigh could not find his straight pins, he would borrow two of the needles, arranging them in the shape of a cross on his lapel for his official tribal and church meetings.

Usually, Sarah and Turner kept very busy when Raleigh was away. At night, they would sit in the cabin, with Sarah engaged in some chore such as sewing while Turner played with his wooden hand-carved toy Indians. Turner's bedtime during the winter months was about 7:00 p.m. As soon as it was dark outside, he began to yawn and flick his quarter moon–shaped eyes. Sarah watched him do this for about thirty minutes before she began preparing him for bed.

Meanwhile, at the militia camp, Raleigh sat by the fire and thought about his family. He wondered if Sarah and Turner were a little afraid at night. He usually burned one lamp in each occupied room in the cabin when he was home. After being away on trips, however, he noticed on his return that Sarah and Turner had double the number of lamps burning in each room. *No*, he thought, *she is not afraid because she is the Beloved Mother of the tribe and is highly respected by the men and women for her ability to protect herself. She can fight any man or animal if necessary.*

Sarah was a beautiful woman. The farm work had toned her body and made her strong. Even with her muscles, however, she was still slim and willowy. Raleigh also admired her toughness and was aware that she always kept a five-inch knife in her apron pocket and tomahawks in the bedroom and kitchen for extra protection.

During tribal meetings, the women did household activities, and the men participated in the meeting conducted by Raleigh. Sarah and the other women also took part in archery and tomahawk drills. Raleigh, years earlier, had ordered that all tribal adults, women and men, learn proficiency with a tomahawk and a bow. The blowgun was not used that much after 1775, but some old warriors taught the skill to young warriors for ceremonial purposes.

It was the evening of December 4, two days before the end of the Virginia militiamen camp. While Raleigh was thinking of Sarah, she was getting Turner ready for bed. At around 7:15 p.m., Turner drank a glass of warm goat milk and ate a molasses cookie before retiring. He then said his prayers.

Lord, now I go to sleep,
I pray my soul to keep.
Bless Daddy at the man minute meeting,
and don't let the hungry people from the
ocean take our land and food. We will
give them some food if they are hungry.
But daddy said that we should not give
up our land. A Cherokee is land-hungry
too, and there is not enough land to feed the
hungry ocean people. They have big
tummies. They eat the land and then eat our
buffaloes, goats, cattle, turkeys, and chickens.
Bless Mommy and all my kinfolks and the
beagles and everybody.
         Amen.

Sarah smiled as she heard his prayer, saying a silent *amen* to herself. She said to her son, "Into bed, Turner. Good night."

Turner gave her a big smile, hugged her tightly, and replied, "Good night, Mommy."

"Good night, Turner."

"Good night, Mommy!"

"Okay, Turner, that is enough for tonight," she said.

Back at camp, at about the same time Turner was getting into bed, Raleigh did what he did best. He told fireside stories about Cherokee and Wiccocomico history. Several minutemen surrounded him as he told stories that he had told them before. No respectable Cherokee would be so impolite as to interrupt a chief or an orator even though only seven acknowledged that they were Cherokee. Cherokee history was Cherokee history, and who could resist hearing the history again and again? Six full-blooded white soldiers sat down with the others and gave their attention to Raleigh. William Scott sat on a log with John West and James Hartless. William Clark, John Clark, David Clark, and John Redcross squatted on the ground. John and James Stuart, Gilbert and James Cottrell, John Bowling, Phil Going, Abraham Warwick, Francis Satterwhite, William Megginson,

Absalom Adkins, John Tyler, and Reuben Banks stood with their eyes fixed on Raleigh as he spoke.

"In the spring of 1756, only 150 Cherokee warriors showed up to do the fighting for the British and colonists. The British believed that the best people to fight the hostile Indians would be other Indians. They were surprised that our people, the Cherokees, were not excited about their war. They thought if they spent money on a fort in Cherokee territory, our people would run to their rescue. Virginia spent one thousand pounds to build the fort. They were insulted when only 150 Cherokee were furnished by the Cherokee Nation to support the British and colonials. Our people had very good smarts and were not going to be controlled by them."

Raleigh and the other Indian men trusted the six white soldiers. Raleigh believed that they had a lot in common spiritually, so he shared the cherished historical information about the Cherokees with them.

"The incidents that opened the Cherokee War started in the spring of 1758. The British recruited hundreds of Cherokee warriors. In April, some arrived at the Virginia Regiment's headquarters in Winchester. The late cold winters and late spring snows in Pennsylvania prevented our Cherokee folk from doing what they do best: scout, raid, and withdraw. They sat around half-starved, waiting for action. While hungry at the main camp, they decided to travel between Winchester and the Cherokee towns. They took barely enough food to support human beings on their way home. As they traveled through the backwoods, they took some horses, which were probably wild and belonged to whoever got them first. According to the white folk, they also harassed some white settlers in Bedford and Augusta counties. In their journey, German settlers, without any reason, killed forty of our warriors in a bloody fashion even though the Cherokees had permission to travel through the area under British command."

Raleigh positioned himself more comfortably on the ground to continue his story. One of the men handed him a tin cup of coffee. "After Braddock's defeat, Virginia offered a bounty for Indian scalps. There has never been a more dastardly deed in the history of the colony than this act of offering reward for Cherokee scalps. Virginia was hostile against Indians and the colonists were trigger-happy. This hateful act of offering rewards for Cherokee scalps caused the bloody war between the Indians and the settlers." Raleigh looked around and asked, "Did they think no one would retaliate? Naturally, our people began to attack Carolina settlements to avenge the murders of our peoples. Tensions increased between Cherokee and colonists. The Carolina officials declared war against us in 1759."

Members of the Amherst Militia made Raleigh feel special as they sat at attention and silently waited for him to continue. These soldiers, some of whom had never heard specifics about the colonial militia's attack on Cherokee towns, had natural interest in learning the martial arts strategies and military campaign histories. An engaging storyteller, Raleigh presented the stories slowly, lowering and raising his voice to keep them interested. His fellow soldiers seemed to be captivated by the way Raleigh spun out the story. His facial expressions and gestures held them spellbound.

"In 1760, around April, Colonel Montgomery, accompanied by 1,600 men, marched through the Cherokee territory. He surprised Little Keowee town and killed every male defender while marching toward his main goal, Etchoe." The men could hear the suppressed anger in his voice, and his eyes flashed in the firelight. "Then the troops moved through the Lower towns. Montgomery discovered when he arrived at Estatoe that it had been abandoned by almost all of its Cherokee inhabitants. He burned Estatoe, Sugar Town, and all the other towns in the Lower Nation to the ground." Unconsciously, Raleigh's right hand tightened into a fist. Some of the men listening to him felt their own resentment rising. "Militia members were ordered to cut down Cherokee fruit orchards, which had taken years to grow, and even to burn their cornfields. The militia troops killed and captured more than one hundred warriors and drove the rest of the population into the mountains. Montgomery thought he was destroying the Cherokees, driving them into the woods and mountains to starve, but what he was really doing was forcing them to relocate and survive in other areas."

Raleigh's voice began to rise, and he shook his closed fist for emphasis. "But our people know how to survive. They know how to be hungry. They can run for miles without drinking water. They thought they were killing our people by forcing them into the mountain. But actually, our people survived by removing themselves and moving into isolated mountains and the piedmont plateaus in Virginia, North Carolina, Tennessee, Georgia, South Carolina, Alabama, and other areas all over the South." Here he drew a ragged breath. The men listening to him were too enthralled to do more than blink. "Montgomery then moved north near Etchoe—located about halfway between Fort Loudoun and Fort Prince George—the nearest settlement in the Middle towns. Here he ran into his defeat. Maj. Gen. Jeffery Amherst had sent about 1,300 troops down by sea from New York. General Amherst is the man who put his name on our county. He sent a battalion of Highlanders and three companies of Royal Scots Greys under Colonel Montgomery. Montgomery and his troops were not aware that concentrated forces of Cherokees were waiting for him. He did not expect Cherokee warriors to be a force to reckon with, and he met stiff and overpowering opposition. They had come into Cherokee territory, and we aboriginal people fight best on our own ground. Montgomery's troops were hemmed in like horses in a corral or rabbits in a rabbit trap. The area had low valleys and bushes so thick that the military troops could hardly see four yards ahead on the trail. There were valleys with very steep banks and ravines. They were all tangled up with the Cherokees in this tight area, which gave our people the advantage. Even a few Indians, given the opportunity to plan the place of the battle, can tangle and tie up a large number of soldiers."

Once again, his voice resonated throughout the camp, inspiring certain militiamen with fierce pride in their ancestors. "As the troopers retreated from the area because the opposing forces were too much to permit them to remain, furious Indians rushed and pummeled them. You know how we are in combat. Almost a hundred soldiers were killed, with twenty Highlanders and nearly eighty Royal Scots, while about forty of our brave warriors fell in battle. Montgomery, withdrawing his soldiers to save their lives, had to destroy some of their provisions during his retreat so that they could free their horses to carry their wounded soldiers back to headquarters." Raleigh started to say more, but his conscience or an inner voice held him back. He wanted to tell the minutemen how the Highlanders and the Royal Scots had been utterly disgraced by the Cherokees in aboriginal highlands and fled the battlefield like rats deserting a sinking ship. He resisted the urge and continued with his story. "The Highlanders and the Scots Greys may have been Montgomery's elite troops, but they had not met the likes of the Cherokees. They should have learned their lesson from our ancestors after the colonists' skirmish with the Cherokees in Richmond in 1656. They must have forgotten how the colonists had to beg for peace. I know this is true because the events surrounding the battle are written in the Virginia Colonial Council's official records."

Noting the looks of amazement in the men's eyes, he said, "I am not making this up! The Cherokees, then called Rechahecrians, whipped Hill's troops, and the Indians that he had with him to help him fight. Their colonial leader, Hill, and his army were near the Richmond James River falls in almost the same embarrassing situation as Montgomery. Cherokees, if allowed to gain the military advantage on their own terrain, make a good fight out of the battle. Montgomery found this out when his men got tangled up in briars and vines on narrow roads above deep ravines. Next, he experienced the menacing way the Cherokees fought with the tomahawk. Well, it was too much for Montgomery and his men."

Raleigh considered whether he should warn his fellow militiamen about the possibility that the British may have written down the Cherokee war strategies and tactics from the battles in 1760–61 and may have trained their current soldiers to use Cherokee martial art skills against their rebellious colonial enemies. "In 1761, Colonel Grant and 2,600 troops, including some Catawbas and Chickasaws, attacked our Middle towns, burning almost twenty of them to the ground. They burned all the plantations and destroyed about two thousand acres of Cherokee crops. Grant drove some five thousand

Cherokee—men, women, and children—into the woods and mountains to starve or survive. He thought they would all perish, but you know our people are at home in the woods and mountains even when they are hungry. You know what happened to some of our people. Many survived as they withdrew to other parts of the South. You and I know that some of them came to Amherst, Buckingham, Albemarle, and Bedford, even over to Amelia and Brunswick counties. We know that these surviving Cherokees are here, don't we? Are they two hundred miles from here? Many are! Are they one hundred miles from here? Many are! Are they ten miles from here? Some are! Are they one mile from here? Some are!"

Just then the six white soldiers, realizing what Raleigh was going to say next, looked at each other and started to shuffle their feet. They told Raleigh and the other men that it was their bedtime. They actually left because they did not want to be witnesses to Raleigh's confession that there were secret Cherokee soldiers in the camp. Raleigh continued resolutely, "Are Cherokees here in this camp?" He continued quietly, "Some are!" They all smiled, including the six white soldiers as they were leaving the scene. Several soldiers laughed loudly, and Raleigh indicated it would be wise to hold down the noise. When the laughter had subsided, he continued, "At the start of the Revolutionary War, the British were able to get the Cherokee Nation's allegiance. It was a mistake for the Cherokee Nation to side with them. The colonists became more determined to conquer the Cherokees. Unlike the Cherokee Nation's agreement to side with the British, we kept our honor by protecting our kin and property. Our Ridge people didn't side with the British regardless of the amount of money they offered to the locals to join them."

Five more militiamen joined Raleigh's history class even though it was getting late. They slipped into the group without Raleigh knowing that they were there.

"Gen. Griffith Rutherford's forces attacked Cherokees from North Carolina and destroyed almost forty Cherokee towns. Our people ran to other areas and hid out in the Blue Ridge and Smoky Mountains. The South Carolina militia under Col.

Andrew Williamson with one thousand soldiers moved against the Lower towns. Under his direction, his soldiers burned the towns, destroying them all. Williamson then joined forces with Rutherford and moved against the Middle towns. From Virginia, Colonel Christian and his Virginian militia closed in on the Overhill towns. Before Colonel Christian arrived, the Cherokees marched to the hills, leaving behind their livestock and farms. More than fifty towns were burned. Those brave Cherokees who escaped were fugitives in their own lands. They survived by eating acorns, chestnuts, and wild game. Some were even refugees with the British. From the Virginia line to the Chattahoochee River, the trail of destruction was ghastly. The Cherokees had to give up and agree to treaty terms."

Raleigh ended his story there. "Before we turn in, boys," advised Raleigh, "let us thank God for his grace in letting some of the Cherokees escape and survive in Virginia and other southern colonies." Raleigh bent his head and prayed.

> Lord, grant your peace to all Cherokees everywhere. Please let all the dispersed Cherokees keep some semblance of the original culture, their homeland. Let us remember Kittowa, the mother town, and all the other towns. Let us not forget the glory that you provided them before their destruction. Let us never forget Kittowa, the Appomattox River settlements, and their happy and sad days. We will never forget the Richahecrians.
> Lord, bless our families back home.
> Amen.

With that, he raised his head and said, "Good night, men!" It was then that Raleigh pulled out his pocket watch—a Repoussé pocket watch, gold and enamel on brass, made in London in 1757—and turned it toward the firelight. He hadn't realized he had been talking for more than two hours! Since it was getting late, and he felt responsible for keeping the men up, he tried to make amends by placing some fresh wood in the camp fire to help provide comfort to the soldiers as they prepared to go to sleep. They exchanged good nights.

As he was leaving to go to bed, John Redcross reminded him, "Remember, up at dawn."

Raleigh went to bed, but he did not sleep well. He thought of Sarah and his family at home, and his mind was overloaded with uneasy fears. He thought about what his fellow worshipers at the small Fairmount Baptist Fellowship had told him. They believed that he had two spiritual gifts, one for healing and the other for discernment. He could sense when something was wrong with his family or band members. He then prayed to God, in the name of Jesus Christ, that they would be protected.

Sarah was awakened at 10:00 p.m. by the barking beagles and the stomping hooves of horses. The horses were moving around furiously in the barn, and she could hear the sounds of their bodies bumping against the barn walls. She looked outside from the bedroom window but could not see anything in the dark moonless night. Silently, she walked across the floor, picked up her tomahawk from the bedside table, and eased into Turner's room. He was sleeping soundly. She stood on her toes and peeked out of his small window, which was near the ceiling and about three feet higher than the window in her bedroom. She did not see anything that alarmed her. The beagles and other animals continued to move around uneasily. By this time, the chickens and guineas had also begun to make loud chucking noises.

She spoke to herself, *I am a Cherokee. I am as good as any man when it comes to protecting my family. I will fight man or beast. I have proven my skill with the beasts. Bears are afraid of me. I am ready to drive this tomahawk stone into the head of any animal, fox, bear, or cougar.* She continued to talk to herself to bolster her self-confidence and dispel any fears. She pushed the solid oak kitchen table against the front door and then sat on it with her weapon in hand. It was amazing that these loud noises did not disturb Turner from his deep sleep. She then cried out loudly,

"I am a Cherokee. I dare you to show your face in this cabin. I dare you to remain on our property. I am ready for you. Come on in, admit your mistake in being on Raleigh Pinn's property and receive your just punishment. God is my protector and Christ is my comforter."

Sarah's face was red and tense, half in horror and half in excitement; she could feel her blood vessels and muscles protruding on both sides of her neck, and the sound of her own heart echoed in her ears. She pushed herself against the door so hard and long that she fell asleep on the table, exhausted.

Sarah opened her eyes and realized that she had slept a long time. The image of the corner grandfather clock's hands pointed to 3:45 a.m. Her neck was aching from the crooked position in which she slept on the table where she had leaned against the hard oak door. With the tomahawk still in her clinched, rigid hand, she gradually remembered the traumatic events that had occurred during the night. Climbing down, Sarah put down her tomahawk and pulled the table from the door.

After removing the cabin door lock and retrieving her tomahawk, she opened the door slowly, and like a sly fox, stepped outside with the weapon firmly in her hand. The morning darkness forced her to go back for a lantern. She stepped outside, with the security of light, and went to the barn. Everything was in order. The hens were awake, but nothing seemed to be wrong, and the hog pen had not been disturbed. Sarah went back inside and checked on Turner to make sure that he was all right. She found him sleeping comfortably, curled up with palms pressed together under his jaw and his two colorful quilts almost on the floor. She pulled the quilts back up over his shoulders, kissed him, and thanked God for his blessings throughout the frightful night.

It was now 4:15 a.m., and she wondered if she should go back to bed or just stay up and make some sassafras tea. She decided to do both. After brewing the tea and drinking two hot cups she returned to bed. Sarah kept the lamp burning after drinking her tea and did not fall asleep right away because her mind was consumed with thoughts of her beloved husband. She was so proud of his love for the Cherokee people, and she recognized that the concern and care for his kin were uncommon. As she reclined on her bed and looked at the ceiling, she wondered how Raleigh attracted so many aboriginal people to the area. Was he inviting Native Americans to come to the Ridge and Stonewall on his hunting trips through the wilderness? Maybe he made contacts during the militia service for the county and colony. People kept showing up here. Some of the strangers spoke a little English and Cherokee. Some spoke very little English and a combination of Cherokee and Algonquian. She was proud that Raleigh understood all three languages.

John Redcross and Raleigh Pinn were dressed in official militia attire as they rode their horses toward Stapleton. John elected to travel to Buffalo Ridge with Raleigh but parted company shortly after reaching there to go to his home in the Buffalo River area. It was December 6. They had been in minuteman training since November 17. Both were excellent soldiers, and the officers and soldiers at their battalion looked up to them because of their reconnaissance, combat, and tracking skills. Even with all the attention the officers gave them, they remained humble because they knew these skills were God-given, not totally something that they learned from men. Their native ancestors had always excelled in these areas, and they too were blessed with the skills.

They wore hunting shirts, short and plain, without cuffs—the standard uniform of Amherst militiamen. Their hat brims were two-inches deep, cocked on one side with a knot of ribbon worn on the left side with a button loop. They looked bereft with short hair. Each had a military-issue rifle and a tomahawk.

"The strangers on the road would not give us any harassment today," said Raleigh. He and John, who was also mulatto-looking, looked noble in their military uniforms and could not be mistaken for either Cherokee or British spies. Fleetingly, Raleigh thought of the Cherokees who were going over to the British side because of several incidents against the Cherokees perpetrated by the colonists in Virginia and the Carolinas.

Raleigh had reason to be on guard, at least until the white colonists realized he was on their side.

Raleigh and John Redcross understood each other well. He spoke some Cherokee and loved their heritage. John Redcross spoke excellent Cherokee and had wholly retained their cultural heritage. They understood each other all too well, and they both often had the same ideas. One of their recent ideas was that they should leave documentation about their Indian background for their descendants and historians. While many of their Cherokee friends were going over to the white side, they did not want to go back to the dust of the earth—from which they came—without leaving as much information as they could about their aboriginal lives.

Raleigh had experienced a full, rich life, and he had been active in both public affairs and tribal business. He looked for every opportunity to leave legal records to document his leadership of tribes on Buffalo Ridge and Stonewall Mill, including real estate records, records of his attendance at tribal marriages, tax records with the mulatto designation, census records, and military records. He imagined that his spiritual presence would follow every event or official action of the tribe even after his death. It would seem that he was peeping over the shoulders of his descendants. His name would be recorded and spoken of for years after his death in Amherst and Buckingham counties.

"Raleigh, how is the plan coming along with the two bands?" inquired John as he shifted in his saddle.

"Great," replied Raleigh. "I think the two communities are managing to stay unified even though they had grappled to intermingle with their white neighbors."

"Are you inviting more Cherokees into the two groups?" John asked.

Raleigh replied in Cherokee, "*Uh uh.*" Yes.

He spoke Cherokee with John but shied away from speaking the language to some Cherokees, because they wanted to appear both Cherokee and white. He did not want the colonists to feel uncomfortable by forcing the Cherokee language on them.

Most people in Amherst County knew what John was. He openly bragged about his Cherokee ancestry. Raleigh, on the other hand, left documents to assert his Wiccocomico and Cherokee heritage for his descendants. Both men felt a closeness with Cherokees/Powhatans or Rechahecrians that were in the East Coast area in 1622, Richmond in 1656, and on the Appomattox River banks around that time. Raleigh and John discussed the future of their friendship and the possibility of their descendants uniting in wedlock in order to pass the strong Cherokee heritage on to their descendants and historians. John agreed with Raleigh that the legacy must remain in Amherst County. By now, they were four miles out from Buffalo Ridge and about a mile away from Stapleton.

When they made it to Raleigh's turnoff at a high point at the Ridge, the sun began to go down on the western horizon. Raleigh and John were looking directly into the sun. As Raleigh said his goodbye to John and began to turn toward the pathway to his cabin, Sarah and Turner heard him and ran out of the cabin to meet him. As they ran toward Raleigh, they were like Cherokee warriors in pursuit of their prey, with the late afternoon sun casting its long shadow straight toward him.

Just at that moment, Sarah realized that the Lord kept his word when he promised her that the shadow would bring Raleigh and her together again, just as Raleigh's shadow had been cast toward her three weeks ago. She did not understand at that time that Raleigh's return trip would allow Turner's and her shadow to point toward him. Sarah jumped on the horse in one motion as her husband pulled her toward him.

By this time, Turner, who had been running behind Sarah as fast as his little legs could run, reached them as well. Raleigh and Sarah both reached down and lifted Turner on the horse. His daddy held him in his left arm while he embraced Sarah, who was sitting behind him, with his right arm. Then, in a moment of embarrassment, Sarah looked up and saw John Redcross on his horse moving along the road.

She squirmed a little and finally managed to look at him. "Hello, John. I was in such a hurry to welcome Raleigh home that I completely ignored you. I apologize for not greeting you."

John, with a huge grin on his face, tipped his hat to her and said, "Your apology is accepted. And now, if you will excuse me,

I need to get home to see my own family. If I'm lucky, I'll get such a greeting when I get home!" Still grinning as he turned his horse, he called back over his shoulder, "Raleigh, I'll come over the day after tomorrow to help you kill those hogs." With that, John spurred his horse into a trot and started whistling as he rode away. It was then that Sarah noticed that John's shadow also came back toward them as he rode toward the setting sun.

They slipped down from the horse and strolled happily toward the cabin, the horse trailing behind them. Raleigh pulled some hard peppermint candy out of his saddlebag for Turner and a ribbon for a hat that Sarah had been making. They hugged him tightly in appreciation for his thoughtfulness. Raleigh led the horse to the barn, removed the saddle, and gave him some hay. He stood there a few minutes looking at his horse's swinging tail.

He laughed at him and said, "You are trying to let me know that you also appreciate my kindness. You and I are happy to be back at the Ridge!"

In his joy to be back home, he thanked God for the haven at the Ridge—a place of serenity for contemplation. He had much to think about, and he needed to spend some time with Sarah and Turner tonight and tomorrow. Since he and John Redcross would butcher four hogs the day after tomorrow, he had only one day to finalize his new plans for the Ridge and Stonewall Mill. He needed to be alone to think carefully and deeply, and he would do so tomorrow on the stump in Pinn Park Cherokee Burial Ground.

The tribal cemetery was always a quiet and serene spot; a private location for thinking, which facilitated wise meditation and planning. It was as if God humbled the thinkers with the presence of the graves of fallen leaders while elevating the thoughts of the present leaders with a touch of his wisdom and omniscience. All major tribal decisions had been made initially at Pinn Park, at least those that required long and serious thought and deliberation.

Raleigh hugged his horse's neck for being so kind in bearing him on the long journey to the Ridge and then went into the cabin to give and receive some more warm and loving hugs.

> For I was ahungered, and ye gave me meat;
> I was thirsty, and ye gave me drink;
> I was a stranger, and ye took me in.
> Matthew 25:35

6

A Compassionate Heart

7 December 1775

It rained during the night and the temperature fell from an average morning reading of thirty-seven degrees to thirty-one degrees in the morning, forming an icy crust on the grass. Raleigh had awakened at 6:00 a.m. because he wanted to have some quiet time with Sarah at the kitchen table before Turner came down for breakfast. As they drank sassafras tea, Sarah told him about the events at the Ridge and Stonewall during the last three weeks. While they reviewed their respective activities during the period of Raleigh's battalion drill, Sarah learned that Raleigh had one very restless night on December 4, two nights before he came home. Shaking his head, Raleigh set down his cup.

"It was crazy. You know how much I can talk when I am telling historical stories. And you know I always get tired when I talk a long time, and I had talked a long time that evening, about two hours nonstop. I should have been in deep sleep when I finally turned in for the night. But I couldn't sleep because I had this force pulling on me. My right hand was clutched tightly although I didn't have a thing in it to grip. I kept looking into the woods because I thought something was out there. Sarah, you and Turner were on my mind. These thoughts created a desire to be home at the Ridge for some urgent reason. I kept turning over and over in my head this urgent need for me to be home on the Ridge. The pressure was especially powerful because I had one more night before I could come home," Raleigh said.

Sarah had been listening intently. She then said, "Raleigh, you don't need to say any more. When I told you about what happened while you were away, I didn't mention everything." Seeing his expression of surprise, she added, "I don't want you to worry about me whenever you are away."

Raleigh sat up straighter in his chair. "Sarah, you need to tell me the whole story! What happened that night?" He leaned forward and looked into her eyes. "I had the feeling that a cougar or bear was trying to get to you and Turner. The dream was about the cougar and the bear, but I could not understand why I was dreaming when I was awake until about four o'clock in the morning! Was it a dream?"

"No, Raleigh. It was your spiritual gift working. I told you that you had the gift of discernment. The Lord revealed to you that I was going through something, and he wanted you to pray for me."

"I did pray for you that night. What happened, Sarah?"

"Well, something was disturbing the farm animals around ten o'clock that night," Sarah remembered. "I looked out the window to see what was going on, but I didn't see anything." She placed her hand on the table that Raleigh had made for her. "I pulled this heavy table up against the door and sat on it. For the rest of the night, I kept my tomahawk in my right hand. That is why you had your right hand clutched so tightly that night. It is your gift working in you as if you were gripping the tomahawk."

"You didn't grip the knife that you keep in your apron?"

"No, I forgot about the knife. I snatched the tomahawk off the table in our bedroom because I knew that it could do more damage if someone or something decided to break into our house!"

It was now 7:15 a.m. and it was getting bright outside. Turner was still asleep. Raleigh thought it best to change the subject, so he told Sarah about his plans to kill hogs tomorrow, reminding her that John would help him. He tried to shake his uneasiness, but he couldn't.

"Sarah, wake Turner up. Then you both can go outside and help me look for tracks in the yard. I know it rained hard last night, so any tracks might have been washed away."

He knew the chances of any tracks were slim; nevertheless, he looked forward to taking them outside to inspect the grounds. It could be another opportunity to teach them Cherokee tracking skills. Sarah's father had trained her well in reading animal and human footprints, but Raleigh often admitted to her jokingly, "You can still use some skills-sharpening training from me, an experienced tracker."

Sarah woke Turner up and told him to get dressed before returning to the kitchen to continue sipping her tea. When Turner came into the kitchen, he found his daddy and mother sitting at the table. He was so happy that his daddy had returned that his eyes lit up and he gave a huge grin. "Daddy, you're home!"

Then he remembered that his father had come home late yesterday, but he had forgotten this during the night. He rushed to his daddy and jumped onto his lap. He had turned six years old this month and it seemed to his father that he had grown much heavier in just three weeks.

"Sarah, what have you been feeding this boy? He is so large. Look at that stomach!" he teased, tickling Turner as he spoke.

Turner laughed, "Mommy gave me some of her molasses bread. It was good. She saved some for you, Daddy. It will make you fat if you eat it. Look how big I am!"

They put on their winter clothes and went outside. Raleigh led the patrol around the cabin and farm. He took the lead point position and Sarah came behind him.

"Turner, you protect your mother by coming behind her. Walk quietly and don't talk! Look on the ground for tracks. I know it's icy and cold, so walk carefully."

When they reached the barn, he found the evidence that they sought. Raleigh made sure that he waited so Turner could find the tracks. He stood near the tracks, which had not been totally erased by the rain, until Turner came near the site.

"Turner, what is this? Is it a bear track or a cougar, or both?"

"I believe it is a bear or a cougar. It is both!" He looked up and grinned proudly, saying, "Daddy, both of the animals were here."

"Apparently a cougar and a bear were outside about the same time," Raleigh explained to Sarah. "Otherwise, you would have heard noises from the livestock at different times. Either a cougar or a bear would have caused the animals to create quite a stir. Since they arrived at about the same time, they probably scared each other off. It's a good thing that the beagles, horses, and chickens made loud noises to warn you about the danger."

After about ten minutes of inspections outside, they went back inside for breakfast. Sarah went straight to the kitchen. She fried some country ham and made redeye gravy—Raleigh's favorite—from the ham grease. Scrambled eggs were waiting on the table. Sarah always cooked three large eggs for Raleigh, and she and Turner ate one egg each. She had already prepared some ashcakes that she kept warm near the fireplace.

She asked Raleigh, "What kind of jam would you like to eat with the ashcakes—blackberry, mulberry, or strawberry?"

"Blackberry, of course."

Then he had a second thought and inquired, "What kind do you want, Turner?"

Raleigh always wanted to make Turner feel important by giving him an opportunity to make small decisions. He knew that Turner would be the chief of the two Cherokee bands at some point in the future and must make wise decisions if the population increased in the two areas and there was a demand for a chief. Raleigh worried at that moment about the big decision regarding the bands that he had to make later that day.

Turner shouted, "Blackberry, of course!"

He loved to repeat whatever his daddy said, and Raleigh knew that when he asked him what kind of jam he wanted. Raleigh reminded him that his decisions were modeled after his own father and therefore were wiser decisions than those that were thought through alone. This concept had been passed down to Raleigh. The decisions that were thought through by two or more tribal members had more power than a decision made by one person alone. At six years of age, Turner was far smarter—two or three seasons smarter—than he should have been.

Raleigh spent time with Sarah and Turner until around 1:00 p.m. Then he told them that he would be back as soon as God gave him an answer to his problem.

Turner asked, "What problem, Daddy?"

Sarah quickly touched his lips and signaled him to say no more. Turner immediately fell silent and held his hands to his own mouth.

Sarah said, "Honey, go on to Pinn Park. We will hold your dinner as long as it takes you to make the decision." She looked at Turner, and he caught the hint.

"Daddy, go on to Pinn Park. I'll get the wood in for the fire—I'm a big boy." He drew himself up to his full height, standing slightly on his toes to appear taller. "We won't eat until you come back from your thinking place. Daddy, we promise we will wait for you!"

As he walked toward Pinn Park on that dreary afternoon with his Bible in his right hand, Raleigh placed his feet down slowly and firmly on the icy trail.

Turner watched his daddy as he left the yard and walked thoughtfully toward the cemetery. He then looked at his mother and asked, "Why is Daddy going all the way to the cemetery? It's so cold out there. Couldn't he think in here where it's warm?"

Sarah tried to find a way to explain to him that Raleigh went to the cemetery alone when he wanted to get in touch with God and feel the spirit of his ancestors.

"Turner, your daddy cannot make big decisions alone. He needs the help of another person."

"Why can't he make the decisions with you and me?"

"He asks us to help him make the small- and medium-sized decisions, but with big, big problems he gets other people to help him. He seeks the help of God and tribal leaders. He seeks God's help first and then he shares it with the other tribal leaders. These decisions are very important because what he decides to do will last for years. You may be a twenty-six-year-old man and remember the decision that your daddy made today!

You may be the chief of the bands and have to make the same types of decisions that your daddy must make today."

She bent down, put her hands on Turner's shoulders, and looked him directly in the face. "Turner, always remember to ask God to give you answers to all of your important decisions in life."

Solemnly, Turner nodded and said, "I will. I will tell God to help me when I say my nighttime prayers."

Raleigh went directly to the stump, his special spot at Pinn Park, and sat there for more than an hour while he meditated on his problem. Then, after he had begun to feel the grace and Spirit of God, he dropped to his knees and poured out his heart to the Lord. With eyes raised to heaven, ignoring the chill of the day, he prayed.

> Lord, I have been distraught for months about the situation in the Lower, Middle, and Overhill towns. Our people have been abused. They have been mistreated. Many of our people were killed and their homes and farms were destroyed and burned. They are hiding out in the hills and mountains along the Blue Ridge and in other areas. Some are scared to come down and go back home. Really, they do not have a home to return to. Their villages have been burned and their crops and orchards destroyed. It would take years to restore the orchards. Lord, they need your help. I need your help to make the right decisions concerning them.
>
> Those who did go back home in 1760 and 1761 were scared that the colonists and militia were coming back to destroy their homes again within the next year. What can I do here at the Ridge and at Stonewall Mill to help them? What can I do for them?

Lord, the colonists took our own Indian land, our reservation, in the 1600s and formed Northumberland County. Our people were dispersed all over the colony. Others were placed in a new Indian reserve, inferior to the good Indian reservation land that they took from the Wiccocomico Indian ancestors. Large numbers of Algonquian people, some mixed with Cherokee, had to become indentured servants to survive in Northumberland County. Now they are doing it all over again in the Cherokee towns. Tell me, Lord. I will wait here with my buried relatives for your answer. Let me know what small part I can play to help them! Before I go to the grave, Father, let me know if I can enter your kingdom with a clean heart and conscience.

 Amen.

He sat back on the stump and opened his Bible to the Gospel according to Matthew. He then randomly turned to chapter 25 verses 34 and 35:

> Then shall the King say unto them on his right hand, "Come, ye blessed of my Father, inherit the kingdom prepared for you from the foundation of the world: For I was ahungered, and ye gave me meat; I was thirsty, and ye gave me drink: I was a stranger, and ye took me in . . ."

Raleigh closed his Bible and meditated over the things he had done through the years for the Cherokee people. After the colonial militias had destroyed Cherokee towns, he provided refuge on the Ridge for some of the Cherokee who escaped. He had later moved some of the people over to Stonewall Mill to spread them out, keeping some hidden for months until he found jobs for them on the area farms. Raleigh and his Cherokee visitors were always apprehensive, afraid that the colonists would come to the Ridge looking for them. Raleigh managed the situation well and settled the people to the satisfaction of both bands. Now he had received word that the people in the Cherokee towns were on edge again; rumors were rampant that the colonists were coming back to assault the Lower, Middle, and Overhill towns again. Should he be a Christian and take more of them? They had been coming to him one by one since the first Cherokee came to the Ridge, but now they were set to flood the Ridge, bringing their hungry, tired, half-clothed bodies. Could he turn them away? Would their large numbers expose the Ridge to the hatred of the colonists?

He had managed to get along with the white people in the past. How long would this last if the new Cherokee crowd settled on the Ridge? Would his presence in the minutemen's battalion protect him from the colonists if they found out that he was harboring a village of Cherokee warriors, women, and children? He doubted that his superior military skills and dedication to colonial freedom from the British or his work in the militia would be enough to carry weight with colonists if they became angry at the Cherokee people at the Ridge and at Stonewall Mill.

Raleigh said, "God, if I turn them away will you receive me into your kingdom when I die? Will you remember that I did not give them food when they were hungry; that I did not take the strangers in when they needed help? Will I lose my reward in the judgment? Tell me, Lord, and I will do what you say! I just ask you to give me the power to hold out to the end."

Raleigh had been feeling guilty for years; ever since he learned about the atrocities of the colonists against his people in Cherokee towns. Feelings of guilt had overtaken him because he was doing well and had some pleasures while his Cherokee people in the dispersed towns were being abused. All the Ridge residents knew he considered it his responsibility to do whatever he could to make his settlement economically and socially successful. God had blessed him with a good station at the Ridge. He knew he had also been blessed by becoming a valuable soldier in the militia and an asset in the minutemen's battalion.

He remembered reading somewhere in the Bible, *To whom much is given, much is expected.* This scripture stayed on his mind as if the passage had been written especially for him. It is true that he had been under great pressure from the whites; they envied his station at the Ridge, a location that was one of the first areas to be settled in Amherst County. The European settlers were moving in, and he felt some of his neighbors' hostility. After they arrived, some colonists began to feel as though they were better than the aboriginal people who had been there for years. Raleigh felt these pressures piercing his body like pins. How long could he keep his neighbors off his property?

He looked like a white man in many ways, but wondered whether the new, darker aboriginal people would give him away and force him to give up all that he had built on both the Ridge and Stonewall Mill. He wondered whether they would learn to speak English quickly before the whites caught on that he had formed the Indian villages.

Leaning forward with his elbows on his knees he deliberated the plight of the Cherokees. Raleigh had learned about the state of affairs in the Cherokee towns in South Carolina, North Carolina, and Tennessee from other Indians, traders, and militia minutemen. The Indian soldiers and traders had seen and heard rumors about Cherokee hiding out in much of southwest Virginia.

Raleigh knew that Cherokees also came to central Virginia from other southern colonies via Pittsylvania, Halifax, Mecklenburg, Henry, and Brunswick counties. Cherokees settled as members of Cherokee villages in many areas. Eventually, most were forced to pass as another race or tribe rather than reveal their Cherokee heritage.

Raleigh thought about the rumor one of the soldiers told him regarding some of these people. "They were hiding out on White Top Mountain. They had their own band, with its own chief, much like the Buffalo Ridge band. Some tribes did not give up their heritage in order to go for white," the soldier said.

Other rumors spread about villages in Brunswick County that had aboriginal people hiding from the colonists as free colored people. These people were reported to be Saponis and remnants of three Iroquois tribes: Cherokees, Nottoways, and Meherrins. The Nottoways, the Meherrins, and the Cherokees spoke an Iroquoian language. Raleigh knew that two of the tribes' members, the Nottoways and the Cherokees, often hunted together in that area. Perhaps the Nottoways had provided a haven for these Cherokees, who may have migrated from Appomattox River settlements. Raleigh reasoned that the Saponis yielded to the other two tribes and learned an Iroquoian language.

Some Cherokees, who had requested the Virginia Colonial Council in the early eighteenth century to let them settle on the Roanoke River for the purpose of free trade, came anyway when the Council refused their request. They resided as white and colored in the Roanoke River area and throughout the area of Southside Virginia. Raleigh knew that his wife's Cherokee relatives, the Evanses, had lived in Lunenburg County in the 1760s in present-day Mecklenburg County before some of the family moved to Amherst County. The Evanses were possibly some of the assembled Cherokees who sought official permission from the Colonial Council in November 1721 to settle along the Roanoke River for trade, about fifty-four years earlier. They lived in scattered locations throughout the area, but united as a tribe in spirit. Like the Evanses, Mecklenburg County had a large number of other residents who boasted of Cherokee ancestry in their family tree.

Raleigh remembered how his father and other relatives in Northumberland County had told him about the regular travel of the Cherokees between the South Point/Wicomico Church location and Accomac. There were almost as many descendants of Cherokee in Onley as there were Accomac Indian descendants. They were all mixed up. The Eastern Shore received the Cherokees when they retreated from Virginia colonists. It would have been more acceptable to the colonists if they settled as white, or even Accomac Indians, but not Cherokee. He wondered if he should do more for the Cherokees at the Ridge.

Raleigh realized that some soldiers were not sympathetic to the plight of the aboriginal people. He knew that some Virginia officials and soldiers hated the Cherokees and wanted to wipe them totally from Virginia. Colonists harassed the

Rechahecrians in the seventeenth century and they used the same tactics on the Appomattox River Cherokee people to separate and disperse them.

Once again Raleigh turned his eyes toward heaven. "God, tell me what to do! What should I do? I need to meet with the council in a few days and I must make a recommendation to the joint council." He pleaded, "Please show me a sign, so I will know for sure what you want me to do."

Just as he finished the prayer, he noticed a small sparrow flying under a large leaf, looking for food. Immediately, almost miraculously, it had begun to snow. This was unusual because it rarely snowed this early at the Ridge. He was hypnotized by the slow descent of each flake. Soon the snow began to fall heavily, silently covering the ground. It was then that he focused on the sparrow again, still hiding under the leaf. Quickly, the snow covered all of its food possibilities.

His mind went back to two years earlier, on a cold, snowy day in February when he met a family of four Cherokees whose leader was called Sparrowhawk. He told Raleigh that he could call him Sparrow or Hawks. They passed through the Ridge area heading toward the James River and they were tired and hungry. He recalled how Sarah had treated them to some of her hot turtle soup and ashcakes. The family stayed a few hours, which was long enough for Raleigh to realize that they had migrated from the Middle town area. They spoke some English but mostly Cherokee. Sparrowhawk felt comfortable enough with Raleigh that he admitted that he was Cherokee, and that some of his kin lived in Princess Anne County on the Virginia coast. He did not indicate that he was traveling to that location. Raleigh, as was his custom, had not told these strangers when they first met that he was part Cherokee. Two hours later, as they had prepared to leave, Raleigh hugged them and told the family that he and his family were fellow Cherokees. His guests admitted that they had known all along that he was Cherokee by the way that the Pinn family received them. As the family had prepared to walk out the door of the cabin into the cold February air, Sarah had given two blankets to Sparrowhawk's wife, mainly for the two scantily clad children. Three inches of snow covered the ground before it stopped. The family left the cabin and has not been seen since.

Could they be related to our Sparrows here at the Ridge? Raleigh was surprised that the thought had not come to his mind when they were visiting in the cabin. *Why did I think of this family now? Was it because it was snowing then as it is today? Maybe I remembered them because I saw the sparrow in the snow and thought of the Sparrowhawks on that snowy day.*

At that moment, he got a cold chill. This was not a chill like one would normally get on a cold and frosty day. This was not the chill that usually came when he sat on the stump in Pinn Park Cemetery on a wintry day and meditated near the graves of his people. This chill was so cold and penetrating that he was ready to go directly to the cabin. He felt sick and needed some of Sarah's herbal tea to warm his now painfully icy body. He felt so chilly that he almost forgot his main mission. As he stood up from the stump, he remembered that God had not answered his prayer yet. He started to sit back down, but his arms and legs had begun to get stiff. His body would not bend to let him resume his seat on the stump.

God wants me to go home, he reasoned. *Is this God's answer, or am I just cold?* He needed some hot tea immediately. Then it came to his consciousness that the Sparrowhawks had been in the same condition as he was, stiff and cold, before Sarah prepared hot drinks for them.

So, God, is this your answer? I will feed the hungry. I will clothe the strangers. I will rest the weary at the Ridge. Just then his entire body straightened up and he felt a warm glow inside as if a fire was burning within his heart and bones. He could not hold his peace any longer about the Cherokee refugees.

As was his custom, he referred directly to his Bible. He opened it randomly and found the book of Jeremiah. He turned to chapter 20 verse 9.

> . . . But his word was in my heart as a burning fire shut up in my bones, and I was weary with forbearing, and I could not stay.

Then he realized why he could not sit back down. *God has given me my answer. He wants me to go home now.* Raleigh knew in his heart that God had inspired him to see the similarities between the sparrow under the leaves and the Sparrowhawks. Both were hungry, tired, and cold, and both needed help. Raleigh squared his shoulders and made a resolution. *I did not help the Sparrowhawks very much then, but I will if they are alive and need my help the next time. I promise you, Lord, that I will help all the Cherokee people who come through the area fleeing from persecution and calamity.*

Raleigh closed his Bible and began to walk toward the cabin. He imagined how Abraham must have felt when God told him that he would bless him and make him the ancestor of a great nation.

When he opened the door of the cabin at 5:00 p.m., Sarah and Turner, who had been gazing at him from the window as he came down the hill, were waiting for him in the kitchen. The food was already prepared and was on the table. He just needed to say grace.

"Raleigh," Sarah comforted him, "I have my special herbal tea for you today because there is a chill in the air." He turned toward her to see how much she knew about his body chill. She had a smile on her face and repeated it again, "I have some hot tea for you because of your chill."

He took his seat and said the blessing. He reached for his spoon and stirred it in his bowl. He shook his head in amazement that Sarah was so wise and knew him so well. He blew air onto the hot turtle soup and steaming ashcakes. *This woman has been living with me for so long that she has also been given the gift of discernment. How did she know I had a chill and needed her tea?*

That night Raleigh fell into a dream of former times. In the dream, he saw scenes of Cherokee living in peace as aboriginal people. They had sprawling settlements in the Overhill, Middle, and Lower towns. In the time before trade routes of whites and Indians went back and forth from Savannah and Charleston to Chota and Tellico, he saw the old towns of Great Tellico, Chatugee, Tennessee, and Chota. He saw the Overhill towns, the Valley towns, and the Lower towns. In the Lower towns, he saw Tomassee, Oustestee, and Estatole. Raleigh tossed and turned in his sleep as he dreamt about the Cherokee mother town, Kittowa. Oh, how he had learned to love the town! His Cherokee ancestors, those who lived in Wiccocomico talked about Kittowa, a precious jewel. Due to her long oppression, the town, like the Pearl among its Ridge people, was loved in a special way by all of the inhabitants of the other Cherokee towns. Kittowa, the ancient town and cream of the Cherokee Nation was as special as the eagle among the birds of the air. She was as gold among precious metals, and as valuable as a pearl made precious out of suffering, like the Pearl people in the Ridge and Stonewall Mill. Then his dream turned into a nightmare.

Raleigh saw enemies assault the Cherokee Nation on powerful horses. Smallpox, with a first name, Genocide, rode on a yellow horse and spread his epidemic throughout the Cherokee Nation. Genocide assaulted great warriors as well as women and children and lingered almost endlessly, waiting until the infected people who resisted death finally died. In the dream, he saw the infected Cherokees view themselves as reflections in the river. When they saw their terrible disfigurement some people shot themselves. Others, proud people, stabbed themselves or cut their own throats. Some threw themselves into the campfire ashes.

The horseman wrestled with the medicine men and the great apothecaries until he had made a mockery of their crafts and blotted out their spotless reputations with herbal remedies. After he had taken their crafts away, the horseman made them run into the woods and mountains in tears. They looked furiously for new herbs to combat the smallpox horseman. The medicine men could not find any ingredients in the trees or in the roots of the ground. Some obsessed apothecaries lost their minds in the woods and mountains, refusing to come back to the village until they had a cure. His dream traveled years into the future and he saw them still in a state of insanity, with long hair, beards, toenails, and fingernails roaming in the wilderness. They were still obsessed with finding cures to whip the lingering horseman on the yellow horse even after he had gone from their area and taken the genocide to other villages.

Raleigh remembered that his people were always combative. They would never give up; it was not the nature of the Cherokees. They could not live without war and combat. If they were not fighting the Tuscaroras or the Shawnees, it would be another tribe. Fighting was a compulsion, and even in this, they had a way of going to the extreme. Now, however, the medicine men had to deal with the smallpox horseman. They could not win this battle against genocide because they could not find the cure.

In the dream he saw another person—a woman—mounted on a white horse. She was thin, almost skeletal in appearance, and dressed in royal garb. They called her the agent of the queen of England. As a representative of the British and colonists, she ravenously sought land. After traveling over the Atlantic Ocean, she was starved and refused to be satisfied until she engulfed the Cherokee Nation. She consumed Raleigh's homeland and Cherokee territory. Even though the queen's agent devoured most of the Powhatan Nation, Raleigh realized that she was still famished and hungry. Her appetite for the land, blood, and scalps of Cherokees could not be sated. She made the colonists fight the Cherokees and even manipulated other people from Europe to move against the Cherokees. Hessian mercenaries and other Germans, Scots, and the Irish were eager to come to Virginia to fight for England.

Raleigh's dream did not reveal the fact that some of the German Nordics were sympathetic to the plight of the Cherokees. Many married the aboriginal people and chose not to return to Germany after the Revolutionary War. They lived in the Blue Ridge area of Virginia and became ancestors to numerous Cherokee descendants. Some of these people chose to assimilate and coexist, whereas other groups did not. In the dream the settlers persisted, overrunning the countryside. The queen's agent had a large empty stomach that could be heard growling throughout the Cherokee territory, from the Appomattox River settlements in Virginia to Georgia. The well-known Cherokee historian and newspaper publisher, Col. E. C. Boudinot, years later spoke of one of the Virginia settlements on the Appomattox River since it was an important part of the Cherokee Nations' early history. The queen's agent made her ravenous presence felt in South Carolina, and from North Carolina to Tennessee. She even traveled all the way to Georgia, making growling sounds that were terrifying and appalling, like a hundred mighty river waterfalls. Raleigh even saw the chief of the ancient town of Kittowa who, after hearing the woman's sound and reviewing his archival decibel records, noted that he could not find a sound in the oration records equal in its shocking magnitude.

There appeared in Raleigh's dream another horseman, a historian, who rode on a great black horse with many other black horses following him. The lead horse represented the black lies on which he rode, and the other black horses were the new or revived lies on which the colonists would mount in the future when the other lies were tired. The lead horse was a black Virginia horse that disputed the skimpy ancient aboriginal history that Native Americans had collected. The rider would take the horse wherever he desired to dispute the Natives' claims that they were as much God's chosen people as the colonists. The historian horseman rode through Virginia proclaiming that only the notations by white historians and explorers would be accepted in this colony, disregarding Native American history and their existence. They would not accept the legend and orations of Cherokee historians that they and their ancestors once lived in Virginia. This horseman led the other two horsemen against the Cherokees, and even ordered the smallpox horseman to kill as many Cherokees as possible, thereby removing any evidence of them having lived in Virginia. The historian horseman's first name was Paper and his last name was Genocide. He asked the British to drive her people, the colonists, through Virginia and take land, scalps, and lives so that there would be no oral or paper records to document the Cherokee's presence in the Old Dominion.

Raleigh continued to dream about future events. The historian horseman also ordered historians, anthropologists, and archaeologists to ignore Cherokee history and legends in

Virginia. He told them that they could not call any person who claimed Cherokee heritage "Cherokee" unless they wore loincloths and had turbans on their heads. The Cherokees had to be humble and poor stereotypical Indians, not those dressing and living like white men in order to stay in Virginia and be documented as Indian. He demanded that civil officials scratch out the word "Cherokee" or "Indian" on official documents and replace it with "mixed," "colored," and "mulatto." Historians were required to be indifferent to Cherokee history, and if possible, make statements in written records that they were all in North Carolina, not in Virginia. The historian horseman's main job was to remove "Cherokee" from the minds and memory of the colonists. He would muffle Native American oral traditions and erase written history of the Rechahecrians or Cherokees in Virginia. The historian horseman would blot out any knowledge of the history of Cherokees on Appomattox Riverbanks, the Peaks of Otter, the Piedmont sections of the Blue Ridge Mountains, Amherst County, and in other locations of Virginia. He would even hide the fact in Virginia history that the Cherokees defeated the colonial soldiers at the falls in Richmond even though it had been recorded in the official documents of the Virginia Colonial Council. As a bold agent of black lies, he even disputed the Colonial Council's records.

The horseman would teach the people to react to Cherokee history in Virginia by saying, "I thought they were all in North Carolina and Oklahoma. They only came to Virginia to hunt. They went back home to North Carolina every night," and other lies. The horseman's trick on the Indians was to make absurd myths appear truthful and to twist history so that it appeared to be a myth. Raleigh dreamed that history officials and scholars would say centuries later, "There are no Cherokee living in Virginia" and "Cherokee have never lived in Virginia because there are no colonial records verifying they were here as poor savages in loincloths and turbans."

His dream presented genocidal fires in which official documents were intentionally and accidentally burned to cinders—records that would document the existence of Cherokee people. He was horrified by visions of courthouses ablaze in various Old Dominion counties with the official records of aboriginal people going up in smoke, as if pleading with heaven for help.

The Cherokee people themselves were forced to tell lies for the horseman. They would deny their own Cherokee heritage because it was proper or acceptable to be another tribe in Virginia. These descendants of Cherokees would state, "Our Virginia ancestors were wrong. They lied when they told their children and grandchildren that we were Cherokees."

Raleigh, still dreaming, wrestled against the information that Cherokee descendants would repeat these lies for the historian horseman. He saw Cherokees with a mixture of black ancestry denying their Cherokee ancestry because it was not proper—according to the historian horseman—to have even one drop of "black blood" in their veins. He saw Cherokee abnegating their heritage in favor of a totally white or black racial heritage. He saw oceans of colonists and their descendants pointing their fingers toward some Native American people and stating, "You are not Indians because you have some black or white blood."

He dreamed about historians canceling or erasing small tribes by using politically expedient phrases indicating that a particular tribe "ceased to exist as an Indian tribe because many of its members intermixed with black people."

The genocide was sweeping and powerful! The horseman was so effective that he made slave masters convince their slaves that even children of an Indian father and black mother—or descendants of Indian mothers and black fathers—were 100 percent black. He dreamed that the slave masters and their white descendants stated that no part of the Indian could be passed on to black descendants because even one drop of the black blood would neutralize all the Indian blood.

In the dream, the horseman was captured in the act of forcing physicians and state officials to expedite these lies by requiring Indian tribal members to be 100 percent black on official records. The lie was so effective that even black people would believe it two centuries later—following the traditions of the slave masters in retaining black slaves who had Indian descent through an Indian father—and deny that they have

Indian blood. People of African and Native ancestry would take on the slave master's brainwashing mentality decades later and remark, "I am all African. I am 100 percent African-American," thinking that they could not be both African and Indian.

Raleigh saw whole generations of racial groups picking up the historian horseman's lies as he rode through Virginia, spreading them like seeds in cornfields. Raleigh saw colonists in the dream saying they were Cherokee and English, Irish and Cherokee, Cherokee and German, Scots and Cherokee. Then these same mixed neighbors pointed at an African and Cherokee girl and made her cry, claiming that she could not own Cherokee ancestry if she had even one black ancestor in her whole family tree.

Raleigh was shocked when he saw the white horsewoman. She had in her hands two scalps. The scalp in her right hand had "Buffalo Ridge" written on it, and the one in her left hand had the name "Stonewall." The name "Mill," the other part of the Stonewall Mill settlement's name, had been left off the scalp in the horsewoman's haste to destroy or disperse the Native American people there. He saw eight familiar names written on scalps as they flew through the air in the hands of the rider; they were Pinn, Beverley, Scott, Redcross, Sparrow, Megginson, Ferguson, and Humbles. The historian horsewoman threw the scalps into the James River, floating toward the Atlantic Ocean. There were some names on the scalps that were unfamiliar to Raleigh like McCoy, Harris, Warrick, Cousins, Banks, Elliott, Chambers, West, Isbell, and many others. He saw another large scalp; it was so large that it rested on the back of the rider's saddle, and extended to the horse's bridle. It had the name "Kittowa" and had words written under Kittowa. They were, "The Pin Indians, the secret society of the Kittowa, will remain a secret because it is destroyed."

He saw in his nightmare a tomahawk coming toward his head and a knife waiting in the background to remove his scalp. The person who held the knife had several names written on his arms. The words on the right arm were "The Colonial Council of Virginia." Raleigh had never been fearful for his own life for he had been honored for heroism and bravery in the militia and by his tribesmen. He was fearless, but this dream implied that the colony of Virginia would destroy his people.

In another scene in the dream, there was another arm threatening his people that bore the strange, unknown name of Pleck. This dream warned him about impending events or occurrences. He sweated for his people, the Buffalo Ridge and Stonewall Mill bands, but could not fight for them in his dreams because the combatants were not real. How could he engage in combat against the unreal forces of the three spiritual horsemen? He surrendered with a great scream that roused Sarah from her sleep. She realized that he was locked in a surrealistic world that she could not enter, and she reached out to him. She saw the bedroom tomahawk in his right hand, ready to bludgeon his dreamworld adversaries.

With a hand on his shoulder, she began shaking him awake. "What's wrong, Raleigh? Raleigh, wake up!" When he didn't respond to her she shook his sweaty shoulders even harder. "Raleigh, you're dreaming. Honey, you're having a nightmare. It is not real!"

She frowned and continued her efforts to draw him out of his dreamworld and back to reality. After what seemed like an hour but was probably no longer than a minute or two, Raleigh—still gripping in the frenzy of his dream and bathing in sweat— slowly returned from his dream to earth. In the confusion in their bedroom, they were both unaware that Turner was also having a nightmare in his room. When he heard his mother's voice trying to wake his father, he jumped out of his bed and ran to Raleigh's quivering arms.

Raleigh gathered Turner closely and asked him, "What's wrong, my son?"

Turner shouted, "Daddy, there is a hungry lady in a white dress over there in my room." He had one arm around his father's neck and the other pointed to his bedroom. "She has blood all over her gown. She has some furry things hanging off her waist, like your rabbit or raccoon skins but black in color, and a knife in one hand and a tomahawk in her other hand. She said, 'I have come over the ocean and I am hungry. I want land and scalps, Cherokee land and scalps!' Daddy, she looked hungry. Go over there and make her leave my room. Make her go back to her home on the ocean." With this, he put his other arm around his father's neck and leaned closer.

Raleigh and Sarah exchanged a glance and reassured him that it was just a bad dream. He and Sarah then led the way to Turner's room, with Turner following at a distance behind. Raleigh looked under Turner's bed and searched behind his cedar chest. He inspected the bed linens and quilts, but they could not find a lady in a blood-stained white dress.

He said, "I think the lady ran out of the house. I'm not sure if she will ever leave the colony of Virginia, Turner, but I know that she has left this cabin and Buffalo Ridge. We will not allow her to stay at the Ridge or at Stonewall."

It was 3:30 a.m. They realized that it was too early to get up for the day so they all returned to the bedroom. Raleigh told Turner to get in the bed with them. As soon as Turner put his head on his daddy's soft pillow, he was no longer fearful. He dropped immediately into a peaceful and well-deserved sleep. Raleigh could not go back to sleep right away because the "vision" he had experienced was too real to only be a dream. It would be months before he would share the devastating contents of the dream with Sarah.

Tossing in the bed, he wondered why Turner had also dreamed about the queen and the scalps. He pondered, *God is surely giving me a warning and some new information to support what I must do. I have to allow some Cherokee people to flee to the Ridge and Stonewall Mill. I must protect them. I will pray for the help of God and seek the assistance of influential, powerful, and understanding Cherokee-connected residents like the Fergusons, Tylers, Megginsons, Isbells, Bollings, and others. They will help me build a fortress around our settlements against future penetration by colonists. Both settlements have suffered enough.*

Before dawn, Raleigh closed his eyes and joined Sarah and Turner in a restful but short sleep.

One hour after Raleigh fell asleep, he and Sarah were up and stirring around the house because they had a busy day ahead. It was hog-killing day, and they had overslept. Sarah hurriedly prepared breakfast since it was a custom to prepare a large breakfast on hog-killing days. As she bustled around the kitchen in a long brown cotton dress and her favorite flowered apron, she thought, *Why, it is a well-known fact that John Redcross is a big eater. He expects a hungry man's breakfast.* She looked forward to the compliments that she always received from him about her food. She fried twelve thick slices of bacon in the large wrought-iron skillet and cooked some of the roof-dried October apples. She melted some freshly churned butter over the apples as they were frying. She also fried ten hen eggs and three guinea eggs. She made some large ashcakes on the fireplace that would hug the working men's stomachs.

John arrived 7:10 a.m., bringing two other helpers with him from Buffalo River. Sarah called to them from the porch as they came into the yard, "Come and get the food while it is hot! What took you so long to get here, John?" This was a silent joke between Sarah and Raleigh because they had to rush themselves to get the food ready since they had overslept. John and his helpers, responding to the mouth-watering aromas coming from the kitchen, hurried their steps and walked briskly toward the house.

They sat at the table as a family. John always called Sarah his kin. They would later be related through marriage of family members, and of course, they were related as Cherokees. They ate their traditional hog-killing-day breakfast slowly, savoring every bite as they wanted plenty of energy to tackle the hard work they had before them. The breakfast fellowship was as much a ritual as it was a good social get-together.

While Raleigh and John were butchering the first hog, the other two men were scalding and scraping the hair off the remaining two hogs. Raleigh had his mind on his dreams last night, and the butchering activities made him think about the scalping policies of the Old Dominion against Cherokees.

Raleigh paused in his work to look up at John. He said, "John, I am going to take them in!"

John replied, "You are going to do what?"

"I must do it. It is on me, and you know I have to do it!"

John knew what he was talking about because he too was aware of the colonists' many atrocities against Native people in general and his Cherokee people specifically. He also knew that this had been on Raleigh's mind the whole time during the last three weeks of the minuteman drills, but John was surprised that Raleigh would attempt such a large endeavor as to invite dispersed Cherokee people to his villages.

Carefully measuring his words, John said, "Once you open the door, Raleigh, they will come. You build the settlement, you open your land, and the poor souls will come, tired and hungry. Can you take all of them?" Then John started to shake his head a little in objection. "But opening the doors for the poor souls in the Overhill and Middle towns, it is too much! They will come! They will also come from the Lower towns when word gets down there through the Cherokee traders or when word reaches the Greenville and Spartanburg area. It will quickly be passed on, up and down to Cheowie and Tomassee, and then throughout all of the Lower towns. Do you want to expose our havens here, our families, to the hateful actions of the colonists? They will not appreciate having Cherokees near them as neighbors, maybe other Indian tribes, but not our fierce fighting warriors. We can get away with being Cherokees because we have learned to act like we are white. They suspect that you are Indian, and they know that I am. But we are few, and we act and dress just like the colonists. You put on your Cherokee council outfit and go down to Stapleton or to the county seat! Just let them know that you are Cherokee while dressed like that. Just do it and see what will happen." His voice rising, John pointed his knife at the animals. "You will be in hot water like these hogs, and somebody else will have the knife on your hide! If they knew that you had a Cherokee council meeting and have brought or are planning to bring more people into the area, our neighbors would be furious. Are you prepared to cause Sarah and Turner to suffer hostility from neighbors when all those people come?"

Still looking John in his eyes, Raleigh said with conviction, "Yes, I suspect that Sarah is already prepared for them. She knows how worried I have been about them." Persuasively, he said, "I will only take my kin and some of the kin of our kin."

"You will have more kin than you ever realized once the word gets out that you plan to take them," John cautioned, shaking his head. "If you are not careful, you could get a large group of kin coming your way from the Lower towns!"

"You are right. We will set limits. Let us give each town a number. Over that number and we will send them on to another village," Raleigh advised.

"That sounds more like it. I'm glad you are coming out of your crazy dream and dropping back down to earth," said a relieved John, who had recently become more cautious in his admissions to everyone that he was Cherokee.

The two returned to work and kept talking. As John cut out the heart of the hog, Raleigh asked him if he were aware of what the colonists were doing to the heart of the Cherokee town, Kittowa.

"Kittowa will always be a town of antiquity in Cherokee history. It is the oldest and will always be there. The whites can't destroy Kittowa, the heart!" John asserted. "The town among all the other Cherokee towns is first in the heart of all loyal Cherokees."

"John, you know how you and I love our nation, how we have kept a part of that nation in Amherst and Buckingham counties. Well, I think we must intentionally and strategically set up towns here that cannot be destroyed by the fires of the colonists. We must keep the Cherokee heritage in the hearts of our people in the Old Dominion, especially since the military and officials are trying so hard to wipe out our people completely from this area. The heritage must be driven deeply into our people's hearts, not just a superficial Cherokee heritage. We must teach them how to love their heritage like we love it." His voice rose with his fervent and quivering passion. "We must bring others in who have that same love and zeal, a love that can never be taken away, not even by death. They must be willing to be humble but with the strong will of a Cherokee. They must be willing to be a member of our villages but holding our Cherokee secrets to their hearts. They must protect the Pearl as they must swear to love and honor God first and be or become a Christian in the Pinn Indian tradition."

As they reached for the next hog, Raleigh continued, "I will make it a condition for admission to Stonewall Mill and Buffalo Ridge. They must hold the heritage dearly in their hearts and be willing to pass it on to their descendants. They must be willing not to switch completely to or to pass for white or colored and deny their Cherokee heritage when the times get bad or the pressures become overbearing. They must brand "Cherokee" on their hearts forever. If the colonists make us white or colored, so be it. Don't let us change our race, don't let us do it on our own out of embarrassment of our Indian heritage. We must document it well that we are real people."

John, inspired by Raleigh's words, nodded in agreement. "That sounds good to me." Then he added more cautiously, "But I still need to think on this."

Relieved, Raleigh said, "That settles it." He felt better after unloading the heavy burden that he had been carrying so long. John was a good listener and also a worthy one; a true Cherokee at heart, and his ears were excellent for hearing important ideas. Even though John said he needed to think about it, Raleigh knew in his heart that John would do his utmost to help the Cherokee cause.

They began to move faster, tackling the task before them with renewed enthusiasm. Now that John and Raleigh had taken care of the real business at hand, the secondary job of hog-killing activities could be completed. They were ready now to assist the other two workers and concentrate on the butchering job with clear minds.

March to join the army commanded by the
Honorable Major General Marquis de Lafayette.
Daniel Gaines, C. M. Amherst
[Colonel of the Amherst Militia]
June ye 21st 1781

7

Shadow of Yorktown

21 June 1781

Raleigh and Sarah have two new children added to their family during the last three years. Anna is a chubby three-year-old child and Eady, not quite a year old, is a healthy toddler. Sarah had been quite busy with the household chores and keeping her children entertained. Raleigh kept himself occupied with farm duties and thoughts of the Amherst militia being called on for extended military service.

Raleigh knew that he was a good soldier and did not need any feedback from militia commander, Colonel Gaines, to confirm this fact. His aboriginal background—both Wiccocomico and Cherokee—excused the need for such conversation. His Christian upbringing, on the other hand, restricted any inward or outward signs of pride. If the Anglican leaders in Wiccocomico knew what his heart was thinking—that he was the best soldier within miles of Amherst County—they would whip him in Jesus's name. Even the Fairmount Baptist Fellowship that he had formed in the village would be shocked at his inward attitude of self-pride. He remembered that, years earlier, it was pride that knocked him in the water at James River and exposed him to ridicule from his horse. How could he ever forget that experience? No, he did not want to go in the self-pride direction again. He would just leave it there.

As he worked in his tobacco field, removing new grassy sections that persistently grew as fast as his tobacco leaves, he wondered what would be next for the militia. *Would I have to leave my farm chores in the hands of Sarah and go to some distant region? When will the orders come to fight the British in a major battle? Will I have to use my combat and reconnaissance skills against my own kin, the Cherokees?* Raleigh knew that he must refrain from relapsing into prideful states against his Christian training, which he had often been guilty of in the past.

He justified his feelings of grandeur by remembering his commanding officer praising his military conduct during practice combat operations. Colonel Gaines told him during the most recent militia drill that he was one of the best reconnaissance soldiers in the Amherst militia, and this gave him permission to be thankful, not prideful, for the colonel's comments.

"This is not pride. It is just a known fact that I am a very good militiaman," he often told his friends. "It is not being proud if my officer evaluated me and I came out shining like gold."

Virginia and other states were attacking and invading Cherokee villages wherever they could be found. The Cherokees had been generally taking the side of the British against the colonists. Raleigh's mind raced with concerns about the Cherokee people. *The act of joining up with the British became the Cherokees' downfall. If their leaders hadn't made the strategic move to side with the British, their villages and crops wouldn't have been burned.*

He tended his tobacco plants carefully. The seeds were planted in seedbeds during the first week of February. When the plants had grown six to eight inches tall around April 15, Raleigh transplanted them to the vast fields of about fifteen acres. Cultivating the soil regularly to keep the dirt loose and free from weeds, he completed his last soil cultivation when the plants were one and-a-half to two feet tall. He usually pruned the upper parts of the plants when the flowers appeared to increase growth in the leaves. Tobacco farming was hard work and required agricultural skills and experience as well as diligence and determination. Raleigh had those qualities, which made him a very successful farmer.

Raleigh could not hoe the grass without thinking about those poor Cherokee men, women, and children hiding in the Blue Ridge. He knew some were along the Blue Ridge near Albemarle, Amherst, Bedford, Roanoke, Culpeper, and other Piedmont counties.

I am blessed to have crops here at the Ridge. They have no crops to hoe! What will I do, if the militia is called upon to go against Cherokee towns? The state militias have attacked the Middle towns twice already, burning scores of villages to the ground, destroying their crops and orchards, and forcing Cherokees to run to the hills and the Blue Ridge Mountains to hide and starve. If our Amherst militia is called on to participate in those military operations against Cherokees, I couldn't go after them. I would be in an awful situation, yet I would have to refuse. The Cherokees are family. We were all intermixed with the Cherokees in Wiccocomico as they hid with our people and other Algonquian tribes in the 1600s and 1700s. It was a rule, a pledge, a given among the Algonquians, especially the Wiccocomicos, that we would never fight the Cherokees. The Pamunkeys violated that rule when they agreed in 1656 to join the colonists with 100 tribesmen and fight the Rechahecrians at the falls in Richmond. The Pamunkeys had already made a pact with the colonists to go to their assistance if enemy forces attacked the colonists. In their defense, I guess they had to keep their agreement even though they were fighting their own kind. However, I haven't made a pact with the Amherst Militia that I would raid the Cherokee towns!

Raleigh had a split personality when it came to fighting. On the one hand, he could teach Bible school lessons at Fairmount Baptist Fellowship each Sunday morning and even occasionally do a little bootleg preaching with the skill of Apostle Paul. He knew the words of Jesus Christ and even did his best to put them into practice in his life. He had a passive, angel-like personality in the church school meetings and in the community. On the other hand when it came to militia combat against the British, he changed his personality totally. He took a 180-degree turn for the worst and became a devilish creature. At almost fifty years of age, he could leap, tumble, and run with Turner and even hold his own with the younger men in the Amherst Militia. Fellow soldiers jokingly referred to him as The Ox. One time, he lifted a large militia mule wagon, and while holding it, slipped a new wheel on the axle. He could throw the tomahawk one hundred feet and split a corn ear hanging on the side of a tobacco barn. Raleigh bragged to his militia comrades that his tomahawk was as accurate as the darts that demons throw at Christians. When in combat, his military demeanor was as powerful as a satanic force. He was gifted with physical strength and warrior skills.

I shouldn't think about enemy combatants I would harm for the cause of American freedom. It wouldn't be Christian. Anyway, I don't need to harbor unnecessarily hostile thoughts about future events. I am not in combat yet.

Raleigh, dressed in his homemade brown cotton breeches and an old store–bought cream-colored shirt, continued to hoe the crabgrass out of the quarter-mile-long tobacco rows. The weather was sultry. His bare feet, digging into the Buffalo Ridge dirt, left lighter footprints than the deeper ones that he made in the sandy tobacco field soil at Wiccocomico. Farmwork provided plenty of time to meditate and he could not get the Cherokee souls out of his mind—the poor, starving Cherokee fugitives.

What will they do in five months when the icy late November air on western North Carolina and southwestern Virginia hills starts howling against their ears, cutting sharply through their ragged clothes, chilling and numbing their bare feet? What will they do when the frost-nipped, shivery air blasts through their flesh and goes to their bones? How will they find enough food and raiment in the mountains?

He finished hoeing the row and began on another one facing the east. The sun was high and he questioned why the heat could not be stored somehow and later shared with the fugitive Cherokees on those mountains in December. His mind raced with other ideas as he hoed the field. He speculated about the kind of tobacco crop he would have at harvest time and if he would even be at home to savor smoking the first leaf of his crop. He always appreciated those first moments when he sat on a newly woven wicker chair and reclined with his pipe while facing the fireplace, leaning back and lighting up the first samples of his recently harvested tobacco crop.

By goodness, this is my best crop, he imagined, as he always believed each year's crop was the best.

As he hacked the grass along the row facing east with a speedy pace equal to the rhythms of his thoughts, he occasionally looked up as if he were expecting something to happen at home or someone to bring some good or bad news from the east. Whether he was thinking about the Cherokees in the mountains or reflecting on his youthful years in Wiccocomico Indian Town, thoughts and reflections were racing through his mind and zapping his energy.

At around 11:30 a.m., Turner ran toward his daddy, gleefully raising a white piece of paper in his right hand and leaving dust trails behind his steps. Turner shouted, "Daddy, Uncle Junior wrote you a letter. You got a letter! You got a letter from Uncle Junior! You got a letter!"

His daddy did not hear what he was saying at first, but by the time Turner was within five hundred yards, Raleigh's ears heard the good news. Raleigh dropped the hoe between the rows and rushed to meet Turner. While still thinking about his crop and making sure his tobacco was top-quality produce, he moved quickly to get out of the tobacco field before Turner's exultant steps plowed against the plants.

He walked to the edge of the field, sat on a rock beyond the rows, and thanked Turner for bringing him the letter. "Son, what do we have here? Is this letter for me? I appreciate you bringing this out to me so fast. This is an important letter from an important person, your uncle. Thank you, Turner."

"Daddy, I ran all the way with it so you could have it in a hurry."

"You did a good job! Let us rest ourselves. You have to be tired with all that running. Just like your daddy is tired from all this hoeing."

He invited Turner to sit on a rock and read it with him. Raleigh seized every opportunity to help Turner improve his reading skills. Raleigh was a good reader, and he learned to write skillfully. He asked Turner to give him the letter because his name was on it. He then opened the letter and reminded him that only the person whose name is on a letter had the authority to unseal it.

"Now that it is open, Turner, I need you to read it with me. Let us read together."

They read the letter together, slowly and anxiously. Raleigh did not let on to Turner that he was somewhat uneasy, full of apprehension and foreboding. He knew that it was not Robert Junior's propensity to write letters. He thought, *Robert can write and read because he too was trained in the indentured servitude institution, yet Junior does not like to write.* His heart beat fast with the suspense of this unexpected letter. He wondered if bad news would greet them. *Is one of our cousins dead in Indian Town or around Lancaster and Northumberland counties? Have the colonists taken more land from the family?* He moderated his pessimism and prayed for spiritual tranquility in the face of possible bad news as he and Turner waded through the letter.

> Gloucester, VA
> May ye 2nd, 1781
>
> Brother Raleigh,
> I just wanted you to know that John and I have been doing well. We are here in an artillery company. We have been here in this assignment several months. I am sorry that we cannot tell you more. Our captain will not let me say any more in this letter. We do not want to give away our position if the British intercept this correspondence to you.
>
> My other boys, Jim and Billy, are with Colonel Morgan's rifle company. I don't get any news on them. I have an idea where they are, but I do not have the liberty to say. I cannot say where because of the security restrictions. I will tell you more if and when I see you.
>
> Pray for our dispersed family. I am praying for the family back home, for the ones in the military and for the dispersed members like you. Pray for Jim, Billy, John, and me, that the Lord will see us through this

war with the British. Anyway, may the Lord's will be done. I will pray for you and yours. Give my regards to the family. Write me when you get a chance.

Your brother Junior

In that instant, he called to mind the unity of his family and how many miles now separated them as the crow flies. After a few seconds his fears abated, but he still worried as a result of the sparse information. He released the built-up tension by verbalizing his thoughts.

"So Brother Robert is in an artillery company. He's where he should be. He could always throw a rock sharper and farther than his brothers, and he could shoot an arrow straighter and farther than my other brother John or me. So his son John is in an artillery section! Who would have imagined that Junior has a son old enough to be an artillery soldier? Time flies."

"Daddy, what is an artillery soldier? What is artillery?"

"Son, artillery is—well, let me see," Raleigh said hesitantly as he scratched his head and leaned toward the ground. He drew a picture in the dirt of a cannon barrel firing.

"I don't understand. What is that, Daddy?"

"Turner, you know that blowgun I have at home? The one that I told you is too dangerous to play with and that I keep hidden from you? The cane stick that I shoot darts from. Remember the one that I pushed a hot iron rod through so that the darts could get through easily?"

"Yes, Daddy, I know where you hid the cane stick that shoots those darts. Mother told me not to touch it when I found it above the open hearth. I know about the cane stick. What is artillery?"

"Son, if I put a small stone in it, about the size of a green pea, and shoot it out of the cane, it will hit you. Well, the cannon are large iron weapons that shoot out large iron balls that blow up when they land. Your uncle and cousin are shooting those balls from the cannon. The cannons are called artillery. They are in an artillery company. An artillery company is a group of men who shoot artillery cannons."

He paused a long time as he tried to find something else to say. "Where in the world are my nephews, Jim and Billy? How long have Junior and his three boys been in the military?" He considered how many more days he had at home before he too would be called into active service.

He and Turner sat on rocks about ten minutes more without a word to each other. Turner knew his daddy well. He was old enough now to understand when to speak and when to remain silent. Turner was a considerate boy and gave his dad quiet moments of meditation as needed.

The scorching sun's position showed that it was nearly lunchtime. Eyes squinting upward, Raleigh could not help but think of war and death. He quickly sidestepped gruesome military thoughts and changed the subject. "Do you guess it's time for lunch, Turner?"

Realizing that his dad had given him liberty to speak, Turner exclaimed, "Yes, sir! Let's eat. We have collards, fried green tomatoes, corn bread, and fried chicken. Oh yeah, we have some hot molasses bread too. Don't forget the cool buttermilk. Yummy! Let's go before the hot food gets cold and the cold food gets warm!"

Raleigh and Turner were relaxing, relishing the lunch that Sarah had prepared with the help of the girls, Eady and Anna, who were holding on to her skirt. Raleigh imagined that someday Anna and Eady would prepare similar lunches for their husbands.

Raleigh jokingly remarked to Turner, "If they keep on helping Sarah in the kitchen, they will become great cooks and have fat husbands within five years after they marry! Sarah had better stop all this cooking around them!"

Raleigh did not realize how important his two girls would be in extending his Native American tribal genealogy. His little girl Eady would grow up and marry into the Beverly clan in Buckingham County on the other side of the James River from Buffalo Ridge. She will take William Beverly, son of Barsheba

Beverly, for her husband. Anna would take Thomas Evans, son of Hannah Evans of Amherst and grandson of Thomas Evans. Hannah had to permit her son, Thomas, to be put into indentured servitude, like many of the aboriginal children of that era. Thomas learned the blacksmith trade in that colonial institution of indentured servitude. It was believed that this family descended from the Evans who had migrated from county to county, having lived at one time in their migrations in Surry County.

Barsheba, like many of the Cherokee Beverly families, had been dispersed throughout Virginia. Before moving to Buckingham County, she resided in Pittsylvania County in the mid-1700s. After the assault by Virginia colonists and militias on Cherokees in Virginia in the early 1700s, her parents, like other Beverly families, are believed to have hidden by dividing their families in various locations so as not to appear as a large Cherokee tribe. When a Cherokee band living in Lunenburg/Mecklenburg area of Virginia along the Roanoke River in 1721 asked the Virginia Colonial Council for permission to settle near the river so that they may enjoy the convenience of free trade, the Council denied them the official opportunity to locate their families on a piece of Virginia land. The word spread throughout Virginia that in order to survive, Cherokee bands must settle as small groups or clans in strategic locations in Virginia and live as white or black farmers, if necessary, to survive.

The Evans families, who resided in the area of the Roanoke River and were possibly represented in the delegation that made the request before the Virginia Colonial Council in 1721, also dispersed their clans. Some of the Evans stayed in Lunenburg, Brunswick, and Mecklenburg counties, while some Evans' families settled in other Virginia localities, including Amherst and Buckingham counties. The Beverly families, for example, resided on lands in Augusta, Caroline, Culpeper, Franklin, Rockbridge, Spotsylvania, and Buckingham Counties. By 1810, of the fourteen Beverly families that lived throughout Virginia, seven resided at Stonewall Mill in Buckingham County.

Raleigh knew that his children would suffer in Colonial Virginia because of their Cherokee and Wiccocomico aboriginal ancestry. Like the Cherokee bands who owned ancestral land in sections of Virginia, his Wiccocomico ancestors were threatened with death and dispersion in the late 1600s and early 1700s if they did not give up their official tribal reservation land in Northumberland. His father, Robert, had warned his brothers and him to watch out for the colonists and new colonial settlers, as they were land-hungry "carnivores" and "herbivores." As Raleigh looked at his two daughters and reflected on their futures, he wondered if their lots would turn out better than his experiences. He left the Northern Neck because he had been warned that the Wiccocomico heritage and ancestry would be like a yoke around his neck, as many of the colonists had made vows to decimate the Wiccocomico bands until they are no more. Even during his indentured servitude and after leaving the Northern Neck, Raleigh knew that he had to look over his shoulders constantly for those "carnivores" about which his father so often warned him. He felt some consolation in the fact that Cherokees, known through the colonies for their tough martial arts skills, intermarried with the Wiccocomico people in Wiccocomico Indian Town, and to a large extent saved the small remnant of Wiccocomico from being removed from Virginia history forever. He would do his part to preserve his people by continuing to encourage intermarriage of his people with the Cherokees.

Raleigh got up from the table and walked to the front porch. His son followed him. Turner, mimicking Raleigh, picked his teeth with a broom straw, and they both sat down and rocked back and forth in the porch rockers. Turner followed his dad's cue by crossing his legs, stretching them out, and placing his feet on the porch railings.

"Turner, did you finish your morning chores before you brought me that letter?"

"Yes, sir. I fed the hogs, cleaned up the barn, and removed the cow chips in the yard. I have to do some more work out there in a few minutes."

"I need your help in the tobacco fields this afternoon. Get another hoe out of the barn and bring one of the rakes. I think we need to get the grass out of the rows because we may get some rain tonight. After spending all morning cutting, we don't want that grass growing back next week."

Raleigh wanted to make sure his boy became a fine farmer, knowing that he would someday inherit this farm. Having been trained in farming, Turner, like his father, loved the earth and the bounty it offered them. Turner rushed to the barn to get the hoe and rake but stopped when he saw a horse and rider on the road. The rider was pushing his horse fast.

Raleigh shouted, "What in the world is that rider trying to do to that animal? Is he trying to ruin the horse? Turner, look at that crazy rider! I had better not ever catch or hear of you driving my horse like that!"

Turner fixed his eyes on the horse and rider, wondering what justification and excuses the rider had for driving him like that. They locked their eyes on the rider and the dust trail that his horse threw behind him. Even Sarah, Anna, and Eady rushed from the kitchen to the porch to determine the reason for the shouting. By this time, they could hear the horse panting, possibly in pain, with each step. They saw the rider move back and forth with the horse's inhalations and exhalations. The chickens and guineas ran for cover, the cow rushed into the barn, and Raleigh's horse stood up on his hind legs and hit the stable fence with his forelegs. The birds in the area scattered from the distant trees.

By the time the horse came to a halt in front of the porch, Raleigh had retrieved his rifle, loaded it with powder, and pointed it at the rider. Being a militiaman, he had been trained for times when he had to be ready to shoot first and ask questions later. Raleigh, skilled in horsemanship, did not sympathize with anyone who mistreated a beast that served at the wishes of the rider. In all of his riding as a farmer and a soldier, as a dragoon and trooper, he never treated a horse in that manner. With his gun pointed at the rider, he was ready to demand justification.

The rider, dressed in a brimmed hat and militia-dress breeches, shirt, and boots, was a stout forty-year-old militiaman who lived near the Rutledge Creek area of Amherst County. After catching his breath, he looked straight at Raleigh, disregarding the fact that the gun was pointing in his direction.

He was a soldier and knew that Raleigh was doing no more than any skilled militiaman would do. As a fellow militiaman and former neighbor of Raleigh's when he owned the farm near Rutledge Creek, he did not expect any apologies for pointing the gun at him.

"Raleigh!" he shouted from his horse, reading from a military order. "You are required to meet tomorrow morning, 6:00 a.m., at the official secret rendezvous at which location and time you will receive further orders. Bring your best gun and militia gear! You may keep your own gun or a new one will be issued to you. If you keep your gun, you will be paid the official sum. By the way, I see you already have your gun in your hand, pointed at me."

Raleigh lowered the weapon, and both militiamen burst out into laughter.

Raleigh knew that he was now being called into active military service. The rider knew Raleigh, and even though he was not supposed to say any more on the military urgency, he felt bound to tell him more because Raleigh was one of the best scouts in the Amherst Militia. He dismounted his horse, put his hand on Raleigh's shoulder, and turned him away so the family could not overhear him.

"Raleigh, we must march to join the army commanded by Major General Marquis de Lafayette. This is signed by Col. Daniel Gaines, our militia commander."

The courier jumped back on his horse and shouted back to Raleigh, "See you at 6:00 a.m." He was off to the next militiaman's house.

Lafayette had always been an inspiration for patriots during the Revolutionary War. He cast a prodigious and monumental shadow among Raleigh's list of role models. Raleigh was familiar with Lafayette's support for Americans against the British. He knew he was the one who convinced his king, Louis XVI, to take the side of the colonists against their British enemies and that he was the reason that French soldiers, ships, military supplies, and funds were directed to America. He was a one-man crusade for America's ambitious war efforts for independence from the British.

Raleigh was ready to go, and he knew all Amherst County's militiamen were equally willing. He walked back to the porch. Sarah and Turner knew that stride. They had seen it when his favorite uncle died in Northern Neck and several times since. The trudge meant that Raleigh was in heavy contemplation. He paced his steps to give himself time to consider all the things happening in his life. He walked slowly to afford himself time to think before he reached the porch. At that point, he would have to explain to his family, in plain rather than military language, that he was leaving. He thought, *What should I tell them? Do I tell them that this is bad? That I am going to participate in some serious battles with the British, not just skirmishes? Should I tell them that I might confront English combatants with my tomahawks? Should I tell all that I think is going to happen? We are going to look for General Cornwallis! That is what we are possibly doing, and they want the great Amherst Militia to help them scout the country. We will find him! I am the best tracker in the country.*

Raleigh remembered Wiccocomico Indian Town. He imagined what the village would look like if the English colonists had just stayed in England. *We would still have our aboriginal customs at Wiccocomico if the English colonists had not invaded our lands. We would have our rich farmland. We could walk out of our yard and fish in the river. Now it is all gone. Why? Because they think they own us. We are not their slaves! I know we are ready to fight a decisive battle in this Revolutionary War. I cannot lie to the family. They deserve to have the whole truth. Or do they? I am not really positive about where I am going or who we are tracking, so why should I act like I know? If Sarah is so smart with those prophetic traits, let her tell the family after I have left the Ridge. After all, she should be able to tell if I am holding back the truth. Let her, Turner, Eady, and Anna predict where I am going and when—or if—I will be back!*

Raleigh walked past his silent family and on to his bedroom. He picked up his Bible, without thinking about it being in English, the Authorized King James Version. Before his family's ears, as if needing to reassure them of his fearlessness, he said aloud, "Cornwallis, look out. We are coming! Wherever you are! This is no hide-and-seek game, for we mean business. You will give up! You will stop pestering our colony. You will stop your English ways of taking our land and thinking you own America." He walked back past his family members, who were still standing on the porch, and headed directly to his favorite praying grounds in the woods.

Sarah had trained the children well and they took their cues from her. She did not stop or say a word to Raleigh when he hurried past them and headed to the field because she discerned he needed time alone with the Lord. He needed to pray for the success of the militia's mission and also pray for the family in his absence. Sarah explained to her children, "Your daddy has gone to his praying spot. He will be so close to the Lord after he has finished his prayer that the Lord's protection will be around the house, family, fields, animals, and God knows what other creatures!"

Putting on her apron, she rushed to the kitchen to prepare some food for Raleigh's trip. Then she looked at Turner and declared, "Get your daddy's gun and other militia gear. Bring the iron militia-issued tomahawk, but also the one that your daddy made out of the hickory branch. You know the one that he made by splitting the living branch toward the top and sticking the sharp rock in the branch. Your daddy is comfortable with both of them in his belt."

Sarah knew that Raleigh had sculptured his favorite tomahawk to fit the palm of his hand. Raleigh watched over the small hickory tree as it grew around the rock and then, at the right time, cut the branch down. Having trimmed it to fit lightly and comfortably in his palm, he could throw that tomahawk at twilight and shut out the light of a candle fly in flight.

"Turner, do you remember the time, two years ago, when your daddy used a tomahawk to kill a copperhead?" Sarah inquired as she began preparing Raleigh's food.

"Yes, Mother. Cocoa spotted the snake that night just as you stepped from the mule wagon. He rushed the snake and grabbed it." Turner thought back to that chaotic scene. He recalled his daddy's tomahawk accuracy when he threw it from a distance of twenty-five feet to the large copperhead and severed it cleanly in two. "Cocoa ran behind the snake as it curled to strike your leg. Cocoa grabbed the snake in the middle of its back and threw it into the air two or three times so you could see it near your foot. When you screamed out, daddy threw that tomahawk straight toward you. I was afraid that you had been hit! He hurled his tomahawk at the center of the snake's back and split it in half. Daddy is good with that weapon!"

"Son, you hurry up and get his weapons. We need to have everything in order tomorrow morning. We don't want your daddy worrying about anything when he gets ready to leave the house."

Sarah was in her usual rhythmic form as she gave various commands to the family. "Girls, let us start cooking some food for daddy. He will be hungry in the morning, and we must pack him a lunch also. Those long marches really jog his appetite. I guess the new adventure is no greater than the long hunting trips he takes all the time. He will be gone for several days to a month or two, or three, or four." She said this to the girls to make them feel as if they too had chores to complete to help Raleigh. Anna pretended to help her mother cook while Eady alternated holding on to the hands of Sarah and Anna as they moved around the kitchen.

> . . . And Joshua went unto him, and said unto him,
> 'Art thou for us, or for our adversaries?' And he
> said, 'Nay; but as captain of the host of the
> LORD am I now come . . .
> Joshua 5:13b–14a

8

Human Hostilities

21 June 1781

Raleigh prayed, "*Lord*, who art in heaven, hallowed be thou name, this is Raleigh again. It has been a while since I came on this ground to talk with you. It seems that I come here when situations in life grow too great for a humble person like me to know how to deal with them. I know that you are on my side in this battle. So I am here just to remind you to protect my family, my extended kinfolk, all the people at the Ridge and Stonewall Mill, all the citizens in Amherst and Buckingham counties, and all the other people that I may have left out. I do not need to ask you to safeguard my fellow militiamen and me during this mission because I feel sure you have already decided to do that. You understand that we are fighting against the evils of the British money, land-hungry citizens, and the Tories. Don't forget us. I pray in the name of Christ. Amen."

Raleigh, head still bowed even though he finished his prayer, did not feel that he was ready to leave his praying ground. Something was missing. He did not have the spiritual assurance that usually gripped his soul at the end of his prayers. This time, he had a hollow, bereft sensation; a strange inkling that God did not hear his prayer. *Maybe God is busy with someone else's prayer. I'll wait a few minutes and pray again*, he reasoned. He reckoned that

God would let him pray again shortly and answer his petition before he walked back home.

He recalled how fast God answered King Hezekiah's prayer after the king turned to the wall and opened up his heart to God. Just then, from the dim recesses of Raleigh's mind, he realized that something was missing in his prayer to God. *Why hadn't God heard me? What ingredients were missing in my prayer? I acknowledged God as my Lord. I admitted that I knew he was holy. I prayed in intercession for others and my family. I closed my prayer with the mention of God's Son, Christ. In Christ's name, I prayed. It was a complete prayer!*

Then Raleigh's heart found the words.

> If my people, which are called by my name,
> shall humble themselves,
> and pray, and seek my face, and turn from their
> wicked ways;
> then will I hear from heaven, and will forgive
> their sin, and will heal their land.
> 2 Chronicles 7:14

Raleigh recalled his past thoughts and behavior as he attempted to sift and remove any impediments that might have hindered the prayer-ending good feeling; he wanted the satisfaction that God heard his prayer. He was no hypocrite; he just didn't pray for the sake of having gone through the ritual of praying. Raleigh usually felt the Holy Spirit when he prayed, even when he left the "sweet hour" of prayer with the word "amen." After sifting the words of the scripture while beseeching God to show him the impediment, he finally received the answer to his prayer. His conscience spoke to him as if it was one of two persons. *Raleigh, you are not humble when you pray. You must, as a Christian,* humble *yourself in prayer! You must turn and seek the* face *of the Lord. You must do what his Holy Word says, not what you* want *to do! Finally, you must turn from your wicked ways.*

He responded to his conscience in childlike humility, *When was I haughty? When did I not attempt to follow the Lord's Word? When was I wicked? Tell me! Tell me! This is not the time for you to start disagreeing with me and getting standoffish! I am ready to go to war and you are getting harder and harder for me to find!*

All right, Raleigh, now that you are in the proper frame of mind to receive the truth, I will give it to you. His conscience revealed: *Raleigh, you hate everything British. You loathe and detest anything British. God made the British people when he made humanity from the dust of the earth. Who gave you the power to pick and choose whom you will favor? I know that some English people stole your aboriginal heritage when they confiscated your fatherland in Wiccocomico Indian Town. You are mad about that! I am aware that your people were dispersed because of the greed of some British people. You grit your teeth in anguish at night when you should be resting! You will lose your teeth over the hatred you have for the people whom you believe helped divide your Native people. I know that the foreigners massacred some of your Algonquian people as well as your Cherokee folks. You are ready to use your tomahawk against any Englishman's head in battle! That is the primary reason you are so excited to go to war: to get* even *with them! You will have sores in your stomach if you don't give it up. You are filled with animosity. Give it up, Raleigh! You, the former sincere young stripling from Wiccocomico Indian Town, have aged into a despicable person like some of the obnoxious colonists that you now hate. Since you are presently close to being spiritually nauseating, you had better be careful that you don't force God to cast you from his presence. You don't want him to leave you, do you?*

No! God knows I don't want to go to battle with the British without God's grace, Raleigh thought.

Each time I attempted to warn you—as your conscience—that you were backsliding from your faith in God, you closed your ears to me. Now that you have finally begun to listen to me today, you want to interrupt some of the things I am ready to say to you. With all that has been said, you do not have the right to decide for Almighty God, for El Shaddai, which soldiers should die in your human hostilities; what you call your Revolutionary War! Look to the Bible in your hands. Open up the cover. Whose name is listed there? Raleigh, speak up! Whose name is there?

Raleigh spoke aloud, "It says, 'Holy Bible, containing the Old and New Testaments of the Authorized King James Version.'"

Yes. You and I heard about the conference that King James called in 1604. During the conference, people requested that the scholars make a new translation of the Bible so that all English people may understand the meaning of the original Hebrew and Aramaic Old Testament and the Greek New Testament. Because of the English scholars, you are able to read the Bible. Raleigh, can you read and understand Hebrew? What about the Aramaic language? Can you understand it? What about Greek? Aren't you glad that the king of England cared enough for you to help you understand God's Word? I am, as your conscience, using English words to speak to you and you are hearing me loudly and clearly. Aren't you thankful for the English culture? Otherwise, you would be an English-illiterate aboriginal resident. You would be wandering, who knows where.

Raleigh, what about this idea you have that you know God is on your side in human hostilities, the human flesh conflicts that you refer to as the Revolutionary War? *You have the same presumption that Joshua had over two thousand years ago when God sent the Captain, Christ, to comfort him. Joshua had the nerve to impute on God the action of taking his side as if he were somebody! God did not need to let the Captain of the Lord of Hosts, Christ, take Joshua's side. As you remember the words of the scripture, Christ spoke on God's behalf when he told him in so many words, 'As Captain of the Lord's army, I have come, not to take your side or your enemies' side, but to take the Lord's side.'*

Raleigh, you like Lafayette's military style. He is French. Why do you like the French? Can you speak French? Is it because the French citizens are helping your country? What do you like about the Germans? The Hessians, the residents of Hess, Germany, are mercenaries. They fight for the country that pays them. They take the highest ground that has the highest pounds. They are on the British side with Cornwallis because Cornwallis has more pounds to pay them than your colonists' treasury. Do you hate these Germans? Some of whom are trying to make a living and earn money to feed their families. Although they are misguided in this present venture, God created them also.

What about the Tories, do you hate your own countrymen? If you encounter Tories in a skirmish, will you kill them with your special tomahawk? Tories have taken the British side while you have joined the rebels' *side, as the British call it, or* patriots' *side, as the Americans call it. Since some of your Cherokee people have chosen the British side, will you also drive your favorite tomahawk into their skulls in battle? Yes, your mind is all confused now! You have two personalities; I am your good spirit and you also have that evil, prejudiced spirit. Those human-initiated hostilities and their horrible results on people have a tendency to develop headaches and heartaches for you, your family, kin, and friends. Yes, you are now mixed up. You ought to be mixed up! The same type of English colonial vindictive behavior that has been and is now being directed against the Algonquian and Cherokee now appears in your character. You are quickly becoming their twin. You must be humble if you want God to hear from heaven and heal your land.*

Raleigh fell on the ground—in the very spot where he had prayed the self-righteous prayer—and prayed aloud a prayer for forgiveness. "Lord, do you want me to give up this combat order to go to Key's Church tomorrow morning to fight Cornwallis? I will do what you say. I will take the chance of being court marshaled for violating my militia oath! Tell me, Lord! Your servant will obey!"

Raleigh received his answer immediately. His good conscience spoke up. *No, Raleigh. You will go on to Key's Church for the militia meeting. You will be a faithful soldier, obey Colonel Gaines's orders, and go wherever he commands your militia to march! Your prayer has been heard. You are humble now because you are afraid of your destiny in battle. God will show his hand in this conflict in spite of horrific human hostilities.*

Raleigh's conscience has just given him a verbal and spiritual whipping. This brought to his remembrance words in the Bible that revealed God as a parent who chastises his children, whom he loves. Now, that "good feeling" to which he was accustomed at prayer culminations had returned to his heart. That precious, Holy Spirit feeling was back!

---

23 June 1781

Lt. Col. John Pope Jr. and Maj. William Cabell Jr., along with five captains, six lieutenants, three ensigns, and 277 noncommissioned officers and privates of the Amherst Militia were on the march to connect with General the Marquis de Lafayette.

Maj. William Cabell Jr. marched with the Amherst Militia to rendezvous with General Lafayette at Williamsburg. His father kept him informed on matters related to logistics even during the forced march. On June 25, Col. William Cabell Sr. wrote a letter with specifics relating to the soldiers' pay to his son, Maj. William Cabell Jr. He stated:

> Sir,—I am just returned home from Staunton, and have to inform you that the militia are to be paid by an Act of the last session: — for which purpose you are to direct the captains to make out pay-rolls at the end of their tour, to commence from the time of their joining the Army; which are to be signed by the commanding officers of the regiment that they are in. They are to receive nothing more for marching to and from than their rations.
>
> Their pay is the same as Continental soldiers and the depreciation of the money to be made up. The Field Officers are to get certificates of the time they are in service from the commanding officer of the regiment they are in—to entitle them to pay also. Tours of duty are fixed by law, at two months from the time of joining the army, and in no case to continue longer, unless the relief should be prevented from coming in time by some unavoidable accident.
>
> The mode of paying the militia is by certificates from the auditors, which are made payable in taxes; for had money been emitted for this purpose, the sum would have been so enormous as to have destroyed the fabrick of our paper money altogether. I hope this will satisfy the militia. We have done everything for them that the situation of our country will admit of.

5 July 1781

Brig. Gen. Edward Stevens commanded one of the brigades of 750 men under the overall command of General Lafayette. The Amherst Militia had been assigned to Brigadier General Stevens's brigade and was in the Williamsburg camp when they received news that Cornwallis was on the move nearby.

General Lafayette had broken camp at New Kent Courthouse on July 5 and marched to a site called Bird's Tavern about sixteen miles from Williamsburg. He left the Virginia Continentals and Militia at this location, as a reserve, while his other regimental forces and rifle company closed in on Cornwallis. When he learned that General Cornwallis and his army were crossing the James River, he thought this would be a chance to put his army in disarray.

General Cornwallis, being a deceptive and cunning commander, also realized that an encounter with the young "boy" Lafayette would put him in an advantageous position. He felt sure that he could whip Lafayette and his Continentals and militia troops if presented with the right opportunity, and he had always cherished an occasion to meet this young French general in a compromising situation. Cornwallis harbored resentment toward the Frenchman for stirring up war fervor among the Americans and their French allies against his British Army.

On the morning of July 6, the brigade soldiers learned that Cornwallis was attempting to cross the James River. The British commanding general wanted to set up his base near a coastal town because he needed to be at an optimal location at which he could receive supplies and troops. Since he suspected that he might also need supporting artillery fire and marines from his naval ships, he intended to set up his British camp in a seacoast town nearby. He also expected additional soldiers and material by ships from General Clinton in New York.

Cornwallis proceeded to trick Lafayette into believing that he had sent most of his army across the James River and that the part that was crossing the James was the rear guard. In actuality, this group of soldiers was only a decoy. The main body of Cornwallis's army was waiting to attack Lafayette. Lafayette decided to move forward to scout out the situation before he attacked the group that he believed was Cornwallis's rear guard. His army attacked Cornwallis in the battle of Green Springs before Lafayette could return to warn his officers that the whole situation was a setup. In the meantime, the Virginia Continentals and Militia served as reserve troops about twelve miles back at Bird's Tavern. Both sides suffered loss of lives and wounded men, with Lafayette's troops having the most dead and injured.

Lafayette would eventually move his army to Williamsburg. He suspected and hoped that he would have another day to confront General Cornwallis's forces.

> And he looked up, and said, I see men as trees, walking.
> Mark 8:24 (KJV)

9

Men as Trees Walking

1 August 1781

General Cornwallis moved his army into the towns of Yorktown and Gloucester and constructed fortifications at a very slow pace, almost as if he were sending a signal to Lafayette that he dared him to attack his army. In the meantime, Raleigh Pinn and his fellow Amherst Militiamen were in Lafayette's camp at Williamsburg.

Raleigh and three other militiamen pulled reconnaissance duty for several days in late July and had been watching Cornwallis's comings and goings as he moved toward his Yorktown camp. Utilizing the skills he practiced in scoping out squirrels, Raleigh found Cornwallis an easy prey to observe as the conspicuous general moved back and forth in his camp. Raleigh realized that he was close to Junior's military compound in Gloucester. The two brothers were now almost together as comrades in combat. He recalled the letter from Robert and realized that maybe he wasn't supposed to write the name of his camp location on it, but he did. It occurred to him as he sat on a wooden box at the center of his compound that Cornwallis had set up camps in Yorktown and Gloucester, close to his brother's camp in Gloucester.

He said excitedly, "He is over there, across the water. My brother Robert and his son John, are over there across from Yorktown. Men, I can guarantee you that my brother will be a thorn in Cornwallis's flesh. He is in an artillery company in

Gloucester near Cornwallis's other camp. We need him over on this side because he is the best cannon firer in this whole command. My brother can throw a rock straighter than you can look straight with your eyes, and his arrow shooting skills are the best in the colony. Now that he has those cannon in his control with his son, Cornwallis's men had better watch their steps with my brother smelling their tracks! With those cannon, who knows what Junior and John can do to the British?"

Capt. Charles Christian, one of his fellow Amherst militiamen, asked, "Is he that good, Raleigh, or is this one of your fish stories?" Raleigh and Captain Christian were friends before they became militiamen. They would later become neighbors on adjoining properties in Amherst County. Captain Christian was tall and slender, a farmer and real estate speculator, and had a likable personality.

"Captain, you be the judge after he starts. Sir, you just wait!" Raleigh asserted. Before his subordinate soldiers, Raleigh called him Captain, but in one-on-one conversations, he called him Charles.

"Raleigh, you know how to stretch the truth in a convincing, symbolic way. I don't know how to explain it, but you give good information when you speak with those stretching analogies. You say your brother Robert will smell Cornwallis's steps like a bloodhound? Will he go after him?"

"You better believe it," Raleigh said assertively. "You don't want to be on the wrong side of my brother. Cornwallis will find out soon that his British forces are on Robert's wrong side. Captain, you see to it that Robert Junior gets those cannon and watch what happens to the general's compound."

Captain Christian agreed. "I trust what you just said, Raleigh. Although you give accurate reconnaissance reports when you return from your militia scouting missions, I am not sure that you are on target with your statement that Robert could destroy Cornwallis's compound with cannon by himself."

"You just keep your eye on his artillery unit when they start firing the balls at the enemy and see what he does! Then make up your mind which soldier is most accurate with those cannonballs." Raleigh caught himself and added, "Captain, sir." He forgot for a moment where he was, that he was in the military and should address his friend as Captain and not talk with him in an informal manner as if he were speaking to a friend from back home.

Ensign Henry Turner spoke up. "Things are going to get hot around here before long. You don't expect all these soldiers and high military officers that are gathering on both sides to sit and look at each other any longer than necessary, do you? The battle is going to fire up soon." Ensign Henry was Raleigh's friend also. They would eventually be neighbors.

At his camp in Williamsburg, Raleigh had plenty of time to think about the war possibilities. Sitting on a stump in the Williamsburg Camp with his fellow militiamen, he thought about Lafayette's confrontation with General Cornwallis at Green Springs and the fact that the young French general was as astute as a Cherokee or Wiccocomico warrior. He said, "Men, if Lafayette had not suspected a trap and ridden ahead of the forces at Green Springs, the whole outfit could have been cut down by Cornwallis's trickery. Amherst Militia, who were held back in ready reserve as Lafayette needed us, could have been drawn into the British army's entrapment and resulting carnage if Lafayette were not so wise. Thank God for him!"

"Raleigh, Lafayette might have some aboriginal blood rushing through his veins," added John Redcross. "For a general, who would have believed he had those scouting instincts? Maybe he is one of those Frenchmen who descended from an ancestor of the tough Scot Highlanders. The Highlanders fight like Indians. How could you explain his reconnaissance skills otherwise?"

The soldiers and officers talked for about an hour and then broke off their conversation as they left to attend to military duties.

"See you fellows later," Raleigh remarked. He remained on the stump and looked toward the town of Gloucester, contemplating what his brother and nephew were doing that very moment.

Even though Raleigh was twice the age of Lafayette, he admired and respected his style. The general's guise was as confident as an aboriginal warrior with discerning attention to detail. Raleigh reflected on his present militia assignment under the command of the French general. *Did God place me here with Lafayette for some special reason? Is this man the instrument to which God referred when he spoke to my conscience, 'You will see God's hand in this conflict, in spite of horrific human hostilities?' Is God showing me his kind hand in this horrible war?*

Raleigh contemplated his future beyond this present campaign. He and his fellow militiamen, who had already seen the allies' dead and wounded bodies at Green Springs that Cornwallis left as if they were rattlesnakes that crossed his path, contemplated how many allies would have been killed if it were not for Lafayette. As the American and French officers were drawing up plans in Williamsburg to close in on General Cornwallis' forces, Raleigh had plenty of time to meditate on his future ventures. *This war is not what I expected, God! What am I doing here, trying to take out my vengeance on England? I am dreading the outcome of these hostilities with England on one side and America and France on the other.*

Raleigh suspected that Cornwallis, with his large number of military personnel and supplies, did not think twice about any threat that Lafayette and the allied forces posed against him. Raleigh and his small scouting squad had supplied intelligence reports to Lafayette's camp officers that revealed Cornwallis's location and the fact that his soldiers were slothfully moving about their Yorktown compound as if the nearby small allied forces in Williamsburg were a joke compared to their English army of several thousand.

Thinking of Cornwallis's military action the week earlier, Raleigh had asked the officers, "Is it a warrior's trap? Is Cornwallis becoming a sly fox in his style, trying to entice us to attack him? Surely he has another trick up his sleeve like the one that he pulled at Green Springs!"

Cornwallis's military attack on them at Green Springs had forced Raleigh to look to his left and right as if he were on the lookout for copperheads. He had become so paranoid that he did not really trust his own militiamen in the camp at night unless he could see their faces. He had a new inclination to keep his hands on his tomahawks. He only removed his hands each time he remembered his prayer in June when the Lord told him that his hand will be seen in this conflict in spite of horrific human hostilities. Each time he remembered these words of the Lord in his vision, he dropped his hands from the tomahawks like they were hot irons in a fire. He would choose God's hands of protection over his own hands anytime.

Raleigh had fond memories of Buffalo Ridge and Stonewall Mill. He whispered a deep, soulful prayer to God on behalf of his people in Amherst County. Then his mind soared like a seagull flying toward the Atlantic coast, toward Wiccocomico Indian Town. He realized that he was less than sixty miles as the crow flies from his ancestral homeland at Wiccocomico. He prayed for his relatives, some of whom still resided there, and for the others who had been dispersed throughout America. They were suffering greatly because of the English colonists' greed for land in the colonies. Raleigh quickly blocked out these habitual images of British atrocities against his people because he did not want God to discipline him again for his racial hatred against the whites from the Isles. Thinking he must get himself together and put his mind on something else, he decided to walk down to the intelligence headquarters to see if he were needed for scouting operations.

As he walked toward the tent, he pondered what Daniel Morgan and his riflemen were doing now. During this time, Morgan had been ill. Gen. George Washington had requested his skilled services, but Morgan sent word that he was ill from previous military action. He indicated that he would have been honored to serve with Commander-in-Chief Washington and that he wished he could join him in future combat operations.

Raleigh's thoughts on Morgan's letter to General Washington brought to his remembrance once more a letter he received from his brother. His brother mentioned that his sons Jim and Billy were in the service of Ranger Daniel Morgan's rifle company.

> *My other boys, Jim and Billy, are with Colonel Morgan in his rifle company. I don't get any news on them. I have an idea where they are, but I do not have the liberty to say.*

Raleigh suspected that his brother had gotten news concerning his son's death but did not want to worry Raleigh with bad news in his letter. A military courier informed officials in Williamsburg recently that several ranger riflemen from Virginia had been killed during Morgan's brilliant victory in Cowpens over Tarleton and 1,100 crack troopers. Cornwallis had sent those troopers against Morgan hoping they would be successful.

As he walked within ten yards of the intelligence headquarters' tent, his eyes became moist in sorrow. He hastily shook his head to clear his vision. *Let me get myself together before the intelligence headquarters' officers see me. I am Raleigh, the one that the militiamen call the tough Injun.*

Raleigh liked the term aboriginal American rather than the word "Injun." The word "aboriginal" connoted first people. *The first people in America were not the people of India, as the explorer termed them. Didn't their ship navigators know they were in America, not India? I don't want to be called Injun or even Indian.*

Then his thoughts moved back to the Battle of Cowpens and the whereabouts of his nephews. He knew about those crack riflemen in Morgan's company. *They were more like the aboriginal Americans. They dressed in long hunting shirts, leggings, and moccasins. Their uniform also included a rifle, a scalping knife, and a tomahawk. Morgan is from Virginia and he must have some aboriginal blood running in his veins. That is the reason he is dressing like we dress. Even our Amherst Militiaman's uniform includes a tomahawk. What a weapon!* Then Raleigh realized that he was trampling on unholy ground again, and in the name of the Lord, expeditiously shuffled his thoughts to less heinous areas. He realized that he was in a war zone, but he did not have to occupy his thoughts on unnecessary killing.

He met Gen. Thomas Nelson, General of the Militia, and Brig. Gen. Edward Stevens, Brigade Commander, as he walked into the tent. He was surprised that the brass leaders were in the intelligence headquarters. General Stevens and General Nelson had reviewed his reconnaissance reports on Cornwallis's operations in Yorktown. They stood over a table with a hand-drawn map of Yorktown spread out on top. While General Nelson leaned forward to get a closer view of the topographical features surrounding the town, General Stevens stroked his black, bearded chin, pointing toward the road leading from Williamsburg to Yorktown.

The action must be getting ready to heat up. Why else would the top brass be here in this tent? Raleigh surmised.

After Raleigh walked into the tent, Lieutenant Colonel Dabney, Commander of the State Regiment, signaled to the generals that Raleigh was cleared for security matters. Lieutenant Colonel Dabney knew Raleigh's brother, Robert, and had received very good reports on him and his son John. He also knew Thomas Pinn, a State Regiment soldier, Raleigh's nephew. Their officer, Captain Yerby, always boasted to Dabney of the Pinns' zest for battle.

Dabney shared some background information with the generals, "Raleigh Pinn comes from a long line of hard-fighting Injuns. They are on our side, thank God! They can be trusted totally." He made this clear because some Cherokees and other Iroquois were siding with the British.

As he continued to praise Raleigh, his brother, and his nephew, Raleigh laughed to himself and thought, *If he and the other field-grade officers only knew how close our Wiccocomico people were to the Cherokees! If they were aware that I am Wiccocomico with some Cherokee heritage, they wouldn't be as positive about my loyalty to the American cause.* Raleigh's loyalty was unquestionably firm, which his faithful service in the militia had demonstrated. Growing quite uncomfortable with all the praise, Raleigh asked permission to be excused, and headed out of the tent. Brigadier General Stevens stopped Raleigh as he moved toward the tent door, "Raleigh Pinn, do you know two soldiers by the name of William and James Pinn?"

"Yes, sir. They are my nephews. Junior's—I mean Robert's other boys. We are from the Northumberland area."

General Stevens apologized, "It was sad to hear about the young Pinn's death in service with Morgan's riflemen company."

Raleigh, shocked, maintained his composure, "Yes, sir."

"He was a fine soldier. I would give anything to have half as skillful soldiers as either one of those Pinn boys. They're excellent riflemen."

"Sir, thank you for your kindness to the Pinn family," Raleigh responded.

"Raleigh, Robert is your brother and John is your nephew also? So Robert has three boys in this Revolutionary War! Robert and John were assigned to Captain Yerby's company over there in Gloucester. Were you aware of this, Raleigh?"

Raleigh cleared his throat and stated awkwardly, "Yes, Robert and John are my brother and nephew. No, sir, I was not aware that they are in Gloucester, close to us. When I received his letter a few weeks ago, he did not tell me where he was for security reasons." He lied because he did not want to get his brother in trouble. *Was General Stevens trying to see if the Pinns are maintaining secrecy?* Raleigh wondered suspiciously. *Did he really know that we are related before today? We are the only Pinns in Revolutionary War service! Does he already know that we are connected to the Cherokees? Why, Billy and Jim are part Cherokee through their mother's side and Wiccocomico and Cherokee on the other side! They are natural fighters in Morgan's riflemen company, with their moccasins and tomahawks. Their mother, Robert Junior's wife, is Cherokee."*

"Raleigh, I am humbled to be in your presence," General Stevens stated sincerely. "You are a good soldier. You have put your life on the line in the Amherst Militia. I make it my job to learn the story on each crack soldier in my outfit. I am going to know the whole story on our best soldiers. You have great Native insight, foresight, and hindsight. I am proud to have you with us here in Williamsburg. We are getting ready for one hot battle, Raleigh. Stay alert and help us."

"Thank you, sir. I will, as much as my Lord will help me."

"Raleigh, are you a Christian?"

"Yes, sir, I am."

"What denomination?"

"Sir, I was Anglican in Wiccocomico. Now, I am Baptist."

Raleigh then begged permission to leave, still not knowing which of his nephews was killed. He had to pretend that he knew about the death already. Otherwise, General Stevens would wonder why Junior had not told him about his son's death. Raleigh knew he would learn in time which nephew died for his country. Either name would be equally shocking and painful.

The pain had already begun pricking Raleigh's heart. His heart and soul were heavy with grief as he walked out of the tent.

"Wait, Raleigh!" Lieutenant Colonel Dabney exclaimed. "You do not have permission to leave yet. We need your reconnaissance service tomorrow night. You report back tomorrow afternoon at four o'clock for the briefing on your scouting mission orders. You and John Redcross will go out together."

"Yes, sir," Raleigh replied, pleased that John Redcross, his friend and one of several Cherokees in the militia, would be his partner on the mission. He remembered he told Sarah a few years ago that he could always trust John to cover his back against the enemy. Raleigh went to his tent. He planned to rest well so that he would have sharp scouting senses during the reconnaissance operations the next day. He wanted to be at his peak level of alertness. He was so apprehensive and disquieted over the report on the death of Junior's boy that he doubted he would have his usual vigilance, precaution, and nimbleness needed to outwit British soldiers serving guard duty for Lord Cornwallis.

August 2

Raleigh and John Redcross reported to the intelligence headquarters for a briefing at 3:50 p.m. When they arrived, they learned that there were two other reconnaissance teams going out with them. Although there were three groups, each team had a different reconnaissance area and mission objective. The Pinn-Redcross team's orders required them to be as "invisible as Indians in the thickets, and secure intelligence on the Cornwallis topographical layout and his soldiers' personnel numbers and fortification while maintaining utmost secrecy in their reconnaissance operations."

Lieutenant Colonel Dabney stated, in his closing exhortation, "Report back to me on or before August 4 with all relevant data: enemy strength, fortifications, location, movement, depth and width of streams, rivers, hills, and ravines. Raleigh, you have your own discretion regarding the date of your return, but in any case, prior to August 4. Do you have any questions?"

"No, sir." Raleigh declared with confidence.

Raleigh and John Redcross moved out from Williamsburg at around 6:30 p.m. along the twelve-mile road leading to Yorktown. Having painted their faces, arms, and chests with a mixture of cooked beef grease, crushed grass, and leaves to help them blend into the forest environment, they wore matching deer-hide breeches and moccasins, and emerald-green cloth formed into turbans around their heads. Committed to secrecy in their reconnaissance operations and avoiding weapons that made loud noises when contacting the enemy, they each carried a knife and a tomahawk. After walking approximately two miles on the dusty winding road, they separated. Withdrawing under the canopy of the shaded thick forest and proceeding cautiously about two hundred yards from and parallel to the road, Raleigh covered the right side and John moved to the left. They maintained the same pace on each side of the road and used bird signals to convey their locations at different intervals as they noted potential ambush sites along the route.

As the sun went down, they breathed easier knowing that each passing hour would bring more darkness to conceal their movements. With darkness now resting on the forest vegetation and road, they faced new hazards. Without the sense of sight while moving stealthily, they depended on their ears as their primary defense against walking into British patrol and reconnaissance teams. Raleigh and John moved slowly and cautiously, walking softly on the leaves and undergrowth. Since noise was their greatest enemy, they made turkey and bird sounds whenever their soft moccasins, crushing brittle leaves and branches, broke the nighttime silence. At around 2:30 a.m., they reached the point near the York River where clusters of trees ran along both sides of the road. Several hundred yards from the bridge where Yorktown Creek flowed into the York River, they set up their resting point. From their hideout behind the trees, they were able to see the candlelight in Cornwallis's compound on the banks of the York River. Raleigh took the first two hours of guard duty while John curled up on a pile of leaves. Looking from the recesses in the cluster of trees, Raleigh maintained complete silence as he peered toward the British campsite.

At 4:30 a.m., John relieved Raleigh and took up his sentry position. Raleigh briefed him. "Those soldiers are walking around over there talking as if they don't have any concerns. They don't think our American forces will be a threat to them, and they have not even sent out scouts during the night. Can you believe that? If they sent some scouts out I would have heard them. No. They don't respect our soldiers."

Raleigh sat down, unrolled his turban and covered his eyes with the cloth as he enjoyed his two-hour turn to rest. John pulled his reconnaissance duty and returned two hours later. He woke Raleigh at 6:30 a.m. Raleigh's military discretionary orders allowed him to decide when to leave his reconnaissance operations. He planned to pull daylight monitoring operations from that spot and then withdraw around 1:30 a.m. the following morning, August 4. Raleigh and John talked quietly as they observed personnel moving about in Cornwallis's compound during the seven-hour period between 6:30 a.m. and 1:30 p.m. He shared information about the Battle at Cowpens with John; information that he secured from a noncommissioned officer in the Williamsburg intelligence tent. A noncommissioned officer had acquired the news from dispatches sent from the front.

"Tarleton's British forces on January 17, 1781, moving from Winnsboro attacked Morgan's rangers at Cowpens, South Carolina." Raleigh told him, thinking about Morgan and his nephews. "Morgan represented himself well in accordance with his reputation for shrewdness. I can see him now placing his riflemen in a skirmish position around his main troops. When General Tarleton advanced on Morgan's main body, after the riflemen discontinued their assault on his British forces, Tarleton was convinced that he would wipe out the Americans. He sent his 71st Highlanders in a left outflanking move against Morgan's formation. Realizing that he was in a critical situation, Morgan sent his Continental Cavalry in on Tarleton's right flank. At the same time, Morgan had his militia dragoons, his heavily armed cavalrymen, to buffet Tarleton's left flank. To top off this offensive, he even had his crack riflemen move in to Tarleton's center to pour on more heat. Tarleton tried to keep his forces calm under the desperate American assault, but his

British forces retreated from the field of action. Colonel William Washington personally chased Tarleton with his Continental Cavalry."

"I thought Tarleton was a better officer than that. Are you sure that you are talking about the British officer Tarleton?" John asked.

"Tarleton has always been known for maneuvering from a hot battle in what I guess he called strategic withdrawal, but I call it just looking out for his hide."

"Raleigh, last week you mentioned that your nephews fought with Morgan. Were they in that battle?"

"I believe one of my nephews went down in one of the battles between Morgan and the British. I don't know if it was Jim, Billy, or both. That must be the reason why Junior, my brother, did not say where his boys were in his letter to me! One of his sons was killed in the Battle of Cowpens, I suspect."

"Why do you think Junior was so secretive about letting you know which one of his sons died?" John inquired.

Raleigh replied, "I don't know. I would like to ask him, but out of compassion, I have intentionally avoided the question. I don't know if Junior's son was in the Battle of Cowpens when he fell to enemy forces or if he fell two months later in the Battle of Guilford Courthouse. What does it really matter? Another fine young man has fallen. As Cornwallis was moving into North Carolina, he continued to chase Morgan's forces. Each time Morgan was able to outmaneuver that sly old fox. Morgan then joined up with General Green and his forces of four thousand. The Americans fought brilliantly until Cornwallis brought in his artillery. Green's forces had to withdraw with all the British artillery balls falling down on them. I have heard that Cornwallis claimed the victory. Our scouting dispatches joked about the severity of Cornwallis's personnel losses, suggesting that one or two more of these so-called Cornwallis victories would bring an end to his army. After the Guilford battle, Cornwallis obviously made up his mind when he retreated to Wilmington, North Carolina, that he needed to move into Virginia."

"He is now camped here in Yorktown as though everything is all right. You and I know that his army cannot sustain those troop fatalities in each battle. He is over there in his compound, licking his wounds," John surmised.

"Now, he is here trying to get some rest." Raleigh added. "He doesn't know what he is in for! We are not going to let him sleep. We will be on his tail every minute of the day and night. We will make him wonder what is behind his walls and over his head. Between Morgan's Indian style of fighting in the Carolinas and Lafayette's Indian style here in Virginia, he will either go crazy or give up. He doesn't have that many more troops to give up, after all those soldiers died in battles such as the Guilford Courthouse battle, which Cornwallis called a victory. Intelligence tells us that he is tired and does not want to sacrifice any more of his soldiers until he gets reinforcement from New York. If he knows what's good for him, he'd better go back to Charleston, where the British can claim a true victory. Maybe he can find some seclusion there while he waits for new reinforcements from his ships. Virginia is the wrong place to lick his wounds. He is in our colony now, and he chose the wrong spot because the Amherst Militia is on his heels."

Raleigh and John began to crawl through different sections of the cluster of trees, as daylight began to expose their position. They hunkered down and observed activity in Cornwallis's compound as well as construction on the periphery.

"Can you believe how slowly they are constructing their defenses around their site? They act like we don't even present a threat to them," Raleigh asserted.

"If they knew what you and I know they would get those lazy troops off their behinds and start setting up their offensive and defensive constructions. When our other forces arrive in Williamsburg, we are going to move against them!" John advised.

"Why do you suppose our officers kept repeating the words 'avoid capture by all means'? If the British captured us, you know that they would interrogate us and attempt to suck intelligence information regarding our Williamsburg site and military intentions. Their intense efforts to acquire secret information would be akin to sucking stuff out of chitterlings at hog-killing time! You know that we wouldn't reveal any secrets about our military operations, except maybe we would give them some manure." Raleigh chuckled softly, and John covered his mouth with both hands to muffle his laughter.

They crawled on their elbows and knees, peering through the vegetation toward the British compound. Because their faces, chests, and arms were camouflaged with brown and green paint that matched the forest colors, they were confident that the British soldiers would not detect their surveillance.

At around 1:00 p.m. Raleigh said, "We are so good at blending in with the topography that even an eagle could not spot us. I know the British wouldn't see us even if they came within two hundred yards. I believe we could even stand up and walk around the perimeter and they still would not see us. You remember, somewhere in the eighth chapter of Mark around verse 23 or 24 that Jesus healed a blind man. The man had only a little faith and he saw only a little bit. He said that he could see 'men as trees, walking.' He might have actually been seeing men working in hay fields and carrying the hay on their backs, but to this half-seeing man, the men appeared to be trees walking. Jesus put his hands upon his eyes again and his sight was restored fully. I hope they don't see us as trees walking in our camouflage. We want to walk and not be seen; not even as trees."

Raleigh had plenty of time to let his mind reflect on important issues in his life at the moment. *Could my nephew have fallen two months after Cowpens in one of the most intensive battles of the Carolinas, possibly at Guilford?* he speculated to himself. He grew a vendetta in his soul, a blood feud, a bitter private war against all that was or associated with England. He hoped his developing blood feud would be kept alive by this painful memory of his nephew falling in battle. Exhausted, Raleigh crouched down under the thick shrubbery, rubbing his hands over his face. He was tired having had only a few hours of rest, but his heart was aching with anger at the thought of losing his nephew because of human hostilities.

"Our family is suffering greatly. The pain is so boundless that the size of the Pearl is grand!" he mumbled as he whispered a prayer to God for his brother Junior and family. He did not have time to contemplate the matter further because he needed to catch a few winks of sleep. Although the rejuvenated vengeance in his heart against the British fired up a burning spirit to pull new missions against Cornwallis's compound, he felt burdened and tired with bereavement and physical exertion. He added, "John, the Lord will bless us because our fight against the British is a noble one. I know we will whip them. My pocket watch says it is now about one o'clock in the afternoon. You take your two-hour nap while I pull guard duty. I will wake you up at 3:00 p.m. Then I will turn in and sleep until about four-thirty. We will then have about two hours of daylight observations before nightfall. Around midnight, we will slip out of this site and head back to base."

Raleigh suffered physical and mental exhaustion. *Why did I feel the need to tell John that the Lord is on our side? God does not take sides on the whims of human clay and combat hostilities.* Then he remembered the biblical words of Joshua to the Captain of the Lord of Hosts, "Art thou for us or for our adversaries?"

Along with other teams, Raleigh and John conducted reconnaissance missions around Cornwallis's site during the next seven-and-a-half weeks. Having observed Cornwallis's operations on the left side, Raleigh and John surveyed the Wormley Creek and Wormley Pond areas on the compound's right side four weeks later. Both areas provided thick vegetation from which they pulled their missions. They mapped key topographical locations, including bridges, ravines, creeks, rivers, and hills. They even infiltrated a cluster of trees near the center of the compound where the British engineers and workers were indiscreetly and lackadaisically building breastworks behind which they planned to place their weapons and cannon.

> Now Jericho was straitly shut up because
> of the children of Israel: none went out,
> and none came in. And the Lord said unto Joshua,
> See, I have given into thine hand Jericho,
> and the king thereof, and the mighty men of valor.
> Joshua 6:1–2 (KJV)

10

The Siege

September 1781

Raleigh knew that something horrendous had seized him and placed his soul at risk with God. It was as if the devil had a siege on his soul and his militia of demons had engaged in small skirmishes against his conscience.

"When will the mighty mammoth battle come? When will I be able to fight off the big waves of racial animosity that my soul has been attracting? Either I win the battle or put out the white flag of truce." He voiced his thoughts to John Redcross on a hot afternoon in early September. With skin paint camouflage and kneeling behind the cover of trees during one of their reconnaissance missions, Raleigh poured out his heart, barely above a whisper, as he deliberated his soul's two natures. There were the bad forces that enticed him to hold grudges against the English people, and his biblical training that grappled with his conscience.

He could not shake the hatred he had for Britain and the swarms of English people she planted in America. Realizing that he held covetous desires for Amherst and Buckingham colonists' fertile farmland during the mid- and late 1770s, he blamed his thoughts on the greedy English people.

"John, if they had not come to America, I would not have caught their fever. Their greed for land was so contagious that their covetousness has even infected me. We aboriginal people know that human beings cannot own land! The land owns us and will eventually capture us when we go to our dusty graves. I blame the English for bringing these crazy ownership ideas to America and infecting us to the extent that even my body has begun to pine away with lust for land. Just as they brought their physical diseases from Europe to America and passed them on to us, they are bringing their moral diseases and spreading the infection everywhere. Now I crave land ownership in my daydreams as much as I desire my wife's body at night. Since I am away from my wife, I struggle to control sexual desires, but those gluttonous cravings for real estate have overtaken my spirit to the point that I have no control. Not only did the English colonists cause me to be vengeful toward them for their ravenous appetites for aboriginal land, now they have infected me with that same disease of greed for land. There is no way to win!"

"I know what you are talking about. I don't have the hatred for colonists' diseases as bad as you, but I have caught that sickness of land hunger you just mentioned. I have it bad like you."

"You don't feel bad that the English settlers have stolen our people's land?"

"Yes, of course I don't like it that they have moved into America and have grabbed every good piece of land that they can buy, steal, and trick from our people. I just do not have that deep anger that you have for those newcomers." John replied. "My Cherokee people didn't like it in October 1768 when Stuart, the British Superintendent of Indian Affairs, forced Cherokees to cede that rich land in southwestern Virginia down near Independence and Hillsville."

Raleigh said, "To top that land-grabbing strategy, two years later, in October 1770, they swallowed up land in Virginia, northeast Tennessee, and the east end of Kentucky. They gave the land cession ceremony a fancy name to make it look legitimate. They called it the Treaty of Lochaber, in South

Carolina. Why would anyone go all the way to the Broad River in South Carolina to meet with the Cherokees to discuss taking land in Virginia, Tennessee, and Kentucky? I was angry when I learned that they had already culminated that tricky treaty. They gobbled up all the area around Grundy, Ervington, Lebanon, Abingdon, Marion, Tazewell, Bland, Newbern, Pearisburg, and Wytheville. They even got that Holston River area in Virginia with its fertile soil. Do you know that the Holston River area was so enticing to deer and other game that the Cherokee chief commanded his people to be careful hanging around that paradise too long because of his fear that they would get lazy? All you had to do was walk over to the riverbanks and you could kill more deer and bear in an hour than two weeks in other areas of Tennessee and Virginia. John, you know that when the British people get in on a good thing, they keep on rolling. Two years later, they came back. Isn't it amazing how they lie back and wait for exactly two years and then close in on the jugular? In 1772, they worked with the governor of Virginia and stole land in Virginia and eastern Kentucky. To keep it from looking like thievery, they called it a treaty. They took a whole triangle of land above Wise, Virginia, in that maneuver.

"Departing from their usual two-year waiting period and actually waiting three years this time British officials eyed another piece of Virginia in 1775 and sent Richard Henderson to close the deal, ripping off more Cherokee land in Virginia, Kentucky, and Tennessee. Eventually, they confiscated the whole tip of southwestern Virginia, including Wise, Jonesville, and the Cumberland Gap area. In taking all the land owned by Cherokee in what they called official treaties or land cessions they made stealing land look legal. What else could our people do but yield to the more dominant British power?

"John, some of our people left the area where they had lived and moved into Tennessee while some came in our direction. You and I know this because we have some of them at Buffalo Ridge and Stonewall Mill. Cherokees who stayed on their land pretended to be black or white. I understand that the colonists are moving into those areas and pushing those so-called white and black people into the woods and mountains. They are trying to eke out a living on land the colonists do not want. Even if we drive the British from America, we would still have a problem because you and I know that the new colonists would not give their land back to the Cherokee people."

"Raleigh, the British acknowledge that the Cherokee are the rightful owners of the land in Virginia and went to great lengths to make negotiations and land extractions look proper and above reproach, but I am uneasy with the way our Cherokee people have been treated. Under the pretext of driving them from Virginia to protect their citizens from fierce Indian attacks, the colonists have dispersed our Cherokee people throughout Virginia and beyond this colony. As you and half of the white citizens in Amherst County are my witnesses, I have never been ashamed of my tribe and I do not mind telling people that I am *Cherokee*!" John stated emphatically. "Through it all, I refuse to hate them because of their mistreatment of our people. You need to be careful that you don't lose your soul with that bitterness you are hiding in your heart. Now, just listen to us. You are forcing me to talk about the English taking our people's land. I thought you just stated that our people never claimed to own land, but God just let them use it while they are alive. Raleigh, you had better deal with your problem or you will end up infecting the whole aboriginal population in Virginia with that bitterness disease."

"What you are telling me is right. Will this ungodly vengeful spirit cleave to me with its tenacious grip until my death becomes the only avenue of escape? The spiritual siege is on and I cannot break out from its hold! Should I give up and forgive the colonists for their evil treatment of aboriginal people? Should I express my heart's desire and fight everyone that I think is responsible for those injustices? The devil wants me to take my tomahawk to the English. After years of warfare in my soul between the spirit and the flesh, I am praying to the Lord to show me a way to deal with this siege on my soul and let my conscience win the battle over the forces of Satan. Will this physical campaign against Cornwallis finally bring an end to the spiritual and mental skirmishes I have been waging against the English people for years?"

"Raleigh, I don't know the answers to your questions. One thing that I do know with surety is that if you keep on with your hateful talk, you will pass that bitterness on to me. I am aware of what the colonists did to our people in Lancaster County. Don't forget that I registered for Revolutionary War service in that county. The more you talk about your fever, what the colonists did against your people in Wiccocomico or our people in the Cherokee territory, the more I start to get hot with the fever."

Raleigh was becoming concerned about the powerful military buildup in their camp in Williamsburg. The Virginia Militia had well-trained militiamen. They were ready for Cornwallis. The soldiers had heard reports that Cornwallis did not respect American state militia and that he belittled their ability to put up a good fight against his veteran British soldiers.

Virginia Governor General Thomas Nelson was the commander of the Virginia Militia, which included over three thousand troops from Virginia. The North Carolina Militia was in reserve and covered the rivers, fords, and passes in its home state to guard against any possibility of General Cornwallis having a convenient and sudden change of heart in setting up camp in Virginia and returning to the south. Cornwallis had set up his camp by August 4 under the skillful reconnaissance and watchful eye of Lafayette's finest soldiers.

The Marquis de Lafayette was not yet twenty years old when he volunteered for service in the American Revolution in 1777. He had a zeal for and wholeheartedly supported the American cause against the British. His wealth and prestige led to Congress commissioning him as a general. His pro-American position was well known throughout France and led to French financial and political support. Lafayette convinced leaders in France to become an American ally in the revolution for independence against the British.

Lieutenant General Lafayette had sent correspondence to the commander-in-chief of the American and French allied armies, George Washington, in early August to the effect that the British general Lord Cornwallis' army was marching toward Yorktown. Lafayette believed that with the right combination and placement of troops at Yorktown, the small combination of American and French forces could possibly defeat the British forces, but he knew it would take a miracle. He needed the assistance of his own French navy to occupy Chesapeake Bay.

Washington left his camp in New York under the control of a small guard to give the British commander the appearance that he was still stalking the British compound. In reality, he had agreed with Lafayette's plan and turned his troops toward Virginia. When British general Clinton finally realized that Washington and his troops were not near New York but were marching to Virginia, he moved quickly to send reinforcements to General Cornwallis in Yorktown. Clinton had hoped to send the reinforcements by ships if they could arrive before the French warships blocked the mouth of the York River near Chesapeake Bay. Meanwhile Lafayette had dispatched a request to French Admiral de Grasse to support the plan by setting up a blockade and commanding the mouth of Chesapeake Bay.

By September 5, Admiral de Grasse had arrived in Yorktown before British admirals Thomas Graves and Samuel Hood arrived from New York. De Grasse maintained a defensive advantage in the Bay when the British ships arrived. After de Grasse defeated the British in this naval operation known as the Battle of the Capes, defeated admirals Graves and Hood sailed back to New York to give General Clinton the sad news.

King Louis XVI, a year earlier, supported the allied American-French operations by sending General Rochambeau to America to lead the first French troops. The allied army of Washington and Rochambeau marched to Virginia. There were 1,400 American soldiers and approximately 5,000 French troops. The allied forces in New York marched an average of about twenty-eight miles a day to reach Philadelphia.

On September 14, General Washington arrived at Yorktown and Lafayette gave him the positive report that de Grasse had achieved his mission: he had outfought the British admirals in the Battle of the Capes.

"The Bay is blockaded and Cornwallis does not have any hope of getting troop reinforcements and supplies!" Lafayette exclaimed.

Now Washington would use the time—while waiting for his marching American and French forces to arrive from New York—to plan a sound military strategy to defeat Cornwallis. When American and French troops reached the city of Annapolis on September 17, some of the troops boarded transport ships that would take them down the Chesapeake Bay. They eventually headed to Williamsburg to join forces with the troops of generals Lafayette, Lincoln, and von Steuben. In the meantime, the other troops with heavy cavalry and supplies, and artillery forces, marched at a steady pace toward Williamsburg.

General Lafayette, Division Commander, and Major General von Steuben, Commander of the Steuben Division, made an outstanding military team. The Prussian officer Baron Friedrich von Steuben first served Washington at Valley Forge as a volunteer. He taught the fundamentals of battle strategies and martial arts with the bayonet. The Continentals were organized in Williamsburg on September 27 with three divisions for the encounter with Cornwallis.

Major General Lincoln commanded the other division known as the Lincoln Division. Each division was set up with two brigades, except for Steuben's Division. Steuben's Division included the Wayne Brigade under the command of Brig. Gen. "Mad" Anthony Wayne. Brig. Gen. Mordecai Gist commanded the Gist's Brigade. General Thomas Nelson, Governor of Virginia, directed the Nelson Division. He commanded the Virginia militia with three brigades and the Virginia State Regiment. Brigadier generals George Weedon, Robert Lawson, and Edward Stevens directed the three brigades in Nelson's division.

Raleigh and the Amherst Militia were in Stevens's Brigade. Steuben's Division also included a fourth group, a brigade of sappers and miners. There were more than a hundred sappers and miners in this group. Soldiers and workers in this outfit were employed in digging saps or trenches and building fortifications. They were essential in undermining Cornwallis's defensive and offensive positions.

On September 28, the allied forces had been organized with the Allied Army Commander-in-Chief, George Washington, leading the assault against General Cornwallis. In addition to the three division commands, Washington had an artillery brigade under Brig. Gen. Henry Knox and a cavalry of regiment dragoons. Lieutenant General Count de Rochambeau proudly represented French military prowess and valiancy as he contributed to the allied forces with his artillery brigade (six hundred men), cavalry brigade of Lauzun's Legion (six hundred men), and infantry brigade (seven regiments of nine hundred to one thousand men each, or a total of more than six thousand men).

As they moved out from Williamsburg toward Yorktown, the main body of American Continentals in the advance formation and the French moved down the "great road" in single column. The Virginia Militia marched in a formation farther to the right of the main body. Both formations were on guard for British ambushes. Washington ordered his troops that, should the enemy attack, they should use their bayonets, the weapon of choice with the French. Von Steuben had trained the American troopers in hand-to-hand martial arts skills of bayonet warfare. They were more than ready for combat after weeks of waiting for reinforcements, artillery, and supplies to arrive from the north.

Raleigh marched bravely in formation with his fellow self-confident, wilderness-hardened seasoned militiamen, especially the gallant Amherst unit. They had been successfully protecting the citizens in their respective counties for years. They did not care about General Cornwallis's lack of respect for state and county militiamen.

Let them attack and we will show them what we have up our sleeves, Raleigh thought as if he needed to reassure himself that the militiamen were ready and able to carry the day. They had their orders and each trooper knew exactly what to do, should sly old Cornwallis command portions of his forces to attack on their right and left flanks.

Raleigh and John, along with other scouting teams, had become familiar with the Yorktown topographical layout. Their reconnaissance of the land and distant observations of British personnel disclosed that some of Lord Cornwallis's men had been wounded, and that he was in a holding pattern waiting for reinforcements and naval support from the York River. The intelligence officers and the division commanders were confounded with Cornwallis's relative inactivity during those last six weeks. Raleigh spoke with John about his suspicions.

"He didn't take advantage of opportune situations in our camp during the early stages of its organization. When we ventured out alone beyond our camp in Williamsburg, his soldiers didn't harass our troops! Could his forces be wounded and tired? Is Cornwallis mentally worn out? Our division commander feels that he is waiting for something that hasn't come yet. Is the general waiting for personnel reinforcements? Are they in need of more artillery firepower or medical care? He must be short of essential personnel and does not want to lose any more officers. It seems like someone or something has cut the heart out of Cornwallis because there is no fight in him. Is he disappointed with his superiors in New York who have been slothful in coming to his rescue?"

"You have been listening to intelligence officers' conversations back there in the headquarters. Between that information and what you and I know from our scouting missions, I can assure you that you are on target with those questions concerning Cornwallis's situation," John surmised.

Raleigh did not believe in shooting sick deer or fowl. He did not even have the heart to kill a bear if it appeared to be ill. "John, it is not fair. This situation with General Cornwallis and his British soldiers is strange. Because the general and his men are tired and possibly injured, I am not as anxious to kill them now compared to my hostile attitude two weeks ago," he admitted as the troops approached Yorktown.

British lieutenant colonel Robert Abercrombie's light infantry brigade, who covered the area to the allies' left and to the British forces' right, was the first to spot the allied forces marching toward their compound. As they sounded the alarm, French general Rochambeau ordered Major General Baron de Vioménil's and Colonel Marquis de Laval's Regiment Bourbonnais to clear the enemy area. This section was covered by British general Tarleton's Legion, but he only sent a token cannon shot toward the American and French forces. The large marshy brook on the left side of Cornwallis's compound served as a barrier to protect the British defenders from the allies.

The intelligence reports on the desperate position of the enemy had now been confirmed. Raleigh asserted, "Earlier, I thought the reason for the British's slow pace in defending their compound was that they did not respect us as a military threat, but now I realize that they were too lethargic to find a better site or to reinforce their present one. I think they have some injured soldiers and low morale."

The British, to their advantage, did not have to work as hard to defend themselves. They had some help from the natural topography. There was a ravine coming around from the York River on the British forces' right side and the allies' left side. Wormley Creek was another defense barrier on their left and on the allies' right side. They had built earthen works to shore up their defenses and had constructed redoubts from which they would fire their cannon toward Americans' positions. While the layout of Cornwallis's defenses was marginally military style, it was not the construction that one would expect of a great commander.

General Lafayette wondered aloud to his officers, "Why, he has had the convenience of eight weeks to set up a better defense. Can you believe this? Are his soldiers apathetic and demoralized? Are they tired mentally or lazy? Have they given up on their war efforts? Have they lost their desire to destroy the Americans' goal for independence?"

American and French officers and soldiers, spellbound, asked themselves and each other, "What is going on here? Did Morgan's Rangers bite at Cornwallis's heels and nip at his flanks in the Carolinas so much that they drove him into such a defensive mode that he was forced to retreat into Virginia?"

The allies quickly began to set up their offensive positions. They had to move quickly to flush Cornwallis out because the allies would not have the convenience of the French naval support on the York River and the Chesapeake Bay beyond the next month, when French admiral de Grasse's fleet sailed back to his naval position in the West Indies. After he left, Clinton could reinforce Cornwallis from the sea with troops, supplies, and artillery. He could even rescue his British forces and take them back to New York. General Washington suspected that General Clinton had already sent ships with troop reinforcements toward Yorktown.

"As long as de Grasse's naval blockade was in force on the Bay, Cornwallis's position was appalling," Washington stated convincingly to his top officers as the allies planned to tighten up the noose around Cornwallis's forces. Placing a siege on his Yorktown position, the allies would wait him out and hope that the British navy from New York did not break the French blockade at the Bay. "The ground forces must close in on Cornwallis before Admiral de Grasse's fleet returns to his assignment in the West Indies."

Raleigh, in all of his life, had never seen such military might and force in one place. His life was passing before him as he observed great military officers, including General George Washington, discussing war strategies while he gazed through binoculars at desperate British soldiers holed up in Yorktown. They were helpless like a rabbit caught in one of his traps at the Ridge.

"They are praying to the same God that I pray to," Raleigh surmised. He had begun to feel sorry for them. The racial hatred in his soul had started releasing its grappling hold on his heart.

Raleigh realized that he had stopped feeding the spiritual monster. *My conscience is in operation. I am beginning to care about those people, the Englishmen.* His new concerns and sympathy for the British were breaking Satan's grip on his heart and soul. His conscience was now putting a siege on his racial hatred of the

English soldiers and colonists, much like the allies had begun their siege on Cornwallis's compound. He compared the change to cutting the tenacious grass from the tobacco rows.

"I must cut the crabgrass of hatred asunder or it will destroy that valuable crop within me, my personal values and personality!"

Raleigh and his fellow militiamen, along with all officers and troops of the allied force, worked on their respective assignments in accordance with General Washington's orders. Between September 28 and October 6, they worked deliberately and quickly. Raleigh and the Amherst Militia troops worked anxiously to set up their tents and encampment area. Every trooper moved with and among other troopers from different military units as if they were one unit assigned together for years. Their officers had already mapped out the exact encampment locations of each unit before they marched from Williamsburg. When they arrived in their assigned locations, they went about their duties of constructing encampments.

General George Washington assigned the French to encampments on the left side, closer to the York River and Yorktown Creek facing Cornwallis's compound. He ordered the American forces to set up their positions on the right side and right center, near Wormley Creek and facing Wormley Pond and the British fortifications. The commanders did not really know what Lord Cornwallis had up his sleeve. Not knowing if he were planning to attack via a loop behind them or even on their flanks, General Washington required all units to make sure that they had the advantage against British surprise attacks.

"Does Cornwallis have some cunning plan? When will his offensive intentions come to fruition?" questioned one of Washington's subordinate officers as his troopers scurried and whisked about the camps, focusing on their assignments. The miners and sappers were digging trenches about four feet deep and seven feet wide in strategic offensive and defensive positions. Their military movements and resolves were exactly opposite to those of the British troops who wandered around aimlessly.

Although General Washington did not have all the details at this time, he suspected that Cornwallis had a serious shortage of field-grade officers. Raleigh and his friend, John Redcross, were cognizant of the intelligence information that allied forces acquired about General Cornwallis's position and personnel. Raleigh suggested to John, "Perhaps this was the reason for that miserable-looking personnel site that exists at Yorktown!"

One officer reasoned to his fellow field-grade officers as he spied through his binoculars, "He does not have any quality leadership."

Washington did not know the reason for Cornwallis's lethargic military activity but presumed he was waiting for British ships from New York to send reinforcements or for rescue. Another possibility for his troops' failure to shore up their defenses was the deficient quantity of his top field-grade officers. Lieutenant General Cornwallis only had one general, Brig. Gen. Charles O'Hara, Commander of the Brigade of Guards.

John reasoned, "Maybe they are waiting for more top grade commissioned officers to help them fight us."

Raleigh said, "You know they are. Wouldn't you wait, if you were Cornwallis, for more brain power to lead your men in battle? Cornwallis is probably burned out now and needs to recuperate from previous battles. He only has Lieutenant Colonel Abercrombie to command his Light Infantry Brigade and a major, Armstrong. Let me see . . . there is that Lieutenant Colonel York that we suspect is commanding the 33rd and his brigade, called the York Brigade. There is a Lieutenant Colonel Johnson directing the 17th and a lower grade officer, Captain Apthorpe, leading the 23rd."

"Colonels de Voit and de Scybothen commanded the two German Auspach Battalions," John added. "Why do you think those Germans like to make words so hard to say and understand? How would you like to have a surname like de Voit and Scybothen?"

"How would you like to have a surname like Redcross?" Raleigh asked jokingly.

"How would you like to have a first name like Raw-leigh?"

"John, don't you dare try to start teasing me. I have two staffs here to assist me: a militia-issued tomahawk and a Raleigh-made tomahawk. You don't want to get on my bad side!"

"You started it, Raw-leigh, by talking about my Redcross name, and I came back at you by giving you some of your own medicine. I am sorry that it is too strong for you to stomach. Maybe I need to scout the area to find some herbs to help you keep stuff on your sick stomach."

"John, what were you saying before you started all this foolishness?"

"I was giving you information about the commissioned officers in that compound. You named some of the people over there under Cornwallis, and I added some that headquarters told me are over there also. I understand from headquarters that the Hessian Command is being directed by Lieutenant Colonel de Fuchs of the prince héréditaire outfit. There are Major O'Reilly with the Regiment de Bose and Captain Ewald of the Yagers Group. There were some other names they threw around in the command center, but with those hard to understand surnames, it is hard for me to remember them."

"With a name like Redcross, those hard-to-understand names ought to be easy for you."

"All right Raw-leigh Pan. I mean Payne, or is it Pin? Maybe it is Row-leigh? Or is it Row- land?"

John continued to fret Raleigh, "I entered the military from Lancaster County, my home area. There are a few Redcrosses in that Northern Neck area, as you know. My name is not so unusual. The Pekwems, on the other hand . . . I mean the Pinns, or is it Pewems?"

"You made your point. I know I have an unusual name, and I don't need you to remind me. Let us get back to the business of determining how many field-grade officers are over there in that compound so we would know what to expect when the battle starts."

John continued, "Lt. Col. Duncan McPherson, Commander of the 71st, with two majors under his command, are there, along with Lt. Col. Thomas Dundas. They are working Dundas overtime because he has two commands, the Dundas Brigade and the 80th. He does, however, have Major Gordon to assist him. There are two other majors in his brigade, Hewett over the 43rd and Francis Needham leading the 76th."

"I actually feel sorry for Cornwallis. He is not the leader that I feared earlier," Raleigh admitted.

Raleigh and John were accurate in their assessment of Cornwallis's personnel. Lord Cornwallis did not have essential field-grade officer strength to command his large group of noncommissioned officers and troops effectively. Although he was waiting for troop reinforcements, he really needed to get additional field-grade officers, both generals and colonels, to shape up the large group of leaderless troops that was already on site. Cornwallis was obviously embarrassed about his troop's pitiable conditions, but he would be the last to fully admit to the tactical misjudgments that put him in his apathetic state. Those previous military campaigns had taken a toll on his forces to the point that they were now wounded, both physically and psychologically.

Raleigh's attitude toward the British had begun to change radically. They were not the "all-powerful invaders" anymore. The British did not look like descendants of the powerful people who stole rich aboriginal farmland in the Northern Neck. "They do not appear to be British kinfolk of the formidable and impregnable foreigners who dispersed our Wiccocomico Indian Town and later became arsonists on homes and crops, hatchet men against their orchards, and murderers in Cherokee towns!" he reasoned as he began to feel compassion for the trapped British soldiers.

General Washington assigned the Amherst Militia and fellow Virginia militiamen in quarters between General Lincoln's headquarters in the front and Lafayette's headquarters to the rear and slightly to the left. These quarters comprised part of the American encampments. Raleigh's group was closest to Wormley Creek and on the side of and in the direction of Chesapeake Bay. The other American encampments, with their artillery pointing toward the British fortifications, were near the center of the siege lines. The French forces had taken the left center and left side of the line, giving the Americans the position of honor to their right. The French lines were closest to the York River. The British fortifications were between the allied forces and Yorktown.

The British forces, in their weak and dire defensive placements, dug two curved lines of ditches around their Yorktown camp. The ditches were about four feet deep and seven feet wide. They had constructed redoubts—temporary fortifications and strongholds used to secure their defensive and offensive positions—with raised artillery emplacements at various points along the trenches and earthen works. They had sharp-pointed branches that presented barricades against allied assaults on their defensive locations.

The inner defensive point, the line closest to British positions in Yorktown, was about a-mile-and-a-half long. The outer line of defense was farther out of the town. This line had three well-fortified and well-armed redoubts near the York River. They were the Fusiliers Redoubt near the north, and Redoubt 9 and Redoubt 10 near the York River to the southeast of Cornwallis's quarters. Cornwallis's quarters were near the banks of the York River and his forces had been placed in this location, close to the York River, so that the British navy ships could provide supplies and troops as needed. Although his encampment site appeared to be a strategic location, he did not calculate the strong American and French forces and artillery batteries on his southern and southwestern borders.

Raleigh kept a journal. *My children and grandchildren will hear about and read about these events decades and centuries hence. They will not believe that I saw all this with my own eyes. The facts in the report will be dismissed as a tale that had been told, contrived by my descendants or me.*

Raleigh, looking toward Cornwallis's compound, spoke to Frances Powell, Richard Lawless, and John Bowling—three of his fellow Amherst militiamen. "Ah, this is both beautiful and sad. The site on the allies' side is amazing and lovely, well-conceived and well-executed. The position of Lord Cornwallis, on the other hand, is surprisingly shoddy in construction! No one will believe our Amherst militiamen's story when we share the details surrounding the situation in which the great Cornwallis had placed himself. Even more, it will be blinked or winked at when our descendants tell our story to later generations."

"How do we know that our descendants will learn about our service in the Amherst Militia? How can we prove that we were here at Yorktown?" asked John Bowling.

"We must keep records—keep a journal, John. There will also be those military rolls with our names listed for pay purposes."

Washington decided to put a siege on Yorktown. Since he had to wait for the artillery forces and equipment to arrive by land, he would just wait it out. His forces would continue constructing the site with fortifications to accommodate artillery batteries.

6–8 October 1781

Already within eight hundred yards of the British positions on the rainy night of October 6, one thousand volunteers, including sappers and miners with digging tools, dug trenches. Raleigh and the other members of the Amherst Militia, as well as troopers from other brigades, assisted the one hundred sappers and miners in the mammoth construction. They constructed a two thousand–foot parallel siege line less than a half mile from the British positions. The allies pulled more than a hundred heavy cannon into their places on fortified platforms.

Raleigh and John continued their reconnaissance missions. They painted their faces and arms in camouflage matching the brown, reds, greens, and yellows of the autumn vegetation. It was much more difficult for them to move about than it had been with the greener August leaves on the trees. Accomplishing their secret missions by nighttime surveillances and low-crawl movements, they always returned to their encampments before daylight. The trees and vegetation along Wormley Creek and Wormley Pond were fair areas behind which to observe military activity in the British compound. Their encampment area was in the rear of the creek and pond areas.

"John, I'll monitor the British redoubt on the far right near the York River. You check out the activity in the redoubt on the left. Since they are setting up their cannon in anticipation of our troops' assault, we have to record everything that they are doing. Let's determine the equipment they have planted in those redoubts and the number of soldiers that have been assigned to each one."

"Let's move out from those trees directly in front of Lincoln's Headquarters at around 1:00 a.m. I'll crawl along the tree line, cross Wormley Pond, and set up my observation post in that cluster of trees. After our recon missions, let's meet back here at about 4:00 a.m. If I encounter any interference with my mission, I will sound out my usual bird signal." John spoke softly. "This is like the time we pulled observations on that bear that killed my hunting dog."

"These observations are a lot more important than bear hunting. This is a human hunt and you know that humans can shoot back. You know how we hunt turkeys. Since we have to see the turkeys before they see us, we have to make it hard for those human beings to see us too. The only difference with this human hunt is that we don't want to alert the whole British compound by shooting at the redoubt soldiers. It is best that we go out without our rifles."

"Raleigh, you and I are comfortable with our knives and tomahawks. If the British soldiers spot us and assault our positions, we can defend better without the rifles. It is nighttime, and like coon hunting, we have the advantage of surprise."

"You are right, John. I will take my favorite tomahawk and the deer-skinning knife, but I hope I don't have to use them." Raleigh, pointing with his right hand, showed John the route that he planned to follow. "I will make my way to the right of Lincoln's Headquarters over there, cross Wormley Creek, low-crawl my way into those trees along the creek bank, and then turn toward those trees over there near the Moores' house. If I am successful in getting that far, I will wait a few minutes and then try to low-crawl over to that cluster of three trees on the edge of the York River. From that point, I could see clearly into that right-hand redoubt."

"If we plan to move out from the trees directly in front of Lincoln's Headquarters at 1:00 a.m. and it is ten o'clock now, then let's get some rest."

"That sounds like a good idea to me, John." He and John moved back toward the American encampment area.

October 7

Raleigh and John went in separate directions as they commenced their reconnaissance operations. After about three hours, Raleigh made his way back to the rendezvous area at around 4:00 a.m. John, having arrived about five minutes earlier, exclaimed, "Raleigh, you got out without any trouble!"

"Of course. What did you think? You know that I am as good as a snake when I low-crawl, and I do my best work at night. I didn't forget our mission requirements: do not get captured."

"What did you see?"

"I saw some soldiers in the redoubt, about three. Each one pulled sentry duty from one of three sides of the four-sided redoubt. I am sure they didn't think we could crawl behind the redoubt, so they didn't man the back side, the side facing their compound. Since they covered sentry duty from only three walls, I guess I could have crawled all the way to the base of the redoubt's rear if I wanted to."

"I saw almost the same thing, Raleigh. I observed three sentries in the redoubt. They didn't pull sentry duty on the side near the York River and the side facing their compound. There were three in the redoubt, but only two were on duty. One soldier watched the side facing our encampments and one observed the side facing the French's encampments. I saw a third man, but he just relieved one of the two on duty. I guess one slept on the floor most of the time. The two sentry soldiers also looked sleepy. I should have just crawled into their redoubt like a snake, from the river side or the back side, and greeted them. I could have opened their surprised, sluggish eyes to the point that they would have fired their rifles all over the place without hitting me. I didn't want them to waste their ammunition because they need to save it for us and the time when we will be ready to move in for real."

Raleigh and John went directly to the headquarters' tent and reported their recon information to the intelligence officer on duty. After the debriefing, Raleigh and John hurried to their tents to get two hours of sleep before the assembly at 7:00 a.m.

8 October 1781

After the formal assembly before their encampment area, at around 7:15 a.m., John Bowling spoke to Raleigh about information that he had just received. "You are one of the best scouts in the colony. You have eyes like an eagle and know what the enemy is doing after each recon mission. I don't understand why you didn't know that your brother and nephew are right over there in the artillery battery section." John pointed toward the American Artillery Park area, in front of the magazine house. "One of the officers told me that you have a brother here, assigned to Captain Yerby's company of Virginia Artillery and in the regiment commanded by Colonel Williams. Let's walk over there and see."

With a cluster of trees between the artillery park and the encampment area, John and Raleigh could not see the artillery soldiers clearly. Walking ahead of Raleigh, John moved with military speed and precision toward the American Artillery Battery Park. As they turned past the wooded area that separated the artillery park from the encampment area, John stopped and held Raleigh's shoulder and pointed. "Is that soldier your brother? The one over there with the quadrant and plummet?"

Raleigh focused his eyes toward the artillery park and saw a soldier bending over a cannon piece and angling his head and eyes toward Cornwallis's compound. He appeared to be calculating a mathematics problem with the quadrant and plummet.

"Yes, that is Robert Junior. What in the world is he doing here? I thought he was across the York River, in Gloucester."

Raleigh turned back toward John and said, "Thanks." He then ran to his brother.

"Junior, what are you doing here? What are you doing with these cannon?"

Robert Junior stepped forward, hugged his brother, and cried, "Brother Raleigh, thank God! Thank God you are here. With this war, I didn't know whether I would ever see you again. You came to see me, didn't you? Or did God bring us together here? Brother, tell me, what are you doing here?"

"I'm here with the Amherst Militia. We were ordered to march to join General Lafayette. I received your letter the same day that my order came to march with the militia."

Robert called out to his son, "John, come over here and speak to your uncle. Where are your manners?"

John and the other artillery soldiers had been participating in a practice drill on cannon operations. John, running from his powder wagon in the rear of the cannon and heading toward the artillery weapons, stopped about halfway between the two points when his father called him. Halting in his steps when he heard his father mention the word "uncle," he held a leather sack with about fifteen pounds of powder in one hand and a lantern in the other.

Turning and walking toward Robert and Raleigh, his father called out, "Stop! Halt! Son, please put that powder down before you come toward your uncle. I am used to the danger of the powder and the lantern coming together, but we don't want to shoot your Uncle Raleigh all the way over to General Cornwallis's compound instead of the cannonball! Put the powder down."

John, placing the powder near the cannon and setting the lantern on the other side, sprinted toward his uncle. John, nearly twenty-two years old and about six foot four in height, was dressed like his father in brown breeches, white shirt, and a black vest. Their pants came down to the knees and they wore black stockings and brown shoes. He embraced his uncle as he greeted him, "Uncle Raleigh! Uncle Raleigh!"

"It is good to see you, John. Your dad informed me in his letter that you were working with him in Gloucester. I am so proud of you and your daddy. I saw Robert calculating the degrees and range for the cannonballs as I walked up a few minutes ago. You need to be aware that he acquired those mathematical skills when he learned the trade of a cooper and shoemaker in indentured servitude. I trust you know that your daddy is a talented soldier. How many other soldiers are able to do those geometrical calculations at the same time that he has to operate those cannons, both while under fire from his enemies?"

"It's true, Uncle Raleigh. I am not as good with mathematics, but I am a sharp science student because I know how to put these chemicals together, bring up this powder and fire cannon number 3," John responded.

Robert, John, and Raleigh spent about thirty minutes in conversation before they realized that the family gathering needed to be put on hold until off-duty hours.

As Raleigh prepared to return to duty, he asked, "Robert, do you remember how tough you tried to be when we were growing up? You always volunteered to break in my new flax shirts for the first time even though the material pricked against your skin. Although you pretended that you enjoyed wearing it before it was washed, I eventually figured out the fact that you were really looking out for me, your younger brother. You sacrificed your body to protect my tender skin. Thanks, Brother." Raleigh looked toward John. "Your daddy is a special brother!"

"He is also a special daddy. During the whole time that Daddy has been doing his job practicing and firing cannonballs, he has been looking out for my safety and showing me how to stay alive when the battle starts."

"That sounds like my brother," Raleigh stated as he turned to leave. "Junior showed that same compassion as he looked out for me when I was young."

"Brother, you better get back to work and quit your bragging about me," Robert advised as he dismissed what Raleigh said.

"I will see both of you later, maybe this evening." Raleigh promised as he waved to them.

"You come back over here at the artillery park, and I will show you the steps that I go through to fire the cannon to do the most damage," Robert told his brother.

Raleigh smiled as he stated, "Yes, I know about your aiming skills. Since your rock-throwing and arrow-shooting were perfectly on target when we were children, I feel sorry for the British targets when you start aiming those cannon at them."

Raleigh headed back to his encampment as Robert and his son returned to their artillery equipment. Not knowing why Robert Junior did not mention his other two sons who were supposedly with the Morgan Rifles Unit, Raleigh did not have the heart to bring up the subject because he feared that his brother was not ready to tell him that one of his sons had been killed in action.

> The sun kept setting, setting still;
> No hue of afternoon . . .
> How well I knew the light before!
> I could not see it now.
> —Emily Dickinson (1830–1886), *Dying*

11

The Battle of Battles

9 October 1781

By October 9, the sixteen-man gun crews were set up and the combined forces of the French and American troops were ready for General Washington's order to begin the assault on Yorktown.

Robert Pinn and John, his son, assigned to cannon number 3, were waiting for the orders to fire their cannon. They were assigned to Captain Yerby's company of Virginia Artillery in the regiment commanded by Colonel Williams. John was a powder boy.

By midafternoon, General Washington walked from the Washington Headquarters Command Post, which had been constructed to the rear of General Rochambeau's Headquarters. General Washington personally fired the first cannon from the American position on the far right to lead off the American assault on Cornwallis. Then the French commander, General Rochambeau, gave the order to his artillery battery to commence firing. The French started shelling the town from the far left, from an artillery position near the York River.

The artillery parks, both French and American, sent cannonballs hurling through the air. With all the firepower and the "fog of war" created by all the cannon smoke, Raleigh could not observe his brother and nephew in action. Even though he could only see shadows of men scurrying around and cannons shooting, he was excited, with apprehension and wonder. With each fiery cannonball from the American artillery park blazing over the sky, he questioned if his nephew provided the powder for that destructive projectile. As their eyes strained to see all of these events at this momentous time in history, Raleigh and John Bowling watched the fiery artillery action from their encampment area while their rushing heartbeats pumped blood-supplied oxygen to their excited and tense bodies. Raleigh's eyes still could not find Robert Junior and his nephew in all the commotion.

"Did Junior fire this one? Did my nephew supply the powder for that one that just went straight for that redoubt fortification?" Raleigh said. He was so prideful because of the Pinn family members' contribution to America's desire for independence. "Our name will go down in history. Later generations will have to be aware of the fact that we were the Pinn Indians, the mixed Wiccocomico and Cherokee aboriginal warriors, fighting side by side with other colonists against Cornwallis. We dare anyone to assert that all Cherokees were against the Americans. They can't imply that all Cherokees are their enemies. The Pinns and Redcrosses are here representing the Nation of Cherokees regally. There are others, Cherokee "Injuns," here in this siege operation." Raleigh talked fast to John in rhythm with the cannonade. "John, my nephew probably put the powder in that great ball that went straight toward Cornwallis's compound. What force! I know John put that powder together. You can be sure that his daddy, my brother, fired it. Look how straight it went toward the British fortifications. They sent the balls low and straight so that soldiers would move around over there before the ball exploded. Look how the soldiers are jumping around, ducking, and running in zigzag motions. Robert Junior's devilish mind is behind that ball. Not only is his aim on target, but he is scaring the soldiers out of their minds. They are about ready to surrender, if my brother keeps aiming like that."

Throughout the night, the allies continued artillery assaults on the British compound and fortifications. Raleigh, hearing the roar of repetitive cannon fire and explosions, had an excuse for not sleeping. He could not sleep anyway because his conscience was troubled by guilt for his past hatred of the British. In Raleigh's mind, finding peace with God was as difficult as Cornwallis's breaking out of the allies' siege of his compound.

There were reports circulating that the bodies of British soldiers in the trenches were torn in pieces, both the dead and the wounded. There were disjointed arms, heads, torsos and legs—most of which had been shot off by allied artillery fire. The Yorktown campaign was conducted generally by fire from artillery batteries rather than by infantry and cavalry units. They shot twelve- and eighteen-pound cannonballs and canister shot. Although some of the cannon barrels would melt if they were fired more than the maximum times per hour, allied forces had enough pieces of artillery equipment to supply enormous firepower throughout the assault on Yorktown. Allied forces fired more than 1,700 shots a day on the British, about one every minute and three-quarter seconds. Peering through borrowed binoculars, Raleigh saw British soldiers jumping and squirming on occasions when cannons were fired. Caught up in a constant state of flux because of the cannonade, formerly brave British soldiers were now reduced to nervous wrecks, waving and shifting their bodies in indecisive movements between cannon shot intervals. Instead of sending each cannonball high and dropping it in one spot, French and American soldiers fired some cannonballs low and direct to cause extreme fear as the projectiles landed and rolled around the British compound before exploding.

Raleigh's mind went back to the time of his prideful and ungodly brazenness. He could not believe that he had exhibited such shameful spirit in his soul against everything that was British, as well as against the will of God. At each moment of cannon fire and explosion on the British compound and fortifications, Raleigh remembered and repented for his sins. He could feel and hear in his mind the enemy soldiers' flesh being torn apart like an old garment being ripped by a seamstress. He imagined their emotional states, their depression, and their concern about their families back in England. He wondered if some had written letters to express their love for their sweethearts and wives. Did any of them write their last will and testaments? He no longer hated the British!

Standing at their encampment area, he and John Bowling watched the cannonade and the carnage in the British camp. "John, are we making widows of those soldiers' wives? What about their children back home in England? We are making them orphans!" He remembered his orphan status when his father died, and he became an indentured servant.

Defectors from the British compound provided corroborating reports that there were torsos and bodies all over the camp. Raleigh supposed that British soldiers were probably too busy sealing up their positions against enemy fire to inter the remains of fallen comrades. The reports further revealed that there were remains of both white and black soldiers in the compound, strewn in the walkways and trenches as wounded and tired soldiers went about their duties, often stepping over corpses. Disease and sickness would soon grip the compound and spread among the troops. Their military esprit de corps had nearly dropped to zero levels.

Raleigh thought he heard German soldiers praying in their section of the British compound. He detected sounds coming from two or three soldiers, who appeared to call on the name of God. Instead of the word "God," it came out like *Gott. Ein feste burg.* He could not understand the words, but he recognized the melody as he used to lead the singing services at Fairmount and knew the short meters and long meters. These words, although foreign, were somehow familiar. Sarah often told Raleigh that he had the gift of interpretation of tongues.

"John, they are speaking in tongues, Spirit-filled tongues, as they cry to their *Gott*! I know what they are doing! I have the Holy Spirit's gifts of interpretation of tongues and discernment, and I can tell that they are not praying, but singing. Those were Martin Luther's words and arrangements, and that is Luther's song, 'A Mighty Fortress Is Our God.' I thought those Germans and Hessians were heathens, but they also believe in God because they are praying and singing Luther's song in their language! They are also Christians, so why are we fighting each other? I wonder how God will deal with their prayers. Will he answer their prayers or our prayers? They are singing.

> A mighty fortress is our God, a bulwark never failing,
> Our helper He a-mid the flood of mortal ills prevailing.
> For still our ancient foe doth seek to work us woe—His craft and pow'r are great, And, armed with cruel hate, on earth is not his equal.

John agreed. "Yes, Raleigh, my ears tell me that they are singing 'A Mighty Fortress Is Our God.'"

"They are praying to the Lord. I would not want to be in the Lord's position and have to choose which side to take. God has to answer conflicting prayers as he has heard French, German, Scot, Welsh, and American soldiers beseeching him to let them win. Since he has received pleadings from the English, Welsh, and Germans to let them defeat us, what will God do? I know for a fact that he answers prayers because I am a witness to God's power. His ears have always been open and his hands have always been ready to help me. But how can he answer these prayers when each side pleads a request that conflicts with the other side's request? If God comes to the rescue of the British, he will not answer our prayer. On the other hand, if he helps us, he will not hear the British, Germans, and others over there."

"Raleigh," John said, "let God deal with those matters. You don't have anything to do with God's responsibilities. Besides, I know you have other matters to take care of rather than trying to help God decide how to answer soldiers' prayer requests."

The allies were spared a higher percentage of fatalities and injuries that normally resulted from direct hand-to-hand and rifle combat. Artillery batteries had begun to take on a greater burden in the offensive against British forces. Regardless, all troopers had begun sleeping with their weapons so that they would be ready in an instant when called on to either charge enemy fortifications or defend their positions.

The allies learned from the defectors that Cornwallis had abandoned his headquarters in General Nelson's home and had crawled into a constructed grotto. The American and

French officers believed that the cave provided the general more security against cannon fire. This great general had been forced to hide like a mole from artillery assaults carried out by the Americans and the French.

11 October 1781

General Washington decided that he must speed up his army's movement toward enemy positions. He would construct a second parallel trench closer to Yorktown to put more direct heat on Cornwallis.

Under the darkness of the night on October 11, construction parties of sappers and miners, as well as other troops, moved within four hundred yards of British fortifications. The men carried shovels, spades, and hoes. They constructed trenches as they ducked under the fiery bombardment of British cannon assaults. By daylight the next morning, the American and French allies had completed a ditch that measured approximately 750 yards, about three-and-a-half feet deep, and seven feet wide.

Since Raleigh, as well as other Amherst Militia scouts, had been put on night reconnaissance missions, he did not work with the trench constructions directly. However, he was curious, so he went to the site and observed the trench construction work that had been completed by the sappers, miners, and soldiers from various units. He always made sure that he knew the topographical layout of the military field and any construction changes before he moved out on his night recon missions. This construction would provide security against Cornwallis's artillery fire. During the next two days, all troops pulled and mounted additional artillery equipment into their newly constructed locations. Washington's parallel, on the right, was not complete, however, because of the firepower that poured down on his men from the British redoubts. Fire from Redoubts 9 and 10 to the east of the British positions forced allied troops back to their previous positions. Washington then halted the completion of new ditches.

Washington ordered a night attack on the two redoubt forts simultaneously. He knew that the allies could not move forward on the British until they took out the two redoubts that retarded the movement. The French troops would assault Redoubt 9, which was somewhat closer to their position, while the Americans planned to move against the closer Redoubt 10.

The Americans closed in on Redoubt 10 by chopping through sharpened logs of the abatis with their axes. Some of the soldiers had ladders to climb the high British defensive dirt walls to the redoubt. Although the French troops waited for others to cut the sharpened logs before they attacked the redoubt, the Americans assaulted the British position at the same time the other troops hacked their way against the sharpened abatis logs. They crawled through the logs, jumped across holes left by allied artillery explosions, and mounted Redoubt 10 walls. Most of the Americans had unloaded muskets so that they could attack by surprise. When a British sentry realized that the Americans were on their fortifications, he sounded the alarm and the British troops immediately fired their weapons in defense of the redoubt. Some American soldiers took rounds to their bodies from British gunfire when they and other troops moved in with their bayonets. Approximately seventy English soldiers supported this redoubt. The surprised and frightened British troops quickly gave up their position and surrendered their weapons. Col. Alexander Hamilton and his men took Redoubt 10 in about ten minutes. The American troops had 120 dead and wounded soldiers.

John Redcross, John Bowling, and Raleigh stood at attention and shoulder to shoulder, with their heads turned toward Redoubt 10 as if they hoped that they would get military orders to help with the American assault. Colonel Hamilton's soldiers demonstrated brilliantly that they could take care of their mission quickly and decisively.

French soldiers and a unit of black soldiers from the Rhode Island Militia under the overall command of Major General de Vioménil, assaulted Redoubt 9 in hand-to-hand combat with swords and bayonets. The Rhode Island Militia captain Stephen

Olney told his men, "If you lose your gun, don't fall back—take the gun of the first man killed."

Raleigh and his fellow militiamen stood near their encampment area and focused their eyes toward the French and Rhode Island units as they attacked Redoubt 9. They were on standby and ready to assist the allies as needed. After about thirty minutes, the French allies and the Rhode Island unit had seized control of the redoubt. They killed and captured the personnel in the redoubt, about 120 British troops.

John Redcross and Raleigh had told their militia officers that they were available should they be needed. Discouraged that they were not called up to assist either assault, Raleigh informed his colleagues, "I would like to have helped those Frenchmen and black Rhode Island soldiers."

"Weren't they daring, the Frenchmen and Rhode Islanders, as they forced their way into that redoubt, took charge with their bayonets and hand-to-hand combat skills, and then told the survivors that they were prisoners?" Raleigh remarked. "I believe we would have been just as efficient, had they called us up."

"Yes, they were great. And what about those Americans? I wish our officers had volunteered our militia to join the assault against one of those redoubts," said John Redcross.

John Bowling advised, "Instead of being irritated about the fact that we didn't get orders to join one of those redoubt assaults, we ought to be thankful we weren't called up. One or all three of us could have fallen in action. A few minutes ago, believe it or not, Sarah could have been a widow and Turner and your girls orphans, Raleigh. You could have been one of Col. Alexander Hamilton's soldiers who died in the American assault on Redoubt 10."

Now that the two redoubts were in the hands of allied forces, General Washington was close enough to fire cannonballs from the two allied-controlled redoubts to every point of the British in Yorktown. With Admiral de Grasse's fleet blocking Cornwallis's chance for escape and supplies from the sea,

Admiral Comte de Barras also arrived with heavy cannon and assaulted Yorktown enemy positions. French and American troopers moved closer and closer to British positions—and to Cornwallis's headquarters.

Raleigh Pinn witnessed all the firepower of the artillery batteries. In the pivotal battle for American freedom, he had been on the world's scene, Yorktown, at the right time and in the right place, and was elated by the opportunity to be there.

On October 17, American and French commanders opened fire on all fronts and from the two closer redoubts. They sent fiery destruction down on Yorktown as Cornwallis attempted to escape with his army from Yorktown to Gloucester where he had a British army compound. Lord Cornwallis had lost all hope of being rescued by naval and marine forces. As his plans were put in motion to escape to Gloucester, a sudden rainstorm during the night made boat travel on the York River too dangerous. General Cornwallis, with this barrier closing off the bleak chance of an escape from Yorktown, abandoned his plans to relocate to Gloucester.

Raleigh suspected that God's hand had intervened in this conflict, just as his hand was present in the rainstorm when Barak, the commander of the Israelite army, went against Sisera, the commander of King Jaban's army. Raleigh remembered reading the astounding Bible story in Chapter 4 of the book of Judges. The commander of the army of Israel and his foot soldiers made a direct frontal assault against Sisera and his charioteers. God intervened by sending a miraculous rainstorm. The flat plain, which had been ideal for chariot cavalry warfare against Israel, became too muddy for the chariot wheels. As a result of the divine downpour, the battle advantage turned in Israel's direction. After Sisera and his cavalry were thrown into confusion and began to dismount from their chariots, Barak and his foot soldiers defeated Sisera and his powerful charioteers. During Sunday school class discussions at Fairmount Fellowship, Raleigh questioned the possibility of divine intervention to cause such a miraculous change of fortune. *How could foot soldiers defeat a chariot cavalry?* He ceased doubting supernatural causes in this incident by reading verse 7 and discovering that God's hand was in the rainstorm that caused the cavalry to fall into confusion.

18 October 1781

During the British and American allies' cannonade, John Pinn and his father worked feverishly at the number 3 cannon. Smoke covered allies and British artillery batteries as both sides bombarded each other. With his quadrant and plummet in hand, Robert tirelessly conducted his geometrical calculations, aimed the barrel, and fired balls at the British compound. While the opposing batteries sent projectiles toward their respective enemies, John scurried to provide powder for his cannon. As rounds came in from the British cannons, one of the exploding balls injured John's right ankle and knocked him off his feet. Dropping to the ground, John grabbed his bleeding ankle with both hands. Robert, leaving his cannon as if it were no longer important, hurried to his son.

"John, are you hurt? Let me move you away from this line of fire." With his muscular forearms, his father grabbed him gently but hastily under his armpits and pulled him from the line of constant enemy fire. As he carried him almost half the distance toward a secure location almost a hundred yards from the previous position, an enemy musket shot penetrated John's left leg. Robert maneuvered his body to his right and tucked his son's body in a position that permitted it to be hidden behind his own torso as he lifted John completely from the ground and carried him to safety. After placing John on the ground, with his own body serving as a buffer against further gunfire, he inspected John's two wounds.

Two soldiers rushed to John's position to provide medical aid. His father reluctantly released and moved away from his son, with the prodding of the soldiers. Robert returned slowly to his cannon, looking back at the medical men as they worked on his son, as if he were not sure whether he should return to his cannon or stay with him. As he realized that he must take charge of his cannon, he instantly called for a new powder boy.

Robert, setting his cannon sight on the likely spot in the British compound from which the line of fire came on his son, wondered if this battle would also take another son. Having marked the suspected enemy fire location, he sent two cannonballs as a return greeting in response to the two shots that hit John. Both balls were aimed in such a pattern so as to permit them to roll and bounce around the British compound as long as possible before connecting with their targets and exploding in the compound.

"This should frighten them and cause havoc long before the balls reach their intended positions. I know vengeance belongs to God, but he will surely forgive me if I kill ten British soldiers for each shot they put in my son! I will ask for God's forgiveness after I finish my cannon assignments. Lord, have mercy on me!" Robert had vigorous thoughts of vengeance and repentance running through his mind while simultaneously manning his cannon.

Raleigh learned about his nephew's injury and rushed down to the casualty area where they had taken injured soldiers.

"John, I know you are hurting, but lie back and let us help you." Raleigh leaned over to hold him down while two soldiers attended to his injuries. "They are trying to take care of your wounds, so please relax and it will not hurt as bad. I am here, and I dare any British soldier to attack you while I'm here! I will pull guard duty here over you and the other injured soldiers, and I guarantee that nobody will dare shoot you."

He stood on watch to protect his nephew and other fallen soldiers against any attacks on the medical compound. Robert Junior worked eagerly at cannon number 3 with a new powder boy, having new determination to take out the enemy compound. With the heavy weight of concern on his mind about his son's medical welfare, he had a new resolve; he must get the British before they get the allies. When his son was on powder duty, he only needed to raise his hand to speed up the powder supply. Now, however, rather than giving hand signals, he called out loudly, "More powder, keep the powder coming." Although aware that he could overheat the cannon barrel by firing too fast, he pushed the cannon to the edge by sending cannonballs at the British compound as often as soldiers brought him powder, balls, and fire.

To keep Robert from losing heart while fulfilling his cannon responsibilities, Raleigh brought him timely reports on his son's welfare.

"John is doing well!" Raleigh shouted over the noise of firing. "The medical assistants are working on him, and they think he should be able to walk after the wounds heal!"

"God does get involved in human hostilities. He intervened in Cornwallis's plans to escape to Gloucester." Raleigh shared his thoughts with John Redcross. "God probably did not want the general to take his army away from Yorktown to regroup and prolong the Revolutionary War in America any longer than necessary. There have been too much killing and injury." Raleigh had a new compassionate heaviness in his heart for Cornwallis and the British troops.

"Raleigh, I don't blame him for trying to escape. If you and I were captured, I know we would figure a way out of captivity."

Raleigh agreed. "It is just natural, an instinct, to escape unpleasant situations. I don't blame him for trying to break out of the Yorktown compound trap because he wouldn't be much of a soldier, even less a general, if he just gave up without craving freedom."

The allies' cannonade had inflicted major casualties on Cornwallis's military personnel and fortifications. Realizing that his security at Yorktown was hopeless since his navy had not arrived with reinforcements or assisted him in an escape, General Cornwallis chose to surrender.

During the early morning of October 19, the allies' artillery batteries increased their barrage of cannonballs against the British compound. At around 9:00 a.m., Raleigh and the allies noticed a strange sight: a young British drummer boy climbed over the earthen works and a large heap of rubbish as if he were rising from his grave, beating his drum. The allied troops did not hear the drum initially as he beat it steadily with almost musical accompaniment to the loud sounds of American and French cannon. It was a ghostly scene, however, as the drum sounded and a British officer appeared, unarmed, holding up a dirty white handkerchief. He waved the handkerchief back and forth, almost to the beat of the drummer boy's percussions. The handkerchief signaled that the British were done—conveying, "We give up!" With each wave, the drummer, before retiring behind the earthen wall, beat the instrument almost in unison with the officer's floating handkerchief signal. An officer of the allies, seeing the young boy and English officer, ordered cessation of all artillery and small arms fire. Then all of the allies heard the beautiful rhythmic music announcing the end of the battle and the beginning of the end of the Revolutionary War.

The morning surrender scene was nightmarish, with the silenced cannon smoke wafting among the rubbish and earthen works. There was the drummer boy with that unforgettable beat and the officer with the dirty white handkerchief waving like a wand among the smoke. Raleigh reviewed the drama in his mind, shivering and trembling as if he had just been brushed by a nippy breeze. He heard the drumbeat and saw the officer's dramatic and theatrical moves, which he vowed to share with his children and grandchildren as long as he lived.

General Washington and General Cornwallis worked out the terms of the surrender. At 11:00 a.m. on October 19, a team of allied officers met in Redoubt 10 to sign the historic surrender. General Washington wrote a short paragraph at the end of the document: "Done in the trenches before Yorktown, in Virginia, October 19, 1781."

At 2:00 p.m. on that day, French and American soldiers lined up on the road leading to Hampton, just outside of Yorktown. The French wore bright blue outfits. The Americans soldiers were dressed poorly, wearing dirty and ragged clothes, with some actually barefoot.

The British soldiers marched out with their arms on their shoulders in accordance with the terms of the capitulation agreement. They deposited their arms in a field directly in front of one of the encampments and American Artillery Park. The French Artillery Park was just left of the American Artillery Park.

After the British forces had surrendered their weapons, they nobly did an about-face military turnaround and moved to the assigned detention camp. All American combatants stood at attention as the surrender ceremony proceeded.

Raleigh and other soldiers looked for the commander-in-chief of the British forces, Lord Cornwallis, but he did not appear in the ceremony. He sent his second-in-command, Brigadier General O'Hara, the only other officer of general rank, to represent him in the dreaded festivities. Even in this demeaning and humbling position, General O'Hara had the nerve to turn up his nose at the ranking officer, General Washington. He preferred to surrender to the French, obviously thinking it unworthy to capitulate to the Americans. Raleigh, guilty of frequent haughtiness himself, had an opportunity to see personal pride on display at a most disturbing and despicable level. Raleigh noticed something that the other militia soldiers might have missed as he shared with John Bowling some background information about General O'Hara's snobbish attitude toward the Americans.

"John, did you see what that uppity low-ranked general did in that surrender ceremony?"

"Yes, the general is a little particular to whom he surrenders."

They were waiting for the end of the ceremonies. Raleigh, leaning in and turning his head slightly toward John, whispered in his ear, "General O'Hara just walked past General Washington as if he were not there and stopped in front of the French general Rochambeau. He prefers to present his sword of surrender to Rochambeau. Rochambeau declined the honor and signals with a nod to the commander-in-chief of the Allied Forces, General Washington. He should have known he didn't have an option to decide who would receive his ceremonial surrender sword. O'Hara went back toward Washington. Washington then declines to accept the surrender sword and orders that it be given to General Lincoln, his second-in-command."

"Raleigh, there was a lot behind that snub! What history lesson did I miss?"

"John, over a year ago, in May 1780, in the Battle of Charleston, General Lincoln had to surrender to Gen. Sir Henry Clinton, not due to a fault of his own. Now the British soldiers are placed in a subordinate position of having to admit defeat in one of the most important battles of the Revolutionary War. To make matters worse, they have to give up, in ceremonial fashion, to the same general, General Lincoln, whom they disdained in Charleston."

"I didn't realize, Raleigh, that General O'Hara's rudeness toward General Washington was the main reason for General Rochambeau's refusal to accept the surrender sword."

Raleigh explained, "Rochambeau realized that General Washington was his superior and had the right to receive the sword. What was noble about Washington's declining to take the ceremonial sword was that he wanted to convey to O'Hara that American and French generals were not pleased with the way that the British leaders mistreated Lincoln during last year's surrender ceremony. The tables have turned on the British and the allies did not want their enemy officers to think they had forgotten about their disrespect toward and humiliation of Lincoln. Washington signaled to O'Hara that Lincoln was to receive the sword."

"Raleigh, you know your military history."

"It's a matter of common sense, etiquette, and respect for your fellow soldier, regardless of whether he is an enemy or ally."

With the surrender ceremony complete, Raleigh was sure that he would be going home. He prayed silent words of thanksgiving to the Lord.

Lord, thank you. Thank you, not so much because we defeated the British but for helping us keep the casualty rate low on both sides. Although they lost many souls, the casualty toll could have been worse as more soldiers could have died and been injured. We could have been here even through the winter if Cornwallis's naval forces had been able to remove the French blockade at the Bay. Thank you, Lord. I know now that you do not take sides! I also know that you are concerned about the wounds of soldiers, regardless of whether they are French, American, or British. You do not like human hostilities. I repent for my hostile attitude. I repent for my hatred of the British. I see them now as your created souls and my brothers. Thank you, Lord! Thank you, Lord!

A detachment of American troops inspected the British compound in the town during the occasion of the surrender ceremony and brought back horrific stories of carnage and misery. British soldiers and workers had left some of their fallen comrades in the open air, unburied for days. There were body parts strewn all over the compound. Local citizens told stories of starving, carnivorous dogs walking around with human body parts in their mouths. These inspections confirmed what Raleigh and other scouts had reported: the British compound had suffered major deaths and injuries, and soldiers had not been able to bury all their fallen comrades in a timely and respectable fashion.

Upon learning about the official inspection report, Raleigh bowed on his knees before he went to sleep and asked the Lord to forgive all the horrible human hostilities that just occurred, as instigated by all sides—the Americans, English, French, Germans, Welsh, Scots, and Native Americans.

Six captains, seven lieutenants, two ensigns, noncommissioned officers, and privates gathered in military formation for the purpose of making out payrolls at the end of their tour, commencing from the time of their joining the army. The commander of the regiment was to sign the list. All officers and troops were excited about the march back to Amherst County and the opportunity to see their wives, children, other family members, and friends. During the last four months, they had been in service for their country, and although they did not regret their service in Williamsburg and Yorktown, Amherst militiamen admitted that the time seemed so long. With their military service completed, they were apprehensive about what they would find back home. For most farmers, the best farm months had passed and the season was lost. Their service would bring some financial rewards, however, as they would receive pay or land bounty for their militia campaign.

When Raleigh walked up to the recording officer at the table, he peeked at the words on the paper on the desk.

> A return of officers and men at present in service from the county of Amherst, together with such as are furloughed.

Captains	Lieutenants	Ensigns
James Pamplin	Wm. Horsley	_____ McCullock
Jn. Diggs	Jn. Horsley	

Raleigh wanted to read all the names, but they ordered the militiamen to keep the line moving. He spotted his name on the second page of the document, halfway down the first of three columns. Raleigh wanted to make sure that his name was not left off the rolls. He remembered when Commander Gaines ordered the militia to march to join Lafayette; the officials had misspelled his name.

He shared his concerns with John Redcross. "The officer spelled my name 'Rolly Penn' when he ordered me to march. Today he almost spelled it correctly as he recorded it on the furlough list as 'Rawleigh Pinn.' That is much better, because

I am a Pinn. Everybody knows that the Pinns are Indians in Virginia, but I would feel better if they dropped the 'w' in Rawleigh. It has always amazed me why the county officials don't like to spell my name correctly. But this is really vain of me to be insolent and haughty at this point in my life. Since God has been good to me and let me live, I must be thankful that I am alive to see my name on the list whether misspelled or not."

"I am glad that you are becoming more humble now, Raleigh. We need to be thankful rather than dwell on petty issues since we have been through a major battle with our British enemies and we came out of it healthy."

"John, I just wanted to make sure my name was there because I have to make sure that the Pearl preserves its heritage. My name on the 'march to join General Lafayette' list and the Yorktown 'furlough' list will preserve my heritage as a contributor to America's freedom. Your name was also on the list, John, on page two, second column. Because you and I are Cherokees, although you have more Cherokee blood than I have, we need to look out for our heritage as there is no guarantee that the colonists would endeavor to keep it for our descendants."

"You are right. I must be more conscious of my heritage. I plan to use every opportunity to let people know that I am Cherokee."

Raleigh, walking with John toward their encampment area, voiced a sigh of relief. "Tomorrow morning at 6:00 a.m., our militia will start our march to Amherst County! Praise the Lord!"

> And fare-thee-weel, my only Luve!
> And fare-thee-weel a while!
> And I will come again, my Luve,
> Tho' 'twere ten thousand mile!
> —Robert Burns, 1794

12

I Will Come Again

October 1781

> That June morning never left me, even though I left Sarah.
> Militia dawn came so early, because for her I left her too soon.
> That morning never left me, although distance was so far,
> Though the kerchief was sad, by it I will hold Sarah at noon.
> That morning never left me, for separation came with war.
> Reunion, come and not part! Thank God,
> for the drummer's surrender tunes.
> —Raleigh Pinn

Raleigh was not a poetic genius, but he wrote these words as he and his militia marched home. Writing in his mind with a pen of love in his heart, he created the lines with the rhythm of the militiamen's march. Each step made his heart warmer and his feet lighter. As he marched west toward Amherst County, he remembered some anonymous lyrics that he read years ago in his indentured servitude class:

> Western wind, when will thou blow,
> The small rain down can rain?
> Christ, if my love were in my arms
> And I in my bed again!
>
> —Anonymous

The four months of separation had been as long in time as the distance between Buffalo Ridge and Yorktown had been in miles. Because of his memory of Sarah, the distance seemed to decrease with each sunset over the four-month period. Along with more than two hundred excited militiamen marching toward Amherst, looking forward to seeing their family members and friends again, Raleigh's mind raced in time with his cadence and heartbeat.

Raleigh wondered how Turner had fared with the tobacco crop. He voiced his thoughts to John Bowling as they marched. "Since I taught him well, that training and Sarah's supervision over the farm probably contributed to a fair crop this year. I don't want to get my hopes up too high because I know that the tobacco crop will not have the size and quality that I always produced. I hope they have saved a few leaves for a good smoke by the fireplace."

"I have a feeling that Sarah made as good a crop of tobacco as you would have made if you were there, Raleigh." John said, "She can't help but be a good farmer because she has been living with you, the best farmer in Amherst County." His cheerful and gracious words were meant to keep Raleigh from worrying about his farm. John continued to praise Sarah. "She is an Evans! What would you expect? They have always been good farmers!"

"I showed them how to bank the sweet potatoes. I would love to get hold of some of those yams. That sweet potato cobbler that Sarah makes—oh my!" Raleigh groaned. "As much as Turner likes to eat Sarah's pies, I wonder if they dried those apples, pears, and peaches on the roof for the winter fruit cobbler? I didn't go to all that trouble planting those vegetables to let them go to waste because I have been taken away from my farm. I am sure that they prepared those pinto, navy, and butter beans for drying as they are essential to carry us through the winter." He was quiet for a moment over the thought of the good food that awaited his return home. "My horse needed new shoes and I should have shod him before I left, but the militia did not give me enough time. Look at me making up excuses and putting the blame on Commander Gaines! I guess Turner cut and raked up the hay and put it in the hayloft. I've got a feeling that this winter is going to be a cold one. We have to get ready for it."

"Why do you think this winter will be a hard one?"

"Look at the way those squirrels over there in the forest are scurrying around and looking for nuts. You have enough Indian in you to know that animals can teach human beings a few tricks about life and the future, if we would only become students and learn the lessons in the forests' classrooms. I need to check the squirrels at the Ridge and Stonewall, to find out if they are storing up acorns. If they are, they would be ready for the snow and frigid chills!"

"Speaking of storing up rations for the winter, why do you think Cornwallis allowed his army to get cornered there in Yorktown without proper provisions and sufficient naval forces as backup for his army?" John asked.

"John, I think his battles in the south took a toll on his supplies and personnel. Why else would a man of his prudent reputation as a military leader allow himself to get cornered like a raccoon?"

"Washington and Rochambeau were smart officers. I think they set up the situations to put Cornwallis in those Yorktown predicaments. It was not an accident that he got himself stuck in the compound near the York River," John suggested.

"Do you think French and American officers, in producing this siege, intentionally forced Cornwallis to live among his fallen soldier's corpses, which would decompose and produce an odor that would be unbearable to all the soldiers? Would they have been that wise or grotesque? If the officers were scholars of history—Latin history—maybe they would have learned this evil strategy from the Romans. Perhaps they read Virgil's *The Aeneid* and learned the devious strategy.

"The British did not have the energy to bury all those corpses. Maybe their great leaders were too preoccupied with our presence on their front and flanks to worry about the luxuries of providing decent burials for their dead. Even some Cherokees in Tennessee are known to get rid of their dead by throwing them into the river. British people often referred to these types of Indian burials as aquatic burials. The British officers, who often called the aboriginal people heathens, should have had the decorum and seemliness to order the interment of those remains in an aquatic ceremony. The corpses deserve more respect than to have those half-living soldiers beholding their fellow soldiers' dissecting, corroding, and dissolving cadavers. The living knows for sure that he is returning to his Potter, his Creator, when his sun goes down. Thus, he has no need for such living remains' grotesque prompting, reminding them of their mortality, as was the case with the decaying remains reminding Cornwallis and his soldiers of their mortality. They could have at least placed palls over their remains. The officers, if they were worth their salt, should have been worried about the psychological effects of all those dead, decomposing bodies lying there on their soldiers. I think it would have even made me give up and surrender with hands up if I were a British soldier and had to smell that stench. There was the York River, adjoining their backyard—why didn't they have the prudence to conduct aquatic burials?"

William Garner, the person to whom Raleigh was indentured in 1754 after he left the home of Richard Seldon, taught him how to improve his reading and writing skills. Raleigh was eventually exposed to the classics and enjoyed the works by Virgil, the Roman poet. His mind went back to Virgil's *The Aeneid*, the Latin epic poem about Aeneas and his adventures. He remembered reading about the Romans and how they sometimes ordered a prisoner, whom they detested, to be tied to a dead body. The prisoner was forced to move around with this useless, constantly decomposing weight attached to his soon-to-be corpse until the repulsive stench from his mortal twin destroyed his emotional and physical existence. He thought about a scene in Book VIII where Virgil poetically describes this cruel punishment.

> The living and the dead at his command
> Were coupled, face to face, and hand to hand,
> Till, chok'd with stench, in loath'd embraces tied,
> The ling'ring wretches pin'd away and died.

At one unfortunate point, as Raleigh marched toward Amherst and talked with his fellow militiamen, he made an awkward step and slid into a mole hole, twisting his right ankle and going head over heels into a ravine beside the road. Four militiamen impulsively rushed to Raleigh's rescue.

After the construction of a homemade crutch to help him walk, he continued his westward stride toward Amherst. Raleigh was afraid to think about anything related to the allies' victory at Yorktown. Each time that his mind began to think, it was encumbered in meditations of pride over the English. Since there existed within his soul a haughty, ungodly temperament, he was afraid to meditate on those thoughts about the Yorktown victory that eventually led to ostentatious conversations with his militiamen.

"After all, I have been through a major battle and have not been injured until this moment. I have lost a nephew in Morgan's Riflemen operations and my other nephew, John, has sustained two injuries at Yorktown—but look at me! A mole has crippled me by his earthen works. What kind of way is this to go home from a major battle? Embarrassing! What are my fellow militiamen thinking about me, their great scout and warrior? I have been injured less than fifty miles from home!"

One of his fellow militiamen, walking in the line to his right, quoted to him Proverbs 29:23: "A man's pride shall bring him low: but honor shall uphold the humble in spirit." The man claimed he was preparing Raleigh for the welcome that the militiamen would receive when they arrive in Amherst County. He continued, "We must be humble as they receive us in Amherst."

Raleigh believed that he was warning him with the first clause, "A man's pride shall bring him low," and not the second clause about honor.

About fifteen miles from Amherst, Raleigh dropped his makeshift crutch and limped on toward his destination—the home on the Ridge! He remembered the warning he just received, however, and made another pledge to God and to himself to retain humble thoughts. As he marched in military formation, he was puzzled how the militiaman knew that God had warned him days earlier about his haughty and prejudiced attitudes toward the British. He felt that he personally would have selected a more appropriate scripture than the one that the militiaman quoted. He thought Proverbs 16:18 was more advisable, considering his recent arrogant attitude: "Pride goeth before destruction, and a haughty spirit before a fall." Repenting for his haughty frame of mind, he also mused, *That mole not only constructed his earthen works but also built a redoubt. How else did he have the firepower to knock me into that ditch?*

Just then he realized that his favorite hickory wood–handled tomahawk was not in his belt. He hollered to John Bowling, "I lost my tomahawk when that mole shot at me from his redoubt, and I jumped into that ditch! I should go back and retrieve it. No, the mole has a right to it. I'll surrender the tomahawk to him because it is his right as spoils of war. Anyway, I still have the military-issued tomahawk. God has been good to me because I didn't have to use either tomahawk throughout the whole Yorktown campaign."

It was almost dark when he turned off the main dirt road and started to limp quickly along the forest trail to his log cabin near Porridge Creek. His dog, Cocoa, a black-brown female beagle, was alerted to his foot being dragged and began barking. When Raleigh mounted the last hill and started descending toward the turnoff, Cocoa ran toward her master. By the time Raleigh crossed over Porridge Creek and began to walk up the trail to his house, Cocoa jumped into his arms and knocked him down. Raleigh was somewhat embarrassed but happy because his dog, rather than an enemy soldier, had pummeled him to the ground.

"First there was the mole and now I have Cocoa!" Raleigh remarked to the dog as if his hunting partner understood him. As he rubbed his injured ankle, he said, "Lord, you are now sending my pet dog against me and abasing me."

He pulled himself up from the ground, tested his ankle, and limped on. When he reached the yard, Sarah opened the door. Turner managed to run under her arm, jump off the porch, and sprint toward Raleigh. As Sarah ran closely behind Turner, he saw both forces storming toward him and knew that he must slow them down before his ankle became totally useless. Pretending that Cocoa tripped him, he sat down and bent over his right leg to prevent Sarah and Turner from hurting the ankle again. Turner leaped onto his stomach and Sarah fell on his chest.

Whew! Raleigh thought, laughing. *This is worse than Yorktown, the molehill, and Cocoa's assault. I am thankful that I survived all five!*

"Daddy, you are home!" Turner shouted as he, now standing, looked down on his daddy. Sarah did not say a word. She just laid on him and gave him a long kiss, as if he needed to be resuscitated from an oxygen-depriving injury. She stood and pulled her husband up by his right hand while Turner grabbed his left arm.

As Raleigh hopped on the trail with his right arm around Sarah's shoulder and neck, she cried but did not say a word. They walked home along the trail adjoining the creek bank without speaking a word. Sarah had a reason for her unvocal and tongue-tied state. She could not speak to Raleigh because she was preoccupied with communication with God as she always believed that recipients of God's blessings must respond in prayer as soon as the blessings flowed. This she did, for the Lord deserved her thanksgivings for her husband's safe return to Buffalo Ridge. She had been sending up supplications to God for months, and now the Lord provided the living proof of his goodness.

When they arrived near the porch, she concluded her prayer of thanksgiving and shouted, "Raleigh is home! Thanks, Lord!" Then she gave him a tight bear hug and helped him up the steps as Turner pulled him up the incline.

As he moved slowly through the front room, Anna ran out of the girls' bedroom with her younger sister Eady trotting behind as fast as her short legs could take her. Sarah had asked Anna to watch Eady before she and Turner had rushed out to meet Raleigh on the Porridge trail. She knew that she could not ask Turner to keep an eye on young Eady, who is almost a year old, because he would surely have deserted her in favor of rushing to greet his beloved dad. Anna, on the other hand, was a levelheaded and obedient three-year-old, and Sarah felt that she, even at her tender age, could be trusted to watch Eady faithfully.

Raleigh, hugging both girls, moved cautiously with Sarah's support. Anna shouted, "Daddy, you home! You home!"

Sarah led Raleigh toward the kitchen and, apologizing for not having supper ready, intentionally stimulated his appetite with the mouthwatering musical sounds of her banging pots and pans. As Sarah cooked dinner, she and Turner asked Raleigh thousands of questions about the war. Raleigh fielded their inquiries as he rested in a kitchen chair, with both daughters sitting on his left leg.

Anna asked two questions that were quite difficult for him to answer. "Daddy, what happened to your ankle in the war? Daddy, who hurt your ankle? Was it the British?"

He was able to dismiss her embarrassing questions by admitting to his family that he had been wrong in his thinking. "Those British soldiers were not as mean as I have always believed they were. They have the same hearts and compassion as we have here at the Ridge."

He told his family how much he missed them during the last four months. "I thank God for his goodness. We could have still been in Yorktown if it were not for the goodness of God. We could have even been the ones that surrendered rather than the British. God was on our—!" He stopped short of saying that God sided with the Americans and their allies.

"I do not understand why God does what he does. All I know is this: we are back home, safe and sound! Thank God. I do not pretend to know why some soldiers win and some lose, but this surrender was a win-win. The British did not have any business over here trying to take our land and control our political futures. God allowed them to save their army in Yorktown and their forces in Gloucester, and he allowed us to come home. Praise the Lord because he is good!"

When the grandfather clock chimed eleven times, Raleigh and Sarah realized that Eady had fallen asleep on his chest. Anna, still resting on her daddy's leg, was snoozing against her mother's chest. Turner, who had been attentive to his father's answers to their questions, had begun snoring in his chair with his head on the table.

After Raleigh and Sarah put their three children to bed, they went to their bedroom to continue catching up on four months' worth of news. Raleigh asked Sarah to update him on the happenings at the Ridge and at Stonewall in Buckingham County. Since Raleigh also owned property in Buckingham County, he wondered about his family members who lived there. Raleigh, for the last three to four years, had begun bringing in the dispersed Wiccocomicos and Cherokees, and the Ridge and Stonewall Mill became their havens. He helped plant the Tylers, McCoys, Coopers, Evanses, and Beverlys (Frank, Jenny, William, and others) at Stonewall Mill in Buckingham County. Other tribal members had begun to trickle into the area from numerous locations.

Raleigh was careful not to talk about the Yorktown siege because he was convinced it was too horrific for Sarah to hear at this point. He might share some of the facts with her later. They continued to talk until about 2:00 a.m., when Sarah began to tell him about some startling visions that she had during the month of October.

"How are the Beverlys doing in Buckingham County, in Stonewall? Did they bring in good corn and tobacco harvests? I understand that Sylvanus Beverly has been doing his part to help our Revolutionary War efforts against Britain by delivering supplies for our soldiers while trying to run his farm."

"Yes, Raleigh, they had a fine crop of corn and tobacco. Because Sylvanus is so frugal and efficient with his time, he and his family even came over to help us with our crops. They have the best farming skills that I have ever seen, with his Cherokee farm training." Thinking about what she had just said, Sarah then clarified her statement. "Of course, they are not the farmers that you are, Raleigh. You know there is something about that Wiccocomico agricultural training that you received over in Northumberland and Lancaster that cannot be learned anywhere else. You know how to make things grow well."

"Well, tell me about things on the farm here."

"Raleigh, you and I will take a walk around the farm tomorrow morning, and I will give you a full report. There are so many things that I can tell you that I would rather not talk about tonight."

"Sarah, were there problems?"

"No. Things went very well here on the farm. I want to tell you some other things that happened, unrelated to the crops."

"Well, go ahead," Raleigh stated, although uneasy as his heart started to flutter in anticipation of some unpleasant incidents in the Ridge. "While you are talking, I will go ahead and dress for bed. Has it been this cold in the Ridge at night, and where is that long nightshirt of mine?"

"You just sit in that chair, Raleigh, and give me your attention for a while."

"I could listen while I get ready to turn in. Well, go ahead and I will just sit here on the side of the bed."

Sarah, sitting down on the edge of the bed with Raleigh, placed both of her hands over the back of his palms and looked directly into his eyes. By this time, she had his full attention. "You would never believe some of the night visions I saw. I observed some meteors flying through the sky on the night of October 6. What was strange about this dream was the fiery meteors could be seen clearly in the cloudy sky. I saw people with hoes and shovels digging graves with a fervor that was as fast, furious, and fiery as the meteors. I saw dead bodies in graves, yet the living kept digging even when there were no new bodies to bury. It was as if they were obsessed with the desire to dig graves. While they dug, the fiery balls flew over their heads. It was like heaven was lightning and people on earth were trying to find holes and rocks on the ground for cover. As if there were not enough heat, they dug like they were seeking coal from the ground for heat. They may have been miners or even gravediggers, I don't know. Then I saw balls of explosive objects coming out of the graves, heading toward human beings and crushing them into pieces and digging their graves at the same time! It was so terrifying that my bedsheets were wet from my sweat, like you when you have been having your nightmares. The balls of fire made gruesome and bloodcurdling noises, and then there were screams, echoes of those screams, and then more screams throughout the night. Just then I saw your nephew John carrying a bucket of something. I couldn't make it out. He was being mischievous and naughty, for each time he came with the bucket, his daddy, Robert Junior, poured it into a hole. Both of them were up to some hideous scheme because they ran a few feet and ducked before there was a great explosion. The meteor blazed through the heavens. Then I saw what their cunning and conniving acts had done! There were bodies, dead bodies, all over the whole earth. Junior, your beloved brother, and John, your sweet nephew, caused the living bodies to break apart into dead torsos, disjointed arms, broken fingers, and beheaded skulls!"

"Sarah, I was waiting for a chance to tell you about that situation. How in the world did you know that Junior and John were in Yorktown?"

"Raleigh, please listen to me and let me tell you what I have been holding within me for almost two weeks. Each time John brought the bucket to his daddy, poured the contents into the hole, and put a torch in it, they both ran or turned away from that thing that they were fixing. Then they applauded as their meteors blasted living beings into heaps of body parts. I tried to stop them, but they kept on doing this throughout the night and for several days. Raleigh, there was no end! They would rest for about an hour, as if what they did exhausted them, and then they were back doing the same misbehavior and demolition. It was as if Satan made them rest for an hour to build up their demonic power to do those dastardly deeds all over again! I saw dead bodies, white and black men, with maggots growing in their flesh, lying out in full view of thousands of scared, nervous human beings. Some had eyes missing and others had been beheaded. People were walking over the bodies and even stepping on the corpses occasionally—their friends should have been digging graves for them, but they just stepped over them like you step over those tree roots behind the barn! Then I saw your brother—your beloved brother, Junior—laughing at and applauding what the meteors had done to the innocent victims. Look at the nerve of him setting a bad example for his son, John, by applauding at the successes of Satan over the will of the Lord. Then, Raleigh, I saw you standing with, I think, John Redcross or John Bowling, in the distant horizon, away from Junior, also clapping each time Junior committed the dastardly acts. Junior, your big brother, had begun to suck you into supporting his mischievous, damaging deeds. You gradually came to your senses and started to show remorse as you began to cry at the appalling scene of the meteors' destruction. I know that this was a dream because you, first of all, would not clap for someone who was doing something mischievous. Also, you normally do not cry publicly, so I know that this dream is not true, but it was so real at the time when I first saw it. It is still as weird now as it was when I saw it. I didn't just see it a short time and then it disappeared. I saw these things for several days. My vision was real! It was somewhat like the scary, otherworldly ones that the apostle John saw on the Isle of Patmos in the book of the Revelation. Raleigh, I saw hunger all over the place. I saw people eating moldy, worm-infested bread at the same time that starving, shriveled dogs—beagles and mixed retrievers, like Cocoa—carried off dead men's body parts. You could count the dogs' rib bones because they were so skinny. They had human parts in their mouths that your devilish brother had just disjointed with his fiery meteors. I questioned the accuracy of the dog visions because I have fed Cocoa well. He is not starving. It couldn't be Cocoa. The vision showed me flies all over the place and men, living men, had ceased to fan them away, as if they were too preoccupied with misery and depression to fight them. The pests seemed to be part of the ghostly setting and were welcome guests in sucking away the horrible smelling flesh."

Raleigh interrupted her. "If I didn't know better, I would say you were with me at Yorktown. Your knowledge of the battle area sounds too familiar. How did you know—?" He halted his question as he realized that his wife was not listening to him.

Sarah, ignoring his question as if he had not said anything to her, tried to keep her train of thought while struggling to paint him an accurate picture of her dreary dream. "I heard thousands of haunting, groaning voices, crying to God for mercy. They pleaded with the Almighty for a miracle, for one more chance to see England, Scotland, Wales, and Germany. These unearthly sounds continued for days. The sounds increased in intensity and loudness each day until they reached such a pitch that they crowded out the sounds of meteors crashing and exploding."

"These things happened for real in Yorktown, Sarah," Raleigh interjected as he leaned closer to her and tried to reassure her that her dream had come to pass. "We heard the British soldiers praying in their compound—"

Sarah, focusing on her dream and insulating herself from Raleigh's distracting comments, closed her ears to his words. "I saw both white and black soldiers trying to climb a tower and some soldiers fighting people in red suits. The black soldiers had large tear-shaped or teardrop insignia on their military hats. I thought they might have been agents of the devil, dressed in red apparel, I don't know. They were with another group of soldiers who spoke a funny language. There were the English and another language group. Both groups were crying out to God for help. The unknown language, the speaking in tongues, came from the soldiers who climbed the tower with the black teardrop soldiers. I interpreted the unknown tongues and heard them say the same thing that the black soldiers said, 'God, have mercy! God, have mercy!' I also heard the red-suited soldiers cry the same thing as they were being assaulted by the two groups. Then I knew that the red-suited soldiers were not the devil's demons because Satan does not cry to God for mercy. He knows that only justice is coming to him, and he certainly doesn't want his justice yet!"

"Sarah, please let me tell you that—"

"Raleigh, you had a part in this dream. You laughed as people were dying before your eyes. You ought to be ashamed of yourself! I saw you smile each time that the demons, your brother and nephew, sent the meteors flying through the sky. After a while, you became guilty and stopped your laughter. You shouldn't have laughed in the first place, and therefore you would not have had the need to feel remorseful! When the meteors fell on victims, I even saw you pat your chest and flex your arm muscles, like a person who has just won an arm wrestling contest. You know, the gestures that you make with your hands when you win an arm wrestling match with your friends on July 4."

"No, honey, I—" Raleigh tried to interrupt Sarah.

She retorted, "No, you shut up! I am talking!"

Amazed that she was this upset with him over a dream, Raleigh thought about the content of her visual experiences. *Sarah is losing her head over unreal dreams that she doesn't really understand. I believe she is trying to get me to interpret them for her, but why doesn't she let me interrupt her and explain the dream? Why is she getting so upset with me? She ought to know that it was just a dream and not a real event, or is it? Could she have been so discerning to have dreamed what I saw with my own eyes and experienced firsthand on the Yorktown battlefield?*

"Raleigh, I have warned you about your hatred of the British, and I have often told you that you were wrong to hold that animosity in your heart. I saw you in the dream enjoying the death of English people! I don't understand how the black people got mixed up in the vision of the English people, but I saw dead African and English people. I warned you that the Lord did not like your attitude. Well, one of those nights after October 6, I saw a vision of you apologizing to the Lord for your racism. You actually apologized for your hatred of English colonists! You repented! Raleigh, I saw a little English boy with a baton and a drum, who looked like Turner and almost his same age, rise from a filthy hole in the ground. Looking like he had risen out of a grave, the boy looked dirty, hungry, and lifeless in his steps as he beat the drum. I couldn't understand the meaning of Turner beating the drum . . . As he beat the drum, the meteors ceased their carnage, Robert Junior stopped making the meteors fly in the sky, and John stopped hauling the buckets with that mysterious substance. I also saw a ghostly man rise out of the same grave that Turner, or the boy that looked like Turner, came out of. There was a haunting haze about that place. Hellish smoke all over the place and burned flesh odors made the scene scary. I may have been dreaming, but it was so real!"

Raleigh, dropping his head into the palms of his hands and crying softly, decided that he had very little to tell Sarah because she knew as much about his physical and spiritual battles in the Yorktown campaign as she did regarding his personal battles with racism and guilt. He decided to just be still and let his wife finish relating her dream.

"Then I saw you and thousands of others applaud when the little boy went back into the grave and the man held up a dull white rag. The man was more bedraggled and befouled than the boy. He was a miserable-looking creature, as if he had been through seven hells and had missed meals for a week and a half. You, however, applauded when the boy went back into that dirty hole and the wretched man came out of the same grave with a rag! Why did you enjoy that scene?" Confident in the accuracy of her visions, Sarah inquired, "Why were you applauding, Raleigh?"

Raleigh tried to answer her questions, but she countered his efforts.

"No, you just listen! I need to tell it all before I forget my visions. Don't interrupt me, Raleigh, dear. Let me finish! I was also able to look into the future and I saw the Pearl, your descendants' heritage, having already suffered for years of past injustices, enduring new colonial attempts at tribal genocide. Descendants of English and other European nationalities went against the Pearl and other Indians. They tried to blot them from existence as *aboriginal* people by saying that they cannot claim that right any longer. They told them that they must choose one or the other, white or black, but not aboriginal American. They had developed a plan to bring about genocide on paper. The officials controlled all legal and official documents to deny the Pearl's existence as aboriginal Americans. They saw to it that all marriages and births delete any mention of the word 'Indian.' They managed to make the word 'Indian' look socially dirty, detestable, and undesirable. If that did not reduce the number of residents claiming to be aboriginal Americans, they developed a caste system, where the Europeans, the whites, were the highest grade of people and all the others were of lesser caste. These people had the power of the dragon, Lucifer, and decided that God made a mistake in his clay sculpturing and coloring. They shouted out that the Potter made a mistake when he put color in the clay. They proclaimed that the white clay was perfect, but the other colors must be placed in a lower caste."

"Sarah, I—"

"They removed any signs of native culture in America. Aboriginal Americans had to take on Anglicized names. Native Americans had to adopt the English culture and speak English. They could not chant and follow the old Wiccocomico or Cherokee ways because of the word they called heathen. Heathen was a detestable word and was to be eschewed by a so-called cultured society. Then they began to place black people in a lower caste," Sarah continued. "Later, they gradually tried to include all aboriginal people in the black caste. Their plan was to make aboriginal people rebel and join the white or black caste and thereby force the native people, on paper, from the earth. After years of old serpent–forced assimilation of native people into the general culture, they then charged that the natives are 'no more' or that they have become mixed with other peoples and 'ceased to exist as a tribe.' The historians and official records reflected Satan's will to make certain people less in value than other people. The gods of this world, the ones who control the philosophies of this world, encouraged light-colored people of the future to mistreat the dark peoples of the earth. I saw the aboriginal Americans being forced to Anglicize their names, much like Nebuchadnezzar made Zedekiah, vassal king of Judah, change his name. His name had been Mattaniah, but

Nebuchadnezzar changed it to Zedekiah. This showed to the world that King Zedekiah was nothing more than a child to Nebuchadnezzar. He received a new name and had to obey his new parent. The new name symbolized that Nebuchadnezzar was boss over the life of King Zedekiah. You remember that the Babylonians did the same thing to the Hebrew youths Hananiah and his two friends. They named Hananiah a Babylonian name, Shadrach."

"Sarah, I want—" Raleigh tried to interrupt, but Sarah kept talking.

"I saw slave masters in America doing this very thing to African slaves, giving them Anglicized surnames. The slaves gave up their proud African names for English names to show that they were nothing more than children to their masters. Their masters did not give them the dignity of calling them by the names of their heritage. I saw aboriginal people being forced to change last names to Anglicized names, much like how your princely family name became Pin and Pinn, instead of Pekwem, after Robert, the Great Man of the Wiccocomico Nation of Indians. You know how they can corrupt a name, like what they did to the Cherokees and that name they gave them, the Rechahecrians. I saw people fleeing Buckingham County. The Beverlys moved to Amherst and other counties. Since Virginia colonists did not want the Cherokees in Virginia, I saw the Beverlys moving to and setting up in distant Cherokee ancestral locations in southwest Virginia."

Sarah's prophetic visions were more accurate than anyone could have expected. Floyd County, on the special Indian Census, in 1900, listed some Beverlys as Cherokees in a tribal section on the census document. These Beverlys had previously lived in Amherst County.

Sarah continued, "I saw your Pearl, your special people—the people that you protected against persecution and scalping for years. I caught a vision of them suffering serious insults, contempt, and disdain. These people—the ones you brought from the Blue Ridge Mountains, from the ancient Appomattox River settlements, and from the Wiccocomico Indian Town—were being persecuted for their knowledge of their royal heritage. They could not claim that they had royalty through the Great Man Robert of Wiccocomico! They could not claim that they were connected to the Wiccocomico and Cherokee people. The history officials said, 'The Wiccocomico tribal members are no more.' They tried to prevent the Pearl from claiming connection to the Cherokees! The history writers echoed the words of the prejudiced officials, 'The Cherokees are in other states but not in Virginia—we sent them out years ago!' They said, 'Aboriginal people are no more—there are no true Indians anymore because they are now white and black.' If they have one drop of black blood, the history people said, 'They are all black.' Why did God allow you to save the Wiccocomico residue? Why did God allow you to bring in Cherokees and place them in strategic positions on Buffalo Ridge and Stonewall Mill? Is God going to leave your Pearl now? Did God bring us this far to leave us? No!"

"Let me explain, Sarah—"

"I saw more," Sarah continued. "They were called names that made them believe that their clay quality and color were less valuable than white clay. As they insisted that they were Cherokee or Wiccocomico, the history people wrote in their records that they ceased to be native because there were only two official groups, white and black. Raleigh, I saw a vision of a little girl crying because an official wouldn't let her retain her heritage. He told her that she ceased to be native because she was either white or black. If they chose the black label, Lucifer made them totally black. The officials said that Lucifer declared that all persons who claimed any heritage on legal paper records in the past with the black label ceased to have any percentage of aboriginal Americans in their blood. The black blood, in their view, was so powerful that it neutralized all aboriginal American blood totally. The officials made black people, the ones they brought over from West Africa, change their names like the native people. I also saw the black people lose their past, their heritage, with this powerful Lucifer-inspired paper genocide. Raleigh, you had better make sure that you leave your heritage with the Pearl. Haven't they been through enough suffering already? Why must they suffer great injustices in the future?

Raleigh, you had better make sure that you leave signs of your heritage with the Pearl! Otherwise, the officials of the future will blot out the Pearl from the earth!"

Sarah's visions of the future continued to be accurate. The western Amherst County band generally formed a separate tribe away from the Buffalo Ridge and Stonewall Mill people, although some of the Redcrosses united with Raleigh's people. Most of the Beverlys, years later, would leave the Stonewall Mill area and join the Beverlys in Buffalo Ridge in eastern Amherst County. By the turn of the century, in 1900, Raleigh's tribe would include the Pinns, Beverlys, Fergusons, Wests, Megginsons, Jenkinses, Chamberses, Cousinses, Isbells, McCoys, Sparrows, Evanses, and others. One of his family members, William P. Beverly would actually set up a Cherokee tribe west of Roanoke in Floyd County and have the tribe recorded officially on the 1900 U.S. Census. This was a new tribe and not connected with the White Top Mountain Cherokee tribe in southwestern Virginia.

"Raleigh, what are you going to do to keep the heritage? How will you preserve the Pearl?"

Raleigh cautiously prepared to speak, expecting Sarah to tell him not to interrupt her again. Surprisingly, she did not restrain him, as if she were now talked out and very anxious to receive answers to all of her questions. Grateful that he could speak now, he looked directly into her eyes.

"Sarah, let me tell you first of all, I love you and never let you out of my heart since that June morning, when Commander Gaines sent me word to march to battle. I just want to let you hear some verses that I wrote for you from the bottom of my heart:

> "That June morn left me not, the memory when I left Sarah.
> Militia dawn came so early, though for her I left too soon.
> That morning never left me, though distance was so far,
> As kerchief was sad, I will hold you under the moon.
> That morning never left me, for separation came with war.

Reunion, come and not part! Thank God, for the drummer's tune!"

"That was beautiful and so romantic, dear. You too have been in my heart and in my mind. It just didn't occur to me to make a poem, as I am not as good with words as you are," Sarah apologized. "You feel my heartbeat and can read my love."

Raleigh continued, "The kerchief in my poem is that same handkerchief that you saw in your vision. The one that the ghostly man was holding that you thought was a rag. The officer came out of Cornwallis's compound with the surrender handkerchief raised high. The kerchief was sad for him, but his raising that kerchief allowed me to hold you now in this house, under that moon. The four-month memory of you, leaving you here, made me sad, but I kept the picture in my mind through our separation due to war. Now the reunion is here, and I pray that we will not part. Thank God for the drummer boy as he beat the tune on the drum to signal a truce. His drumbeat that stopped our cannon fire was a beautiful tune. The boy that you thought was Turner was really a boy almost his age and looked somewhat like him as he walked bravely from the camp's trenches. With all the cannon fire going toward Cornwallis's compound, this young boy stepped forward, beating that sweet music. I thought of you, my darling, because I knew that I was going home when the surrender officer came out of the trenches as the drummer boy went back into the hole. What you thought were meteors in your vision were not meteors but cannonballs that our artillery companies fired on the British. We also sent other types of artillery rounds into their camp."

"I saw your brother and nephew. What was that all about?" inquired Sarah.

"You saw Junior and John in those visions as they were firing cannon rounds. John was the powder boy on gun number 3 in the Virginia Artillery. Don't get mad at them because of their work and the bravery of other artillery soldiers. They prevented the deaths of many infantry and cavalry soldiers who would otherwise have had to engage the British enemy in hand-to-hand combat."

"Why did I see gravediggers?"

"Our Yorktown battle was primarily one controlled by artillery companies. Although you thought they were meteors in the sky, they were really cannonballs. You saw the sappers, miners, and soldiers digging the trenches to protect us from Cornwallis's artillery fire. You thought we were gravediggers, but we were digging furiously so we could hide from the cannonballs and gunfire. We were firing back but from behind the trenches."

Sarah was dismayed. "My previous visions and dreams have been accurate. Raleigh, why did I have so many points wrong this time?"

"Sarah, all that you dreamed were true. You saw the dead people lying on the ground and the living soldiers walking over the deceased soldiers. That was true because they actually left some of their dead soldiers and workers out on display, unburied. Not only that, but many British body parts were strewn all over the place. Yes, you were right. We learned after the surrender, from local people in Yorktown, that there were hungry dogs walking around with human remains in their mouths."

"What about the tower vision?"

"The vision you saw of soldiers going against a tower, white and black soldiers trying to climb a tower, is accurate. Only it was a redoubt. A redoubt is a temporary fortification that the British soldiers used to secure their compound and to protect it from enemy invaders. The people you saw were French and American troops going against Redoubt 9. The Americans assaulted Redoubt 10. What you saw was a vision of a unit of French soldiers and a unit of black soldiers with teardrop insignia on their hats from the Rhode Island Militia as they assaulted Redoubt 9, just as the Americans did against Redoubt 10, and engaged in hand-to-hand combat with swords and bayonets. I just hope those brave black Rhode Island militiamen don't get passed up for recognition by the colony of Rhode Island for their heroic action that night. Sarah, really, I don't need to confirm to you that your visions are correct because you know that God gave them to you. If God gave them to you, you know that they are on target. I am just confirming the truth of your visions, as everything that you have told me this morning and all during the night is correct. My job of dream interpretation is very easy because you saw everything so vividly and accurately."

"Raleigh, I'm sorry for my rude attitude toward you as I told you about my visions. I was angry with you for your behavior on the battlefield and the way you laughed when your artillery soldiers fired on British soldiers. I was in such a hurry to tell you about the vision that I didn't give you a chance to interrupt me. I guess I had taken one of those haughty attitudes that you get sometimes."

"Sarah, you know you don't have to apologize to me because we love each other so much that we have never felt a need to express apologies formally. Now, regarding the Pearl, based on the confirmation of your previous visions that you revealed this night, I am confident about the truth of your Pearl visions. I am sure that you are accurate about the Pearl. I will just leave it there and pray that God will take the bad—the demon-spirited efforts of people to hold back our people—and make it good in the long run. You always go into the kitchen, take the sour lemons, and make delicious, sweet, cold lemonade. In a similar fashion, God will take our people's painful history and turn it into a good heritage. You know that the Pearl originates in the oyster as a result of the oyster's suffering. The more suffering, the lovelier the Pearl is. I am aware of all of the suffering, the dispersion, the poverty, the nakedness, the hunger, and the loneliness. God will not put more on us than we can bear, praise God! I will just commit the Pearl matter to God's hands and care. I will never forget what you just told me about your visions concerning the Pearl and will keep the visions in my mind, heart, and soul. I will pray to God to take care of our people and deal with the Pearl's enemies, according to his divine will. I am aware that some colonists in Wiccocomico wanted to rid all tribal members from the soil forever. We are not destroyed as they hoped. I will do everything within my power to leave legal documentation and records for the Pearl. Just this week, before I left Yorktown, I made sure that they had my name on the furlough list. I also saw John Redcross's name on those documents. I do not want anyone telling the Pearl a hundred or two hundred years hence that I was a deserter from the militia. I came to Yorktown on the Order List of Commander Gaines and I left Yorktown on the Furlough paper. I was there. Junior and John were there. Thomas Pinn, my other kin from Wiccocomico, was in the Virginia State Militia. And there were also Junior's two sons, Billy and Jimmy, who fought with Morgan's Rangers and Riflemen in the Revolution. I have been faithful to America, and our family has been faithful to our country even though our country has been somewhat stingy toward us. They can talk about the Cherokees siding with the British, but I and other aboriginal people took the road less traveled. I dare the historians to try to say all Cherokees and Wiccocomicos allied themselves with the British side."

"It is now 5:00 a.m. Where did the time go? Raleigh, you have to be tired with all that walking you have done yesterday. What time should we get up?"

"At 7:00 a.m. I need to check on the farm and see how much work you and Turner have been doing on the place. Sarah, come closer. I have missed you dearly."

"Raleigh, you are going to be pleased with the tobacco crop this year and the other harvests. Our family came over to help us—the Pinns, the Beverlys, the Megginsons, the Fergusons, Jethro Ferguson and his gang, and others. The Beverlys, Sparrows, and McCoys came out of hiding to help get the crops in and ready. We even have six large banks of sweet potatoes. The beans have been dried. There are great quantities of all of your favorite varieties. You are going to have some good fruit cobbler this winter. Turner and I dried apples, pears, peaches, cherries, mulberries, and blackberries."

"Sarah, you have managed the farm well in my absence."

"You don't know how much I have missed you, physically and emotionally!" Sarah admitted. At 5:40 a.m., Raleigh and Sarah stopped embracing and went to sleep.

After breakfast, Raleigh sat beside Sarah in his favorite chair near the fireplace, with his legs crossed and resting on a stool, smoking his Ridge-grown tobacco from his special pipe. Anna,

Eady, and Turner reclined in front of the fireplace. Raleigh meditated on Sarah's Pearl visions and made plans to bring other Cherokees to the Ridge and Stonewall Mill.

Raleigh always evaluated the quality of his crop by placing the first tobacco sample in his favorite pipe and smoking it leisurely by the fireplace. Since the tobacco had been fire-cured slowly, he respected the tender care that had been given to the plants by smoking it unhurriedly. Tobacco buyers came each year to inspect his crop and make a bid. Because he had a reputation for growing, harvesting, and curing fine tobacco, he was always cunning enough to bluff buyers into giving him a top bid from the start rather than wasting his time. Since his products were esteemed to the point that the buyers came to his farm to bid—even buyers representing English markets—he did not have to go to the cooperative tobacco auctions.

"Sarah, do you realize that I am so proud of you? You have managed this farm well. In my absence, you worked and supervised other workers to the extent that you have brought in great crops. I shouldn't have worried in Yorktown about how you and the family would have survived if I had been killed. You did well, dear! Maybe I need to go to Yorktown next year at about harvest time!"

Sarah, realizing that her husband was congratulating her for the way she ran the farm in his absence, smiled appreciatively and remarked, "Raleigh, you know nobody can beat you in growing tobacco."

This she said apologetically because she did not want him to think she had managed the farm better than he would have if he had been there. "You are the best in Virginia. We just watered and harvested the crop after you planted and tended it. Don't you remember those hot days when you toiled endlessly in the sun, hoeing the soil? Actually, you came in from weeding that scorching day when the militia messenger on that fast stallion came from Commander Gaines, with the command that you go join General Lafayette."

Sarah and Raleigh put on their coats and headed outside. Walking with his head down and his memory fresh, Raleigh thought about that June day when Commander Gaines ordered him to report to the assembly area for the march to join Lafayette. After he and his fellow militiamen had been ordered to march in June, Raleigh became very concerned about the conditions of his farm produce and tobacco crops. Although he did not doubt Sarah's ability to work on the farm, he still worried about the produce and farm animals.

So that his absence due to his service as a militiaman would not ruin him financially, family and tribal members volunteered to help Sarah and Turner bring in Raleigh's crops. The volunteers harvested Raleigh's tobacco crop between the first and second week of July. A total of twelve men and women alternated by helping Sarah cut the tobacco stalks and place them on sticks. They left the harvested plants in the fields to dry for three days. Sarah supervised them according to the standards, timelines, and procedures that Raleigh would have expected if he were in the fields. It did not take long for the volunteers and Sarah to realize that Raleigh had an excellent crop. Since the large crop needed three new fire-curing barns built quickly, she summoned the Ferguson clan, whose carpentry skills were legendary. Jethro and the Ferguson clan were well known in the area as descendants of Scots, Pocahontas, and the Cherokees. Although other volunteers helped with the carpentry work, Jethro was the lead carpenter in constructing the barns.

There were others in Buckingham—the Megginsons and Fergusons—who proudly proclaimed openly that they had Pocahontas and Cherokee aboriginal blood running through their veins. Although treated in business as white people, the Fergusons and Megginsons' skin complexion sometimes called their white designation into question under the heat of the July sun. Jethro worked on the barns during the last week of June and the first week of July. By mid-July, his skin was very different from the white-appearing complexion that he displayed at the May Day program in the Ridge. Eventually, Jethro Ferguson, his sons, and descendants would be classified as free mulatto aboriginal citizens in Prince Edward and Buckingham Counties. Some of his descendants married white women while others had Native Americans or mulatto spouses.

Raleigh preferred the fire-cured method for his tobacco crops in Buffalo Ridge. His father, Robert, had been a great fire-cured tobacco farmer, as well as the two men under whom he had been apprenticed as an indentured servant in Northumberland and Lancaster Counties. With this solid experience and training, Raleigh brought excellent tobacco-growing skills to his farms in Buffalo Ridge and Stonewall Mill. He liked to give the tobacco ten to fifteen days of slow smoke cure to keep from scalding the leaves. Raleigh remembered that it was easy for his father to come up with the required Northumberland County court-ordered tobacco poundage in the 1730s when he was fined on the occasion when he missed four consecutive Sunday church services at the Anglican Church at Wiccocomico.

"Dad was the best among the crops of excellent tobacco farmers! I believe that they searched for something to fine my daddy so that they could get some of his savory, fragrant tobacco. Who ever heard of courthouse officials fining a person for missing four Sundays of church unless it was my daddy with his aromatic tobacco crop?"

Sarah led Raleigh around the farm as her husband inspected every section, with Turner and Cocoa following them. After checking on the livestock and the hay in the barn loft, he walked down to the spring to see if it had been cleaned. When Sarah led him to the new tobacco barns that had been constructed side by side, Raleigh examined each barn as if he had to put his stamp of approval on them. Then they walked over to the edge of the field and sat down on an oak log. He held Sarah's hands and smiled appreciatively while she held her breath for Raleigh's evaluation.

"Sarah, they are good, solid buildings. You have done well in the Ridge in my absence. Since I couldn't have managed the place any better than you did here, I ought to march off to another Yorktown." Raleigh mentioned Yorktown jokingly because he didn't know how to commend her any higher than by admitting what an excellent job she had done.

"Don't you dare think of leaving me again! I am not sure my heart could stand any more of those dreadfully realistic dreams while you are away." Sarah, pleased with Raleigh's assessment of her farm skills, beamed and wisely returned praise to Raleigh. "Raleigh, you did well at Yorktown. We, the whole family, including our Cherokee and Wiccocomico families, pitched in to help harvest the crops. Everyone is so proud of you. The locals cannot threaten us now like we are stepchildren in Amherst. We are relatives of an American patriot! What a heritage! The Pearl can claim heritage and blood with the Pinns, the aboriginal patriots of Yorktown!"

> I shall be telling this with a sigh
> Somewhere ages and ages hence:
> Two roads diverged in a wood, and I—
> I took the one less traveled by.
> —Robert Frost, 1916

13

The Road Not Taken

November 1795

Raleigh was the main speaker at Fairmount Fellowship Service on the first Sunday after his return from Yorktown. He looked forward to addressing the small group of church members, who had been traveling from house to house to worship each Sunday. Today, however, they held the service outdoors, near the ancestors' burial ground. It happened that it was also the very spot where Raleigh had prayed to God that day after he received orders to report to his militia headquarters. Although Raleigh had been trailblazing on routes less traveled, the road to the Ridge had lately begun to be a very popular place for tired and weary aboriginals who had been uprooted from native habitats by combative environments. They ran to the Ridge as a God-anointed, mighty fortress and a village of refuge. The trail to the Ridge was becoming a beaten, no longer grassy road.

Raleigh had hoped to build a permanent house of worship in the Ridge for the tribal residents. As a result of his long hours of solitude during the siege on Cornwallis's compound, he developed building plans to satisfy his burning desire to construct a church close to his ancestors' burial ground near Porridge Creek.

"Thank you for permitting me to address you this morning. I will not take long as it is cool in this Ridge, and I do not want you to catch a cold because I talked too long. I prayed to God on this very spot, on the bright green June grasses that have now turned death-brown in color. I could have been dead and buried in Yorktown instead of standing on this dead grass. The Lord has smiled on me and brought me through one of the most pivotal battles of the American Revolution. I know you are wondering why I went to war because I have, in the last few years, spoken against killing people. Christ told us that we should not kill. Well, first of all, let me explain why I chose to take this path in the war because we know that some of our native people have refused to side with the colonists to help them fight their own kind, the British. I am aware that some of our aboriginal people have even sided with the British to fight the colonists, as the lesser of two evils. I, however, went in another direction. I took routes less frequently traveled by our aboriginal people. Please open your Bibles and let us go the Epistle to the Colossians, Colossians 3:17:

> And whatsoever ye do in word or deed, do all in the name of the Lord Jesus, giving thanks to God and the Father by him.

"Years ago, I would have fought the colonists eagerly. Why? I was upset with them because they settled on Wiccocomico Indian Town land. Not only that, but they stole my father's land, took me from my mother and siblings after Dad died and caused me to be placed in indentured servitude. I was so angry with the colonists because they changed our whole way of life. Our livelihood was no more because we couldn't hunt and fish like our ancestors did in the bygone days before the colonists came, when land was open and free. Why did they have to take our rich farmland? I don't need to remind you how incensed I have been against those cunning colonists! I stored up this animosity within my heart and soul for years, and the heat of this burning racial hatred almost destroyed me. You remember how cranky I was at times for no apparent reason. It was that racial hatred burning within me! I had to take another road, a route that was different from that of my ancestors. Otherwise, I would have followed a pathway straight into moral and physical self-destruction. Most of our ancestors were dispersed and destroyed because they resisted colonial aggressors. Because I have been grappling to resist, I let malice toward colonists capture my soul. I am tired, not just physically but spiritually. My soul has been engaged in a spiritual battle with combatants wearing the uniforms of good and evil. The warfare action has beaten me down like an old man.

"I have been forced out of Wiccocomico Indian Town and would have been dispersed from Buffalo Ridge if I had not joined the Amherst Militia. I will not give the colonists a reason to wipe us off the Ridge and out of Stonewall Mill. If I had not gone to Yorktown, they would have had a reason to say I was siding with the Cherokees and British against the colonists. I have played the game that the colonists play. I will also buy land. They seem to be following me, wherever I go. The colonists were in Wiccocomico, so I came to the Ridge; and now they are near the Ridge. I realized quickly that I must join them, be like them. Otherwise, I would be manhandled like an outsider. You know what happens to outsiders. They disappear.

"The Bible tells us about a man named Haman who hated the Jews. You can find the story in Esther, chapter 3 verse 8. When King Xerxes of Persia promoted Haman and gave him great power in Persia, he said he did not like the Jewish people because they had different ways, laws, and customs from the Persians' ways of living. The true motive behind Haman's desire to kill all the Jews was that Mordecai, also a Jew, refused to bow down and worship him. Haman then convinced the king to pass a law to have all the Jews killed in all Persian provinces. Just because one powerful man did not like the Jews' ways and customs, he concocted a plan to destroy all the Jews. We indigenous people know better than to insult God by bowing down to human beings. Can you believe that they called us savages when we, as civilized people, have never desired to worship human clay? Does this story sound familiar? Cherokee and Wiccocomico peoples are being destroyed because our ways are not like the colonists' ways. We refuse to bow down to the white men from England"

Several older members in the audience shouted words of encouragement during his talk. "Amen."

"I took a different road. I took the trail with the least resistance, to help my people. If it were just up to me, I would be dead and in my grave now because I refused to bow down to the colonists. The Lord has been talking to me and showing me the things that I must do to help you in the Ridge and Stonewall Mill, our scattered people in Wiccocomico, and the Cherokee who are hiding out along the mountains. The Pinns here are direct descendants of Wiccocomico ancestors, and there are some Cherokees here in the Ridge from the Middle towns, Overhill town, and other locations. We have here—as well as others in Stonewall Mill—band members who are descendants of the Appomattox River Cherokees who were driven from their settlement. The Ridge is a new ground for the Wiccocomico people, but it is not new for the Cherokees because the Ridge has been written in the mental annals of Cherokee leaders for generations. This place has been a retreat, a place of refuge, for the Rechahecrians, and it has been a refuge for Middle and Overhill Cherokees. Even some Lower town Cherokees in Georgia and South Carolina know about this small mountain, the Ridge.

"What has changed now is that you have been able to live here openly, no longer in secrecy. Why? Because I have been like a limber tree that bends with the windy storms of life. Instead of resisting the colonists, I decided to love them, work with them, and even make their enemies my enemies. That is why you are able to live, work, and worship on the Ridge. We have learned how to love, not hate, our neighbors. We are not going to give present-day Hamans a chance to kill us off because we refuse to bow down and worship them. Just as Queen Esther went to the king with a plea that her people should be spared and defeated Haman, I went to Yorktown with the colonists to show them that we on the Ridge are not really different from the colonists. Based on my Amherst Militia service and Yorktown campaign participation, I dare the colonists to try to make our Ridge people look different, like Haman declared about the Jews!

"I feel that most of you understand why I decided go in another direction from other groups of Cherokees. Because of generations of new settlers on our aboriginal property, we have lost land, warriors, and family members. Enough is enough! I have been traveling a different road for several years. Since you, as tribal members, have been faithful and followed me on this rarely traveled trail, we have continued our travels together. There are some disadvantages with our new march. We are traveling in the same directions as the colonists, and as a result, we are going to lose some of our aboriginal ways. In the future, some history writers might claim that we are no longer Indian. Since this is about survival as a people, let them say whatever they want to say! Just as Esther in the Bible felt that the survival of her Jewish people was more important than anything else, I also believe our people's survival is important.

"When Militia Commander Gaines ordered me, along with my fellow militiamen, to report to his temporary headquarters for an assignment, I consulted the Lord. I didn't seek your advice. I didn't ask Sarah what action I should take. I did what I always do when I have an important personal or tribal matter to consider. I went to the Lord, my Master, in prayer. As your tribal chief, I went to God in prayer by way of the greatest Chief, Christ, 'the chiefest among ten thousands.'

"I came up here in the Ridge, on this very ground, on this spot, and fell to the ground. I came up here to ask God to take our side against the British. The Lord gave me a verbal tongue-lashing. He brought to my awareness my hateful and prejudicial thoughts and ways. He reminded me that I was a vengeful person. He alerted my conscience that I was a racist against anything that was English. In this very setting where I prayed a self-righteous prayer, I asked God to let us win the war against the British army. God showed me that he had something 'against me,' like he was disappointed with the church in Ephesus in Revelation 2:4. I beseeched God's forgiveness immediately. I thought he was going to whip me good on this very spot at that very hour for my self-centered prayer. Repenting, I prayed and prayed and prayed for the Lord to spare me and forgive my haughty and sinful spirit! The idea that I had devised this prayer—that God should side with the Americans against the British—was unimaginable!

"I couldn't pray right after that ungodly petition. I was tongue-tied! You know I have never been tongue-tied. This time, this prayer, however, I could not find the words to communicate with the Lord. I felt like Isaiah in chapter 6 of the book of Isaiah, when in the presence of God, he felt like a sinful stranger in the midst of a Holy God. Isaiah said, 'Woe unto me, I am undone!' I too felt like cow dung in the presence of God when I asked the Lord—like I was some important somebody—to take 'our side' in the war. Then the Lord told me in a small matter-of-fact way that my prayer was wrong!

"I said, 'Lord, do you want me to give up this combat order to go to Key's Church tomorrow morning? I will do what you say. I will take a chance on being court marshaled for violating my militia vow! Tell me, Lord! Your servant will obey!'"

Forty-five people sat on the ground listening to Raleigh as he spoke from his heart. Observing a real live Yorktown campaign hero, their own chief, they attended to every word that flowed from his mouth. He appeared larger than life, wearing a black hip-length coat, white shirt, brown breeches that came below his knees, leg stockings from his knees down to his buckled black shoes, and a hat that had been folded back and buttoned on one side. He had removed his hat and laid it against his heart when he commenced his speech, as if he wanted to let them know it was coming from the deepest recesses of his soul.

"I thought I heard my spirit tell me, '*No*, Raleigh. You will go on to Key's Church for the militia meeting. You will be a faithful soldier, obey Commander Gaines's orders, and go wherever he commands your militia to march! I have heard your prayer. You will see my hand in this conflict, in spite of horrific human hostilities.' I can hear those words as clear as if God spoke to me this minute. That is why I went to war! He told me what I had better do, and I did it! He promised me that I would see his hand, his good hand, in spite of the 'horrific human hostilities.'

"John Redcross and I were not different from most other aboriginal men just because we fought in the Revolutionary War, as did a few other aboriginal Cherokee militiamen from Amherst County. We just have the distinction of being known publicly as Native Americans. There were others who were aboriginal Amherst militiamen but were quiet about that fact. We went in a direction that was not common—the different route," Raleigh explained to his listeners to defend the pro-American position that he took. "I could not stomach the opposition of the Tories and the British in this war. I saw what the British had done to those lands and people of Wiccocomico Indian Town and other areas in the East Coast. The English people consumed our land over there in Wiccocomico, aboriginal property that my great-grandfathers, grandfathers, and father cultivated. Now the nerve of the English—they followed me here to Amherst and presently endeavored to control our fortunes and futures. No way! I was glad to take up arms against them. I am aware that some aboriginal people placed their trust and hope in the cause of the British and the Tories. My mind recorded their historical tendencies to take land and kill aboriginal peoples. John Redcross also felt the same way. His people have also suffered under the English in Lancaster County and also here.

"Please don't let me get started on this subject about the British. God has already whipped me for my combative attitudes against them. I have sworn to love the English as well as all of God's special peoples, the clay people of all shapes and colors. My descendants have been told, and will be told, never to harbor animosities against persons of other colors, religious denominations, and heritages. The Pearl must respect all God's creatures! Just as we are made up of various colors, we must be careful. Otherwise, we might find ourselves fighting against God if we take the intolerant route of racial hatred.

"At first I went to battle against the British because of their hateful ways toward the aboriginal people. In time, however, as a soldier, God dealt with me and now I love them as well as all other peoples. I have white blood running through my veins as well as native color and heritages. My descendants should know and others will know in the future that the clay color does not influence the quality of their souls. They might eventually have all colors running through their blood. The one thing that the Pearl has as a heritage is the commonality of aboriginal Cherokee and Wiccocomico! I have made sure of that! The unified tribe will pass on our legacies as one heritage. They will marry aboriginal Cherokee and Wiccocomico people. I have not restricted the tribe members from marrying black or white people because that would be against God's law! No mortal creature can possibly win any war, battle, or skirmish against the will of God. God's power is too great for mortals to go against his will. Although the colonists might attempt to blot out our people's aboriginal background in their history records and through other genocidal techniques, the Pearl will always know about its aboriginal heritage. Even some aboriginal people—acting on the whims and even long-term planned philosophies of the prejudiced colonists—may attempt to deny the rightful history of the Pearl in the colony of Virginia, God and the Pearl know who and what we are! Colonists must be careful that they do not cross the line and become combatants against the Lord!

"I will make sure that I leave as much of the special heritage behind before I press my dying pillow. With the help of God, I will bless the Pearl with our rich history on official documents and other records that I am leaving to them. Sarah told me about her recent visions and how some people will assault the Pearl. She looked into the future and observed the Pearl's enemies. She saw the baser sort colonists' twisted genocidal strategies for the future. I am countering their devilish and deceiving philosophies. The Bible presents Satan—who is known also as adversary, devil, and slanderer—and how he will send his agents, his angels, and messengers to hurt and buffet innocent people. The Pearl is prepared since we have already come out of suffering and war. The Wiccocomicos have endured adversities of every type imaginable. The Cherokees have experienced untold hardships. Like a tree that has been tried through the wind and doesn't break under the fiercest of storms, so I am preparing the Pearl for perseverance and resistance to the pressures of life."

The Buckingham members, who had also come over to the Ridge from Stonewall Mill to welcome Raleigh back, supported his words throughout his speech. "Praise the Lord! Amen."

Raleigh continued, "The colonists and even other natives may become victims of Satan's assaults and commit paper genocide against aboriginal people. They may even massacre members of the Pearl. Still, those who survive will have our heritage in their hearts. Even if their hearts are cut out, the spiritual heritage, that aboriginal heritage, will live on through the ages. They cannot dilute it, drown it, burn it, cut it, or bury it. God, through others and me as his instruments, has protected the Pearl. I went to Yorktown to help give it a heritage. Generations will know that the Pinns are Native Americans on military documents and on marriage documents. They can't erase it. Some of these special people have escaped from the Middle towns, and they have withdrawn from the Overhill towns. They have departed from Wiccocomico Indian Town land, territory that is no longer theirs to claim. Others are remnants of the Rechahecrians and the Appomattox River settlements. They retreated to the Ridge and to Stonewall Mill. The Pearl will live on until God calls it home! It is one of his special people, who—like primordial trees—has come through the storms of the ages, bent but not broken."

By this time, every person in attendance was standing and had begun to respond to Raleigh's words with rhythmic responses. During this particular service, Raleigh was their unofficial preacher, and they gave him as many amens as they would have shouted in support of their pastor.

"First, the Pearl must bear this covenant with the Lord forever. Members must *love* the Lord with all their hearts and *love* their neighbors as they would want others to *love* them."

"Amen!" responded the audience in unison.

"The Pearl cannot conceal or shroud prejudice against any person or group of people. If you show prejudice against others, the Lord will place a spiritual siege on you, and you will suffer guilt, like the physical siege we placed on Cornwallis at Yorktown. The only way out was for him or his agent to come out of hiding with his hands up, with the handkerchief of peace waving the surrender prayer and begging for peace! If you show respect for people based on their skin color, the guilt over time will force you to come out with your hands up and apologize for your prejudice."

Raleigh spoke this of Cornwallis, not because of any known prejudice that the British general possessed, but as an analogy to his own hostile heart and the Lord's siege on his soul. Raleigh believed that the Lord had placed his soul under a spiritual siege at Yorktown until he quit his racist hatred of the English people. Raleigh had to yield up his bigoted attitude against English people.

"Don't let God put a siege around your spiritual and social positions! Treat other races and heritages like you would want to be treated. Follow the Golden Rule."

The members replied loudly with encouraging words of amen.

"Second, the Pearl must *live* quietly and peacefully, and attend to its own business. It shall be a good neighbor even if its neighbors don't return the good. Even when colonists mistreat you, *live* quietly and peacefully with others and yourself. Even when other tribes mistreat you, live quietly and peacefully with them and yourself."

"Amen," the audience replied in unison. "Praise the Lord!"

"Third, the Pearl must *educate* itself, through occupational skill preparation and mental improvement. We are not savages, and we must refrain from ways of life that tend to confirm the 'savage' image that others have of us. You must have a strong work ethic. I have tried to set a model for you of what hard work and determination can accomplish through the help of the Lord."

"Praise the Lord," the crowd replied.

"Fourth, the Pearl must *rise up* in defense of America should a new adversary attempt to take away or encroach on America's institutions. America shall be defended with words, and if absolutely necessary, with arms. The Pearl shall fight when called on by America's leaders to *rise up*. I have freely set the example with my response when Militia Commander Gaines called on me to go to battle and to all those other campaigns in which our militia participated. You must do the same. The Pearl must endeavor to *purchase* land and build home**s**, if possible. As we cannot truly own land—God is the owner—you must lease the land. Ritually speaking, you must retain it as a legacy for your family. Aboriginal people have roamed too long in this colony, but now the time has come when we must stop being nomadic people. The Pearl has laid down roots in this section of Virginia. Let us not follow the tradition of our ancient ancestors by roaming, roving, and rambling from place to place. We are in a new era, and we must live as the white man lives! He buys and sells land. In the future, they will say that you did not live here because you did not have a permanent place of abode. If you don't have a piece of paper—what they call deeds—you are just unwelcome guests, or a hunting tribe passing through**,** not landowners."

"Amen," one of the attendees stated in support of the chief.

"We know, as aboriginal people, that human beings cannot own land. The land is there as a welcome host to receive our decomposing bodies. The land will be here even after a thousand generations come and go. But it would not be good English manners to suggest to the colonists that the idea of a deed is stupid! That would be impolite. The colonists like to say that native people are passing through because they do not have permanent housing. Colonists assert that we never really lived in Virginia unless we have an English-style physical structure on land that we 'own.' I say they do not use the word 'own' to mean the same way native people use the word. We count 'owning' land to mean 'renting' from God until he calls you home. Colonial settlers really believe that they can own land, not that the land will own them when they go to the grave! Since the colonist occupies the same spot for his home and therefore thinks he somehow is a better person than a native person who migrates from place to place, we must do the same to be respected as stable aboriginal citizens. Let us not prolong the colonists' opinion of us, that we are vagabonds and wanderers. You know how much land Cherokees claimed as their hunting ground in Virginia and other states. Well, the colonists like to say that Cherokees don't live here in Virginia because some of our people don't build rock or wood homes like they do. They claim our people are all in North Carolina and other colonies. Can you believe that, Buffalo Ridge Cherokees? Stonewall Mill Cherokee members, what about those words that we don't live in Virginia?"

The whole assembly broke out with loud sniggering and chuckling as they thought about the foolishness in the colonists' statements that Cherokees are no longer in Virginia. They had already heard the news about the colonial officials' desire to trade with the Cherokees for land in Virginia. They wondered why the colonial officials would be as stupid as to negotiate for land with a people whom they did not believe had a rightful title to the land in the first place.

"Who are the colonists trying to fool by saying that Cherokees are not in Virginia?" Raleigh wondered out loud. "They know that Cherokees lived in, are living in, and will live in the future in Virginia. They are just trying to set up a myth for their children to pass on, that 'Cherokees never lived in Virginia.' The only way they can pass this myth on is to negotiate with Cherokees and gain the land as quickly as possible so that they can then say that they, the English, have always owned this land. Their children and grandchildren might be so vain as to believe their mythological lie."

The congregation raised their hands in praise to the Lord for Raleigh's words. "Thank you."

Raleigh ended the Sunday service speech. The large attendance by tribal members made it look almost like a regular united tribal meeting of Buffalo Ridge and Stonewall Mill bands. The main reason for the strong church attendance was the fact that the tribal members from Stonewall had heard that Raleigh was back in the Ridge and would be speaking at Fairmount. He was their chief and their hero. He had done what others had only thought about accomplishing or hoped to do in some distant future—he served America as an aboriginal soldier with the American Militia.

Tribal members had also heard about the heroic exploits of his brother, Robert Junior, and his three sons, John, Jimmy, and Billy. They praised God for the whole Pinn family, including

Thomas Pinn, and thanked him for Raleigh, their chief. The members heard Raleigh loudly and clearly, and assured him that they would not hesitate to rise up when called upon by America. Even though Raleigh predicted that they, the Pearl, would be mistreated by racists and baser sorts in America, that fact still did not entitle members or give them leave to disregard America's call to *rise up*. They promised to do all those things that Chief Pinn requested of the Pearl as well as to pass on to their children these expectations.

"Finally, Pearl, as Paul tells us in Colossians 3:17, 'And whatsoever ye do in word or deed, do all in the name of the Lord Jesus, giving thanks to God and the Father by him.' Make sure that you mold and fashion all that I requested you to do by the Word of God, as stated so beautifully by Paul in the Epistle to the Colossians, chapter 3 verse 17. The Lord showed me his hand in Yorktown. I wondered how he could answer my prayer for protection and the prayers of Amherst militiamen and other American and French soldiers while hearing the petitions for protection from English, Welsh, Scot, and German soldiers. How could the Lord possibly bless the combatant groups at Yorktown? God, however, did bless us by giving us peace. He allowed Cornwallis's haughty spirit to yield in the act of surrender! The Europeans went back to Europe, and we Americans went back to our home cities, towns, and villages. Our prayers were answered, so don't tell me that the Lord can't perform powerful miracles. God can do great wonders for the Pearl, and we must be ready to give God the praises, as Paul tells us. Since my conversion to Christianity in the Anglican Church of Wiccocomico years ago, I have endeavored to obey the Word of God. Now I'm a Baptist. Be you Baptist, Methodist, Anglican, or whatever group, you must serve God through the Lord Jesus. I expect the band members to be Christian! I have been through high waters, muck, and mire, and I am still here praising the Lord. I look back on my past and I see trials and tribulations from my youth and throughout my adult years."

As Raleigh spoke, his words flowed from his tongue like those of a Baptist preacher; full of love for the members, high praise for God's blessings, and strong exhortation to his hearers.

"To make sure that we have a permanent settlement here in the Ridge, we need a church, a symbol of our personal, heartfelt faith in the Lord. We must build a house for the Lord, for the peoples' heritage, the Pearl, or at least the Buffalo Ridge part of the Pearl. We are tired of moving from house to house for worship service. If the Jews could build their temple thousands of years ago, you know we can build a small church on the Ridge today." Raleigh looked toward Stonewall Mill tribal members and suggested, "The Stonewall Mill group will also deal with their spiritual and building needs as the opportune occasion presents itself. David made it clear to the Israelites that the time was past due for building a temple for the Lord. The Israelites loved the Lord and were tired of worshiping their God in tents." Raleigh continued, "Since you were able to build several tobacco barns within a few months, I know you can build places of worship for our people."

The members agreed that the time was overdue to build a church in the Ridge. Since the burial grounds had been there for generations and tribal members had been worshiping from house to house for a long time, the men agreed to meet on a yet-to-be-announced Saturday with tools, lumber, and logs to construct the church. The ladies planned to bake, boil, stew, and roast enough food so that their hardworking men would not get famished.

Raleigh would, over a period of almost twenty years, set the standard for land ownership by purchasing and selling hundreds of acres of land on different occasions. Tribal members continued to purchase land and construct physical buildings in the Ridge and Stonewall Mill. The Pinns, Fergusons, Bollings, Scotts, and Beverlys led the list of tribal members who became great landowners in the Ridge. The Fergusons, Megginsons, McCoys, Tylers, and Beverlys also became real estate holders in Stonewall Mill. Some of the Buckingham County (later Appomattox County) Stonewall Mill Fergusons, Megginsons, and Tylers had genealogical connections with Pocahontas, and like her other descendants, were financially prosperous. As tribal members, they also wholeheartedly supported their chief's endorsement of land ownership and building construction.

The church building too would be a centerpiece of Christian worship in the community, just as the Jerusalem temple had been a physical symbol of the Jews' spiritual faith in God.

Praying the closing prayer, Raleigh thanked the Lord for his blessings in allowing him to return to the Ridge and for his family and friends. He did not have the audacity to thank God for the British's surrender, for he realized that there was a deeper theological and providential issue that was best left in the hand of the omniscient and omnipotent God, Jehovah. Although Raleigh did not say it aloud in prayer, he did thank God softly in the deep recesses of his heart for his miraculous rainstorm when Cornwallis tried to retreat to Gloucester. That was one storm he was glad happened, but he could not really admit to God openly that he was thankful. He was afraid of getting on God's bad side for implying that God chose America over England. He just said in closing his prayer, "Thank you, Lord! Amen."

Sarah called on the members to sing the closing hymn as God had anointed her skillful singing tongue with blessed words from Martin Luther's pen. "Let us all sing Martin Luther's 'A Mighty Fortress Is Our God.'" She stepped forward, after having been standing with the audience, raising her right hand and directing the audience as they lifted their voices together. Sarah's choice of a closing selection was very appropriate. Raleigh, on the other hand, wondered why Sarah chose that particular hymn and if she knew the story of that song at Yorktown.

With her discernment gift, she knows more than she admits, Raleigh surmised to himself.

> And I will give it you for an heritage: I am the Lord.
> Exodus 6:8

14

The Pearl: The Heritage

1782

Raleigh could not possibly forget that morning after he returned to Buffalo Ridge from Yorktown. Sarah, by way of her spiritual vision and discernment gifts, shared with him the appalling and harrowing mental pictures that permitted her to transcend time. She was carried into the future, to places where her descendants were experiencing social and physical discrimination.

I promised Sarah that I would give the matter over to God in prayer, Raleigh meditated. *I told her that I would just commit the Pearl matter to God's hand and care. I also pledged that I would never forget what she told me concerning the Pearl visions.*

Raleigh vowed that he would keep the visions in his mind, heart, and soul, and prayed that God would take care of the problem. He also told her during those early morning hours that he would do everything he could to leave legal documentation and records for the Pearl.

I must do everything within my power to document our presence in Virginia. In the meantime, I have committed the matter into God's hand for him to do his part. He contemplated confidently in his mind, heart, and soul that when he gave a problem to God in prayer, that settled it. He knew that he would not have to lose any sleep tossing the Pearl matters around, over which he had little, if any, control.

He had heard Cherokee stories about evergreens and animals, after creation—pine and cedar varieties of trees and holly—stayed awake at night to keep watch. Of the animals, the owls and panthers had watch duty during the nights. Raleigh thought about God's creation and preferred to leave matters beyond his personal control in the hands of God, not animals and trees. He preferred to sleep during those quiet hours with confidence that God was on sentry duty, not trees, owls, and panthers. He was aware the Cherokee people were taking on animal surnames like Panthers (Panters), Owls (Howells), and Squirrels (Sorrells). Raleigh and John Redcross were well aware that Northumberland had many family members with the Sorrell name.

It would be utterly impossible to sleep without the protection of God. With all of the burdens that I have on myself, as a result of being the tribal chief and the head of the Pinn family, my eyes would never close in peace. Without God's harbor and port being there against those storms, I would be shipwrecked. Without God as my militia general, I would have fallen in battle years ago. I prefer to trust that God is looking out for me, not holly or evergreen trees or even owls or panthers.

Since he trusted God to do his part against those things that Sarah saw in the future, Raleigh climbed out of bed, said good morning to his wife, and began putting on his clothes.

Sarah knew that her husband had not forgotten those promises that he made to her that early morning after their all-night discussion about the past and future. She made her way to the kitchen where Raleigh had already begun to make a fire in the large, charcoal cook stove. Sarah began preparing him a full, hungry-man breakfast to keep him through the trip. He planned to get an early start for his horse ride to Amherst Courthouse. He was extremely excited to have the opportunity to pay his personal property taxes. This was another form of credential or voucher to document his life in Amherst County and his legacy for the Pearl.

During the two-hour trip to Amherst, Raleigh's mind flowed with vivid and colorful thoughts about the past. He smiled as he wondered why Sarah was so smooth in peeking into the future, those visions a hundred or two hundred years into the future, while lately he was barely able to get rough recollections of the past. Riding on a horse allowed a rider to meditate without worrying about where he was walking. His horse had a way of knowing where Raleigh wanted him to go, and therefore, his master was free to think rather than concentrate on the rocky road.

How is it that Virginia colonial officials can enter into land treaties with Cherokees, while at the same time, culminating the land cession contracts, saying to the general public, "Cherokees have never lived in Virginia"? What intelligent official would be so witless as to pay for, or contract for whatever reason, land boundaries between the Cherokees and the colonists if the purchasing party didn't believe that the ceding party had lived on, owned, and had a right to the land in the first place? Here are the colonists, culminating land cessions by signing in the appropriate sections, while at the same time thinking to themselves, "Cherokee, you know you never lived here!" Sarah's visions are on target. The colonists have a devious scheme. They want to get the land from the Cherokees, the aboriginal protectors of the land, and then years later say to Cherokee descendants, "Look here, we own the land. Your Cherokee ancestors were never here." Ah, the colonists' genocidal plan is masterful!

I am going to keep the Amherst County clerk busy with my constant purchasing and selling land, recording tribal marriage records, paying tax bills, and filing other legal documents. I will let the legal system back me up. I'll make sure that I create a lot of official paperwork in the courthouse. Now let them try to tell the Pearl that Raleigh Pinn never lived here in Amherst County. Now I dare the colonists to erase my name from the Yorktown furlough roll! I will leave the records of my land ownership in Buffalo Ridge and Stonewall Mill. There will be all those land transactions for the Pearl, the marriage documents for the Pearl, and all the personal property records in both areas. There are and will be marriage records of tribal members in Stonewall Mill and Buffalo Ridge. There are the many records of the Stonewall Mill people marrying the Buffalo Ridge people, and vice versa. The Pearl has kept and will keep the courthouse clerks busy!

I can't believe those treaties with the Cherokees! They are getting rid of Cherokees. They want their land while they plan to shoo them away from Virginia, North Carolina, South Carolina, Tennessee, Kentucky, and Georgia! Shoo, like they are nothing more than fowls! Go away! Get out!

The colonial officials, with Stuart, went to all that trouble to contract with Cherokees for the land in 1768 in North Carolina and

Virginia. Then they came back in 1770 and contracted with Cherokees in Lochaber, South Carolina for land in Virginia, West Virginia, Northeastern Tennessee, and the eastern end of Kentucky. Then in 1772, with the Governor of Virginia, they returned to get another piece of land in Virginia, West Virginia, and Eastern Kentucky. In 1775, they came back with Richard Henderson and contracted with the Cherokees for more land, with Kentucky, Virginia, and Tennessee! Can you believe that?

Raleigh had almost begun to think aloud, and was occasionally speaking audibly when he reached the base of the western side of Buffalo Ridge heading toward Amherst Courthouse. *The colonists are trying to make it appear to future colonists that they owned the Cherokee land all along. They are going to say one hundred to two hundred years hence that Cherokees only traveled through Virginia. How can the Cherokees only just pass through Virginia when they whipped the bottoms off the colonial soldiers in Richmond Falls in 1656? They actually occupied the land there. This battle almost escaped the view of Virginia archives were it not for the Colonial Council being in session and the battle events being recorded in the Colonial Council official minutes.*

When they received word of the buildup of Cherokees at the falls, military leader Hill and his army, with a hundred Pamunkey allies, went against that larger force of Cherokees. The colonists lost the battle and sued for peace. Because the events happened when the Council was in session, they actually recorded the events in the official Colonial Council records. I'm surprised that the colonists would be so stupid as to allow their whipping to be recorded! It is like a child publicly summoning all the children in the neighborhood to witness his mother whipping him for misbehaving. Even his mother would have retired him into the smokehouse for the private lashing. The colonists must have lost their heads, in the wake of the large Cherokee force, and ran in panic to the Colonial Council for official help. God is good in preventing this piece of history from going unnoticed. Now let them say that Cherokees were just passing through Richmond!

I guess they will say the aboriginal force was another tribe, other than Cherokees. They recorded the tribe's name as Rechahecrians. They probably used this name since they did not know how to spell or pronounce the tribe's true name. They heard the correct pronunciation,

Tsa la gi, *but called the people* Che-ro-kee. *I hope they get the name of the aboriginal force in Richmond Falls correct. Whether they get the name correct or not, the effect is still the same: they got whipped by the Rechahecrians. A Cherokee by any other name is still a Cherokee!*

Anyway, unless aboriginal people build houses with rocks and logs, as is the habit and fashion of colonial settlers, they will say they "did not exist in this colony." I expect that colonial writers will adopt the political philosophies of the locals. What if the Cherokees are really living in the colonists' neighborhoods, attired like them and living in homes similar to theirs? They will say, "They don't really exist because they aren't wearing loincloths and chanting." They, along with their historians, will deny that Cherokees ever lived in Virginia. Sarah assured me of this fact when she saw those visions, the future.

Raleigh's stallion, moving back and forth, right and left, entranced him, in a rhythmic mood, to construct a poem to the rhythmic movements:

> "I am traveling to Amherst to document my stay,
> Though some say, 'Aboriginal Pinns were not here!
> Colonial English only in Yorktown saved the day!'
> My Pearl will have written and prepared records to share.
> Oral legends will cease to be the most effective way,
> Because The Pearl's Wiccocomicos and Cherokees care!"

Raleigh filled out the tax record himself. He did not glow with pride like he did years earlier when God had to let his horse whip him because of his arrogance. He was somewhat gleeful when the official let him fill out his own personal property record, knowing the official had to write the records for most other customers. There was one section, however, that the official had to complete himself.

He wrote, *Rawley Pinn 1031.* Raleigh did not understand the code, and being the curious Pinn that he was, asked, "What is the meaning of the number?"

The clerk noted, "The '1' means 'white (free) tithe,' '0' for 'slaves,' '3' for 'head of cattle,' and '1' for 'horse.'"

"I understand." Then Raleigh paid his assessment tax, walked out of the courthouse, and mounted his horse. *The clerk thinks I'm white? That doesn't really matter because how does a clerk really know what racial blood runs through my veins? How does he even have the audacity to attempt to assess my genealogical racial composition based on a quick glimpse of my physical features? Only Jehovah, my Creator and Sustainer, can do that! I wonder how many racial category options he has on that list from which he can choose.*

Slave, 0. That is correct. God would never let me purchase a slave. The very minute that I should venture to deliberate on purchasing another human being to help me work on my farm, God would not only command my horse to whip me but also direct mole holes and everything else in his arsenals against me. It is impossible for a man to presume to own a slave, and it is almost impossible for a man to believe he can really own a piece of land. The land is there to receive us as our grave. The land will eventually possess us.

It is just an anthropological impossibility from the Creator's perspective, Raleigh thought deeply, realizing that God, in Genesis 1:26, "gave man dominion over only the fish of the sea, and over the fowl of the air, and over the cattle, and over all the earth, and over every creeping thing that creepeth upon the earth." God did not give human beings leave to turn fellow beings into slaves.

So "3" means three cattle. That is correct! The "1" means one horse. That too is correct. I plan to come here each year, Lord willing I live and see how long that first number, race, stays at "1." The other numbers are within my control. The second number, well, I will never own a slave! It will always be "0." The third number, the Lord willing and I live, I hope to increase that number, or it may decrease. The fourth number, well, I may get another horse for Turner, making two horses. Raleigh hurried toward home, realizing that he had a two-hour trip ahead. He knew that he had to make many such trips to the courthouse to pay personal property and real estate taxes. He would also see to it that his name was listed on family and tribal marriage licenses.

I must see to it that the marriages between members in Stonewall Mill and Buffalo Ridge document the communities' social, religious, tribal, and family connections, and the high rate of intertribal marriages. I will do my best to make sure that my name shows up on legal records until my Maker calls me home. I need to show Turner and other family leaders how to mark their presence on marriage, land, death, census, and other written documents. The Pearl must be protected against the coming genocidal philosophies and activities.

On the return trip to Buffalo Ridge, Raleigh's concentration focused on the sad and tragic condition of Cornwallis's compound, the dead soldiers and workers, some of whom were not buried. He speculated that God may have given the British and Americans a preliminary warning of what would come on both forces should they continue to pursue those horrible hostilities. He did not have his Bible with him as he rode through the Glades area of Amherst County, but a Bible verse came to his memory. He reminded himself to look up the Bible scriptures concerning the nation of Judah and how their disobedience against the law of God led them into captivity.

The nation of Judah suffered grievous deaths prior to their actual captivity. Some of their dead bodies were not buried. There was some mention in the scriptures about their carcasses becoming food for the dogs or beasts of the earth. The Pearl must be very careful. They must obey the words of the Lord and the rules that I set forth in my covenant for the tribe. As long as they love the Lord and treat their neighbors as they themselves would like to be treated, the Lord will keep those horrible ills from their presence. Actually, the Lord will bless the Pearl as he blessed the Israelites with their heritage.

When Raleigh returned home just after midday, he greeted his family hurriedly and went directly to the front room and retrieved his Bible. He anxiously thumbed through the pages with a troubled, apprehensive, and distressed countenance while Sarah looked on, waiting for him to explain what he was seeking in the Bible. He found a passage that he had not anticipated before he connected with the one that he had in mind at first. Raleigh read Jeremiah 14:16 aloud.

> And the people to whom they prophesy shall be cast into the streets of Jerusalem because of the famine and the sword; and they shall have none to bury them . . .

The Pearl needs to read this! They must stay close to God. He perused further and came across the primary section for which he had been searching, Jeremiah 16:4:

> They shall die of grievous deaths; they shall not be lamented; neither shall they be buried; *but* they shall be as dung upon the face of the earth: and they shall be consumed by the sword, and by famine; and their carcases shall be meat for the fowls of heaven, and for the beasts of the earth.

Raleigh read aloud, as if he wanted Sarah to serve as his witness before the Pearl that they must obey God's words.

"Raleigh, you have done your part. You have already told them that they must obey God's commandments. You warned them bluntly that they must love the Lord and their neighbors. Why are you so distressed? God will not punish you should they disobey the statutes of the Lord. If they fail to heed your words concerning God's laws, then they too will suffer the punishment that Judah suffered."

"I am not that worried about the Pearl," Raleigh declared unconvincingly.

"Yes, you are! I see your countenance. You are stressed. You have that Pearl stress, those facial features that habitually let me know you are consumed with Pearl-related issues. Keep in mind what God's word says. Just as there are predictions of punishment for disobedience, there are also prophecies of protection."

"Where did you find that?" Raleigh inquired.

"Look in chapter 54, somewhere there, in those verses." Sarah knew which verse he could find the "protection" passage.

She, along with Raleigh, has been keeping the family together with the scriptural promises of God. She remembered the chapter, verse, and actually had the exact words committed to memory. She just did not want to overshadow Raleigh with her confidence, for he was the biblical scholar in the family.

"Here it is. I found it! Listen to what it says, Sarah. I want you to commit this to your memory. It is one of the most important biblical passages concerning the future of the Pearl. Listen! It is in Isaiah, verse 17: 'No weapon that is formed against thee shall prosper; and every tongue that shall rise against thee in judgment thou shalt condemn. This is the heritage of the servants of the Lord, and their righteousness is of me, saith the Lord.'"

Sarah said excitedly, her voice rising, "That is the passage! Read it again, Raleigh."

"Listen, Sarah, or you may miss the full import of the words! Isaiah 54:17. Isaiah chapter 54 verse 17," he repeated, as he did not want Sarah to forget the verse.

> No weapon that is formed against thee shall prosper; and every tongue that shall rise against thee in judgment thou shalt condemn. This is the heritage of the servants of the Lord, and their righteousness is of me, saith the Lord.

"Raleigh, you said it! That is the verse I think you need to give to the Pearl as encouragement. You cannot be negative all the time. It is proper to warn them about the consequences of disobedience but also give them some carrots. You know how your horse loves to eat carrots. He actually responds to your commands better when you give him a carrot or a pat on his back or jaw when he obeys you. When you get mad at him and whip him, you don't always have the best results. That is why you don't fuss about him anymore!" Sarah instructed cautiously, as she wanted to stay within proper bounds with her husband, as a good, submissive wife. After speaking, she immediately realized that the horse analogy did not quite fit with human beings and regretted that she brought it up.

"Heed, Sarah, it says here that 'No weapon that is formed against.' The Pearl shall prosper. Well, it didn't say the Pearl, but if the Pearl obeys the laws of God, it means the Pearl."

"Yes, Raleigh, the Pearl will have God's anointed protection all around them if they obey the statutes of the Lord. No weapon in the hands of any beings, whether human or spiritual demonic beings, shall prosper. They may try to kill them in battle, burn them in an arson attack, and remove their legacy by erasing their heritage on legal documents and in oral history. Keep in mind, no weapon shall prosper. There are going to be some new racial and ethnic weapons that the European colonists will devise that are unheard of now!"

"Yes, Sarah, the Lord will provide his Shekinah glory on the Pearl, that special protection all around them if they obey the commandments, statutes, laws, and words and all the other rules of the Lord that the Good Book mentions. No weapon in the hands of any mortal creature or evil spiritual being shall flourish, advance, or make headway. Even though the Pearl's adversaries may aspire to assault them in armed battle, the Pearl will come out victorious. Their spiritual or physical adversaries may endeavor, in a flagrant manner, to reduce to ashes or cremate The Pearl, but their activities will be useless as weapons. You remember the three Hebrew boys in the fiery furnace! No weapon, even fire, harmed them. They were burn-proof! They may attempt to burn records of the Pearl's heritage. They may burn the courthouses. They might be more devious and flagrant in their misdeeds against the Pearl. They might ignore our Cherokee and Wiccocomico history in the Virginia annals. The historians' dodging efforts of commission and omission will not be prosperous. The people—the assailants—who attempt to go against the Pearl will not prosper. All of this is based on the Pearl keeping close to the Lord and obeying his statutes. The European settlers' hateful weapons, whether through removal and destruction of their meager records of our people or through intentional or unintentional omission by historians, regardless, they will not fare well or profit. Neither will their agents who use those dreadful instruments!"

> The woods are lovely, dark and deep,
> But I have promises to keep,
> And miles to go before I sleep,
> And miles to go before I sleep.
> —Robert Frost, 1923

15

Documents, Past Tense

1794

Raleigh was gratified with his land purchase from Charles Christian. He negotiated ninety acres on the south branch of the Buffalo River and Braxton Ridge on June 21, 1788, to add to land he owned in the area already. He was committed to purchasing land so that he could document his life in Amherst and Buckingham Counties. He realized that he had a long way to go to fulfill his goal of leaving legacies on paper.

I want to buy more land in Buffalo Ridge rather than in Buffalo River, but I have to wait for the right time, place, and price. Raleigh was pleased with his hard work and frugality in acquiring the fifty pounds to buy the ninety acres from Charles. He wanted to have his tribe in the area of the Ridge close to Stonewall Mill. The colonists must not be privy to his plan before time; he hoped to purchase some land later in the Ridge so he could leave a lapse of time between his earlier purchases of land in Buckingham County and Amherst County. The people, the Buffalo Ridge and Stonewall Mill bands, must be close enough to maintain frequent relationships. The Ridge land area must be extended to make way for new Cherokee coming into the hills. At first, Sarah thought he was crazy trying to accommodate those dispersed aboriginal masses, but now that things were coming to fruition, she actually began to see the wisdom of his plan. The Cherokees were coming to the Ridge from all over.

The news had been passed as far as the Lower towns and Middle towns, and the fringes around those locations. A white trader told Raleigh in 1782 that he had spoken with a stressed, dispersed Cherokee who had been hiding out in the foothills near Spartanburg. The Indian had indicated that his people were hiding out along the hills and foothills in South Carolina, North Carolina, Virginia, and other colonies. They were uncomfortable because they did not know when the colonial militia would return to hunt them down. The traders overheard the homeless creatures talk about plans to move into the Ridge area over the next few years. The trader told Raleigh to be careful because they were coming toward his area. The trader did not know that Raleigh was actually prepared to receive them. Not only was Raleigh on standby to host them when they came, he had actually contrived the plan to plant them in incremental waves.

On March 21, 1794, he completed the transaction for four hundred acres on Porridge Creek and Mill Creek on the eastern side of Buffalo Ridge. He acquired the land for only fifty pounds. Talk had begun to spread among the colonists that Raleigh had become a land speculator and was giving up farming.

"Let them think I am giving up farming, Sarah! I am still farming, but I am buying land too. I hope they think I am doing it for the money. What they don't know is that the Lord has been blessing us with successful harvests each year. The burden is on me to help the dispersed souls. As they work on my land, I can make more money to buy more land to bring in more aboriginal people. I will give them a piece of the land for a token amount. How else could I bring them in without settling them when they arrive?"

Raleigh was not acquiring the land for his son, Turner, because he had begun training his son to make his own way in life by buying his own land. Raleigh's land deals, farming strategies, and social plans favored the Pearl, not his own wallet. He paid his taxes faithfully between the 1780s and 1802, as reflected in the Amherst County land tax record books. He paid his personal property taxes in the same county continuously with official records revealing his personal property holdings.

Raleigh felt the happiness that came with true success. Training his son to follow in his footsteps, Turner accompanied him on each of those land transactions. His keen eyes watched his father's negotiations like those of an eagle. Raleigh made sure that Turner shadowed his goings and comings. Turner's father wanted to make sure that Turner thought about him and his land transactions after his father had been buried in his grave.

Surely, he will keep my legacy going! Raleigh thought as he hoped Turner had learned this particular apprentice trade, as if he needed to reassure himself that his bumblebee-like work ethics over the last two-and-a-half decades had not been developed in vain.

As they walked home from the Mann property, Raleigh explained to Turner what had just happened. "Turner, do you understand what happened in our transaction with Mr. Mann?"

"Yes, Daddy, I guess, somewhat. Why didn't you pay him the money, the fifty pounds? How can you own the land when you left the money at home? You only gave him five pounds."

"That's a good question, son. I gave him 10 percent of the total price. Remember, he gave me this piece of brown paper with the words:

> Paid five pounds for four hundred acres, March 21, 1794. Bal. of 45 pounds due March 22 or soon thereafter.
>
> James Mann

"We will go to the Amherst Courthouse tomorrow to record the transaction. James Mann and his wife, Jane, will be there. I will take care of the matter then. That is smart of you to notice that, Turner! That shows you are a chip off the old block. Let's hurry home to tell your mother what we just did."

"Sarah, I did it! I just completed the deal about an hour ago. We have that quiet, secluded, hidden land that I dreamed about in 1774 or 1775. Remember when I first whispered to you my plan for the dispersed people? You first thought I was stretching myself out too far. Well, I got all that land for fifty pounds, the same amount that I paid to Charles in 1788 for just ninety acres. It has good timber and the Porridge Creek also runs along on it. The land is close to the ancient aboriginal burial ground. Oh yes, the church can have a solid building now. This land also has better soil! I really believe James Mann knows what I am doing, that I am setting up a relief area for the needy. Why else would he allow me to have that much land, four hundred acres, for only fifty pounds? I think he suspects that I am going to bring in the Indians. I hope, rather I pray, he respects me enough to keep his mouth shut and not let the colonists learn of his suspicions. The local colonists would string me up if they thought I was making an Indian town close to them, here in the Ridge. Anyway, honey, I did it. Four hundred acres of rich soil for fifty pounds!"

"Raleigh, you don't have to convince me how cunning you were in getting that good land. I know that you always manage your funds well. You have your mind fixed on hiding out more of those poor dispersed Cherokee souls. Turner walked outside to the barn to get everything ready for the next day's trip to Amherst. He was almost twenty-five years old and still anxiously showed his father that he was wise enough to transact legal, Amherst County Courthouse land business by himself. He knew his daddy would not permit him to conduct the land deal, but he wanted to be present to watch his father as he completed the real estate negotiation and settlement."

"Sarah, what do you have for supper?"

"You and Turner will just have to wait until I fix it to find out."

Raleigh wiped his mouth as if he were ready to eat now and walked toward the barn to help Turner.

That night, Raleigh dreamed about the marriages that he had witnessed and for which he provided surety. As the tribal leader, the brides and grooms always made sure that he witnessed the process and gave his consent, even though Raleigh was not always the father of the bride or groom.

He thought he was making a pact with the Buckingham Beverlys in the 1770s. He promised the Beverly family's leaders that his children and tribal members would intermarry with their Buckingham families. He encouraged them to move in stages to Amherst County in general and Buffalo Ridge in particular. Some Beverly residents would stay in Buckingham County for a decade or two while their other family members settled in Amherst County. He supervised the marriage between Frances Beverly and Mary Williams, daughter of Nancy Williams, on November 29, 1792. He dreamed that he had met with Thomas Evans's father, a descendant of a long family line of Cherokees, to plan the wedding between Thomas and his daughter Anna. They would eventually marry on November 2, 1795, with Raleigh and Sarah attending the ceremony.

He reminisced about the time when he and John Redcross discussed the marriage of James Pinn to John's daughter, Nancy. John wanted to keep aboriginal blood in the family and promised Raleigh to let his descendants marry Raleigh's family members when the time was ripe. Redcrosses would intermarry with Pinns and Beverlys for generations.

There were several weddings that Raleigh facilitated, and there would be many more, an almost uncountable number of marriages of his family to Cherokee spouses after his death. Raleigh would still get the credit for the alliances between these aboriginal couples because his prodigious and colossal shadow would protect and shield the Pearl through many centuries. His presence would be felt in members' hearts through their faith in God. As an aboriginal citizen, he and his father did not worship the sun, the fire, the rain, or the earth, but the Creator, Jehovah. Raleigh made sure that his descendants maintained their Christian faith. He also passed down to his issue and progeny a contagious spirit of love for the family and aboriginal heritage.

Raleigh's dreams would vibrate through many centuries. His life would influence the native milieu for generations. His life would have the most influence on future generations of many native leaders. He was a retainer of Wiccocomico and Cherokee traditions, a peacemaker in spirit, a fighter in the flesh. How else could he have masterminded this timeless preservation, the Pearl? He did all this without going to war against his colonist neighbors on the Ridge and Stonewall Mill! He did this without worshiping idols while burning sweet grass and sage. Oh, he did smoke his pipe with his homegrown tobacco, but it was in worship of God for his love and bountiful harvest. The tobacco smoke went up from Raleigh's mouth and lungs toward the ceiling, like the Israelite priests when they burned incense in the temple and the smoke went toward heaven.

Raleigh continued to dream. *God made our lungs and breathed into us the breath of life. I smoked and prayed to God, with the circles of smoke ascending to heaven's atmosphere and proclaiming, "Thank you, God, for my bountiful fruit, grain, and tobacco harvests!"* He dreamed about Turner courting the young Joicey Humbles and wondered what his intentions were with her. Raleigh had already done his genealogical homework on the Humbles family line. He knew that Joicey was an aboriginal of America, having a family who descended from a long line of Native Americans out of Charles City back in the early 1700s. Like Raleigh's indentured servitude as a young Native American child in Northern Neck, Joicey's mother, Martha, residing in Amherst County, had ancestors who had also been placed in indentured servitude in Charles City County. Raleigh knew the Humbles family well and had researched their stock. They were mixed Cherokee Iroquois and Algonquian from that Charles City area. They too were connected with the Rechahecrian people who mixed with the Algonquian residents. Martha had recently had a child named Susanna in 1790. Raleigh also wondered if that child would also marry a local aboriginal tribal member when she comes of age. Raleigh did not know at the time that his hunch was on target, as Susanna, at age 17, would marry John Redcross's son, John Junior, on February 13, 1807.

These clear thoughts and images came freely in Raleigh's repose. He had a talent for looking back in his dreams and seeing images that most people would have long since forgotten. These dreams of events from the past had a way of coming to his consciousness, whether stimulated by some previous day's events or some other triggering incident. Apparently, Raleigh had those dreams on a regular basis because he remembered things from the past with such clarity, as if they had been repeated to him frequently. Even listeners to his dream tales were suspicious that he rehearsed them in dreams every night as a way to remember them so vividly. Some of his nightmares were horrible enough that the average man experiencing such images would go into shock or perhaps be led to an asylum for the mentally insane. In Raleigh's case, he believed that all nightmares, as well as the pleasant dreams of past events, were given to him for a purpose. They stimulated within his mind the development of directions and strategies to meet some kind of goal or objective that he must achieve in his lifetime.

Raleigh tried to slip out from his past-tense dreams and use aboriginal instinct to peek into the future. He struggled as he tossed and turned in his bed. Sarah, realizing that he was dreaming, shook him as he went through jerking movements in his intense efforts to change tenses. He could not, however, go from the past to the present tense. Finally, after Sarah's numerous attempts to halt his dreams, he slipped into the present tense. He did not wake up completely, however; he just entered into another dimension. Half asleep, he continued to think about Turner courting his girlfriend, Joicey.

Then Sarah, realizing he was speaking now, listened. She heard him ask, "Why did Turner court a Humbles?"

Sarah shook him until he awakened. Then she asked, "Why are you inquiring about Turner's reason for marrying a Humbles girl?"

"I know why! She has aboriginal ancestry," he said to Sarah. "Turner only needs to look at her mother, and he will have his answer. Look at native customs. I wish he would marry that girl! She is a little plump but beautiful to look at. Look at her beautiful hair and lovely skin color. What's wrong with Turner's eyes? I know what's wrong. He is looking at all those other pretty girls. He has been peeking at the girls in two of the seven Beverly households in Buckingham County. I must stop taking him with me when I go near those Beverlys' cabins. I guess my great job of building tribal connection between the Pinns and the Beverlys is hurting Joicey's chances with him. I must spread out and increase the contacts among the tribe members. We need to get other families together, increase the variety. We don't want too much inbreeding, as we need to get closer with the Fergusons, Jethro and his gang. The Fergusons in Buckingham and Prince Edward Counties go back to Gaelic origin. The rumor is that they were connected with the Farquharsons and came from the ancient Chattan clan. Some say that they are Scots from the Scot Highland clans. I wonder if they are related to those fighting Highlanders who went against the Cherokee towns several years ago. I get a feeling that some Fergusons were in that unit of Highlanders. It would be interesting if we discovered that the Highlanders drove Cherokees from Cherokee villages in the South and West this way and their Ferguson descendants later ended up marrying the very Cherokee family members that their ancestors drove to Buffalo Ridge and Stonewall Mill! They were enemies in one generation and bed partners the next two or three generations . . ." Raleigh gradually slipped back into his sleep mode while smiling in his sleep and even giggling loud enough for Sarah to notice him.

Sarah stared at him from her fully awake position for several minutes. She sat on the side of the bed with her upper torso turned back toward Raleigh and gazed at him. She continued shaking him to force him to wake up, but after seeing his wide smile, she decided to let him enjoy his dreams for a change.

He resumed his dreams about the colonial assaults on Cherokee villages. *I have taken some of those dispersed Cherokees that they stirred up. All they did was go down there and burn their villages and towns, and kill some of their warriors, women, and children. Like a great stone falling in the Great Wiccocomico River, the riffles from the stone's impact go all the way to the Atlantic Ocean. Those militias just moved the people out of their Cherokee towns. The ones that they did* not kill, they drove them in all directions, like the water riffles running from the shock of the stone.

His mind went back to stories his daddy told him about the Wiccocomico dispersions. He wondered what happened to Jane Pinn. As an aboriginal woman who was too old to be in indentured servitude, she was passed around from house to house. *Why did the colonists break up our Indian reserve? Why did they chase the Pinns all over the place? That poor woman, Jane, had to live with John Pasquett for two months in 1763, and then Ann Nickens kept her for a while in 1764. The Wiccocomico Parish paid different people to look after her. They ordered that the goods that Jane Pinn owned that were in John Pasquett's hands be sold to the highest bidder. Why didn't they just let her live as a native and why did they try to force acculturation on her? I will not force Cherokee souls to adopt the colonists' ways. They need to adopt some local ways so that they can survive, but as far as assimilating totally, no.*

Then Raleigh's dream returned to Stonewall Mill, in as vivid imagery as those dreams of Wiccocomicos. *The Megginsons have some intermixture of Pocahontas's blood. The Cherokee McCoys, almost pure bloods, are hiding out in Stonewall and the Ridge. The Isbells are also over there in Stonewall Mill. They act like colonists, with royal ancestry lines going back to Europe, but you know that they have some Native blood down the line. They are more comfortable talking about Cherokee culture than I am, and I have some Cherokee blood. Why else would they hang so closely with the aboriginal girls in Stonewall Mill? Some of those people, the Fergusons, and Megginsons, are mostly aboriginal residents. The Cherokee Bollings have that Pocahontas blood too. They are connecting with our people in the Ridge and Stonewall. The Bollings are crazy about land, like the colonists. They love land more than I love land.*

What Raleigh did not know at the time of his present-tense slumber was that John Bowling, three years later, on January 27, 1797, would purchase 156 acres of land adjoining his other property near Charles Christian and his acres on the Buffalo Branch and Braxton Ridge. He was correct when he dreamed that the Bollings (Bowlings) "are connecting up with our people on the Ridge . . ." The Bollings were uniting with Raleigh in land connections.

The present tense held on to Raleigh's dream and did not let him slip into the past nor the future. His mind was so fixed on the Bollings, Fergusons, Megginsons, and others that his cognitive capacities grew exhausted to the extent that he moved into a subconscious state. He not only stopped dreaming, but his memory and cognition closed down to permit him a partial night's sleep. He had to be alert tomorrow for the courthouse meeting. He was the tribal storyteller, the historian, and those recurring dreams of the past permitted his brain to perfect his long-term memory and storytelling efficiency. As Raleigh slept like a baby in his mother's womb, he smiled in perfect contentment, conscious of the wall of protection that God had constructed around the Pearl and him as its leader. He had miles to go before his Maker would tell him to sleep on. Until then, he needed to work in the daylight and get a bit of sleep at night.

In his subconscious mental state while sleeping, he smiled as he experienced a momentary future tense vision of James Mann and June shaking his and Turner's hands to close the land transaction the next day. Sarah noticed his smiling face as he slept when she climbed out of bed quietly at five thirty to fix his breakfast. She started to stir him, but his primrose sunbeam countenance restrained her. She saw something around his head, which appeared in the dark room to be a halo. The luminous cloud that she thought to be a halo or a regal crown was in fact fireplace light reflecting from the bedroom dresser mirror. She knew her husband had a Wiccocomico chief in his ancestry and this princely heritage only accentuated her convictions.

Sarah was also aware that Raleigh had been anointed for some special mission of helping the dispersed, homeless creatures who were heading toward the Ridge to hide out in those lovely dark and deep woods. The Ridge was a hiding place for those seeking refuge; a scenic paradise for persons desiring peace and relaxation, and an agricultural oasis for farmers who had a mind to work. The Ridge and Stonewall Mill were somewhat like the Holston River for the Cherokees. With all the game and rich land in the vicinity, it was easy for farmers to survive without working very hard. Raleigh, on the other hand, made the land fertile for farming and attractive for game. He could be called an arsonist because he occasionally burned trees in some areas to facilitate grass growth. He was a very hard worker on his farm as noted by the number of trees that he cut and stumps that he removed to clear the land for planting. To new guests and visitors to the area who were not aware of Raleigh's energetic efforts and work ethic in developing the land, the Ridge was a paradise and an enchanting natural habitat.

Raleigh had a craving to help orphans and homeless people because he himself had been taken from his home in Wiccocomico and lived in two different homes as an indentured servant. Sarah knew that he was dreaming good dreams, experiencing pleasant thoughts for a change, instead of nightmares. She decided not to awaken him from those precious moments. He would complete the land purchase this morning, and the new property would be there as a refuge, a haven for deserving souls. Those purposeful dreams, visions, and nightmares were what actually led Raleigh to purchase the land. The new aboriginal settlers would work on the farm, learn farm production and retail skills, understand real estate transactions, and ultimately move out on their own in an educational, vocational, and supportive native environment.

> Your old men shall dream dreams.
> Acts 2:17

16

Dreams of the Distant Future

1794

One week later, on the night of March 29, Raleigh's mind and soul captured the most picturesque, graphic, and intense vision of the future. The grandfather clock had just chimed out 3:00 a.m., the period when he was in his deepest rest, when his subconscious state fostered physical passivity and his mental and spiritual persuasions were most active for new, peculiar, and extraordinary dreams.

Raleigh and Sarah had been working feverishly to prepare their new land, the old four-hundred-acre Mann Place, for spring planting. Physically worn out, they welcomed deep sleep. Sarah was too tired to assist Raleigh in awaking from his nightmares, should they agitate and rattle him.

His mind and spirit carried him six to eight generations hence. He saw happy children, boys and girls, holding hands. He could not see things clearly, but it appeared that they were playing marriage games on a hill covered with fragrant blue, white, purple, and yellow violets. He saw friendly, bright-hued butterflies and bees encircling them, as if they too were participating in a marriage-related game of pollinating flowers. The scene was blissful and timeless. It seemed that they were rollicking and disporting themselves gaily on the hillside in peaceful, gregarious communication, and he recognized the children as descendants of tribal members. He delighted in the colorful futuristic scene until he noticed a stranger standing near the edge of the dark, shaded woods. The man—known in

Raleigh's vision as Pleck and wearing specs—stepped forward like a military leader, with his right palm near his eyes while straining to see the children. He grinned at the sea of couples like a Cheshire cat, and he demanded that the striplings halt their play, raise their right hands, and call out their surnames.

Raleigh's visions allowed him to look through time, almost a century and a half, and focus on vague details of key generation histories. With labyrinthine, tangled mental images, as if he were looking down the rocky pathways of time through clouded binoculars, he saw both sad and pleasant optical apparitions. It may have been Sarah's visions thirteen years earlier, in the early morning hours after he returned from the Yorktown campaign, which predisposed these sights. She told him about the visions that she had seen regarding tribal members, the Pearl. Now his subconscious, automatic tribal chieftain impulses, during rest and repose, precipitated powerful images through time.

He saw numerous pairs of children. As he adjusted his sights on one of the couples holding hands, he noticed names inscribed on the backs of their hands. The word "Pinn" had been branded on the girl's hand and the name "Beverley" had been placed on the boy's hand. Raleigh looked through the sea of couples for other familiar names. He beheld pairs with familiar and unfamiliar combination of names. There was a play section with couples named McCoy and Banks, Isbell and Ferguson, Pinn and Twopence (Twopins), Elliotts and Wests, and Chambers and Warricks. There were couples with other combinations: Jenkins and Beverley, Cousins and McCoy, Scott and Pinn, Jordan and Beverley, Megginson and Ferguson, and Humbles and Evans. He spotted surname admixtures of Sparrow and Pinn, Jewell and Pinn, Pinn and Ferguson, Tyler and Adcock, Ferguson and Tyler, Bolling and Cousins. There were other couples unified with the names Redcross and Pinn, Beverley and Ferguson, and Scott and West.

Raleigh noticed another group of stripling couples rowing across the James River from Stonewall Mill. The surname mélange included Isbell and West, Ferguson and Isbell, Beverley and McCoy, Megginson and Beverley, and McDaniel and Ferguson. The Stonewall Mill couples landed their canoes on the Stapleton banks and ran all the way to Buffalo Ridge. They joined a group that included an aggregation of Thomas and Rose, Rose and Ferguson, Redcross and Woods, Hutcherson and Ferguson, Johnson and Jordan, Johnson and Banks, Robinson and Megginson, Cheagle and West, Beverley and Redcross, Chambers and Warrick, Sorrell and Pinn, Powell and Sorrell, Coopers and Harris, Harris and West, West and Chambers, and Chambers and Pinn. Then the surnames on their arms all ran together as they, hopping and skipping in a circle around a post, lifted their palms in the air at the command of the man on the fringes of the trees, who had an official-looking white satin banner across his shoulder. Dressed in a black tuxedo and top hat, his banner brandished and flaunted unfamiliar words: "State of Virginia, Records Official." His official formal attire, appearing out of place in this rural setting, only added to his dream's suspense.

The Top Hat official came from the shaded wooded area and sat on a log. He had a writing quill in his right hand and a blank scroll in his other hand. He rested the scroll on a large stump. Raleigh knew that large stump; it was the same stump on the old Mann Place from which he and Turner had felled a tree two days earlier.

"Raise your right arm and let me record your surname! Lift it high and hold it there until I tell you that I have written it on my Virginia Archival Rolls." Pleck ordered the children to stay in place with hands up, as if they were being robbed, until he had documented their names.

Raleigh tried to wake up so he could chase the Top Hat official away from his Pearl. He moved from one spot in the bed to another. He shifted his body but was unable to break out of his deep sleep. Sarah too was in a state of exhaustion from the land-clearing activities.

"Let me up! Where is my tomahawk?" He forgot he had lost his favorite tomahawk on the marching trail. Then, vaguely remembering that in his dream, he shouted, "Sarah, hand me my military-issue tomahawk! I will split that tall black top hat without even touching his head. That will send him skipping!"

Raleigh was unaware of the official's ultimate purpose on the Ridge. If he had been cognizant, he would have been angry in his sleep about the fact that the Top Hat man wanted to categorize his Pearl by surnames and place all Indians in the black stratification. He wanted to take certain rights away from the darker people in Virginia. Raleigh always acknowledged that some aboriginal people were generally dark. If Raleigh had known what was really happening in his visions, he would have been really perturbed with the official's mission of trying to be a little god. Even though God created human flesh and souls, the Top Hat man desired to place value on clay pigments. Raleigh probably would have inquired about the stranger's authority, if he had been privy to the situation. "Who gave you the omniscience and omnipotence to evaluate human clay? Are you saying dark is bad or of less value than light clay?"

He would have prayed to God, *Let me at him! His racial philosophy is evil. He is an agent commissioned by the spiritual principalities and powers of Satan! Lord, please awaken me so I can chase him out of the Ridge.*

An angel came to Raleigh with words of wisdom so that he could reduce his stress level. Raleigh began to relax as his spirit comforted him.

"Raleigh, you must relax. Calm down! There are certain things in life that are beyond your control, as there are issues and social events within the spiritual realm. Satan's agents have been controlling very strong, spiritually evil and malicious forces. You have about as much power to deal with those agents as you have in deflecting mid-July sunrays in your tobacco field. Give it up, Raleigh. This philosophical racial evil is beyond your purview. It is not new. There is nothing new under the sun. Racial hatred has been around for generations. Even your aboriginal contemporaries harbor racist ideas. Some value light complexion more than dark-skinned hues. Others favor the dark, pure-blooded Indian. Your native people also harbor these feelings, so why worry over the Top Hat stranger? Let it go and give it to God! These evil philosophies have been on earth since creation, and you can be assured that they will be here as long as you and your descendants live through many, many generations. You do not need to wake up, just sleep a while and leave those high evil spiritual realm issues to God's discretion!

At that moment, Raleigh, deeply involved in his dream, looked down toward the James River and Isbell's Ferry Landing at Stapleton, a short distance from Stonewall. Ferguson, Isbell, and Megginson officials from Buckingham County (later Appomattox County) walked off the ferry with their horses. They mounted those animals, as if every second wasted meant life and death, and galloped toward Buffalo Ridge. When they reached their destination at that spot, they gathered all the Stonewall Mill couples and told them to follow them back to Stonewall Mill. They then charged the stranger not to record any names of Stonewall's children.

Ferguson and Megginson stated that they were of the lineage and heritage of European, Pocahontas, and Cherokee/Rechahecrian. Ferguson charged him.

"Don't you ever record any information on our people for which you intend to do harm. Their color and heritage, whether Native, European, or even Negro, will not be recorded for ill will as long as we live."

"I am sorry," the stranger apologized as he thought that the Fergusons and Megginsons were full-blooded white people. "I thought the children were trying to go for white. You know we do not want them to marry any of our folk. You know what I mean."

Ferguson exclaimed, "No, I do not know what you mean! The best thing you can do is to leave this Ridge and go back to Richmond. If Raleigh were living, he would pepper your rear end. Since I do not have any authority here in this county, it is best I leave. Raleigh was the chief of the Stonewall band and the Ridge people. John Turner, his great-grandson is chief now, and it behooves you to leave quickly while you are in possession of all of your body parts!"

The Top Hat man started to leave, but as he walked away, he wrote a name down quickly from the Buffalo Ridge group: "Beverley." He was trying to write other children's surnames down on his scroll as he retreated. He tripped and lost his quill in the grass. Ferguson shouted to him words to the effect that,

"If you don't leave, I will request Appomattox's Commonwealth Attorney Isbell to investigate the legality of your authority here, interfering with Stonewall Mill and Buffalo Ridge children!"

He left abruptly, as if he did not want to engage in political skirmishes with the powerful, wealthy, and influential Pocahontas people in the Virginia Senate. He looked back and shouted "I have other racial tricks in my hat, just you wait!" as he left the Ridge. "I will be back to Amherst County. You can be assured of that!"

Ferguson yelled back, "I dare you! I dare you to even contemplate putting your signifying hide in Buckingham County. I know what you are doing with your scroll-recording antics. Try it and see what happens!" The Virginia official knew that the Fergusons had clout with the Virginia Senate.

Raleigh did not really understand all of his visions. The Top Hat stranger had begun building contrived evidence to imply certain surnamed people were really Indian and black and should not be permitted to marry people of the white race. He would later go so far as to harass and threaten county clerks, physicians, midwives, ministers, and others, and he even threatened to imprison people who helped people of color marry white people. Raleigh was privy to these facts during the continuous barrage of visions.

Raleigh did not realize that Dr. Isbell, an Appomattox physician in Stonewall Mill, would never permit any of his patients to be discriminated against, especially those who were of the Pearl. Actually, he fathered several children by Judith Ferguson, children who were descendants of Stephen Ferguson. Stephen was the son of Jethro Ferguson, a skilled master carpenter and descendant of Scots and Cherokee/Rechahecrian people in the area. Little did Raleigh know that Jethro Ferguson—the man who built the Pinn's tobacco houses while Raleigh was with the Amherst County Militia in Yorktown—would later have a son, Stephen, to unite with the tribe. Stephen Ferguson would become one of the ancestral pillars of the Pearl. The Top Hat man dared not record the name Ferguson, McCoy, Megginson, and other Stonewall Mill tribal members on his sinister scroll.

Some Beverley families migrated from Buckingham County (current Appomattox County) to the western Amherst County band. Rockbridge County also had families of Beverlys in its midst, yet Pleck dared not record Beverley on the Buckingham County roll because he feared the warning from the influential Fergusons, which was still resounding against his ears. He, however, dared to add Beverley on his scroll in Roanoke County and Washington County. He somehow missed the fact that a census taker had recorded the Beverlys on the Floyd County 1900 U.S. Census as a Cherokee tribe. The Floyd County Beverlys were so bold as to insist that the census officials list them as *Cherokee* on a separate Indian Tribal Population Census form.

The registration official later corresponded with and traveled to counties in Virginia, building his rolls of native people who should not be permitted certain social advantages that were afforded to whites. He was not brazen enough to list any surnames that were directly connected with the politically potent Pocahontas lines. He intentionally avoided recording names that were tied with Pocahontas's descendants. He did not have the courage to add the Ridge's Bollings to his scroll from Amherst County because of the mammoth influence of state's leaders who were partial to the Bollings, also a common surname of Pocahontas descendants. He recorded the name slyly as Bolden and Bolin in Lee and Smyth Counties in Southwestern Virginia.

The Ridge band's Sorrell family surname was listed on his genocide rolls in Amherst County, as well as on the rolls of Rockbridge County, Augusta County, and Westmoreland County. The Ridge's surname Wood also made the list in Amherst County and Rockbridge County. The Top Hat official left off or missed the prominent Cherokee surname Owl, or the anglicized Howell, in Appomattox County, but he did add it to the rolls of Charles City County and King William County.

The angel continued Raleigh's sleep therapy and counseling services. "Raleigh, when you wake up, you must develop a plan to advise the Pearl to tread lightly. Teach them to refrain from being hotheads. You have been a good example by toning down your negative demeanor. If you can do it, your tribal members certainly can learn how to think before speaking or acting. In heated situations, tell them to count to ten before acting. Genocide has taken your aboriginal family and friends for centuries partly because of their hotheaded attitudes. Don't freely hand excuses to your enemies to kill, imprison, enslave or banish you. You make it hard for your enemies to destroy your legacy and heritage. You have been ready physically to fight Virginia officials, as you feel that the officials and historians are actually spiritual agents and instruments of perverse and crooked world philosophies. You cannot fight spiritual forces with physical muscle because these human philosophies have been propagated for thousands of years, actually throughout the ages. Satan's agents will be here for centuries. Look what the colonial militia did to Cherokee towns in the 1760, 1761, and again in 1776 under the pretext of fighting the enemies of the colonies. The Cherokees, by favoring the British, handed the so-called excuses to the colonists to burn their villages and kill their people. Granted they were weak excuses, but still they served the colonists' purpose for instigating and committing aboriginal genocide. Now aboriginal groups have adopted those cruel racial philosophies to appease the instigators, incubators, and propagators of those bigoted ideologies. Native groups now value racial hues based on the colonists' evaluations.

"Raleigh, you are not aware of another coming evil that will be directed against aboriginal people. The slave mentality will permeate future cultures. The colonists made slaves of not only Native Americans, but great African descendants, some of whom were from kings and princes in African antiquity. All Africans will be devalued, just because of the horrible stench left from the slave institution. You think slavery is horrible! It is incomprehensible how society will put down descendants of slaves, just because of the social stigma resulting from that evil institution of slavery. Native groups will also encounter the same human forces that incubated slavery. Please encourage Turner to refrain from the evil practice of enslaving human beings!

"There will come a time, soon after you follow your ancestors to the grave, when Cherokees will again be assaulted. As a stone generates ripples in a lake, so will be the force of this genocidal assault on Cherokees within three to four decades. Turner will see these spiritual and physical evils in his lifetime. Some Cherokees will flee from the colonial militia in all directions, like water withdraws from the stone when thrown into a river. You might as well tell Turner and other natives to expect them in large numbers in this part of Virginia. They are coming from North Carolina, Georgia, Alabama, and Tennessee. They will flee from an evil philosophy called the Removal. The miserable creatures will come your way, hungry and homeless, fleeing human beings' attempts to control their affairs. Raleigh, don't get caught up in the evil social institution of slavery. You dare not own a slave, as no human being can own what God has created! Go to sleep, Raleigh. Rest in peace. You need your rest. Your life has been a hard row to hoe. Hold fast to your faith in God. Tell your descendants to value themselves for what they are, not what others think they should be. Don't get caught up on the world's value system, where more esteem is placed on one particular ethnic group over another ethnic group, or a certain color over another hue. Teach them that they increase in value as the people face trials and tribulations in this life. They will be strong and sturdy for the harsher tests of the ages. Just as an oyster builds up protective defenses against a grain of sand or other foreign matter entering its shell and pressing against its sensitive body by forming a hard pearl covering over that invasive object, your descendants must do the same. As the oyster makes a valuable pearl out of suffering, your tribe's preciousness will increase through suffering and become a more precious Pearl.

"Tell them to refrain from getting caught up in the racially divisive philosophies of the ages. If aboriginal groups reject your people because of their heritage or color, be peaceful and content. They will sell their souls, should they beg to be accepted or become companions of those purblind and dogmatic aboriginal groups. Stay as far from those status-seeking groups as possible. Leave them alone. Move away from them and their sinister locations. They are fighting God and his creation. No man or group has the power to evaluate God's clay creations. You sleep, Raleigh!"

Even during this subconscious state, Raleigh had the graceful etiquette to thank God for those moments of heavenly counsel. He exclaimed aloud, "Thank you, Lord!" Sarah was still fatigued and worn out and did not hear Raleigh's thanksgiving shout.

His mind had been occupied in future tense apparitions and visualizations for two hours and thirty minutes. It was now 5:30 a.m. He turned over to his left side, placed his palm-to-palm hands between his pillow and mattress, and slipped into blissful, tranquil, and placid slumber. He had a slight smile on his slumbering face as Sarah awakened and observed his praying palms mirroring his soulful peace and contentment. At that moment, Sarah knew he had been talking with the Lord through visions and dreams.

> Who, when he had found one pearl
> of great price, went and sold all
> that he had, and bought it.
> Matthew 13:46

17

One Pearl of Great Price

1812

"Your grandfather Raleigh endured major hardships so that the Pearl may survive. He was there for tribal members' marriages and funerals. He purchased and sold land at an almost feverish pace so that he could leave his aboriginal presence in history. He fought in major militia battles, one of which was the great Yorktown campaign against British general Cornwallis. Your grandfather Raleigh pressed his pillow of death over a decade ago and joined his ancestors, a route that you and I must take in time."

Turner Pinn recited the story of the Pearl's history to his daughter, Polly, who was seven years old, going on eight. She sat on the floor near her father's knees. Being one of the older children, he wanted her to understand the irreplaceable position that his father, Raleigh, had in the tribe. Joicey, his wife, sat patiently and attentively as Turner spoke of the royal heritage of his people. Polly and the other children sat around the fireplace and listened to him. Raleigh, or "Rolly" as some family members often called him, age four, John, age five, Saunders, age six, and Segis, age seven, sat on the bright cedar floor near their dad's left side. Maria, age ten, leaned on a floor pillow near Turner's right side. This was the side to which the elder Maria was placed. Polly earned the position of being the tribal storyteller-elect because of her firm attentiveness and astute interest in her father's heritage stories. Although all the children were listening to Turner as he unfolded the oral heritage of their people, Polly knew that her dad's eye contact with her meant that she would be the chief communicator and the legacy preserver designee. The children, as well as those siblings not yet born, would give heed to future stories just as he rehearsed it to their sister Polly. The other children would be Martha Jane, Betsy, and Lavinia. They too would be able to pass the information on to their children. Polly, however, would become the official tribal storyteller.

"The swamp was very dreary and cold. The people had, by this time, adjusted to the sad and solitary scenes. This had become their home. They had to hide out in the swamps, the dismal swamps, to flee the meanness of the new invaders, the colonists from Europe." Turner enjoyed telling his family about the historic past of the Pearl.

"Polly, your Cherokee ancestors migrated from the west to the Ohio upper waters over a period of many years. They built the Grave Creek mounds near the Ohio River. They migrated eastward over the Allegheny Mountains to Central Virginia to the Peaks of Otter. They moved on along the Appomattox River and had settlements on the riverbanks, and they had their own Cherokee chief. They lived peacefully, except for occasional battles with the northern Indian tribes. We were in a friendly relationship with the Powhatan Indians. God created the aboriginal people from the ground. We were God's special people. We have been protecting his earth because we knew that he removed us from the ground."

Turner continued telling the Buffalo Ridge and Stonewall Mill bands' story and rehearsing their rich legacy since Wiccocomico. "In Iroquoian, our people named themselves *Ani-yun-wiya*, which means 'real people.' The Cherokees always felt that we were and are God's special people. We don't think we are better than anyone else, but we know that God took great care in making us from the dirt. The Wyandot or Huron—who spoke almost the same Iroquoian language as our people and lived in the Great Lakes and St. Lawrence Valley—called the Cherokee people *Uwatayo-rono* or 'cave people' and *Entari ronnon*, which means 'mountain people.' So, Polly, don't forget that you have been formed from clay, anointed clay, created by God."

Turner pointed out that the Cherokees are special. He remembered that his father, Raleigh, more than three decades earlier, used a Bible to make key statements. He picked up the same family Bible and turned to the very familiar section, the Second Epistle to the Corinthians, chapter 4, verses 6 and 7:

> For God, who commanded the light to shine out of darkness, hath shined in our hearts, to give the light of the knowledge of the glory of God in the face of Jesus Christ.
>
> But we have this treasure in earthen vessels, that the excellency of the power may be of God, and not of us.

Turner tried to model his father's style of passing down the living aboriginal heritage. He strained to employ identical tones, styles, and words as those that Raleigh used as he struggled to remember what and how his chief, Raleigh, had passed the stories to his ears. As the current chief, he had the burden to see that the heritage was passed on to the next generation, just as his predecessor had done supremely in his lifetime. Then he put the Bible down and picked up two straight pins.

"Polly, don't forget that you are a precious instrument from your Creator. You are made from clay but have the real treasure not in the clay but within the clay. You have this royal Cherokee heritage, priceless, perfected through the travels of the people, their victories in battle and wars, their sufferings and struggles. We are an amalgamated people, Cherokees/Rechahecrians and Wiccocomicos, composed of the defeated and the victorious peoples. 'We have this treasure in earthen vessels, that the excellency of the power may be of God, and not of us.' Polly, as stated in 2 Corinthians 4:7, let your life, everything you do, show the power of God. Don't let any people—regardless of the color of the clay from which God made them— think that they are better than you are. Help them understand that they are not any better created than you are. God just used lighter or darker clay. Regardless of the color or hue, they are still made out of clay."

Turner called to mind at that moment how his father had a smooth way of preaching as he passed the heritage down to clan members. With glimmers from his father's past methods of making points concretely, he placed two straight pins in his right hand and asked Polly, "What are these?"

"They are pins."

Her father asked her again. "What are these?"

"Pins."

"What are they, Polly?" he asked again. The other children wanted to join the guessing game, but Joicey placed three fingers of her right hand to her lips, signaling them to keep quiet. They complied.

Polly, catching on to her daddy's style of instruction, responded excitedly, "They can be used to stick you!" She sensed that she was closing in on the right answer.

Turner asked her again, "What are they, Polly? You are close."

Polly smiled and stated, "A cross! Put them together and you have a cross."

"You are right, Polly. I wear this type of cross to formal tribal meetings. Why do you think I wear the cross?" questioned Turner. "I know the answer is hard to come by, but I will give you a little hint, like my dad gave me. They represent two things that are special to your grandfather and me."

"The cross reminds me of Christ!" She smiled in assurance that she had the correct response.

"Yes," responded Turner, "but what else? What people are loved with a special love?"

"You have Christian love."

"What people are loved with a special love, Polly?"

"They are the Buffalo Ridge and Stonewall people!"

"You are right, my daughter. You are so right. You too must love them if and when you become their chief or leader. They are special. They have suffered and are in need of protection. The strong must bear the infirmities, or sicknesses, of the weak."

Turner continued his oral history lessons. "When you put the two pins together, they mean more than straight pins to stick in something. They mean closeness and togetherness. They mean unity. They represent this special relationship between the Ridge and Stonewall clans. They are images of two things: our love for God and the love we hold for our fellow man. We wear the two pins as one unit, crossed, representing the cross of Jesus Christ, the symbol of our Christian faith. The pins are crossed, representing the unity that exists between two Cherokee bands, the Ridge and Stonewall people. They also represent unity between the Cherokee and Wiccocomico peoples. The two pins together also symbolize the two bloods that flow through our veins, Cherokee and Wiccocomico."

Turner continued his oral history exercise with his daughter, the potential chief of the united band. He endeavored to be at least half as effective as his father, Raleigh, in passing on the oral stories to Polly and his grandchildren. He prayed that God would give him long life so that he could be a voice and not just a shadowy presence over the next generation—his grandchildren.

"Daddy did not live to share this with you. If Daddy were living, he would really bring out the exciting parts of our history! He was good with historical stories. It was as if you were really there when the events happened. Polly, if only you could have looked on your giant granddaddy! I don't mean he was that tall, even though he was about six feet. I mean that he was a great man of stature." Turner realized that some of his words were probably over Polly's head. She was only seven years old, a little more than his age when Raleigh first started telling him about the band's rich aboriginal legacy.

Turner often questioned whether he would be as great a chief as his father was during his lifetime. Actually, Raleigh's presence was still being felt in the Ridge and in Stonewall over a decade after his death.

Turner reminisced, "Daddy told me that he will be with me in spirit even when he has gone to be with his fathers. As a child, I always wondered how he was going to die in the Ridge and travel all the way to Wiccocomico to be buried with his father and grandfather. Now I realize that he meant he would sleep with his ancestors, in death, in the ground. I still could not understand back then how he was going to protect me on top of the ground when he was buried down in the ground. Now I know that he was talking in symbolic language. He could not be buried with Grandfather Robert, his dad, in Wiccocomico Indian Town, but he was interred here in the Ridge, in the Indian burial ground near the church. The burial ground is older than the church. Dad said he did not know how far that graveyard went back, but maybe as far back as the first time Cherokees traveled through and lived in this area.

"Dad said he would always be here to help me. I guess he meant in spirit, by way of the prayers he sent up on my behalf before he died. I really miss my dad. We have some major issues now and some coming in the future that dad could handle easily, if he were here. He told me about some of the things that were coming to pass in my lifetime. God, I don't know if I can be as strong as he was in dealing with those new issues that are coming. Dad assured me that he and mother had seen them in visions of future events. They were horrible! They were gifted in visualizing things before they even happened. I think they were like Joicey and me when it comes to being mated together. We are equally yoked, and they were made for each other too."

Turner thought about his marriage five years ago, in 1807, and felt sad that his father and mother were not able to attend the wedding. "Only William Sale, Dad's friend, was witness to our wedding. Daddy knew that Joicey would be my wife because he often told me that she was a plump girl, which meant in Daddy's language that she was really comely and eye-filling. He thought she would make me a fitting wife. I remember how pleased Mother and Dad were when Anna and Thomas Evans married in 1795. Thomas's father, Benjamin, and his mother could not be there as witnesses, but Dad and Mother were there, proud as peacocks.

"The Evans family members were well-known Cherokee people in Amherst County, and this marriage was in line with their Cherokee heritage and followed the tendency of Wiccocomico and Cherokee/Rechahecrian people to marry other Cherokees. Some of the Evans family members came from Mecklenburg County to Amherst County sometime after the early 1760s, although the area where the Evans lived was originally a part of the Lunenburg County territory, around Stith's Creek, joining Miles' Creek and the vicinity. They lived privately and later openly Cherokee, as well as other residents in that area.

"Almost ninety years ago, in 1721, our Cherokee people had been living around the present territory of Lunenburg County, in an area that is now Mecklenburg County, not far from the Roanoke River. Although they had been living in sparsely populated areas, the Cherokee people—some believed to be the ancestors of the present-day Evans and some of the other Amherst County Cherokees—decided that they wanted to live openly as a Cherokee tribe for the purpose of trade and boldly appealed to the Virginia Colonial Council for permission to dwell along the Roanoke River. The Council acted on their formal request and responded to the effect that it was not convenient to allow them to live there as a tribe because they might disturb the Northern Indian hunting tribes. The Council pretended that they were worried about tension between the Cherokees and the Northern Indians that could result, but they were really threatened by the prospect of the Cherokees' bold presence as a large tribal settlement in Virginia. The Colonial Council's response came to the petitioners as an eye-winked signal, and the Cherokees understood it clearly. The Council spoke in code, to the effect that the Cherokees could stay in sparsely developed areas in Virginia, with dwellings here and there, but not to try to form Cherokee settlements like the large villages in the Lower towns, Middle towns, Outer towns, Overhill towns, or even like the settlements on the Appomattox River in the 1620s. Cherokees mastered the strategy perfectly in that they continued to live in Virginia and became known as Cherokees only to their respective small hamlet residents, much like the Evanses in Lunenburg County and our people here in the Ridge.

"Those areas near the Roanoke River were loaded with Cherokees, much like those in Amherst and Buckingham

Counties, as their craftiness in living in recessed forest areas and sparsely developed hamlets protected them from assaults by colonists. They lived behind closed doors and among their own kind as Cherokees but acted as just regular white colonists. That is why my daddy knew where the Cherokees dwelled, including the Evanses and the Redcrosses. Now the Evanses and Redcrosses are a part of our family, not just because of recent intermarriages with the Pinns. My deceased mother, Sarah, had Evans and Redcross connections, and now the Evans' and Beverlys' blood runs deeply through our veins. Daddy told me that Charles, Major, and Sarah Evans sold their 120 acres in Mecklenburg County in the early 1760s and moved to Amherst County. He also said that the Redcrosses were interconnected with the Evans family during this same period.

"When you see a Pinn family, you can be assured that there would be some Evanses, Redcrosses, Beverlys, Fergusons, Jenkinses, Sparrows, and others around the corner or living just over the next hollow. Look at how they clustered up in the Amherst Militia! There they were, the names Pinn, Evans, Bollings, and Redcross. You go to the courthouse, look up the land records and, behold, their land bordered each other, but to deceive the more prudent colonists, they separated their land plats by permitting colonists to buy land in between. Even in these cases, they live no further than a hill holler from each other."

Turner talked on, not sure if all his children understood what he was saying. He knew, however, that if he told this story repeatedly over decades, his children would not only remember the heritage, but understand the facts behind the great history.

"Raleigh's presence at the Cherokee nuptials was obvious as he looked on during James Pinn and Nancy Redcross's marriage back in 1799, and he made sure that the county records listed his name. He was there for James Pinn and Nancy Redcross, daughter of John Redcross. He was listed on the document as James Pinn's witness, not parent. He presented himself at the marriage of William Beverley and Eady Pinn, my sister and your aunt, in 1800. This too was an arranged marriage to carry on the Cherokee line with the Beverlys. The Pinns and Beverlys have been close over the years. The Beverley families followed daddy from Buckingham in stages, first one family and then another. He gradually started a Cherokee village in Stonewall Mill. He didn't let the locals catch on or be privy to what his heartfelt plans were. I have to think through every step I take with the tribe. Because the copperheads are out there, hiding in the grass, I have to look down to protect my path, look back to see where I came from, look toward the future to get my bearing, and look up to clear everything with God.

"Daddy stayed in contact with God, as I always saw dad on his knees, praying to the Almighty. There were times when I wondered why a grown man, the great tribal chief Raleigh, had to drop to his knees like a child at nighttime prayer. Even though it took me years to discover the secret, I finally found out why he was so successful with everything he touched: he stayed on his knees! Daddy always said that the humble would be exalted, and the Lord exalted him and our family. He often referred to the Pearl as our family too, and since he loved the Pearl as much as he loved our kin, God also blessed the Pearl. Daddy believed that God called him to this special project of protecting the Cherokees, and he had to yield to the call.

"The Cherokees were miserable, hungry, homeless aboriginal people, constantly coming to the area and looking for a place of refuge. Daddy gave up land, food, raiment, and money to assist, shelter, and protect them. I think Daddy had read the Old Testament and followed the model of the Jewish people. He made the Ridge and Stonewall Mill two villages of refuge, like the cities of refuge in the Old Testament. He always told me that the Pearl was more valuable than money and land, but I never could understand what he meant until I grew older, when he revealed to me how valuable the Pearl really was. Now I am a believer that he had found something priceless! He showed to me words from the Bible to back up his actions: 'When he had found one pearl of great price, he went and sold all that he had and bought it.' Daddy spent a lot of money to help the Pearl, to purchase it. Now I must appreciate its value even more because of Dad and Mother's blood, sweat, and love. It is priceless now!

"I just hope that I can lead this tribe half as well as my father did. He always had that Wiccocomico ruggedness, its strength. I thank God that both groups believed in the one God, Jehovah. The Anglican Church in Wiccocomico taught my father very well. Dad had strong faith in God and assured me that his God would look out for the Pearl and its leaders. He rehearsed to me what his father, Grandfather Robert, explained to him. 'Never give up in life. If you have a God-anointed purpose, trust God to get you through. There are times when you have to sacrifice treasure, time, and talent to keep your focus, but don't give up. Then there is the work part. You have to labor and toil to achieve your life's purpose. Success may require that you have major exertion, stress, and pain, but don't give up. God will be with you if the purpose is united with the will of God. No person or thing can counter the will and work of God. The primary thing is to not give up.'"

Turner strayed from Raleigh's farm practices, as he purchased slaves. Because Raleigh was not alive to warn him that he was straying from his father's belief that the labor and toil must always come from family members and hired servants, not from slaves, Turner made the colossal mistake during his lifetime of developing farm plans that were not in line with his father's wishes. Raleigh believed that God's purpose and plan do not allow or support slave labor.

Looking into Polly's eyes, Turner continued his storytelling. "Polly, I remember, when I was about seven years old that I fell into the James River after leaning over our canoe to untangle my fishing line. Dad allowed me to struggle in the water until I had begun to panic. Then he shouted, 'Son, remember, you have to trust in yourself, your ability to work your own arms and feet, and you must have a strong work ethic. You have to risk leisure in the water. Leisure will contribute to your body drowning in the James.' He was calm, but I was panicky. I could swim a little but quickly began to question my ability to survive in the water. Dad, on the other hand, had confidence in me. He always told me to try to make it in life on my own, and if in trying I failed, he would be there to help me. I didn't know then what he really meant. Anyway, I am struggling in the James and

I can see a watery image of Daddy leaning over the canoe, but only talking and not reaching out his strong arms to help me at all! I got so mad and began struggling, kicking my legs and arms harder and saying to myself that I want to get back into that canoe. I learned to trust in my own abilities, not in Daddy's skills. I somehow managed to get back near the canoe, and then Daddy extended his arms and pulled me in.

"After shaking the water off and thinking about what just happened, I realized that Daddy was really there with me. He was my encouragement. He had, over a seven-year period, begun to make a strong effort to build up my self-confidence. Anyway, he always told me that should I not be able to achieve any goal that I set for myself, he and God would be there to inspire me. The key point that he always meant was that I must try hard first. Without exception, he demanded that I show him that I had self-confidence, put forth work or effort, and risk any and all resources to make sure that I achieved my goal. That achievement spirit is still with me, Polly. Now I know why Daddy didn't jump into the James River to rescue me. He said that any problem had the greatest likelihood of solution when the owner of the problem first assumed the personal mission of solving it. Daddy was a great swimmer. He first learned how to swim in the Wiccocomico River. He knew I was going to assume the responsibility of getting out of the water and trusted in my abilities even if I had moments of doubt, and he patiently taught me a life's lesson during that emergency.

"Now, Polly, I understand what he meant when he told me that I could be the chief. He did not have to be there in the shadows. I wondered, *How can he help me, if he is not standing near me when I need him?* I learned the great lesson of life when he first trained me to make it on my own, while at the same time, he taught me from the Bible, in word and deed, how the Word can be a lamp unto my feet. Before he died, Daddy told me that he had sent up prayers to God on behalf of the Pearl and me. He let me know that he had all the confidence in the world in me, in my work as a tribal leader. I couldn't reason how he had so much confidence in me when I didn't have it in myself. He taught me about life that day in the James River, in the tobacco field, at the kitchen table, around the open hearth. He really knew he had my ears as he and Mother talked about the issues of life while sitting at the table and near the fireplace. He told me that when everything else fails, he and God would be there. He did his part in training me. Now that he has joined his ancestors, his prayers are with me because he sent them up before he died. I am anointed with heavenly warmth because he sent up his nightly prayers on my behalf.

"Polly, I am working hard to teach the customs and heritage of our people to the Pearl. You must do the same if you are to become a leader. Anyway, you have your training requirements with your children. I have much pressure on myself. I must aspire to do right by The Pearl, otherwise I will come up short with The Pearl, God, and Daddy. Daddy had such confidence in me and I do not want to disappoint him. Polly, I know the dead do not have any power in the grave because Daddy taught me that from the Holy Word. I know I cannot disappoint Daddy because he is sleeping with our ancestors, but I just don't want to come up short before his shadowy spirit. His presence is here in our history, our customs, our traditions, and our heritage. Don't you feel it, Polly?"

"Yes, Daddy! I hope my children will feel my spiritual presence when I join my ancestors in the grave."

This response from Polly assured Turner that she had been listening attentively to him and that she understood most of his explanations. "They will, Polly. I am pleased with your interest in our history and culture. You must pass it on, just as it was handed down to you. Don't let the heritage be lost!"

Turner used every opportunity to teach the Pearl's heritage to his children. "Our fathers, who owned the land, were invaded by light-skinned, light-colored clay people from lands beyond the ocean. They were lighter than we are and their skin is not dark in the summer sun. They came in large canoes from England and tried to conquer our people."

Turner instructed Polly in the tribal history lessons for another thirty minutes. Then he reminded her that it was her bedtime. "Are you sleepy, Polly?"

"Just a little. Please keep on telling the story about the big word people, the Wiccoco people and the Re-cha-hec wild people."

"Who else is sleepy? I don't want to put you children to sleep by my long talking. I know these stories may be too much for you now, but if I repeat them every year or two, you will understand them fully."

Maria had almost fallen asleep in her mother's arms by this time, while Raleigh, John, Saunders, and Segis had curled up on the floor in fetal sleeping positions.

"I am not sleepy, Daddy, keep on telling us about the wild people," Maria, half awake, stated.

"They were not wild, Polly and Maria. The colonists were the ones who thought Indians were wild and vicious because they dressed and acted differently than they dressed and acted. They could not ever spell our tribal name correctly. Our people were Cherokees, but the settlers thought they were *Recha* people. Some colonists, who knew who they were, preferred to call them Recha instead of Cherokee. The others called them Chalaque, referring to their foreign speech."

Joicey, who listened patiently as her husband went through his ritualistic orations, became the timekeeper and declared, "Children and Daddy, time is up for storytelling. Lamps go out in five minutes!" Realizing that some of the children did not hear her because they were asleep, she clapped her hands five times and said loudly, "Lamps out in five minutes! This is the last time, children and Daddy! Lamps out in four minutes."

By the time she stated the last "lamps out," all the children had awakened and were moving hastily toward their bedrooms. Turner stood up and began stretching his arms toward the ceiling and yawning drowsily, as if he too had begun getting sleepy.

> Beneath those rugged elms, that yew-tree's shade,
> Where heaves the turf in many a mold'ring heap,
> Each in his narrow cell forever laid,
> The rude forefathers of the hamlet sleep.
> —Thomas Gray, *Elegy Written in a Country Churchyard*

18

Sacred Ground

The long columns of sainted aboriginal remains, submerged and immerged in rich Buffalo Ridge soil, attested to the hallowed, God-fearing spirit of the founders of Fairmount Church and the greatness of the interment site. Those fallen bodies lay resting as if to remind all wise living beholders that physical life is vanity. The entombment site had been there as long as anyone could remember. Raleigh, one of the early ancestors, founded the resting place for tired souls there when he first settled in Rutledge Creek and in the Ridge. Raleigh was interred there and he could no longer speak on some of the now lost secrets of the site's genesis and inauguration. The people in the Ridge were never slaves, as the location had served as a haven for homeless and fleeing Cherokees and Wiccocomicos. This was possibly the last permanent abode for the first mortals. It was a village of refuge for Raleigh, who was really more of the Wiccocomico tribe than Cherokee. No one would argue, however, that Raleigh had a greater abundance of the latter's heritage burning in his chest. The site probably contained remains of several tribes whose hearts were surrendered in like fashion to the Cherokee spirit. Turner adopted the spot for melodic chants with its usual private and reclusive environment, just as Raleigh came here for Christian prayer as well as native chanting. He felt the spirit of the Creator as he chanted before the burial site, just as his father must have done for almost three decades when he sang there.

Tribal members also sought out the quiescent and placid setting at Fairmount Church and the Cherokee interment site, also known as Pinn Park. There is no other place within miles of the Ridge more seemly to reminisce, chant, pray, or meditate than the highly concealed and obscured Pinn Park. Tribal members have used the site for years to rest their burdened bodies on oak logs or stumps near the columns of ancient graves of fallen trailblazers. Innumerable individuals have utilized these serene and pastoral quarters to help facilitate solutions to their problems. Raleigh wore down the grassy trail from his cabin to the site due to his frequent traversing. Raleigh courted Pinn Park's spiritual atmosphere on occasion of all great tribal and personal matters that required serious contemplation. He meditated there as long as mandated and waited on the Lord for permission to leave with solutions to life's problems.

Turner Pinn often resorted to the site when he had been "whipping the donkey." Just as Balaam in the Bible whipped his donkey when his beast tried to warn him against evil deeds that he was committing against the Lord, so Turner was pestered by his conscience because he owned slaves, a fact that was against his father's wishes. He had raging battles within his soul between good and evil. Turner purchased a slave in 1811 and would own four slaves by the mid-1800s.

Raleigh always believed that human beings did not have divine permission to own slaves. He stated on numerous occasions, "No human being should dare own another God-created being." Without Raleigh's guidance, Turner violated his father's wishes that his descendants should refrain from buying and using slaves. Turner's father always suspected that some of those poor miserable African souls were descendants of African tribal royalty, as he himself descended from royal Wiccocomico aboriginal heritage and possibly also Cherokee royal ancestry.

Raleigh endeavored endlessly to retain his regal heritage, and he did not look kindly on anyone who tried to take away another person's ancestral legacy and independence. He knew that those slaves, after one or two generations of institutional acculturation, lost much of their African tribal heritage. Raleigh always seized opportunities to share a history lesson with his family to protect their history.

Here is one such lesson: "Our Native Americans were keenly aware that African visitors came to the Americas before the first Caucasian explorers. They did not, however, attempt to control the lives of the aboriginal people like the colonists," Raleigh often told his family as he repeated the oral history lessons. "Some of those dark-skinned visitors may have remained long enough to mingle their blood with our peoples. Whether they were Moors or another African ethnic group, they came."

Raleigh shared this with his children so that they would not be naïve enough to place dark-clay human creatures below those of lighter hues made by the Creator.

"Whether they were chocolate, brown, or black, the fact that they came over the ocean meant that they were ahead of the others. Africans valued life by placing esteem on the earth, the animate, and the inanimate. Life was not worth living if that required them to deny the very earth from which their clay composition and hues came. The Africans were in unison with the earth like our people are. They were the first to forge iron from the ground, cultivate some seeds, and develop music. I have heard about their great cultures: Ghana, Songhay, Timbuktu, and Mali. Numerous Negro peoples were a part of and influenced the great cultures of Egypt and Ethiopia. Negro explorers and slaves were with the first Spanish and Portuguese visitors to the Americas, and some stayed while others went back to their native lands. We must be respectful as some of their blood may be flowing through our aboriginal American veins. Devaluing those dark souls because of their skin hue will, in effect, lower our own self-esteem. We are somewhat dark like those souls and we must not let the colonists' color consciousness and social values affect our ways.

"In African countries white colonists are sometimes viewed with the same level of disdain due to their light, pale color, as local colonists viewed dark people in America. I am diverting this oral history lesson to deal with a current problem in America. This institution of slavery has taken a hold on the throats of the dark people. The colonists tried to enslave our aboriginal people, but we knew every molehill and rabbit hole in the area. They knew that it would be futile to attempt to corral us and therefore sought the hardworking, earth-bound African people—those great ironworkers, stonemasons, planters, and boatmen—who were removed from their natural lands in Africa. The colonists sought free labor even if it meant buffeting the Holy Spirit's warnings to their hearts."

Raleigh shared this history lesson not as a part of the usual aboriginal oral family history but as a hint of caution to his children and a word to the wise against ambitious ideas of owning human beings. Native Americans respect the earth, including animate and inanimate materials that have been formed by their Creator from the soil.

Several Buffalo Ridge tribal members participated in the slave merchandising institution, including James and Turner Pinn. Aboriginal members of the western Amherst tribe also owned slaves during the early to mid-1800s.

Raleigh maintained that the land, especially the Ridge soil, was sacred. In his eyes, the land was blessed with beauty because it yielded not only plant food in the ground, like sweet and white potatoes, turnips, beets, and onions, but also innumerable vegetables above ground. He was a seasoned, successful farmer, as reflected in his skillful work with the soil and plants and his harvests always provided quality produce for the household as well as for the market. His market revenue tendered sufficient pounds to support his family adequately, with revenue left over for investment. He entrusted his funds in land, as he had observed the way British settlers in Wiccocomico drooled over the prospect of acquiring colonial property. Raleigh also noticed Amherst and Buckingham Counties colonists' envious reactions at the prospects of real estate ownership. These continuous observations branded powerful impressions in developing Raleigh's personal values to the extent that he almost became a greedy real estate entrepreneur himself. Raleigh made up his mind that he would not let the colonists' slave institution epidemic spread to Buffalo Ridge and infect his God-anointed conscience as long as he lived.

Raleigh regarded the earth as a foundation on which a skillful builder can construct a fine home and considered Buffalo Ridge soil an ideal spot for his home and eagerly sought out real estate for that purpose. There were sloping hills and flat lands with plentiful game. He enjoyed looking down from the Ridge on the winding James River with its magnetic power to attract creatures of the earth—deer, bears, beavers, and others—as well as its hospitality in hosting fish of all types. He could think of no other topography that was closer to its Creator in all of Amherst County or even Virginia, including that Cherokee aboriginal haven, the Holston River section in Southwestern Virginia.

He felt that the earth's plant life and plentiful supply of water had natural ways of attracting all varieties of game—deer, rabbits, raccoons, bears, and other animals—to its bosom. Raleigh knew enough about agriculture to recognize that the death of these same creatures provided excellent fertilizer for crops. Actually, he did a superb job of communicating to others that the earth's food cycle has to be respected.

Chief Raleigh stressed to his family, in his later years, the sacredness of the earth in welcoming aged and sickly human remains to its abode for honorable repose. He often stated, in his usual Anglo-adopted style of speaking: "Those carnivorous vultures, the buzzards, have other, less noble animal sacrifices to consume. Therefore, mother earth steps forward and invites human victims to her restful embrace."

Turner's mind took him back to his father's funeral service during which the preacher stressed the importance of the earth. "Earth to earth, ashes to ashes, dust to dust."

His mother, Sarah, deposited a rose petal on the casket in the grave when the preacher said "earth to earth." Turner dropped a rose petal on the preacher's "ashes to ashes" command, and finally, Sarah deposited the last petal with the words "dust to dust." Turner remembered and meditated on his thoughts during the interment ceremony. *My heart also seemed to float down on the coffin as the petal floated, flipping to the left and back to the right, as if it did not want to make contact with the top of the casket. I could not understand why my father chose to retreat to the ashes, to the earth, and to the dust when he was really needed back here in Buffalo Ridge. Why did he have to go at that time? Why couldn't God let him stay a little longer?*

Then Raleigh's words from the past came to him. "When people die, mother earth steps forward and invites human victims to her restful embrace."

Turner realized that his daddy faithfully sought the sacred earth, the substance created by God and from which he made man. Earth was there to remind his tired soul to return to its genesis and Creator. The soil existed as a reminder to the living souls in attendance at the committal ceremony that the current funeral ceremony was a stunning dress rehearsal for their own future funeral services.

Turner thought about the words that the Fairmount Baptist preacher spoke, which were used by Anglican, and later Episcopalian, leaders:

> "Lord, thou hast been our refuge, from one generation to another. Before the mountains were brought forth, or ever the earth and the world were made, thou art God from everlasting, and world without end.
> Thou turnest man to destruction; again thou sayest, Come again, ye children of men.
> For a thousand years in thy sight are but as yesterday; seeing that is past as a watch in the night."

Then the preacher stated,

> "Forasmuch as it hast pleased Almighty God, in his wise providence, to take out of this world the soul of our deceased friend and tribal chief, Raleigh, we therefore commit his body to the ground, earth to earth, ashes to ashes, dust to dust, looking for the general resurrection in the last day, and the life of the world to come, through our Lord Jesus Christ."

I wonder if Daddy in his earlier days, as he disliked anything that was British, would have appreciated the use of the Old English words at his funeral. I am satisfied that he was pleased with the preacher's selection of words since Daddy had "mellowed" his disposition toward "everything that was English." He began to appreciate, in time, English people for their major contribution to the colony of Virginia and America. He dealt with his ethnic hatred of the English people. The Lord allowed him to return to himself, his Maker, with a clear conscience and a love for his fellow man. Thank you, Lord, for allowing him to join his ancestors with a clean heart. Thank you for giving my daddy the hope of resurrection. He always said that he was "looking for the general resurrection in the last day, and the life of the world to come, when Christ will, in his second coming, judge the world, and the earth and the sea shall give up their dead."

I am glad that the ground cannot grasp my father's remains forever. Daddy and I used to despise the job of removing tree stump roots that had grown around a large rock. I understand that the earth grapples with forces that try to take away that which belongs to her. Earth, you will give up Raleigh in that great resurrection day! He has to come forth to meet his Savior, Jesus Christ! You will give up those souls in the cemetery who sleep in Christ Jesus!

It was a sad, cloudy day as we left the interment site at Buffalo Ridge's cemetery. Mother walked from the gravesite, as if an anvil was weighing down her heart. There were moments when I could hardly hold her up. Raleigh was her life on earth. She couldn't bear to leave him there in the ground even though the site was his favorite place for repose and meditation. Mother said that he wouldn't have to "tread the pathway from the cabin to the burial ground anymore for prayer. He will have a permanent place there until the great day of resurrection. He will be comforted in his grave with the hope that God will not leave him there."

He remembered two years earlier, in 1810, when the U.S. Census taker visited his home in the Ridge. He asked Turner for certain vital information.

"I have a household of eight people. They are my six children, my wife Joicey, and me, Turner Pinn."

"I don't need to know their names," he remarked.

Turner sensed the census taker was surprised that a man of color had been so prosperous, so he proudly stated his children's names anyway. "My six children are Segis, Maria, Martha Jane, Polly, Saunders, and John."

Turner thought, *He may have wondered whether we were Caucasian, Indian, or black. I am dark brown and was much darker in the summer when he came to take the census. I volunteered information to let him know that our aboriginal people, dark as we are, go back for thousands of years in Northumberland and Lancaster Counties in Virginia, and along the southeastern area of America. I told him that we were both Wiccocomico and Cherokee Indians. Daddy didn't like that "Indian" word, but I figured the census worker would not understand the words "aboriginal American." I have worked hard in the Ridge to support my large family and I give praise to God for His blessings. It has not been always easy for me, but with God's help, I have survived.*

Turner continued to follow in his father's footsteps as he trod the pathway to the cemetery to pray, meditate, and chant. He also went to certain locations in the general area for health herbs, just as his father and mother did for decades.

Turner meditated on the Ridge's herbal traditions. "The sacred ground within miles of the grave has the 'balm of Gilead' herbs. The Ridge's herbal plants are essential for Cherokee *nun-wa-ti* medicine. Whether we used the azalea or rhododendron's twig, peeled and boiled, in a poultice, to rub on rheumatism or cherry bark tea for coughs and colds, the Ridge provided the 'balm of Gilead.'"

After the family finished eating lunch, Turner asked Joicey to get the family ready for an herb-hunting trip. "We will leave in about fifteen minutes. Make sure that you bring the four baskets that Mother Sarah made. Bring two of the large cane strips baskets and two of the honeysuckle vine baskets. Bring the cane ones, the red ones that we dyed with the pokeweed berries."

As they were walking to the woods, with Turner and Joicey leading the way and the children following, Turner began his lecture on the Ridge's tribal herbal heritage. Turner felt that this was fitting as a start to the botany lesson.

"My daddy, Raleigh, and mother, Sarah, were skilled medicine makers. When Daddy went hunting or while he and mother were farming, he killed two birds with one stone. What I mean by this saying, 'two birds with one stone,' is that my parents were able to hunt medicine plants while doing other jobs, like hunting, picking apples, or farming. He would be on the lookout for herbs in the bushes or woods. Other times, urgent times or when he had used up the herbs, he went to the woods for particular plants, roots, berries, nuts, and tree bark.

"Children, back when I was about nineteen, George Washington and his staff started an Indian policy called 'civilization.' They saw aboriginal American people, us, as something bad, uncivilized, and even thought our cultures were old-fashioned and useless. They believed that their ways of life were better than ours and demanded that we give up our lifestyles in favor of their ways. Keep in mind now, they were the new people, the settlers, and they were asking—no, demanding—that we, the aboriginal people, drop our ways. The guests were telling the hosts what we must do or else. Some of the whites even recommended that our native people marry colonists so that our race and ways would disappear!

"This is one of the reasons that you are here today in the woods. Children, I need to show you what our people have known for thousands of years and the colonists still do not know. Your daddy wants to make sure that you do not give up the old aboriginal ways, the medical herbal secrets. I promised my daddy, and he promised his daddy, and his daddy promised his daddy before him. You understand what I am saying. We promised our ancestors that we would pass the Indian ways on to our descendants. We will not give up our aboriginal customs even if the Great White Father Washington wants us to. We do not need to marry white people to hide our race and ways. History needs to know about our glorious, wise ancestors.

"Our people are one with the earth. The colonists demand we give up our ways if we want to have peace with them. How can we give up customs that mirror the unity between our people, the soil, and the plants? When we are sick with a cold, we can go to mother earth and she tells us to choose the best remedy. We have so many earth choices. Mother Joicey can pull some onions from mother earth and make a poultice. If she couldn't find an onion, the soil would speak up and say, 'Here is some garlic. Make a poultice for the body to cure the croup.' Or she could select locust honey and cherry bark and mix up a fine tea for that cold and cough. She could get some mustard and make a poultice for the croup. Mother could grind up poplar root and bark for a tea for that fever or cook some poplar bark for cough syrup. Even the peach trees will call to you to select its bark for your cough or make peach tea for the fever. The cherry bark tea will also cure your fever. Children, I need you to pass this on to your children and they to their children. Don't you forget what I am telling you! You cannot break the oral heritage cycle. You must pass it on!

"Even dogs, bears, deer, and other animals are one with the earth. They know which plants are meant for their body's ills also. We once had a dog, Cocoa. A swarm of hornets landed on her body, on her nose, and side. As a child, I watched her from the front porch. Do you know what she did? Polly? Saunders? Segis? John?" Turner asked.

Saunders shouted, "She ate some plants! Daddy, she looked for some medicine to help her!"

"Yes, Saunders, she did, but how?"

John questioned, "Laid on the ground, in the dirt?"

Raleigh listened attentively as he looked toward Saunders and nodded in support of his answer.

"Wallowed on the ground?" Segis exclaimed.

"John and Segis, dogs lie and roll on the ground sometimes when they have bruises and cuts because they know that God has some stuff in the dirt that will heal the wound. This dog did more than wallow. What else did she do?"

Polly stated, doubtfully, "Laid down on the tobacco plants?"

"You are all correct! Cocoa went to the tobacco field and wallowed all over my daddy's tobacco plants. I started to chase him out of the field, but daddy Raleigh made me stop. He said, 'Turner, Cocoa is teaching us a life's lesson in herbal medicine. He got stung with the hornets, didn't he?' I answered, 'Yes, Daddy.' He said, 'Then, leave him alone because he is showing us what we should do when the hornets sting us.'" Turner then asked, "When you get stung, Segis, what would you do to stop the pain?"

"I would wallow in the tobacco field," Segis asserted.

"No, you are a human. You would not wallow, but you would come in the house and tell us, and we would put some tobacco juice on the stung places. Our Indian people are close to the earth. I said 'Indian.' My daddy did not like to use that word because he said we are not Indians. He told us that India is near China, and we are not people from India or China. Some people say we look somewhat like the Chinese, a little darker, but we are not Indians! Our people are one with nature and the earth. The earth will cure you of all your physical ills, if you will only allow your body to be in balance with the earth. Just as God's spirit will help you with your spiritual ills, God has given the soil, plants, and animals all that we need to be healthy,"

"When Cocoa had bowel problems, he ate grass. Do you know why?" Joicey inquired.

"The earth's plants were there to break up the bowels," Saunders replied. He remembered that his mother made him eat okra when he was constipated. "Mother, you always give me boiled okra, that slimy stuff, when I stop up."

"What does it do for you, Saunders?"

"It helps me, Mother. I am not stopped up anymore!"

"Why do I give you blackberry and mulberry cobbler when you are stopped up?" Joicey asked.

"To help my stopped bowels, you give me blackberry and mulberry cobbler."

"It is the blackberry and mulberry seeds that make you go, not the cobbler. I also give mulberry bark tea to all of you at times. Guess why?" Joicey continued.

Segis raised her hand and stated, "To help our bowels."

"Yes, children. You understand how important plants are to our bodies. The earth and soil know what our bodies need and want to give us those plants to ease our pain," Joicey said.

Turner continued his life's lessons. "Dogs and bears are in oneness with nature. Nature, through God, tells the animals what to do for their sick bodies. Animals have instincts. Nature gives us plants to help us control our bowels when they run. What plant can we eat to stop runny bowels?"

Polly shouted, "Dogwood tea and grape leaf tea."

"You are correct, Polly," Joicey said. "I give you creasy greens, turnip greens, and pokeweed. These plants help keep your bowels regulated. They also give you strength from the soil. There are other plants out there that the earth gives us for our protection. We will tell you what they are at the right time. We don't want to clog up your mind now with too much stuff. Do you remember, Daddy told you to bring certain types of baskets on our herb-finding trip today? He did this to show you that the earth is good to us. She gives us honeysuckle vines for some of the baskets, cane for other baskets, and oak branches for other types of baskets. Daddy also gave you a hint about the color. He reminded you how we tinted the baskets. We use certain plants from the earth to put color on the basket, like the pokeberry dye. We also use walnut dye and many other plants for our baskets. Daddy uses different plant dyes to tint the oak and pine furniture that he makes. Children, the earth is inviting you to choose plants for your health, food, weapons, and tools. Today, each of you must pick at least three plants that we have talked about and place them in your baskets. We will not go home until you find the right plants, those that we have talked about today. The earth is calling on you to store up medicinal herbs for those times when you need them."

"Children, you are smarter than the colonists on these matters of herbal health," Turner explained. "Most settlers don't know about plant uses for medical cures, those that you have just learned about the last hour. Can you believe that George Washington wants us to put away our customs and adopt their ways? If we lose our oneness and balance with mother earth, we will be lonely and sickly. If we have been rude to her and separated from her during our lifetime, how dare we knock on earth's grave door for rest when we are sick to death? Native people are close to the soil, to the air, and to the river. Saunders, do you know what I plan to do with that large pine log behind the barn?"

"I thought you were going to make firewood out of it."

"What am I doing with the great poplar log beside it?"

"You are making a canoe out of that one."

"Yes. I am going to make a canoe out of the pine log also."

"Daddy, I didn't think pine logs could be used for canoes. You and I have been chipping out and burning the poplar one to make a canoe to take the trip down the James River. We have worked on that one for almost a year, slowly hollowing it out. When it is ready, we will travel down the James to the tribal meeting at Stonewall Mill."

"Children, for your information, there are several trees in the Ridge that are good for canoes, just as there are several types of wood that are good for bow and arrow making. I normally use locust wood, but I also could just as easily use other types of durable materials. There are many types of fowl feathers that we can use for the tails of arrows. When turkey or chicken feathers are not available, I may use other fowls' feathers. Our people have always known how to listen to the earth for cues. Listen children, listen carefully, and you will hear different leaves say to us, 'I can ease your toothache pains.' You listen and the earth will tell you to find dandelions. You dig up some roots and chew them for a toothache. You can even chew the dogwood bark for headaches. It will help most aches, including backaches. You are not old enough yet for backaches, but wait a little while. I know you wonder why I don't cut down dogwood trees when I am clearing planting fields. Well, they have been loaned to us from the earth to help our ills. You can even make a tea from it for diarrhea.

"There are also some rattlesnakes and copperheads among the trees and plants. God gave us the plants and trees, but he wants us to have common sense when we use them. With the black walnut tree over there, there are some good and some bad. It has ingredients in it to relieve your toothache, but you have to be careful with the bark because parts of it are poisonous. I don't want you striplings fooling around with it unless you are with me. You know what I am talking about. We all love poke salad, but Joicey makes you children get out of the way when she is preparing it. Why do you suppose she is so nervous? There are some poisonous parts in it—the roots and stems. Your mother cooks the small, young leaves. She boils them over and over and over. Then she fries the boiled greens in bacon grease."

Polly, holding on to her daddy's leg, said, "Daddy, poke salad is good. I love it."

Turner responded, "Yes, we all enjoy the greens. They are almost as good as cress greens. You just have to pick the leaves, wash and cook them very well, and then fry them in the bacon or ham grease. The black walnut tree gives us good nuts, beautiful wood for furniture and flooring, dye, and medicine for pain, but parts of it are very poisonous. You have to be careful with the poke and the black walnut, just like the black widow spider. It has a colorful red hourglass, but if you touch it, you will definitely find out that there are danger zones. The spider's bite will make you sick. That is why you need to stay close to mother earth and listen to her as she tells you the sweet secrets of earthly existence. The earth has been set apart for us to enjoy and go back to when we die. We should never worship any material on, from, or in the earth, as that would be against the Lord's second commandment: 'Thou shalt not make unto thee any graven image.' The Lord made the land and set it apart for us. Children, stay close to the earth, as close as you see Mother and Daddy hugging it. Children, your mother and I have completed our earth lesson. Children, as soon as you find three herbal plants for your baskets, we will head home. So, start looking!"

> "Polly Pinn a free woman of colour aged
> twenty three years rather dark mulatto
> complexion about five feet nine inches in
> height, has a mole in the left hand
> near the wrist, born free."
> —Amherst County Courthouse, 27 October 1828

19

Free People of Color Registration

November 1830

"Family, our people, the purer bloods, were sometimes darker complexioned with straight black hair. Since census takers couldn't say some of our folk were Caucasian or black, they started calling us mulatto. This is strange, because at times, like the last two decades when my daddy and I paid Amherst County personal and real estate taxes, they listed us as white. We, the Pinn line, are generally almost full Indian. Your beloved mother Joicey is lighter complexioned, although she has some white and Indian in her. White people don't quite get that we existed since antiquity. They unwisely think that, in 1608, when John Smith and the other English explorers visited our Wiccocomico people, along with the Chickacone and the Onawmanient, that this was the beginning of our chronicle."

Turner had so much to share with his family. Even though his children were much older now and could absorb more information than they could as young children, he still had to be prudent in how he told the tribal histories. Chief Pinn had to keep up their interest throughout the narrative, as well as to interject key words to help them retain the essence of the oral histories in their memories.

Turner Pinn spoke to tribal members at Fairmount Baptist Church near the bank of Porridge Creek at around 1:30 p.m., following the first Sunday morning worship service in November. Fairmount held their worship services twice monthly, on the first and third Sundays. The weather was partly cloudy with a strong chill as the wind blew leaves strongly against the log church. The wintry breeze forced the crisp leaves to make tapping noises on the church's logs and window panes, as if the ticking sounds highlighted the timely importance of the tribal meeting occurring inside. Approximately forty-six adult members remained after the third Sunday worship service for the tribal meeting. He had to bring his followers up on the county, state, and national social issues. Those issues that related directly to the Ridge and Stonewall Mill needed special mention.

The tribal members, dressed in their best Sunday clothes, sat patiently and attentively as they listened to their tribal chief, Turner Pinn. Standing in the center of the sanctuary in front of his audience, on floor level, he wore a black suit with a white shirt that he buttoned at the neck and a bow tie. He was tall, lean, and distinguished as he opened the meeting. He commenced the lecture with some tribal history, or edifications as he called it, before he led into the meat of his talk, the "admonitions."

"The Cherokee people, the other part of our mortal dust, existed long before Hernando de Soto's expedition, when he explored the Cherokee towns. Some of our Cherokee people lived in the towns, in close existence with their family and friends, while others lived in single and small group homes beyond the main Cherokee towns. Our people were not just in the North Carolina and Tennessee Middle, Valley and Out towns. They lived in Tennessee Overhill towns, and the South Carolina and Georgia Lower towns. They dwelled in isolated homes in the wooded forests, even beyond the major Cherokee towns, wherever they had land to settle on and were free from problems with the colonists. They were even in Virginia and on many occasions, in order to survive, they had to act like they were white or black. My daddy knew the ones in Virginia that were related to us. Some of our family moved back and forth from

Southwestern and Central Virginia, in Floyd and other towns in Southwest Virginia. They kept up their family connections with their people in major towns and in the outlying areas.

"Our people now have so many colors. Some tribal members are mixed bloods, some are almost pure blood, some dark-complexioned pure bloods, while others have lightened up because of the Caucasian mixture. Your mother Joicey can verify that! Even though she has some white within her, she is almost all-Indian in attitude and behavior. You just let her get angry with you because you tread on her bad side and watch what she does. The aboriginal response, the intolerance with foolishness from others, would show its ugly head in her action toward you!"

The tribal members laughed, but quickly settled down as they were not sure how much liberty that Chief Pinn meant for them to take after his rather amusing remarks. They remembered that they were in a tribal meeting, as well as in a church building, and immediately displayed their serious side.

"Family, we are aboriginal people, from antiquity. You can look at Joicey's family line on all sides. Look at my line, my paternal and maternal grandparents. You cannot miss the aboriginal connections! Daddy and Mother had dreams and visions years ago about what the European people would do to us after they settled firmly in America. My parents dreamed of the future, our present time and beyond. They had a feeling that European settlers were going to interfere with our rights, as they would try to change our aboriginal ways. Those colonists, as my parents predicted, have already begun a process to call all our people colored, those who are not of so-called pure European blood. All free non-whites, blacks, and Native Americans have been lumped into this colored category whether they have some European blood or not. Now there is this devious scheme to dump all races or ethnic groups into only two groups, either you are white or colored.

"Decades ago, Daddy and Mother were able to peep into the future, and they told me that this would happen. I expect that the colonists will eventually move Indian and all other non-white people from the colored to black classification. The color changes that they are concocting are not the issue that upsets me. Given the fact that many of our purer blood people are dark, what makes me mad is the fact that they are trying to make 'black' equal to 'slave' descendants. They are trying to put all dark people on a negative social level, that of being a slave. None of our people here in the Ridge or in Stonewall Mill or in Wiccocomico has ever been children and grandchildren of slaves, so why throw us into that servant category?

"I had to report to the courthouse in late September 1828. The clerk wrote down the fact that I was a 'free man of dark-brown complexion.' They wrote other stuff, like the fact that I am tall, 'five feet ten inches high, aged forty-six, and born free.' He even added the statement that I had a 'scar over the right eye.' They knew that they had better write on that courthouse register paper the note that I have always been free. I didn't want to lose my religion by fighting in that courthouse and give them a reason to lock me up.

"My daddy has always been free. My granddaddy has always been free, although my daddy served periods of indentured servitude during his early years as a Wiccocomico aboriginal child. My great-granddaddy and all his ancestors have always been free! Our people have been free since antiquity! Now I have to carry this paper, this pass, around like I am a freed slave! I know how upset daddy would be if they tried this when he was alive. I know what they did! They waited until daddy died, that great Revolutionary War soldier, and then made that law. They didn't enact them until he went to the grave to join his ancestors. The officials knew that he had a reputation for having descended from Wiccocomico aboriginal royalty and fought for America's freedom from England. They had to get him out of the way before they dared ask aboriginal people to justify why they were walking around Virginia as free people.

"I was not freed a little before 1806, the date that the law specifies to consider people of color really free. I have always been free, both by ancestry and deep in my heart, and I do not need a 'pass' to let people know that I was free before 1806. Like the eagle among the other birds, my ancestry and my heart testify to my freedom. They can't make me leave the colony and they better not try to make any of you, my children and tribal members, leave the colony. Colonists should think twice before tampering with the Pearl, with the idea of forcing any of you to leave the colony. We've always been free, children and descendants of people who have been free since antiquity, and they only need to look at me and know that I am real aboriginal American!

"I took you, Saunders, with me that day to the courthouse, as I remember it to the day, on September 26, 1828. I let them register you because I didn't want a slave-hungry colonist, weeks later, laying his devilish hands on you, as if you were a slave or a freed slave, demanding to see a 'pass' that you may not have had in your pocket at the time. I saw what the official wrote on you, Saunders. He said you were a free man, dark in complexion, about six feet tall and twenty-two years old. He even recorded that Saunders did not have a scar on his head, face, or hands. Can you believe that? He tried to notice marks on us, like he was getting ready to capture us if we broke their laws or something. I don't know what they were doing! They knew that the Pinns, Beverlys, Sparrows, and others have been free since antiquity. We don't need 'passes.' This is a sad age to live in!"

The tribal members leaned forward in awe and respect for the deep knowledge that Turner possessed. Even though they had heard this talk before, their chief's words were different and just as interesting and fresh today as when they first heard his lecture. Turner looked at Polly and then turned to the audience as he continued to speak.

"Polly, in the last part of October, you had your turn to register in Amherst County. Do you know why? It was to let the European descendants know who the aboriginal people are and who the freed slaves are. Eventually, these two groups will become one group, Negro or black. They have the idea that non-whites, whether Native Americans or free Negroes, should not be free to walk around Amherst County, or even Virginia, without official records housed in the county clerk's office. Why should we, aboriginal American citizens, present a 'pass' to document our aboriginal freedom to these newcomers, the settlers, to certify that we have legal permission to exist in Amherst County? The aboriginal people of Virginia are the hosts, not the visitors, so why did the colonists become the hosts and we the guests? My daddy fought in Yorktown to win freedom for America from the British. Can you believe this? Now those very relatives of British people—that daddy, his brother Robert Pinn and his three sons, Thomas Evans, John Redcross, Sylvanus Beverly, Jacob and John Banks, and others fought—are demanding that we explain why we have the right to be here and own land in Amherst County, as if we are dirty objects that they would rather not have around.

"Members, you may not know, but I think I told you many times that more than some twenty years ago, Virginia's legislators passed a law, in 1806, to get rid of the free Negroes in the state. The colonists were getting scared of freed slaves, the fact that they were getting too plentiful. They had brought them to our land in great numbers and later realized that those slaves who received their freedom presented a problem for the colony. This law led to this 'pass' system. All Negro slaves who were freed by their slave masters after May 1, 1806, and stayed here in this colony more than twelve months after freedom must give up their freedom. They could be put back into slavery by being sold again. The money from a slave sale would go to those so-called county poorhouses for their maintenance of poor people or the re-enslaved souls would have to work for the poorhouses in the counties.

"It is sad that they would use such a law, putting freed slaves back into slavery, under the pretense of helping the poorhouses' officials acquire funds to operate their houses to help the poor. Have you ever heard of such going around the barn to do what they could have done by just going through the barn in the beginning? If the state leaders didn't want to free those African people in the first place, why did they allow slave masters to free them in Virginia? It is sad that they would go so far as to develop a sneaky plan to make freed Negroes hurry up and get out of Virginia, or else. If, after twelve months of freedom in Virginia, the freed persons had not left the colony, the souls would be re-enslaved. They would make profit off the backs and sweat of re-enslaved, God-created beings.

"The overseer of the poorhouse had the power to make money by putting the freed slave back into slavery. To keep from 'whipping the donkey' or feeling guilty, to keep from whipping their consciences because they were re-enslaving free men and women, the officials pretended that they would use the money for the purpose of the needy. What does securing money for a poorhouse have to do with re-enslaving poor, innocent human beings who want to stay in Virginia?

"Guess what? In 1826, Virginia realized that they made a mistake with that stupid legislation and the state legislators changed the law. The poorhouse officials lost their power to catch freed slaves who remained in Virginia beyond a year, and the county sheriff replaced the poorhouse overseer as the person who had the authority to capture and sell a slave who has been free for more than twelve months.

"Now the law makes us, aboriginal Americans, somewhat like freed slaves. We too as free non-whites, have to get a pass to explain to the whites that we have legal permission to be in Virginia! My daddy and mother saw these evils coming years ago—that officials would try to make us feel like we owe them something. Their visions have come to pass, as we, Virginians who descend from people of antiquity, are now made to feel like we don't have a right to be in this colony. I dare them to find records of the Pinns being slaves, and I challenge them to attempt to put our people—Beverlys, Sparrows, Fergusons, Evanses, Bollings, McCoys, Cousinses, and other Pearl—in that awful social slave institution. Have you ever heard of such deception with that pass or registration law? The level of their cunning is amazing!

"First, I registered to make sure that it was all right for the other Pearl to participate in that new registration process, and a few days ago I also asked Joicey to register. The official wrote down in his court records the fact that Joicey was my wife and that she was of rather light complexion, stout built, born free, and aged about forty-five. I know that official spotted her stocky, pretty build. I should have taken her to the courthouse last month with me when I registered, to look at the roaming eyes of that record official."

The audience burst forth with loud laughter, and just as quickly as they laughed, they stopped. They were careful not to disrespect their chief's lecture.

"I sent the rest of my family—William, John, Raleigh, Polly, and Martha Jane—to register on the 27th of October 1828. Tribal members, you listen to me! Due to the fact that this register and other court records will follow our descendants through hundreds of years, my daddy told me to make sure that I document the Pearl on as many of the white people's official documents as I can. I promised him that I would do this and you owe it to Raleigh and me to keep the Pearl's documentation going through the generations! You hear me!

"I will meet soon with the tribal clan leaders of Stonewall Mill and Buffalo Ridge to give them more details about this law. I know daddy always kept both groups informed, as his daddy stayed alert to the connivance of the colonial officials. I have already told some of the Ridge's members to go register and I will order the other family members to go to the courthouse over the next two or three years. The Stonewall Mill family members have to go to Buckingham Courthouse to register. We will not have as much hostility directed at our group in Buckingham County because my daddy was and I am close to many of those officials who know that we are royalty, and that our people descend from great Cherokee, Wiccocomico, and Powhatan peoples. Actually, there are a bunch of people of influence in Buckingham who are going for white but pride themselves in being descendants of Pocahontas and Cherokees. Some of the Megginsons, the Bollings, and the Fergusons are connected with aboriginal people. I feel sure that they would protect our people over there because we all are related to each other. In Amherst County, and to an extent even in Buckingham County, we still must be careful as registrants, and we need to spread it out so that the colonists do not think I am forming a Cherokee or Wiccocomico tribe here in the county. We should not go in waves, but register one, two, or three at a time."

Maria—who married Bartlett "Sparrowhawk" Sparrow on December 28, 1827—eventually registered on October 11, 1831. Turner's other three daughters, Segis, Betsy, and Lavinia, went to Amherst with Maria and registered after Christmas on the same date, December 28. The registration clerk at the courthouse continued to note distinguishing characteristics of the registrants. He recorded that Lavinia "was the daughter of Turner Pinn, very light complexion for a Negro, or perhaps more properly a very dark mulatto, five feet eight and three quarter inches high, about sixteen years of age with a scar on the back of the right hand occasioned by a burn." They were beginning to put Native Americans into the Negro category.

The Beverlys, Sparrows, and Pinns continued their intermarriage traditions. John, the son of William Beverly and Eady Pinn Beverly, married Lavinia, daughter of Turner and Joicey, before Christmas on December 21, 1860. William Beverly's first wife was Eady Pinn. He married his second and present wife, Judith Sparrow Beverly on July 4, 1827. Segus Sparrow, daughter of Bartlett and Maria Pinn Sparrow, married F. C. Beverly, son of Rita Beverly of Appomattox County. Jonathan Beverly was the strong Beverly clan leader who kept an eye on the Beverly clan for Chief Turner Pinn. He passed tribal news on to Polly Beverly's family members, including Aldridge, Anthony, Mary, Henry, Lucy, and Elizabeth, or Betsy as she was called, and the rest.

Jonathan Beverly showed his shadow on official court records when Chief Turner could not be there. Polly Beverly did her best to pass down strong tribal heritage and history to her family, just as the other Polly, Polly Pinn, would as she grew in knowledge, age, and wisdom.

They named their children after ancestors, occasionally throwing an aboriginal first name on one of the children in the family, like Pocahontas, Powhatan, or Delaware, to leave cues for later generations. The name "Pinn" gradually became synonymous with pure Native American, as they were hailed proudly among the aboriginal people as the only officially recorded "Native American" Yorktown battle revolutionary soldiers. "Raleigh" became a common name among the Buffalo Ridge band. The first name "Turner" also gradually grew in popularity among the clans, as clan leaders were also pleased with Turner's leadership over the Pearl.

The family members continued to document the Pearl's activities on official court records in obedience to the wishes of Raleigh and Turner. During tribal meetings, Turner emphasized the importance of registering at the courthouse even though it was demeaning to the Pearl members. Although the Ridge registrants normally did not have to have their bodies checked for distinguishing characteristics, Turner thought their inspections were going too far anyway when they checked their bodies for identification marks. This registration of free colored people would continue for decades. The inspecting official checked Delaware Scott, the son of Judith Scott, for example, by examining his face, head, and arms for scars in 1849. Three years later, in 1852, he had begun checking his breast for scars in addition to his face, head and arms. Those decades were dreadful times for these aboriginal people because the Buffalo Ridge and Stonewall Mill Pearl members were not criminals or freed slaves that necessitated those officials to inspect them like they were animals. Turner, well aware of the unstable conditions in America for aboriginal people, held his disgust within, as he, the tribal leader, did not want to give the court officials reasons to arrest him and persecute the Pearl.

Turner continued his talk. Although it was now about 3:45 p.m. and the people had begun to get hungry, tribal members still focused their attention on their chief.

"Georgia legislature recently, in 1828, passed a group of laws that increased the state's control over the Cherokees. These laws were designed to destroy the Cherokee as a nation, with the ultimate purpose of securing their land rich with minerals and other resources. These laws were really unconstitutional since only federal laws applied to Native Americans. President Jackson, however, did not interfere with Georgia's connivance. George Gist or Sequoyah, that same year, invented and used the new written Cherokee language in his Cherokee newspaper, *The Phoenix*. Most colonists still believed that Indians were wild and uncivilized." Turner knew that they also thought this way about his people and therefore walked cautiously through life.

Raleigh had trained Turner well. There is a common word among aboriginal peoples for a deceptive, devious person, *seente,* meaning "people who are like snakes." He always warned him as he was growing up that he had to watch for *seente*, rattlesnakes and copperheads along Buffalo Ridge's pathways, which he always followed up with a smile and a wink. Turner knew his daddy was telling him metaphorically to keep his vision sharp and walk clear of trails full of the social snakes in society. As a result of his wise training, he trod lightly and carefully on social pathways in Amherst and other areas of Virginia. Realizing that the Ridge and Stonewall Mill had prime real estate, Turner did not want to give county officials legal reasons for closing in on his property and lands belonging to the Pearl.

> This is to serefy that I do give leave
> for Richard Tuppence to git lisons to marry
> my dorter Polly, being of lawful age this
> twelfth day of June 1829. —Turner Pinn

"Richard, when you married Polly a few months ago, I told you that we had to document the marriage. I asked John and Thomas to write the note for me and take it to the courthouse since I have trouble writing. I wish I could speak, read, and write like my daddy, Raleigh. I just made my X by my name on the note that Thomas took to the courthouse."

It is amazing that Turner did not sign his name. He chose to affix his X to documents, rather than write his name clearly. Having descended from ancestors with literary skills—Raleigh, Sarah, and his father's father and mother—it is a mystery why Turner did not write his name on documents.

"You know that I am not much of a writer, even though my father and mother were very good at writing words. I like figuring numbers."

Turner continued, "Times are getting hard now for our people. We are losing our rights, many of those rights that my daddy, Raleigh, fought for years ago. As a result of Nat Turner's slave rebellion, the winds are blowing coldly on the Buffalo Ridge band. The Virginia General Assembly recently made new laws that restrict the rights of Native Americans and free blacks to meet or assemble in public.

"Now, the Ridge and Stonewall Mill people have to watch out when we meet in public. The colonists think we are going to start an insurrection against the whites. Why would we, who have lived peacefully side by side with the colonists for years, be suspected of scheming against the colony? I told you years ago what daddy forecasted concerning these times. We have been suffering and we are going to suffer even more as an aboriginal people. The colonists are dumping us into the African slave category—black—and in the process, they are taking away the few rights that we once had.

"As I told you, George Washington, a few years ago, encouraged Native Americans to marry white people so that we could change our dark color and adopt their English ways. Some of our people followed this plan and are going for white. Daddy and I have never gone for white even though the tax people called us white on those personal property tax records. We have not sought out those light-colored people to make us some light-colored children. Stephen Ferguson married a white woman—you older tribal members know him from his daddy, Jethro Ferguson, the skilled carpenter who built tobacco barns for us when Daddy was in Yorktown fighting the British. I don't know whether Stephen married her because he loved her or because he wanted to obey George Washington and mix up his aboriginal Cherokee and Pocahontas-Powhatan blood with some of the Caucasian Scot and English blood.

"You know the Selbys. Susan is with us today in this meeting. Her family members feel comfortable with us and are down to earth with aboriginal people. Stephen married Susan Selby. A few years back, four or five angry Prince Edward County white citizens charged the Selbys, in court, for letting 'colored people' hang out at their place. It has gotten so that now white people have to be careful in hanging out with people who are as light as they are. Jethro, a skilled carpenter, and his family are loaded with both Scot and Irish ancestry, probably from the Highlander clan in Scotland. Those Highlanders follow customs like our aborigines. Some of those clan members, after a child is born, will wave the child over the fire as a religious purification ritual. They don't burn the child, but just follow the ritual. They are clannish and understand our aboriginal clan members' ways, although a few whites in Prince Edward did not see the clan connection between the Selbys and Fergusons. You know how clannish the Fergusons are. When one of the clan members moves to a new location, the whole gang goes with the one who moves."

The tribal members burst out in laughter and applause. Several shouted out, "That is true! Amen. Amen."

Susan dropped her head in embarrassment and a beautiful smile spread across her freckled, blushed countenance. Jethro, his wife, Elizabeth, and Stephen applauded and "amens" added to the thunderous commotion in a meeting that had been generally serious and formal in structure.

"The Fergusons, as they will attest, are probably related to the other Scots-Irish Fergusons along the Appomattox River in Buckingham County, but their aboriginal skin tones show off their pretty skin tones in the midsummer sun. They look as white as the Selbys and other Fergusons look in the winter, but let the summer come! The summer grabs their skin and says loudly, 'You are aboriginal people, not all white, so don't forget it!' Now why would those local citizens in Prince Edward County, four or five in number, take other free white people, maybe even their kin, the Selbys, to court for hanging around with other clannish white and Indian people, Stephen Ferguson's folk, who just happens to look 'Indian' in the summertime? The only difference is that Stephen and his family admitted that they have 'Indian' in their blood. The sun helps them prove it in the summertime. Just having some aboriginal blood makes them undesirable to some white people.

"With the new Virginia laws on free blacks, this racial stuff has been stirred up and all colored people have been thrown into the stirred-up mess. They are ready to put the Selbys in shackles for their clannishness with other clannish people, just because the Fergusons are temporarily dark-skinned during the mid to late summer. Our people across the James River in Stonewall Mill, with their blood now also flowing through the

Ridge people's veins, are filled with ancestry from the Cherokee tribal members who lived on the Appomattox River. Look at the Fergusons, Megginsons, Elliotts, and others. Some are going for white while others go for colored. You know why they are colored, it's because of the new laws that say you must be all white or you must be all colored. Watch it now because the colored people are soon being translated to black because of Virginia's laws and officials. Watch them try to write the 'black' word on your documents, whether you are as white as the Buckingham and Prince Edward Counties' Fergusons and Megginson or not. This whole dire situation, this hatred against colored people here in Virginia, Georgia, and throughout Eastern America, is based on greed. They don't want to give those free blacks any kind of advantage, just as they also could care less for the Native American aborigines.

"Anyway, what I was saying is that this new law restricting the free people of color, or free blacks, from assembling in public is not going to affect the Buffalo Ridge people or the Stonewall Mill group. Stonewall members are being protected by influential so-called white political figures in Buckingham and the state of Virginia. Now in Buffalo Ridge, even though we are mixed up with the Stonewall Mill folk in a tribal way, we must still face the music alone in Amherst County. We must be prepared to stir up trouble in Amherst County if the officials try to restrict our public attendance at Fairmount Baptist Church or at tribal meetings. You don't suppose that they are wise to what we are doing, assembling monthly and calling tribal meetings? Do you think that they can really stop our tribal meetings? No! They know they are not going to stop our church meetings! They can forget that idea, if they have it in their mind. I think we are secluded well enough in the Ridge to do almost whatever we want to do up here. I am not going to worry about the officials. Amherst officials know the Ridge people are Indians anyway. They are not going to bother us unless they think we are taking sides against what the federal people are doing with the Cherokees in Georgia. Some kindhearted white officials here don't like what the federal people are doing against the Cherokees in Georgia any more than we do. They are sympathetic with the Cherokees down there because so many whites here in Central Virginia are mixed up with the Cherokees."

Turner asked one of the members to stand up and give a report regarding problems in the Cherokee Nation. It seems that he had recently returned from Richmond, Virginia. He purchased a *Cherokee Phoenix and Indians' Advocate* newspaper at Pollard and Converse's Store in Richmond. They were the official distributors in Virginia for the Cherokee paper. With the large pockets of Cherokee single and village homes in outlying areas throughout the state, Virginia's Pollard and Converse establishment was one of the eleven authorized American subscription agents. This paper could also be secured from traveling native and white traders as they passed in the vicinity of Buffalo Ridge. The traders probably picked up the weekly newspaper from agents James Campbell in Beaufort or Moultrie Reid in Charleston, South Carolina. The subscriptions could also be secured from agents in Nashville, Tennessee, or Mobile, Alabama. The Ridge and Stonewall Mill residents did not have any trouble acquiring this newspaper. They always had Cherokee guests traveling through the Ridge area, and naturally, the Ridge leaders extended the usual aboriginal hospitalities. Turner considered himself as knowledgeable concerning what was going on in the Cherokee Nation and with officials in the national government. As chief, he spoke Algonquian Wiccocomico and some Cherokee. He used this newspaper to learn Cherokee, as the paper printed the news in both English and Cherokee using the new Cherokee symbols. Although Turner could not read and write English well, he was not totally illiterate. Actually, he was highly respected by citizens within and without the tribal community for his mathematical skills in calculations. Real estate dealers had to be careful with Turner, The Pin Indian, as he was known. It seems that whether he was buying or selling land or selling his farm products, he always landed firmly on his financial feet. He was among the most progressive businessmen among free people of color in Amherst County. Turner felt more comfortable having one of the young literate members read to the assembly the state of affairs in the Cherokee Nation. He asked Polly, his daughter, to review the *Phoenix* and share some of the important points to the audience.

"The Cherokee paper quoted an article from another newspaper, the *Southron*, which revealed white people's indifference and dislike for Cherokee landholders.

> A Milledgeville, Geo. Paper, the *Southron*, of the 10th ult. has an article alluding to the bill which has been reported to the House of Representatives of Georgia, providing for the extension of the jurisdiction of the laws of the state to the territory occupied by the Cherokees. 'They are not citizens of the state,' says the editor; 'they are not the owners of the land they occupy...' They must be driven from the soil for which they have an inherent attachment, and driven at the point of sword and bayonet; for they have no right, nor title, to their present homes. The plan is one that might easily be carried into execution by a few divisions of Georgia militia . . ."

As Polly read from the paper, Turner signaled her to stop reading and then continued his address to the assembly. "Do you see what I have been telling you in the Ridge and Stonewall Mill? You cannot set up an obvious tribe because they are waiting to take away any land that belongs to Indians, especially if Cherokees are connected with it. Daddy told me that there is something about Virginia's colonists that leads them to dislike Cherokees, even though every fifth person in Amherst County that breathes the air near you is probably part Cherokee and will admit it. Actually, every fourth person is probably Cherokee but the 25 percent might not own up to it because of the outside pressure against persons that are Indian. Some white citizens are sleeping with Cherokees and don't know that their wives or husbands have aboriginal blood flowing through their veins. Those estranged Indians, those that live in outlying areas of Virginia, in hidden single homes or little settlements, such as in the Piedmont area of Virginia, like here in Amherst County in the Ridge, have to keep a low profile. They see what is happening in the Cherokee Nation. The more they hear about Georgia, South Carolina, North Carolina, and Tennessee, the tighter their lips are in holding back the hot secrets of their Tsalagi heritage. The old ones saw what occurred to those great villages in the Lower towns, Middle and Out towns, and Overhill towns in the 1700s. The militias went against those towns, burned their homes, orchards and crops, and killed warriors, women, and children.

"Several of you old ones know about those mean-spirited deeds because you or your parents fled from those atrocities, either in 1760–61, or in 1776. State militia also went back and assaulted those villages several times again after 1776. The militiamen chopped down fruit orchards that had been nursed for years and set ablaze beautiful, ripe cornfield and other crops meant to sustain the townspeople through the winter and spring. There are people who escaped to the hills and came along the mountains or Piedmont to what are now the counties of Bedford, Buckingham, Amherst, Albemarle, and other locations. Some of you are direct descendants of those great aboriginal people. You young ones hold on awhile, and you will see this current Cherokee problem with the Cherokees in Georgia and other surrounding states chase more Cherokee people toward Virginia. We have recent arrivals from Cherokee towns among us now. I will permit them at an appropriate time to tell you about their former experiences that led them to withdraw from the hot spots. In light of what is happening now in Georgia and other areas, you need to know what can happen here if we do not behave privately. In protecting those fleeing people and our land, we have kept our lips closed too long. We are damned if we do tell the secrets to tribal members and the secrets are exposed to citizens outside the tribe. The citizens in this colony would come down on us if they knew that we have deceptively split our people into two groups, Stonewall Mill and Buffalo Ridge to hide the fact that we have a fairly large tribe here. We are, however, damned if we don't tell the members within our group all the secrets of our people because then they will lose their God-given heritage.

"It has all been about registration. As you have settled in at the Ridge and at Stonewall, Daddy strategically placed you on lands that kept you hidden for a while and then you came out. We worshipped God and called on Yo-He-Wah. The locals did not understand that the Cherokees have generally adopted the white man's culture. In the Ridge, we did not jump to George Washington's suggestion that we assimilate with the whites so that we could get rid of our aboriginal ways. We are still free colored people. We did not adopt the white man's God because our aboriginal people have always worshipped one God. We have never bowed to objects, the sun, or fire. Some European and Middle Eastern cultures still worship objects instead of God, and they have the nerve to call us heathens. We know that Yo-He-Wah created us. We know that Jesus Christ is His Son.

"We have some Hebrew influence, as some of our people abstained from certain types of prohibited foods. After we learned more about Christ, we realized that certain food restrictions did not apply to us. Our people have had Hebrew-type cities of refuge, where people may flee from their enemies, if they are innocent. The Ridge has been, to an extent, a village or hamlet of refuge to those dispersed Wiccocomico and Cherokee people. We have our purification ceremonies, and our religious burial rites. Our women and men wear aboriginal jewelry much like the Jewish men and women wore. We divide our clans just like the Jews did in the Old Testament. Many of our people have been given biblical first names, like Jethro, Shadrack, Stephen, John, Sarah, Mary, Peter, Thomas, Martha, Daniel, and others. We even have our people who can see into the future, those who see visions and dream dreams. We have medicine people who have gifts of healing and skill in making herbal medicines. We do not eat unclean food or meat that has died through sickness. We are not heathens.

"I have been telling you to register all activities like marriages, land purchases, and sales. Don't be shy when the census takers come around. I know we have to be secretive, but now I am telling you to loosen up. You tell the census takers how many children you have. Those records will be valuable hundreds of years from now. It will show that we were here in the Ridge, free people of color, not slaves but *free*.

"We are civilized people, but the colonists think we are civilized because we act like the whites. Aboriginal people have always been civilized, as we have had our own healers and medicine makers. We have a beautiful language and a great tribal structure. We have a strict, social body of rules that is much like the Jews' commandments. There was a time when aborigines would not eat the dirty, unclean hogs like the whites, but now we are free to eat the hogs. We place rocks and stones over our graves while the colonists just bury their people in a hole and cover them up without stones. I am sorry to admit that we have gradually adopted the white man's ways when it comes to eating hogs and burying our dead without stones on the grave. I cannot lie about this, as you can look out from this building and see the burial ground. We do not pile up stones over our graves anymore!"

Jethro Ferguson and his wife Elizabeth, along with their son Stephen and his wife Susan, worshipped with Fairmount this Sunday and remained for the afternoon tribal meeting. Jethro sat on the second bench to the right of Turner and listened alertly, realizing that the chief's every word provided covert and overt messages for the clan leaders' consideration and possible action, and that he must not miss its import. He leaned forward in his best Sunday light brown pants, dark brown vest, and yellow-brown coat. His bright white shirt was almost hidden as his broad, light-brown-and-white necktie stood out front, as the chief talked in the center of the floor, near the communion table. Jethro's black turban had been unwrapped and placed neatly in his lap. He and other men followed Turner Pinn's signal when the chief ceremoniously unwrapped his blue-black turban before commencing with his address before the tribal members. Jethro's wife, Elizabeth, strikingly beautiful and complementarily attired with her husband in her modest brown-and-yellow dress flowing below her ankles, attended to the speaker's words like a princess observing a regal event.

Turner, with his unwrapped turban folded neatly over his left arm, used his right hand and arm to make nonverbal signs to dramatize his words of admonition. "We worship God and would never steal land from the colonists, like they take property from us. Who is uncivilized? Not us! We would not covet and steal their land for gold, like what they are doing in Georgia with Cherokee land. Even the white man admits that we are the most civilized tribe around. They will not, however, give us credit for being more civilized than they are or even equal to them in civilization."

These words, like others during his speech, supported the Golden Rule of treating others as you would want to be treated. Turner made it clear that the tribal members must never steal land from others. He as well as his father always believed that soil does not belong to human beings anyway, and therefore they have no reason to covet, as it is forbidden in the Ten Commandments. The chief's every word carried meaning. With the statement "equal to them in civilization," Turner conveyed the eternal principle that human beings are created equally, and therefore no individual has the right to esteem himself more importantly than another person.

"I will prove this to you from their words. Polly, continue reading from the *Cherokee Phoenix and Indians' Advocate* newspaper, an article in the paper written by a white man."

Polly read from the article.

> "The Cherokee perhaps have doubtless assimilated nearer to the manner and customs of their more favored [white] neighbors than any tribes, who have come in contact with civilization— the very circumstance of their refusal to migrate hence, while the removal can be effected of tribes less enlightened, is altogether in their favor . . .
> *Cherokee Phoenix and Indians' Advocate,*
>
> New Echota, Wednesday, February 11, 1829, Vol. 1.— No. 48. Page 1."

Turner continued lecturing. "The white man is admitting that the Cherokee would be stupid to leave their rich lands in Georgia and other areas and go to some undetermined, forsaken land yonder somewhere! We must not be stupid when we buy land. Make sure it is documented or registered in the courthouse because some people out there are greedy for land. We are not stupid people!"

Turner, with these words, sent home the message to his members that they should never concede or give up their property to others, if at all possible. It was their land to use and colonists must not be permitted to take it.

"When the census takers visit your home, make sure that you let them know that you own your property, that you are free people of color, that you are not white, and that you and your ancestors have been in this colony since antiquity."

Stephen raised his hand for permission to speak. Turner looked at him and nodded.

"That *Cherokee Phoenix* paper has an interesting science article on 'Motion of Animals.' It was written on the back page and last column of that paper. If you are not careful, you would have missed reading it. The writer listed the motion of serpents, Pholas shellfish, crabs, marine birds, horses, tigers, crocodiles, reindeers, armadillos, and eagles, to name a few. One creature that the writer mentioned was an oyster. You know how our tribal members respect the oyster as well as the eagle. The oyster especially got my attention. He said in the article about the motion of animals that the only impulse an oyster has is to open and shut its shell. Well, we all know that that one motion, opening and closing its shell, is essential for survival. That same motion is also the reason that the oyster gets in trouble and suffers for it later. The sand particles slip into its shell and press against its tender body, irritating it to the point of much suffering and distress. In its pain, the oyster produces watery substances that cover the sand or other impediments. So without the impediments to irritate its body, the oyster would not produce a pearl!"

"It is amazing how the Pearl is mentioned in our meeting, without fail. Thank you, Stephen, as I forget to lecture on the word Pearl and its meaning in my talk. I am about to close our meeting, and Stephen has figured out a way to bring up the

Pearl. During our next meeting, I will speak on that subject. I know Stephen wants me to discuss the Pearl now, but the hour is late. I thank you for your patience with my long talk. Please forgive me and know that I love you and the tribe. Otherwise, I would not have kept you this long. I believe it is time that we go home. This country—the nation that my daddy loved to the point that he was willing to fight for peoples' freedom by taking up arms during the American Revolution—is against its aboriginal citizens. Do we have to take up arms again to retain freedom and our rights to our land and happiness? I hope and pray not! We must revisit issues related to our freedom in the Ridge and Stonewall Mill, and the Pearl. The next meeting will be in two weeks from today, same time and same place, and our agenda will include the Pearl."

Turner, hitting the tomahawk solidly against the table, then proclaimed, "Meeting adjourned."

> God grant me the serenity to accept
> the things I cannot change;
> courage to change the things I can;
> and wisdom to know the difference.
> —Reinhold Niebuhr

20

The Census

June 1840

Polly, the tall, slender, thirty-five-year-old daughter of Turner Pinn and mother of John Turner Pinn, was the attractive dark-complexioned wife of Richard Two Pins. She wore her waist-long, coal-black straight hair in two braids and resembled a Cherokee princess as she and John Turner, her fifteen-year-old son, walked toward the front yard gate. John Turner was of average height with straight hair and a bright complexion. This walk was a daily ritual for them at 5:30 p.m., as John Turner stopped working on his chores at the farm and Polly finished cooking supper. They strolled down to the gate and waited for Richard, who worked as a boatman, a navigator, on the James River and arrived at their Ridge farm at around 6:00 p.m. Polly, like her ancestors before her, used every opportunity to teach her child about the rich history of her free colored people.

"John Turner, your grandfather, Turner Pinn, reminded us that the census takers will visit our home every ten years and that we must let them know that we are free people of color so these facts can be recorded in American records. I wonder if my daddy knew ahead of time what they were planning to do with the Cherokees with that 1835 Cherokee census and military roundup of aboriginal people. With that census, they were ready to drive the people to some barren land yonder beyond nowhere. The things that the officials did to the Cherokees after that census have made our people on the Ridge and at Stonewall Mill very jumpy. They get suspicious about strangers who want to know information concerning who lives in our house and their ages, how much land we have, and other facts."

Richard came from a long line of family navigators who operated boats on the bays and rivers in Eastern Virginia. Short in height and with almost blond curly hair, he looked like a white man as he came up the road from the James River. Polly was tall, dark-skinned with long, shiny black hair. When Richard turned from the Ridge road and opened the gate, Polly ran to his open arms as he dropped his lunch bucket. They still displayed their honeymoon affection after eleven years of marriage and sixteen years of courtship. Regardless of differences in their physical appearances, they maintained such mutual love and affection that visitors on the road would think that they were still in their first year of marriage. Although they did not know this at the time, Polly would die young and leave her husband and children behind, so the couple instinctually relished life with each other while it lasted.

The three family members walked back toward the house slowly as Polly continued her talk with John Turner. She enjoyed the times when her husband could be with her to hear her lectures. She had an overpowering need to tell all she could remember about her history to her son and husband. Richard too sensed Polly's urgency and need to pass information on to them, as if she had hints that she would not be on earth very long.

"My daddy and your grandfather told all the tribal members to cooperate with that 1840 census taker this summer, just as he did in the summer of 1830. I remember so well that time when this stranger knocked on our door in 1830, at around 10:30 a.m. because the sun flashed in my face when I opened the door, and he stood there with his back to the sun. He stated that he was taking census information for Amherst County and America. I told him to stand there on the porch until I ran to the barn to get Daddy. Mother Joicey stayed in the kitchen and waited until Daddy came around the side of the house and greeted him on the porch steps. Then mother and the rest of the family came out to observe the funny-looking stranger. He had big eyes and only asked the questions that were on that paper form he had. I remember that he was a nice man even though he looked scary with those thick eyebrows and large eyes. I am glad that Daddy's farmwork kept him close to the house that day. Otherwise, that man would have had to return when the man of the house was there. I was twenty-five years old and you, John Turner, were only five years old when the census taker made his census visit to our house in 1830.

"This year, he will probably be a white man with a tablet in his hand, like ten years ago. John Turner, you or your daddy would know what to tell him if I am not here at the time. You know how I am always working hard on the farm in the morning hours and part of the early afternoon period. I have to help your daddy at the farm because he cannot work on the ferry all day and then try to take care of what chores you and I do not complete. Tell the census taker, if he shows up when I am down on the lower ten acres, that we are free people of color and have been free since God created human beings. Let him know how many people are in our home, that we own the land, and that Richard Two Pins is the head of the family. Watch him when he writes your daddy's name, because he is surely going to misspell it. Colonists tend to write it Tuppence, Toppence, Turpin, and many other spellings. Tell the recorder that it is Two Pins, but he will probably write it Twopence."

"Mother," John Turner asked, "do I tell them that I am John Turner Pinn or John Turner Two Pins? You know the white people always write our surnames incorrectly. Granddad told us how important these census records are for us, when we get old and for later generations to see. They like to make us Pen, Pin, Pan, Pann, Pain, and even Pence. Why can't they just write it P-i-n-n? Or even Pekwem, the original spelling from Wiccocomico Indian Town? Or even the early Anglo version of Pekwem, 'Pewem'?"

"You tell him that you are John Turner Pinn, if he asks for it, since you were born before your daddy and I married. It is all right for you to keep the name, as it is a royal name in history and carries weight with aboriginal people much like the name pharaoh with the Egyptians. There are many Cherokee people who love the name 'Pin' so much that it is equal to the word 'pure Cherokee.' They are known as Pin Indians, or Keetoowah, and are proud of their heritage from antiquity. You keep your name. Your daddy is proud of the name Two Pins, and he too takes pleasure in his name's heritage in Algonquian and Cherokee history. He, of course, does not mind you going by the Pinn name because he often remarked that he would like to have people call him Richard Two Pins or Richard Pinn, either one. He tells me privately that he would not mind having the name Pinn. Actually, your dad is kind and self-confident enough in his position as the head of this household that he has given me permission to retain my royal surname, Pinn, on official documents."

Polly continued, "John Turner, do not speak out your name unless he asks you because he probably only needs the name of the head of the household, not my name or your name. He only needs the number in the household and each person's age. They are busy and are in a hurry to go on down the road to the next house. They don't have the time to be nosy even though they like to peek into the house to see how well-off we free people of color are. Watch his eyes and notice how he is looking for stuff to see. If he had the time, he would set up our parlor room for his spy shop, but thank God he has to rush off to get the census information at the next house. They are not paying him to be nosy, but I do feel that his boss knows how to hire eavesdropping, meddlesome people to be census takers. I guess I am still suspicious about census takers after they made that Cherokee census in 1835 and later used it to march our people off to Cherokee Territory in Oklahoma. They took all of their land and told them to 'shoo.' When they got to Oklahoma, the officials noticed that some of the Cherokee people who were on the 1835 census were not there in Oklahoma. Did they think all those people would be so stupid as to walk all the way to Oklahoma and not try to escape? Let them try to use this 1840 census to round us up to inquire about how many of the Buffalo Ridge and Stonewall Mill people or their ancestors have escaped and hidden in our refuge villages from the assaults on them in 1760–61, 1776, and even during the late 1820s and mid-1830s, during all that talk about moving them to Oklahoma. I trust Daddy's opinion that the census taker will be all right, and we do not have to fear him. I guess Daddy knows that Grandfather Raleigh was a Revolutionary War soldier and an Amherst militiaman, and the white citizens would not have the nerve to remove our people to Oklahoma. We are Virginia aboriginal people who fought for the freedom of our colony and America from the British. They wouldn't dare! John Turner, don't be afraid."

"Mother, what does he look like? Would you tell me so I can spot him when he comes into the yard?" John Turner inquired. "I hope he can sprint to the porch because Sassy will surely try to bite him! Should I tie up Sassy, or just make him keep his eyes on our dog while he is getting his census information? This would keep his eyes occupied on Sassy and give him less time to engage in snooping behavior. That would be a way to make him hurry up and write down the facts and get away from Porridge Creek. I know if I untie Sidney, the census man would leave our yard twice as fast as he would normally!"

Sidney was a black cocker spaniel, much larger than others of his breed, and had an appetite for strange visitors' shanks—visitors that she suspected Polly and Richard didn't like. The canine had the ability to read the minds of Richard and Polly and attack strangers that she believed were her masters' adversaries. Sidney was bad news for the Pinns' well-known reputation for hospitality to visitors in the Ridge, and for that reason, her masters were forced to keep her tied to the sycamore tree near the north end of the yard. John Turner had a habit of setting Sydney free whenever his father was not home.

"Mother, can I untie Sidney, just in case the census man has some tricks up his sleeve with these census questions? May I?"

"No, son. Daddy said the census man would only do his job. You remember that Daddy told us the Israelites made a census of the twelve tribes of Israel. This is almost what this man is doing for the history of the colony and America. When your

Granddaddy Turner comes over tomorrow, I will ask him to tell you why he believes the census man is alright."

"Yes, Mother. I will not turn Sidney on the man unless I catch him throwing out more questions than he is supposed to ask for that census."

"No, son," advised Richard. "Our house in the Ridge, as well as all the homes up here, is a place of refuge, and we cannot mistreat strangers. Remember what the Bible says about strangers. They might be 'angels unawares.' You wouldn't let Sassy and Sidney put their teeth into an angel's shank or thigh, would you?"

"No, sir, Daddy. I will protect the stranger. I will tie up the dogs when the census man comes into our yard."

As they talked, Richard opened the front door and Polly went toward the kitchen. John Turner walked with his daddy around the house to the water pump. Richard and John Turner washed their hands and faces quickly in preparation to eat, smelling the beef pot roast, red potatoes, string beans, boiled buttered corn, and, of course, ashcakes.

Turner said, "Polly, I am glad you reminded me about the 1840 census taker. I told you and the tribal members a year ago to expect his visit this year, but I clean forgot it. You love the Ridge and Stonewall Mill people, don't you? As busy as you are working six to eight hours on the farm, cooking three hot meals a day, and attending to other chores around the house, you must be exhausted at bedtime. You have time, after all this activity, to remember facts that I should be reminding you, not you bringing it to my memory. The thoughts, about this new decade, 1840, warn me that I am getting older. I was born in 1770 and here it is 1840 already. Where has the time gone? I will be seventy years old this year, the Lord willing, and it seems like yesterday when Daddy Raleigh and Mother Sarah celebrated my fifth birthday in 1775. That day was one of the happiest days of my life, with the licorice sticks and birthday cake. God has been good to me to allow me to live to greet my seventieth birthday.

The Lord has blessed his grace on your mother Joicey too. She has turned sixty years old and she is still in excellent health. Where have the years gone?"

"Daddy," Polly inquired, "do we need to remind the tribal members again about their need to be careful? Remember the problem that almost occurred ten years ago when all the new visitors to this area started crowding up together in our area and you told them to follow Raleigh's pattern of splitting up the Buffalo Ridge and Stonewall Mill group. The people were not in our tribe but lived in our area."

"Daughter, you are so alert. Do you remember that situation? I thought I had kept that problem secret from the tribal members."

"I heard you and mother talking in the bedroom. You told Mother Joicey that you were worried about all the people piled up together in the village since all of the members were not a part of our tribe. You were willing to cover for your tribal members against accusations that we were starting a Cherokee tribe, but you could not justify all those people living near each other with those Cherokee names, whether all were Cherokee or not. You were afraid that the white people would attack our village and round us up like they were planning to do with the Cherokees in Georgia."

"Yes, that was a close situation. Some of those aboriginal people who lived near us in 1830 left our area and traveled to other areas. Some are now living close to each other in the Buffalo River area of western Amherst County. This year we will not have that great crowd of people—Patterson Johns, Rachel Peters, William Cato, James Johns, William Suthards, Albert Terry, Joel Brannum, Benjamin Whiteside, Elizabeth Long, and John Arnold.

The census-taker misspelled my son's name. He had called him 'Rowland,' when I know we told him that his name was 'Raleigh' Pinn. The colonists messed up my daddy's name the same way. They called him 'Rawley,' 'Rolly,' and who knows what other spellings. Who else was living near us back then? Who else was there, Polly?"

"Daddy, you forgot us, Richard Two Pins was next, and then you, Turner Pinn, Bartlett Sparrow--"

"Now I remember, next Jack Helton, and there were others, but some are not here now. It is just our tribe, William Jackson, Charles Beverley, John Cousins, Samuel Scott, Rowland or Rawley Pinn, my son, William Harris, you and your husband Richard Two Pins, Bartlett Sparrow, and Ezekiel Humbles, Joicey's kin. There are others here with us this year, including Jonathan Beverley and those new refugees. If the 1830 census taker did not figure out the fact that we had a group of Indians congregated together up here, maybe we can survive this 1840 census taker. We have fewer homes with aboriginal people now and those recent refuges from Georgia, Tennessee, and North Carolina are hiding way back in the woods, up near Icey Mountain and on back."

"Daddy, you kept your promise to Granddaddy Raleigh to protect the Cherokees and provide a village of refuge in Buffalo Ridge and Stonewall Mill. You have done an excellent job and have not lost one soul to the people in the South who are probably still looking for them. They looked at their 1835 census roll in Oklahoma and realized that all those people who were missing must have either died on the trail to Oklahoma or escaped to the hills. Do we have to worry about the Scotts, Beverlys, Sparrows, Elliotts, and others possibly being forced to Oklahoma from Buffalo Ridge and Stonewall Mill?"

"Let them try to come up here for us and see what will happen to their rear ends. We are a part of this colony. Cherokees were tricked in these treaties into giving up their Virginia colony land. We have been going as white and colored people publicly and Cherokee privately. The white people know we are Cherokees when we go to Stapleton and Amherst. We just can't act like we are too proud and too strong up here as a village. That is why we separated the Stonewall group from us, or rather Daddy made arrangements for the six Beverly families to leave Buckingham County in waves. First, most of the ones in Stonewall Mill stayed there for a while and then gradually moved on toward Buffalo Ridge. Some of our people on the Ridge moved to Stonewall Mill. Even Saunders, your brother, and family moved over there. We don't want too much attention since the Pinns have the disadvantage of attracting white people's curiosity, with our well-known aboriginal Pinn heritage.

"Whether they are residents of Stonewall Mill or Buffalo Ridge, it does not matter. We as a group are not escapees from Georgia, so we don't have to worry. We have made arrangements to keep those who escaped, those who have been hiding during the last ten to twelve years, back deep in the woods until the threat of the census taker has passed. Each tribal resident up here and at Stonewall Mill knows how to tell the census taker that there are some houses deep in the woods, but we are not sure if anyone lives in them, with all those 'rattlesnakes and copperhead snakes in those mountains.' They would not need to repent the next Sunday at Fairmount because they would not have lied to the census taker. They just warned him about the snakes and the fact that it may be a long, dangerous walk for nothing since the houses are probably not occupied. That is the truth! The occupiers would leave the house and hide even deeper in the woods. They all have dogs and those beasts would alert them to strange, nosy people coming their way. They would have plenty of time to cut and run into the woods," Turner remarked jokingly as he winked at Polly and laughed.

"Daddy, that would not be lying, and require Sunday repentance because there wouldn't be anyone in the houses. Our folk would tell the truth, since there wouldn't be anyone occupying the cabins. I don't blame the census taker if he decides to forget about going into those deep, dark recesses to look for free people of color that he thinks are Cherokee but wants to protect his legs against poisonous snakebites. So that is how you and the rest of the aboriginal people kept suspicions out of the mind of the 1830 census taker, by hurrying him up with that census taking and kept him away from the large group of people—you told them about the snakes!" Polly smiled in amusement. "Did you do the same thing with the 1830 census taker in Stonewall?"

"Yes, it was a different census taker in 1830 at Stonewall than the ones who visited Buffalo Ridge because the Beverlys kept us informed. He was not the same one who came to Buffalo Ridge. If our snake story worked in the Ridge, since there are snakes up here and it was no lie, we used the same line with the Stonewall Mill census taker in 1830. The Humbles watched out for the escapees and kept them from the nosy officials. The McCoys have been laying low for years over there. The McCoys are pure Cherokees, straight from Cherokee territory, while other McCoy in our bands descend from people who have been in our area before the first census in 1790. In a few years, they will be free to set up open residences in Buffalo Ridge. In the meantime, he and his large family need to keep a low profile. They are close to the Cousins here in Amherst County and the Cousins spread out eastward in counties beyond Buckingham County. They are clannish and like to hang around with the Fergusons in Stonewall Mill. The Harrises are getting close to the Coopers and Bankses in Buckingham County. Francis Cousins, James Cooper, and Jacob and John Banks were all in the Revolutionary War. Some of those folks will probably join us in a few years on Buffalo Ridge, but for now, we need to discourage too many new Cherokees. The Coopers and Bankses are all mixed up with Algonquians and Cherokees. Our Cherokees are known for being an intermixture of the people they defeated as well as the people that defeated them. The Elliotts are laying back and plan to move into our bands soon. They are related to Pocahontas and the Cherokees. We are going to have quite an array of colors in our two groups, like a rainbow after a great rain.

"The storms in Georgia, and the roundup of our people in Alabama, Tennessee, and North Carolina, are driving all colors of people our way. Look at Anthony McCoy's people, pure-blood dark people with straight black hair. Look at them hanging around with the half-white, Scot Highlander Cherokee with Pocahontas mixture. What a rainbow of colors that is going to come out of those storms that forced them together! The Harrises are Cherokees and they have a Tsalagi princess among their clan. She evaded the forced march to Oklahoma and has now joined our Harris group. The Harrises like to hook up with other Harrises when they go into a new area, and her action in joining the Harris family follows that tradition. You know the Harris family that came from the Albemarle side of Amherst County. The young royal united with the group with the same surname. We believe the Harrises fled the Etowah River area of Floyd County, Georgia, and it is said that they are full bloods.

"The McCoy clan probably came from the Chickamauga County area of Tennessee. They are still a little fidgety and like to hop around to evade any people who may be looking for them. Some of their people were in Amherst County as early as the first U.S. Census in 1790, as an ancestor was listed as A. Coy. Their movement from place to place fits into our refuge strategies anyway as we move new tribal members around so that the white citizens won't know what we are planning up here in the Ridge and over there at Stonewall. We are not really sure which McCoy clan they evolved from, but we are sure they are at least half blood to full blood. The Fields beyond the Stonewall Mill area claim to be Cherokee and possibly fled from the same location in Georgia. They too are full-blood Cherokees. When we give refuge to the fleeing souls, we don't make them prove their blood level before we take them in, as it is not important to us. The fact that they are Tsalagi, I don't care if they are quarter blood or full. They need food, a place of lodging, and a chance to reestablish themselves in our havens of safety. I think you have met the Harris princess, but you did not know that she was a Cherokee princess and might not remember her being in one of our tribal meetings. So don't breathe a word of this to anyone, not even to your brothers and sisters, you hear?"

"I won't speak a word of what you just told me, Daddy."

August 1840

The census official completed his census recording at Turner Pinn's house and sought information about occupants in the next house. Turner, noting that Polly Beverley and her family lived there, cautioned him about the snake problems in the Ridge.

"We who live here know how to walk through the pathways along Porridge Creek, but I think the giant copperheads know how to block the road or slip up behind you before they put their venom into your leg. As you go up higher in the mountain from Polly Beverley's house, be careful because the rattlesnakes are going to be more plentiful the higher you get among all those rocks. If you are lucky and don't get treated like a stranger by the copperhead snakes, you need to look on both sides of the road as you move toward Bartlett Sparrow's house. As you climb higher to each of those houses there in the Ridge—you have Jonathan Beverly, Samuel Scott, William Harris, George Jewell, Anthony Beverley, and then Bartlett Sparrow—hurry up and finish your work before sundown because if the snakes don't come out to greet you, the bears will surely come out to see who you are."

The man thanked Turner. "The snakes must be bad up here because you are the sixth person who told me the same thing about the poisonous snakes."

"I know you like your job with this census-taking. You have to be a good walker to do a good job, so don't let those snakes bite you and damage your leg muscles and nerves for the rest of your life. You are a young man with a long life ahead and a lot of census-taking decades ahead of you. I don't want to see you crippled up doing this very important census work for America."

The census taker, a tall, freckled-faced, red-haired official, seemed to perspire more because of Turner's cautious warnings rather than the physical exertions of traversing the Ridge. "You mentioned some strange surnames up there. Are there any Indians residing in those hills? You mentioned the Harrises, Beverlys, and Sparrowhawks. I just left a bunch of Beverlys and they looked Indian and you are saying there are more up there in those thickets on the mountain? I don't mean anything by this, but are you related to the Indians? Because you look like some of those free colored people out there in Southwestern Virginia."

"I am a Pinn, and the Pinns, civilized free people of color, are in Coastal Virginia and even in Southwestern Virginia, just like the Beverlys. We are civilized up here, so you only need to fret about those snakes and bears, not friendly aboriginal people. By the way, I did not say Sparrowhawk, I told you where the Sparrows live. I don't know how you got the word hawk added to sparrow. There are some real hostile Indians called Sparrowhawks, but they have been sent to Oklahoma Cherokee territory. We are friendly people up here in the mountains. The only things the residents here don't like are strangers who are nosy, but I don't think you need to worry about getting on their bad side because you would not have the time to be nosy. If you don't travel fast and make your rounds, darkness will set in and you'll be forced to spend the night in the Ridge. I know you don't want to do that. Anyway, you could take your time and get half of the houses this afternoon and come back tomorrow to finish up, but I guess you know what you need to do. Please forgive me for being nosy about your job because nobody likes nosy people. I don't want to hold you up and make you spend the night with the bears."

Turner pointed up the hill and advised the official, "Go up that way to Polly Beverley's house. You can finish up with Polly Two Pins's house on the other end of the circuit. Call out 'census taker coming' when you get in hearing distance of Richard and Polly Two Pins's yard because they have two very bad dogs, Sidney and Sassy. Those canines have a habit of slipping up behind strangers and trying to bite their shanks and thighs if they don't get a warning first. Good luck and hurry up!"

As the census taker came within hollering distance of Bartlett Sparrow's house around 3:30 p.m., he cried out, "Census taker is coming! Census taker is coming in your yard!"

Turner Pinn did not tell the official that the community residents were interconnected and that every tribal member is close to or is related to other tribal members. He could have told the stranger that Bartlett Sparrow was his son-in-law and had married his daughter Maria Pinn in 1827, but his father always told him to never volunteer information when it is not requested because the "unsolicited facts could come back to haunt you later." That small piece of information could be added to other data and help the officials conclude that a Cherokee tribe had established itself in the recesses of those woods. Virginia did not want the Cherokee to set up a tribal settlement on the Roanoke River in the early 1700s, so the nonaboriginal residents would be furious if news got out that Raleigh and Turner had constructed one in the Ridge.

Maria saw the stranger from the backyard and called out to her husband, Bartlett, who was hoeing in the vegetable garden on the west side of the house. Bartlett, who had been through this once already in 1830, dropped his hoe, wiped his sweaty face with his shirt sleeve, and pulled his handkerchief from his back pocket. After taking off his hat and mopping up the remaining sweat from his face, head, hair, and neck, he hurried from the field to intercept the official. Although he and his wife knew what and how much to say to him, he was worried that his children would volunteer unnecessary and secret information to the census taker.

As Bartlett rushed toward the stranger from the field and Maria moved toward the official's direction from the yard where she had been washing clothes, six children came out of nowhere and sprinted toward the stranger. Bartlett, who was twice the distance from the stranger than Maria and the children, surprising even himself for a forty-two-year-old man, outran his family. Breathing hard while extending his right hand for a handshake, he greeted his guest.

"My name is Bartlett Sparrow. Welcome to my farm."

"Hello. I am a census official, and I just need to ask you a few questions for the national government. I won't be long. Did you say your name is Sparrowhawk or Hawkins?"

Bartlett was sharp on his feet and realized what the census taker was doing here. He knew that the official was aware that aboriginal people anglicized their aboriginal names, especially when they did not want white people to know that they were Native Americans.

"No, my name is Bartlett Sparrow. I am the owner of this farm."

"How long have you lived in these hills? Are you white or colored?"

"I have lived here for over twenty years, but my people have been free people of color for centuries. Our ancestors were here when the colonists came over from England."

Maria, James, Simpson, Turner, Cyrus, Mary, and Joicey, stood quietly while the stranger wrote the information that Bartlett gave to him for the census. They had been told already, almost a year ago, to keep quiet when the census stranger came to the Ridge and to let Bartlett speak for the household.

"So you are free colored people. I am going to ask you some questions." He wrote 'Bartlett Sparrow' and moved his eyes and pen along the paper past the 'free white persons' section to the 'free colored persons' section.

"How many free colored males under ten years of age?"

Bartlett stated, "Two: Simpson and Turner."

"How many free colored males ten to twenty-four years of age?"

"One."

After he recorded Bartlett's eight family members, the official remembered his time restrictions and asked him, "How far is it to the next house?"

Bartlett picked up a long oak stick from his yard and graciously presented it to the census taker.

"Just a rock's throw, but I advise you to take this big stick to protect you along the pathway because those copperheads look just like the ground. You think you are getting ready to step on leaves and dirt and realize that the stuff is really a fat curled up copperhead or rattlesnake. You are getting into high ground now—rattlesnake territory."

"Thank you for the snake stick. I heard that it is bad up here. I have to go. Thank you for the idea of the stick."

The census taker moved away at a quick pace, head down, eyes on the ground, and stick in a swinging position until he disappeared from Bartlett's sight. He admired the census taker's courage and commitment to his job responsibilities.

Richard and Polly Pinn's son, John Turner Pinn, had straight coal-black hair, as well as the other children. Polly Beverley's children, looking like aboriginal children in an Indian village, probably gave the official an opinion that the Ridge was supporting a Cherokee village. It was ironic that the official noticed, in particular, the strong Native American features of John Turner Pinn at Polly Pinn's house and Martha Ann

Beverly at Polly Beverley's house, two mothers with the name, Polly. Seventeen years later, John Turner Pinn and Martha Ann Beverly, united in holy matrimony and would report to the Amherst Courthouse on March 20, 1857, to register as free people of color. The official recorded the following:

> JOHN TURNER PINN a free man of colour and a light mulatto – age thirty-one and about five feet and eight inches tall – Born in Amherst from ancestors free before the first day of May 1806.
>
> MARTHA ANN PINN a free woman of colour – a light mulatto – straight black hair about thirty-five years old and about five feet five inches tall – scar on right hand – dark spot on each cheek –– Born in Buckingham and descended from ancestors free before the first of May 1806.

    The officials at Amherst Courthouse did not catch on that this union, as well as other unions between the Ridge and Stonewall Mill tribal members, had been planned as far back as the 1700s. Raleigh was the mastermind, and it was no surprise to him that Amherst County residents in Buffalo Ridge and Buckingham County residents at Stonewall Mill would unite in marriage, generation after generation. The court clerks, however, did not make the connections to conclude that there was a large Cherokee village uniting eastern Amherst County (Buffalo Ridge) and western Buckingham (Stonewall Mill, later Appomattox County) with the James River running through their center to disguise their unity.

    Raleigh—having joined his ancestors for almost forty years at Pinn Park Cherokee Burial Ground—prayed years earlier for an understanding heart and grace to put together the great tribe, the Pearl, much like Solomon's prayer for wisdom. God had answered his prayer in this symbolic Native American court registration in 1857 and would continue to bless the Pearl from generation to generation with other symbolic events to bring to the remembrance of tribal members God's protection of the Pearl.

As Robert Pinn found serenity in his prayer for peace in 1733, Raleigh, his son, found serenity through his prayers. Turner Pinn, Raleigh's son, found serenity through his prayers. Turner's daughter, Polly Pinn, found serenity through her prayers; John Turner Pinn found serenity through his prayers; and Martha Jane Pinn West—John Turner Pinn's daughter and Willis West's wife—also found serenity through her prayers.

> For I know the thoughts that I think toward you,
> saith the Lord, thoughts of peace, and not of evil,
> to give you an expected end.
> Jeremiah 29:11

21

Shalom

February 1850

Fairmount's morning service ended at 1:45 p.m., approximately an hour and a half after the prayer service started. There were almost 150 members and visitors in attendance for the regular worship meeting, mostly members of the Buffalo Ridge community and some members who live in Stonewall Mill, just across the James River. The other worship service participants were church visitors but tribal members from surrounding hamlets. All participants wore their best Sunday clothes and sat in their usual pew seats. Fairmount members traditionally sat together with their respective family heads, usually the father or grandfather, and the head patriarch always signaled to family members what they should do next. Since the patriarchs were generally well versed in the Holy Scriptures, they were the ones who initiated the verbalized "amen" at various points while the preacher delivered his sermons. If he misquoted God's word or made a remark that was not supported by the Good Book, he could not expect to get "amen" support for his sermon during the next minute or so. It was as if the patriarchs were scrutinizing each additional sermon sentence to evaluate the degree to which the minister had gotten back on track. In time, if the sermon was worth its salt from a theological perspective, he could be expected to get plenty of "amen" responses—as the family patriarch first, their respective family members next, and then visitors always provided a chorus of "amen" in support of the preacher's messages.

It was time for the 2:00 p.m. Bible study as the class teacher, John Turner Pinn, stepped forward to the lectern, the same one behind which the minister had used for his forty-minute sermon during the regular worship service less than an hour ago. John Turner—dressed in his black suit with vest, white shirt, and wide black-and-green striped tie, high-topped jet-black shoes that were almost as dark as his leiotrichous hair—held his black derby hat in his left hand. He placed his worn brown Bible on the communion table to the left of the lectern and then invited the Bible students to join him in prayer.

"Lord, may the words of my mouth and the meditation of my heart be acceptable to you, oh Lord, my strength and my redeemer. Amen."

"Amen," followed the congregation in supportive expressions of unity.

"Please open your Bible to Jeremiah, chapter 29 verses 1 to 11," John Turner requested and gave them a moment to find the book, chapter, and verses.

"Now I need a volunteer to read these verses." As a skilled teacher, he did not want to embarrass nonreaders in attendance by forcing them to read. He also realized that the large participation of Bible study class members meant that they attended the class and trusted him to not call on them, even those participants who could not read, as some of his best scholars during question-and-answer sessions were actually nonreaders.

Stephen Ferguson raised his hand slightly and signaled the teacher that he would be willing to read the verses. John Turner nodded to him, and Stephen rose and reached back for his King James Version Bible. He read the verses from Jeremiah 29:1–11 and sat down.

"Well done. Thank you, Brother Ferguson."

John Turner commenced with the Bible study class, picking up where he had left off two weeks before. He reminded them about the Jewish captives' condition as noted in the text.

"Jeremiah's letter warned the Jewish captives in Babylon against their false prophets' deception and urged them to wait patiently for God's time. Too often during times of distress today, as in the times of the Judean captivity, there are those leaders who demand rebellion against the authority in power even though their present dire circumstances came about as a result of their own sin and idolatry. Some prophets told them that they would return to Jerusalem soon, within two or three years, but Jeremiah, writing from Jerusalem to the Judean captives, advised them that they had to stay there for seventy years before God would permit them to return to their homeland."

John Turner Pinn had a spotless reputation in the Ridge for his Christian character and biblical knowledge. Although he was only twenty-five years old and had limited training in reading and writing, he mastered the practical side of God's commandments. He not only knew the Word of God, but applied it in his teaching and everyday practice while at the same time imparting his sagacious insight with tribal members. John Turner, as he was called in the community by both names, a skillful and profitable carpenter and farmer, provided a better-than-average living for his wife and five children. His estate, land, home, and personal property were more than three times the average value of other tribal members and more than twice the estimated worth of the white residents in Amherst County.

As he believed that God's word required him to manage his financial talents frugally, John Turner perfected the application process by working hard, trusting in God's word to bless his work efforts, and giving up worldly enticements to waste money on nonessential items in life. He always advised his Fairmount Bible Study class members to follow his acronym, TRWS: *Trust* God to bless their life's efforts; *Risk* or forego unnecessary pleasures in life in favor of channeling additional time, human talent, and financial resources in a fertile manner; *Work hard* to achieve personal goals; and relax in soulful *Peace* with your life's lot.

Residents of the Ridge respected John Turner for his success as a carpenter and farmer and his Bible teaching skills. They were well aware that he had accumulated almost $5,000 toward his personal estate. One of his teaching strategies was checking for class members' attentiveness to and understanding of his instructions; one example is when he used the word "peace" in the TRWS acronym. His class members wondered how he got the S instead of a P for peace in the TRWS strategy, and one student actually asked him how he got the acronym TRWS. John Turner then responded cheerfully.

"I am glad you are listening to me! I left the P or peace out because the S has a better sound flow, TRWS, instead of TRWP. Remember, in the Hebrew language, *Shalom* or *Salem* means "peace." So, you have TRWS. *Trust* God, *risk* needless pleasures in life, *work hard*, and then go in *peace* while trusting God to provide the *shalom*. Why let life make you sweat when you have done the three—*trust, risk, and work*? Shalom to you, brothers and sisters!"

Bible school class members selected John Turner as their teacher more than two years ago, as they saw his fiery zeal in following God's commandments and his knowledge of all sixty-six books of the Bible. Because students knew that he was a fair and kind neighbor, each word that issued from his mouth during his discussions and question-and-answer sessions took on special meaning. His students esteemed their teacher as a worthy servant and messenger of God.

"My great-grandfather, Raleigh Pinn, and my grandfather, Turner Pinn, resisted battle cries from tribal members in the Ridge and Stonewall Mill whenever colonists mistreated them. We have heard stories about how some clan heads wanted great-grandfather and grandfather to take up arms against the colonists because of the way some of the local outsiders treated our Indian people. Just like during the days of Jeremiah and his advice to the captives in Babylon to be calm and not rebel against King Nebuchadnezzar, Raleigh Pinn and Turner did not let unwise clan leaders influence them as tribal chiefs to resort to rebellious acts against colonists."

John Turner continued his Bible teaching. "The year was around 596 BC when Jeremiah heard from the Lord, like our ancestors received words of wisdom, and then wrote a letter from Jerusalem to the three thousand exiles in Babylon. The passage, chapter 29 verses 5 to 6, reads,

> Build ye houses, and dwell in them; and plant gardens, and eat the fruit of them; take ye wives, and beget sons and daughters; and take wives for your sons, and give your daughters to husbands, that they may bear sons and daughters; that ye may be increased there, and not diminished.

"The main idea that the book emphasized is the assumption that Nebuchadnezzar was being used by God as his agent to punish the people of Judah because the exile to Babylon was the work of the Lord as a result of Judah's disobedience and idolatry. They were to settle down in their land of captivity and go on with their normal lives in the foreign land as if they were back in Judah. The captives were even to pray for their captors, as Jesus in Matthew 5:44 told his disciples to 'pray for those who spitefully use you and persecute you.'

"This has been the habit for Jewish people throughout history, as they had a way of enduring exile in foreign lands in peaceful existence while at the same time looking with faith in God to the future. Throughout history, Jews have adjusted to their country of captivity with the hope of being restored to their homeland.

"Students, what other groups, other than the Jews and African slaves have endured such hostility from their enemies as that directed against the American Indians? No other group to the degree of these three! Our ancestors always reminded tribal members that we are clannish like the Jews and have many of their customs. Forefathers told our members to be patient and not rebel, as they advocated shalom and demanded peace as Proverbs 15:1 exhorted, 'a soft answer turneth away wrath.'

"How could they fight against the colonists with their potent iron weapons and gun powder? My great-grandfather Raleigh decided that—since he could not whip the new colonial settlers—he would join them. He became an Amherst militiaman and later participated in the Battle of Yorktown against the great English general Cornwallis.

"Raleigh learned wisely from his daddy, my great-great-grandfather Robert, as he gave up the ghost while being pressured by new land-hungry colonists who were pushing his Wiccocomico Indian Town tribal members off their reservation land. Great-grandfather Raleigh, deciding that he was not going to fret, battle, and die over land like his daddy, Robert Pinn, left Wiccocomico Indian Town and came to Stonewall Mill and Buffalo Ridge. Our esteemed ancestors, having read this same biblical scripture from the book of Jeremiah in their lifetime, knew what to do: they remained in peace with their enemies to the point that their enemies decreased their level of hostility with the passage of each new moon.

"Our ancestors heard from God, and rather than fighting the colonists, bought land, built houses, and dwelled in them. They planted gardens and ate the produce from them. They married and had children. They did not, like many Indians in this colony and other colonies, take up arms against the newcomers. Verses 5 and 6 seemed to have been written directly for our people in Buffalo Ridge and Stonewall Mill. Did our people marry and have children? Yes, we did! Back in 1810, in Stonewall Mill, the Beverlys had seven families, half of fourteen Beverly families in the whole colony of Virginia. Of those seven families, there were more than sixty family members. They had children, all right! William Beverly over there had fifteen members in his family back then, and Betty Beverly had fourteen. Charles Beverly had a dozen in his household."

There was a loud explosion of laughter from the seventy-five students participating in the class. The adults realized that their ancestors modeled the biblical advice perfectly, as the two tribal communities were bursting at the seams with homes and inhabitants.

Bartlett Sparrow, now fifty years old and keenly aware of tribal members' fertility practices in the Ridge, remarked: "We did a darn good job. Excuse me for saying this in the church. I mean, we did a right good job of obeying those commands. Just look at all these houses hidden along the Ridge and at

Stonewall Mill, including those that you know are way back in the woods, and just notice how many people are here today for this Bible study! I would say our forefathers and present parents have been right active in begetting, excuse me, uh, uh, rather they have been active in reproducing. Just focus out there at the Fairmount graveyard and at the large number of gravestones and sunken places in the ground. You need only to look at our teacher, John Turner, barely twenty-five but with a whole bunch—I mean—a whole bench full of children."

Bartlett, pointing to Turner Pinn's family as they sat in their pew reinforced his point. "Look at their mother, Martha Ann, and notice all her children: James, William, Jesse, John, and Robert."

She wore an ankle-length emerald-green dress. Her brown high-top shoes could be seen only when she lifted her dress two or three inches to pat her feet during devotional singing in the previous church service. An attractive, regal woman, she had been leaning forward as she listened to her husband's class teaching. She quickly drew herself back against the pew. She did not like to be placed out front in public settings, as Bartlett's remarks had directed all the class members' eyes toward her. Therefore, she reclined on the bench in her reserved, humble, and shy manner. With nowhere to hide, her bright facial complexion turned fiery red and drew even more attention.

The students smiled at her as they knew Bartlett's comments were meant to be complimentary—lauding John Turner and her for their obedience to God's words in being fruitful—and not derogatory.

Bartlett promptly retrieved the audience's attention when he stated, "God's word in Genesis 1:28 commanded us to multiply. I have done my best to see that happen. The Good Book says, 'Be fruitful, and multiply, and replenish the earth.'" He spoke about Martha Ann Beverley Pinn while she sat with her five children on the third bench, on the row to the left of her husband, John Turner Pinn, who had been speaking from the lectern. This was the same lectern from which Fairmount's preacher spoke on first and third Sundays at 12:30 p.m. The Bible Study class was always held at 2:00 p.m., right after the preaching service.

William Beverly, who is around eighty years old, was there with his second wife, Judith Sparrow Beverly. They married in Nelson County on Independence Day, 4 July 1827. William, after losing his wife, Eady Pinn Beverly, married Judith.

Martha Ann usually lined up her children by ages. She sat near the center aisle, followed by James, William, Jesse, John, and Robert. Bartlett Sparrow's remark about the couple's sexual productivity—asserting that Martha Ann and John Turner missed only one year procreating since their marriage—was akin to the 'pot talking about the kettle.' Although he did not produce children annually, Bartlett had more seeds than John Turner as he and Maria filled two rows on the right side of the church. Maria Pinn Sparrow, Bartlett's wife, age forty-five, daughter of Turner Pinn, sat with her children: Mary, James, Simpson, Turner, Cyrus, Joicey, John, and Lavania. Their daughter, Segis, sat with her boyfriend, Frank C. Beverley, son of Rita Beverley of Appomattox County. They would have a marriage ceremony on March 15, 1855.

Maria Pinn Sparrow was a Bible scholar and an inquisitive student who frequently asked helpful questions to assist her nephew, John Turner, as he endeavored to enlighten all participants in the living Word of God. The Sparrows were also known for doing their part in populating the Ridge. William Sparrow, age forty-five, sat with his family of twelve members on rows five and six, to the right of John Turner's lectern.

"Look at verse 7. Who can tell me what it means?" John Turner inquired. He was a practical-minded instructor, not only teaching the Scriptures from a content and knowledge level, but also conducting the class with a desire to move the members in a conduct-oriented, application phase after the class has ended. He wanted class members' behavior to benefit from class participation, not just cognitive, theoretical analyses of the verses.

"Tell me what it means to us in 1850, not in 590 BC. I want to know what this scripture is telling us today."

Anthony McCoy of Stonewall Mill responded excitedly, "It says to 'seek the peace of the city whither I have caused you to be carried away captive, and pray unto the Lord for it: for in the peace thereof shall ye have peace.' This means that we must pray for our communities, because we cannot truly pray in the Holy Spirit sincerely if we disobey God's word. God told us through the prophet Jeremiah to seek peace now that we have gathered in these secluded hamlets. Since it was God's will that we have been brought here, we must live peacefully with each other and our white neighbors. Because we have built homes, married wives, and produced children, we, including our forefathers, have obeyed these requirements. We have built homes and married wives, generally, of our own people, aboriginal women, like the Jews had to marry Jewish wives." He paused, but continued after a moment. "There is, however, another part to God's requirements. He wants us to live peacefully, and in the process, our Lord will hear our prayer requests. If we behave, God will not turn a deaf ear to our prayers but will bless us with further peace. On the other hand, if we stir up discontent and strife against our neighbors here in and outside these hamlets, we can be assured that God will not hear our prayers. We know this command is justified because we have followed it, and as a result, have lived peacefully in this colony with our tribal neighbors and white colonists. As a result, God has blessed us with homes, land, and gardens, more land and great farms, and a horn of children, more children than we ever imagined. We have sought peace and the Lord has given us more peace than we, as free people of color, aboriginal people, have ever expected. We are surrounded by some people who don't like colored people, yet through the will of God and our obedience to his word, we are not engaged in combat against our white neighbors. How could this happen unless God was with us? Tell me, how could we possibly have all this land up here and not have white land-grabbing, baser sorts taking it, unless God has been standing guard to protect us? What about Samuel Scott's prosperity, with his personal worth totaling more than $7,000, and other tribal members up here and at Stonewall Mill? God has been good to us."

"Great answer, Brother McCoy. I cannot add to or take away anything you just said. Thank you for a job well done," John

Turner commended. "It is great to have you and others who have come from Stonewall Mill to join us in the Bible study class."

Anthony McCoy, seventy-seven, sat with his wife, Susan, who is ten years younger than him. Their other children and grandchildren, sitting on their pew, were Sophia, forty-two; Delaware; Amanda; Macca; and Henry. Albert McCoy, age thirty-two, came with his father, Anthony, and sat on another pew. Albert sat with his wife, Mary, and five children: Martha, Mary, Charles, Peter, and Benjamin. Martha covered her breasts with a shawl as she nursed Benjamin. The McCoys, brown-complexioned full-, half-, and quarter-blood Cherokees with straight black hair, sat on their pews, proud to be affiliated with the Buffalo Ridge band of Cherokees. The Ridge and Stonewall Mill had become their villages of refuge as they had trickled into the area over the last forty to sixty years from areas believed to have been Chickamauga County in Tennessee and Covewhulla Creek section of Georgia, with each new visitor strategically summoning two or three others from Tennessee in cycles of every few years. They abided by the plans established and enforced by Raleigh and Turner Pinn, as the chiefs did not want to cause any discontent among white residents in Amherst County due to too many Cherokees coming into the area at the same time. The forefathers believed in God's word by keeping the peace and they practiced shalom commands daily. Both bands' populations were bursting at the seams and placing their peace in jeopardy, as the colonists were starting to become suspicious of the large number of strange Indian-looking people around the area.

"Don't let me hear of you, class members, disturbing the peace next week or even next year. From as far back as our oral history takes us, we do not know of any major peace disturbances that occurred in opposition to God's word. The closest thing that we can come to non-peaceful action was that Yorktown Battle in 1781, but my great-grandfather Raleigh had permission from God to fight against the British. He would never have gone into any battle without the Lord's approval, so you must follow in his footsteps and seek the will of the Lord in your life before you do anything to disturb the tranquility of God's universe."

John Turner flipped the page to what he thought was the heart of the chapter. "Let us read verse 11 silently first, then one volunteer will read it aloud, and lastly we will all read it in unison."

After a minute, Albert McCoy's daughter, Martha, raised her hand, and asked shyly, "May I read the verse, Mr. Pinn?"

"You have permission, and thank you."

"Verse 11: 'For I know the thoughts that I think toward you, saith the Lord, thoughts of peace, and not of evil, to give you an expected end.' May the Lord bless us as hearers. Amen."

"Thank you, Martha. You are a good reader, considering the fact that you are only ten years old. Let us give her our applause, as well as her father and mother, Albert and Mary, for their good training work with their oldest daughter."

The class applauded longer than usual, as they were very proud of Martha, looking like an angel in her white cotton dress and black-and-white high-top shoes. She sat near the large potbelly stove and the flickering blazes had thrown beams of light against her face while she read verse 11 slowly. The applause reflected appreciation of her reading, just as the stove's rays reflected radiance on and magnified her cherubic countenance.

"Who can tell me what this verse means, first for the Judean people, and then for us today in 1850?" John Turner looked around at the fifteen or so raised hands. "Let me see, well, there are so many hands. I need someone to tell me which one went up first."

Anderson Beverly, his wife Pamilia, and three-year-old son Chalman sat in the second from the last pew near the back of the church. Anderson said, "I believe I saw Stephen Ferguson's hand shoot up first. Nobody can beat him in raising hands because of his carpentry skills with those hammers every day. John Turner, did you have to ask whose hand went up first? You were wasting your breath! You knew before you asked the question that it was Stephen."

Stephen was the husband of Susan Selby and the son of the late Jethro Ferguson. He and Susan huddled together, ages sixty-two and fifty-seven, respectively, holding each other's hands and looking like a romantic teenage couple. They were known for their fertility when other couples, around their same ages, had long ago ceased to reproduce. Their youngest children, Judy, as she was called, age fifteen, sat on the pew on her daddy's right and Susan, age twelve, leaned on her mother's left arm. Stephen was one of Stonewall Mill clans' leaders. Giving due credit to his Christian name, as well of his father Jethro's biblical first name, Stephen was a true scholar of the Good Book. With his sharp knowledge of the Word and his snappy hands, he was a clear choice to win the battle among "hand raisers."

"If we were not in this sacred place, I would swear from my view in the back here that I saw Judy lend some assistance to her daddy's arm as it shot up in the air," John Turner teased Judy. "Brother Ferguson, help me out here. Enlighten the class and me with your deep words of edification."

"Class, I apologize for the edge I have of being the first to raise my hand because I do get encouragement and pressure from both daughters. All the way over here, from the time we left home, while riding the ferry across the James River and during the three-mile wagon trip up here to the Ridge, my girls, Judy and Susan, made it clear that they expected me to be a good student today. So with this twin assault against me, you must understand why I raised my hand so fast and spoke up. Now, what was that question, again?" he asked.

John Turner repeated the inquiry. "Can you, Brother Ferguson, tell me what verse 11 means, first for the Judean people and then for us today in the year 1850?"

"The verse says, 'For I know the thoughts that I think toward you, saith the Lord, thoughts of peace, and not of evil, to give you an expected end.'"

Stephen placed the Bible on his lap and looked up, first toward John Turner, and then to his left and right as he began to give his answer. "God is saying to the people that he knows what he is doing, as Creator and Sustainer of the world. I am a carpenter and have plans each time I go on a new carpentry job. God has plans too. He has our lives mapped out and he does not plan to leave us, just as he did not bring the people of Judah all the way to 590 BC to leave them in Babylon. He assured them of this when he said that he has peaceful thoughts and not evil thoughts. His thoughts come before his plans. When I go to work, I have plans, and then I complete those plans that I thought about earlier. God told the captives in Babylon that he would finish that plan that he has for the captives—plans for peace. This means that he would free them in the future, but they must keep the faith in him to bring the prophecy to completion."

"You did an excellent explanation of that verse, Brother Ferguson. Now that you edified us and we know about 590 BC, what about AD 1850? What is verse 11 saying about us in the Ridge and Stonewall Mill today? I will give you a hint about what I am looking for in particular. What did Great-grandfather Raleigh tell us about peace and the Pearl? He passed a story down by way of his son, Turner, who lived to tell us what Patriot Raleigh said. What did Grandfather Turner tell us a few years ago about the Pearl? I know Grandfather Turner is here today, all eighty years of wisdom, but he is not permitted to help you with the answer."

"Thank you, brother teacher, for the hint. I know what you want me to say. As a carpenter, I have learned certain rules of life. I learned them from my father, Jethro, who was an excellent carpenter. He taught me some basic rules for success and often reminded me to follow those principles to have peace in my carpentry trade. Each time that I hit my thumb with the hammer, cursing and using God's name in vain did not help me have peace from my thumb's pain. Since it was my fault that I messed up my thumb, because I did not follow sound carpentry rules, I had to learn to just stop the bleeding, block out the pain, and profit from the principles that kept my daddy's thumb healthy. I had faith that if I followed the carpentry safety rules, I would eventually experience peace." He glanced at his daughters and wife in turn, and then continued.

"God informed Judah in captivity, by way of the prophet, that they disobeyed his commandments, broke his covenants over many generations, and even ignored his promises to send them into captivity if they did not obey his laws. Jeremiah assured the people that his long-range plan was to bring them peace from captivity, even though they had disobeyed him for generations.

Even though they must wait seventy years for freedom from Babylon, they could still have peace of mind and spirit in their daily lives as they maintained that faith in God to keep his promise. Our Wiccocomico and Cherokee people have suffered for centuries, and have survived colonists' efforts to wipe Indian people from the face of the earth. They have chased us off our God-given land, beaten up and left us to die, burned our homes and villages, destroyed our crops and orchards, and forced us to go hungry for days and weeks. We have seen Indian children who survived, existing as orphans, sent into indentured servitude. Like the Jewish people in Babylon, we too wondered why God was punishing us, even though we knew that punishment and chastening bring about patience, make us pray, and lead us to work for peace. Amid the cries from some unwise tribal members, who advised various extreme steps against the colonists, our sages kept calm like Jeremiah in 590 BC. Our tribal wise men trusted in God to give us peace, even during and after the Wiccocomico Indian Town's destruction and the colonial militia's assaults on Cherokee villages in the 1760s and 1775. They kept their faith in God, Jehovah Shalom, or God of Peace, to bring them peace at some point in the distant future." He paused for a breath, but he had more to say.

"My daddy, Jethro—who built your Great-granddaddy Raleigh's three new tobacco barns while he was fighting General Cornwallis at Yorktown in 1781—told me a story about a pearl, a narrative that he first heard from the Patriot Raleigh. Raleigh had grown up in Wiccocomico Indian Town and knew about oysters' pearls. Apparently, Raleigh shared the story with his son, Turner, and Turner passed the story on to you. It seems that sand and other harmful objects occasionally slip into the oyster's shell and irritate its tender body. Through suffering, God gives the oyster the ability to endure hardship and troubles, those foreign objects that invade its territory within the shell. The oyster endures the pain on its body by keeping calm and secreting a substance around the sand or other foreign objects. Trusting that the secreted substance will get hard over time while having faith in the substance to protect its tender body against those prickly foreign objects, the oyster has peace even in pain, while waiting for the pain to stop. The pearl covers the invading object and protects the oyster from the prickly intrusion. The long periods of suffering, through peaceful coexistence with the prickly object, became the reason for the oyster taking on a precious gem in its shell, a pearl. The greater the pain, the greater the amount of secreted substance the oyster produces."

Many of the parishioners nodded at him encouragingly to continue.

"We can learn about the level of the oyster's suffering by examining the size and quality of the pearl. That little oyster had the faith to keep on producing the secretion, in pain, over time, while staying in perfect peace with the pearl-enclosed foreign object. What faith the oyster had! It sought peace in its habitation. We as Cherokee people have sought peace in our habitations, at various times in history. We kept up our faith in God that we or our seeds would have peace in time. We built houses, even though the colonists like to say our houses were not really houses. They said this so that history would forgive them for taking our land. All of you here, even the striplings, know what they asserted: 'The land was just Cherokee hunting land because we didn't see any brick homes or wood constructions like we build on the land. That proves that they never lived here in Virginia. They just came, hunted, and went back to their Cherokee territory nightly in other colonies.'

"Well, we've got news for the colonists! We came, built homes, married wives, and had children in Virginia. Many of those houses, unlike the colonists' homes, were small, wooden structures, caves, longhouses, and other constructions. This scripture here told us to keep calm and make peace with the newcomers who want to make us captives or drive us from the colony. The sages knew that, in time, our people would have peace. In reality, they already had peace of spirit because they had faith in God to keep his word. That faith gave us the present peace as well as assurance that God would bring that final peace that comes after death, which surpasses all understanding.

"Turner told us that his mother Sarah saw visions of colonists asserting to the world that Cherokees never lived in Virginia. She dreamed that unscrupulous officials and historians would sink so low as to deny that her children, grandchildren, and great-grandchildren had royal aboriginal heritage. In time, however, Sarah experienced peace, because she realized that God is in charge of the future and that genocide would not prevail. She told us that she saw the scripture from Isaiah, chapter 54 verse 17, that assured her that 'no weapon formed' against her people would prosper and that this is the 'heritage of the servants of the Lord.' With this dream, she enjoyed some semblance of comfort on earth as she looked forward to joining her ancestors and the perfect Prince of Peace, Christ.

"Our ancestors looked forward to Jehovah Shalom. Just as the Jews waited peacefully for God to bring them true peace from Nebuchadnezzar and captivity, we now experience peace because of the Pearl, with the understanding that full peace might not come in our lifetime."

Stephen interrupted his own storytelling. "Mr. Teacher," Stephen begged, "I don't want to steal your thunder any further, as I know you are ready to seize this golden occasion to deal with the Cherokee and Wiccocomico heritage, the Pearl. You have, through your skillful teaching style, set up this opportunity to discuss the Pearl, and I would be remiss if I didn't yield now to your instructions."

Judy and Susan, jumping up from their pew and applauding wholeheartedly their father's excellent responses to the teacher's questions, led the response as the whole class stood with thunderous handclapping and hurrahs, and exploded into cheers for Stephen. The church, rocking under the movement of so many at once, reminded the students of the shouting occasions that occurred at the annual revivals in September.

"Thank you, class. Thank you for giving a well-deserved expression for Mr. Ferguson's great answers. Thank you, clan leader Ferguson. Grandfather Pinn—Chief Pinn—you are up next, after that great explanation by clan leader Ferguson. As Bible class teacher, I yield to you, Granddaddy. Since we are required to make the Pearl explanation officially, at least one time in each decade, I believe now is the time. The opportunity has been brought on by Mr. Ferguson's answers to my question. Please, Grandfather Pinn, explain the Pearl."

Turner Pinn—who sat on the front pew with his wife, Joicey, age seventy, John Pinn, age thirty, Lavania Pinn, age ten, and Samuel Pinn, age six, wiping his eyes with his handkerchief quickly—felt uneasy because he was in a dewy-eyed, unprepared state. His friend, relative, and clan leader, Stephen Ferguson, had set up the perfect occasion for the Pearl discussion even though Turner Pinn's red and watery eyes revealed his uneasiness. Since the chief is expected to maintain his composure at all times, he realized that he must act like he was in meditation, until such time that he was prepared to stand up.

"Grandfather Pinn, I mean, Chief, we need your services!" John Turner pleaded. Then John Turner realized that his grandfather was crying. He suspected that his tears resulted from all of Turner's painful mental images of atrocities that the Cherokee and Wiccocomico people have endured over the centuries. John Turner surmised that his granddaddy was tearfully happy that this study group, almost instantly, had arrived at such a high level of readiness for new wisdom on the Pearl.

Chief Turner Pinn became sentimental over the fact that the Pearl kept the peace over the years, even under circumstances caused by colonists' hostility, resentment, and verbal and physical hostility. Peace seemed to be the philosophy of the Ridge, as Polly Pinn, his daughter and John Turner's mother, was at peace as she had departed to join her ancestors and the Prince of Peace. He wondered why he had been permitted to live a peaceful life, longer than his daughter, since he was already past the "three scores and ten years" point. He meditated over this Bible study session and how his grandson conducted the Bible study so wisely. What would he say to the group? How could he simplify the abstract concept of the Pearl so that even the youngest generation of participants would comprehend it at a level that would support memory for a lifetime, hopefully at a level of understanding equal to that of Stephen Ferguson? How would he explain the Pearl in a way that connected with Stephen's answers?

The whole class sat forward in silence and respect as they waited for the Chief to stand, at which point all attendees would jump up and come to attention until he signaled them with the lowering of his right hand to be seated. Class members were wise enough to keep their seats, as they did not want to be so presumptuous as to assume that Chief Pinn was ready to stand. The decision to stand and explain the Pearl was his alone, not the Bible study teacher's determination.

Turner sat, eyes closed and head bowed in meditation. Joicey, despite concern that her husband's deep meditation prevented him from knowing that his grandson had yielded the floor to him, also bowed her head but kept her eyes open as she occasionally looked toward her husband. She wondered why he did not stand and address the class, considering that he always longed for the opportune time to discuss the Pearl.

The lull in all activity, other than the intense breathing from class members and visual expressions of anticipation and wonder, lasted for several minutes. Then Wyatt Jewell, age ninety-nine, broke the placidness when he raised his small frame in a tortoise-like fashion, slowly but noisily, from his seat between Mary Beverley and George Jewell. With all the students' eyes on him, he meandered deliberately toward the lectern. After begging for permission to address the assembly, with his raised right hand slightly pointing toward John Turner, who was now seated on the front pew, he broke the silence.

"Inasmuch as I am the oldest person in this meeting today, although not the oldest tribal member in the Ridge or Stonewall Mill, I beseech Bartlett Sparrow to stand here on my left to help steady me while Judah Scott, wife of the late Samuel and mother of Delaware Scott, position herself to my right." He summoned William Beverley, eighty years old, and his wife, Judy Sparrow Beverly, age seventy, to form a line to his right.

"Stephen, would you and your wife, Susan Selby, join me to my far left." He waited. "Jonathan Beverley, you and John Cousins need to come up front also."

Standing in a semicircle near the lectern and facing Turner Pinn, he said, "Everyone, please stand up and receive our leader, Chief Pinn!" Bartlett Sparrow held him steadily.

Every person in the assembly stood up and applauded continuously until Turner Pinn stood up and walked toward the front of the church. When his hands touched the lectern and he had positioned himself behind it, Wyatt and his line of receivers, who represented family members in attendance at the Bible study class, walked back to their seats and the audience sat down.

Turner, wiping his misty eyes from which he had successfully kept back the tears, spoke slowly and softly. "Patriot Pinn, after he returned from the Yorktown Battle in 1781, where he had been a leading scout and reconnaissance militiaman, spoke to us in this very church or on this same spot in which I am now standing." He talked while occasionally looking down at the floor, as if remembering what his father may have been feeling almost seventy years ago and putting himself in the mood to speak.

"Members, greetings to you. Thank you and our teacher for this occasion to discuss the Pearl. It is miraculous the way we arrived to this point in the Bible study. First, our teacher dealt with the lesson on Jeremiah 29, verses 5 and 6. As Teacher John Turner has directed us to this point and Brother Ferguson has so wisely explained his questions, I am elated to follow them with the Pearl discussion.

"Thank you, Wyatt, and those tribal members who came forward with him to receive me with such pomp and circumstance. I am just plain old Turner Pinn. I don't know how long our Creator will allow me to tread my clay feet on his dusty earth. Given the fact that I am just clay, I am special because God's breath is inside me and I am a living being. I am also special, as you are, because of the Pearl.

"The Pearl is the spirit, with a small s, not the capital S of Holy Spirit. The Pearl, with a capital P, is the spirit of the ages, the ghost of the ages, as the Germans like to refer. The Ridge and the Stonewall Mill people are special not only because we were and are created and sustained by God, but because we, like God's chosen people in captivity in Babylon, have the spirit of the ages. Our ancestors obeyed God and built houses, grew gardens, took wives, and had children. Our ancestor, the Great

Man Pewem of Wiccocomico, if he were here, could connect the spirit of the ages before his time with our time and we could see the Pearl clearly. We have suffered like the oyster with impediments of sand or other foreign matter, with the colonists invading our habitat and causing pain to our bodies. Our Indian people have, in the process of doing what Jeremiah 29 told Judah to do, experienced impediments to our habitats. Early colonists invaded our Wiccocomico Indian Town reservations and moved our people further inland. Then newcomer colonists also came, like grains of sand against the oyster's tender body, and pressured us to move further inland. How could we have peace with the newcomers, with these impediments pressuring our habitats? If we continued to move each time we faced irritations, we would never have a heritage, but if we stayed we had to suffer genocide by death or by assimilation. We either had to adopt the colonists' ways and forget our heritage or resist the colonists' ways and face further dispersions like the ones that our ancestors faced at Wiccocomico Indian Town.

"The only option that we have, if we want a heritage, is to stay, dig in, build houses, plant gardens, marry, and have children. I know the colonists don't want us to remain, but we must stay. Now, here is where the Pearl comes in. When we stayed on Buffalo Ridge in the late 1700s, we faced pressures from the newcomers from England. Since the two groups could not occupy the same space, we found the space first and dug in the Ridge and Stonewall Mill. I know they came against us with all types of pressures, but Raleigh's spirit of love allowed him to love his enemies. He built a protective barrier of love around those impediments to protect his tribe against painful and potentially destructive impediments. He acted like a colonist but stayed Cherokee and Wiccocomico. While inviting new Cherokees to join his beloved Wiccocomico and Cherokee heritage, he accepted his lot in life, the suffering and mistreatment as an aboriginal resident by loving his neighbors, not fighting them. The little oyster could not have peace within its shell while, at the same instance, fighting the sand or sticks that slipped in. Raleigh wrapped a partition of love, peace, and prayer between the tribe and the colonists.

"Raleigh Pinn knew the story of the Rechahecrians, the Cherokees in Virginia at the fall near Richmond in 1656. Daddy told me how the colonists, as impediments, irritated him so much that he wanted to come out of his own shell. They tried to dislodge the seven hundred Cherokees at Richmond falls when the Colonial Council in session at the time, after learning of the Cherokees being so close to them, ordered colonial soldiers to go against the Cherokees to dislodge them. They even followed a much-used tactic practiced today when they asked other Indians to join them in fighting the Cherokees. The Cherokees could have run from their shell, but they stayed.

"Let me say here, before I go further, that you must expect this colony, Virginia, to keep you under pressure until you deny your Cherokee ancestry or leave the colony. They will even use other Indian tribes to help dislodge your heritage or physical presence. You must still love the colonial officials and even those naïve aboriginal pawns that they use to help them. The love that you show them, in effect, builds up the size and quality of the Pearl.

"The more pressures you have over the ages, the more love and kindness it takes to protect you against the mental and physical pressures that they are bringing on your tribe. The threat of taking away your heritage is painful. We constantly face pressure when the officials encourage us to act like and marry colonists, and in the process cease to be Indian. The added pressure that we always face is that, if we do not marry the colonists, they threaten us by stating that we never did exist in Virginia: 'only colonists lived in Virginia, not Cherokees.' 'Only Cherokee hunting parties roamed in Virginia.' 'Cherokees did not live here because they went back to other colonies every night.' They have done and will continue to do everything possible to see that our history in Virginia is not recorded for posterity. Never forget that impediment on our tribe. It is the hatred for Cherokees, anything Cherokee in Virginia. They will either make you leave the colony or make you deny your Cherokee heritage. The Pearl, the love in spite of the hatred, wraps around the impediment, and protects you over the years against your soul's destruction, that is, malicious hatred against colonists. Why should we deny our history, our heritage in Virginia, just because colonists don't like the word Cherokee? They even dislike the word Wiccocomico. The colonists in the Northern Neck tried to remove all Wiccocomico. Live with the genocide, the hatred, the land stealing, and the mistreatment by insulating the impediments with love.

"Almost seventy years ago, I was a young boy when I saw my daddy, Chief Raleigh, talk on this spot before they built this church. He told us what the Pearl is and what it is not. He told us that the Pearl is the *love* that we have in our heart for the Lord and for our neighbors, even the irritating colonists. He told us that we cannot hide or shroud prejudice against any person or group of people. He used the example of General Cornwallis. I remember that one so well. He said that just as Cornwallis's army had to surrender at Yorktown and come out with his surrender flag waving, we have to give up hatred in our hearts. We must surrender and come out with our hands up, apologizing for our prejudice. Human beings cannot hate fellow humans. Daddy admitted that he had hidden hatred for British colonists, and he could not have any peace until he surrendered his soul to the Lord and allowed peace between the colonists and himself. He warned us that God would put a siege around our spiritual and social positions when we mistreat other races and heritages. Follow the Golden Rule.

"Second, he told us that we must *live quietly and peacefully*, and attend to our own business. This action would help build protection and a buffer around impediments in life. Daddy told us that even when other tribes mistreat us, we should live quietly and peacefully with them and ourselves. This was sound advice! How could we have existed up here in the Ridge, Indian people, free people of color, looking like Indians with straight hair, talking with different dialects and keeping strangely to ourselves? We didn't have the protection of a missionary church organization to protect us as a buffer from the colonists. We didn't have a missionary group to tell us how to be an Indian group. We knew how to live and let live, even when in pain because of our neighbors. Through it all, we survived. Daddy promised us that if we followed the five principles, we would have peace.

"Let me not get ahead of myself. Third, Daddy made us promise to take up arms against anyone who takes up arms against America. '*Rise up in defense of America,* should a new adversary attempt to take away America's freedoms,' he said. Raleigh fought against the British, and as a result, he insulated himself and the tribe against accusations that our people were not patriots. The Pearl is precious in the Ridge.

"Fourth, he made us promise to *get education,* a trade, like what he earned in his indentured servitude. He survived by learning a trade and reading and writing better, and thereby improving his ability to make a living. This tended to keep the peace in the Ridge. Daddy didn't let the colonists cheat him on produce purchases and land deals.

"Fifth, speaking of land, he encouraged us to *purchase land* and build homes. Since human beings do not own land, as we cannot really own the land, the ground from which we came, and as it will receive our bodies when we die, we still should go through the motions and acquire land deeds. 'Don't let the colonists say that we never lived here. Don't let them commit genocide on us by saying that there is no paper evidence that we ever existed,' he said. The insulation against annihilation from the Ridge is to purchase those deeds so that you can have peace up here. This is the protection from pain. Daddy told us not to let the colonists call us vagabonds, wanderers, and ramblers. He ordered us to get deeds. When our ancestors' descendants show our land records to the colonists' descendants two hundred years hence, they cannot say we did not exist as free aboriginal people. If they try to say that we didn't exist as aboriginal Americans, they would be deluding themselves. They will be lying to their souls and putting it under a siege like the one in which Cornwallis was caught in 1781 at Yorktown. Cornwallis surrendered the battle but didn't come out of his hole in which he had hidden. The colonists who refuse to believe that we existed, with all of our documentation, will be greater pretenders under siege like Cornwallis at Yorktown.

"Finally, he spoke to us from Colossians 3:17, 'And whatsoever ye do in word or deed, *do all in the name of the Lord Jesus*, giving thanks to God and the Father by him.' Pray to God and give him thanks for his blessings in placing us in a contented, peaceful state on earth and at peace with our lot and our neighbors, regardless of how prickly they may be.

"Now, after thousands of years, we have survived in America, and who knows how many hundred years we have existed in this colony of Virginia? What other object, other than the Pearl, could have protected us from the sand and foreign substances in life? The Patriot Pinn's Pearl kept us safe, through it all. We are here even though some colonists don't want us here. We can prove our heritage as well as or better than any Indian group in the colony, as the Patriot made sure to leave a legacy. He reminded us almost seventy years ago how he made sure that they knew that he was both Wiccocomico and Cherokee and how he demanded that they include those facts on records. He assured us that no sensible person with the Pearl—the historical spirit of suffering and resisting—could ever say we are not aboriginal Cherokee and Wiccocomico. To close this talk, since it is now almost five thirty, my daddy had added protection against colonial genocidal attempts. He told us not to cast the Pearl at people who were too hoggish to receive it as worthy and priceless, as they would consume or trample it. Either way, it would be a conscious or unconscious attempt to destroy the Pearl rather than appreciating the special tradition of peace, love, and kindness that has blended our people for centuries in America and Virginia.

"Don't beg anyone to accept you as aboriginal Cherokee and Wiccocomico. You and your Creator know who you are, and therefore, it does not matter if you are appreciated or not. Let the Creator attend to people who dislike you because of your race, and you deal with matters within your human realm, issues with more magnitude and solemnity. You let God deal with people who are opposing you and working in those dark spiritual and satanic realms. If the future is to be in any way like our glorious and exciting past, with the pain, and the Pearl getting larger and more precious with the passage of each moon, we can be assured that the present and future life will bring new impediments into our habitat. Shalom to you, whether those stumbling blocks, obstacles, and burdens come as the results of social genocide, physical attacks, or historical genocide. Whether you face these pressures today when you leave this church or two hundred years hence, go in peace. Shalom."

The assembly sprang up, clapped, and stomped their feet in acts of acclaim to and praise for Chief Pinn. Turner sat down as his wife, Joicey, reached for his face with both palms, looked directly into his eyes, and said, "I love you, my chief."

John Turner, wiping his wet jet-black eyes with his handkerchief in amazement and joy for his grandfather's wisdom, went to the lectern and announced, "In accordance with our custom that no speeches may follow the chief's annual or ten-year generational lecture, I now declare this Bible study class over, even though I would love to compliment the chief for his timely speech and his skillful ability to connect Jeremiah 29 with peace, progeny, and the Pearl."

Did John Turner know that he would receive the tribal chief torch from his grandfather in several years and must give the next generational speech on the Pearl in that very location? Was he aware that his unborn daughter, Martha Jane Pinn, would bring a new aboriginal name into the tribe—West, a popular English and Cherokee surname? He suspected that his descendants would pass on the legacy of the Pearl, but he did not know that his daughter would marry Willis West, son of Willis West Senior and Betsy Beverly.

Did John Turner know that new Cherokee family members over the next century united in holy matrimony with tribal members and produced a stronger Cherokee heritage? Did he have any idea that this little girl, Judy— who assisted her father, Stephen Ferguson, during the question-and-answer session— produced a son, Joseph Peter Ferguson, who married Ann Megginson's daughter, Isabelle? Did he know that Peter and Isabelle had a child named Augustus Ferguson, who wedded Nannie West, daughter of Willis West and Martha Jane Pinn?

Martha Jane was the daughter of John Turner Pinn and Martha Ann Beverly, daughter of Polly Beverley.

It is amazing—the tribal connection! Patriot Pinn, back in March 1794, dreamed about the rainbow of tribal nuptials through the ages. His dream about the intricate tribal marriages had already become a reality in 1850, and it was obvious that the pattern would continue.

It is doubtful that John Turner, in 1850, realized the major influence that Patriot Pinn made on the legacy of Buffalo Ridge and Stonewall Mill people, the history of Amherst and Appomattox Counties, and the heritage of Virginia in general. Little did he know that these special aboriginal people continued Patriot Pinn's Pearl through many generations and centuries— or did he?

Shalom.

> Is it possible?
> Is it possible?
> So cruel intent,
> So hasty heat, and so soon spent,
> From love to hate, and thence for to relent?
> Is it possible? Is it possible? . . . All is possible!
> —Sir Thomas Wyatt, Is it Possible?

22

Is It Possible?

April 1855

Turner Pinn summoned a meeting with three of the Stonewall Mill clan leaders to assess their ongoing progress in producing diversity in the Cherokee/Wiccocomico bands on Buffalo Ridge and Stonewall Mill. Stephen Ferguson, Anthony McCoy, and William Beverly had been informed about the meeting during Sunday's church service on Buffalo Ridge. The meeting had been scheduled for Monday, April 9, under the great oak tree on the western bank of the James River near Stapleton, where the Porridge Creek runs into the James River. The meeting was set to begin at 2:00 p.m.

At about 12:35 p.m., Stephen pushed his canoe from the Appomattox County riverbank and rowed about a hundred yards to the island in the middle of the James River. He had some difficulty sculling his beech bark canoe over to the island, as the muddy, chestnut colored waters were turbulent and roaring. He did this to test the waters rather than to attempt a direct voyage to the meeting site at a greater angle from the Appomattox County shore to the Stapleton bank. He realized that he would have an easier go of it if he departed from the island and moved with the flow of the water at a much straighter angle to the Stapleton rendezvous location on the left side. As predicted, his excellent sculling skills and the raging water flow brought his canoe quickly and roughly to the Amherst County bank at Stapleton. Stephen was the first of the three clan leaders to arrive at the designated site.

Turner, the Chief, arrived on his stallion about ten minutes after one o'clock. He dismounted his horse and greeted the standing Stephen with his usual, "*O siyo.*" Hello.

Stephen responded, "*Do hi quu, ni hi na hv.*" I am well, and you?.

The chief replied, "*O s da.*" Good.

The Chief invited Stephen to sit down on an oak log near his canoe. "Stephen, I am glad that you arrived before Anthony McCoy, as I have a serious tribal matter to discuss with you."

Stephen lifted his humble, respectful head and looked his chief in the eyes. "First, I need to tell you that William Beverly expressed his regrets that he could not attend. He has gotten a bad spring cold. I told him that I would pass on to him the information from this meeting when I get back. I will stop by his house before I go home to tell him what we discussed."

"I would be grateful to you, if you don't mind. I don't want to canoe through those rough waters anytime soon."

"Now, Chief, you said you have a serious matter to discuss with me?"

"Yes. Let me get to the matter before Anthony gets here, as it will save some time. I understand that your daughter had a son a few months ago. I realize that you and your wife Susan have the freedom to permit your daughter to have a child, as it is your business. I am just the chief, and as your chief, I need to know where you and your clan are going with this heritage thing. Do you know who the father is? Does he fit into our predetermined scheme of things for the tribe? I am sorry . . . I regret to have to inquire into this matter, but it is both a religious and a tribal issue."

"Chief, the father of Judith's son, Joseph Peter, is Dr. Isbell. You know him. Frederick is the doctor over in Appomattox County. He is white, but the way he acts among our clan members, I am sure he has some aboriginal blood in him. As far as our tribal 'scheme of things,' it just happened. Judith fell in love with him and she got herself with child. Dr. Isbell could have killed the baby before it was born, but he told Judith and me that he loves her and his Maker too much to take the life of their child. He did not consider the idea. I guess that answered the religious part of your question. It would be against God's will to kill the child of Dr. Isbell and Judith. What do you think?"

"Well, first of all, I suspected that this would happen. I guess you and Susan did not see that young Frederick getting carried away with Judith for the last three years. I predicted that Dr. Isbell would come over to our side soon, seeing that he and his people are as clannish as we aboriginal people are. I did not think that he would actually father a child by Judith and not destroy the baby before he was born. He must be telling the truth because you said that he told you he loves her. I think he is showing his heartfelt love of God and Judith by keeping the child. I heard that Dr. Isbell has been getting carried away with your daughter's beauty. You know that she has that Cherokee blood mixing up with Susan Selby's European blood. Susan is a very pleasant lady for eyes to behold! I guess if anyone is at fault, it is me since I did not advise you against marrying Susan way back then. You used the same excuse that you are stating now about Dr. Isbell's folks. You told me then that Susan's people like to hang around with our native people and that her people act just like us, that they are 'clannish.' I remember when some of the people in Prince Edward County took your in-laws, Susan's people, to court for hanging around with our Native people. The neighbors tried to charge the Selbys with associating with colored people! The judge threw the charge out of court. Even the judge sided with your in-laws. The judge also knew that you and our other family members are aboriginal people.

"If fault is to be sought in that matter, it should stop with me. Now that you and Susan gave birth to Judith and Susan, and as they are naturally beautiful girls, what can we expect but to have all those male colonists languishing and panting in the worse way for them? As your Chief, I should have put a stop to that Dr. Isbell two or three years ago at the Isbell store. I saw how the eyeballs of one of the colonists almost left his eye sockets when

Judith innocently raised her arms and yawned. Can you believe this? She was not even safe when she did something simple and innocent like raising her arms to yawn. That is why we have that tribal rule in place now against tribal women raising arms while yawning. It is impolite. You know that we do not think it is ladylike for our girls to yawn in public! I saw those colonist boys looking and drooling over Judith one day down at the Isbells' store. I am not surprised at the fact that he is interested in her. So he loves one of our beautiful girls. I admit I did notice Frederick looking at Judith. He didn't look at Judith in an unseemly way. So he does love her?"

"Chief, as far as the matter goes about the tribal issue, Dr. Isbell comes from a long line of European royalty! When Judith told me that she was three months pregnant, I was very upset. I was ready to aim a bow and arrow on Frederick's bottom when she started crying and shouting that Frederick is 'royalty.' She pleaded, 'Don't shoot him, Daddy, he is descended from kings and queens, barons, dukes and duchesses, counts, princes in England, France, Scotland, Norway, please don't shoot him!' I wondered what his royalty had to do with me wanting to put one of those royal Cherokee arrows in his bottom.

"Then it came to me, the royalty stuff! Look at all the importance we have been placing on the Cherokee royalty in our tribe and the Wiccocomico connection with the Great Man of Wiccocomico, Robert Pekwem. During our 1850 annual tribal meeting, I vaguely remember one of our clan leaders stressed the importance of documenting native royalty among the Cherokees and Wiccocomicos in our tribe. Remember, the Harrises had that Harris princess that came into our area and joined her family, our Harris clan, fleeing from all that 'removal to Oklahoma' talk. Every year you give a short lecture on our aboriginal royalty for the benefit of our young and old people. Judith was sitting with me and my wife. Susan was also on the church bench with us during that particular meeting five years ago. We, the chief and clan leaders, planted the idea in Judith's mind that it is all right to have children by a father with royal blood, regardless if it is Cherokee, Wiccocomico, English, Scot, or whatever.

"That is why she kept holding my arm as I wondered if I should put the arrow in the bow string. Judith said, 'Don't shoot him, Daddy,' as if her son, Joseph Peter, would lose his royal father. At the time, I did not think his connection with European kings and queens mattered in the least. Now that I have had time to think about it, it does fit into our 'scheme of things.' Your father, Chief Raleigh, said a long time ago that we should leave a paper trail, writings about our history to prove to later generations that we existed. He said that we cannot really trust the colonists to keep those records to give our side the advantage. We can now say that our people go back to earlier times because the Isbells and Fergusons have records. Our native people did not write things down until a few years ago with the invention of the Cherokee Sequoyah syllabary. Before that, we did not write down all the ancestors that came before my great-grandfather. The Europeans, on the other hand, kept perfect records of who begat whom. Did you know that Frederick is the ninth great-grandchild of Sir Thomas Wyatt, the renowned poet? He was the one who wrote 'Is it possible?'

> Is it possible?
> Is it possible?
> So cruel intent,
> So hasty heat, and so soon spent,
> From love to hate, and thence for to relent?
> Is it possible? Is it possible? . . . All is possible!

"The poem is about a lover recounting the fleeting fancy of his fickle mistress. Judith at first did not want to have anything to do with that Frederick, but when he promised to support Joseph and any other children that they would have, then she had a change of mind. He said that he would treat his children like little royal blood heirs. He would give them land and build houses for them. That fits into our plans. As Chief Raleigh always said, we need to have children and build stone and wood houses so that colonists will know that we have been here in Virginia," Stephen said.

"Daddy Raleigh at first respected the colonists, and over a period of time, after they started stealing our rich, fertile Wiccocomico aboriginal land, he changed his attitude from appreciation to dislike," Turner said. "Later, he relented and began to love the English colonists as God's children. This change for the better came about after something he saw in that great battle at Yorktown. He saw some black Rhode Island militiamen assault a British barrier at Yorktown without any fear. He was very impressed with their character and determination to get the job done. They defeated General Cornwallis's soldiers stationed in that wooden barricade. Daddy Raleigh realized that all people, regardless of their colors or political views, are to be valued and loved. That war did something to Daddy Raleigh. That Wyatt poem makes me think about how Daddy relented, after first hating the English. He actually relented before he died. Maybe that Wyatt fellow wrote that poem for Joseph Peter and his tenth great-grandson's tribe. We should love all people regardless of their colors. We can learn a lesson from people more than ten to twelve generations past.

"My father, Raleigh, had a vision way back that the new colonists did not care to document that we were here in Virginia," Turner stated. "He said that colonists believe that unless the Injuns had a physical building on their own property, they did not really live here. They had to own the land. Otherwise, they were just passing through Virginia. Our people had to have physical houses built exactly like the English people, or else. If they didn't, then colonial historians refused to write down words that showed to later generations that we were really here."

"I know Dr. Isbell will keep a good record of his son, Joseph Peter," Stephen attested in support of his daughter's boyfriend. "All of his uncles and aunts will also write down words that say, 'The Fergusons were here in Appomattox County, free native people.' I dare the jealous colonists to mark out the history records of the powerful Isbells, Fergusons, and Megginsons at the courthouse. That Dr. Isbell's line goes way back to influential people. Sir Wyatt went with King Henry and Anne Boleyn on several trips. Ann Boleyn, at that time, was the king's mistress first, and then Anne married the king later, in January 1533. Dr.

Isbell's ninth Great-grandfather Wyatt served in her coronation in June of that year. Frederick is related way back to King Henry and Anne."

Chief Pinn and Stephen had been meeting informally on the banks of the James for almost an hour when they noticed Anthony rowing his canoe toward them. He was trying to rotate the rowing blades ninety degrees at the end of each stroke, allowing the blades to extend away from the canoe as he rotated them. They wondered if they should go out to help bring Anthony in, since he had begun rowing from the Appomattox County side of the river at a rough angle across the flow of the water. After a few minutes of battle between the boatman and the raging James River, Anthony gained control of the canoe by sheer sculling skills. After three or four minutes, his vessel flowed onto the Amherst County river edge.

Anthony floated up to the bank, placed his oars on the canoe seat, climbed out, and pulled the craft completely on land near Stephen's canoe. Anthony then bowed slightly to his chief while shaking his hand, and said, "*O si yo.*" He then greeted Stephen with a hello and a handshake. Stephen responded with an "*O si yo*" in return.

Stephen could hardly wait to tease Anthony about his brief difficulty in the James, fighting the swift water flow. "Anthony, I thought you were a better boatman than what I just saw out there in the middle of the James! I assumed you had our Cherokee canoe sculling skills. What happened a few minutes ago? Chief Pinn and I were about to jump into my beech bark canoe and come out there to steady your boat!"

"Stephen, if you could have come across the water any better than I did, prove it now! Here is my canoe, mount up and row across to Appomattox. Teach me how to cross the river against those waves. I need a how-to-row lesson from you so I can learn how to get back after this meeting with the Chief."

"I am just teasing you, Anthony! You did better than I did when I traversed over to the island about an hour ago, then I rowed with the water at a slight angle to the left. I had a time getting down here from the island! Mind you, I am not trying to tell you how to maneuver your boat back home. But if I were you, I would walk upstream with that canoe for about a mile or two and then ride with the flow, rowing at an angle slightly to the right all the way to your departing spot over yonder."

Chief Pinn, realizing that he needs to speak up and provide some closure to his arguing clan members' conversation, suggested, "Both of you should walk together with your canoes on the edge of the James, about a mile upstream, and then you two can ride with the waters down to your getting off points over there. Stephen, you will reach your point quicker, but maybe you and Anthony can help each other until you get off at your spot. Anthony, with your sculling skills, you should make it with ease down to your docking station."

"Chief, that sounds like a good idea," Stephen responded. Anthony, suspecting that Turner was trying to mediate the conversation between the two clan leaders, brought closure to the matter by agreeing with the chief.

"Great idea! We will walk up along the edge of the river about a mile, and then row on the Appomattox side of the island so you can get off at your spot, Stephen, and then I should be able to have a smoother and straighter ride down to my spot. I hope the return trip is smoother than my trip over here. I had the strangest feeling that something eventful happened or will happen on this day, April 9, either in the past, today, or in the future," Anthony said. "I was struggling to get over here when my mind tried to tell me about a great struggle between two powers. I don't know what the canoe episode on the James River between 1:30 and 2:00 p.m. has to do with some future fateful event in either Amherst County or Appomattox County. My discernment tells me that something great is going to happen soon! It took me ten minutes longer to get across that river, and that is unusual! What does ten minutes of time have to do with answering my uneasiness about that future event? Men, this is strange! You should have been with me on that river out there during the whole voyage over here. My spirit was caught up in the past, present, and the future. I wonder what is going to happen here in ten days, ten months, or ten years. What is going to happen? I am usually correct in my predictions, so I had better write this day down as keepsake."

It is amazing how accurate Anthony's premonition was! It would be ten years to the date, Monday, April 9, 1865, when a very dramatic event would occur. Between 1:30 and 4:00 p.m., Gen. Robert Lee would sign a surrender treaty with Gen. Ulysses Grant at the McLean House in the town of Appomattox, about ten or fifteen miles as the crow flies from Stapleton.

Chief Pinn moved in a half-circle and declared, "Meeting in session!"

They always met in a semicircle with their backs to the west and their countenances facing east, toward Stonewall Mill on the eastern side of the river. This ceremony reflected their ritual of facing east when major business transactions occurred in the tribe, with their backs toward Buffalo Ridge symbolizing the fact that the chief left the Ridge, the major band. By all participants facing in the direction of their sister band in Appomattox County (formerly Buckingham County), their semicircle posture represented the unity between the two bands.

Across the James River, in Appomattox, exactly ten years later to the day, Gen. Robert E. Lee and Gen. Ulysses S. Grant negotiated the terms of surrender which led to the end of the War Between the States. Anthony's unusual struggle in the water represented the struggle that General Lee endured up to the 4:00 p.m. closure to the surrender treaty. It was around 4:00 p.m. that General Lee finally shook hands with General Grant. Lee bowed to the other officers and he and Colonel Marshall left the room. It would be a supreme moment in the nation's history. Anthony was not able to tell Chief Pinn and Stephen the date and details of the future event, but his premonition was on target, almost to the day and hour of the actual momentous event.

As the Buffalo Ridge and Stonewall Mill bands were always free people of color, aboriginal people of America as far back as antiquity, and had never been in that horrible institution of slavery, the surrender event in Appomattox would still have a powerful influence on all peoples in Central Virginia and America in general. Anthony never did feel comfortable in his spirit as he remembered the almost traumatic, life-threatening episode on the James River and the foreboding revelation.

Ten years later, almost to the day, Stephen's grandchildren, two of Judy's children, would have a fateful moment with soldiers of the Confederate Army. Stonewall Mill band legend revealed a slight confrontation between the Ferguson boys and several soldiers as they were marching through Appomattox in their retreat from Richmond to Lynchburg. It seems that Stephen's grandsons were standing behind a fence that ran along the road on which the Confederates were marching when some of the soldiers—hungry, dirty, and raggedy— saw the two boys resting against a fence and eating large pieces of ashcakes. The soldiers begged for a little piece of the corn bread. The Ferguson boys, not realizing the state of hunger that existed among the soldiers of the Confederate Army, responded with a resounding negative statement. "You are not going to get any of this ashcake!" they said. The soldiers kept on marching up the road, tired and limping along while looking back at the boys to see if they changed their minds about giving them a piece of the delicious-looking treat.

The Fergusons' influential position in the community had an impact of making the boys independent thinkers. Their social status in the neighborhood permitted them to behave like white youths even though they were free people of color. The boys' harsh answer probably resulted from the generally hateful impression that the Ferguson family had about Lee's soldiers. Some of the tribal members' ancestors had been caught up in the horrible institution of indentured servitude, and they were very sympathetic to the African men and women who were being kept in slavery. The Ferguson boys saw the little slave boys working under cruel conditions and believed that the Confederates were fighting the Union soldiers to keep the Africans in slavery. The tribal bands disliked the Confederate soldiers because they somehow connected the war efforts of Lee's soldiers with the strength of the institution of slavery.

"Men, I summoned you to this meeting because you know how our people have begun marrying spouses other than tribal members. As chief, I need to assess what is going on and determine if these matrimonies fit into our tribal schemes. You know that the Pankeys have gotten connected with some of those descendants of passengers who came over on the *Mayflower* ship and lived at Plymouth, Massachusetts. They were the Cookes, Francis Cooke. His descendants were some of the Pankeys, Cookes, and Chamberses. The Pankey line goes all the way back to France, back to Jean Panetier or Pankey, who lived between the late 1600s and the early 1700s. They lived in Saintonge, France. He was a man named Jean, but they called him John. I guess he changed the sound of his name because he was embarrassed with having a female first name. The Pankeys over there just had a little child that year. That little child goes all the way back to France. I meant to ask you clan leaders what you think Chief Raleigh Pinn would say about all this marrying and having babies with the colonists from Europe."

Anthony asked, "What does this have to do with me, Chief?"

"I need to talk to you three clan leaders on the Stonewall side—well, two leaders, since William Beverly cannot be with us today. He is my brother-in-law, as his first wife, Eady, was my sister. Please make sure that you give him a briefing on each thing that we discuss today. I don't need to talk to Saunders Pinn in Stonewall because he is my son and from my line.

"I need to know to what degree you, as pillar leaders of the tribe, are maintaining our tribal integrity. Keep a record of all Stonewall tribal marriages and give me a report each time one of our men and women marry. I need to know whether a man, a Buffalo Ridge Beverly boy, for example, is proposing to join up with a Stonewall girl. One of you needs to go to the Appomattox County courthouse and make sure that your name, as clan leader, is on that piece of marriage document. You remember how Daddy Raleigh always stood in the shadow of those recordings at various courthouses. He was called a surety. He would make sure if you were a relative, like a bride's father, that the clerk scribes the correct name on the court paper. You must continue to practice this, to be responsible for one another. If you cannot go to the courthouse, then send one of your fast young boys over to the Ridge to tell me and I will come over to Appomattox Courthouse. I will let them mark my name down as surety. That way, we leave a discrete but powerful record for later generations that we were a close knit tribe. Nobody can say we were not in America as aboriginal people. We are united in a tight-knit bond, regardless if the James River runs between our two land bodies! Later generations of tribal descendants will know what we were doing, standing behind that bride and groom at the courthouse.

"Both of you know how Chief Raleigh always had his name put on those marriage licenses, whether the couples were on the Amherst or Buckingham County side. He was there in Amherst County when his daughter Anna Pinn married Thomas Evans, the blacksmith. He was instrumental in encouraging the courtship of his daughter Eady Pinn and William Beverly. Look at all those Beverly children they had. Now their children's children are populating all over Stonewall and Buffalo Ridge. They are crossing the James River and moving to Amherst County. My father, Raleigh, approved the marriage between Frances Beverly and Mary Williams. He was there to leave evidence on the marriage license that this was a tribal marriage. I don't have the time to name the different couples that had his permission and blessing to marry."

Anthony said, "I promise to let your know if any of my clan members are getting married. If I cannot be there in the shadow of their filling out those papers, I will send a messenger to tell you to hurry up and come."

"*Wa do*, Anthony," Chief Pinn said. "Stephen, you think you can monitor this on your end of Stonewall?"

"By all means, Chief!" Stephen asserted, knowing all along that he was more than excited about being in the shadow of those marriages of his clan members. He would make his way to the courthouse, no matter what came up. Even if he were sick, he would get Susan to place him in a buggy and drive him to the town of Appomattox to put his name on the court papers. To Stephen, it was an honor to leave his name at the courthouse to prove that he was an important man in the tribe at Stonewall Mill.

Little did Stephen and Anthony know that a fire would burn down the Appomattox County Courthouse in a few years and some of those archival papers would be lost from the eyes of descendants and historians forever.

"Now, men, clan leaders, listen to me. We have to keep in mind the type of men and women that are marrying each other. Are they marrying responsible partners? Partners who will be there for the long term? The men and women must be people who will protect the family over time as well as people who will look out for the Cherokee tribe's welfare. Who knows? He might end up being called on to be the chief. If the chief cannot take care of his own house, how can he lead the tribe?

"Is the bride from good stock? The same goes for the man. Did the girl know what kind of Cherokee or Wiccocomico family the spouse came from? Were the grandfathers warriors and hunters, or did they make the clothes and cook the food in the house with the women? Did the women go hunting for household food? How much royal ancestry has been passed down through the line of the husband or wife? These things are important to me as chief of the tribe. They were important to Chief Raleigh! Clan leader Stephen Ferguson will share with you, Anthony, the story regarding Judith. Keep in mind, Anthony, that at one time, Daddy Raleigh did not look kindly on any of the tribal members going out of predetermined and socially permissible aboriginal families for a partner. If one of our people liked the looks of a colonist's son or daughter, or one of those pale faces' sons or daughters happened to be in love with one of our aboriginal people's son or daughter, Chief Raleigh would not have approved them. Later, however, after Daddy went off to that battle at Yorktown, my mother said that Daddy changed his attitude toward the colonists. The colonists could even date or marry one of our people or one of our people could go over and marry one of their people. Daddy changed his opinion. Any man or woman marrying into our tribe, white or aboriginal, had to be a partner with some right breeding! That family had to have some good breeding and, and, you know what I mean. Stephen just gave me some background on Judy's man. I know you are aware that Stephen's oldest girl's son is part colonist. If you ask him, Stephen will tell you who her child's father is. But for now, I just want to know what is going on with your clan and the breeding that is going on."

Anthony said, "Chief Pinn, as you know, my son, Albert, married a Ferguson and her line goes all the way back to Scotland, the Scot Highlands. The Fergusons have that long line from kings and queens, barons, dukes and duchesses, all the way back to the fifth century. Their royalty has gotten connected with royalty from Italy, England, Spain, France, and who knows where else. Those royals like to find other royals to marry, and it does not matter what country they come from, as long as they are royals.

"I wouldn't be surprised if my son's wife's parents and kin investigated my ancestors' background all the way to Tennessee and determined that our people were fierce warriors in battle against our enemies. Our people whipped those clannish Royal Highlanders in one of those great battles that they fought against our people about a hundred years ago. The Highlander soldiers who marched with the British troops in the 1700s against Cherokees probably took back to Scotland the stories about how fiercely our people fought. Their descendants heard about Tennessee Cherokee warriors and came across the sea to America to find us, to marry our women and men. Those Scots and Englishmen are more clannish than we McCoys are! All of the colonist people who descend from people who were in Scotland, England, France, and other places, some places that I cannot say the big words of names, are real clannish. Years ago, before they came to America, they lived in great stone houses that are called castles in Europe. They have three or four floors on top of each other, held up by stones and rocks. The walls are made of solid stones. Today, the colonists have small houses compared to those castles in their homeland beyond the Atlantic Ocean.

"Chief, you know the McCoy men are good fighters and carpenters. On the carpenter side, we like to build houses with wood, with one or two floors. We can even put stones on the walls, but we prefer not to build more floors than two or three. Stephen knows what I am talking about, the clannish style! His wife's people, the Selbys, travel like gypsies. Where one Selby goes, the whole gang follows. If they go to the well to get some water, the rest of the gang goes over to get the dipper and put it into the bucket. If one yawns, all the others yawn!"

Stephen laughed behind his right palm held to his face and comically acknowledged the truth of Anthony's words. He lifted his left hand and said, "Anthony, you have stopped working as a carpenter and have gone into court jester work, telling jokes. Chief, Anthony and I know how important it is to leave a legacy for our band over there in Stonewall, and we know you are doing the same up there in the Ridge. You have a responsibility to protect our tribe, and we are behind your efforts. Please know that all the Stonewall clan leaders are walking the extra mile to protect our tribal history and heritage."

Chief Pinn said, "The colonists who came to America from Europe and their descendants—some of whom are living today in Amherst and Appomattox counties—enjoy trying to make us feel like we are the new people in America. They like to make us think we have to look up to them, as if we are the dark-complexioned visitors and they have been here since antiquity. They have it backward! We also know from our teachings at Fairmount Church that we must not be respecters of persons, that we should love everyone regardless of his or her background, color, and wealth. But we know that we have to do a better job of teaching European social skills to our children. We must train our people to develop *etiquette* in society and proper manners. We are not *heathens*, as the baser sort colonists prefer to refer to us, often using the 'heathen' word. Wouldn't they be surprised to know that many of our tribal members have direct and indirect connections with the great kings in Europe? Albert's wife, Mary, with some of her French royal ancestors speaking in the spirit through her, likes to use this French word with our Stonewall children. Just before we eat with or in front of the colonists in public, she says, 'Make sure we all follow proper *etiquette*!'

"Anthony, your son Albert, because of his wife's ancestors, has connected those Scot Highlanders and Englishmen with the Buffalo Ridge and Stonewall Mill bands of Cherokees. Can you believe that descendants of those Highlanders and Englishmen who fought against Cherokee towns in the 1700s are back here now as family and not enemies?"

Stephen continued to give the story about the Fergusons, based on what Dr. Isbell told his daughter about the royal families in Scotland and England. These facts were generally corroborated by the information that Albert shared with him about Mary's ancestors.

"Way back, about three hundred and ten years ago—say, about 1541—John Ferguson was born. His daddy was Robert Ferguson. Robert Ferguson of Craigdarroch, Glencarin, Dumfriesshire in Scotland was married to Janet Cunningham. Robert's mother and father were Thomas Ferguson and Margaret Crichton. They married around the year 1508. That Crichton family was descended from royalty. Margaret's father was 2nd Lord Robert Crichton of Sanquhar, Scotland, and his wife was, as I remember, Marion Maxwell. Robert Crichton 2nd Lord had a father named Robert Crichton of Riccarton and his grandfather was called Robert I Crichton of Sanquhar in Sanquhar Castle, Dumfriesshire, Scotland. His great-grandfather was Sir Robert Crichton of Sanquhar, Sheriff of Dumfries. I think the Sheriff's great-grandfather, William De Crichton of Crichton Castle, Scotland, married royalty. That line descended from many royal folks. There was Alexander I "the Fierce," King of Scotland, who married wife Maceth around 1103 in Scotland. His father was Malcolm III Canmore "Longneck," King of Scotland. His father was King Duncan I of Scotland. If you keep on going back in time, I have lost track, but I think King Duncan I had a great-grandfather named Malcolm I of Scotland. Royalty was way back in that family. Constantine I of Scotland is way back there, around A.D. 850.

"If my memory was as good as all the information that that boy, Dr. Isbell, told me and I had the time to tell it all, we would be out here all day, all night, and into next week. You have to let me go home for supper, at least. With all that royalty between Dr. Isbell and the Fergusons, I would never get back over to Stonewall. There is not enough dry wood on this riverbank to use for firewood for a campfire to take us through the night and into next week. That Styrbjorn "the Strong" Olafsson, Prince of Sweden, and wife Thyra Haraldsdatter, Queen of Norway, brought in the Norway and Sweden families to Stonewall. Then there were the Denmark royals, the King Harald III "Bluetooth," King of Denmark, around A.D. 910. By the way, around the same time as the King of Denmark, there was the royal Lady of Leinster of the Highland in Scotland, around A.D. 950.

"Chief, you started this long discussion. I have to keep going before I forget what I had planned to say. I have rehearsed this a long time, about three weeks. You know, King Henry I of Selby in Yorkshire, England, married Matilda, Princess of Scotland in 1100 in Westminster, London, England. Charlemagne of France or rather Charles the Great, Emperor of the Holy Roman Empire, reigned in the mid- to late A.D. 700s. There is that Berenger II, King of Italy, born about 928 AD, who died in Germany. He is in this family also! King of France, Hugh Capet and his son, the Pious King of France, Robert II, is in that Capet line. The Balls are in this family line with the Fergusons also, Gen. George Washington's mother's sister's side. The Isbells are not directly related, just indirectly, to President Washington, being his great-great-uncle . . . I have lost track! He is in there somewhere!"

Chief Turner spoke up. "I do not want to try to remember all those long, strange names. Our oral traditions require us to remember our aboriginal ancestors back ten or more generations. Now you want me to add all those European names. You want me to remember British people who might have had children who fought our ancestors in the 1600s and 1700s. They followed our people to Wiccocomico. Then they came to Amherst and Buckingham Counties. They also fought our ancestors in the Cherokee villages. Some of those Highlander royals sent their royal Scot Highlander to assault our Cherokee towns. It is amazing what God can do to a people over two or three hundred years! It is said that a day is as a thousand years and a thousand years as a day with the Lord. So those hundred plus years since the Highlanders fought our people and now marrying and having children in Stonewall in 1855, those years amount to be about a fraction of a day with God. It is awesome how God can turn hate to love in a fraction of a day! One minute they are archenemies, fighting warriors in Cherokee towns, and the next minute or the next hour or two hours, a fraction of a day with God, they are in love with our women or men in Stonewall Mill. Only God has the power to do this! Leaders, clan leaders, this meeting is closed." The chief stated. "I came here to meet with you, with a heavy heart. I had planned to give you a tongue lashing for all these courting that I have heard about going on in Appomattox County between the aboriginals and the colonist newcomers. I have always wanted our people to marry and have children with our own tribal members. Today, you clan leaders have more wisdom than your chief! You are planning what I believe God has planned for our people to keep them from disappearing in history. Since both bands' tribal members are intermarrying, Buffalo Ridge will have little royal aboriginals and European royals as well.

"The baser sorts in Amherst County would love to blot us out from Amherst history. They have begun calling us people of color. The next thing they will do is to start calling us blacks, like their slaves. We have never been in slavery! Whenever our native people have been enslaved, they escaped. We know every molehill, hollow, and cave in this country! How can the newcomers try to enslave people who have been in American since antiquity? Now they think calling us colored will make them feel important and make us think we are less than they are! I can see that your people in Stonewall Mill, your white royal kinfolks, have begun protecting your backs against those baser sort folks. It is amazing what a river, the James River, named after the King of England, does to both protect our people and be the cause of division. As the river served to divide our one peoples into two different locations, it protected our tribe for over a century against enemies who did not want us to form a large tribe of Cherokees on the Amherst County side. Now our band on the east side of the river lives a different type of social life. Some of you can marry white European people and still be Cherokees and Wiccocomicos. In Amherst, we stay with our own people, Cherokees and Wiccocomicos. The descendants of European colonists now want to call us colored. They haven't quite figured out yet that we are the same band, just divided by the James. On the other hand, our Bible, the King James Bible, tries to bring us together. True believers in God are not 'respecters of persons.' One would think the name James would work the same way with the James River.

"Speaking for my daddy, Raleigh Pinn, I want to thank both of you for your wisdom in encouraging marriage between the two people, the aboriginals and Europeans. I know that William Beverly feels the same way I feel, as he is my brother-in-law. He married my sister. Daddy Raleigh wanted clan leaders to train their people to keep written records of our aboriginal history. Those Europeans really know how to save the names of folks begetting other folks. This king begat this prince and this prince begat the 'Fierce King' of whatever. If they know how to remember all those begetters in England and can still remember those names after traveling across the Atlantic Ocean, they can be entrusted with our oral heritage and certainly write down our more recent history. Thank you on behalf of Daddy. *Wa do!* See you on Sunday at Fairmount. *O s das v hi ye i!* Good evening!"

Chief Turner mounted his horse while Stephen and Anthony pushed their canoes into the water and stepped into the crafts. They waited with their paddles, holding them in an upward position, giving the signal of respect to Turner Pinn. They waited for their chief to leave first, then pushed off from the bank and rowed in a slightly straight line up and against the raging river until they reached the island. They turned about a hundred yards above the island and allowed the fast flowing water to move their canoes at an angle toward the Appomattox side of the river. After a short time, Stephen stepped out of his canoe and pulled it on the bank. He waved to Anthony as he flowed on down the river toward his stop.

"Make sure that you stay close to the bank!" shouted Stephen jokingly over the noisy, rapidly flowing James. "I don't want to have to come down to get you out of that water when your craft turns over and drags you all the way down to Bent Creek!"

"Yes, please don't hold your breath until I lose control of this canoe. I will just have to come back up there later with my shovel and bury you!"

At that moment, while Stephen pulled his canoe further inland and Anthony continued his jerking movement down the river, both clan leaders looked toward Stapleton at the same time and spotted their Chief on his horse. He had turned around, come to attention, and looked at both men, as if to say, "I will not leave until I know both of you have stepped on the Appomattox bank and are safe from the rapid river water."

After Anthony stepped out of his canoe and onto the bank, Turner then turned his horse in a military manner in the direction of Buffalo Ridge. He thought to himself, *I would like to see those newcomers' historians try to erase us from Virginia history. They like to say, 'When did the colonists first see those Stonewall Indians?' They have their new tradition now of not letting our history start in America until they come over here by ship, build their houses, and then record words on a piece of paper: 'I saw this Indian and that Indian in this village and that village.'*

Our people can say, 'Not only can the newcomer colonists say they saw us or our ancestors, here in the 1600s and 1700s, but they can even say and write down on paper that they married and/or had children with those Indians!'

The Pankeys, Fergusons, McCoys, and the Cousinses can even say that some of the **Mayflower** *passengers who left Plymouth and moved down here in the early 1600s, 'saw our aboriginal ancestors in Buckingham County.' They can also say that some of the passengers and descendants married and/or had children with them. Our tribal history started long before the colonists arrived and we have colonial relatives who are eyewitnesses to assert it!"*

Turner reminisced about his father. He wondered how it were possibly that his daddy's attitude relented from the cruel intent against the English settlers for years to that of peace, with almost perfect peace with the colonists. Turner spoke out words of thanksgiving on his horse! "Daddy actually had compassion for those Englishmen and Germans at Yorktown as they sang that song *Guide me, O Thou Great Jehovah*." Then he wondered how Sir Thomas Wyatt had the wisdom to write that poem about his daddy. He remembered the words and spoke the words repeatedly and loudly, as if he were trying to remember them for Joicey as soon as he got back to the cabin.

"Is it possible?
So cruel intent,
So hasty heat, and so soon spent,
From love to hate, and thence for to relent?
Is it possible? Is it possible? . . . All is possible!"

How did my daddy, Pinn the Patriot, *know that his Pearl would be so valuable? Did he really know that they would suffer from European colonists' persecution? Did my father have any idea that these colonists' descendants would marry and have children with descendants of the people that they previously persecuted? Patriot Pinn's Pearl, what a heritage!*

Turner, after the thirty-minute horse ride on the three-mile Buffalo Ridge road, approached his cabin as the sun was going down on the western horizon. He looked toward his home and saw Joicey waiting on the porch, waving at him.

I need to tell Joicey to remind me ten years from today, on April 9, 1865 *to see what happened in Amherst County, Appomattox County, or in the James River. Anthony was so sure today that something weird or monumental will happen in ten months or ten years exactly from hence. If the Lord will, and Joicey and I live, I want to see how prophetic Anthony's spirit was while he was rowing on the raging James today.*

Epilogue

Members of the United Cherokee Indian Tribe of Virginia, Inc. (UCITOVA) trace their ancestry back to Northumberland County, where the "King of Wiccocomico Indian Town," Robert Pewem/Pekwem/Pinn, is recorded as their first ancestral chief and patriarch. As English settlers encroached on the Northern Neck Indians' reservation, Chief Pinn's great-grandson Raleigh Pinn—who with other relatives served briefly as indentured servants—left the area in search of new western land for their people and mingled with other Indian tribes, including the Cherokees. Raleigh, who had both Wiccocomico and Cherokee heritage, used his training as a Native American farmer and experiences with white settlers as an indentured servant to become a successful farmer in Amherst and Buckingham Counties.

Amherst County court deed records from the late 1700s to the early 1800s detail his land transactions. Raleigh Pinn was also a militiaman with the Amherst County Militia, eventually serving in the Revolutionary War at the Battle of Yorktown. Even though Raleigh Pinn successfully assimilated in many ways into the white culture, he continued to honor his Native American heritage. He formed two bands of mixed Cherokee and Wiccocomico on lands he owned; one in Stonewall Mill in Buckingham County and one in Buffalo Ridge in Amherst County, separated by the James River. Raleigh Pinn—strategically parting the bands so as not to alarm local colonists with one large Cherokee settlement—served as chief of both Cherokee groups for many years.

Four hundred plus years later, suffering and sorrow have continued to attach to UCITOVA's joy and jubilation, but

Raleigh Pinn's *Pearl* still endures. Surviving the effects of war, Native slavery, economic and social ostracism, and historical and racial genocide, more than seven hundred card-carrying UCITOVA members exist today. In a state where the dominant culture's official and unofficial racial integrity and genocidal strategies have been used for centuries in attempts to blot Native Americans from Virginia's archival records, UCITOVA still survives!

Some of UCITOVA's officials believe that state politicians turned over the approval process to the eight tribes so that Native Americans can take the blame for continuing Native American genocide, knowing that a proverbial "foxes in charge of the hen house" state would exist. Since the eight tribes are taking their time admitting new Virginia tribes while they are actively seeking U.S. congressional approval as federally acknowledged tribes, UCITOVA and other Native Virginia tribal applicants have been stalled while they write state-recognition procedures. Virginia's officials could honestly say, "It is their fault, not our fault. We admit that we mistreated Native Americans in Virginia for generations and we have already apologized for our ancestors' behavior toward them. The officially approved tribes are in charge now, not us!"

The state-approved tribes have highlighted to U.S. congressional committees the mistreatment they have received at the hands of Virginia's dominant culture. The fact is that they do not have sufficient documentation to seek Bureau of Indian Affairs' (BIA) approval because of Virginia's official genocidal policies regarding Native Americans for generations. Therefore, they indicate that they have no other choice but to seek U.S. congressional approval. UCITOVA officials feel that state-approved tribes should seek approval through Congress, if that is the only means to achieve federal approval. In the meantime, since 1992, for twenty-two years, the Council on Indians have been writing and rewriting Virginia's acknowledgment process for new tribes at a high bar, on the BIA format, a level that they themselves admit they could not qualify if they were to reapply today. During the period of the development of the acknowledgment rules and procedures, the Council on Indians has approved three additional tribes within the last four years.

UCITOVA's officials and members admit that their ancestors were correct when they suspected statewide genocide. They believed that colonists would "put up other Indians to do the destruction that they themselves were unable to do—just as they forced a Virginia Indian tribe in 1656 to help their soldiers fight Cherokee forces who had settled at the falls in Richmond, Virginia." The Pearl, UCITOVA, continues to experience roadblocks in its four-hundred-plus-years epic tradition of suffering while trying to survive as a tribe.

What would Raleigh Pinn—Revolutionary War patriot and Amherst County militiaman, realtor, farmer, and tribal leader—say and do if he were aware of what was happening to his Pearl in Virginia today? If Raleigh and other UCITOVA Revolutionary War ancestors only knew about the genocidal strategies that have been put into play since their deaths and up to this point in Virginia history—how their great Commonwealth, for which they went to war against British and Tory enemies was treating the Pearl/UCITOVA—what would they think?. If they were able, they would turn over in their graves in Pinn Park Burial Grounds!

RECOMMENDED READING

A List of Militia Ordered into Revolutionary Service from Amherst County, Swen Library, The College of William and Mary. Williamsburg, VA.

Egloff, Keith, and Deborah Woodward.1992. *First People: The Early Indians of Virginia.* Richmond, Virginia: Virginia Department of Historic Resources.

Forbes, Jack.1988. *Black Africans and Native Americans.*"Native Americans as Mulattoes." New York: Basil Blackwell, Incorporated.

Grainger, John D. 2005. *The Battle of Yorktown, 1781: A Reassessment.* Woodbridge, Suffolk: Boydell and Brewer Limited, 2005.

Hamel, Paul, and Mary Chiltoskey. 1975. *Cherokee Plants: Their Uses—a 400 Year History.* 1975. Hamel, Paul B. and Mary U. Chiltoskey. Sylva, N.C.: Herald Publishing Co.

Higginbotham, Don. 1961. *Daniel Morgan: Revolutionary Rifleman.* Chapel Hill: The University of North Carolina Press.

Huston, James A. 1991. *Logistics of Liberty.* London: Associated University Presses.

Ingram, Scott. 2002. *The Battle of Yorktown.* Farmington Hills, MI: Blackbirch Press.

Johnson, Henry P. 1881. *The Yorktown Campaign and the Surrender of Cornwallis 1781.* New York: Harper & Brothers.

Kent, Zachary. 1989. *The Story of the Surrender at Yorktown.* Chicago: Children's Press.

Ketchum, Richard M. 2004. *Victory at Yorktown.* New York: Henry Holt and Company.

Lee, Susan, and John Lee. 1975. *Events of the Revolution: Yorktown.* Chicago: Children's Press.

McLeroy, William and Sherry. 1993. *Stranger in Their Midst.* Heritage Books: Bowie, MD.

Parris, John. 1950. *The Cherokee Story.* Asheville, North Carolina: The Stephens Press.

Potter, Stephen. 1994. *Commoners, Tribute, and Chiefs.* Charlottesville, VA: University of Virginia Press.

Purdue, Theda. 1989. *The Cherokee.* New York: The Chelsea House Publishers.

Starr, Emmet. 1968. *Old Cherokee Families—Old Families and Their Genealogy.* Norman, OK: University of Oklahoma Press, 1968.

Sutton, Karen. 1997. "Red, Black and Revolutionary." Thesis Paper, University of Maryland (Baltimore).

The Patriot Resource. The American Revolution. Accessed October 3, 2006. http://www.patriotresource.com/battles/yorktown/.

Thornton, Russell. 1990. The Cherokee: A Population History. Lincoln, Nebraska: University Of Nebraska.

Ulmer, Mary, and Samuel Beck, eds. 1951. *Cherokee Cooklore.* Cherokee, NC: Cherokee Publications.

Underwood, Thomas Brian. 1961. *The Story of the Cherokee People.* S.B. Newman Printing Company.

Unger, Harlow G. 2002. *Lafayette.* Hoboken, NJ: John Wiley & Sons, Inc..

Welch, Douglas. 1982. *The Revolutionary War.* New York: Galahad Books.

UNITED CHEROKEE INDIAN TRIBE OF VIRGINIA, INC. (UCITOVA)

Horace R. Rice, Ed. D.

The United Cherokee Indian Tribe of Virginia (UCITOVA)

Introduction	403
Brief History of UCITOVA	435
1600–1790	440
1790–2000	452
2000–Present	494
Works Cited	519
About the Author	529

Buffalo Ridge	Native Americans of the Buffalo Ridge region, including Stonewall Mill and Buffalo Ridge residents, who inhabited the region in the early to mid-1700s.
Blue and Green	Mountains and River—merging the two (2) colors; representing unity of the two (2) peoples for a period of over four hundred years.
1607/1608	Period when English colonists made contact with Powhatans (Algonquian-speaking people). They visited the Wiccocomico area in 1608.
1656	Year when English colonists lost their battle with Rechahecrian/Cherokee Indians—who settled near the falls in Richmond, Virginia—and sued for peace.
Kituhwa	English spelling for historic chief or mother town of the sixty or more towns of the Cherokee people.
Wighcocomoco	One of the early spellings of Wiccocomico Indian Town in Northern Neck, Virginia—Northumberland/Lancaster Counties.

Ya (na)s se Cherokee spelling for "buffalo." Represents chief historical region of the UCITOVA people.

Buffalo Buffaloes inhabited the Buffalo Ridge region prior to and during early colonial settlements.

Crossed pins Symbol of two (2) regions (Buffalo Ridge and Stonewall Mill) coming together, separated only by the James River. Also represent their belief in Christ and early influence of the Anglican/English Church, and reflect tradition of Kituhwa or Pin Cherokee and Wiccocomico connection. Straight Pin crossed in shape of a Christian Cross.

Pearl Symbol of suffering. Just as an oyster suffers and forms a pearl, the UCITOVA people have suffered (invasion, dispersion, forced indentured servitude, Indian slavery, and paper genocide).

Rechahecrian English word for Cherokee in the 1600s.

The United Cherokee Indian Tribe of Virginia (UCITOVA)

Introduction

Amherst County residents have always known that people of Cherokee heritage reside in the county[1] and Virginia, in general. In 1896, Whitehead wrote an extensive article on the "Amherst County Indians, Highly Interesting History of an Old Settlement of Cherokees" (*Richmond Times,* April 19, 1896). A large percentage of the current residents claim some Native American ancestry, mostly Cherokee. Whitehead, in 1896, "regretted that so little is known and so little has been published by the present generation of the history of the county in our State."[2] He criticized state historians for their failure to record data on the Native American population. He noted that other "adjoining states" were documenting their history. "If the same effort had been made by historical societies or other organizations after the Revolutionary War, that is now being made to get a correct history of the Confederate War, the effort would have brought out facts about our ancestors that would challenge the admiration of all who feel an interest in

---

[1] Edgar Whitehead, "Amherst County Indians, Highly Interesting History of an Old Settlement Of Cherokees," *Richmond Times* (Richmond), April 19, 1896.

[2] Edgar Whitehead, 2.

Virginia history," he wrote. He then proceeded to write about the Cherokees of Amherst County, information that historians in Virginia had failed to record. As opposed to other states that have cherished their Native American history, Virginia's official indifference toward Native Americans—especially Cherokees—has made it very difficult for researchers to present an accurate and continuous chronology of Virginia's history.

Tooker, in *Problem of the Rechahecrian Indians of Virginia* (1898), took a similar view regarding Native American history, Cherokee history in particular, and the slackness or weak efforts of historians in Virginia to document the same. He noted, "The main reason why we know so little about them [the Rechahecrians or Cherokees] is because no one wrote in the colonial days with the descriptive minuteness of Captain John Smith, and he had no followers after his death."[3]

Tooker indicated his purpose for writing the paper on the Rechahecrian Indians. He noted that it was not with the "intent of discrediting their now accepted identification with the Cherokees nor to argue against the classification of the term Rechahecrian as one of the early synonyms for this nation [Cherokees], but rather to draw attention to the mixed character of the Indians who were originally designated by the term as verified by some data hitherto overlooked and traditions ofttimes quoted, but never analyzed nor compared with the historical memoranda now to be presented." He concluded with the present facts and tradition that "many of the Indians were originally Powhatans," who were forced from Virginia by angry colonists after the "terrible massacre of 1622–23." These Indians fled the area and joined the northern branches of the Cherokees, and in time, became "so amalgamated with them" that they soon lost their Powhatan language and tribal connections. He noted that traces of their former language still existed in the "Cherokee tongue." The connections between

---

[3] William W. Tooker, *Problem of the Rechahecrian Indians of Virginia* (Washington, DC: Judd And Detweiler, 1898) 261, 383.

the Cherokees and Powhatans are strongly supported by Native American descendants in Virginia and other states.[4]

Tooker agreed with Horatio Hale's view[5]: "As the Cherokee tongue is evidently a mixed language, it is reasonable to suppose that the Cherokee are a mixed people and probably, like the English, are an amalgamation of conquered and conquering races." His data supported John Haywood's research[6] on Cherokee traditions and orations regarding their "wanderings" and migrations. One of the traditions placed the Cherokees near the upper waters of the Ohio River as they migrated from the west, "where they erected the mounds on Grave Creek in West Virginia, gradually working eastward across the Alleghany mountains to the neighborhood of Monticello, Virginia, and along the Appomattox river. From that point, it is alleged, they removed to the Tennessee country about 1623, when the Virginians suddenly and unexpectedly fell upon and massacred the Indians throughout the colony. After the massacre, the story goes, they came to New River and made a temporary settlement there, as well as one on the headwaters of the Holston; but owing to the enmity of the northern Indians they removed in a short time to the Little Tennessee and formed what were known as the Middle settlements."

Tooker also mentioned the work of J.W. Powell. Powell, in the *Seventh Annual Report to the Bureau of Ethnology*, indicated that "The Cherokee bounds in Virginia should be extended along the mountain region as far at least as the James River, as they [the Cherokees] claim to have lived at the Peaks of Otter, and seem to be identical with the Rickohockan or Rechahecrian Indians of the early Virginia writers, who lived in the mountains beyond the Monacans, and in 1656 ravaged the lowland country

---

[4] Horace R. Rice, *The Buffalo Ridge Cherokee: A Remnant of a Great Nation Divided* (Bowie, MD: Heritage Books, Inc, 1995), 15-16, 28-30, 35, 41, 45, & 62.

[5] Horatio Hale, ed., *Iroquois Book of Rites* (Philadelphia, PA: D. G. Brinton Library of Aboriginal American Literature, 1883) 42.

[6] John Haywood, *Natural and Aboriginal History of Tennessee* (Nashville, TN: G. Wilson, 1823).

as far as the site of Richmond, and defeated the English and Powhatan Indians (should be Pamunkey) in a pitched battle at that place."[7]

C.C. Royce, in commenting on the work of Haywood, concluded that the "story is of the vaguest character."[8] Royce did not consider or have knowledge of the information to which Tooker referred—"data hitherto overlooked and traditions ofttimes quoted, but never analyzed nor compared with the historical memoranda"—and that Tooker presented in his research on the Rechahecrians. Royce, however, with the knowledge and information that he had available, did support the opinion that the Cherokees may have lived in Eastern Virginia based on the orations and legends of other Indian tribes who had contact with the Cherokees. Regarding the Cherokees living in Virginia, Royce stated, "Either the tradition is fabulous or at least a portion of the Cherokee were probably at one time resident of the eastern slope of Virginia." Royce, however, did not conduct extensive research on the issue of the Rechahecrians or have the Tooker information.

Tooker noted that the Rechahecrians first appeared in written records in 1621 in Capt. John Smith's "General Histories," where he quoted the observation of John Pory, the Secretary of the Colony:

> A few of the westernly Runnagados had conspired against the laughing king [of Accomac on the eastern shore], but fearing their treason was discovered, fled to Smith's Isles where they made a massacre of Deere and hogges; and thence to Rickahake betwixt Cissapeack [Chessapeack] and Nansamund where they are now seated under the command of Itoyatin.[9]

---

[7] J. W. Powell, "Cherokee Indians--Rites and Ceremonies," review of Seventh Annual Report, by John Wesley Powell, *Report of the Bureau of Ethnology* no. VII (n.d.),79.

[8] C.C. Royce, "Cherokee Nation Of Indians," *Annual Report to the Bureau of Ethnology* V (1887), 136, 137.

[9] William W. Tooker.

Tooker mentions the above piece of written history about this band of Rickahake Indians as information that had been entirely overlooked by other writers. He felt that there is more in these few words of history than appears in the first reading. He explained:

> These 'Runnegados,' were from the westerly parts, and being able to cross the Chesapeake Bay is surely evidence that although 'they want Boats to cross the Bay,' as stated by Pory, they traveled in canoes, either stolen or furnished them by the Powhatans. Their retreat to a refuge between an Indian town called 'Chesapeack' and another known as 'Nansamund,' where, as stated in 1621, they were 'still seated, shows that they then had no settled abiding place, but were, as related, 'Runnegados,' or unruly Indians, gathered together from various tribes—Powhatans and others—living previously in the hills to the west of the then known territory of Virginia. The 'islands' designated as 'Smith's Isles' are still so called, and are situated about two miles to the eastward of Cape Charles. The place where they were then seated, 'Rickahake,' as near as we can locate it from Smith's map, was probably on the borders of the 'Great Dismal swamp,' in Norfolk County, Virginia. Having been seated there in the dreary recesses of Rickahake for a time, probably increasing in numbers by the influx of refugees, with occasional sorties for the purposes of plunder, would naturally give them and all predatory Indians in the vicinity the appellation of the 'Rickahakians,' and as such they became well known to the Virginia colonists. The main reason why we know so little about them is because no one wrote in the colonial days with the descriptive minuteness of Captain John Smith, and he had no followers after his death. It must be admitted from the evidence presented that the term Rickaheke is of Algonquian origin, and undoubtedly descriptive of the locality where bestowed, at or near

the 'Great Dismal Swamp.' While its translation will have a bearing on the inquiry, it is perhaps well to give it. The term is composed of two elements, which an eminent philologist terms adjectivals and substantivals; the latter is really a locative, while the former, on strict analysis, can be shown to have a verbal origin. Making allowance for the consonantal interchange, due to a misapperception, mishearing, or otherwise on the part of the first observer of the initial sounds of the name, it will be immediately observed that the adjectival Rickah or Rechoha is paralleled in the Delaware (Zeisberger), Nechoha, 'Alone;' Nechohaneu, 'he is alone;' Nechohani, 'I am alone;' Chippeway (Schoolcraft), Nizhiki; Otchipwe (Baraga), Nijike, 'alone;' Cree (Lacombe), Kikotis, 'solitude;' Micmac (Rand), Nedaje, 'lonely.' Therefore, by this derivation, Rickah with its locative Rake, 'land or place,' connotes the 'lonely place' or 'the place of solitude,' which, together with its English plural termination, viz, Rickah-ak-ians, gives us 'the people of the lonely place,' a descriptive term that is quite well exemplified in its English appellative of the 'Great Dismal swamp.'[10]

Tooker stated that the evidence noted above documents the fact that Toyatin, or Itoyatin, and his followers of Rickahake were the main characters in the massacre of forty-seven Virginians in March of 1622–23, although it seems to have been instigated by Opechancanough of the Pamaunkey. He then moved to the question, "Who were the 'Westerly Runnegados' under the command of Itoyatin, and what was their relationship to the Cherokees of later times?" He indicated that Capt. John Smith, in 1608, encountered a hunting tribe called Hassinnungaes by his Patawomek interpreter. *Hassinnungaes* is an "Algonquian term that denotes 'the people of rock holes,' i.e., 'a people who live in caves.'" Tooker mentions that Lederer (1669–1670)

---

[10] William W. Tooker

learned that "over the Suala mountains lay the Rickahocans." This term is believed to refer to the Cherokee nation.

Tooker sums up his point:

> We find that if these Rickahocans of Lederer were originally those of Rickahake under Itoyatin and were the Indians driven out of Virginia by the colonists about 1623 and who were again the invaders of 1656, as mentioned by the early Virginian writers and by Powell, as the foregoing would seem to make them, we can then account for the association of the Cherokees of Haywood's traditional story with the Powhatans of eastern Virginia.

The association between the Cherokees and Wiccocomicos in the Northern Neck of Virginia during the 1600s and 1700s follows this pattern also (John Pinn's Revolution War Pension Application. Pension application of John Pinn R8264, statement by Pinn transcribed by C. Leon Harris.).[11] The Cherokee Iroquois and the Wiccocomico Algonquians came together as a hybrid people on a long-term basis as documented by the existence and survival of UCITOVA in Buffalo Ridge and Stonewall Mill.

Tooker noted, "Their traditions (Iroquoian linguistic family members) are replete with accounts of these war parties against the Oyada or Cherokees. They called the Cherokees by way of derision We-yau-dah and O-yau-dah, meaning a people who live in caves."

He concluded with the discussion of the Hassinnungaes as the most northern branch of the Cherokees and that this supports the tradition relating to the Cherokees building the Grave Creek mound in Marshall County, West Virginia. "At all events, they (the Cherokees) had then worked eastward across the Alleghany mountains, rendering it possible that they were along the Appomattox river in 1621, from whence, with the Powhatans, their near neighbors, they attempted the attack

---

[11] John Pinn, *Southern Campaign American Revolution Pension Statements: John Pinn*, 1842.

upon the King of Accomac, and, after assembling at Rickahake, were at last, in the year 1623, according to tradition and history, driven out of Virginia and over the mountains."

Mooney, in *Myths of the Cherokees*, wrote the following piece of colonial history relating to the Cherokees in Virginia:

> The Cherokee were the mountaineers of the South, holding the entire Allegheny region from the interlocking head-streams of the Kanawha and the Tennessee southward almost to the site of Atlanta, and from the Blue ridge on the east to the Cumberland range on the west, a territory comprising an area of about 40,000 square miles, now included in the states of Virginia, Tennessee, North Carolina, South Carolina, Georgia, and Alabama.[12]

Mooney supported Tooker's view that the Rechahecrians were the Cherokees:

> It was not until 1656 that the English first came into contact with the Cherokee, called in the records of the period Rechahecrians, a corruption of Rickahockan, apparently the name by which they were known to the Powhatan tribes. In that year the Virginia colony, which had only recently concluded a long and exterminating war with the Powhatan, was thrown into alarm by the news that a great body of six to seven hundred Rechahecrian Indians—by which is probably meant that number of warriors—from the mountains had invaded the lower country and established themselves at the falls of James river, where now is the city of Richmond. The assembly at once passed resolutions 'that these new come Indians be in no sort suffered to seat themselves there, or any place near us, it having cost so much blood to

---

[12] James Mooney, *Myths of the Cherokee* (Washington, DC: Bureau Of Ethnology, 1902), 14.

expel and extirpate those perfidious and treacherous Indians which were there formerly.' It was therefore ordered that a force of at least 100 white men be at once sent against them, to be joined by the warriors of all the neighboring subject tribes, according to treaty obligation. The Pamunkey chief, with a hundred of his men, responded to the summons, and the combined force marched against the invaders. The result was a bloody battle, with disastrous outcome to the Virginians, the Pamunkey chief with most of his men being killed, while the whites were forced to make such terms of peace with the Rechahecrians that the assembly cashiered the commander of the expedition and compelled him to pay the whole cost of the treaty from his own estate. Owing to the imperfection of the Virginia records we have no means of knowing the causes of the sudden invasion or how long the invaders retained their position at the falls. In all probability it was only the last of a long series of otherwise unrecorded irruptions by the mountaineers on the more peaceful dwellers in the lowlands. From a remark in Lederer it is probable that the Cherokee were assisted also by some of the piedmont tribes hostile to the Powhatans. The Peaks of Otter, near which the Cherokee claim to have once lived, as has been already noted, are only about one hundred miles in a straight line from Richmond, while the burial mound and town site near Charlottesville, mentioned by Jefferson, are but half the distance.[13]

All Cherokees or Rechahecrians were not removed from Virginia, but continued to live in Virginia in a somewhat acculturated state, a survival skill that the Cherokees have been known to master. They lived a lifestyle that was similar to that of the white man. Some Cherokees stayed in Virginia during the 1620s while others returned to the Commonwealth

---

[13] James Mooney, 1902, 29.

of Virginia later. Virginia had been home to some Cherokees since or before the 1600s.

Col. E. C. Boudinot, in the *Journal of the American Geographical Society of New York*, on the Indian Territory and its inhabitants, stated that "the Cherokees once had extensive settlements on the Appomattox River in Virginia, and formed the principal tribe in the Powhatan Confederation. That chief was a Cherokee."[14] Former Chief Jonathan Taylor, Eastern Band of Cherokee Indians in Cherokee, North Carolina, noted that a number of local surnames in Amherst and its vicinity are the same surnames as those owned by Cherokees in Cherokee, North Carolina. He indicated that "before the removal, our people were in Virginia, Alabama, Kentucky, Tennessee, North Carolina, South Carolina, Georgia, and part of West Virginia."[15] During a meeting with the author in Cherokee, North Carolina, Chief Taylor indicated that "a McCoy," a common UCITOVA surname, was represented on his tribal council. He explained, "We have a McCoy that is the chairman of our Council."

Burk noted, in *The History of Virginia from Its First Settlement to the Present Day*, that while the 1656 Virginia Assembly members were engaged in "wise and benevolent projects," they received news that six or seven hundred Rechahecrian Indians, from the inland or mountain areas to the west, had fortified themselves near the falls of the James River near Richmond "apparently with the intention of forming a regular settlement." The assembly members were also informed that neighboring Indian tribes were on the move with the new settlers, the Rechahecrians, a fact that seemed to indicate that the neighboring Indian tribes were involved in treachery against the colony. The colonial assembly members were alarmed by the Rechahecrians' strong fortification in a location that provided opportunities for ideal defensive and offensive operations against the colonists. It appeared that this was the same location that another tribe

---

[14] E. C. Boudinot, "The Indian Territory and Its Inhabitants," *Journal of the American Geographical Society of New York* V, (1874, January 01), 220.

[15] Horace R. Rice, *The Buffalo Ridge Cherokee: The Colors and Culture of a Virginian Indian Community* (Madison Heights, VA: B R C Books, 1991), 42.

had occupied previously and resulted in great expense and trouble to the colony in removing them. When they were removed, the government kept this site free from intruders until the present time. Now that the site has been occupied again by "a powerful band of hardy warriors, who perhaps were only the advance guard of a more formidable and extensive emigration"—it caused great concern among the colonists. The assembly responded to this threat by a "prompt and vigorous" proclamation for the removal of the new intruders:

> Whereas information hath been received, that many western or inland Indians are drawn from the mountains, and lately set down near the falls of the James river, to the number of six or seven hundred, whereby upon many several a considerations being had, it is conceived great danger might ensue to this colony: The assembly therefore do think fit and resolve, that these new come Indians be in no sort suffered to seat themselves there, or any place near us, it having cost so much blood to expel and extirpate those perfidious and treacherous Indians, which were there formerly: It being so apt a place to invade us, and within the limits which in a just war were formerly conquered by us, and by us reserved at the conclusion of peace with the Indians.
>
> In pursuance thereof, wherefore, and due respect to our safety, be it enacted by the present grand assembly, that the two upper counties, under the command of captain Edward Hill, do presently send forth a party of one hundred men at least, and that they shall first endeavor to remove the said new come Indians, without making war, if it may be only in case of their own defense: Also strictly requiring the assistance of all the neighboring Indians to aid them to that purpose, as being part of the articles of peace

concluded with us; and failing therein, to look duly safety of all the English of those parts . . .[16]

Col. Edward Hill was appointed to lead the removal of the intruders. Along with a troop of one hundred men, he had hoped to dislodge them with peaceful means only. If he could not satisfy his mission by peaceful means, he was ordered to seek the assistance of all the neighboring Indians. He was forced to seek the assistance of Totopotomoi, King of the Pamunkey Indians. Totopotomoi provided the aid without hesitation; and marched with one hundred Pamunkey warriors. Totopotomoi and his army were no match for the "new come Indians" and he died with "a greater part of his followers, gallantly fighting in this obstinate and bloody encounter."

Underwood, in recording the official history or records of the Cherokee people in *The Story of the Cherokee People*, noted that the earliest contact with British settlements occurred in Richmond, Virginia. Underwood supported the Virginia Assembly's documentation when he wrote that the first known contact the British settlements had with the Cherokees occurred at Richmond, Virginia. The colonists had been at war with the Powhatan tribe at the James River Falls for a considerable time. They had no sooner driven out the Powhatans than the village site was reoccupied by a large force of Cherokees. The Cherokees replaced the Powhatans in their village site after the British had spent time on its effort to dislodge the Powhatan tribe. They became very alarmed and called in over a hundred Pamunkey warriors "to help them destroy the new intruders." "The combined forces" marched against the Cherokees, but received such a beating that the English colonists were "forced to sue for peace."[17] The connection between the Cherokees

---

[16] John Burk, *The History of Virginia from Its First Settlement to the Present Day* (Petersburg, VA: Dickson & Pescud, n.d, 1816).

[17] Thomas B. Underwood, *The Story of the Cherokee People* (Muskogee, OK: S.B. Newman, 1961), 20.

and Powhatans are strongly supported by Native American descendants in Virginia and other states.[18]

Historical records do not provide many details of the events surrounding and following the battle in Richmond due to "scanty" state records on Indian affairs. Based on the minutes of the second session of the assembly, we learned that the powerful Rechahecrians defeated Colonel Hill and his followers in the battle to dislodge them. Colonel Hill's properties were secured to pay some of the cost incurred in the failed expedition against the Rechahecrians. Burk could not tell us whether Hill's offense was "cowardice, or a willful disobedience of the instructions he had received. There is, however, reason to believe that he was defeated, and that the Rechahecrians maintained themselves in their position in Richmond at the falls of the James River by force: For the governor and council were directed by the assembly to make a peace with this people, and they [further] directed that the monies which were expended for this purpose, should be levied on the proper estate of Hill."

> *On a debate and consideration of the charge and defense of Colonel Edward Hill, by the general and unanimous vote of both houses, without any contradiction, he hath been found guilty of those crimes; and witnesses there alleged against him; and for the vindicating themselves from any imputation of his crimes and deficiencies, they have ordered, that his present suspension of all offices, military and civil, that he hath or may have continue; and of what's already expended in procuring a peace with the Rechahecrians, and if the governor and council shall find any nearer way of effecting thereof, that it shall be acted at the said colonel Hill's proper cost and charge.
>
> * A literal transcript from ancient records.

---

[18] Horace Rice, 1995, 15-45.

While it is an accepted fact by many historians and Cherokee leaders in North Carolina and Oklahoma that the Rechahecrian and Cherokee are one and the same people, a few Virginia historians still have some confusion regarding Cherokee history, or the Anglicized word "Cherokee" in the Commonwealth of Virginia. This is partly due to the myth that Cherokee never crossed North Carolina and Tennessee lines into Virginia, or if they did, all Cherokee were driven from the Commonwealth of Virginia by the colonists; "that they, the Cherokee, are all gone and did not come back into Virginia." It is as if Cherokee came to Virginia and inspected the Colony, but went back to other states at nightfall. They ignore the documented treaty history between the Cherokee and the British and the Cherokee and colonial governments that shows large tracts of land owned and ceded by the Cherokees in Virginia (Royce, *Map of the Territorial Limits of the Cherokee Nations of Indians*;[19] Pendleton, *History of Tazewell County and Southwest Virginia*;[20] & Mooney, *Historical Sketch of the Cherokee*.[21]

Some historians ignore or are indifferent to the official Virginia Assembly records that verify the presence of the Rechahecrians in Virginia. Burk discussed the "scanty materials"[22] which the state has in its possession regarding Indian affairs. Burk agreed with Whitehead's view (1896) that early Virginia leaders dropped the ball on documenting Virginia Native American history.

The other major Native American tribe, in addition to the Cherokees, from which the UCITOVA people descend, is

---

[19] C.C. Royce, *Map of the Former Territorial Limits of the Cherokee "Nation of" Indians* (Washington, DC: Geographical Map Division, Libary Of Congress, 1884). Repository: Library of Congress, Geographical Map Division, Washington, DC.

[20] William C. Pendleton, *History of Tazewell County and Southwest Virginia, 1748-1920* (Johnson City, TN: The Overmountain Press, 1920), 28.

[21] James Mooney, *Historical Sketch of the Cherokee* (Chicago, IL: Aldine Transaction, 1975).

[22] John Burk, 106.

Wiccocomico ancestors. Bush, in *The Bulletin of the Northumberland County Historical Society*, noted:

> The chiefdoms of what are now Northumberland and Lancaster counties were peripheral areas during the first three or four decades of English settlement in Virginia. The Cuttatawomen, the Wiccocomico, the Sekakawon (hereafter termed the Chickacone), and the Onawmanient (also known as the Machodoc) were far from the Jamestown area, where Powhatan and the leaders of the Virginia Company were facing off. Indeed, in the early seventeenth century, the Potomac Algonquians worried more about the southward expansion of the Susquehannocks.
>
> The Indians of the lower Northern Neck, however, were not left completely alone. As early as the summer of 1608, John Smith led an expedition up the Potomac both to explore the region and to gather intelligence on the various chiefdoms. His party probably made contact with the Wiccocomicos, the Chickacones, and the Onawmanients. The latter two chiefdoms may have received orders from Powhatan to give the English a hostile reception in 1608, and the Onawmanients did ambush the English party on June 16, 1608, near the Nomini Bay.[23]

Stephen Potter, writing on the Wiccocomico, noted:

> Although not specifically mentioned in the accounts of the first exploration of the mouth of the Potomac River, the Wicocomocos were also visited by Smith's

---

[23] Richard C. Bush, "Native Northumberlanders," *The Bulletin of the Northumberland County Historical Society* XXXV, (1998), 8.

party (not to be confused with another Indian group of the same name).[24]

Potter further stated:

> The Grand Assembly passed an act requiring that 50 acres (20 ha) be set aside for every bowman among the tributary Indians and the sum total of land be surveyed for each Indian group (Billings, 1975: 68). Exercising their newly granted authority as a frontier county to treat directly with local Indians, the Northumberland County commissioners did more than simply oversee the surveying of the Indians' lands. They moved the Chicacoan and Wiccocomocos southward, out of their former territories along the Coan, Potomac, and Wicomico rivers prime agricultural and waterfront land that was settled or coveted by the English. In the process the commissioners combined the two chiefdoms into one group. That done, they made Machywap, werowance of the Chicacoans and "so ancient and known a friend of our English Nation," leader of the combined group (Potter, 1976: 72).[25] The more numerous Wiccocomocos objected and threatened to kill Machywap. The county commissioners, in turn, threatened to treat those Wiccocomicos who did not acknowledge Machywap's authority as 'Enemies of our English Nation.' Ultimately, the Wiccocomocos prevailed, and by 1659 Machywap was deposed.

---

[24] Stephen Potter, *Commoners, Tribute, and Chiefs* (Charlottesville, VA: University Of Virginia, 1993), 10-11.

[25] Stephen Potter, "An Ethnohistorical Examination Of Indian Groups In Northumberland County, Virginia, 1608-1719," (PhD diss., University of North Carolina, 1976), 46, 47, 72-77. M.A. Thesis, Department of Anthropology, University of North Carolina.

Thereafter, the combined group was known as the Wiccocomicos.[26]

Potter, in the *Bulletin of the Northumberland County Historical Society*, discussed the ongoing saga and conflicts between Wiccocomocos and their desire to retain their rightful ownership of their reservation land and the colonists, who desired to possess the fertile property:

> Although Lancaster County was formed from Northumberland in 1651 (Hiden 1957: 12), and included the land along the North bank of the Rappahannock River, Northumberland County still retained jurisdiction over the lands of the combined Chicacoan and Wiccocomoco Indians. Today the area that was once their "reservation" is predominantly within the northeastern corner of Lancaster County...
>
> At the Grand Assembly for March 1658/9, an order for patenting the land of the Wiccocomico Indians was granted to Governor Samuel Mathews. This order was supposedly 'grounded upon the desire of the said Indians to surrender the same to his honor,' the governor (Hening 1823(I): 515). In April 1660, Pewem and Owasewas, two of the "great men of the Wiccocomico Nation of Indians" complained to the commissioners of Northumberland that two whites, Robert Jones and George Wale, were trespassing upon their land (Appendix: Documents 15, 16, 17, 18) . . . In November, 1662, the Wiccocomico Indians sold the disputed neck of land to Robert Jones for twelve match coats (Appendix: Document 20).[27]

---

[26] Stephen Potter, 1993, 195-196.

[27] Stephen R. Potter, "The Dissolution Of The Machoatick, Cekacawon And Wighcocomoco Indians," *The Bulletin of the Northumberland County Historical Society* XIII, (1976, January 01): 10, 12, 13.

> According to John Gibbon, a visitor to the area in 1669–71, Machywap's successor was a Wiccocomoco named Pekwem (also spelled Pewem), whom he called "the king of Wickicomoco" (Potter, Stephen, 196). However, the Northumberland County commissioners evidently refused to recognize Pekwem as the werowance since he is referred to in all the court records as simply one of "ye great men of the Wiccocomico Nation of Indians."[28]

Stephen Potter presented a thorough discussion of the destruction or dissolution of Wiccocomico culture and socio-economical ways of life in the Bulletin of the Northumberland County Historical Society, 1976. He indicated that the General Assembly passed an act in 1652 that set aside fifty acres of land for every bowman. This act was designed to protect the lands of the tributary Indians; a total of 4,400 acres for the 88 bowman or approximately 352 tribal members.[29]

> The tract of land surveyed for the eighty-eight Chicacoan and Wiccocomico bowmen and their families consisted of 4,400 acres (1,782 ha) lying on the south bank of Dividing Creek, between the Corrotoman River and Chesapeake Bay. Although the act of 1652 guaranteed tributary Indians the right to their lands, particularly those set aside for them, the legislation was ignored more often than it was enforced. No sooner were the Wiccocomicos settled on their new reservation than they were in court complaining that two Englishmen had "intruded upon their Land—whereby they [the Wiccocomicos]

---

[28] Stephen Potter, 1993, 196.

[29] Stephen R. Potter, 1976, 8, 12, 13. Stephen Potter provided a thorough analysis of the Wiccocomico tribe and the "dissolution" of its people between 1608-early 1700s.

are made incapable of providing food for their livelihood.[30]

John Gibbon's observation in 1669–71 that Pekwem or Pewem was king of the Wiccocomico Indians supports the traditional view of UCITOVA that Robert Pinn (I), anglicized surname from Pewem, was the king. Robert Pinn is one of the major ancestors of the UCITOVA Indians. The Northumberland County court, in 1669–70, recognized Robert Pewem as the Great Man of Wicocomico, not as one of the great men of Wicocomico.[31] The order required that white citizens give the guns back to the Wiccomico Indians, via of the "Great Man of Wiccomico Indian Town." Robert Pinn I is believed to have been born after 1600. He appeared on public records earlier in *Northumberland County Record Book 1662–1666*, Northumberland County and in Gloucester County/York County.[32] Ruth and Sam Sparacio's book, *Deeds and Wills, Abstracts of Northumberland County, VA*, noted Robert Pinne's real estate transaction.[33] Apparently this Indian of Wiccocomico Indian Town was already quite influential as a businessman.

Robert Pinne, Northumberland County Order Book abstracts during the 1652–1665 session, February 10, 1662, made his mark as a witness on a deed document with John Clarke and Dennis Clarke. Robert Pinn was already a great leader in the Northumberland County area and respected by the county

---

[30] Stephen Potter, 1993, 195-196.

[31] Northumberland County Clerk of The Court, *Northumberland County Record Book 1662-1666*, vol. 1678-79, (Heathsville, VA: Northumberland County Court, 1678–79).

[32] Polly Cary Mason, ed., *Records of Colonial Gloucester County* (Baltimore, MD: Clearfield, 2003) 32. Robert Pinn's name noted in Deed transaction with other witnesses on 30 April 1649.

[33] Ruth Sparacio and Sam Sparacio, eds., *Virginia County Court Records: Deed & Will Abstracts of Northumberland County, Virginia, 1662-1666* (McLean, VIRGINIA: The Antient Press, 1993), 6.

court officials. During the same court period, April 20, Pewem "again" complained about Jones trespassing on his land.[34]

Bush noted that Robert Beverly's 1703 estimate indicated that there were only ten members of the group [Wiccocomico Indians] left. He stated:

> We can speculate on several factors that, in combination, would bring about the virtual disappearance of Northumberland's native population. The first is migration by those who were unable to adapt to the complexities of cultural coexistence and therefore moved beyond the frontier of English settlement to join Indian chiefdoms there. The second is assimilation, whereby Indians who had grown up in English households and worked for English masters chose to abandon the culture of their parents and blend into the society of the new arrivals." (As we have seen, even William Taptico, "King of the Wiccocomoco Indians," had chosen to adopt the material life of the English even as he sought to preserve some vestige of Wiccomico identity.). The third factor is disease. Although there is only modest evidence of Virginia Indians suffering pandemics caused by bacteria for which they had no immunity, it is hard to believe that they did not.[35]

In 1648, the Indian reserve was eliminated by the colonists to form or create the county of Northumberland (Doran, *Atlas of County Boundary Changes in Virginia—1634–1895*, 1987).[36]

There was another factor that affected the socio-economic lifestyle and survival of the Wiccocomico during the dramatic period between 1608-early 1700s. The Wiccocomico, like other

---

[34] Northumberland County Clerk of The Court, *Northumberland County Record Book 1652-65*, vol. 1652-65, (Heathsville, VA: Northumberland County Court, 1652-65).

[35] Richard C. Bush, 1998, 19.

[36] Michael Doran, *Atlas of County Boundary Changes in Virginia--1634-1895* (Athens, GA: Iberian Publishing, 1987).

Native Americans in Virginia, were subjected to removal from their reservations/settlements by slave traders. C. S. Everett, in a book edited by Alan Gallay, presented a historical perspective on a rarely discussed topic, *Native American slavery*. It has been common for historians to inform the public about the slave trade involving Africans, but the topic of Native Americans slavery in Virginia has been ignored by many of those historians.

> From 1610 to 1646, colonists engaged local tribes in three major wars. During this time enslavement was generally punitive retribution. In several instances, though, Virginia exported Indians, suggesting an existing external market for American slaves. Evidence quite strongly indicates that "many" local Indians were readily enslaved and exported during the course of the Third Anglo-Powhatan War (1644-1646). With the existence of an external market for Indian slaves, financial incentive may have played as much a role in slavery as did colonial vengeance. One wonders how knowledge and profit related to this market informed Virginians' notion of slavery during this era, widely acknowledged as the formative period of African slavery in North America...
>
> In the Third Anglo-Powhatan War, during William Berkeley's first tenure as Virginia governor, countless Indians were enslaved and a good number exported, defraying the colony's expenses in prosecuting the war. Combined with relentless colonial military action, slaving subdued the Powhatan tribes. Other tribal nations gambled that they could avoid enslavement by becoming tributaries of Virginia...
>
> Despite the guarantees of freedom by the Treaty of Necotowance, Virginias persisted in the enslavement of local Indians, particularly children, which threatened to drag the colony back into war...

> Imagine the displacement and sorrow for homes and lives lost, the deculturation and reculturation that comes with being lifted out of town and country, bound by strangers and carried six, seven, or eight hundred miles to a strange country, forced to labor in other men's fields for other men's benefit. This sort of slave traffic ran into, through, and out of the Old Dominion. And a good number of Indians remained in Virginia as slaves.[37]

Bush indicated that "there is no question that white Northumberlanders employed their Indian neighbors and perhaps even possessed them as slaves." He noted the inventory of Symon Overzee's estate revealed that he had "2 Indians, a boy & a girl servants," but another view of the scene indicates that they [the Indians] were "slaves."[38] The Wiccocomico Indians were, as Bush noted, forced to change their Native American lifestyle and assimilate into the colonist culture or migrate to other areas beyond the domains of the English.

The foregoing facts have been included as background information or introduction to the UCITOVA tribe, a people that have suffered and endured persecution in various forms in Virginia for over four hundred years. They are descendants of the Rechahecrian (anglicized to Cherokee) and Wighcocomico (anglicized to Wiccocomico) peoples.

While Amherst and Appomattox Counties have a large number of their citizens who claim Cherokee ancestry, only

---

[37] C.S. Everett, *Indian Slavery in Colonial America*, ed. Alan Gallay (Lincoln, NEBRASKA: University Of Nebraska Press, 2009), 70, 71, 97, & 108. Everett mentioned the pro Native American slavery positions taken by officials and judges in Virginia, and the roles of two judges, Robert Carter and John Smith, in the dispossession of the Wicocommicco tribe in neighboring Lancaster County. He made reference to a case in Virginia regarding the Wiccocomicos, the Nickens family, and the "Inhuman practice" regarding said family. The Nickens were relatives of the Pinns in Wiccocomico Indian Town.

[38] Richard C. Bush, 1998, 16.

the UCITOVA people have huddled together over the last 250–400 years as a tribe, both informally and formally, to protect themselves against annihilation in Virginia as a Native American group. The Wiccocomico people—who were intermarrying with the Cherokees in Wiccocomico Indian Town to preserve its Native American identity against the encroachment of the English settlers during the 1700s (John Pinn's *Revolutionary War Pension Application*)[39]—continued their existence in Amherst County and Buckingham (Appomattox) County in the second half of the 1700s until the present time. John Pinn, one of the three Wiccocomico tribesmen who served in the American Revolutionary War at Yorktown, indicated in his pension application that he "is a descendant of the Aborigines of America—that his father was a mustee and his mother a Cherokee, who were inhabitants of Lancaster County (formerly Northumberland County), Virginia, at a place called Indian Town" [Wiccocomico Indian Town]. John Pinn was probably named after his grandfather, John, the son of Robert, the Great Man of Wiccocomico. John Pinn's father, Robert 2, was probably named after his grandfather, Robert, the Great Man.

The Wiccocomico have not disappeared or "faded away" as Native American people—perhaps they would have been annihilated in Northumberland and Lancaster Counties if the leaders had not removed themselves and joined other tribal groups. They have increased their number from the ten in Wiccocomico Indian Town as noted by Beverly in 1703 to 350 to 600+ relatives in UCITOVA, in Central Virginia alone. Actually, three Pinns from Wiccocomico Indian Town served in the American Revolutionary War (Raleigh, his brother Robert, and Robert's son, John) at the decisive Yorktown Revolutionary War battle. There were six Pinns altogether in the Revolutionary War (In addition to Raleigh, Robert and John, Robert's two

---

[39] John Pinn, *Southern Campaign American Revolution Pension Statements: John Pinn*, ed. C. Leon Harris, Transcriber, and Annotator (Suffolk County, MASSACHUSETTS: Commonwealth Of Massachusetts, 1842). Pension application of John Pinn (Pinn) R8264, statement by Pinn transcribed by C. Leon Harris.

other sons fought with Daniel Morgan's Riflemen in Cowpens, South Carolina, as well as other campaigns). Thomas Pinn (one of Raleigh's brother's son?) was also a soldier in the American Revolution.[40] The Pinns were the only minority soldiers with the "N.A.," Native American designation in the Daughters of the American Revolution report (*Minority Military Service Virginia*, DAR).[41] While there were other UCITOVA Native American patriots, only the Pinns were decisively noted in military records. The Pinns—contrary to the desire of some colonists in Wiccocomico Indian Town—were not destroyed but migrated to other areas beyond heavily populated English settlements and increased their tribal numbers. Although some of the Pinns escaped colonists' efforts to steal their Wiccocomico reservation land by moving on to Central Virginia, other natives of Wiccocomico experienced Native American slavery, forced indenture servitude of children and adults, and other crimes against them physically, economically, culturally and psychologically.

The U.S. Census Bureau indicated that 19 percent of Virginia's Native American population—1,836 of 9,211—registered as Cherokee.[42] With almost 20 percent of Virginia's Native American population stating that they have Cherokee ancestry, why have Virginia's historians and officials taken the position that all the Cherokees have left Virginia, or as some people feel, that they were never in Virginia in the first place? Their attitude reflected their indifference to Cherokee history; it is as if they refused to believe that remnants of Cherokee people are in Virginia. The prevailing myth that all the Cherokees have been moved to Oklahoma or to Cherokee, North Carolina—perpetuated by the well-documented history of the removal to Oklahoma, strong Native American historical

---

[40] Eric G. Grundset, ed., *Forgotten Patriots* (Washington, DC: National Society Of Daughters Of The American Revolution, 2008), 525.

[41] John Pinn, *Southern Campaign American Revolution Pension Statements: John Pinn*, 1842

[42] Russell Thornton, *The Cherokee: A Population History* (1990: University Of Nebraska, 1990), 199.

records collected over time in the states of North Carolina, Tennessee, Alabama, and Georgia, and an almost shocking absence of official Cherokee records in Virginia—have made it very difficult for Cherokees to claim their rightful heritage in Virginia. Do Virginia historians and officials really believe that Cherokee ancestors in Virginia and other states would have misled their descendants by giving them or passing down an incorrect name for their tribe?

During the early periods of American history, Virginia colonists were involved in aggressive efforts to remove Native Americans from their newly found territory, not in efforts to record and preserve their heritage and history. Virginia, officially, has not been a Native American–friendly state—even throughout the colonial period when colonists supported a heinous policy of putting a bounty on Native American scalps (*Journal of Cherokee Studies*, Fall, 1976, 98),[43] and up through the Eugenics and Racial Integrity era of Dr. Walter Plecker in the early to mid-1900s.

Thornton[44] discussed the assaults and genocide of Cherokees during the mid-1700s. The Cherokee Nation had several divisions. The Lower towns were situated along rivers in what is called South Carolina. The Upper or Overhill towns were located in eastern Tennessee and extreme North Carolina. In the center were the Middle towns. The British considered the area two separate divisions. To the west were the Valley towns—in present Southwestern North Carolina and Northeastern Georgia. In the center of the area, but to the east, were the Middle towns, along a portion of the Little Tennessee River and its tributaries, in the western part of what is now North Carolina. The northern and eastern portion of the Middle town area was sometimes designated as the Out towns, since the area was geographically isolated from the main body of Cherokees.

Thornton noted that conflicts between the European colonists and the Cherokees had a major influence on the decline

---

[43] Raymond Evans, "Notable Persons in Cherokee History: Bob Benge"," *Journal of Cherokee Studies*, Vol. 1, No. 2, (1976), 98.

[44] Russell Thornton, 1990, 10-38.

of the Cherokee's population history, particularly the "wars" of 1760–61 and 1776. When some Cherokee allies were slain by Virginians and Cherokees began to attack Carolina settlements, tensions increased. The Carolina government declared war against the Cherokees in 1759. Colonel Montgomery, with over 1,600 men, marched through the Cherokee territory twice in 1760. He surprised a Cherokee village, Little Keowee, killing every man of the defenders. Then he destroyed the Lower towns, burning them to the ground, cutting down the orchards and cornfields, killing and taking more than one hundred men, and driving the whole population into the surrounding mountains. It is likely that the scattered remnants of the Cherokee towns removed themselves to isolated areas in present-day Virginia, West Virginia, North Carolina, Tennessee, Georgia, and other areas all over the South, in retreat from the militia and for survival.

In 1760, Montgomery next moved north to the Middle towns and Upper towns. Here he was more or less defeated by the concentrated forces of Cherokees. In 1761 Colonel Grant and 2,600 soldiers, including some Chickasaw and Catawbas, dealt another blow to the Cherokees, burning fifteen Middle towns to the ground, as well as all the plantations and destroying some 1,400 acres of Cherokee crops. Grant drove some five thousand Cherokees—men, women, and children—into the woods and mountains to starve or survive. In a short period of time, the "rest of the Cherokee population fled to what western towns and Overhill settlements remained, where there were barely enough food for a third of the total Cherokee tribe."[45].

At the start of the Revolutionary War, the British had managed to get the allegiance of the Cherokees against the American colonists. Eventually, thousands of American colonial troops attacked Cherokee towns from several quarters. James O'Donnell indicated that the Carolinas and Virginia agreed to attack all the towns. While Georgia could not participate in the master plan, South Carolina would attack the Lower towns, and the two Carolinas would annihilate the Middle and

---

[45] Ibid., 36.

Valley towns. Virginia would move against the Overhill.[46][47] The Overhill towns' Cherokee residents did not resist the Virginia Militia and therefore avoided all-out bloodshed.

American colonists did not anticipate that these assaults would force escapees from Cherokee towns to remove themselves to isolated areas in North Carolina, South Carolina, and Virginia—areas with which they were familiar—and cause them to settle in these locations, sometimes living as Cherokees or, during warfare adversarial periods, as "friendly" Indians, other than Cherokees. They often settled in new areas as "white" people or free "colored," as they were termed by the local white populations, in order to survive economically and to hide out from the persecutions related to their previous alliance with the British and their attacks on settlers. Rather than destroying the Cherokees, the colonists chased survivors from their destroyed towns and allowed them to acculturate into other communities throughout the southeast, including Central Virginia. These colonists' efforts at neutralizing the Cherokees only forced them to find more room to spread out in other areas and states;[48] they, in effect, forced them to hide and change their strategies for survival. They would continue to live as Cherokees in these new locations. On the surface with the white population, they would go through the motions of appearing acculturated, but with fellow Cherokees and family members, they would intensify their efforts to retain their Native American customs, folkways, and culture. Some Cherokees would not admit that they were Cherokees, but pretended to be a member of a friendly tribe, or even colored or white, unless they knew that the white residents would not persecute or reject them for being Cherokees.[49]

Some family members boldly asserted their Cherokee ancestry even during periods of Virginia history when the word

---

[46] James H. O'Donnell, *Southern Indians in the American Revolution* (Knoxville, TENNESSEE: University Of Tennessee, 1973) 43-44.

[47] Russell Thornton, 1998, 10-38.

[48] John Pinn, *Southern Campaign American Revolution Pension Statements: John Pinn*, 1842.

[49] Horace R. Rice, 1995, 55.

"Cherokee" could have negative effects on their physical and financial security (Rice, 1995, Sandidge Interview, page 55). Buffalo Ridge band members on the Amherst side of the James River generally did not tell strangers that they were Cherokees. This secretive approach could have been due to the fact that they were members of a hybrid band, Cherokees and Wiccocomicos. Oral local legends revealed that Wiccocomico descendants in the Ridge had to "look over their shoulders" for several decades because of their perceived threat that Northern Neck colonists planned to annihilate all remaining natives of Wiccocomico Indian Town. The eastern Amherst County Native American tribe, Buffalo Ridge band, kept the secret from strangers but boldly asserted who they were to other Native Americans. William E. Sandidge, clerk of the Amherst County Courthouse for more than fifty years, did not press band members to indicate their official tribal association. During an interview with Mr. Sandidge and his son at his home on January 25, 1995, Mr. Sandidge shared the following information with the author:

> The Indians on the east side of Amherst County [UCITOVA] did not specify what tribe they were but the Indians on the west side claimed to be Cherokee. The records at the courthouse were not segregated by race. They were mixed up like they are today. My father was clerk of the court for thirty-three years and his father was the clerk for seven years. I was born in 1904. I have lived in Amherst all my life. My grandfather was the clerk of the court from 1893–1900. My father was clerk from 1900 until 1933. I started in 1933 and worked until 1983.[50]

William Sandidge and his two clerks of the court ancestors, three generations, knew about and processed official court documents (deeds, marriage records, wills, tax information, etc.) for the Buffalo Ridge people for ninety years—from 1893 until 1983. His declaration that Buffalo Ridge tribal members

---

[50] Ibid., 1995, 55.

were "Indian" is expert testimony, based on his family's occupational longevity as clerks of the county court. Amherst County Court is filled with thousands of Buffalo Ridge band members' interfamily transaction records and documents. The "Sandidge, Clerk" name and title has been affixed on the bottom of most of those documents for three generations. Mr. Sandidge's statement concerning his extended family's influence in Amherst County's Courthouse did not, in the opinion of the author, come off as a boasting declaration. This was Mr. Sandidge's way of asserting that he knew what he was talking about regarding the UCITOVA band, as he spoke as a former clerk on behalf of his father and grandfather and ninety years of official legal records.

Another policy caused the Cherokees to disperse from their Cherokee towns and move secretively in all geographical directions. The Cherokees, in 1838, numbering approximately seventeen thousand, were rounded up like cattle in their smaller and reduced Cherokee territory and forced to move westward to Oklahoma (Thornton, 117).[51] This single federal order to remove the Cherokee—also known as the Trail of Tears—changed the proud indigenous tribe into an indigent destitute people. Numerous captives escaped. Eluding the troops by hiding in the hills, even with calls by Chief Ross to return to the main body, they remained as a defiant band that refused to cooperate with the forced removal to Oklahoma (Moulton, 1978, 97). Many Cherokees left the area when the talk about removal started. Others escaped during the roundup of Cherokees for the forced removal to Oklahoma. They hid out in the forests and moved in all directions from the troops like water ripples when a rock falls into a pond. Some roamed along the Blue Ridge Mountains and came into Bedford County (Charles "Greyhorse" Harmon, *Forgotten Patriots*, DAR, p. 519, Cherokee Indian), Buckingham County, and Amherst County;[52] some even settled in the Northern Neck area of Eastern Virginia. They lived along the piedmont region at the base of the Blue

---

[51] Russell Thornton, 1990, 117
[52] Eric G. Grundset, 2008, 519

Ridge Mountains and survived as white or free colored people. A large number of free colored people showed up in Central Virginia during the 1820s to 1840s.

Albert McCoy, son of Anthony McCoy, moved into the Buckingham County area (Stonewall Mill) prior to 1840, as his name appeared on the 1840 Buckingham Census. Was Albert the *A. Coy* that was listed on the Amherst County Census, 1810 (NARA microfilm, M252, 71 Rolls, Bureau of the Census, Record Group 29)? Some tribal descendants believe that some McCoy family members lived in Tennessee prior to Albert McCoy's arrival in Stonewall Mill; and that he was the same "A. McCoy" in the 1835 roundup census of Cherokee people scheduled to be moved to Oklahoma but escaped.

> "One fullblood, one quarterblood and nine halfbloods. One slave. A farm and two farmers. A mechanic. Nine read English and one reads Cherokee. One weaver and two spinners. They owned a ferry boat. From James W. Tyner, *Those Who Cried, the 16,000*, published by Chi-ga-u Inc., 1974, page 169).[53]

Albert McCoy's family had difficulty speaking fluent English as indicated by some of their descendants. Raleigh Pete Carson, a descendant of the McCoy and Ferguson clans, stated (Rice, 1995, pages 146–148) that the McCoys were full-blood Cherokee and they had trouble speaking English. He noted that his great-grandfather, Lafayette McCoy, was a carpenter and casket maker. "He was a full-blooded Cherokee Indian. He could speak very little English . . . We were told that Fayette never cut his 'coal-black' straight hair, parted in the middle with two plats, with red ribbons on it. He wanted to remain as he was, a Cherokee Indian . . . His dialect was not clear. He was such a Cherokee that he didn't learn English . . ."[54]

---

[53] James W. Tyner, *Those Who Cried: The 16,000* (Muskogee, OK: Muskogee, Ok, 1990), 169.

[54] Rice, 1995, 146-148.

New names suddenly appeared on the Census rolls in the 1850s in counties in Central Virginia. Some ancestors of UCITOVA members were previously residing in areas where the Rechahecrians lived, often with the same surnames that were owned by Cherokees who came into the area from Southwestern Virginia, North Carolina and Tennessee. Some of the surnames and some early locations/residences of family members are noted: the Bankses (Goochland, York, Surry, and Southhampton Counties); the Elliotts[55] (Norfolk and Surry Counties); the Pinns (Northumberland and Lancaster Counties); the Evanses (Lunenburg and Mecklenburg Counties); the Scotts (Norfolk and Henrico Counties); the Sorrells (Lancaster County and Northumberland County); and the Sparrows, (Northumberland, Norfolk and Princess Anne Counties).[56] They and other families joined their cousins, who were already in Central Virginia, descendants of Cherokees from the Appomattox River areas, Rechahecrians (survivors from the battles of 1760–61 and 1776, and escapees from the forced removal to Oklahoma); and Wiccocomico from Wiccocomico Indian Town, and escaped Wiccocomico slaves and released indentured servants of Northumberland and Lancaster Counties.

The Cherokee population was reduced further in Virginia through a new strategy, "paper genocide." Dr. Walter Plecker, the Director of the Virginia Vital Statistics Department, stated in *The Virginia Medical Monthly*, November 1925, on the subject of "Racial Improvement," that "America was claimed by the great Nordic race as its final and chiefest possession; as the great haven of refuge from religious and political persecution where the most hardy, most enlightened and best equipped of Europe's people could establish a great country for their race."[57]

---

[55] Ibid., 1995, 152.

[56] Paul Heinegg, *Free African Americans of North Carolina, Virginia, and South Carolina from the Colonial Period to About 1820* (Baltimore, MD: Clearfield Company By Genealogical Publishing, 2005), 93-104, 453-458, 942-947, 462-480, 1030-1050, 1072-1073, & 1073-1076 (Names included large percentage of Native Americans).

[57] Walter A. Plecker, "Racial Improvement," *Virginia Medical Monthly* January 1925.

Dr. Plecker, in *Virginia's Vanished Race*, 1947, continued his paper genocide of Native Americans in Virginia by discussing the reduction of some Native American tribes. He concluded that "in the early days the Indians resisted the whites and were crushed; the free Negroes yielded, prospered, and absorbed the Indian remnants."[58] This statement reflected the then-official policy of Virginia, that the Indians are "no more, as they have become 'Negroes.'" It also forced many Virginia Native Americans to deny any African American ancestry. These types of statements from state officials had the effect of causing Native Americans to dislike any tribal member who admits having African American ancestry. Native tribal members with Negro ancestry—even with Negro and European ancestry in their genealogy—turned off and offended other Virginia Native Americans, due to the heavy, anti-Negro toxic eugenic atmosphere in the state.

After brutal campaigns by Virginia officials against Cherokees and other Native Americans during the 1600s, 1700s, and 1800s, Dr. Plecker continued his campaign in the early to mid-1900s—where the earlier political and military officials' genocidal policies left off—by engaging in paper genocide of Native Americans. His campaign was an aggressive state policy of paper genocide as opposed to the earlier periods of aggressive militia assaults on Cherokee villages in Virginia and other states, and to the ongoing passive silence with the pen on the part of historians in refusing to follow neighboring states in documenting Native American history aggressively. Of the Cherokee residents who remained in Virginia after the colonial assaults on their villages, their descendants had to face the paper genocide; the aggressive pen by Virginia Vital Statistics officials in calling Native Americans "Negroes;" and the passive efforts of historians in failing to pick up the pen and record the true history of Native Americans for posterity, especially Cherokee history. How tainted are the Native American historical records that do exist, as a result of Virginia's anti-Cherokee campaigns, indifference to Cherokee historical recordings, the state-endorsed eugenics movement and other Racial Integrity efforts?

---

[58] Walter A. Plecker, *Virginia's Vanished Race* (Richmond, VA, 1947).

Descendants of the Wiccocomico tribe joined and became acculturated with Cherokees prior to and after Cherokee removal to Oklahoma and united with UCITOVA in Central Virginia. Native American tribal rolls in Oklahoma included Pinns/Panns/Pans/Pens/Penns/Paynes who were removed from the East to the West. Others were able to remain in the east, some as Native Americans and others, if necessary, as white or black residents. Who are these people who were resilient and refused to go away? How did they keep their Native American culture in spite of the fact that English settlers followed them from Wiccocomico Indian Town to Central Virginia and encroached again on their lands? How did they survive under the rigid Virginia eugenics and racial integrity policies? This report is a summary of two people; two tribes that joined forces in the middle-to-latter part of the 1700s—the smaller Wiccocomico band and the larger group of Cherokee people—and deceptively separated the united group into two groups, one on each side of the James River, to protect its sovereignty against encroachment by settlers. Their descendants continued the Stonewall Mill and Buffalo Ridge Band of Cherokee, united and operating under the present incorporated name, United Cherokee Indian Tribe of Virginia, Inc., UCITOVA.

Brief History of UCITOVA

The Cherokees in the Ridge and Stonewall Mill, united as the Buffalo Ridge Band of Cherokee and now known as the United Cherokee Indian Tribe of Virginia, Inc., are survivors. Matching the tradition of Cherokee people in general, their Native American ancestors assimilated into the general environment by becoming successful farmers, carpenters, military minutemen/Revolutionary War soldiers, teachers, nurses, physicians, attorneys, judges, and midwives. They refused to be stereotyped as "poor Indians," isolated in the Ridge, although some were poor and some were living in remote areas of the Ridge. They were, however, united with the nucleus group. They assimilated in the community, for purposes of survival as a Native American tribal band in a hostile environment, and became "colored

Indians" to some, and "white" or "colored" to others. Among tribal members and residents of the community who could be trusted or entrusted with the fact, they boldly stated that they were "Cherokee Indians."

UCITOVA's ancestors dressed like the rest of the general population—except during official tribal meetings and other formal functions—as they did not want to draw undue attention to themselves. They had numerous historical examples of what undue attention could do to Cherokee groups, as they heard oral legends about the incidents with the colonial militia actions of 1622, 1760–61, 1776, and 1838 against Cherokees. They pledged that they would make adjustments in their environment to avoid removal, assimilation and/or annihilation. UCITOVA's ancestors refused to draw attention to themselves by looking different, thus setting the stage for manipulation as helpless people by outside forces.

There have been some hints of Native slavery in UCITOVA, Mary Catherine Bolling noted that she heard her "grandmother talking about slavery. She told us children how the people were mean to our people during slavery." She indicated that her "grandmother was Mary Catherine Beverly." A review of Catherine Beverly Bolling's grandmother's 1850 U.S. Census reveals that her grandmother (Catherine Beverly) was a free 16 year old mulatto in the household of her mother, Mary Ann Beverly, age 43. Mary Ann Beverly, head of the household, had a son, William J. Beverly, age 14.[59] She stated that she was "named after [her] grandmother."[60] Mary Ann Beverly was not a slave as records reveal that she owned 55 improved acres and 65 unimproved acres and a total land value of $400.[61] Mary Ann Beverly was the daughter of William Beverly and Eady

---

[59] Bureau of Census, National Archives, *Census, United States, 1850, Eastern Amherst County, Virginia* (Washington, DC: National Archives Microfilm Publication, 1850), Roll M432_933; Page 84A; Image 169.

[60] Horace R. Rice, 1991, 104-106.

[61] McLeRoy, Sherrie, and William R. McLeRoy, *Strangers in their Midst*, ed. McLeRoy, Sherrie, and William McLeRoy (Bowie, MD: Heritage Books, Inc, 1993), 120.

Pinn Beverly. Mary Ann Beverly was a progressive head of her household. Catherine Bolling may have heard her grandmother, Catherine Beverly, and great-grand mother, Mary Ann Beverly, discuss Indian slavery, as the Beverlys have always proclaimed that they were aboriginal people of America. Although some of their Native ancestors may have been enslaved as Indian slaves, UCITOVA ancestors and descendants were never enslaved during more than two hundred and fifty years of recorded existence in Central Virginia, as they owned their land, paid taxes, and fought in all major American wars.

The Daughters of the American Revolution has published a book that includes many names of Revolutionary War soldiers and sailors.[62] Numerous Revolutionary UCITOVA War ancestors have been included in the publication: Sylvanus Beverly, Rawley Pinn, John Redcross, John Banks, Jacob Banks, John Fields, James Cooper, Francis Cousins, James Couzins, Thomas Evans, William Jackson, Robert Pinn, William Pinn, Thomas Pinn, George Tyler, and others (*Forgotten Patriots*).[63] There were other 1700-era patriarchs and matriarchs who were Tribal Pillar ancestors in Stonewall Mill and on Buffalo Ridge.[64] These leaders were united in their conviction to survive as free, aboriginal citizens in Amherst and Buckingham County (Appomattox County in 1845).

They were Native American Cherokee and Wiccocomico, a remnant of a great nation divided through war, disease, and political alienation. A longitudinal, global view of UCITOVA's recorded history from the 1600s until the present time reveals their close-knit culture, medical and pharmaceutical practices,

---

[62] Eric G. Grundset, 2008.

[63] Ibid., 2008, 509-528.

[64] Horace R. Rice to United Cherokee Tribe Of Virginia (UCITOVA), Madison Heights, VA, *Basic Facts on UCITOVA--Statistical Analysis of Family Relationship between UCITOVA Tribal Pillars/Revolutionary War Ancestors*, (Madison Heights, VA: Unpublished, 2009), 30. The statistical analysis (SPSS) of family relationship (Intermarriage) between UCITOVA Tribal Pillars/Revolutionary War patriots and present generation tribal members.

love for God and Jesus Christ, religious fellowship, intermarriage patterns, kinship connections, and Cherokee and Wiccocomico military combat and farming skills. They were and are as much and more real "Indian" genetically and at heart than many reservation Indians who are kept together by outside federal reservation regulations. UCITOVA's members had instinctual intermarriage over a period of more than four centuries and strong commitment to "family" and to "passing on" their Cherokee-Wiccocomico heritage to descendants.[65] The early ancestors and the spiritual forces for survival kept the people together, even after the death of strong leaders of the tribe. The band refused to die or "fade away."

The leaders encouraged family members to stand on their own two feet. The "nobody owes you anything" philosophy prevailed and still prevails in the tribe. They have not sought handouts, money, or land from others. Actually, they were engaged in real estate transactions, often purchasing and selling hundreds of acres at a time, in the Ridge long before many of the European settlers arrived in the early 1700s to mid-1800s in Buffalo Ridge.

They were atypical Indians because they did not allow themselves to be classified as an isolated, withdrawn, socially introverted band in the Ridge and in Stonewall Mill. If these Native American people had not been respected by average colonial citizens during the 1700s to mid-1800s, they would have been manipulated, removed from the area, or placed in slavery by land-hungry white residents. These tribal ancestors modeled the possibilities, the vocational potentialities, which exist for a dedicated, united band of family members. Since the late 1600s in Wiccocomico Indian Town, they believed in education, vocational training, maintaining their faith in God, and the principles of hard work.[66]

---

[65] Rice, 1995, 111-210.
[66] Northumberland County, *Court Clerk, Northumberland County Order Book, 1729-37*, vol. 1729-37, (Heathsville, VA: Northumberland County, 1729–37), 109.

The following longitudinal overview documents the UCITOVA band's close tribal relationship and Native American customs. They were and are a remnant of a great and powerful Nation. The Cherokee had a great fall, but some of the broken pieces of the Nation have survived through persecution and dispersion. The Cherokee Nation of Oklahoma, the Keetoowah Band of Cherokee Indians in Oklahoma, and the Qualia Band in Cherokee, North Carolina, all federally recognized tribes, are big pieces of the "Nation." There are many other bands that are as much "Cherokee" as they are, although some of these smaller bands may not have as much historic tribal documentation as the Buffalo Ridge Band. They are nevertheless still Cherokees. These bands are scattered along the bases and ridges of the Allegheny and Blue Ridge Mountains, and have been forced to flee to other states beyond the original Cherokee settlements and boundaries. In 1993, thirty-nine Cherokee bands held a Unity Council meeting in Jasper, Tennessee. Samuel Penn, UCITOVA Chief, attended one of the three-day sessions.[67] The bands are living testimonies of Cherokee persistence and its instinctual, moral, and intestinal fortitude. They are living reminders of the great Nation, whose broken pieces can survive even when the main part of the Nation has been broken, who can still live without being connected to a head or under one leader. UCITOVA is one of those bands (Ross, Chief of the Keetoowah Band, Letter to UCITOVA in support of UCITOVA's state-recognition efforts, February 14, 1994).[68]

---

[67] Samuel Penn. An Attendee at One Of The Sessions, *Unity Council Meeting of 39 Cherokee Bands* (Jasper, TENNESSEE, 1993). Chief presented oral report of the meeting at next regular UCITOVA meeting.

[68] John Ross, Chief, and Keetoowah Band Of Cherokee to Author and UCITOVA Chief, February 14, 1994, *Letter of Support for UCITOVA State Recognition.*

1600-1790

In 1600, the Wiccocomico (anglicized Wicomico) tribe had 130 warriors and approximately 500 members (Bush, 1998, 4).[69] John Smith and the English party probably made contact with the Wiccocomicos, but the Wiccocomicos were not involved with the Chickacones, Onawmanients, and other Powhatan tribes in conspiracies against Smith. Their relative passive actions, even though the tribe was the second largest tribe in number on the Northern Neck, did not save them from encroachment on their lands by English settlers. Their Wiccocomico Native American lifestyle was seriously curtailed by the annexation or formation of the new county, Northumberland, from the Chickacoan District in 1648 (Doran, 1987, table 3).[70] The Indian reserve was eliminated to form Northumberland County. English settlers began to move into the area. In 1610/1611, Strackey noted that the Wiccocomicos had 435 members;[71] however, by 1669, Hening indicated that the population had decreased to 235.[72] Beverley (1705) noted that the Wiccocomicos in 1703 had only ten members officially.[73] Robert Pinn 2's family probably made up almost half of those ten tribal members left in Indian Town. The settlers' encroachment forced a new way of life for the Northern Neck aborigines. Raleigh, one of Robert 2's sons, left the Wiccocomico area and brought a portion of the dispersed Wiccocomico tribal members in Amherst County (Buffalo Ridge) and Buckingham (Stonewall Mill) County, by assimilating with the Cherokees in those areas.

---

[69] Richard C. Bush, 1998, 4.

[70] Michael Doran, *Atlas of County Boundary Changes in Virginia--1634-1895* (Athens, GA: Iberian Publishing, 1987), Table 3.

[71] William Strachey, *The Historie of Travell into Virginia Britania (1612)* (London, ENGLAND: Hakluyt Society, 1953), 45-46, 64-69.

[72] William Hening, ed., *Statues at Large: A Collection of Laws of Virginia*, vol. 1, *Laws between 1819-1823*, (Richmond, VA: George Cochran, 1823), 274-275.

[73] Robert Beverley, *The History and Present State of Virginia* (London, ENGLAND: R. Parker, 1705).

Bush, in *The Bulletin of the Northumberland County Historical Society*, vol. XXXV B 1998) noted that the land fights between the original owners and the settlers had the attention of the Virginia authorities. "Gov. William Berkeley [through the peace treaty of 1646] sought to regulate English access to unsettled land to ensure that the natives would be able to provide for themselves undisturbed." The treaty, however, did not restrict some Englishmen from settling on Wiccocomico lands without negotiating and paying for the land according to the treaty.[74]

In order to work their new land and provide the necessary domestic services, the settlers began to capitalize on the Wiccocomico Indians' corrupted lifestyle by hiring out their children. Bush noted that laws were eventually passed to "limit the period of servitude by an Indian servant (either as a slave or as an indentured servant) to the time served by an English servant"[75] (Hening, Statutes at Large).[76] Later, the Assembly passed another law to deal with the abuse of Indian indentured servants by colonists. The law prohibited masters from transferring children, who had been approved by the court to be entrusted to their care, to other whites, for whatever reason. The law also freed male children at age twenty-five.[77]

A 1672 law empowered and authorized the county courts:

> To place out all the children whose parents are not able to bring them up apprentices to tradesmen; the males till one and twenty years of age, and the females to other necessary employment till eighteen years of age and no longer, and the church wardens of every parish shall (be) strictly enjoyned by the court to give them an account at their orphans courts of all such children within their parish.[78]

---

[74] Richard C. Bush, 1998, 10.
[75] Richard C. Bush, 15.
[76] William Hening, 1823, 138-143.
[77] Ibid., 544-456.
[78] Ibid., 298.

Several Pinns, ancestors and relatives of the UCITOVA members, were caught in this indentured servant scheme to force children to work on the settlers' large farms; in some cases, tribal land that had been confiscated from their parents and grandparents. Since their parents could not follow their Native lifestyle on their lands, some Pinns were forced into hard times and had to let their children become indentured servants.

The Pinns did not always live in a "hard times" setting. Robert Pinn (1), Wiccocomico tribal leader, was a major land owner and engaged in real estate transactions in 1662.[79] His name was listed on a Gloucester County land description as early as 1649.[80] In 1679, the Northumberland Court ordered white settlers, who had taken guns from the Indians at Wiccocomico Indian Town, to return them to the "Great Man Robert [1] of Wiccomico Indian Town."[81] UCITOVA tribal members have heard about this Great Man of Wiccocomico, their ancestor, as their oral heritage relayed stories of their royal and princely status as *Pinn Indians*. The Virginia Assembly recognized "Great Man" as a term used by tribal members to refer to the king of a tribe.[82] Robert Pinn, the chief or king of the tribe, was probably born between 1600 and 1630. Although the settlers confiscated Indian land, the English court's justice system apparently made decisions that were often in favor of Native Americans. Robert Pinn displayed confidence in the court system as he was often a plaintiff against white settlers. The Lancaster County Court also ruled in a Pinn's favor against white defendants:"()mas Pinn, servant to Mr. John Pinckard being blind is ordered to

---

[79] Northumberland County Clerk of The Court, *Northumberland County Record Book 1662-1666*, 9 Feb. 1662, 6.

[80] Polly Cary Mason, ed., *Records of Colonial Gloucester County* (Baltimore, MD: Clearfield, 2003), 32.

[81] Northumberland County Clerk Of The Court, *Northumberland County Record Book, 1778-79*, vol. 1678-79, (Heathsville, VA: Northumberland County Court), 23.

[82] William Hening, 1823, 395.

bee discharged from paying levies (Lancaster County Order Book 2, 1680–86)."[83]

Sutton, in *Red, Black and Revolutionary*, noted that John Pinn 1 was the son of "_____ Pine" [Pinn] (1997, 24). This "____ Pine" was probably Robert Pinn 1. Sutton indicated that John Pine 1 was the father of Robert Pin 1 (24), probably Robert Pinn 2, grandson of Robert Pinn 1.[84][85]

John Pine was very active in Northumberland County during the early 1700s as noted by his frequent name notations in the county order book. Some of those referrals, for example, were:

> PINE v STOTT. John Stott being returned arrested per copia att ye suite of John Pine for [blank] pounds of tobacco and not appearing. Attachment is therefore granted against his Estate returnable to next Court.[86] Lancaster County Order Book, 1702-1713, September 14, 1704.
>
> To Mr. John Pine for three tithables over charged last yeare.[87] November 8, 1704

---

[83] Clerk and Court, eds., *Order Book, Lancaster Count*, vol. II, *Book 2*, (Lancaster County, VA: Lancaster County, 1680–86).

[84] Karen E. Sutton, "Black, Red and Revolutionary: Free African Americans of Lancaster And Northumberland Counties, Virginia In The Era Of The American Revolution," (PhD diss., University of Maryland, 1997), 24. Master's Project submitted to the Faculty of the Graduate School of the University of Maryland in partial fulfillment of the requirements for the degree of Master of Arts, History.

[85] Northumberland County, *Court Clerk, Northumberland County Order Book, 1729-37*, vol. 1729-37, (Heathsville, VA: Northumberland County, 1729–37), 109.

[86] Court Clerk and Lancaster County Court, eds., *Lancaster County Order Book, 1702-1713, Order Book 1702-1713*, (Lancaster, VIRGINIA: Lancaster County Court, 1702), 101.

[87] Court Clerk and Lancaster County, eds., *Lancaster County Order Book*, (Lancaster, VIRGINIA: Lancaster County Court, 1702–1713), 108.

John Pine - 7 Tithables[88] November 8, 1704

Pine v Batteman – Ordered that ye Petition exhibited by John Pine on ye account of Isaac Batteman be dismist, the matter lying before ye Vestry.[89]

Pine v Stott. The two actions brought to this Court by John Pine against John Stott are dismist, neither party appearing. March 14, 1704/5[90]

Pine v Chittwood. The action brought to this Court by John Pine against Thomas Chittwood is dismist, not appearing.[91] March 14, 1704/5

Fox v Pine. John Pine being arrested to this Court att the suit of Capt. William Foxx for the sum of [blank] pounds of tobacco and not appearing, order is therefore granted against the Sheriff upon whose petition an Attachment is granted against the Estate of John Pine returnable to next Court.[92] June 14, 1705

John Pine, like his father, Robert 1, was in court on a regular basis bringing charges against or being charged by colonists that had been allegedly encroaching on his property or possessions. The Court generally administered justice fairly, whether aboriginal or colonial plaintiff or defendant, based on the judges' various court decisions as rendered and noted in the Lancaster Court Order records.

Since the Anglican Church had become the state church in the colony of Virginia, in the Northern Neck of Virginia, church wardens had the power to tax all church members, through

---

[88] Court Clerk, ed., *Lancaster County Order Book, 1702-1713*, (Lancaster, VIRGINIA: Lancaster County Court, 1702–1713), 108.
[89] Ibid., 110.
[90] Ibid., 113.
[91] Ibid., 117.
[92] Ibid., 131.

PATRIOT PINN'S PEARL   445

the court, who did not attend church regularly. Robert Pinn 2, a successful farmer and church member in the Wiccocomico Parish Church, was fined by the court for missing more than a month from the Wiccocomico Parish Church (Church of England):

> "08/16/1733 Robert Pinn of Wiccocomoco parish being presented by the Grand Jury for absenting himself from his parish Church for one month is fined five shillings or fifty pounds of tobacco and that Said Robert pay the said fine to the Church Wardens of the said parish."[93]
> *Northumberland County Order Book 1729–37*, 109

Sutton indicated that Robert Pinn [2] had five children:[94]

Robert Pin 2 [or 3], born about 1730
Rawley Pin 1, born about 1733
John Pinn 1 1732
Sally Pinn, married Amos Nickens 1
Ann Pinn, married _____ Kesterson

The Pinns' genealogy then would be as follows:[95]

---

[93] Northumberland County Clerk of The Court, ed., *Northumberland County Order Book 1729-1737*, (Heathsville, VIRGINIA: Northumberland County Court, 1729–1737), 109.
[94] Karen E. Sutton, 27
[95] Ibid., 24.

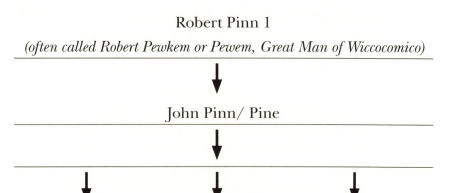

Robert 2's children were:

Robert 3, Rawley, John, Sally, Ann

In 1743, the Lancaster County Court ordered Robert 2's children into indentured service:

> Robert Pinn [3], orphan of Robert Pinn [2] (deceased), is by the court bound to Thomas Doggett of the County til he attains the age of twenty-one years and that his master is to teach him to read and write and the trade of a cooper and find and provide him sufficient wholesome and cleanly diet, lodging, and apparel and at the expiration of the servitude to say and allow him as is appointed for servants by indenture or custom.[96]

In 1751, the Court of Lancaster, violating the law against transferring an Indian indentured servant from one master to another, ordered (June 14, 1751):

---

[96] Clerk and Court, eds., *Order Book, Lancaster County,* January 1743 (Lancaster County, VA: Lancaster County.

> Robert Pinn [3], son of Margaret Pinn, is by court bound to William Downing and Helen his wife til he attains the age of twenty-one years; his master is to teach him to read and write and the trade as a shoemaker and to find and provide with sufficient wholesome and cleanly diet, lodging, and apparel and at the expiration of the servitude to say and allow him as is appointed for servants by indenture or custom.[97]

On May 7, 1764 the churchwardens of North Farnham bound Thomas Pinn to William Dowman, the same man to whom Robert Pinn was bound in Lancaster County on May 11, 1751 Orders 1764-5, 227.[98]

The *Northumberland Order Book (1753–1756*, 25 August 1754, p. 213) noted that Rawley and Robert Pinn (3)'s brother, John Pinn, was placed in an indentured servant status.

> 25 August 1754—To Ezekil Hayden of Lancaster County for taking up John Pinn, a servant man belonging to Rich Hudnall of this County, 90 lbs. Tob., O.B. 1753-56, 213.[99]

Raleigh Pinn, the brother of John and Robert (3) and the last son of Robert (2) (deceased) and Margaret was indentured by Northumberland Court Order. Margaret, a widow, because of poverty, was forced to let her last son go into servitude, only her two daughters remained at home.

> "25 Aug. 1754—To William Garner of this County for taking up Rawleigh Pinn, a servant boy belonging to

---

[97] Clerk of Court, eds., *Order Book, Lancaster County*, (Lancaster County, VA: Lancaster County, 14 June 1751).

[98] Paul Heinegg, 942.

[99] Court Clerk, *Northumberland County Order Book 1753-1756*, vol. 1753-1756, (Northumberland, VA: Northumberland County, 1754), 213.

Richard Seldon of Lancaster County, 90 lbs. Tob. OB 1753–56, 213."[100]

In 1774, Raleigh Pinn (mulatto), who had moved from Northumberland County and a state of indenture servitude, showed up on the Buckingham County Tithable Roll, in Stonewall Mill, present-day Appomattox County.[101] Raleigh later settled on Buffalo Ridge in Amherst County, while at the same time owning property in Stonewall Mill, Buckingham County (part of the Appomattox County in 1845), across the James River from Buffalo Ridge. Later, he was ordered into service in the Revolutionary War.[102] He would serve at Yorktown in the final major battle of the war (*Minority Participation in the Siege of Yorktown*, National Park Service, Colonial National Historical Park, Yorktown Battlefield September 30, 2000):[103]

> When the war broke out, there were about 200,000 Native Americans living east of the Mississippi River, making up about 85 nations or tribes. While in some areas of the country, loyalties of these nations were split (particularly among the Iroquois in the northeast), historians estimate approximately 13,000 warriors fought for the British in the course of the conflict, far more than allied themselves with the Americans.

---

[100] Court Clerk, *Northumberland County Order Book 1753-1756*, vol. 1753-1756, (Northumberland, VA: Northumberland County, 1754), 213.

[101] Woodson, Robert F, and Isobel B. Woodson, eds., *Virginia Tithables--From the Burned Record Counties* (Richmond, VIRGINIA: Isobel B. Woodson, 1970).

[102] Order Roll. List of Militia Ordered into Service from Amherst County, June 21, 1781, Military Roll, Major William Cabell, William Cabell Papers, Swem :library, William And Mary College, Williamsburg, VIRGINIA.

[103] National Park Service and Department of the Interior, *Minority Participation in the Siege of Yorktown* (Yorktown, VA: National Park Service, 2000), 1.

At Yorktown, individuals of the United Cherokee Tribe of Virginia fought with General Washington's army. Today, on the anniversary of the start of the siege, descendants of one of these soldiers, Rawley Pinn, join the National Park Service in recognizing his participation . . .

The James River is in the center of the picture. Amherst County is on the left and Appomattox County is on the right. Buffalo Ridge (not shown) is on the left and Stonewall Mill (not shown) is on the right.

Long before the war, Raleigh had already begun fighting a battle in Amherst County and Buckingham County (later, in 1845, this area of Buckingham County became Appomattox County). He fought a battle to form two villages of Indian people, one in Buffalo Ridge and one in the Stonewall Mill area. The major part of this battle was to protect his bands from outside forces, the English settlers, who were moving into Amherst and Buckingham Counties. He had seen how the Northern Neck settlers, hungry for land in the New World, had destroyed Wiccocomico Indian Town, his home. He saw his proud adult relatives lose their Native American way of life, and he experienced Indian children losing their independence and becoming indentured servants on some of the land previously owned by his parents and ancestors. He therefore invited some of his relatives from Wiccocomico Indian Town to live in the Stonewall Mill area as well as in Amherst County (Buffalo Ridge area). They would live with other Indians, Cherokees, just as Raleigh's ancestors intermarried and socialized with Cherokees in Wiccocomico, and thereby protected their heritage and race from total annihilation. He had learned the white man's ways as an indentured servant to English settlers. He continued to learn the white man's lifestyle by working side by side with them in his role as a military minuteman in Amherst County and later as a soldier in the Revolutionary War battle at Yorktown. His brother's three sons also distinguished themselves as soldiers at Yorktown and rifle marksmen service with Daniel Morgan's Riflemen.[104]

He now knew how to protect his tribe; he separated the band into two bands, one on the east side of the James River and the other one on the west side. By this time, the Cherokee people had used this strategy of dividing its numbers and settling in remote areas. In the 1700s, some Cherokees, after being dispersed from their settlements in Virginia and other states, came back to Virginia in small groups or bands. The Cherokees, for example, requested permission from the Virginia Colonial Council to settle on the Roanoke River so that they "may enjoy convenience of free trade" (*Colonial Council minutes*, #343, 3 November 1721).[105] The Council officially refused to grant Cherokees, as a tribe or band, a chance to become residents on the Roanoke River because their presence there "might disturb" other Northern Indian hunting tribes (#344). The Cherokees, however, disregarded the official response and came back to

---

[104] John Pinn, *Southern Campaign American Revolution Pension Statements: John Pinn*, 1842).

[105] Minutes Clerk, ed., *Colonial Council Minutes, 1721*, (Richmond, VA: Virginia Colonial Council, # 343, 1721).

the area in small groups, sometimes as white residents and sometimes they even permitted people to call them colored or mulatto, as the game was survival. The Evanses, for example, lived in Lunenburg County (land later included in Mecklenburg County) near the Roanoke River and several Evans family members later moved to Amherst County.

Some Evans family members are believed to have been descendants of the group of Cherokees who sought permission to set up a Cherokee settlement near the Roanoke River for trade purposes in 1721. Many of Amherst, Brunswick, Lunenburg, and Mecklenburg Counties' Evanses—believed to be descendants of the Lunenburg/ Mecklenburg Counties' Cherokees who sought Colonial Council approval to set up a band of Cherokee—still retain their Cherokee heritage today. Being denied settlement access to the Roanoke River site, they followed the Cherokee tradition of remaining in and/or coming back into Virginia and living as Cherokees in isolated homes or small communities because to settle in Virginia as a large, threatening, Cherokee tribe would open up the colonists' fear of "savage Indians" living in their neighborhoods. Sarah Evans, Charles Evans, and Major Evans of Lunenburg County (present day Mecklenburg County), sold 120 acres on Stith's Creek [DB 8, page 356]. These were the children of Charles Evans, born around 1696.[106] Lunenburg County Deed Book 8, page 357, noted that Major, Charles, and Sarah Evans made their X mark on the document at the time of the sale, October 10, 1764.[107]

Sometime after the land sale, Sarah and several of Charles Evans's other children moved to Southside and Central Virginia. It is believed that Sarah had already met Raleigh Pinn before moving to Amherst County, as there were some Pinn and Redcross family members living in the Lunenburg and Mecklenburg County area and vicinity.[108]

---

[106] Paul Heinegg, 466.
[107] Clerk Of The Court, ed., *Lunenburg County Deed Book*, vol. VIII, (Lunenburg, VA: Lunenburg County, n.d), 356.
[108] Paul Heinegg, *945, 947, 969*.

Raleigh was enumerated as head of a household of eight mulatto members in his household in Amherst County in the 1790 census.[109] Raleigh used this survival strategy by separating the members on both sides of the river. Each group was represented by some Beverlys, Pinns, Fergusons, McCoys, Bankses, and other surnames. They also married the Redcrosses and Evanses, and other "well-known" Cherokees in the area.[110] Raleigh Pinn, Silvanus Beverly, and Jacob Bands, in addition to Thomas Evans, John Redcross, John Cousins, William Jackson, Thomas Pinn, and others were UCITOVA Revolutionary War ancestors.

As a soldier in the Amherst Militia and at Yorktown, Raleigh served with other Cherokee people. Some of Raleigh's relatives would later marry into these Native American soldiers' families.[111] Since Cherokee people are an amalgamation of the conquerors and the conquered, the Pinns followed this tradition and provided a small number of mixed Algonquians/Cherokees to the larger group of Cherokee.

1790–2000

Raleigh Pinn's influence over the UCITOVA people today, even after two-hundred-plus years since his death, is still powerful. Raleigh was the founder of the band, and he wrote the book on tribal survival techniques. He managed to keep his name and his tribal members' names on official county record books—much like his father, grandfather, and great-grandfather did in Northumberland and Lancaster Counties. Raleigh left his name on census records and also served in the Amherst Militia and Revolutionary War, leaving military records for tribal documentation. He chose secluded, beautiful areas in Buffalo Ridge and in Stonewall Mill to set up his tribal habitations.

---

[109] Bureau of The Census, *First Census of the United States, 1790*, vol. 1st Census, (Washington, DC: Government Printing Office, n.d), 47.

[110] Edgar Whitehead, April 19, 1896.

[111] Horace R. Rice, *Basic Facts on UCITOVA--Statistical Analysis of Family Relationship between UCITOVA Tribal Pillars/Revolutionary War Ancestors.* 2009.

Walker noted that "according to the scouts sent out by the Assembly, pioneers had begun to move into the present Clifford and Sweet Briar areas and some had settled along Buffalo Ridge and Tobacco Row Mountain, sometime between 1710 and 1720.[112]

Raleigh presided as the first recorded tribal leader. He frequently attended weddings of tribal members.[113] He served as the mentor for groups, both in the Ridge and in Stonewall Mill, from the time of his arrival in Buckingham and Amherst Counties until his death after 1800. His name did not appear on courthouse real estate deed records after 1801[114] and his name as tribal leader was also absent from wedding records as a parent or witness after 1801.

Polly Beverly, daughter of William Beverly and Eady Pinn—who lived in Buckingham County (Appomattox Stonewall Mill area) but moved to the Ridge, across from the James River—served as the Beloved Mother of the tribe until the mid-1800s. Turner Pinn, Raleigh Pinn's son and a prosperous farmer, served as a leader for the band while his daughter, Polly Pinn Two Pins, or Two Pence, wife of Richard Two Pins, later served as the Beloved Mother of the group. Her son, John Turner Pinn, Turner Pinn's grandson, was the tribal leader in the Ridge until Willis West, Betsy Beverly's son, came of age to lead the band.[115]

---

[112] Frances M. Walker, *The Early Episcopal Church in the Amherst-Nelson Area* (Lynchburg, VA: J.P. Bell, 1964), 33.

[113] Clerk of The Court, ed., *Amherst County Marriage Book*, vol. Book I, (Amherst, VA: Clerk Of The Court, n.d). Some of the court recordings for Tribal Members' ancestors that Raleigh attended: Beverly/Williams, 29 November 1792; Evans/Pinn, 2 November 1795; & Pinn/Redcross, 27 August 1799.

[114] Clerk of the Court, ed., *Amherst County Deed Book*, vol. Deed Book I, (Amherst, VA: Amherst County, n.d), 330, 341, 363. Some of Raleigh Pinn's numerous Deed recordings in Amherst County on Buffalo Ridge.

[115] Clerk of Court Amherst County, eds., *Amherst County Deed Book*, vol. LXI, (Amherst, VA: Amherst County Court, 1909), 570. Deed for the Second Fairmount Baptist Church, to Deacon Willis West, church official (trustee).

Willis West, great-grandson of William and Eady Pinn Beverly, was a deacon and Sunday school superintendent at Fairmount Baptist Church on the Ridge. Fairmount Baptist Church (the First Fairmount), an old and historic church on Buffalo Ridge, was probably started by Raleigh Pinn in the mid- to late 1770s. The historic Pinn Park Cherokee Grounds cemetery is near the site of the First Fairmount on the Ridge. It is believed that Raleigh and other early tribal pillars and members are interred in Pinn Park.

Elizabeth "Betsy" Beverly (born 1837) was daughter of Polly Beverly (b. 1805), granddaughter of William Beverly (b. 1770) and Eady Pinn Beverly (b. 1780). Betsy was the mother of Willis West and Benjamin Beverly.

In the 1830s, however, the U.S. Census in Amherst County revealed that a large group of Native Americans and white citizens lived in a general vicinity to each other, including Patterson Johns, Rachel Peters, William Jackson, William Cato,

James Johns, Williams Sutherds, Albert Terry, Joel Brannum, Charles Beverley, Henry Evans, Benjamin Whiteside, Elizabeth Tony, John Cozens (Cousins), Samuel Scott, Roland "Rolly" Pinn (Turner Pinn's son), William Harris, John Arnold, Richard Tuppence, Turner Pinn, Bartlett Sparrow, Ezekiel Umbles (Humbles), Jack Helton, Sicely Napier, Jeffery Johns, and Frederick Beverly.[116] By the 1840s, white settlers continued to purchase land from these Native Americans and build dwellings between them. During the 1840s, Samuel Scott, William Harris, George Jewell, Madison Beverly, Anthony Beverly, Bartlett Sparrow (*1840 U.S. Census*, Amherst County, page 222), with Ezekiel (H)Umbles and Richard Tuppence (page 226) (with his wife Polly Pinn Tuppence) and Turner Pinn and Polly Beverly (page 225) were living in the same tribal setting or area (clustered together in a residential clan connection) and listed as free colored individuals.[117]

It is obvious that, by the 1840s, the Jacksons, Beverlys, Cousinses, Scotts, Pinns, Harrises, Tuppences, Sparrows, and Humbleses continued to remain in a tribal group in the eastern section of Amherst County, known as Buffalo Ridge, and others of this group had relatives who lived in Stonewall Mill (Buckingham County, later Appomattox County).

Census records show these families, the larger group, which had been clustered together in 1830 for a short period, had dwindled by the 1840 census to the ten primary Amherst County surnames represented in the genealogy of most of UCITOVA's members. The other Native Americans included in the 1830 census community had moved by the 1840 census, some of them probably relocated to other locations for survival. The later

---

[116] 1830 United States Federal Census: Amherst County, Virginia, Family History Library Film, Series: M19; Roll 194, Page 525, Federal Census M19: Roll 194, Library Film 0029673. Film included the names of neighboring Native Americans clustered together, including Turner Pinn.

[117] 1840 United States Federal Census, Amherst County, Virginia, 1840, Census, U.S. Census 1840, Roll 550; Page 225; Image 457, Nara National Archives, Washington, DC, Family History Library Film 0029683.

census records after 1840 show a progressively larger number of nonfamily members settling in these previously "closed" areas. These Native Americans were prosperous farmers in the Ridge. Turner Pinn, Raleigh Pinn's son, the second chief or leader of the Buffalo Ridge Band, owned two slaves during the 1840 census period. Earlier, he owned four slaves in 1829 while Samuel Scott also owned slaves (McLeRoy and McLeRoy, 1993, 32[118]; Rice, 1991, 24).[119] These people and others, those wealthy enough, followed the slave-owning customs of Cherokees in other areas of the southeast. UCITOVA band members became very serious about assimilating into the general environment, and like other Cherokees during this period of time, acted like wealthy white people in their business ventures.

In 1829, the *Cherokee Phoenix and Indian's Advocate* was a popular newspaper in Virginia. Due to the many Cherokee language readers in central and other areas of Virginia, Editor Elias Boudinot listed twelve agents that were authorized to sell the *Phoenix* newspaper in the United States. One of the twelve agents was Pollard & Converse in Richmond, Virginia.[120] This was during a period when Cherokee were very restless about white politicians' talk of moving Cherokee from the Cherokee Eastern territory. Joining fellow Cherokee who were already in Virginia, people came from the official Cherokee territorial limits out of fear of being taken to other areas. Virginia had a large number of Cherokee subscribers to the *Phoenix* paper. These people were descendants of Cherokees who did not leave Virginia in the early 1600s, as well as those Cherokee people who fled from the colonial militia assaults on their Cherokee towns in 1760–61 and 1776 and joined their relatives in Virginia.

It is possible that the historic Fairmount Baptist Church that was built in Nelson County, near the northeastern end of Buffalo Ridge, may have been named after Fairmount Baptist Church in Buffalo Ridge in Amherst County. The Nelson

---

[118] McLeRoy, Sherrie, and William R. McLeRoy, 1993, 32.

[119] Horace R. Rice, 1991, 24.

[120] Elias Boudinot and Ed, "Agents for The Cherokee Phoenix," *Cherokee Phoenix and Indian Advocate* I, (1829, February 11): 1.

County Fairmount Church was built in 1849 near the site of Key's Church, originally built around 1765 by the Anglican/Episcopal Church.[121] Walker noted that during the Revolution, Key's Church served as a meeting place for minutemen and messengers to and from the army. It was also a recruiting station for Revolutionary War soldiers. Col. William Cabell wrote in his diary that he met with recruits "when they rendezvoud at Key's Church." The First Fairmount Baptist Church in the Ridge was already built when the Nelson County Fairmount Baptist Church was rebuilt from the ashes of Key's Church. Raleigh, who had engaged in rendezvous at the Nelson Key's Church as a soldier, may have attended the Key's Anglican or Episcopal Church when he left the Anglican Church in Northumberland and Lancaster Counties. As already noted, this denomination forced his father, Robert, to pay a fine for missing more than a month from worship services. It is possible that friends of Raleigh, after his death, may have named the Nelson church in 1849 after the church in Buffalo Ridge.

Deacon Maloney O. Ferguson, grandson of Willis West and a descendant of Raleigh Pinn, was a strong leader of the tribal group between the 1940s and late 1980s, serving as chairman of the Deacon Board and Sunday school superintendent. He held the same spiritual leadership offices that his grandfather, Willis West, had held years earlier. M. O. Ferguson was firm like his grandfather. The religious leaders held strong power over church members and political influence in the communities of Stonewall Mill and Buffalo Ridge. Usually, they had as much or more influence than an officially elected town mayor. They controlled the people spiritually and brought civil control to the communities.[122] Christian spiritual faith played a major part on the social structure of the villages, and therefore, ministers, deacons, trustees, and other lay leaders exerted informal leadership over the people, not just on Sundays, but throughout the week.

---

[121] Frances M. Walker, *The Early Episcopal Church in the Amherst-Nelson Area* (Lynchburg, VA: J.P. Bell, 1964), 36, 37.
[122] Horace R. Rice, 1995. 132.

Raleigh Pinn planted and supported the tribal group in Stonewall Mill, even though he left that community as a land owner and moved to the Ridge. Yet, he would canoe across the James River to provide moral and financial support to his relatives as needed. Turner Pinn, Raleigh's son, continued to be the patriarch of the two bands for many years in Buffalo Ridge and in Stonewall Mill, after Raleigh's death. Turner Pinn gradually controlled the Amherst group and extended more self-control of the Stonewall Mill group to clan leaders William Beverly, Stephen Ferguson, and Anthony McCoy. After 1810, some members of the *seven* Beverly families in Stonewall started moving over to Buffalo Ridge. The three clan leaders served as unofficial leaders of the Stonewall Mill Band between the 1840s and 1870s. William Beverly, in 1860, was listed on the U.S. Census in Appomattox as a ninety-year-old "mulatto."[123] He had been a strong leader of the Beverly clan for years.

The Beverly family has a rich place in Cherokee history with the Ridge and Stonewall Mill bands, and other Virginia locations. The *1810 U.S. Census* (Virginia) presented the following breakdown of the Beverly/Beverley families in the state of Virginia (all were listed as "mulatto"):

County	Number of Families
Augusta	One
Buckingham (portion later annexed as Appomattox, 1845)	*Seven*
Caroline	One
Culpeper	One
Franklin	Two
Rockbridge	One
Spotsylvania	One

---

[123] Bureau of the Census, *U.S. Census 1860*, (Washington, DC: Government Printing Office, 1860), M653, 1438 Rolls. William Beverly was listed 90 years old, Mulatto.

The Stonewall Mill area and vicinity of Appomattox County claimed half of all of Virginia's Beverlys/Beverleys in 1810.[124] During the 1830 U.S. census taking process, Buckingham County Beverly families generally did not participate, as they were concerned about the "rumor" about the possible removal of Cherokee from the East to Oklahoma. While seven Buckingham County Beverly families submitted their demographic family data to the census takers in 1810 and ten Beverly families in 1820,[125] only one Beverley family, William Beverly, son-in-law of Raleigh Pinn, participated in the 1830 U.S. Census Buckingham County reporting.[126] The only other area county Beverly participant was Cornelius Beverly of Campbell County. The other Beverlys in the area were very cautious and secretive about their family business, as they suspected that officials were trying to collect census information to move Cherokee from Virginia to Oklahoma. By 1840, after the threat of Virginia Cherokee removal had passed, six Buckingham Beverly families "came out of the woods" and again participated in the census reporting.[127]

Most of the Central Virginia Beverly families descended from the Appomattox Beverly clan and are believed to be related to most of the state's Beverlys/Beverleys. The Southwestern Virginia Beverlys are possibly related to the Central Virginia Beverlys and some of the Blevins/Bevins/Bivins are believed to be kin to the Beverlys/Beverlys. Most Beverlys in Southwestern Virginia claim descent from the Cherokees. This is as noted by a census recorded on the *Twelfth Census of the United States*.[128]

---

[124] Janice Hull, ed., *Index to the United States Census for Buckingham County, Virginia* (Buckingham, VIRGINIA: Historical Buckingham, Inc, 1996), 93, 116.

[125] J.E. Robey Felldin, ed., *Index to the 1820 Census of Virginia* (Baltimore, MD: Genealogical Publishing, 1976), 32.

[126] Jackson et al, ed., *Virginia 1930 Census* (Bountiful, UTAH: Accelerated Indexing Systems, Inc, 1976), 21.

[127] Janice Hull, 93, 116.

[128] 1900 United States Federal Census, 1900, Burks Fork, Floyd, Virginia, Roll: 1708; 1A; Enumeration District: 0012, Nara, 1900. T623, 1854 Rolls, Microfilm: 1241708.

William Beverly's entry on this special tribal section of the census, at the end of the county census data, noted that he and his two other family members were of the Cherokee tribe. William P. Beverly was the son of Madison Beverly, one of the residents in the tribal families huddled together near Turner Pinn's band in Buffalo Ridge in Amherst County in the early 1800s. In 1860, William P. Beverly, son of Madison Beverly, was sixteen years old when the census taker recorded the household information.[129] Madison Beverly lived in Amherst County in 1840.[130] He later moved to Botetourt County and his information appeared on the 1850 U.S. Census,[131] and several other locations during the remainder of the second half of the 1800s (U.S. Census, 1860, Montgomery, VA; U.S. Census, 1880,[132] Alum Ridge, Floyd County, VA).

William P. Beverly continued his documentation of his tribal identity in the Burk Fork District of Floyd County as he maintained his Cherokee connection. Madison was probably deceased by this time. The census enumerator listed William P. Beverly and his two children as members of a "Cherokee tribe," in a special "tribal" section on the census report entitled

---

[129] 1860 United States Federal Census, Montgomery, Virginia, 1860, Family History Library Film: 805363, Montgomery, Virginia U.s. Census, Roll: M653, 1363; Page 768; Image: 266, Nara, Washington, DC, Nara Microfilm Publication M653, 1,438 ROLLS.

[130] 1840 United States Federal Census, Amherst County, Virginia, 1840, U.S. Census, Amherst County, VA, 1840 Census, Amherst County, VA, Roll 550; Page 313; Image: 443, Nara, Family History Library Film: 0029683, Nara, BUREAU OF CENSUS.

[131] 1850 United States Census, Botetourt, Virginia, 1750, Census, Botetourt, Virginia, 1850 Census, Botetourt, Virginia, Roll: M432_936; Page 131A; Image: 500, Washington, DC, Nara.

[132] 1880 United States Federal Census, Floyd County, 1880, Alum Ridge, Floyd, Virginia, Family History Film: 1255365, Page 264A; Enumeration District: 025, Washington, DC, National Archives. Madison, as a Cherokee Native American, chose to move around Central and Southwestern Virginia. Eventually, his son, William, settled in 1900 as a Cherokee in an "Indian Tribe" Enumeration in Floyd County, Virginia.

"Indian Population," separate from the rest of the citizens (U.S. Census, Floyd County, 1900, 21 June 1900). The Beverlys in Appomattox and other areas have always been known as and told their children that they were Cherokee.

The Beverlys on the Ridge married other Cherokee on the Ridge. Obadiah Knuckles once lived in the Ridge and his daughter, Roqueen "Rosa," married Benjamin Beverley, the son of Betsy Beverly, and great-grandson of William and Eady Pinn Beverly. Rosa Knuckles Beverley's brother, Calvin, indicated in *Cherokee By Blood*.[133] that he was Cherokee and descended from the Redcross line, via his mother, Susan. Calvin had moved to Jonesboro, Tennessee, and married Luthena Tyree, a Cherokee (*Amherst County Marriage Book 3*, page 108, 2 July 1881).[134] Many Tyrees in Amherst County are Cherokees (Rice, 1995. 219). Two other daughters of Obadiah Knuckles married into the Beverly family. Benjamin Beverly's grandson, Ben Alton Beverly, is Past Tribal Advisor for UCITOVA. The Southwest Virginia Beverlys and other Virginia Beverlys have Cherokee heritage (Santini Interview in Rice, 1995, 30).

The *Report on the History of the Buffalo Ridge Band of Cherokee*, 24 January 1994 (Rice), has a section on the people who cried out from many states, including Virginia and West Virginia, to the claims court that they were eligible for some of the funds that were being provided to Cherokee people from the Eastern United States. The claims court, however, denied Calvin Knuckles and many other applicants in the early 1900s because they remained in areas that were not a part of the Eastern Cherokee territory at the time of the removal to Oklahoma (the British and colonial land treaties of the 1700s which the Cherokees had sectioned off former tribal land and ceded the land to Virginia and other states). The court used the criteria that the people, to be eligible, must have lived in the reduced

---

[133] J. Wright Jordan, ed., *Cherokee By Blood: Record of Eastern Cherokee Ancestry in the U.S. Court of Claims, 1906-1910, Applications 23801-27800* (Bowie, MD: Heritage Books, 2007), 258.

[134] *Amherst County Marriage Register*, Book 3 (Amherst, VA: Amherst County Court, 1881), 108.

area of the Cherokee territory, not the original large area owned by the Cherokees prior to the 1830s. Applicants had to prove that they were in that reduced land territory or were related to people who were removed to Oklahoma or to those who escaped to the Cherokee, North Carolina area. This logic or rationale for deciding who was eligible for the funds had some major faults: it excluded many of the Cherokees who did not live in the reduced Cherokee area at that time, but had remained in Virginia, South Carolina, Kentucky, or West Virginia, for example, on their farms. Why should Cherokee land owners in Virginia give up their rich farmland because the official Cherokee territory had continued to shrink as a result of deceptive land cessions? Many Cherokees remained on their original lands and lived as Cherokee, or as white or colored, if necessary, to survive. In areas other than Central Virginia, many Cherokee people were forced to live as colored people.[135]

Vivian Santini, a well-known Cherokee and Northern Tsalagi Tribe of Southwest Virginia chief, has conducted extensive research on the Cherokees of Southwest Virginia, Tennessee, and North Carolina. She indicated that her people are Cherokees and Powhatans and that they have Pocahontas ancestry. She noted that the Bollings in Virginia are related to Pocahontas and Cherokees, and that they are also her ancestors. UCITOVA's Bollings also have Pocahontas heritage. Santini stated that some of her ancestors' land were taken in Southwest Virginia and some relatives, after their land seizure, were listed as "black" on official rolls in Virginia, including the Wilsons and Neels.[136] The paper genocide in Virginia had the effect of taking hold of the myth that all Cherokee had been moved to Oklahoma and Cherokee, North Carolina, and that anyone who proclaimed to be Cherokee must really be "colored." Therefore, some Virginia officials listed them as either "colored," or "white," but not "Indian."

---

[135] Clerk Of The Court, ed., *Washington County, Virginia Marriage Book*, (Washington County, VIRGINIA: Washington County Court, 1792–1900).

[136] Horace R. Rice, 1995, 30–31.

The Virginia statute of 1705 seems to have begun the paper genocide of Native Americans. On the question of "who shall be deemed mulattos?" Hening recorded:

> Be it enacted and declared, and it is hereby enacted and declared, 'That the child of an Indian and the child, grand child, or great grand child, of a negro shall be deemed, accounted, held and taken to be a mulatto.'[137]

Forbes indicated that he "discovered that Native American descendants had been legally defined as *mulattos* in Virginia in 1705, without having any African ancestry". These Indian people in the Ridge and in Stonewall were usually placed in the mulatto classification. Forbes noted that the census periods of 1800, 1810, 1820, and 1830 classified non-whites, including Indians, as free persons of color. The Native Americans of Robeson County, North Carolina and all Virginia counties were classified as colored. The 1840 census also classified most non-whites as free colored. He noted that the entire Cherokee Indian population of Carroll County, Georgia, was included as colored persons, with names such as Rattlesnake, Ekoah, Watta, Tah-ne-cul-le-hee, Wasotta . . .[138]

Forbes added:

> In Virginia one finds that all the Indians of the Central Tidewater counties were classified as 'M,' including the residents of the Pamunkey and Mattaponi reservations, with a few exceptions in King William County where one or two were classified as 'B.' The same pattern appears in Norfolk County, Virginia, where many members of the Nansemond Indian group living near Portsmouth were classified as 'M'.

---

[137] William Hening,1823, 252.
[138] Jack Forbes, *Black Africans and Native Americans: Color, Race, and Caste in the Evolution of Red-Black Peoples* (New York, NY: Blackwell, 1988), 190-200 of 352 pages. "Native Americans as Mulattoes.

Persons who can be identified as Chickahominy Indians or as ancestors of the present-day Chickahominy are uniformly classified as mulattos. A similar trend occurs in King William, King and Queen, Caroline and Essex Counties.

Even the Pinns—who are well-recognized Indians in America, descendants of the Wiccocomico and Cherokee "aborigines of America"—(National Society, Daughters of the American Revolution, *Minority Military Service Virginia 1775–1783*, 22–23;[139][140] John Pinn's Pension Application; on Cherokee removal rolls as Panns, Pans, Pins, Pinns, Penns, Paines)—have been consistently classified as M even though Raleigh Pinn's family of "7" was noted as white in the First Census of the United States, Heads of Families—Virginia, 1783 (*Virginia, Compiled Census and Census Substitutes Index, 1607–1890*)." Later, his household of "8 souls" was placed in the mulatto category.[141]

The Evanses and Redcrosses, with whom the Pinns and Beverlys intermarried during and after the late 1700s, were "well-known Cherokee Indians in Amherst County" (Whitehead, 1896). Dock Jenkins, a tribal member of UCITOVA and a descendant of the Pinn and Beverly families, had to struggle to keep the "Indian" as his racial classification, against the campaign of Dr. Plecker's racial genocide (U.S. Census, Amherst County, 1920); birth certificate listed parents, Ivanhoe and Cora Beverly Jenkins and Dock Jenkins as "Indian and white."[142] All Jenkins family members on the 1920 census page were listed as "Indian" Native American: Felix Jenkins, Cora Beverly Jenkins, Dock Jenkins, Robert Jenkins, Wm. Jenkins, Gracie Jenkins, Laura Jenkins, and Luther Jenkins. John Pinn (a relative), mulatto, was listed as a boarder in the home. Fellow relative neighbors were also listed as Indian: Ivanhoe Jenkins' whole

---

[139] Daughters of the American Revolution, *Minority Military Service Virginia*, vol. 1775-83, (Washington, DC: DAR, n.d), 22, 23.
[140] Eric G. Grundset, 2008.
[141] Ron V. Jackson, 1976.
[142] Horace Rice, 1995, 195A.

family of eight members and Ollie Wright and his two other family member (U.S. Census, 1920, Amherst County).

Due to the laws on the books in Virginia and the paper genocidal practices of Dr. Plecker and other county officials, Dock Jenkins threatened to take a local newspaper editor to court, if his Negro classification of his race were not retracted from an article that the newspaper had written. He stated:

> I am a certified Indian. It is on my birth certificate "White/Indian", District number 50, File Number 14150, 28 Oct. 1912). The news people called me a Negro, but they retracted it after they were informed and saw proof that I was an Indian.[143]

The period between the 1860s and 1990s in Virginia was stormy and stressful for UCITOVA and other Native American tribes, even for Indians who were not connected with tribal groups. While other individuals and Indian groups were buckling under the aggressive, anti–Native American policies in Virginia, and actually finding it easier to "go for white," UCITOVA people were clinging together in their communities and trying to survive with interdependent agricultural, scholastic, religious, and social activities (Rice, 1995, 1880 U.S. Census, Stonewall Mill, page 1, line 33).[144] McLeRoy and McLeRoy, in *Strangers in Their Midst*, wrote:

> Turner Pinn's ownership was the longest and extended over a decade, from four slaves in 1829 to two in 1840. Luther Porter Jackson speculates that these were 'true' slaves utilized by Pinn on his expanding farm.[145] [146]

---

[143] Ibid., 196
[144] Ibid., 121
[145] McLeRoy, Sherrie, and William R. McLeRoy, 32.
[146] Luther Porter Jackson, *Free Negro Labor and Property Holding in Virginia, 1830-1860* (New York, NY: Macmillan, 1942), 215.

Turner Pinn also employed and provided income for his family members on his large farm. Ann Megginson—mother of Isabelle Megginson Ferguson, wife of Peter Ferguson—was also a farmer with nine children and one servant. She employed more than one hundred farm workers (William Clifford Megginson interview, Rice, 1995, 201), many Native American family members and some white employees. She had a servant in the home to assist with the household chores.

Joseph Moore, father of Ann Megginson's children, deeded additional land to Ann and the children in 1893 because of his affection for Ann and the children.[147] Joseph Moore was born in 1841 (according to the 1850 Appomattox Census, 235, he was nine years old in the home of his father, Blake B. Moore, age thirty-four, and his mother, Elizabeth M.). Joseph's deed was dated 24 August 1887 and directed to Ann Megginson and her children, Norvell, Norman, Rosa A., Ida B., Clinton, Clifford, Norman, Hattie, and Ada. Joseph stated that the land had been given to him by "his father Blake B. Moore, by deed dated 17 March 1868 . . ."[148]

Ann lived next door to Joseph Moore, the father of her children. Joseph Moore lived with his father, Blake Moore, as noted in the 1850 census, and with his grandfather, William Moore, as documented in the 1860 census. Blake Moore's property value was listed as $1,000 in 1850, and by 1860, it had increased in value to $21,705 (1850 Appomattox census; 1860 Appomattox census). Joseph Moore's grandfather had an estate value of $25,000 on the 1850 census and $100,000 on the 1860 census. Joseph Moore learned farming skills on his father's farm and later by working on his grandfather's farm. Ann and her children would eventually inherit some of the Moores' real estate. In 1883, Ann's daughter, Margaret Isbelle Megginson,

---

[147] Clerk Of The Court, ed., *Appomattox County General Index to Deeds, 1892-1915*, (Appomattox, VIRGINIA: Appomattox County Court, 1892–1915), 154.

[148] Clerk Of The Court, ed., *Appomattox County Deed Book*, vol. 1, (Appomattox, VIRGINIA: Appomattox County Court, n.d, 24 August 1887), 270.

married Joseph Peter Ferguson, the son of Frederick Isbell, a white physician. Dr. Isbell was a descendant of European royalty via his mother's line, the Lees. Some of the Isbells' Native Americans listed on the Cherokee rolls in Oklahoma in the early 1900s are possibly related to Appomattox County Isbells,[149] as well as ancestors and relatives of the Fergusons, Megginsons, and other close and distant descendants.

The Bollings, Megginsons, Fergusons, Blairs, Elliotts/Elletts, and others Pocahontas descendants in Appomattox have been proclaiming their Native American heritage for years.[150] M. O. Ferguson, Ann's great-grandson, indicated in 1984 that his great-grandmother's children were "by Joe Moore" and that Ann was Cherokee and had royal background. He did not make his point clear to the author regarding the royal background. Did the deceased Ferguson mean the Megginsons or the Fergusons who have royal heritage from England, Ireland, and the Scot Highlands, or was he referring to their heritage from Princess Pocahontas? M. O. Ferguson also related that Joseph Peter Ferguson, his grandfather, was the son of a physician. He noted that Dr. Frederick Isbell supported his grandfather (Joseph Peter) and his grandfather's brothers and sister. He stated that Dr. Isbell gave land and support to Judith Ferguson, his great-grandmother, and her sons.[151] Mott Ferguson, son of William Ferguson and nephew of Peter Ferguson and Isabelle Megginson Ferguson, noted in the *Iron Worker* magazine,[152] that he was "remembering that his grandfather [Dr. Isbell] was a physician, thought he would like to be one too . . ." Judith Ferguson and Dr. Frederick Isbell were the parents of William Ferguson, Mott's father.

---

[149] Prepared By The Commission and Commissioners Of The Five Civilized Tribes, *Index to the Final Rolls of Citizen and Freemen of the Five Civilized Tribes in Indian Territory* (Washington, DC: Secretary Of The Interior, 1907).

[150] Rice, 1995, 16, 29, 31, 62, 121 & 152.

[151] Ibid., 1995, 38, 62, 63, 71, & 130.

[152] W.D. Lawrence, "The Fergusons--five Brothers Of The Lynchburg Plant," *The Iron Worker* no. 1934 (1934, October 1).

Margaret Isabelle's husband, Joseph Peter, and her son, Augustus Ferguson—both successful farmers—provided employment to tribal members during hard times. Peter and Augustus are believed to be descendants of or related to Pocahontas (Robertson, p. 34),[153] but like some of the Megginsons, also claimed the Cherokee side. In addition to the Pocahontas tradition, there is a tradition that Ann Megginson's mother was possibly a slave or descendant of a slave. Joseph Peter Ferguson and Margaret Isbelle Megginson united in marriage or intermarriage, as numerous other Ferguson/Megginson intermarriages strengthened the connection with Princess Pocahontas and Cherokee heritage.[154]

Some Appomattox Stonewall Mill tribal members had more political insulation against paper genocide than their Amherst County Buffalo Ridge relatives because "important people in high places" kept their names off Plecker's *black* list in Richmond. Dr. Frederick Isbell, a physician and father of Judith Ferguson's children, and his relatives, the Appomattox County court clerk and commonwealth attorney, managed to keep the Fergusons, McCoys, Megginsons, Beverlys, Tylers, Bankses, and others off the Plecker list. In Amherst County and other counties, however, Dr. Plecker, the Registrar of Virginia Vital Statistics Office, required clerks to watch certain surnamed families who were trying to pass as *Indian* or *white*. He noted in a December 1943 letter that:

> The Virginia Bureau of Vital Statistics, through the exceptional, pains-taking, and laborious work of the highly trained genealogist whom it is fortunate in having, has made a study of groups and families of the principal borderline aspirants for racial change. The chief sources of information are the early birth and death records, made by tax assessors from 1853

---

[153] Wyndam Robertson, *Pocahontas, Alias Matoaka and Her Descendants* (Baltimore, MD: Genealogical Publishing, 2010), 34.

[154] Jamerson et al, ed., *Appomattox County Marriages, 1854-1890* (Appomattox, VIRGINIA: 1979), 26, 27.

> to 1896; marriage records from 1853 to date; United States Census reports for 1830, 1850, and 1870, especially a list by races, now in the State Library, which have been studied back to 1808; and, not of least value, their own proclamation of race made by applicants for registration as voters, made soon after the War Between the States, to United States military authorities, now preserved in the State Library . . .
>
> Public records in the office of the Bureau of Vital Statistics, and in the State Library, indicate that there does not exist today a descendant of Virginia ancestors claiming to be an Indian who is unmixed with negro blood . . .[155]

Dr. Plecker, in "Eugenics in Relation to the New Family and the Law on Racial Integrity," a paper read before the *American Public Health Association* (Second Edition, Issued by Bureau of Vital Statistics, State Board of Health, Richmond, VA, 1924), presented the following introduction:

> Owing to the unusual demand for this booklet by high schools, colleges, physicians, dentists, ministers, and others, the first edition of 35,000 was exhausted within a few weeks and the second edition of 30,000 is issued."
>
> "Virginia teachers are specially requested to ask for their quota for older pupils. Hundreds of letters

---

[155] Dr. Walter A. Plecker to Local Registrars, Physicians, and Et Al, Richmond, Virginia, *Letters to Local Registrars, et al*, (Dr. Plecker, VA State Registrar, 1943).

of approval have been received [in support of this pamphlet].[156]

Dr. Plecker noted the following:

> An Act to Preserve Racial Integrity...
> Be it enacted by the General Assembly of Virginia, That the State Registrar of Vital Statistics may as soon as practical after the taking effect of this act, prepare a form whereon the racial composition of any individual, as Caucasian, Negro, Mongolian, American Indian, Asiatic Indian, Malay, or any mixture thereof, or any non-Caucasic strains, and if there be any mixture, then the racial composition of the parents, and other ancestors, in so far as attainable, so as to show in what generation such mixture occurred, may be certified by such individual, which form shall be known as a registration certificate. The State Registrar may supply to each local registrar a sufficient number of such forms for the purposes of this act; each local registrar may personally or by deputy, as soon as possible after receiving such forms, have made thereon in duplicate a certificate of the racial composition as aforesaid, of each person resident in the district, who so desires, born before June fourteenth, nineteen hundred and twelve, which certificate shall be made over the signature of said person, or in the case of children over fourteen years of age, over the signature of a parent, guardian, or other person standing in loco parentis. One of the said certificates for each person thus registering in every district shall be forwarded to the State Registrar for his files; the other shall be kept by the local registrar.

---

[156] Dr. Walter A. Plecker, Registrar, and Virginia Bureau Of Vital Statistics. "Eugenics In Relation To The New Family and the Law On Racial Integrity" (paper read before the American Public Health Association, January 01, 1924).

Every local registrar may, as soon as practicable, have such registration certificate made by or for each person in his district who desires, born before June fourteen, nineteen hundred and twelve, for whom he has not on file a registration certificate, or a birth certificate.

It shall be a felony for any person willfully or knowingly to make a registration certificate false as to color or race. The willful making of a false registration or birth certificate shall be punished by confinement in the penitentiary for one year.

For each registration certificate properly made and returned to the State Registrar, the local registrar shall be entitled to a fee of twenty-five cents.

No marriage license shall be granted until the clerk or deputy clerk has reasonable assurance that the statement as to color of birth man and woman are correct. If there is reasonable cause to believe that applicants are not of pure white race, when that fact is stated, the clerk or deputy clerk shall withhold the granting of the license until satisfactory proof is produced that both applicants are "white persons" as provided for in the act. The clerk or deputy clerk shall use the same care to assure himself that both applicants are colored, when that fact is claimed.

It shall hereafter be unlawful for any white person in the State to marry any save a white person, or a person with no other admixture of blood than white and American Indian. For the purpose of this act, the term "white person" shall apply only to the person who has no trace whatsoever of any blood other than Caucasian; but persons who have one sixteenth or less of the blood of American Indian and have no other non-Caucasic blood shall be deemed to be white persons. All laws heretofore passed and now in effect regarding the intermarriage of white and colored persons shall apply to marriages prohibited by this act.[157]

Appendix: Howe, in his *History of Virginia*, 1845, wrote, "There is the remnant of the Mattoponi tribe of Indians, now dwindled down to only fifteen or twenty souls. Further up on the Pamunkey, at what is called Indian Town, are about 100 descendants of the Pamunkeys. Their Indian character is near extinct, by intermixing with the whites and negroes" (pp. 349–350).[158]

In support of Dr. Plecker's efforts, some Virginia historians and officials waged paper genocide campaigns against Native Americans, by asserting that all Native American populations had some percentage of Negro ancestry. Their campaigns had the effect of putting aboriginal people on the defensive socially and forcing Native Americans to claim that they were white or to deny any black connections. So much of the historical writings between the late 1800s and mid- to late 1900s were saturated with politically expedient eugenic jargon, and therefore current prudent historians have to read Native American writings/history of this period with cautious skepticism. Were they authentic historians, political agents, or a combination of both? Were the writings tainted due to political pressures on historians to endorse or slant their historical narratives in the direction of the influential eugenic movement at that time? Why were writings slanted in the direction of implying that Native American ancestry is a negative characteristic; Native American/European ancestry is a better category; and Native/European/African American ancestry is a very negative attribute?

---

[157] Walter Plecker, Director, and VA Bureau Vital Statistics, *Virginia Act to Preserve Racial Integrity* (Richmond, VA: Virginia General Assembly, 1924), 29.

[158] Henry Howe, *History of Virginia* (Charleston, SC: William Babcock, 1852), 349-350.

UCITOVA's ancestors and descendants have been careful to not "put down" or belittle various racial groups because they believe that God created all beings equal. They do not believe that they should deny black ancestry when someone says, "You are Black Indians." Even when the particular tribal members do not have any record of African American ancestry, they usually responded with the statements:

> "No. We are 'Indian.' I have always said we are Indian."[159]

UCITOVA has many tribal members who are Native Americans and European Americans, especially those who have European ancestry via descendants who came to America on the *Mayflower* in 1620, and others who came to Virginia between the 1600s and the mid- to late 1800s from Europe. Their descendants would not even attempt to respond to a discrimination-motivated question regarding their African ancestry, just as they would be the last persons to boast, if you asked them, about their direct lineage with European royalty (kings, queens, dukes, barons, etc. of England, Ireland, Scotland, Germany, and other countries). There are other members of UCITOVA who have Native American, European American, and African American ancestry.

UCITOVA members are unique among Native American bands because, based on research on Native American Revolutionary War patriots in their genealogy, as of a 2009 SPSS analysis report (Rice, 2009, *Basic Facts on UCITOVA—SPSS Data Analysis*, Table 1, Graph 1), of the then 648 tribal members' records analyzed, 269 have three or more Native American Revolutionary War soldiers in their genealogical family tree, eighty-eight have two Native American Revolutionary War patriots and thirty have one Native American Revolutionary War patriot, making a total of 387 out of 648 tribal members' records analyzed. Regarding the number of members who descend from Cherokee/Wiccocomico pillars from the 1700s to early

---

[159] Horace Rice, 1995, 165.

1800s, seventy-two members have one Cherokee/Wiccocomico pillar; eighty-five have two Cherokee/Wiccocomico pillars from 1700s to early 1800s; and 419 have three or more Cherokee/Wiccocomico pillars from 1700s to early 1800s. There were a total of 576 tribal members out of 648 who descend from pillar ancestor or approximately 89 percent who can claim one or more pillar ancestors from the 1700s to early 1800s. This analysis reveals that there has been a high rate of tribal intermarriage among pillar ancestors and their descendants, as well as Revolutionary War patriots, most of whom were Native Americans, over several centuries. The researcher did not analyze (or count) Revolutionary War patriot ancestors who were of European ancestry (who sided with the Americans) but whose descendants were later included in UCITOVA's tribal genealogical trees.

The New History of Virginia by Phillip Alexander Bruce of the University of Virginia noted: "By the date, 1736, war, disease, and intemperance, had reduced Indian tribes to very thin ranks. The Pamunkey on York River could only show a roll of ten families. This was the remnant of Powhatan's powerful kingdom.[160]

Alexander Francis Chamberlain, PhD, Assistant Professor of Anthropology, Clark University, Worcester, Massachusetts, in his article "Indians, North Americans," in the *Encyclopaedia Britannica*, eleventh edition, vol. 14, pp. 460–464, made similar slanted, discriminatory statements as others above concerning Virginia's Native American tribes. He stated the following: "No pure bloods left. Considerable negro admixture," and of the Pamunkey, he stated: "All mixed bloods; some negro mixture."[161] These writers seemed to have been caught up in the genocidal mood of some Virginians as their pens were tilting and slanting

---

[160] Bruce et al, *The New History of Virginia*, vol. 1st ed (Chicago, IL: The American Historical Society, 1924), 334.

[161] Chamberlain and Alexander F, *Indians, North American*, 11th ed, Vol. 14 (Cambridgeshire, ENGLAND: Encyclopaedia Britannica, 1911), 460-464.

toward racial discrimination trends as they recorded Native American history in the Commonwealth.

On page 468, he noted: "In some regions considerable intermixture between negroes and Indians has occurred, e.g., among the Pamunkeys, Mattoponies, and some other small Virginia and Carolina tribes." It is also thought probable that many of the Negroes of the whole lower Atlantic Coast and Gulf region may have strains of Indian blood.[162]

John Garland Pollard, in his pamphlet "The Pamunkey Indians of Virginia," says: "There has been considerable intermixture of white blood in the tribe and not a little of that of the negro; though the laws of the tribe now strictly prohibit marriage to persons of African descent."[163]

Dr. Plecker continued, in the pamphlet, to talk about the admixture of Negro blood in the Indian tribes of Virginia, including the Pamunkeys, Mattoponies, Chickahominy, and other tribes. He reiterated that they should not be registered as white nor given licenses to marry white persons.

In 1892, James C. Pilling, in *Athapascan Language*, in discussing the Pamunkey Indians, noted that "there has been considerable intermixture of white blood in the tribe, and a little of that of the negro, though the laws of the tribe now strictly prohibit marriage to persons of African descent." He noted that the tribe refused to accept "a colored teacher, who was sent to them by the superintendent of public instruction to conduct the free school which the State furnishes them. They are exceedingly anxious to keep their blood free from further intermixture with that of other races, and how to accomplish this purpose is a serious problem with them, as there are few members of the tribe who are not closely related to every other person on the reservation. To obviate this difficulty the chief and councilmen have been attempting to devise a plan by which

---

[162] Alexander F. Chamberlain, *Science*, vol. 17th ed (New York, NY: 1891), 32, 468.

[163] John Garland Pollard, "The Pamunkey Indians of Virginia," *Smithsonian Publication* (1894): 33.

they can induce immigration from the Cherokee Indians of North Carolina."[164]

The paper genocide of Native Americans was skillfully put into effect by some educators and officials during the period between the 1860s and 1970s. The laws of the General Assembly and aggressive fervor of historians and court and county officials kept the heat on non-whites in Virginia. These aboriginal people had to apologize for being Native Americans. They were encouraged to proclaim that they were more "white and Indian" in order to protect their family against the discrimination that had been directed against colored or black residents. State and local laws and so-called scientific or historical writings had the effect of forcing Native American people to deny any blood quantum above one-sixteenth Native American, thereby making them legally "white" on court and census records.

Those who refused to deny their Native American ancestry and/or refused to deny some black ancestry were forced to have black or colored placed on their official records. The laws and writings, in effect, created a psychologically conducive atmosphere to erase Native American or Indian classifications from all paper documents in Central Virginia and the State of Virginia. The UCITOVA people always believed, during these seven to nine decades, that the Indian, mulatto, and colored designations on records and documents would, over time, preserve for their descendants the fact that they were "non-white," or Native Americans. They believed that persons with "White" on records throughout their genealogy line would have difficulty proving that they had any trace of "Indian" in them.

Since 1790, some Virginia officials have managed to force UCITOVA people to become free colored, mulatto, colored, or black. Several census takers listed band's members as IN (Indian). Today, UCITOVA has to document that they are Native Americans, over the obstacles of contaminated records; racial integrity files in high official places; physical genocide against Native Americans since 1622, including the legal taking

---

[164] James C. Pilling, "Athapascan Language," *Bureau of Ethnology, Smithsonian Institution* (1892): 10, 11.

of scalps; indifference on the part of some Virginia historians to record Native American history accurately, especially Cherokee history in Virginia; and psychological and paper genocide against people who claim Native American, Native American/white, and Native American/white/black ancestry.

Gabrielle Tayac, in "Eugenics and Erasure in Virginia," summarized some of the damage that has been done on Native American history (20).

> Even lesser known is the way some states used eugenics laws to terrorize American Indians, driving families underground and trying to wipe out tribal identities. The after-effects live on, denying many historic tribes access to federal recognition. One of the best documented examples is Virginia's eugenic-inspired campaign of racial intimidation, lasting from 1924 to 1967, and directed for most of the period by the arch-bureaucrat Walter Ashby Plecker.
>
> The term eugenics is attributed to Francis Galton, a cousin of Charles Darwin, who stated in 1883: "We greatly want a brief word to express the science of improving stock . . . especially in the case of man." Derived from the Greek words for "good" and "origin," eugenics provided a scientific justification for imposing racial hierarchies. The shadow side of the work of Gregory Mendel, who showed how traits were biologically inherited, eugenics promulgated the false notion that different races had fixed inherent traits of morality, intelligence and strength. Two centers of the movement were Germany and the United States. In Germany it became entangled with myths of Nordic and Aryan supremacy. In the U.S., it focused on preserving the "old American stock" and inspired anti-immigration laws. . .
>
> Eugenicists generally placed African Americans at the bottom of the hierarchy and so-called Caucasians at

the top. American Indians were viewed as having a primitive constitution that could be passed through generations—and through intermarriage.[165]

Dr. Plecker wrote two letters to the local registrars, physicians, health officers, nurses, school superintendents, and clerks of the courts. He wrote one letter in January 1943 in which he requested the following actions and information:

> Please report all known or suspicious cases [of people who were claiming on documents to be [Indian] to the Bureau of Vital Statistics, giving names, ages, parents, and as much other information as possible. All certificates of these people showing "Indian" or "White" are now being rejected and returned to the physician or midwife, but local registrars hereafter must not permit them to pass their hands uncorrected or unchallenged and without a note of warning to us. . .[166]

Some of the people and counties that Dr. Plecker included in his January 1943 letter to "local registrars, clerks, legislators and others responsible for, and interested in, the prevention of racial intermixture" are as follows (only some counties in Central and Southwestern Virginia are noted below):

---

[165] Gabrielle Tayac. 2009 (Fall). "Eugenics And Erasure In Virginia," *National Museum of the American Indian* 10 (3): 20.

[166] Walter A. Plecker, 1943.

County	Family Surnames
Amherst (Migrants to Alleghany and Campbell)	Adcock (Adcox), **Beverly** (this family is now trying to evade the situation by adopting the name of Burch or Birch, which was the name of the white mother of the present adult generation), Branham, Duff, Floyd, Hamilton, Hartless, Hicks, Johns, Lawless, Nickles (**Knuckles**), Painter, Ramsey, **Redcross**, Roberts, Southards (Suthards, Southerd, Southers), **Sorrells**, Terry, Tyree, Willis, Clark, Cash, Wood
Bedford	McVey, Maxey, Branahm, Burley (see Amherst County)
Rockbridge (Migrants to Augusta)	Cash, Clark, Coleman, Duff, Floyd, Hartless, Hicks, Mason, Mayse (Mays), Painter, Pultz, Ramsey, Southerds (Southers, Southards, Suthards), **Sorrells**, Terry, Tyree, Wood, Johns
Roanoke County	**Beverly**. (See Washington)
Washington	**Beverly**, Barlow, Thomas, Hughes, Lethcoe, Worley.

*Many names above correspond to popular Cherokee surnames (Rice, 1995).

Several UCITOVA surnames are noted in the list. Some of the Beverlys—who had seven Beverly households in 1810 in Buckingham County (later Stonewall Mill section of Appomattox County) and a total of almost sixty Beverly family members (1810 U.S. Census, Buckingham County)—moved to Buffalo Ridge in Amherst County. One hundred and thirty-three years after the 1810 census, Dr. Plecker's paper genocide letter attempted to blot out the Beverlys' rich Cherokee heritage. These aboriginal descendants with a proud Cherokee and Wiccocomico heritage in Central Virginia had to be on guard because Dr. Plecker attempted to erase Native American identification from the Beverly name and family in his racial and eugenics genocidal policies. The political and social eugenics atmosphere in Virginia is likely the reason for Madison Beverly and other Cherokee migrating from county to county. Their migratory behavior in 1800s is similar to the behavior of the Wiccocomico during the 1600-1700 dissolution of their tribal reservations, the Indian slavery in Virginia, and the indenture servitude institution in Northumberland and Lancaster counties. Cherokee and Wiccocomico tribal members were well aware that their physical and cultural presence was unwanted in the Colony, and chose to walk lightly among non-native residents in the dominant culture.

Some names were not listed—for example, the Native American Fergusons continued to marry Native Americans as well as white people in Appomattox during the period of Dr. Plecker's racial integrity investigations and classifications. It is believed that state senator Samuel Ferguson, for example—a descendant of Pocahontas and/or related to some of UCITOVA's Fergusons' ancestors and the Isbells of Appomattox—protected the Beverlys, Pinns, McCoys, Bankses, Isbells, Elliotts, Megginsons and other Appomattox Stonewall Mill residents. Actually, it seems that the county clerk did not even bother to collect and send any Appomattox County names to Dr. Plecker. If the county clerk did send a list to Dr. Plecker, the State Registrar was probably so threatened by the politically powerful descendants of Pocahontas and other Appomattox officials—some of whom were also Cherokees who lived in Appomattox County—that he did not publish Appomattox County's list of names in this December 1943 letter. These people continued to marry fellow Native Americans and occasionally white residents without interference from Dr. Plecker and other Richmond officials. Some "light-skinned" students even went to school with "white" students.[167] Others in Stonewall went to the "colored" school with other Fergusons. The mass race hysteria was controlled somewhat in Appomattox County to the point that Stonewall Mill UCITOVA family members were not provoked into signing away their dignity on public documents. If they chose to be labeled colored or black, it was their choice, not the officials' choice. Actually, some white residents, as well as family members, worked for UCITOVA employers during the early 1900s.[168] UCITOVA has a large percentage of members with Native American-European American ancestry. Actually, a large percentage of residents in Amherst County claim Cherokee ancestry. Lois Smith, former Director, Amherst County Historical Museum, informed the author that "there are a lot of people in Amherst County who claim to have Cherokee ancestry. One day recently, for example, I went to the restaurant for lunch. While talking with people in the restaurant, I told them that we were going to open the exhibit on Indian artifacts. Several residents in the restaurant responded to this by stating that they have Cherokee ancestry. It is amazing how many people apparently are Cherokee."[169]

UCITOVA ancestors and members knew that they were Cherokees, and other Native Americans and non-Indians recognized them as such in the community (Rice, 1995, Interviews on pp. 132–207). They had strong Cherokee medical, pharmaceutical, social, and kinship tribal customs that continued throughout the three-hundred-plus years of tribal history. Several book—written by the author: *The Buffalo Ridge Cherokee: Colors and Culture of a Virginian Indian Community*, 1991;[170] *The Buffalo Ridge Cherokee: A Remnant of a Great Nation*

---

[167] Rice, 1995, 161.

[168] Ibid., 1995, 160.

[169] Lois Smith, Citizens in Amherst County claim Cherokee ancestry Horace Rice, Amherst Historical Museum, Amherst, VA, August 5, 1992.

[170] Rice, 1991.

Divided, 1995;[171] and *A Report on the History of the Buffalo Ridge Cherokee, United Cherokee Indian Tribe of Virginia, Incorporated*, 1994[172]--provide detailed information on UCITOVA's history, kinship and marital relationships, Native American customs, medical and pharmaceutical practices, and social relationships. *Strangers in Their Midst*, by McLeRoy and McLeRoy, a book on the free people of color in Amherst County who had to register at the court house between 1822 and 1864, has a wealth of information on Amherst County UCITOVA ancestors, many of whom once lived in Appomattox County and moved to Amherst County. McLeRoy and McLeRoy noted:

> In 1924, the Virginia Legislature passed the Racial Integrity Act, which stated that only those with one-sixteenth, or less, Indian heritage and with no other non-Caucasian blood could be considered 'White.' The Act, which remained in effect until the integration movement of the 1960s, bothered many people—especially those many prominent Virginians who claimed descent from Pocahontas and were therefore, legally, 'colored.'[173]

The most outspoken proponent of the law was Dr. Walker Ashby Plecker, Virginia's Registrar of Vital Statistics from 1912 to 1946. In a virtual one-man campaign, Plecker undertook to erase the state's contemporary Indian heritage, which he felt had been so substantially diluted with Negro blood that few true Indians still existed. What was his basis for this theory? In historic antebellum records—such as the county registers—those of Indian blood were described officially as *free Negroes* or *free colored*. In Amherst County, some Beverly(ley)s, Elliotts,

---

[171] Rice, 1995, 132-207

[172] Horace R. Rice, "A Report on the History of The Buffalo Ridge Cherokee, United Cherokee Indian Tribe of Virginia, Incorporated" (unpublished manuscript, 1994), Microsoft Word; copies of birth certificates, marriage data, land deeds, etc.

[173] McLeRoy & McLeRoy, 24.

Evanses, Pinns, Nuckles (Knuckles), Carters, Coopers, Cousins, Coys (McCoys), Evanses, Pinns, Fergusons, Fields, Humbleses (Umbleses), Isbells, Jenkinses, Johnsons, Pinns, Redcrosses, Sorrells, Sparrows, Tuppences (Twopences), Tylers, Warwicks, Wests, and others were placed in non-white groups.

Appomattox County officials, in 1845, the year of its formation as a new county, recognized and embraced their free people of color. A. A. LeGrand, Commissioner of the Revenue, Appomattox County, noted, "This page embraces the free people of colour" (of the 35 names noted on the document, 21 are ancestors of the Buffalo Ridge and Stonewall Mill band and are noted below):

> Jackson, John; Ferguson, Stephen; Green, James; Ferguson, Petres; Ferguson, Peter; Ferguson, Jos.; Humbles, Royal; Cousins, Wm.; Fields, Wm.; Ferguson, Jesse; Humbles, Ezekiel; Ferguson, Charles; Ferguson, David; McCoy, Anthony; McCoy, Tamenus; McCoy, John; Humbles, Dudley; Humbles, Sam; McCoy, Albert; Beverley, Wm., Sr.; and Beverley, Wm., Jr.[174]

Some of those names listed are Pillar ancestors and others are Secondary Pillar ancestors. They all were recognized for their contributions to Appomattox's development as a new county in Central Virginia.

The Commissioner wrote: "This is to certify that the foregoing list of Taxable Property was taken partly by Mr. John T. Bocock, late Commissioner of the Revenue for the 2nd District of Buckingham, and partly by myself..." The above Free People of Color had been tax-paying residents of Buckingham County (2nd District or Stonewalll Mill area) and Appomattox County officials wanted to make the fact clear that they respected their presence and "embraced" them as fellow members of the new County of Appomattox.

---

[174] A.A. Legrand and Commissioner of the Revenue. Appomattox County, *Embracing the Free Persons of Colour* (Appomattox, VA, 1845), 1.

Some white and black residents believed that these strange people had a "secret." They believed that the Band members were trying to start a "third race" in Central Virginia. They did not realize that there actually existed a third race, *Native Americans*, and that UCITOVA was almost destroyed by the reckless practices and policies of Virginia officials who demanded that there exist only the white and black races. UCITOVA kept the secret from some outsiders but used the "secret"—the intermarrying among tribal members—as motivation for tribal members to keep the native heritage alive.

Isabelle Ferguson Fields, a UCITOVA tribal member, was a teacher of the Indian/or colored children on Buffalo Ridge during the 1944-45 school year.[175] Isabelle Fields—wife of George Fields, a World War II recipient of the Asiatic Pacific Theater Ribbon with one Bronze Star[176]—gave some hints about the secrets of the tribe. She shared private papers about their tribal European royal ancestry. Isabelle Fields[177] and Raleigh Pete Carson,[178] her father's first cousin, decided to open to the author some of the tribe's historical European royal connections. Pete Carson noted in his letter to Isabelle Fields and the author:

> The Ferguson family once owned [much of] Appomattox [County] as long as there has been a Virginia . . . Our ancestors may have been some of the prominent names connected with English dignitaries [royalty] . . . We are part Cherokee . . . A large amount of records were destroyed by fire [at the Appomattox Courthouse].

Isabelle Fields and Raleigh Pete Carson opened the door to the author about very private ancestry secrets of many of the tribal ancestors. It was a well-kept secret among the band

---

[175] Rice, 1995, 168, 55.
[176] Department Of The Army, *Enlisted Record and report of Separation Honorable Discharge* (: Department Of The Army, 1945).
[177] Horace R. Rice, 1991, 77, 61-63
[178] Horace R. Rice, 1995, 146-148.

members in Appomattox—as well as in Buffalo Ridge—that the Fergusons, McCoys, Pankeys, Isbells, and others relatives have direct genealogical connection with European royalty via marriages between and/or children of tribal ancestors and European colonists. The Panetiers or Pankeys came to America from Nassigny, Allier, Auvergne, France, in the late 1600s. Jean Panetier (Pankey) died in July 1717 in Manakin Town, Goochland, Virginia. The Pankeys eventually settled in Appomattox County. There are other band members who have family genealogical records that reveal direct connection with Donald, King of Scotland, born 1034 in Perth, Scotland; and Bethoc Beatrix, Princess of Scotland, born 984, in Perthshire, Scotland. Native Americans intermarried with and/or had children by colonists, some of whom had royal connections via France, England, Scotland, Ireland, Germany and other European countries.

Tribal members were reluctant to talk about their connections with European royalty because they did not want people to think they were trying to be more important than other Native Americans, white people, mulatto people, and African Americans. Some tribal members have kept many of the European royalty connections secret, only revealing the information to mature family members (regarding direct genealogical connections, location of ancestors' birth, country, city or town of residence in Europe, name of castles, for example, in England, etc.).

Historians often ask, "When did the colonists or explorers first see the Native Americans or their villages?" This is often a way to verify that Native American communities/cultures existed in America in pre-colonial or colonial times. UCITOVA's ancestors were not only seen by European colonists, but colonists married and/or had children with Cherokee/Wiccocomico women and men. UCITOVA leaders are able to document some members' genealogical descent to European ancestors back to the ninth century AD; Wiccocomico royalty back to the 1600s via the Pinns (Pekwem); Cherokee royalty via the Harrises; and Princess Pocahontas connection to a minor extent via the Fergusons, Megginsons, Bollings, and Elliotts in Appomattox

County. UCITOVA's Native American ancestors left valuable records to document their aboriginal existence in Buffalo Ridge in Amherst County and Stonewall Mill in Buckingham/Appomattox County (land records, marriage records, military records, will records, and others).

Cherokee names are prominent in Amherst County. They stand out much like the names on the *Index and Final Rolls of Citizens and Freedmen of the Cherokee Tribe in Indian Territory*;[179] [180] and in the telephone directories in and around Cherokee, North Carolina.[181]

McLeRoy and McLeRoy noted:

> He (Dr. Plecker) had particularly harsh words for many families in Amherst and Rockbridge counties who claimed to be Indian . . .[182]

Dr. Plecker finally resigned after remarking privately that he had known he had been acting without legal grounds. Modern historians have described his actions, and the effects of the Racial Integrity Act, as akin to the Nazis' attempt to purify the German race.

The racial purity leaders harassed Native Americans in 1942 when the General Assembly Virginia passed the Code:

> It shall be a felony for any person willfully or knowingly to make a registration certificate false as to color or race. The willful making of a false registration or

---

[179] Prepared By The Commission and Commissioners Of The Five Civilized Tribes, *Index to the Final Rolls of Citizen and Freemen of the Five Civilized Tribes in Indian Territory* (Washington, DC: Secretary Of The Interior, 1907).

[180] Horace R. Rice, 1995, 90-94.

[181] Southern Bell Telephone Company, *The Southern Bell Telephone Book* (Asheville, NC: Southern Bell, n.d, 1993-94).

[182] McLeRoy & McLeRoy, 1993, 14.

birth certificate shall be punished by confinement in the penitentiary for one year. (The Virginia Code 20-51. *False registration or certificate*)[183]

Virginia continued to engage in illegal, official paper genocide against Native Americans as late as 1954, when they resurrected racial aggression toward Indians.

> 1.14. Colored persons and Indians defined. -- Every person in whom there is ascertainable any Negro blood shall be deemed and taken to be a colored person, and every person not a colored person having one-fourth or more of American Indian blood shall be deemed an American Indian: except that members of Indian tribes existing in this Commonwealth having one-fourth or more of Indian blood and less than one-sixteenth of Negro blood shall be deemed tribal Indians.

Virginia Senators and Delegates regretted the passage of the 1924 Law and the resulting damage on Virginia's Native Americans' self-esteem and culture. The House of Delegates, on Friday, February 2, 2001, approved a resolution "expressing regret for Virginia's eugenics policies and forced sterilizations between 1924 and 1979. In 1924, the state passed two eugenic-related laws, the Racial Integrity Act, which made interracial marriage illegal and resulted in many American Indians being defined as *black*, and another act regarding sterilization" (*The News and Advance*, 3, Feb 2001, 1). "It was racism, pure and simple," Del. Mitch Van Yahres said of the Racial Integrity Act, which he noted was used to give "a respectable veneer to racist

---

[183] Virginia General Assembly, Senate (SB 219), *The Racial Integrity Act* (Richmond, VA: Virginia General Assembly, 1924). Racial Integrity Laws were included in the Act (RIA) for purposes of protecting white resident against the perceived threat of race-mixing.

doctrine."[184] He further stated, "Virginia's eugenics laws were models for Adolph Hitler's policies." He added that "Nazis used that as a defense during the Nuremberg trials, that they were just adopting policies already sanctioned by a government in the U.S."

During the 1950s and 1960s, UCITOVA members began to migrate from agricultural-related occupations in the country and moved to Madison Heights and Lynchburg. Some members left the home church in Stapleton and joined other churches in their neighborhoods. In Appomattox County, Stonewall Mill, this same trend of mobility occurred as members left Mount Zion, Mount Airy, and Springfield Baptist Churches and joined other churches in their new areas.

As the people became more prosperous and moved out from the ancestral farming areas, it was obvious that the Band required a stronger force than just kinship control, Cherokee heritage, and church affiliation to keep the Band together as a unit. Two sticks tied together are much stronger and harder for an outside force to break than two sticks separated. Therefore, in 1991, the Cherokee leaders held an emergency meeting to discuss the problem: economic opportunity and acculturation trends had begun to pull the close-knit Stonewall Mill and Buffalo Ridge groups apart. The band members were moving out and settling in new areas as a result of financial upward mobility and/or a desire to be successful in new careers. Although Cherokee people were known for their ability to become acculturated, the leaders did not want to see occupational success and mobility pull members away from the Band geographically, culturally and socially.

UCITOVA ancestors and descendants—who experienced several centuries of paper genocide (on census records, marriage records, tax records, and other documents)—now have to document or prove to the state of Virginia that they are Native Americans. This is ironic because the state, which committed paper genocide and other discriminatory practices,

---

[184] "Expressing Regret for Virginia's Eugenics Policies," *Lynchburg News and Advance* (Lynchburg, VA), February 2, 2001.

is now asking UCITOVA to use present and scanty official records to make their case. As a result of Virginia's officials doing a very good job of frightening brides, grooms, and mothers of newborn babies from recording "Indian" on official documents, UCITOVA has to go the extra mile to expose the "ugly" practices that covered up the "Indian" in tribal members. Virginia only accepted two races, *white* and *black*, and generally nothing in-between. The officials made every attempt to erase the strong and overwhelming amount of Native American evidence of UCITOVA's aboriginal people. After frightening Native American brides and grooms and mothers of newborn babies to self-report their race as one of two options, black or white, Dr. Plecker used these same reports years later to prove that these people and their descendants were "blacks" or "white," and not "Native Americans."

What the officials did not know about these people was the fact that Raleigh Pinn, equally aggressive in keeping the records alive— and each descendant after him— passed the precious Native American customs and pride on to their descendants and strictly advised them to keep the Native American culture alive in the family. Raleigh and Sarah Evans Pinn were literate and made a point of passing down their heritage by leaving their legacy on signed documents for their ancestors (Amherst Deed: March 18, 1800, Raleigh and Sarah Pinn "signed their names rather than making their marks.")[185] Mary Elizabeth Pettigrew West, for example, told her descendants to retain their Native American status:

> I always reminded my children and relatives to put down 'Indian' on their documents for race. They were Indian. It wasn't anything to be ashamed of. They had Indian in them![186]

---

[185] Court Clerk, ed., *Amherst County Deed Book I*, vol. I (Amherst, VIRGINIA: Amherst County Court, 1800), 161.

[186] Horace R. Rice, 1995, 162.

Ben "Buck" Beverly noted:

> My father always talked about the fact that they were Cherokee Indians. He talked about it all the time. He said he was Indian and we were. He said, 'Don't let anyone tell you differently.' People used to say that we were white. I said, 'No, we are Indians.' I have always said we are Indians.[187]

Stanley "Duck" Harris, a retired four-term member of the *Amherst County Board of Supervisors* and UCITOVA tribal member, indicated that his grandfather, William Harris and his grandmother, Pauline Harris, had a strong Cherokee heritage. He stated during an interview with the author, on July 31, 2001:

> Pauline was a Cherokee Princess who evaded the *Trail of Tears* and came to Nelson County. My aunts, Rachael and Jennie, my father's sisters, told me this [the princess connection]. What I understand is that they didn't want her to go on the trail to Oklahoma. So she came into Nelson County.
>
> The Coopers came to Amherst County from Caroline County; some of the family went to Tennessee. My grandmother on my mother's side told me that there was a large family of Coopers. Some Coopers married McCoys and Fergusons. The Coopers were Powhatan and they married Cherokee.[188]

Stanley Harris' statement supports many of UCITOVA ancestors' claims that Cherokees appeared on the census rolls in 1830 and 1840 from other areas of the Cherokee territory, as well as those Cherokees who appeared in Amherst County after the colonial assaults on Cherokee villages in 1760–61 and

---

[187] Ibid., 165.

[188] Stanley Harris, family Native American genealogy Horace R. Rice, Madison Heights, VA, July 31, 2001.

1776. William Harris appeared in a tribal relationship in the village, with other UCITOVA ancestors in 1840 (Amherst County Census, 1840). The marriage of Coopers and McCoys followed the pattern that had begun with other tribal members; Cherokees were marrying Algonquians throughout the counties of Amherst, Appomattox, Lancaster, and Northumberland (John Pinn's declaration about his parents' Cherokee/Algonquian connection in his *Application for Revolutionary War Pension*, 1842).[189]

Rev. Luther and Betty Banks McCoy and Family. Andrew Johnson, Rev. McCoy's brother-in-law, is standing in the background near his horse.

These people— a remnant of a broken and divided Cherokee Nation—kept their Indian appearance by controlling the members. It was easier to maintain group cohesion in Buffalo Ridge by "going for colored," since they could not claim "Indian" on official documents.[190],[191] The "rush off and marry white residents" mentality had been discouraged by the UCITOVA elders for generations,

---

[189] John Pinn, *Southern Campaign American Revolution Pension Statements: John Pinn*, 1842
[190] Horace R. Rice, 1995, 191-192
[191] Ibid., 1995, 37, 159-161.

although some of the members were often classified as white. Reverend Lucas, in 1888, a new minister at Fairmount Baptist Church on the Ridge at the time, returned a marriage certificate to the courthouse for an Amherst County band member who married an Appomattox County band member (Wm. L. McCoy and Belle Banks, 2/20/1888, Book 3, 177 see family picture above).[192] The court clerk assumed that the couple was white, since he could not determine the color of the new minister. Their marriage record listed them as white, even though the Ridge members were generally considered colored, Indian or mulatto by outsiders.

Some of these people whose ancestors were Native Americans and European American did not really look "colored," but were forced at every opportunity to have colored placed on their legal documents. Some residents objected to this paper genocide. As late as the 1920 U.S. Census in Amherst County, Courthouse District, UCITOVA members' ancestors were listed as Indian on the census reports (Ivanhoe Jenkins, Felix Jenkins, and Ollie Wright families).[193] Dock Jenkins and his wife, as well as some of the Wright descendants are registered UCITOVA members.

As late as the 1980s, 1990s, and 2000s, many UCITOVA members were still marrying UCITOVA tribal members[194] or descendants of UCITOVA ancestors, and attending numerous family reunions each year. Most members of UCITOVA have standing invitations to attend any family reunion of the Beverlys, McCoys, Sparrows (Sparrowhawks), Megginsons, Elliotts, Fergusons, Pinns, Chamberses, Carters, Bankses, Wests, Cousinses, and others. Because family members are so interrelated genealogically, any surnamed individual will generally be admitted in the door of the reunion, just on the surname alone.

It had been said that it took a miracle to keep these people close and united this long, and that historians should "be

---

[192] *Amherst County Marriage Book*, vol. 3, 1888), 177.

[193] Census, 1920 United States Federal, 1820, Census Enumeration, Court House, Amherst County, Roll T625_1879; Pge: 1B; District 10; Image 7, Nara, Washington, Dc, Ancestry.com 1920 United States Federal Census [database On-line] Provo, UT, USA. ANCESTRY.COM.

[194] Horace R. Rice, 1995, 127.

thankful." The leaders, however, realized the urgency of the times and, in 1989–1990, began to discuss the possibility of setting up an official and structured tribal organization rather than the informal, natural family connections that had previously prevailed with strong charismatic leaders.

The elders/representatives—from the clans of the Fergusons, Beverlys, McCoys, Pinns/Penns, Chamberses, Elliotts, Wests, Woods, Megginsons, Sparrows, and others—met in 1990 and formed the structure for the corporation. The Band was formally incorporated in 1991, after almost four hundred years of informal and recorded tribal history. Samuel Penn was elected the tribal chief and representatives from several families served as pillars or members of the executive council.

Since that period of formal organization, UCITOVA has been holding monthly meetings and communicating via newsletters, postal mail, telephone calls, and e-mail to members on a regular basis. The members have continued to attend formal family affairs, reunions, church services in their traditional churches, and other events.

Funeral services of UCITOVA members, or relatives of UCITOVA members, still attract large numbers of UCITOVA's members. Eulogistic service programs reflect surnames that are unique to Cherokee people in Virginia and in Cherokee, North Carolina, Tennessee, and Oklahoma. Birthday parties for senior family members, funeral services, recognition programs, family reunion events, and annual tribal activities include family members who descend from the same early ancestors. The UCITOVA chief sends an official UCITOVA Resolution to deceased UCITOVA members' families and funeral services, to be read prior to the minister's eulogy. The Resolution is read by the respective church clerk. It states, "Whereas _____ was a member of the United Cherokee Indian Tribe of Virginia, a tribe with more than four hundred years of recorded history, and whereas _____ was a faithful member . . . and whereas his/her tribal registration number _____ . . ."

2000–Present

Today, after more than four hundred years, almost seven hundred UCITOVA members—descendants of aboriginal people of America and some European colonists who arrived in America during the 1600s–1800s—are still remembering their noble Cherokee-Wiccocomico heritage in Central Virginia. They have been knocked down, bullied, and harassed. They have not, however, stayed down. They are proud of the royal history that their ancestors passed down to them and they refuse to give it up. It is only by standing back and looking longitudinally over the years can researchers and genealogists understand the miraculous events that have occurred as remnants of a great Cherokee Nation have been and are still banding together, with the assistance of Wiccocomico and European ancestors. They are stating, "We are still here, Cherokees, in Central Virginia. And we are a part of that great Nation that divided!"

In 2001, UCITOVA officials had its membership rolls reviewed by a certified genealogist. "After reviewing about 397 individual membership folders out of approximately 450 for the United Cherokee Indian Tribe of Virginia (UCITOVA)," Phillip Wayne Rhodes, a certified genealogist, wrote, "Each folder included, for the most part, an individual family record, a chart showing genealogical descent of the individual, and documents relating to the individual and his or her family group (marriage records, birth records, death records, etc.)."[195] He concluded his report with a summary.

> The primary purpose of the collection of family and personal data by UCITOVA appears to be to document tribal Cherokee ancestry. The fact that this one group of individuals in the twentieth century can document their Indian ancestry well into the seventeenth century is of great historical significance. The accurate recording of such vital information is

---

[195] Phillip Wayne Rhodes, *Genealogical Research; UCITOVA Data* (Lynchburg, VA, 2001), 2.

extremely important to this generation as well as to future generations. It is doubly important that future generations be able to locate the information so carefully researched. Whether UCITOVA intends on releasing the information in published form is not the important issue here. It would be of great benefit to the general public to have this information available, but that decision is left to the officers and members of UCITOVA.[196]

Phillip Wayne Rhodes, C.G.

The band had 450–500 members on official tribal rolls during the time of Mr. Rhodes' research. Today, over five hundred out of almost seven hundred members can document two or more *1700s to early 1800s Native American* tribal pillar ancestors, in some cases four or five of those pillar ancestors are listed in tribal members' genealogical family trees. Most of the remainder of UCITOVA members can document genealogical descent from one or more *secondary pillar Native American* ancestors (those ancestors immigrated Cherokee areas in Virginia and other states and settled with Buffalo Ridge and Stonewall Mill bands during and after the 1830s).

The United Cherokee Indian Tribe of Virginia, Inc., has its tribal office in Madison Heights, Virginia. Madison Heights is a town in Amherst County, between the city of Lynchburg and the counties of Appomattox (formed from sections of Buckingham, Campbell, and Prince Edward counties), Bedford, Campbell, Nelson, and Rockbridge. Most of the ancestors and descendants have lived in and most are still presently residing in Appomattox (Stonewall Mill and vicinity) and Amherst Counties, and in the city of Lynchburg. While UCITOVA members' ancestry is predominantly Native American, some members are Native American-European Americans due to Native Americans ancestors' intermarriage with European colonists as early as the 1600s (from England, Ireland, Scotland, France, Germany, and other European countries). Some UCITOVA members

---

[196] Ibid., 2

have *Native American, European American, and African American* ancestry as a result of genealogical connections with European and West Africans (West African ancestry during years after 1865). UCITOVA members' intermarriage with the clannish Scot Highlanders has made the very clannish Native band even more protective of its clans' heritage and genealogical connections. Even though the band does not restrict intermarriage with other ethnic groups, including people of African descent, it has been very zealous for over four centuries in encouraging tribal members to endeavor to keep the membership predominantly Native American.

UCITOVA's ancestors have fought for the United States in all major wars, from early times until the present time. More than 80 percent of the females on UCITOVA's tribal roll that contains almost seven hundred male and female members—those of legal age— are eligible to join the Daughters of the American Revolution (DAR) as a result of their ancestors' participation in the American Revolutionary War. Although they would be eligible for membership, only nine tribal members have actually applied for and been granted membership in the DAR. Three of the nine tribal members have served as officers in two local DAR chapters in Central Virginia. One of the three officers has served as Regent/President of a local DAR chapter.

The U.S. National Park Service of the Department of Interior recognized Raleigh Pinn's service with the Amherst Militia at Yorktown by inviting a UCITOVA delegation to Yorktown on September 30, 2000. During the event, the program's master of ceremonies noted:

> At Yorktown, individuals of the United Cherokee Tribe of Virginia fought with General Washington's army. Today, on the anniversary of the start of the siege, descendants of one of those soldiers, Rawley

Pinn, join the National Park Service in recognizing his participation."[197]

The Virginia Pinns (Raleigh, his brother Robert, and Robert's three sons, and Raleigh's nephew Thomas Pinn) have the distinction of being the only Virginia soldiers and sailors listed as Native American in the National Daughters of the American Minority Soldiers pamphlet; although there were other UCITOVA Native American ancestors in the war, they were not specifically noted with the NA designation for Native American on Revolutionary War records.

At least ten Revolutionary War soldiers are ancestors/relatives of UCITOVA's present membership.

In 2001, Dr. Robert Maslowski, an anthropologist and archeologist, wrote:

> The United Cherokee Indian Tribe of Virginia (UCITOVOA) is a tri-racial band with demonstrated Cherokee ancestry located in Amherst County, Virginia. According to the genealogical records some members of the band can trace their Indian ancestry back to the late 1600s . . . This tri-racial ancestry actually fits in with the observations of Mooney and others about the nature of the Cherokee . . .
>
> Corn was a main ingredient in the diet of the Buffalo Ridge people and hunting is an important source of food for some members of the United Cherokee Indian Tribe of Virginia. One traditional Indian recipe for ashcakes has been handed down through some of the Buffalo Ridge families. Ashcakes were made by digging a hole in ashes, placing a ball of cornmeal in the hole and covering it up until it was cooked. Herbal teas especially sassafras were also frequently used and

---

[197] National Park Service, U.S. Department of the Interior, *Minority Participation in the Siege of Yorktown: Cherokee* (Yorktown, VA: National Park Service, 2000), 1.

blackberries, walnuts and chestnuts are frequently gathered by members of the Buffalo Ridge Band.

The Cherokee have the best documented use of plants for medicinal purposes of any tribe in North America . . . The Buffalo Ridge Cherokee have used many home remedies for the treatment of diseases and health conditions. Many of these remedies have been passed down through oral histories and have Indian origins. As an example Betsey Beverly treated serious asthma problems by taking her child's clothing off and placing him on a plank 'over the creek early in the morning.' The child did not experience any more problems with asthma after using the remedy. She used the practice of cold plunge baths in a running stream which was a universal Indian panacea for strong sickness of almost any kind. Mooney mentions that this treatment was used by the Cherokee during the smallpox epidemic of 1738 or 1739.

Cherokee tried whenever possible, to promote peace and harmony. This atmosphere was conducive to trade, political relations, and intermarriage with other groups. From the time of first contact with whites, the Cherokee were a willing people and were able to cross the long bridge to a superior civilization in a very short time. Two things that made this transition possible was intermarriage which allowed leaders to move easily between both worlds and the other was the development of writing by Sequoyah, which made teaching everyone possible. (Bettis 1975: xii)

Dr. Rice (1991, 1995) has compiled a wealth of oral history and genealogical information on the Buffalo Ridge Band. His oral histories mention several instances of medical practices and foodways that have Indian origin, but these were not treated in any detail. To get a clearer picture of the Band's Indian ancestry it might be beneficial to do an anthropological study of specific medical practices and foodways to document their origins and relationships to specific Indian Tribes Such a study would include oral histories from the older Band members who still use herbal medicines and cook traditional foods.

Another avenue of research that may add to our knowledge of the Buffalo Ridge Band would be historic archeology. Early cabin sites should be located, dated and recorded for future research. The Buffalo Ridge Band lived in Amherst County for over 200 years and if a number of old cabin sites can be found and investigated, historic archeology could provide insight into the social status, ethnic origins, changes in material culture, and changes in foodways of the Buffalo Ridge Band.[198]

The Amherst County Board of Supervisors, on February 4, 2003, submitted and passed a resolution recognizing UCITOVA as Native American and the Band's contributions to Amherst County:

> *Whereas* UCITOVA's ancestors were aboriginal Native American people of Virginia (Cherokee and Algonquian); and Whereas the United Cherokee Indian Tribe of Virginia, Inc. ancestors engaged in early land transactions (buying and selling) in Amherst County in the 1700s; and *Whereas*, the United Cherokee Indian Tribe of Virginia, Inc. had ancestors who were American Revolution soldiers, and *Whereas*, the United Cherokee Indian Tribe of Virginia, Inc. ancestors have been recognized by the National Park Service for their participation in the Yorktown Battle against British troops; and *Whereas*, the United

---

[198] Robert Maslowski, *Overview of the United Cherokee Indian Tribe of Virginia, Incorporated (UCITOVA)* (Milton, WEST VIRGINIA, 2001).

> Cherokee Indian Tribe of Virginia, Inc. has members that have participated in major wars supporting the United States, and . . . *Be it resolved* that the Amherst County Board of Supervisors recognizes the United Cherokee Indian Tribe of Virginia, Inc. membership for their support of Amherst County and their desire to preserve their Native American Cherokee culture and heritage.[199]

As of 2015, after more than four hundred years of good times and bad times for Cherokee and Wiccocomico tribal members, two decades of waiting for recognition as a state-approved tribe, UCITOVA is not a state-approved Native American band! The general consensus among historians and average citizens in Central Virginia is that UCITOVA has members who generally have Native American and European ancestry as well as members who have Native American, European American, and African American ancestry, and some members who have Native American and African American ancestry. In a state that has been saturated with so-called historical writing about Native American history, with a pro-eugenics philosophy, some of Virginia's state-approved Native American tribes have been socially programmed to deny, or at least not mention *African* ancestry in their genealogical tree. They know that the eugenics movement theorized that if a Native American had European ancestry, the fact was hailed as a positive racial attribute. On the other hand, eugenics philosophers somehow believe, in non-scientific terms, that "African blood neutralizes any Native American and/or European ancestry" that exists in the genealogy of a European or Native American.

It is obvious among history scholars as well as average Americans that Virginia officials have been unfair with their Native American recognition criteria. Dr. Plecker's eugenics philosophy—although he admitted that he acted illegally

---

[199] Amherst County Board of Supervisors, *Resolution in Recognition of the United Cherokee Indian Tribe of Virginia, Inc* (Amherst, VA: Amherst County Board Of Trustees, 2003).

with the Racial Eugenic campaigns—is still being felt today on Virginia citizens' stereotyping of who Native Americans *are* and *are not*. The eugenics social forces are alive and doing well in Virginia! Those philosophies say: "While European American ancestry in your Native American documentation is not a negative, any mention of African American ancestry in your Native American family tree will definitely be a negative and hurt your cause in documenting a Native American tribe!" Some state-recognized tribes have been forced to play the *race* game well by remaining silent on noting any ancestry other than Native American and European American.

Racial discrimination against Native American tribes who acknowledge some African ancestry tends to bring more negative social stigma on those members in comparison to tribes that privately acknowledge the fact that they have some African ancestry, but maintain the secret. As it is generally accepted by most historians that there are probably few, if any, tribal bands in the Southeastern and Eastern United States with members that have full blood (Native) ancestry and no traces of African ancestry, it is obvious that the Dr. Plecker's Racial Integrity campaign during the early to mid 1900s was effective in continuing racial discrimination against Native American. Dr. Plecker's destructive strategies and actions against Native Americans during the early 1900s were more recent extensions of cruel tactics that Native Americans' colonial enemies utilized during the 1600s, 1700s and 1800s.

Exodus 1:8 (KJV) says, "Now there arose up a new king over Egypt, which knew not Joseph." Joseph was the hero of Egyptians and Israelites. One may wisely ask, "How could the Egyptians leaders forget the economic and cultural accomplishments of Joseph and the Israelites in Egypt?" Today, in the twenty-first century, one could also ask wisely, "How could Americans, in general, and Virginians, specifically, ignore the contributions of Raleigh Pinn and other UCITOVA Native American Revolutionary War patriots to American's independence and nation building? Based on Virginia leaders' indifference to the great achievements of UCITOVA's ancestors in America and the Commonwealth of Virginia, and their refusal to recognize

UCITOVA as one of the state-approved tribes, one would expect that they, like the pharaoh of the book of Exodus, have forgotten their history lessons or have become indifferent to the achievements of Buffalo Ridge/Stonewall Mill/UCITOVA's ancestors in Virginia history. State officials have been placing a moratorium on recognizing UCITOVA!

It seems that, for more than twenty years, the state House and Senate leadership has hesitated to let the UCITOVA Resolution for State Tribal Recognition go to the General Assembly for a vote. With credit given to the members of the General Assembly, each of the two times a Resolution has come up for a vote by the General Assembly between 1992 and 2013, the House of Delegates and the Senate have voted to approve it. Each time, however, there has been political maneuvering by persons/ groups with vested interests in keeping the Resolution from moving to the governor for his signature. In 2013, after the Resolution had been approved by both the Senate and House of Delegates (HJ 744, vote 92-yes, 3-no; SJ300, vote 40-yes, 0-no), certain officials encouraged the legislators to wait until the next year when they will have a newly written tribal recognition procedure to follow. Why should UCITOVA wait until the Council on Indians develops their strict tribal recognition procedures? UCITOVA was the first tribe to apply for state recognition in 1993, after the first eight tribes were approved. Three tribes have been approved since 2010, but UCITOVA continues to be ignored by certain officials and the Virginia Council on Indians.

Last year, Virginia officials and the Virginia Council on Indians supported the development of new tribal recognition procedures, much like the federal BIA criteria, with a *bill* rather than a *resolution*, making tribal recognition much more difficult. With these new requirements, few of the current state-recognized tribes could meet the *new standards* for state recognition if they had to apply for recognition as new applicants.

The genocidal practices continue today, as some Virginia leaders and historians are dropping the ball again on Virginia's history. They are missing an opportunity to inform the Nation that Virginia was the very first colony in America to make direct contact with Cherokee. Virginia is missing an opportunity to document the fact that the Cherokee and Wiccocomico are still alive and doing well in Virginia—that "Virginia Cherokees have *not* all gone to North Carolina and Oklahoma." Some historians have naively stated that Cherokees are not in Virginia and/or that "Wiccocomico do not exist today, as their descendants have been destroyed in the Northern Neck by the European colonists and they are no more!"

UCITOVA is living proof that Cherokee and Wiccocomico united in Virginia, in spite of Virginia's official genocidal practices: destroying two Wiccocomico reservations; enslaving Wiccocomico Indian Town's members and exporting them to other colonies and countries; requiring the aid of tributary Indians to fight the colonists' Indian enemies (which resulted in the loss of life of many of those tributary tribal warriors); designing and implementing the devious indentured servitude institution by which adults and children lost much of their Native American culture and economic livelihood; and other racial discriminatory acts over the centuries. Cherokee and Wiccocomico migrated from those hot spots and appeared gradually on Central Virginia U.S. Census rolls. After more than three centuries of struggles to retain their culture and life, descendants of Revolutionary War patriots, Pillar Tribal ancestors, and Secondary Pillar patriarchs and matriarchs face discrimination from some present-day Virginia officials. It seems that the dominant culture is saying, "How dare you attempt to survive after all that your ancestors have endured over the centuries!" "Your tribe has a nerve; trying to continue to cling to your Cherokee and Wiccocomico Native American culture and heritage!"

UCITOVA has as much tribal documentation as most of the current state-approved tribes. On May 14, 1992, Secretary of Health and Human Services, Howard Cullum, wrote a letter to UCITOVA Chief, Samuel Penn, with notification that June 12, 1992, had been set for the first meeting with Virginia Council on Indians in the Cabinet Conference room, Richmond, Virginia. Secretary Cullum enclosed in his letter the 1989 *recognition criteria* that VCI adopted and a request that UCITOVA bring "evidence of [the tribe's] genealogical connection with the Cherokee Tribe of North Carolina." Since 1992, UCITOVA has been forced to jump through mythical hoops based on Virginia's traditions and myths. The system implies, "You cannot be a Cherokee band unless North Carolina Cherokees say you are." Why has Virginia abdicated or surrendered its sovereign authority to North Carolina or Oklahoma to say who are *Cherokees* in Virginia. The Commonwealth of Virginia made significant contacts with Cherokees who resided within its midst long before Oklahoma and North Carolina. Virginia's Native American history, if allowed to be recorded accurately, can assist North Carolina and Oklahoma Cherokees in understanding their own rich Cherokee aboriginal history.

UCITOVA was invited by Virginia Senate Joint Resolution #15 (1992) to seek state recognition. The General Assembly voted unanimously to ask the Virginia Council of Indians—composed of one representative of each of the eight state-recognized tribes and other members of the Council—under the Department of Health and Human Resources, to study the Buffalo Ridge Band's documentation, and "complete its work in time to submit its findings and recommendation to the Governor and the 1993 Session of the General Assembly." More than 1200-1500 pages of documentation of the Band's history were presented to the Council (the author of documents included most of the materials in his 1995 book, *The Buffalo Ridge Cherokee*, Heritage Books). The council, however, determined that it could not recommend state recognition, although the Secretary of Health and Human Resources supported the Band's report that Cherokees were in Amherst County and Southwestern Virginia. The department, following its usual procedure of taking the recommendation of subcommittees, however, abided by the recommendation of the Virginia Council on Indians and declined to recommend approval to the governor and the Virginia General Assembly.

During the 1992–93 period when UCITOVA was being studied by the Council, Wilma Mankiller, Chief of the Cherokee Nation of Oklahoma, had written letters to several state governors, including Virginia, warning them about "illegal Cherokee" tribes, and advising them that Cherokee recognition should come from the federal government, not the states. Virginia's officials and governor, for whatever reason, possibly yielded to the influences of outside and internal pressures and denied UCITOVA state recognition.

June Weeks, Executive Director of the Alabama Indian Affairs Commission (an Indian affairs office similar to the Virginia Council on Indians), responded to Chief Wilma Mankiller's letter to the Alabama governor, with a letter to the effect that the state of Alabama recognizes that it has three Cherokee tribes within the state and has every right to recognize its Native American people (March 12, 1993). June Weeks indicated that the Echota Cherokee Tribe of Alabama, the Cherokees of Northeast Alabama, and the Cherokee of Southeast Alabama were state-recognized tribes.[200 201] The state of Georgia also recognized its Cherokee residents during this same period of political disagreement and concern on the part of the Cherokee Nation of Oklahoma as to who should recognize Cherokee bands, the state or the federal government.

June Hegstrom, former Chairwoman of the Cherokee of Georgia, noted that the state of Georgia recognized two Cherokee tribes and one Creek tribe. Georgia, disregarding Chief Mankiller's wishes, voted to approve its Cherokee tribes while Wilma Mankiller was in the Georgia General Assembly chamber.[202] The states who recognized their Cherokee bands believed that they, more than the federal government, are closer to their state Native American history than the federal government. Those state-approved tribes could later apply for federal recognition. It is not known how the Virginia Council on Indians or the governor responded in writing to Chief Mankiller's letter. VCI has taken a strong position against state

---

[200] Jane Weeks, Executive Director, and Alabama Indian Affairs Commission to Guy Hunt and Governor Of Alabama, March 12, 1993, *Letter to the Alabama Governor in response to Cherokee Chief Wilma Mankiller's letter to the Governor*, (Montgomery, AL: Alabama Indian Affairs Commission, 1993), 3 page letter and 1 page attachment.

[201] Rice, 1995, 131.

[202] Ibid., 131, 132.

recognition for UCITOVA since Wilma Mankiller's interference in 1992–93 with Virginia's tribal recognition process, contrary to the actions of other states' Indian councils. The Council's actions and inactions over a period of more than twenty years have the effect of destroying a Native American band with very rich and historic documentation. UCITOVA's officials were disappointed with the Council on Indian's disapproval of their application for state recognition in 1993. Some UCITOVA leaders feel that Virginia officials were picking up where Dr. Plecker left off and continuing genocidal practices against the tribe by ignoring UCITOVA's rich and extensive documentation.

UCITOVA chief Samuel "Mountain Wolf" Penn stated in 1991:

Samuel H. Penn, UCITOVA Tribal Chief

> My grandmother Penn, my grandfather was deceased—she always told me that we were Indians. They grew up in the Stapleton area and attended Old Fairmount Church. My paternal grandparents and

great-grandparents are buried in Penn Park, at Old Fairmount Church, on Buffalo Ridge.

"My research into my family history has revealed that my ancestors were Indians. The census records and their physical appearance verified that they were in fact Indian. The oral tradition among our relatives, that lived near Old Fairmount as well as those that moved away from the area, indicated that they were members of the Cherokee Tribe.[203]

Chief Penn noted:

Our ancestors began a great journey in Amherst County, over two hundred and fifty years ago. The raw history cannot be disputed. Cherokee Indians lived, worked, and died [buried at *Pinn Park Cherokee Grounds* during 1700s---] on Buffalo Ridge in Amherst County. With more than 1500 pages of collected research and information, we attempted to achieve state recognition, but were told that we didn't have enough information and documentation.

We refuse to be held back . . . There is no way that we are going to allow bureaucracy to wipe out two hundred and fifty years of rich oral and physical history with the stroke of a pen . . . The time has come that no one has to hide his or her heritage! Our ancestors endured this because they had no other choice—hiding their true identity because of fear of being set aside or considered outcast. Our ancestors kept the tradition and tribe going since the 1700s, with their strong kinship and marriage structure. They must have known that at some point in history, someone would stand back, look over the two centuries of rich tribal history, and document their activities and facts about the Buffalo Ridge Band

---

[203] Horace R. Rice, 1991, 42.

> of Cherokee. They are firmly rooted . . . I encourage all members, present and future, to read the material on the Buffalo Ridge Band and gain knowledge of the rich history that has been placed on the shelf for the past 250 years . . . So without remorse, pave a course down the muddy road so future generations can hold their heads high and be proud of the ancestors of Buffalo Ridge and Stonewall Mill, and the rich heritage that they left to us.[204]

John Ross, chief of the United Keetoowah Band of Cherokee Indians of Oklahoma, one of three federally recognized Cherokee tribes, indicated in a 1994 letter to UCITOVA that the Keetoowah Band is in "complete support of the Buffalo Ridge Band of Cherokee (UCITOVA) in its efforts for state recognition." He further stated that "the Cherokee social structure provided political alternatives to groups with differences of opinion from the main or governing body of Cherokee."[205] Contrary to Chief Mankiller's view, Chief Ross clarified his opinion that bands of Cherokee in different states have every right to exist and have their own governmental structure without yielding to other Cherokee bands.

UCITOVA had hoped to gain state approval before applying for federal approval, as their officials believe they have documentation to meet each of the *federal recognition criteria*. During the years since 1992, UCITOVA has complained to the Council on Indians and the secretaries of Health and Human Resources (Howard M. Cullum and Preston Bryant) about the unfair response regarding the tribal documentation that has been provided to the VCI and the Health and Human Resources office. During 1992, there was commotion and talk in the Virginia Health and Human Resources Office about "black Indians trying to get State Recognition." This is contradictory as

---

[204] Horace R. Rice, 1995, 191-192

[205] John Ross, Chief, and Keetoowah Band Of Cherokee to Author and UCITOVA Chief, February 14, 1994, *Letter of Support for UCITOVA State Recognition*.

UCITOVA Native Americans' membership roll has no record of African ancestors among its members in the period of over two hundred years prior to 1865. Even if UCITOVA had African/Native American ancestors included among those early Pillars/Revolutinary War patriots, that fact would not negate the fact that UCITOVA is a legitimate aboriginal band. In early January 1993, UCITOVA's chief, Sam Penn, received a copy of VCI's minutes from December 21, 1992. VCI noted that it believed that UCITOVA descended from many "non-intermarrying persons of non-Indian descent, that the petitioning group was not a historical tribal entity . . . but rather organized as a 'tribal' entity in 1991."

The VCI implied that the tribal members were not really a typical tribe, with intermarriage among its members over several generations. UCITOVA's officials have noted that its members have similar intermarriage patterns as federally approved tribes. If UCITOVA members—who descend from documented ancestors as far as *four hundred years ago*—had closer Native American intermarriages than those that existed, some of those marriages would have been too close to be legal (*The Buffalo Ridge Cherokee*, Rice, marriages, genealogy list, etc.; Rice, 1995, 43–226).[206]

UCITOVA members believe that the *non-Indian descent* statement seemed to be language to the effect that UCITOVA has some "black and/or other ancestry within its band." Cherokees throughout the Southeastern United States intermarried with colonists on a regular basis. Since all or most of Virginia's state-approved tribes have some black and white ancestry within its midst, actually most Southeastern Native American tribes, why are Virginia officials overemphasizing *non-Indian descent* in response to UCITOVA's request for state recognition? UCITOVA officials admit that some tribal members have ancestry from England, Ireland, Spain, France, Scotland, and West Africa, but the primary ethnic and racial ancestry is Native American and has always been Native American since antiquity. These intermarriages occurred with European colonists beginning

---

[206] Rice, 1995, 43-226.

in the 1600s, which followed the traditions of Cherokees throughout the Southeastern United States. There were some cases of intermarriage between tribal members and African Americans after 1865, but, as noted already, UCITOVA's members are predominately Native American Cherokee and Wiccocomico.

One would think that VCI and Virginia officials would be proud of the survival of this band for over a four-hundred-year period, as only a few state-approved tribes have been able to document their survival over so long a time. It is obvious that individuals or groups who use racially stereotyped jargon to refer to Native Americans, such as "Black Indians" or "Indians intermarried with slaves," are keeping Dr. Plecker's self-admitted, illegal strategies alive in the twenty-first century. They are also resuscitating colonists' practices that were utilized in the 1600s through the 1800s to neutralize Native Americans rights as tribal members or land owners of aboriginal, ancestral or reservation land. Those colonists captured aboriginal natives and exported them to other areas, colonies, and nations as Native American slaves. They also claimed that Native American land owners intermarried with "blacks" or "white" residents and therefore were no longer entitled to native tribal lands or the right to be classified as Native Americans.

Today, one Virginia state approved tribe is a Bureau of Indians Affairs candidate for federal tribal recognition. That tribe has every right to be federally recognized based on its well documented, long and continuous Native American history in the Commonwealth; regardless of early 1900s and twenty-first century strategies used by some individuals or groups, with vested interests, who proclaim that the tribe has some "black" ancestry. Those critics who use that jargon are playing the Plecker "race game" card to delegitimize the Pamunkey Indians. The same strategy is also being utilized by some Virginia officials to stop UCITOVA's efforts for state recognition.

UCITOVA tribal leaders and members believe that Virginia officials continued genocidal policies when VCI stated in its minutes that UCITOVA "started as a 'tribal' entity in 1991." With the hundreds of pages of documents that UCITOVA provided to the VCI in 1991–1993 (including documents in *The Buffalo Ridge Cherokee, the Colors and Culture of a Virginian Indian Community*, 1991, and reports that were later included in *The Buffalo Ridge Cherokee: a Remnant of a Great Nation Divided*, 1995, a history of UCITOVA)—why have Virginia officials refused to recognize UCITOVA as a state-approved tribe after more than two decades?

The House of Delegates and Senate approved a General Assembly resolution in 2013 to recognize UCITOVA but General Assembly leaders and Virginia Health and/or Human Resources/ Natural Resources officials objected to the resolution being sent to the governor for his signature. They encouraged the General Assembly to wait until they complete their twenty-plus year's development of a tough, BIA-type of recognition procedure for state Native American recognition (recognition of Virginia Indian Tribes, Office of the Secretary of Natural Resources, January, 2014). This is also ironic, as most of the VCI's state approved tribes have appealed to the U.S. Congress to grant federal recognition—due to a lack of proper documentation in a state with Native American history that has been saturated with eugenic influence and the fact that they cannot pass the strict BIA federal recognition standards. Why have the Health and Human Services/Natural Resources officials and VCI been so strict on UCITOVA, a band that has met the standards that were in place twenty-two years ago, during the twenty-plus year period when VCI members and officials were in the process of writing and making the procedures harder for state tribal acknowledgment?

UCITOVA's tribal representatives complained over the years that Virginia officials were being unfair to its tribal members, as the band met the procedures and there were not any appeal processes in place. These double standards on the part of the VCI and state officials—admitting three tribes within the last ten years with no more documentation than UCITOVA, having most of VCI state-approved tribes with no more documentation than UCITOVA, and stalling with double-standard practices over the twenty-plus-year period by ignoring UCITOVA's rich tribal history—are exposing UCITOVA to a thick and toxic eugenics atmosphere and placing the band in a state of genocide. One would think that the Commonwealth of Virginia and America would be interested in Virginia recognizing this unique band of Native Americans, not trying to blot them from Virginia's Native American rolls forever!

Since 1992, when UCITOVA first applied for state tribal recognition and during the twenty-plus years of seeking tribal recognition, three UCITOVA's Native American centenarians have died—with rich tribal knowledge and oral heritage that had been passed on to them from the 1700s and 1800s.[207] Two tribal officers—vice chief[208] and a tribal advisor[209]—and other members have also died, while excitedly waiting for state tribal approval. As the years have passed, tribal members' hopes for recognition have been dashed, and they feel abandoned, persecuted, and ignored by state officials and the Commonwealth of Virginia.

Chief Mountain Wolf Penn stated that there is no way that a stroke of a Virginia official's "pen" is going to hold back UCITOVA's "rich oral and physical history." Presently, state recognized tribes are being held back for federal recognition due to centuries of illegal Racial Integrity pecking order efforts. Virginia has been saturated by the racial eugenics pecking order mentality and it seems that Native Americans are being threatened at every level of the "pecking order;" from federal officials to state officials to tribal officials representing their respective tribes on the VCI to tribal bands seeking state recognized approval.

UCITOVA tribal officials have suggested that Virginia could recognize the band as a state-approved tribe, grandfathering the tribe under the 1989 state-recognition procedures in place when the General Assembly approved it in 1993 and 2013. The only other state option, an unfair and devious approach, is to continue the crime of ignoring UCITOVA and its rich history as a Native American band; thereby prolonging the

---

[207] Rice, 1991, 107-109, 104-106, 127-128.
[208] Ibid., 1991, 120.
[209] Rice, 1995, 88-90, 163-165.

eugenics and genocidal practices that have been committed since Virginia became a colony; practices for which the Virginia House of Delegates has already apologized (*Resolution*, February 2, 2001).[210]

Jose R. Martinez Cobo, in a United Nations' Economic and Social Council Commission on Human Rights, *Study of the Problem of Discrimination against Indigenous Populations*, Final Report, noted:

> The right to define what is an indigenous person be reserved for the indigenous people themselves.
>
> The Indian people of the Americas must be recognized according to their own understanding of themselves, rather than being defined by perception of the value-systems of alien dominant societies.
>
> The World Council of Indigenous People declares that indigenous peoples are such population groups as we are, who from old-age time have inhabited the lands where we live, who are aware of having a character of our own, with social traditions and means of expression that were linked to the county inherited from our ancestors, with a language of our own, and having certain essentials and unique characteristics which confer upon us the strong conviction of belonging to a people, who have an identity in ourselves and should be thus regarded by others.[211]

---

[210] General Assembly of Virginia, ed., *General Assembly of Virginia--2001 Session House Joint Resolution No. 607* (Richmond, VIRGINIA: General Assembly Of Virginia, 2001). Expressing the General Assembly's regret for Virginia's experience with eugenics, House Joint Resolution No. 607.

[211] Martinez Cobo, Jose R, *Study of the Problem of Discrimination against Indigenous Populations, Final Report*, (New York, NY: United Nations Economic And Social Council Commission On Human Rights, 1982), 5.

The UCITOVA people knew that they were aboriginal Americans, born of parents who have been free people since antiquity (John Pinn's Pension Application noted that he descended from *Aboriginals of America*). Polly Beverly, a member of the Stonewall Mill clan, moved from Buckingham County—later known as Stonewall Mill, Appomattox County—to Buffalo Ridge in Amherst County. Her son, Aldridge, registered at the Amherst Courthouse as a free person of color on February 17, 1851. The registrar wrote:

> Aldridge Beverly . . . son of Polly Beverly, born in Buckingham County, VA, bright mulatto strait black hair . . . born of parents free prior to the first of May 1806.[212]

Five years later in 1856, Aldridge registered again at the Amherst Courthouse, in obedience to Raleigh Pinn's wishes that band members continue to document and keep paper trails of their aboriginal status in America:

> Aldridge Beverly, a free man of color, born in Buckingham County, a bright mulatto, straight black hair . . . born of female ancestors free prior to the 1st day of May 1806.[213]

While initially disagreeing with the requirement of colonists' descendants that they must register as *free persons of color*, Polly—a descendant of Raleigh Pinn's daughter, Eady, and his son-in-law, William Beverly—and the Buffalo Ridge and Stonewall Mill band members reluctantly registered at the Courthouse. The Beverlys, Pinns, Sparrows, Fergusons, McCoys, Harrises, Scotts, Cousinses, and others knew that forced county registration was one of a number of ways they could prove to later generations that they were descendants of Virginia aboriginals who have been free since antiquity. The Pinns, almost singlehandedly as

---

[212] McLeRoy & McLeRoy, 1993, 78.
[213] Ibid., 1993), 88, 89.

a family, saturated the Amherst Court House with hundreds of Deed records and Personal Property records from as far back as 1700s (Some of the Deeds: 21 June 1788, Book F, page 283; 16 April 1792, Book G., Page 94. 192 acres; 22 March 1794, Book G., 400 acres, page 436; 15 October 1798, Book I, page 369; 7 May 1841, Book W, page 82; 1 February 1842, Book Y, page 362–363; and Personal Property: 1782, Frame 4; 1799A, Frame 455, 1805A, Frame 71; 1807B, Frame 151). While other UCITOVA ancestors owned land and paid personal property taxes in Amherst County and in Stonewall Mill as early as the 1700s, the major land owners in Buffalo Ridge were Raleigh Pinn, Turner Pinn, James Pinn, and Thomas Pinn. One of the major land owners in Buckingham/Appomattox County, in addition to Raleigh Pinn, was Jethro Ferguson, father of Stephen Ferguson. Jethro, his wife, Elizabeth, and Obadiah Jenkins, for example, sold seventy-six and a half acres of land to John Owens and his heirs on February 2, 1822 in Prince Edward County. This portion of land was probably a part of the section of Prince Edward County that became a part of Appomattox County in 1845 when it became a new county.[214]

After more than four hundred years, following Virginia's colonial contacts with Wiccocomico and Cherokee and centuries of shabby Native American historical record-keeping and paper genocide by colonists and their descendants, Native American descendants today must attempt the difficult and time-consuming task of retracing their historical steps in order to satisfy state and federal recognition criteria, steps that include documentation which have been intentionally erased by the dominant culture in Virginia. State-recognition officials, in one breath, appear to imply, "I dare you prove that your people were here when the first white man arrived in Virginia, according to our criteria for recognition!" In the other breath, elected officials or designees apologize, "We regret that we mistreated your Native American people by dispersing and killing warriors and family members, taking aboriginal lands, and deceptively

---

[214] Clerk of Court, *Prince Edward County Deed Book, 1822*, (Farmville, VA: Prince Edward County Court, 1822).

recording you as black, colored, and mulatto." These official colonial and state actions had the effect of turning history into a myth over time; thereby making it almost impossible for affected tribal entities to document their continuous existence over three to four centuries.

Del. Mitch Van Yahres noted, "It was racism, pure and simple." As political leaders in the past have apologized for the rough treatment of Native American people over several generations,[215] calling it "racism, pure and simple," officials need to be cautioned to handle indigenous Native American groups with *care*.

One would think the Council on Indians, composed of aboriginal bodies like UCITOVA, would empathize and understand the dilemma in which UCITOVA has been placed, as they experienced similar roadblocks when they sought state recognition and as they seek federal recognition. Dominant cultures need to be very careful how they handle indigenous cultures, as it is virtually impossible to put the egg back together again after they have spent years of reckless mishandling of their histories. Using the analogy of the nursery rhyme, "Humpty Dumpty," to emphasize the point, an indigenous tribe, like an egg placed on a wall, faces certain disaster from a fall. These contradictory expressions by Virginia officials are akin to saying, "Even though we are so sorry that we broke the Humpty Dumpty egg, we will not attempt to put it together again, and we dare you to attempt to repair what we have broken!" While continuing deeds of mistreatment through the present time and failing to atone for its cruel treatment of indigenous cultures, Virginia's statement of remorse is no apology at all.

There seems to be no incentive on the part of many dominant cultures in the world to come to the rescue of fragile, historic and indigenous groups—many are hundreds of years old—to prevent falls that would be totally destructive to their survival.

---

[215] General Assembly of Virginia, ed., *General Assembly of Virginia--2001 Session House Joint Resolution No. 607* (Richmond, VIRGINIA: General Assembly of Virginia, 2001). Expressing the General Assembly's regret for Virginia's experience with eugenics, House Joint Resolution No. 607.

UCITOVA is one of those indigenous bands that is fragile and should be handled with care; otherwise, it too will be lost from history books forever.[216] After twenty–two years of indifference to and centuries of hostility toward UCITOVA's ancestors and culture, the dominant culture's leaders in Virginia, through their refusal to support and pass legislation for state recognition (or, more accurately, refusing to send the *passed legislation* to the governor for his signature), are continuing a four-hundred-year tradition in Virginia of committing *tribal genocide* on the historic indigenous band.

---

[216] Horace R. Rice. "The Socio-psychological Effects Of Dominant Cultures On Dominated Cultures: A Comparative Analysis Of The Acts Against And Effects On Congolese Batwa and Cherokee Indians" 2007, 1, 2, 6-9. Lynchburg College, Randolph College and Virginia University of Lynchburg sponsored an Ota Benga Conference. The author discussed the Congolese Batwa and Cherokee Indians, who experienced similar fates because of the dominant cultures' aggressive acts in their respective areas.

WORKS CITED

"Agents for The Cherokee Phoenix." *Cherokee Phoenix and Indian Advocate.* I, (1829, February 11): 1.

Amherst County Marriage Register. 1881. Amherst, VA: Amherst County Court.

Amherst County Marriage Book. Vol. 3, Amherst, VA: Amherst County Court..

Amherst County Marriage Book. Vol. Book I. Amherst, VA: Clerk of the Court, n.d. Recordings for Tribal Members' ancestors: Beverly/Williams, 29 November 1792; Evans/Pinn, 2 November 1795; Pinn/Redcross, 27 August 1799.*Amherst County Marriage Book.* Vol. 3. Amherst, VIRGINIA: Amherst County Court, 1881.

Amherst Militia. 1781. Military Roll. Major William Cabell. Swem Library, William And Mary College. Williamsburg, VIRGINIA.

Army, Department. 1945. Enlisted Record and Report of Separation Honorable Discharge: Department Of The Army.

Appomattox County Deed Book. Vol. 1. Appomattox, VIRGINIA: Appomattox County Court.

Appomattox County General Index to Deeds, 1892-1915. Appomattox, VIRGINIA: Appomattox County Court, 1892–1915.

Beverley, Robert. 1705. *The History and Present State of Virginia.* London, ENGLAND: R. Parker.

Beverly, Madison. 1840. U.S. Census, Amherst County, Va. 1840 Census, Amherst County, Va. Nara, Family History Library Film: 0029683. Nara, BUREAU OF CENSUS.

———1850. Census, Botetourt, Virginia. 1850 Census, Botetourt, Virginia. Washington, DC. Nara.

———1880. Alum Ridge, Floyd, Virginia. Washington, Dc. National Archives. Madison, as a Cherokee Native American, chose to move around Central and Southwestern Virginia. Eventually his son, William P., settled in 1900 as a Cherokee in an "Indian Tribe" in Floyd County, Virginia.

Beverly, William P. 1900 U.S. Census, Burks Fork, Floyd, Virginia. Nara, 1900. T623, 1854 Rolls. Microfilm: 1241708.

Boudinot, E. C. 1874. "The Indian Territory And Its Inhabitants." *Journal of the American Geographical Society of New York*. V, 217-224.

Boudinot, Elias, Ed. 1829, February 11. "Agents For The Cherokee Phoenix." *Cherokee Phoenix and Indian Advocate*. I: 1.

Bruce, Phillip, Lyon Tyler, and Richard Morton. 1924. *The New History of Virginia*. Vol. 1st ed. Chicago, IL: The American Historical Society.

Bureau of Census, National Archives. 1850. *Census, United States, 1850, Eastern Amherst County, Virginia*. Washington, DC: National Archives Microfilm Publication.

Bureau of the Census. *U.S. Census 1860*. Washington, DC: Government Printing Office, 1860. William Beverly was listed 90 years old, Mulatto.

Burk, John. 1816. The History of Virginia from Its First Settlement to the Present Day. Petersburg, VA: Dickson & Pescud.

Bush, Richard C. 1998. "Native Northumberlanders." *The Bulletin of the Northumberland County Historical Society*. XXXV: 3-19.

Census, Bureau of The. *First Census of the United States, 1790*. Vol. 1st Census. Washington, DC: Government Printing Office.

———Census, U.S., 1840. U.S. Census, Amherst County, Va. 1840 Census, Amherst County, Va. Nara, Family History Library Film: 0029683. NARA, BUREAU OF CENSUS.

———Census, U.S., 1860. Family History Library Film: 805363. Montgomery, Virginia U.s. Census. NARA, Washington, Dc. NARA Microfilm Publication M653, 1,438 ROLLS.

———Census, U.S., 1880. Alum Ridge, Floyd, Virginia. Washington, Dc. National Archives. Madison, as a Cherokee Native American, chose to move around Central and Southwestern Virginia. Eventually, his son, William, settled in 1900 as a Cherokee "Indian Tribe" in Floyd County, Virginia.

Chamberlain, Alexander F. 1891. *Science*. Vol. 17th ed. New York, NY.

Chamberlain, and Alexander F. 1911. *Indians, North American*. 11th ed. Cambridgeshire, ENGLAND: Encyclopaedia Britannica.

Clerk, and Court, eds. *Order Book, Lancaster County,*. Vol. II, *Book 2*. Lancaster County, VA: Lancaster County, 1680–86.

Clerk, Court, and Lancaster County Court, eds. *Lancaster County Order Book, 1702-1713.* , *Order Book 1702-1713*. Lancaster, VIRGINIA: Lancaster County Court, 1702.

Clerk, Court, and Lancaster County. *Lancaster County Order Book*. Lancaster, VIRGINIA: Lancaster County Court, 1702–1713.

Clerk, Court. *Amherst County Deed Book I*. 1800. Vol. I. Amherst, VIRGINIA: Amherst County Court.

――― *Lancaster County Court, 1702-1713*. Lancaster, VIRGINIA: Lancaster County, 1702–1713.

―――.*Northumberland County Order Book 1753-1756*. Vol. 1753-1756. Northumberland, VA: Northumberland County.

Clerk, Minutes, ed. *Colonial Council Minutes. 1721*. Richmond, VA: Virginia Colonial Council, 1721.

Cobo Martinez, Jose R. 1982. *Study of the Problem of Discrimination against Indigenous Populations, Final Report*. New York, NY: United Nations Economic And Social Council Commission On Human Rights.

Commissioner, Prepared By the Commissioners of the Five Civilized Tribes. 1907. *Index to the Final Rolls of Citizen and Freemen of the Five Civilized Tribes in Indian Territory*. Washington, DC: Secretary Of The Interior.

County, Northumberland. *Court Clerk, Northumberland County Order Book, 1729-37*. Vol. 1729-37. Heathsville, VA: Northumberland County.

Court, Clerk. ed. *Amherst County Deed Book*. Vol. Deed Book I. Amherst, VA: Amherst County, n.d. Some of Raleigh Pinn's numerous Deed recordings in Amherst County on Buffalo Ridge.

Court, Clerk, Amherst County. 1909. *Amherst County Deed Book*. Vol. LXI. Amherst, VA: Amherst County Court. Deed for the Second Fairmount Baptist Church, to Deacon Willis West, church official (trustee).

Court, Clerk. 1822. *Prince Edward County Deed Book, 1822*. Farmville, VA: Prince Edward County Court.

Court, Northumberland County Clerk. *Northumberland County Order Book 1729-1737*. Heathsville, VIRGINIA: Northumberland County Court.

Court, Northumberland County Clerk. *Northumberland County Record Book 1662-1666*. Vol. 1678-79. Heathsville, VA: Northumberland County Court, 1678–79.

Daughters of the American Revolution. *Minority Military Service Virginia*. Vol. 1775-83. Washington, DC: Daughters of the American Revolution.

Doran, Michael. 1987. *Atlas of County Boundary Changes in Virginia--1634-1895*. Athens, GA: Iberian Publishing.

Evans, Raymond. 1976. "Notable Persons In Cherokee History: Bob Benge." *Journal of Cherokee Studies*. Vol. 1, No. 2: 98-106.

Everett, C.S. 2009. *Indian Slavery in Colonial America*. Edited by Alan Gallay. Lincoln, NEBRASKA: University Of Nebraska Press. Everett mentioned the pro Native American slavery positions taken by officials and judges in Virginia, and the roles of two judges, Robert Carter and John Smith, in the dispossession of the Wiccocomico tribe in neighboring Lancaster County. He made reference to a case in Virginia regarding the Wiccocomico Nickens family, and the "Inhuman practice." The Nickens were relatives of the Pinns in Wiccocomico Indian Town.

Felldin, J.E. Robey.ed. 1976. *Index to the 1820 Census of Virginia*. Baltimore, MD: Genealogical Publishing.

Fields, George W., Jr. 1945. *Enlisted Record and Report of Separation Honorable Discharge*, 2 November 1945.

Forbes, Jack. 1988. Black Africans and Native Americans: Color, Race, and Caste in the Evolution of Red-Black Peoples. New York, NY: Blackwell. "Native Americans as Mulattoes."

Gaines, Daniel, C.M. Amherst Militia. 1781. Military Roll. Major William Cabell. Swem Library, William and Mary College. Williamsburg, VIRGINIA.

Grundset, Eric G., ed. 2008. *Forgotten Patriots.* Washington, DC: National Society of Daughters Of The American Revolution.

Hale, Horatio, ed. 1883. *Iroquois Book of Rites.* Philadelphia, PA: D. G. Brinton Library Of Aboriginal American Literature.

Harris, Stanley. Family Native American genealogy. Horace R. Rice, Interviewer. Madison Heights, VA, July 31, 2001.

Haywood, John. 1823. *Natural and Aboriginal History of Tennessee.* Nashville, TN: G. Wilson.

Heinegg, Paul. 2005. Free African Americans of North Carolina, Virginia, and South Carolina from the Colonial Period to About 1820. Baltimore, MD: Clearfield Company By Genealogical Publishing.

Hening, William, ed. Statutes at Large: A Collection of Laws of Virginia. Vol. II, A Collection of Laws of Virginia, 1660-1682.

Hening, William, ed. 1823. Statutes at Large: A Collection of Laws of Virginia. Vol. 1, Laws between 1819-1823. Richmond, VA: George Cochran, 1823.

Howe, Henry. 1852. *History of Virginia.* Charleston, SC: William Babcock.

Hull, Janice, ed. 1996. *Index to the United States Census for Buckingham County, Virginia.* Buckingham, VIRGINIA: Historical Buckingham, Inc.

Jackson, Luther Porter. 1942. Free Negro Labor and Property Holding in Virginia, 1830-1860. New York, NY: Macmillan.

Jackson, Ron, ed. *Virginia, Compiled Census and Census Substitute Index, 1607-1890.* Bountiful, UTAH: Accelerated Indexing Systems.

Jackson, Ronald, Gary Teeples, and Daryl Schaefermeyer, eds. 1976. *Virginia 1930 Census.* Bountiful, UTAH: Accelerated Indexing Systems, Inc.

Jamerson, Vicki, Edith Nash, and Clyde Nash, eds. 1979. *Appomattox County Marriages, 1854-1890.* Appomattox, VIRGINIA.

Jenkins, Dock, Ivanhoe Jenkins, and et. al. 1820. Court House, Amherst County. Nara, Washington, Dc. Ancestry.com 1920

United States Federal Census, Provo, UT, USA. ANCESTRY. COM.

Jordan, J. Wright, ed. 2007. *Cherokee by Blood: Record of Eastern Cherokee Ancestry in the U.S. Court of Claims, 1906-1910, Applications 23801-27800.* Bowie, MD: Heritage Books.

Lawrence, W.D. 1934, October 1. "The Fergusons-- Five Brothers of the Lynchburg Plant." *The Iron Worker.*

Legrand, A. A., and Commissioner of the Revenue. 1845. *Embracing the Free Persons of Colour.* Appomattox, VA.

Lunenburg County Deed Book. Vol. VIII. Lunenburg, VA: Lunenburg County.

Maslowski, Robert. 2001. Overview of the United Cherokee Indian Tribe of Virginia, Incorporated (UCITOVA). Milton, WEST VIRGINIA.

Mason, Polly Cary, ed. 2003. *Records of Colonial Gloucester County.* Baltimore, MD: Clearfield.

McLeRoy, Sherrie, and William R. McLeRoy. 1993. *Strangers in their Midst.* Edited by McLeRoy, Sherrie, and William McLeRoy. Bowie, MD: Heritage Books, Inc.

Mooney, James. 1975. *Historical Sketch of the Cherokee.* Chicago, IL: Aldine Transaction.

———1902. *Myths of the Cherokee.* Washington, DC: Bureau of American Ethnology.

National Park Service, U.S. Department of the Interior. 2000. *Minority Participation in the Siege of Yorktown: Cherokee.* Yorktown, VA: National Park Service.

O'Donnell, James H. 1973. *Southern Indians in the American Revolution.* Knoxville, TENNESSEE: University Of Tennessee.

Pendleton, William C. 1920. *History of Tazewell County and Southwest Virginia, 1748-1920.* Johnson City, TN: The Overmountain Press.

Penn, Samuel, An Attendee at One of The Sessions. *Unity Council Meeting of 39 Cherokee Bands.* Jasper, TENNESSEE, 1993. Chief presented oral report of the meeting at next regular UCITOVA meeting.

Pilling, James C. 1892. "Athapascan Language." *Bureau of Ethnology, Smithsonian Institution.*

Pinn, John. *Southern Campaign American Revolution Pension Statements: John Pinn.* Edited by C. Leon Harris, Transcriber, and Annotator. 1842. Suffolk County, MASSACHUSETTS: Commonwealth Of Massachusetts. Pension application of John Pinn (Pinn) R8264, statement by Pinn transcribed by C. Leon Harris.

Pinn, Turner, and Polly Beverly. 1840. Census. U.S. Census 1840. Nara National Archives, Washington, Dc. Family History Library Film 0029683.

Pinn, Turner. Family History Library Film. Series: M19; Roll 194, Page 525. 1830 Federal Census M19: Roll 194. Library Film 0029673. Film included the names of neighboring Native Americans clustered together.

Plecker, Walter A., Registrar, and Virginia Bureau of Vital Statistics. "Eugenics In Relation To The New Family And The Law On Racial Integrity." Paper read before the American Public Health Association, January 01, 1924.

———Walter A. to Local Registrars, Physicians, andet al. Richmond, Virginia. *Letters to Local Registrars, et al.* Dr. Plecker, VA State Registrar, 1943.

———Director, VA Bureau of Vital Statistics. 1924. *Virginia Act to Preserve Racial Integrity.* Richmond, VA: Virginia General Assembly.

Plecker, Walter A. January 1925. "Racial Improvement." *Virginia Medical Monthly.*

Plecker, Walter. 1947. *Virginia's Vanished Race.* Richmond, VA.

Pollard, John Garland. "The Pamunkey Indians of Virginia." *Smithsonian Publication.* (1894, January 01).

Potter, Stephen.1993. *Commoners, Tribute, and Chiefs.* Charlottesville, VA: University Of Virginia.

Potter, Stephen R. 1976. "The Dissolution of The Machoatick, Cekacawon and Wighcocomoco Indians." *The Bulletin of the Northumberland County Historical Society.* XIII, (1976, January 01): 5-33. Stephen Potter provided a thorough analysis of the Wiccocomico tribe and the "dissolution" of its people between 1608-early 1700s.

Potter, Stephen. 1976. "An Ethnohistorical Examination Of Indian Groups In Northumberland County, Virginia,

1608-1719." PhD diss., University of North Carolina, M.A. Thesis, Department of Anthropology, University of North Carolina.

Powell, J. W.. "Cherokee Indians--Rites And Ceremonies." Review of *Seventh Annual Report*, by John Wesley Powell. *Report of the Bureau of Ethnology*. no. VII (n.d.).

Rhodes, Phillip Wayne, ed. 2001. *Genealogical Research of UCITOVA*. Lynchburg, VA: Written Summary to UCITOVA.

Rice, Horace, ed. 1994. "A Report on The History of The Buffalo Ridge Cherokee, United Cherokee Indian Tribe Of Virginia, Incorporated." Unpublished manuscript. Microsoft Word; copies of birth certificates, marriage data. land deeds, etc.

———1991. The Buffalo Ridge Cherokee: The Colors and Culture of a Virginian Indian Community. Madison Heights, VA: B R C Books.

———1995. The Buffalo Ridge Cherokee: A Remnant of a Great Nation Divided. Bowie, MD: Heritage Books, Inc.

———United Cherokee Tribe of Virginia (UCITOVA). 2009. Madison Heights, Va. Basic Facts on UCITOVA--Statistical Analysis of Family Relationship between UCITOVA Tribal Pillars/Revolutionary War Ancestors. Madison Heights, VA: Unpublished.

———"The Socio-psychological Effects of Dominant Cultures on Dominated Cultures: A Comparative Analysis of the Acts Against and Effects on Congolese Batwa and Cherokee Indians." 2007. Lynchburg College, Randolph College and Virginia University of Lynchburg sponsored an Ota Benga Conference. Dr. Rice compared the Congolese Batwa and Cherokee Indians, who experienced similar fates because of the dominant cultures' aggression in their respective areas.

Robertson, Wyndam. 2010. *Pocahontas, Alias Matoaka and Her Descendants*. Baltimore, MD: Genealogical Publishing.

Ross, John, Chief, Keetoowah Band of Cherokee. 1994. Letter to Author and UCITOVA Chief, February 14, 1994. *Letter of Support for UCITOVA State Recognition*.

Royce, C.C. "Cherokee Nation Of Indians.1887. " Review of *Cherokee Nation of Indians*, by Charles C. Royce. *Annual Report to the Bureau of Ethnology*. no. V (1887, January 01).

———*Map of the Former Territorial Limits of the Cherokee "Nation of" Indians.* Washington, DC: Geographical Map Division, Library Of Congress, 1884. Repository: Library of Congress, Geographical Map Division, Washington, DC.

Senate (S.B. *The Racial Integrity Act.* Richmond, VA: Virginia General Assembly, 1924. Racial Integrity Laws were included in the Act (RIA) for purposes of protecting white resident against the perceived threat of race-mixing.

Service, National Park, and Department Of The Interior. 2000. *Minority Participation in the Siege of Yorktown.* Yorktown, VA: National Park Service.

Smith, Lois. 1992. Interview. Large number of citizens in Amherst County claim Cherokee ancestry. Amherst Historical Museum, Amherst, VA, August 5, 1992.

Southern Bell Telephone Company. 1994. *The Southern Bell Telephone Book.* Asheville, NC: Southern Bell. 1993-94.

Sparacio, Ruth, and Sam Sparacio, eds. 1993. Virginia County Court Records: Deed & Will Abstracts of Northumberland County, Virginia, 1662-1666. McLean, VIRGINIA: The Antient Press.

Strachey, William. 1953. *The Historie of Travell into Virginia Britannica (1612).* London, ENGLAND: Hakluyt Society.

Supervisors, Amherst County Board. 2003. *Resolution in Recognition of the United Cherokee Indian Tribe of Virginia, Inc.* Amherst, VA: Amherst County Board Of Supervisors.

Sutton, Karen E. 1997. "Black, Red and Revolutionary: Free African Americans Of Lancaster And Northumberland Counties, Virginia In The Era Of The American Revolution." PhD diss., University of Maryland. Master's Project submitted to the Faculty of the Graduate School of the University of Maryland in partial fulfillment of the requirements for the degree of Master of Arts, History.

Tayac, Gabrielle. Fall 2009. "Eugenics and Erasure In Virginia." *National Museum of the American Indian* 10 (3) 20.

Thornton, Russell. 1990. *The Cherokee: A Population History.* Lincoln, Nebraska: University Of Nebraska.

Tooker, William W. 1898. *Problem of the Rechahecrian Indians of Virginia*. Washington, DC: Judd And Detweiler.
Tyner, James W. 1990. *Those Who Cried: The 16,000*. Muskogee, OK: Muskogee, OK.
Underwood, Thomas B. 1961. *The Story of the Cherokee People*. Muskogee, OK: S.B. Newman.
Van Yahres, Mitch. "Expressing Regret For Virginia's Eugenics Policies." *Lynchburg News and Advance* (Lynchburg, VA), February 2, 2001.
Virginia, General Assembly of, ed. *General Assembly of Virginia--2001 Session House Joint Resolution No. 607*. Richmond, VIRGINIA: General Assembly of Virginia, 2001. Expressing the General Assembly's Regret for Virginia's experience with eugenics, House Joint Resolution No. 607.
Walker, Frances M.. 1964. *The Early Episcopal Church in the Amherst-Nelson Area*. Lynchburg, VA: J. P. Bell.
Washington County, Virginia Marriage Book. Washington County, VIRGINIA: Washington County Court, 1792–1900.
Weeks, June, Executive Director, and Alabama Indian Affairs Commission to Guy Hunt and Governor Of Alabama, March 12, 1993. *Letter to the Alabama Governor in response to Cherokee Chief Wilma Mankiller's letter to the Governor*. Montgomery, AL: Alabama Indian Affairs Commission, 1993.
Whitehead, Edgar. 1896. "Amherst County Indians, Highly Interesting History of an Old Settlement Of Cherokees," *Richmond Times* (Richmond), April 19, 1896.
Woodson, Robert F, and Isobel B. Woodson, eds. 1970. *Virginia Tithables--From the Burned Record Counties*. Richmond, VIRGINIA: Isobel B. Woodson.

ABOUT THE AUTHOR

Horace R. Rice, a native of Pacolet (Spartanburg County), South Carolina, has been working in the field of public and higher education in Virginia since 1965. His mother, a quarter-blood Cherokee, was born in Cherokee County, South Carolina, near Pacolet.

He earned a Bachelor of Arts degree from Johnson C. Smith University in Charlotte, North Carolina (1965), a Master of Education degree (1970), and a Doctor of Education degree (1980) from the University of Virginia in Charlottesville, Virginia. His areas of specialization were administration and supervision, counseling, and educational research. Dr. Rice has worked in the education field as a government teacher; elementary, junior high, and high school principal; and school division assistant superintendent.

He is an army veteran sergeant, serving as a reconnaissance scout on the Korean DMZ—a hostile fire zone—in 1968–69. He is an ordained minister and has been a church pastor since 1976. He is the author of numerous books/articles on Native American history, including the *Buffalo Ridge Cherokee: A Remnant of A Great Nation Divided* (1995, Heritage Books, Inc.).

Willie Ann McCoy Snead, daughter of Rev. Luther McCoy

Eddie Ferguson, son of Augustus and Nannie West Ferguson

Raymond Ferguson, Jr., son of Raymond Ferguson, Sr. and Ruth Johnson Ferguson.

Captain Andrew McCoy, Jr., West Point graduate and pilot. Died in an airplane crash. Grandson of Rev. Luther McCoy.

Dr. Brenda Cherokee Morse Taylor, descendant of the Pinns, Beverlys, Sparrows, Hughes, Giles, and Morses.

Lynchburg, VA Mayor signing Daughters of the American Revolution Native American Month Proclamation. Standing: Three UCITOVA and DAR members: Blondie Ferguson Anderson, Holli Rice and Gloria Ferguson Rice. Center: Mayor Joan Foster.

Raleigh Pete Carson   Joseph Ferguson

Stapleton, VA

James River in Stapleton, Virginia. **Buffalo Ridge** is three miles west of the river in **Amherst County** and **Stonewall Mill** is two to three miles east of the river in **Appomattox County** (Founded 1845, formerly part of **Buckingham County**).

Ezra Ferguson's Family

Back Row: Mary (wife), Ezra, Winston (Mary Ferguson's brother), Annie Ferguson McCoy (daughter), and other children. Second Row: Thurman, Percy, Josephine Ferguson Jackson, Mabel Ferguson Freeman. Front Row: Susie Ferguson (died 10 yrs.old) and George (died 2 years old). Children not pictured: Coleman, Boyd, Albert, and Fannie Ferguson Banks.

Above: Clockwise: Herbert Chambers, Bernetta Chambers Pinn, Leroy E. Chambers and Lelia Warrick Chambers

Onie Sparrow, Grandson of Willis and Martha Jane Pinn West

George and Isabelle Ferguson Fields

Ferguson Family, descendants of Raleigh Pinn and Jacob Banks, Revolutionary War Soldiers

Shirley West Christian and Samuel H. Christian

Stapleton, Virginia

Maloney O. Ferguson, Alma West Ferguson and Family in 1952. Alma West is a descendant of the Pinns, Wests, Elliotts, Beverlys, Scotts, Wards, and Humbles. M. O Ferguson is a descendant of the Fergusons, Selbys, Megginsons, Pinns, Beverlys, Wests, and Elliotts.

Made in the USA
Columbia, SC
13 August 2018